WHO WILL SURVIVE?

Russ Corey—Financier and founder of the Moon's first self-sufficient outpost. *Hestia* will be safe haven for the few who can reach it in time.

Marc Seavers—Hero of an Antarctic disaster, now assigned as Mission Commander for the great escape from Earth.

President George Starling—Leader of the most powerful country on Earth—but even his armed forces will turn against him when personal survival is at stake.

Vasily Tereshnikov—Commander of the escape ship *Pegasus*, yet secretly under the orders of Russia's premier.

Thousands of men and women will sacrifice their lives to save a fraction of the human race . . . but who will survive?

MARTIN CAIDIN

EXIT EARTH

BAEN BOOKS

EXIT EARTH

Copyright © 1987 by Martin Caidin

A Baen Books Original

Baen Publishing Enterprises
260 Fifth Avenue
New York, N.Y. 10001

First printing, April 1987
   Second printing, April 1988

ISBN: 0-671-65630-9

Cover art by David Mattingly

Printed in the United States of America

Distributed by
SIMON & SCHUSTER
1230 Avenue of the Americas
New York, N.Y. 10020

This book is for me
and
ROB NEWMAN
and our
LONG VOYAGE HOME

Book I

DUSTBIN

1

Russ Corey stood on the brink of a cliff ledge eighty feet above the rock floor of the great cavern. Eighty feet straight down and if he miscalculated so much as an instant he'd smash himself to spattering gore. He looked straight before him, across the cavern to the opposite walls glistening with condensation, reflecting the blue-yellow radiance of the artificial sun overhead. A sudden babble of argument and concern drifted up to him from far below. He lowered his gaze to look past his feet at the small human figures staring upward at him. Bird's-eye puppetry. The brief thought amused him.

A single voice shouted upward. "Russ, for Christ's sake, use the safety net! This is crazy!"

Russ Corey gave himself the luxury of a smile that flickered and was gone. That was August Mason shouting from below. Mother Mason, who worried about the health and well-being of Russ Corey. Well, that was really a full-time job. No wonder Mother was neurotic; just thinking about the edge of fine madness along which Corey moved was enough to turn him into a nervous wreck. Corey picked out Mason's face from the others. Even from this height he could read the con-

1

cern on his aide's face, the one hand held over the eyes, the nervous fluttering of his other.

For a moment Corey didn't answer. To hell with the safety net. Screw that stuff. He didn't want any exit doors beyond his own skill and timing. Anything less would take away the whole purpose of this moment. Russ Corey looked directly at Mother Mason. "Fuck the net!" he called down.

Then he forgot the issue. Slowly he raised his arms until they stretched fully outward to each side of his body. He breathed deeply and steadily of the thick air, feeling its rich heaviness as his chest rose and fell in perfectly timed movement. He flexed his fingers to test his arm muscles, then brought together the fingers and thumb of each hand. He arched his back slightly and his powerful leg muscles tensed as he rose slightly on the balls of his feet, balanced like a great upright cat.

He took a deep breath and held it, lips pressed tightly. Again he looked straight ahead, through air to the glistening rock walls. Feathery white and brown flashed for a moment as his falcon wheeled before him, inviting him with a single plaintive screech to fly. Russ Corey smiled easily this time and then he sprang up and forward, hurling his body from the edge of the cliff to the certain death waiting far below.

He snapped his arms down and hard against his sides as his body fell in perfect balance toward the lethal rock. His hearing at such moments was incredibly, exquisitely sensitive and he heard the sudden intake of breath from those looking up as he plunged headfirst. God, he loved this moment! His entire future could now be measured in the briefest of seconds. He still must pass the test. He heard the shrill cry from below, not so far away this time.

"For God's sake—!" Another sound, the screech of the falcon, closer, diving with him. Only thirty feet left now. He snapped out his arms again, the great feathery wings arched perfectly in position, catching the rushing air with a gusting sigh. As quickly as his arms moved his feet snapped apart to angle the tail pinions into maximum lift. With a sigh of a hundred hushed violins,

2

the song of the wind, he transformed his death plunge into a marvelous sweeping curve. His head came up, the pressure on his arms grew to a terrible intensity, and he knew if a single tendon failed it would spell his doom.

Russ Corey did not fail and neither did his body. Every muscle and tendon and nerve straining to the perfection of the moment, performing as he commanded, his body raced over the rock floor of the cavern, his chest bare inches above the surface. Now he had all the speed and lift he wanted and he twisted his arms and angled his feet to alter the curvature of the wings, to change their camber, to twist the tail pinions into another command of lift. His body ascended another few inches above the rocky surface, then several feet, and suddenly the center of lift moved along his feathered arms and he flashed upward. With a sudden cry of joy, a shout instead of words, he again twisted his arms and beat them fiercely in great curving movement. Feathers rolled and twisted and flexed and spiraled the air about him and back along his body and he flew with the falcon; bird and man in a single flashing lunge, and the man grinned as he and his feathered brother soared within the great lunar cavern.

Russ Corey swooped and plunged, banked steeply and moved his arms closer to or farther from his body to change his lift, arcing downward, crashing against the air with fierce flapping energy, savoring the incredible feeling that had haunted men from the first time they looked into the skies and comprehended, finally, that their feathered cousins truly flew from the lifting force of air.

He soared into a loop, changed his mind at the top of the arc, twisted his body suddenly so that he slipped into a spiral and dove straight down before lifting a wing to roll into a gentle climbing bank. He thought suddenly: *Earth. How bizarre that we had to leave the birthworld so we could cross an ocean of vacuum. No lift there for our wings. No magic of flight* . . . Theirs had been a test of distance, endurance, brainy accomplishment. Men rose on glorious pillars of blinding

3

flame, shrieking like a billion dinosaurs. Up and away from birthworld and not until they rode precisely on invisible rails of centrifugal force were they moonbound. Sealed in metal craft they threw themselves away from Earth like a metal toy at the end of a fist-clutched string swung around and around by a smiling child. Then they shut down their roaring fires and floated impossibly, tin cans falling toward the waiting airless world of ancient dust and time-frozen lava and crater-smashed surface.

They cocooned themselves in clumsy suits, tiny planets to seal out the hard vacuum, and they moved with childish delight despite the cumbersome protection they needed to keep their pressure-filled bodies from exploding in vacuum. There could be no living on this gritty surface of eternal silence where never grew the first blade of grass, and they had no mind to test their skills against the naked harshness of space.

They brought with them tiny packages of enormous energy. Shaped charges, explosives, boring and tunneling devices took them deep beneath the surface of the moon like angry wasps claiming ownership of all this world. Down they went, into sloping corridors, and they emplaced their explosives, and all across the tightly rolling surface of the airless world deep rocks and magma clanged like bells from the fracturing and splitting and hollowing out of the new caverns. They sealed the caverns, brought in pumps and machinery, powerful artificial lights and artificial suns, they brought in plants and liquid nutrients and seeds and all the things they needed to create a new place to live. Here, in a world of gossamer gravity and air as thick as they wished, they brought to man a perspective he had never known in his long history on the third planet from the sun.

Men had never before *lived on a world other than Earth*. They made of Earth a stranger. That had been the driving goal of Russ Corey ever since—but he forced away those thoughts. Not now, not here, not before the anxious eyes of his own people, these men and women *and the children* who had come here to live and move into a future they had yet to carve out of time and inertia and needs and goals yet to be determined.

4

But Corey couldn't resist the grin of his own inner thoughts. In a fleeing tendril of judgement and memory he recalled his own admonition that life on the moon, *within* the moon, must have its moments other than grim dedication. He had to make the moon singularly attractive, create its own siren call. Man lives by crooked grin and chuckle as much as he does by grimly set jaw and earnest words. They had been several months into their first permanent lunar colony when Russ Corey selected four of his people to return for a visit to Earth. He selected them with the greatest of care. Three of them slender and gentle of body, the fourth a strapping oak of a man of great body girth and weight. They rode the shuttle to Earth and everyone remaining on the moon waited anxiously to hear of their reactions.

The next night they set up the videophone contact between Earth and the lunar caverns. Russ Corey had made certain of the time lapse. "I don't want open communication except on an emergency channel between us and down there," he told Jim Stuart, his communications chief. No one had yet recognized that Corey had even created the phrase *down there* in reference to Earth rather than the *up* there, so that even in their minds they would not have to crane back their necks to visualize the world of origin. There were all manner of psychological quirks and he played them all to the hilt. Now, with the four "returnees" back on Earth, he had set into motion another train of events that, if all went as he'd planned, would generate its own positive results.

"What's it like back home?" The anxious questions poured forth in a tumultuous eruption from the group crowded into the comm room beneath the lunar surface. "How's it feel? Did you walk under the sky? Could you remember the clouds?"

They weren't prepared for what they heard. Corey had told Milt Irving, the heavyweight of the group, to be sure to let the others speak first. "It's *terrible* down here," they said in weary, nearly broken voices. "We can hardly breathe. Sally, here, has been in bed ever

5

since we arrived. Her chest, well, she's pulled muscles and she's been on oxygen and—"

"And the *bugs*," cried the youngest. "I'd forgotten about the bugs. Mr. Corey was nice enough to arrange a picnic for us, and we brought a wonderful meal with us on the bank of a river so we could watch the sunset, and my God, we're swollen from head to foot, and we haven't stopped sneezing . . ."

Of course they were bitten. The bank of a river in a marshy area at twilight. Feeding time for gnats and mosquitos and God knew what else. Hordes of them came to feast on the unsuspecting human visitors. They were stung and bitten and chewed upon and angry welts sprang up along their tender skin. "We had to leave the food and everything and run for our lives," Harold, the youngest, went on in a voice of mixed anger and complaint.

"You should have been with us the next morning!" Michael cried in a half-shout. "Gee, I'd forgotten about allergies, I guess. I mean, in the morning I couldn't even *breathe*. I was all stopped up and coughing and my eyes were swollen and . . ." He took a deep breath and they could almost hear his wail a quarter million miles away without the electronic transmission. "I want to go *home!*"

Home. An airless, barren, grit-covered globe no wider in diameter than the distance from Los Angeles to New York. *Home*. Wailed piercingly by a miserable youngster. Corey had almost banged a fist into his palm with pleasure. Milt Irving wrapped it up without ever knowing the role he played. The video camera swung to bear on Milt, almost spread-eagled in a chair of deep cushions. "What's wrong with him?" someone asked from the group.

"It's my heart," Milt said slowly and with infinite weariness. "I mean, everything here is so *heavy*. I can hardly move. The heat, it's like a blanket over you. It smothers you. And my hearts been pounding ever since I got here. It's like my blood is made of liquid lead, y'know? Like it can hardly move through my body. If I stand up and walk around too much I start to faint."

6

Big, strapping, muscular, powerful Milt Irving. A seventeen-year-old in a seventy-year-old body. Desperate to go home. To the moon. *Up there*.

"All is perspective," Russ Corey had said so many times there was no counting of the phrase. "Perspective and timing, and we need both together." Many men spoke philosophically of such things and historians noted duly their sparks of wisdom and confined them with pithy sayings into forgotten books on dusty shelves. Not too many men given to such proclamations are billionaires. Few who speak in this manner are terribly powerful and ruthless and haunted by dreams *and* have the financial and industrial might to alter the rolling swerve of a planet's destiny. Russ Corey said what he wished to say and he had the means to bring his philosophy to life.

He swore he would personally stand on the airless satellite circling the Earth and he would look across space, down through space, at the blue-white planet floating in velvety blackness, the gleaming orb that had always been the sole home of mankind. That Russian, Tsiolkovskii, had said it very well back at the turn of the century. Something about the Earth being the cradle of mankind, but that man couldn't live in a cradle forever.

As far as Russ Corey was concerned, his own soul ravished by a love long lost to him, snatched from him at the prime of her life, they were all long past that moment to launch the great trek Outward. He became the singular driving force to return his country to the moon. Project Apollo had been a splendid beginning, but it fell to the weaknesses and the curse of financial anemia and men froze their dreams in the coin of their time and the shining spacecraft became the dulled pyramids of the modern age. Corey controlled a global empire with a value no one could measure with any true accuracy. It encompassed multiple billions. It reached throughout the world. He met with Jonathan T. Bailey, then president of the United States.

"We've got to go back to the moon. *Now*," he said with an intensity that surprised his old friend.

7

"There's no way," Bailey told him. "We can't afford it. The deficit is destroying us. It's political suicide—and as far as the country is concerned, it's financial ruin. Besides, no one *needs* the moon any more, and—"

"Bullshit," Corey snapped. "Why don't you tell me we all ought to live by a ledger sheet and shut down the goddamned churches? We sure as hell don't *need* the churches, do we? They don't produce a goddamned thing, and we're talking billions every year in lost taxes. Why don't you go after their hides?"

"Because I intend to run for office again and be the president of this country for another four years," Jonathan T. Bailey said smoothly. He sipped from a heavy glass of bourbon as smooth as his voice. "*And* I've got the church vote with me. That good enough reason for you?"

"*No*."

"In your own precious idiom, then, Russ, that's tough shit." Bailey tossed off the rest of his drink and leaned forward to his old friend. "You have any idea what it would cost to go back to the moon?"

"Not just go back," Russ Corey told him. "Go back and dig in. Yes, I know what it will cost. Using the boosters we've developed for the stations, and especially the straight-shot boosters that can lift from a runway directly into orbit, it will cost on the order of twenty billion dollars."

The president chuckled and slapped his desk. "The way twenty billion rolls off your silver tongue," he laughed, "makes my heart sing." He poured again into their glasses. "For Christ's sake, have another drink."

"What if it cost this country only eight billion?"

"What?"

"You heard me, damn it."

"You couldn't do diddly crap for eight billion and you know it."

"I'll put up the other twelve billion, John."

"You're shitting me."

"While I'm drinking your bourbon? Never."

Bailey sipped slowly, thinking back on all the impossible things he'd known Russ Corey to do in a lifetime

8

of friendship. He wouldn't be in this office without the help of the man "drinking your bourbon," as he put it.

"You'll do that, Russ?"

"My word on it."

"I could get it through. On that basis. Everybody on the Hill loves a bargain."

"Do it. Set up the machinery. Get me the people to work with. I'll take care of the rest."

Thoughts of the past wisped through his mind as he soared and floated in the dreamlike magic of feathered flight in the great lunar cavern. He was immensely pleased with their growing self-sufficiency, although that was never stated for the record. Intense genetic science and limitless solar and nuclear energy, plus all the water they could ever need squeezed and smashed from lunar rock, combined with one-sixth Earth gravity to establish a thriving and unprecedented agricultural system. The moon was never quiet with the relentless gouging and carving of new caverns and corridors. Russ Corey knew far better than most men that he must present the moon as a viable producer of goods unavailable in quantity anywhere on Earth, and that the lunar colonies needed products the terrestrial industry had to sell or trade.

No finer vacuum industry existed anywhere. Hell, the surface of the moon was one entire vacuum and all its advantages were right there for the asking. In the minimal surface gravity and vacuum, Corey Industries produced electronic components that only a few years before had been impossible dreams. Earth science, computers, industry, all of them, would almost kill to obtain the lunar products. The special laboratories produced medicines, enabled extensive microbiological research in unprecedented safety.

Russ Corey turned the lunar adventure into a profitable undertaking against the dire warnings of all the know-little but loudly preaching soothsayers. To get his goods from the moon back to Earth he went *back* in time, to the 1970s and '80s, to develop a long-quiescent project: the electric rail gun. In the frictionless lunar surface vacuum he built sealed containers accelerated swiftly on magnetic levitation, along the mile-long rail guns, and hurled his merchandise at six thousand miles an hour, burning the equivalent of household electricity, for the long fall back to Earth.

He no longer bothered with the industrial developments of Hestia, the main lunar base complex. He left industry, mechanics, agriculture and all such details to his teams. Instead he labored to alter the concepts of billions of people about the values *to them* of the lunar facilities. The failures of the Earth space stations were his greatest and most unexpected ally. The huge stations, successors to the American Skylab and the Russian Salyuts and Mirs of early years, dribbled away their promises. Keeping them structurally sound was a nightmare. Holding down the leaks, sealing in their liquids, preventing mechanical breakdowns and deterioration under the whiplash of a naked sun: all these and yet more problems made of the space stations an economic and industrial disaster rather than the long-cherished fulfillment of promises. Corey made certain the channels of media he controlled—and they were considerable—never let up on the pressure of space-station clumsiness, trouble, failure, and staggering cost that was measured in tax dollars thrown down a hole higher than the sky.

Russ Corey thought now of distant Mars as his own personal dream, but every time he had the opportunity he came here to Cavern Fourteen. As he was here this very moment, birdman extraordinary. He had personally strawbossed Number Fourteen. Extra sealant for the walls and the flooring and the overhead. Doors of thick metal, double chambered for doubled strength. Oxygen and nitrogen pumped and squeezed into the chamber until he achieved pressure six times greater than on the surface of their birthworld. He grew vines and created gardens and the plants cleansed the air and made it sweet, and the delicate flowers that grew best under flimsy gravity flourished and bathed them in gentle fragrance. Flight Bowl was his joy.

With the air pressure at ninety pounds a square inch,

thickly fluid and heavy, the lifting capability of a wing moving through such viscous atmosphere became almost magical. But there were other marvelous advantages unattainable on Earth. The lunar gravity was but one-sixth that of the birthworld. There Russ Corey weighed one hundred eighty pounds. Russ Corey on his adopted world weighed only thirty earth pounds. And he was as strong as ever, despite the ghostly diminution of his weight. Inserting that strength and the science of synthetic feathers into the soupy air in Flight Bowl enabled Corey to become what had forever eluded man until this moment: a creature of true, self-sustaining flight.

Corey beat his winged arms steadily, climbing until he felt the warmth of the "artificial sun" gleaming near the cavern roof. He made a circle of the upper reaches and held his arms steady, angling the wing camber to spill lift, bringing him into a wide descending spiral toward the floor. He would make his approach into the face of strong air currents churned by a great shrouded fan so that he would land "into the wind" as birds did from instinct.

"Down below!" he shouted in his curving descent. "Birdman landing!"

He caught a glimpse of Vicki Correnti in a bright red feathery ensemble, waving to him. "All clear, Russ! Come on in!" He continued his circling descent, judging his approach with practiced eye and memory, and then he brought down his legs and moved his body from horizontal to near vertical, his powerful arms churning a storm of downbeating air from the glassine feathers. With a final thrust of energy he angled his armwings to create the sudden ground/air cushion to bring his feet lightly to the rocky surface.

Vicki came to him immediately, her hands curling away the velcro strips binding his feathery covering to his body. A flight attendant took their feather gear to be hung on racks in the drying room. Nature accommodated birds with wet feathers. Not so with upstart men. Attempting flight with wet synthetic feathers guaranteed a crumpling fall from any height.

11

Vicki brushed her lips against his cheek. She was always beautiful, but more so at such a moment when everything she did was action and movement. Short, curly black hair, startling white skin, and wine-red lips bobbed before him. "That was beautiful, Russ. Just beautiful. It's the best I've ever seen you."

He nodded to acknowledge her praise. *She* was the best manflier he'd ever seen, and accolades regarding flight came rarely from her. He should have known better. "Your start, however—"

His eyes flicked upward. "You mean from the ledge?"

"Yes. You're an unmitigated idiot also, Russ Corey. A Grade-A, homogenized blithering numbskull. If the pressure was one pound less than ninety—" She took a deep breath. "Damn you, that would be a very stupid way to go."

"Yeah. Like Icarus. Next you'll tell me," he gestured to the dazzling globe suspended high above them, "that I flew too close to the sun like our Greek hero of mythology. Singed my feathers, I guess."

"Singed your *ass*, maybe," she cracked. "But I won't tell you that. I'll let you buy me a drink to soothe my frazzled nerves." She shuddered from a sudden chill. "You damn fool, I— "

"Private or public drink?" he said smoothly. She knew from those few words the subject of Russ Corey and personal danger was done, finished, over with. *Drop it, lady,* she warned herself. Then aloud, with a smirk: "They have showers in the lounge?"

He laughed and took her arm for the long walk to his quarters. They could have taken the maglev shuttle, but walking on the moon when you had strong muscles and a featherlight body was a joy. The corridors curved and wound gently between numbered caverns and communities. Every effort had been made to eliminate the constant presence of surrounding rock. Every corridor had running water and riotous flora, and their presence served a master well beyond psychology and fresh air. Every corridor was an extension of their round-the-clock farming. Every corridor produced food as well as natural air scrubbers, and every corridor had its touch of luxuriant lunar flower that grew nowhere else on the moon *or* the Earth.

Every corridor for personnel movement, that was. On the next level below were the massive tunnels. These served the construction and survival needs of the Hestia base and the continually expanding communities. They ran plumbline straight between the different base stations, and contained supplies and materials that would last the lunar stations twenty years if every source of supply from the birthworld were suddenly severed. In the light lunar gravity men could move even the heaviest loads on man-powered railcars. At specified "chokepoints" in the underground system new caverns blossomed with construction and drilling equipment. Corey kept his teams always digging horizontally, but vertically as well. His advanced chemical explosives gave him the equivalent of small nuclear weapons to create "instant caverns" but without the associated nuclear radiation or its problems. Far beneath every living and work community on the moon there had been "boomed out" the great caverns for future development. In the interim they were filled with water or converted to near-jungle growth that required no further tending.

"You will never know when things go wrong down on Earth," Russ Corey drilled into the hundreds of people already living in the scattered but connected lunar communities. "When things go from bad to disastrous it will happen before you can do anything about it, and likely you'll never know about it until after it's happened. So you've got to think at all times that you're cut off from Earth, that the ships won't be sailing between us and them, that you *must* live on the food, water, energy, industry, medicine, and recycling of what we have here. Don't think I'm talking about a nuclear war. Your problems won't necessarily come from anything so dramatic. A long famine, an economic disaster, or a shift in the social and political climate could dry up all funds to support what we have here on the moon. Think about that. Think about it a lot. *And always be prepared for it.*"

None of those thoughts attended their dreamlike walk

13

from the Flight Bowl to his quarters. Corey, noted Vicki, was still infused with a quiet exhilaration about his flight. Without conscious thought he took her hand in his. A shock like an electric jolt ran through Vicki's body. Never had she known this form of gentle sharing from Russ Corey. This same man with whom she had made love, sometimes for the sake of his physical relief, sometimes in wild lustful abandon, at times even for sexual and sensual exploration, had never once exhibited a single emotionally warm *touching*. She kept her own movement as light as his, holding firmly but not daring to squeeze his hand in hers, lest the moment vanish suddenly with his realization of his own tenderness. From which he would recoil, and not even God would tell her why, as if his hand were suddenly burned. But the feared withdrawal never came as they wound their way along the corridors, as they went through airlocks standing like sentries between corridors branching away from one another.

Then they were at his quarters, though she preferred the term apartment to something so, well, *official* would do nicely, thank you. Inside, the corridor door closed behind them and a red strip glowed warmly by the door control. No one *locked* their quarters within Hestia. The glowing strip said it all. *This place is occupied. Do not enter without permission*. In this subsurface world where trust was as critical to survival as air to breathe, violating that glowing strip of privacy would have been sacreligious.

He walked toward the shower, shedding clothes as he went. His last covering had fallen to the floor in that slow-motion drop of low gravity when she regained her senses, emerged from the euphoria that swept with them into his apartment. "Russ . . . you want a drink before you shower?"

He stopped and half-turned, splendid and nude, his hand half-raised in a gesture of acknowledgement. "Soon as I'm done, if you would," he said with a nod and started again for the shower.

"The usual?" she called, a bit louder this time.

14

He disappeared around the corner and his voice came back strongly to her. "You got it!"

She stood for several moments, as if she could still see him before her. She could scarcely take her eyes from the man when they were together. So often did she find herself staring at Russ, as if he were a dream come true, that she had to learn *not* to stare in her swirling emotions of love, respect, desire, awe . . . she could have made a list a page long. There were *so many* personalities within Russ Corey. She knew more than most men, certainly more than any other woman, and yet she had never shaken the feeling that he permitted her more than a peripheral glance at his real self, that she was afforded a rare visitor's status, but nonetheless denied full entry into the *person*. Physically, Russ was enough to quicken the senses of any real woman, and for someone who responded with her whole being to a man she wanted, at times she felt almost hypnotized by his presence and, to no lesser extent, simply by knowing how truly extraordinary he was.

The usual adjectives of "handsome" or "macho" didn't apply to Russ; he was so far beyond those socially insipid yardsticks that they never entered her mind. When she looked at Russ Corey she didn't see parts or pieces but *the man*.

She laughed to herself with the thought. Here she was in a luxurious apartment two hundred feet below the surface of the moon, her own world an impossible quarter million miles away, with a man in the shower who'd just finished flying like a bird—*as* a bird, she corrected herself—who'd just walked across his living room stark naked and as unconcerned about her presence as if she wasn't there, and she was in his kitchen squeezing cold oranges to get fresh juice for a screwdriver *just* the way he liked it. An added fillip was the vodka. He insisted that the best of the Russian vodkas didn't touch the smoothness and quality of Suntory, a Japanese brand. *Whatever*, she shrugged.

She listened to his sounds from the shower, saw in her mind's eye the needle spray icing into his skin. The man was tall and at first he appeared to be slender and

15

it was deceptive, for Russ had enormous shoulders and corded muscles and seemed half again as wide as he should have been. He seemed to be all knotted muscle and painfully bunched tendons and scars everywhere. God had carved his face with a crude hatchet. It didn't belong on a man. Mount Rushmore, maybe, because only stone could have done full justice to the scars that marred and streaked his face. Squared jaw, slightly hollowed cheekbones, deep eyes, a thick shock of unruly hair, ears with cuts and nicks as though made of ceramic vigorously slammed with a hammer, and— Her thoughts returned to his eyes.

A shudder rippled her thoughts and her skin. Nothing she had ever seen on *two* worlds matched those eyes. If someone encountered only his gaze and not a single other part of him, his presence was devastating. He had eyes that seemed to grip you physically, that could lift you into the air and shake you like a rag doll. Eyes that evinced scorn when they wished or sent their own message of gentle touch—*you're safe; no need to be afraid*—if that were his meaning.

From the first time they'd met she knew this was a man to whom the use of power was as simple as punching out numbers on a telephone. Tap, tap here and tap, tap there, and men across an entire world reacted and moved the mountains *he* wanted moved. He wielded power with a casual contempt, like the artist who knows without the slightest concern that his brush will produce a masterpiece.

Funny; she had never heard Russ speak to her with the voice that overwhelmed, frightened, even terrified grown men. Men and women exposed to his voice when he was all business or power-wielding likened it to an aural steel or titanium, or some other slashing force. Yet, Vicki smiled to herself, no one could ever recall Russ Corey raising that voice in anger. "I don't need anger," he told her when she queried him on this matter. "At least not for effect. I mean, not for what I mean to happen. That sound crazy? It isn't. Put it this way, Vicki. I never raise my voice to or get angry about someone I do *not* like. I wouldn't waste the effort."

That, she said to herself with a mixture of trepidation and laughter, made those moments when he terrified her a bit more bearable. That, and the realization he would have been stunned to know Vicki had *ever* been the least frightened of him. Because, he might have reasoned if ever she brought up the matter with him (and she would have died before doing *that*), he was a man given to quick wit and humor, and easy laughter. When he laughed aloud his mirth came soft and disarming, a gentle brushing aside of whatever grim moment might be at hand. He laughed because the impulse at whatever pleased him was never contained. The laughter of Russ Corey was as natural as that of a child.

Then there was that other Russ Corey. The brilliant scientist of a dozen disciplines. The master of a dozen engineering and scientific fields. In a world that had come roundly to condemn smoking (which he found ludicrous in the face of devastating air pollution), he could hardly be found without his thin dark cigar clenched in his strong but crooked teeth, or using it as a miniature baton to emphasize his speech or instructions. In his younger days, Vicki learned (and she had researched this man very thoroughly), he had been a brilliant geologist and mechanical engineer, a man with almost a mystical sense of the structure of the Earth, and the moon as well. He became a leading scientist in the planetary sciences. He'd trained his body as hard and constantly as his mind. He needed his physical conditioning so he could with some degree of safety and promise of survival parachute into remote regions or live in the wilds for his studies, ascend high mountains or dare the bubbling cauldrons of angry volcanos. Skill, daring, training, science degrees; they had all been part of his gambit to lock a seat on lunar expeditions. To no small degree his fortune contributed to what he wanted.

How he had amassed his enormous financial and industrial wealth was a tale only Vicki knew. She had been a NASA astronaut and he had flown in Earth orbit with her, and they had traveled to the moon together, and something unspoken passed between them. She did not believe, *could not* believe, that he lived without

17

a woman dominant in his life. But no one knew and she dared not inquire, so she did what a wise woman does who finds herself attractive, for whatever reason!, to so incredible a man. *Go with the flow, honey,* she told herself, and something wonderful took place: she became "his woman" without a word ever spoken of the matter. That didn't mean, however, she couldn't entertain her curiosity of the "other man," the professional, the giant of the industrial and financial worlds.

"Vicki!"

His sudden call came with unexpected abruptness. Just her name from the water cascading over his body. Not a summons; an invitation of one word only she understood completely. She slipped from her clothes, lithe and sinewy, and took up his drink in one hand to join him in the shower. He grinned at the drink. "You're getting to read my mind," he said pleasantly. She handed him the glass and he turned to keep the shower spray from the screwdriver, and he drank long and fully and when he lowered the glass it was empty. "You'll need all that energy," she told him, her hands sliding along his body, inviting hardness and lustful love. He paused only long enough to place the glass on a shelf and they slipped into each other's arms, kissing deeply, and they had no further need for words.

God, how she loved moon gravity! Her arms circled his neck and she raised up her body and he supported her beneath her buttocks, and it was easy and gentle and sure because she weighed only feathers, and slowly and marvelously she impaled herself on him and they made incredible love. When they were done and the glow diffused them both she nibbled on his ear. "I wonder," she whispered, "what the poor flatlanders down below are doing?"

He laughed, easy and warm and satisfied. "If they're trying *this*," he said slowly and comfortably, "they'll damned well have a terrific backache in the morning."

He slid into a deep nap on the floor. No, she corrected herself, on the living carpet she had designed herself. She was an engineer and a test pilot and a

18

scientist and an astronaut, and the single greatest contribution she had made to living on the moon had been her *carpets!* She had calculated lunar gravity and the mass of different materials. When they planned living quarters for the moon bases she had balked at his plans for hard floors. "You've got to make some things *comfy*," she said.

"Comfy?" he echoed.

"Don't say it like it's a dirty word," she giggled.

"What's comfy, then?"

"Luxuriant, deep carpeting. So deep you feel like you're walking on air. So soft you're floating. It makes every apartment a dream to move around in."

"You're not much of a homemaker," he said critically. "I'm living with fractions of pounds for Earth transfer and you're into knee-deep shag. What do you suppose we exchange for the weight and bulk? Food? Medicine? Computers? What?"

"Look, you're setting up a plastifoam processing plant in Hestia, right?" He nodded. "And you can make the stuff so it's got a furry feel." She laughed again at his look. "Well, it *does* feel like fur. Even if it feels like a synthetic fur."

"Okay."

"You put that on a floor and it feels like a cheap rug," she went on. "A really cheap rug. Everything is hard right beneath it. It's like being in a cheap motel room."

"When were you ever in a cheap motel room?"

"A disastrous love affair when I was sixteen, and I'll thank you not to pry. But the carpeting was disgusting and *that's* what we'll have on the moon."

"You have a better idea." Not a question; a statement. "All right, go to it. But stay within the weight and volume restrictions, don't interfere with any other operations, and don't bug me about it again. When you're ready, show me."

Marvelous, she thought. Her plan was simple. The plastifoam came in sheets. The material was absolutely airtight. She had the technicians in the plastifoam plant sew long sections to her exact specifications. Once the instructions went into the computers the machines spit

19

out exactly what she wanted: double-layered plastifoam carpets that fit exactly into the rooms for which it had been cut to size. The carpeting went down, looking all the world like wrinkled skin, disgusting to the eye and repelling to the touch. Then she had air pumped into the space between the two layers, air that stayed in place within the baffles sewn by computer into the layered plastifoam, and *presto!* An incredible living carpet that, in one-sixth gravity—well, no one said it better than Russ Corey the first time he walked that carpet in his bare feet.

"It's like walking on a room filled with tits," he said with a straight face.

She'd made her fame on the moon. And they were the first couple to make love on the lunar living carpet.

He slept through the urgent call signal. Vicki had turned down the volume on the communicator panel, but the bright orange flash that designated a priority message brought her hand with trained swiftness to the response control. She scanned the illuminated bars and pressed PRINTOUT. Immediately the screen flashed the message and simultaneously released a printout on plastiform. She tapped in RECEIVED and took the message extending from the printout slot. It didn't make much sense to her, and rarely did a message come to the Hestia base in code. She knew as much as anyone else among the command and control staff the communications systems and its form for messages, but now she was baffled. She toyed with the printout in her hand, started several times to awaken Russ and each time decided to let him sleep on. A priority message from Earth really didn't mean that much. There was very little that could be decided in a rush when the two worlds remained a quarter of a million miles apart, and anything to do with Hestia base maintenance or support or operations would never have been directed to Russ Corey. Long before now it would have been received, appraised and action started on, on . . . well, whatever it was.

It's just one more enigmatic piece to the biggest

puzzle of all, she mused. She studied Russ in deep sleep on the carpet. She loved this man in a way she'd never thought she could give of herself to any other being. She was grateful for his obvious affection for her, but was it also love? She didn't know and she wouldn't dare to risk a wall between them by insisting upon a declaration. That would have been stupidity beyond all common sense. And Russ Corey had already revealed to her more about himself than anyone else on two worlds knew. So, puzzle or not, there'd be no rocking any boats on her part.

She stood up slowly, deciding to let him sleep another ten minutes while she exposed her body to the solar tanning studio installed in every apartment. She eased into the room, nude, standing on the pedestal that rotated her slowly for full exposure to the ultraviolet rays. Eyes closed, fingertips braced to each side, she gave her body quietly to the tanning radiation. But her mind raced, and she found herself rushing backward in time to when she'd first learned things about Russ Corey that left her gaping, speechless. She was aswirl with mixed emotions: impressed, even overwhelmed, repelled, frightened, and almost crushed with life's own cruelty to this man.

"I didn't know you were married." She rushed after her own words. "I mean, once *were* married." She hated herself for stumbling.

"No sweat," he told her to soothe her obvious discomfort. He went reflective for a while, then obviously came to a conclusion within himself to share with at least one other human being what had been his past, what had happened to him, what sculpted him from the granite of life to become so incredibly wealthy and powerful. His hand patted hers. She dared not grasp or squeeze for fear of—God; she'd been right. His was a gesture and not a clasp. His hand withdrew slowly, almost of its own accord, as he plunged back through his memories.

"One girl. Girl and woman, both. Teri was both," he said slowly, looking off into some distance where only

21

he could return. "I didn't simply love her. All the right words fit. I loved here recklessly and wildly and completely and I couldn't love her enough. Every new day was a challenge to love her even more than I had the day before." Another long silence and his words came unbidden, freed of some terrible restraint that had so long imprisoned them within his mind.

He sighed. "Teri of the golden hair and violet eyes and all that beauty and a mind of," he stumbled for a moment before continuing, "crystal wonder. It's the only way I can describe her and still I can't do her justice." He offered a thin smile to Vicki and she wanted desperately to cry and desperately she fought not to.

"We were married an incredible, breathless two years when she was struck down. They've got a fancy name for it. It's burned into my brain. Amytrophic lateral sclerosis. What they call Lou Gehrig's disease. It hit her like an explosion without sound. That's what it was like. Maybe that was better, although I can't believe anyone that incredible could be . . ." He glanced for a moment at Vicki. "I don't know if there's a God but if there is I'd do everything I could to kill the son of a bitch with my own two hands."

He looked away again. "Almost in a few days and nights—it seemed like that, anyway—she lost the ability to coordinate her own body. A prison was being built around her and somewhere in that prison she was trying to get out, and she couldn't and . . . I was out of my mind. I wanted to kill anything and everybody, take the goddamned disease myself, but it doesn't work that way." Another silence. "The doctors had nothing to offer but bullshit. The few who were honest could only promise her a slow and horrifying ending to which you wouldn't condemn a dog. She didn't want to live any more because she knew what was happening, what *would* happen. She preferred to die a thousand times before she would let herself become a human garbage heap."

He looked along the horizon, seeing the past again in his mind and his heart. "She begged me to take her to the mountains. I did. I took her to an airport in Colorado and I got a small plane and I had to carry her into her seat because she couldn't walk. I landed twelve thousand feet high in the Rockies. She wanted that. I didn't realize for a long time afterward she knew her lungs, her muscles, couldn't handle the thin air. She was pulling the switch I didn't have the guts to pull for her.'

He swallowed hard. "When I carried her from the plane she pointed to a ledge we could see high above us. 'Up there, Russ. Take me up there. Please.' That's all she asked. I carried her there and wrapped her in blankets and held her as tightly and as gently as I could. You could *feel* the pain from her, it was radiating outward from her body, but she never mentioned it. Never complained. That night we had company. The moon. It seemed to hang in the sky just for her. Enormous and pale orange and right over the mountains. Sharp and clear. You could almost reach out and touch it. It was bitter cold and her lungs were knives tearing into her but she didn't move, just lay there against me. Finally she moved her arm and I don't know where she got the strength but she lifted her arm and she pointed at the moon.

"She said to me, 'That's where I'd like to go.' What the hell could I say *to* her! I don't know where the words came from, but I told her that if that's what she wanted, she would. Go to the moon.

"She began to shiver. I don't believe it was the cold. It came from inside. Everything breaking apart, coming to pieces. She said to me, 'I'm going,' and I could hardly hear her words, she was so weak. And then she said, God help me, she smiled when she said it, she said, 'Tonight. Tonight I'm going there. I love you, Russ.'"

Vicki hadn't dared to move or breathe.

"Then she died." He forced something back in his throat before going on. "I stayed with her all night on that ledge. In the morning I carried her body back to the airplane and I flew out. I had the human part of her, the body, cremated."

Suddenly Vicki understood what no one else in this

23

man's life knew. He had taken a tracked crawler by himself from the moon base, violated all his own rules by going out into the vacuum alone. He was gone for three days, and now Vicki understood. *Oh, God* . . . Somewhere out there on the moon, under the skies where the stars shine hard and brilliant and steady, in the sky where Earth herself is a blue marble rolling through an endless black velvet, under that celestial canopy he had buried beneath the surface of the moon the mortal ashes of his beloved.

"I had a promise to keep," he said to her that night when his soul sundered and she had the first deep look within. "But how the hell could I keep it? Get Teri to the moon, I mean. It wasn't enough just to send her ashes there by rocket. Sure, I had enough money and enough pull in the administration to get a research payload up there. That wasn't good enough. I had to carry her there just as I'd carried her up that mountain for her to die."

He shrugged and a smile appeared briefly. "I didn't have enough money, enough pull, whatever it took, to do the job then. So I decided to get what I needed. Any way I could." He looked at Vicki and she saw raw power, unstoppable, even death, in his look. "It didn't matter to me how I did it. And there was one way, the best and the fastest way, to get what I wanted. A single business that did a half trillion dollars' worth of business every year. Beyond the law, mostly untouchable, as mean and rotten and dangerous as any in the world."

Vicki's brows arched. "That would be drugs, wouldn't it." Statement; not a question.

"You bet. I put together the finest and most technologically advanced hit team you can imagine. We had it all. We started coming down on the biggest operators. One in each part of the world. We took everything they had, all their money *and* their drugs, and we set up big buys for their customers, and then we hit them, too. As fast as we brought in the money I moved it into the aerospace and computer industries. It's hard to believe. We moved eighty billion dollars in the first year and

24

suddenly I had the muscle to start my program to get this country back on the moon."

"You must have pleased a lot of people with what you were doing. You were breaking up drug rings and—"

"Pleased some, pissed off most of them, killed as many as we could. Our government made secret deals with us. Information, CIA and other reports from around the world. We lost some good people but we must have run up a kill ratio of a hundred to one. When I had enough to do what I had started, I dropped out of the business, turned it over to my best people, and they set up an international force with Interpol. They're still pretty good at it."

"What happened next?"

"It was horsewhipping and horsetrading time. I met with the right people, bought the right people; I even fronted for some major government contracts. Out of it came the new ships, the new engines and the fuels. Think of it as stoking the fire and helping fuel the machine. That's all there was to it."

The hell it was. She knew better. She was one of the astronauts swept up in the surging heave of the United States to return to the moon. She knew a lot more than most. She and the other members of the new spacecraft wondered where the hell the new push was coming from. They didn't really care because they were wildly exuberant about their new roles, brought in as members of the design teams. New engines, new propellants, new systems, new this and that, an incredible breaking wave upward and outward that by comparison made the old Apollo the crude beginning it truly was. His true role unknown, Russ Corey moved among them. They knew him only as a mining engineer brought into the team to oversee construction of the first deep lunar installations. They never knew it was this same mining engineer who manipulated and pressured and bribed and blackmailed and did whatever was needed to get a powerful force to the moon. They landed robots by the hundreds. Construction equipment drilled and hammered and bored and gouged and clawed into the moon. Rumor had it that small nuclear explosives had been used to rip out the big caverns deep under the moon. The rumors were never proved, and to counter the stories that refused to abate about nuclear radiation on the moon, Russ Corey arranged for a nuclear reactor aboard an unmanned supply ship to crash and explode onto the lunar surface. It hit the moon deep within the Tycho crater hundreds of miles from the Hestia base already spreading laterally as well as deeper into the moon, and it created enough confusion to move the screams and objections to the back pages of the newspapers.

Russ Corey was with his teams on the moon, and he made his soul journey in the tracked vehicle, alone with his memories and the ashes of his love, and he seemed then to be at some sort of peace within himself. He moved in his most trusted lieutenants to run his industries back on Earth. He planned to never again walk the surface of that planet.

Now he flew as a birdman and he slept deeply on the air-cushioned floor of his apartment deep under the surface of the moon. Vicki heard the timer in the solar cubicle and returned to the living room. She stood quietly by his body on the floor. She knew she must awaken him. She didn't know he was awake.

"Your skin glows," she heard him say. She saw his eyes capturing her. "You're very beautiful, Vicki."

"I . . ." A hand fluttered. Her own; she hated that sort of indecisive gesture. "I was going to wake you."

"I know."

"Oh?" She showed her surprise.

"There's a problem."

"But you were asleep! How could you know—"

"It shows. In your face." He raised himself to a sitting position, arms about his knees, studying her. "What is it?"

She brought him the printout. "I don't know what it means," she told him.

He read the message. DUSTBIN. ONE NINE TWO XRAY NINE SIX.

"Damn."

"What is it, Russ?"

He ignored the question. "Call ops for me. If there's no shuttle Earthside in the next three days, tell them to pull out all the stops and get one ready." He shook his head, anger showing in bunched muscles along his neck and shoulders. "Tell them I'll be on it. Oh, yes: no word to *anyone* about this. And we'll be taking the bird down to Scobee Field."

She couldn't believe what she was hearing. Russ . . . going *Earthside?* And based just on this cryptic message? What in the hell was Dustbin? And those code numbers and letters? What were they? And what was—

He saw her confusion. "Don't push it, Vicki. Please do as I've asked."

"I will, I will," she said quickly. "I'm sorry. It's just that all this is so—"

"No explanations now, Vicki. I've got to go back for a meeting. One on one."

She held rigidly to her silence. She was bursting with questions but she stilled her voice. He saw it all, understood. "For your ears only, Vicki."

Afraid to speak, she nodded.

He was slipping into his jumpsuit. "I've got to meet with George Starling."

No holding back the question now. "The president? The president of the *United States?*"

"Yeah," he tossed over his shoulder as he went through the door into the corridor. The door closed. He was gone.

2

*I*cy green water slashed with gale force against the upwind sides of the starboard hull. *Spirit* heeled sharply, and within the cabin Marc Seavers grinned with the unexpected blow that threw him off balance. *Spirit* was a gleaming catamaran of blue and gold fully seventy feet from one sleek end to the other, designed

27

to take anything short of a typhoon and come out racing. But now the gods tested her. The cat's structure trembled from pointed rakish bows to double sterns, the water just choppy enough and the wind strong enough to create a perfect imbalance of forces. The sleek catamaran cut water and tried to hold course from her hull pressure and speed, fighting the wind whipping and carving hollows beneath the hulls as water tore away. Seavers glanced up as if he could see directly through the rounded Fiberglas shape of his cabin; in his mind's eye he did just that. He "saw" clearly the two masts straining from the forces of their sails before the angry wind. A touch of caution came unbidden to his mind and he offered up a sardonic grin to his natural instincts of safety and survival. Unseen and utterly alone in the vast expanse of the Pacific Ocean, he extended his right hand and offered up his middle finger to the gods who dallied and raced along this great liquid bulge of the planet.

No hand held *Spirit* on her course. Seavers' seeming recklessness was more indifference than any measure of courage. He'd been tested and scarred and proven his steel many years and on many occasions before this moment. He knew no fear of what the growing storm might do to the catamaran or to him. He had long been beyond fear. The accelerating fury of wind and ripping sea could well break up *Spirit*, tear sails, snap a mast; whatever. Marc Seavers braced himself in the cabin, perfectly content with his gamble that the three computers he'd designed for this twin-hulled challenger of the deeps would sniff out and judge and feel and taste and respond to every slash and cut and parry of the ocean and all it had to offer. Or to throw at him. Three *America Cup* computers—he'd liked his touch in their naming—measured the myriad and constantly changing forces of the ocean and slavishly attended to their duty of adjusting sail and heading and correction for wind and sea.

Marc Seavers had designed those computers and he'd installed them in *Spirit*, their electronic systems linked to controls and gears and pushpull rods and cables so that with the memory of the man who'd programmed them they would survive the growing fury or they would, like their human charge who didn't really give a damn, drown and sink forever into what might as well have been a bottomless ocean. The catamaran took a particularly nasty jolt, the sharp prows bursting high out of water and the double-hulled structure groaning and flexing as the computers made thousands of judgements and measurements every second to bring the double nose back on the course the man had punched into the electronics. Seavers fell against his bunk. Balancing himself instinctively, he looked into the rounded face of the porthole opposite him and saw not water, but needles of spray wind-whipped horizontally as it flashed through his view.

"Do your worst!" he shouted. "Give it everything you've got! I'm ready for you, you bastards!"

The wind shrieked at him and every inch of *Spirit* trembled. Seavers smelled and tasted sharp salt in the air and on his skin; hell, the salt was everywhere, the cold hovered and prodded against the survival gear encasing his body. A man could freeze to death in this icy, salty wind, but Marc Seavers wouldn't freeze. *No such luck*, his inner voice said, unbidden. But it was true. With his layered clothing proven in the utterly savage cold of the Antarctic night, no damned Pacific breeze was going to ice his skin and bones, no matter how fierce its blow. Besides, going out from freezing would have been too easy. Quitting. It was a hell of a thing to be thirty-three years old and in terrific physical shape and not give a damn about living or dying. He offered up a mental shrug to the seesaw battle in his mind. *That's the way it is*, he heard that inner voice again, but this time it seemed to be taking a devil's advocate position and arguing against his instincts for survival. *Jesus, you could go bananas fighting with yourself like this*. Again the thought intruded into his carefully disciplined routine of either concentrating only on what he was doing or merely going blank. It didn't always work. He'd been trained and triple-trained and disciplined for the mental work ethic as long as he could remember, and no level of personal disaster, even with what had come so close to crushing him, could turn off his mind for long. *Shut up!* he cried within his mind, but the self-admonition failed in its intended effect, and his suddenly administered try at shutting off his thoughts seemed to blow away in the icy gale, as if the howling winds might be blowing into the cabin and through his skull as well.

He braced himself again through a long shuddering swing of the big catamaran, muscles flexing, knees bending just right as the cat slammed down on the water, slewing suddenly, then obeying the thrust and pressure and push of its sails as the superfast computers dueled furiously with wind and seas. Marc Seavers sighed to himself. He didn't want to live, there was too much pain, but he had too much appreciation of life just to slap a .38 muzzle against the side of his head and blow away his skull and brains. That was too easy. Even the thought of suicide repelled him, churned both stomach and mind. The pain inside him wouldn't go away, but neither would the real Marc Seavers, to whom life had always been the arena for contest and winning. No; he might set up risks that *seemed*, if not suicidal, at least so gravely against his survival that he had a good chance of placing himself in a position from which he might not be able to extricate his physical self, and then, no matter what he did, he could accept death knowing he'd fought it right down to the wire. But he *must* fight. *Even if I've stacked the deck against me*, he grinned ruefully.

He hated this side of himself that so enjoyed the battle. He *couldn't help* fighting with all his might, with every fibre of his being. He cursed himself anew and turned to the electronics rack before him, slipping off his right glove so his forefinger could tap the buttons in the sequence he wished. He had the crazy fleeting thought that part of his genetic memory must have included cousins from the Norse gods. Faint images of Valhalla and Asgard ghosted through his mind. He could almost hear distant strains of Wagner.

Next I'll be hearing music from "Ring of the Nibelungs."

He conjured a mental scene, if somewhat gauzy and ephemeral, of Wotan drifting across the rainbow bridge into the realm of the gods in their castle of Valhalla. *Sure, that's all I need, warrior maidens and dead heroes tramping through my brain. Or what's left of it* . . . Well, it was music that he wanted and it lay here before him in the electronic rack waiting for the finger jabs to bring it alive. He thrust from his thoughts mythic grandeur so he could concentrate on the music he'd planned for just this moment.

His finger stabbed the SELECT button for the first tape. Kitaro's *Oasis*. He'd start off this session, when the winds peaked to their strongest and the ocean hurled daggers at him, with music that reached gently out to him. From *Morning Prayer* through *Aratanaru Tabiji*, Kitaro's *New Wave*. Not of water *per se* but of spirit. Hell, that's appropriate, he conceded, considering the name of this split-tailed tub. He knew the other numbers by heart and knew also that his conscious appreciation of what he'd be hearing would perk up when the strains of *Shimmering Horizon* mixed with the scream of wind.

He depressed the second button for another Kitaro series with the simple title of *Ki*. Enough selections in here to bring even more meaning to what might be his final moments. *Stream of Being* to *Endless Water* and finally to *Cloud in the Sky* as the final number. "Leave it to the Japanese to make it only *one* cloud," he grumbled aloud and went on to the third tape.

Daniel Kobialka's *Mind Dance* offered a *Bolero Medley* that would set the stage for two music passages he had always loved: *Clair de Lune* and then *Song for Lisa* that Debbie loved so much and—

Oh, Jesus. You son of a bitch . . . A cry of anguish burst from him and he bit down so hard on his lip from inner pain that blood spilled down his chin, salty as the air and the sea but hot and angry. A face swam before his eyes and he bit down again until his teeth raked his lip and through blurred vision he glanced down and saw his own blood on his survival suit. He wiped his lips with the back of one hand, feeling needles punctur-

31

ing him from head to foot, a measure of physical pain that might blot out the anguish of his heart. His eyes raised to heaven. "Please, God, not again. Let it be, let it be . . ."

He gritted his teeth, felt *Spirit* groan from another barrage of roaring wind, and went back to the music selection rack. His finger stabbed the title *Deep Breakfast*. What a damned dumb name for one of the most stunning musical passages he'd ever heard. He had thought Ray Lynch was crazy until he understood the meaning of the composer, who had once told a friend: "You must be starved, old friend. Come into my apartments, and we'll suffer through a deep breakfast of pure sunlight." Good enough, Ray Lynch, wherever and whoever the hell you are.

That would be enough to mix mind and music with wind and water; from this moment on he wanted the sound to come louder and louder to crash over and against and through him. He worked the computer control for the music rack so that when *Midnight Blue* slid into position and tore from the powerful speakers imbedded in the cabin and the hull, all about him on the decks, he would be inundated with the crystal, soaring voice of Louise Tucker. For an unguarded moment his memory hurried back in time and he barely snatched control from the face that rose in his mind.

Flashdance clicked into position. Irene Cara's voice would go right through him with the opening number, and he tapped buttons rapidly so that after each successive number on the tape, *What A Feeling* would play before the next number in line. Power and energy and life would surge from the speakers to tear over him, to make him one with the moment and the danger.

Then the entire sound track from *Close Encounters*. The whole works, every inch, every decibel, soft to furious, childlike and steamy to raw power. His finger stabbed and the electronics obeyed and the next tape moved into its slot.

He laughed aloud as he brought into position a long double tape of *Star Wars* and *The Empire Strikes Back*. He didn't know *why* he'd insisted to himself that he must include this music. The magic of a much earlier age and the magic of imagination and power all rolled into—well, into whatever it was that called to him.

His laughter ebbed when he came to Vangelis' *Chariots of Fire*. That was so goddamned real to this very moment . . . That's not what bothered him, he admitted to himself. It was the composer. And it wasn't this tape. It was that *other* one Vangelis had done. Every time he heard it the music hurled him violently back to the horror and agony of those months of bitter survival in Antarctica. How the hell had Vangelis even selected the *name*? A dazzling and shattering strain of memory and cold and isolation that he called *Antarctica*. Memory and cold and misery, to be sure, but isolation is a relative affair. He and the others had been isolated from the world when disaster struck their research base at the bottom of the world, but they weren't isolated from cold beyond belief, from savage pain and purple limbs that rotted away, and their worst fear was their own isolation from sanity. Isolation lay in the frozen corpses. Isolation lay in timelessness of a wind that woman-screamed and in cold that mocked all their struggles to stay warm enough just to survive. Marc Seavers would never forget the moment when the clouds broke for a few hours. Against all the dictates of common sense warning him to conserve his energy, not to exert himself, not to break the seal leading to the grinding teeth of polar cold, against every shred of sanity, he went outside. The temperature was somewhere about a hundred degrees below zero; he didn't know. The gauges had frozen and cracked at that point. But it didn't matter. Bundled and wrapped until he moved like a stumbling potato sack he went through the zigzagging tunnels, the frozen snow beneath him crunching, the sound of crystals breaking and screaming in tiny voices, and he went up the spiral stairway, his mouth and nose covered so his own exhalations would help warm the air he must breathe, because they were out of the cool oxygen by now, and in this murderous temperature cool oxygen was pleasantly *warm*. But he forced his way up and around and managed to grind open the hatch to the outside world and by some miracle even the winds had died down so that the air was frozen transparent but the flinging knives of wind-lashed cold were absent for this briefest of respites.

Marc Seavers looked out from the bottom of the world to a sight few men had ever seen. He knew he was on *top* of a world with its gravity gone crazy. An image flashed into his mind of a huge globe and a sliver of a man standing upside down along its icy bottom staring outward—down? up?—at stars unbelievably clear and shining without the first shimmer or twinkle and then the brightest star in all that firmament rose upward from the horizon and began to race across the blackness in which the distant suns hung suspended like ornaments. He blinked and he stared at the brilliant light sailing impossibly through the space ocean to follow an invisible curve and then he realized he was looking at one of the great shuttle spacecraft launched into polar orbit from Vandenberg Air Force Base in California.

Unbidden, spontaneous, explosive, a cry of *"Heyyyy!"* burst from him, his voice snatched up by the cold and flung away across ice and snow, and as if in answer the first sharp blade of a renewed wind stabbed at him. He ignored the teeth of cold trying to tear at his flesh. By the time the light fell ever smaller to disappear around the far side of the planet the wind was howling and another killer storm rampaging toward him. He fought his way back to the entrance and under the thick padding his face was grinning, for he felt a warmth that could never come from the outside but only from his heart.

Life. Damn, he'd seen life hurtling above, and within that shining light there were power and warmth and men and women, and he knew that despite their knowing they could do nothing to help the isolated band imprisoned and buried within the Antarctic winter, they would have looked down. To hell with not *seeing*. He *knew*, and somehow he knew also that they sensed, there was this life down here, hanging on, grim and tenacious, specks of human determined to fight, to last out the worst nature had to offer. He dogged the hatch behind him and wound his way carefully down the spiral steps to the ice-buried base camp, and when he returned to the almost graven images staring at him, they thought he'd snapped, had gone crazy, because Marc Seavers was grinning and his face was bright and alive, and only a crazy man could grin after the Antarctic earthquake and shifting of mountains that had trapped them at the bottom of the world where no ship could move, no airplane could fly, where even their radios were dead and the rest of humanity was a billion miles away. Marc Seavers came back from topside with his grin. . . .

He stared at his finger in the shuddering, careening cabin of *Spirit*, the finger poised over the button that would slide the haunting, icicle-tinkling strains of Vangelis' *Antarctica* into its numbered slot. My God, he'd been back there. . . . A shudder spasmed his muscles and he shook himself like a wet dog to shove away the moment, and his hand moved and poised over the last button. A smile creased his stubbled face.

This was more like it. His select, chosen finale. The creation long ago of Alan Hovhaness, a celebration of life and surging energy, of wonder and . . . *And God Created Great Whales*. A magnetic capture of Kostelanetz and great whales recorded in the deeps, woven together with the magic of imagination and music, captured here for him. His finger stabbed the button and the tape clicked into place. Done, by damn.

Seavers stood as straight as the thundering wind and ocean would allow him. He breathed deeply and checked the harness secured about his body on the outside of his survival suit. He fought his way to the hatch, braced himself, and shoved it aside. Wind screamed at him and spray slashed at him and he grinned anew because he loved the sea and found no enemy here. He secured the hatch, grasped the guideline and made it to the two posts he'd built into an afterdeck of the catamaran. A blast of wind threw him against one post with a painful jarring. He winced with the sudden pain in his shoulder, grasped the post and snapped a steel hook from the post to his left-side harness. He did the same by his

35

right side and now he was part of *Spirit*, linked by steel hook and cable to the wildly lurching catamaran crashing through the swells and hammered by the shrieking wind.

The music began, the haunting strains of Kitaro mixing with turbulent water and howling gale. He'd set the amplifier for full power, more than a thousand watts erupting from the speakers all about him, and he forgot the cold and the slashing salt knives and he knew no fear, none, though he knew his life might be measured in hours. His face began to bleed from the cutting edge of wind-driven salt and water and as fast as the thin haze of red appeared the same wind and water drove it away. He gave himself to sky and ocean and his music and his mind began to drift, a deep mindsigh of peace that no one else in all the world could even begin to understand. And it didn't matter.

The ghostly remains of a distant star slid into grey horizon and brought darkness to the ocean world. Marc Seavers had about him the running lights of *Spirit* and ghostly phosphorescence of the broiling sea and he drew to him the long night to come, the fury of the elements. He slipped into what might be an unbidden, unplanned cleansing of his soul, alone, alone in the midst of the largest ocean on the planet, and the music swirled about and enveloped him and he slipped away into his past. There was release there.

And there was pain.

He slid back through the memory corridors of his subconscious, the journey unbidden, unwanted but totally beyond his control. There appeared a flashing mixture of images from within the base, the contorted features of Carl McIver who'd gone mad and attacked their generating plant with an axe. For a fraction of an instant the tableau was there, McIver, the axe bloody from the three people he'd killed; and Seavers could *feel* his hand sliding down to his boot and the heft of the heavy knife he always carried there. No gun. What the hell would a man be doing in the confines of a buried Antarctic station with a *gun*? Yet before him was a madman who'd snapped from the forces that tore at men's souls and if he ripped up that generating station then they would *all* die, and in a single instant and flowing motion the knife was out of its boot sheath and became a flash of light in the air and buried itself up to the hilt in McIver's neck. He toppled in slow motion, much slower than the blood that spurted out in a long glistening line from his neck and *stop it!* Seavers' mind shouted to another part of itself, and he had the feeling that sombody, something was saying, *what the hell; that's not important, anyway,* and that was warning enough of what might yet come, but what could he do about his subconscious having its own way?

Whatever was that voice, it was right. Antarctica was not very important. One hundred and twenty men and women were in that base when the tearing *CRACK!* of the earthquake shattered much of the station and severed power cables and smashed communications, tore down antennae, swallowed up their tracked vehicles, turned the ice runway into tumbled huge cakes and spears of killer ice and condemned them all to die because they faced a storm that would last for over a month. No way to get out and no way for anyone to get in and the power was almost gone and they were frightened, and that storm that would last a month howled and gibbered for twice that time and most people gave them up for dead.

That wasn't important. What mattered was that the storm ended finally and the first teams flew down to the bottom of the world and reported to a stunned and jubilant nation that of the hundred and twenty souls given up for lost, Marc Seavers against all odds had kept his team alive and that seventy-nine men and women were coming out. The first reports twisted and seemed a bit distorted from the hysteria and joy mixed in with their details, but clearly it was this one man to whom they owed their survival. The name of Marc Seavers leaped onto the headlines and splashed across television screens and everyone dug frantically for pictures and film of the man hardly anyone in the public arena knew. Stocky, rugged, five-foot-ten and two hundred five pounds of solid meat and tendon on the wide-shouldered frame of an athlete and navy diver, sharp and piercing dark eyes beneath a shock of unruly black hair. *And* a brain, a navy scientist, *by God!* And he'd commanded a destroyer and he'd also been a submarine commander, and a leader of research submarine expeditions, and the country lavished its attention on a bona fide, genuine, twenty-four-karat honest-to-God *hero*, who was known to be a quietly religious man and his wife, and wasn't she beautiful? Deborah, and two daughters, Karen and Missy—

Well, how had he pulled off the impossible? The first evacuees of the forever night of Antarctica were those with arms or legs that had been cut away with saws and knives so they could survive their gangrene, and there were a few with chest ailments and another with a bad heart, those came out first, and they all spoke of this incredible Marc Seavers. *How did he do it?*

Oh, he was an incredible bastard. Meaner than a starving mule or an angry water buffalo. Newsmen blinked. "But that was the only way. He was cruel to us. He as soon punched out a woman as a man. We were miserable and weak and we just wanted to die and he wouldn't let us do that. He was almost savage in his treatment of us, the way we had to help ourselves and one another. He made us keep work schedules and we all learned how to be doctors because our doctor was dead and . . ." Leadership, courage, strength, belief in God, belief in country and in his family: all of it made his indomitable spirit. One man looked into the face of a television camera. He forced himself up on one elbow from his stretcher at the evacuation airfield. "I hate Marc Seavers. I had to hate him. That's where I got my strength. He *made* me and the others hate him. That's why we're alive. I'd follow him to hell anytime. I've been there the last couple of months. I hate him and I love him . . ."

Commander Marc Seavers, U.S. Navy, was the last man to leave the broken, crumpled remains of the Antarctic science station. He sat in the navy transport plane and he sat numbed, wrapping this new time about his body and his soul, because he didn't have to *do* anything now, he didn't need to think or survive or be a leader, it was all done and every passing minute brought him miles closer to Deborah and Karen and Missy who were waiting for him at Pensacola Naval Air Station in Florida where it was warm and there was a beach and . . . He slept almost all the way home, and he woke only when it was time to eat. They made him drink and eat because they feared for his health even though the doctors were stunned with his excellent physical condition. But hardly anyone talked with him because Marc Seavers didn't want to talk or think. He hurt, a wonderful deep ache that warmed him body and soul in his incredible reaching out from within for his wife and his children.

His old mentor and friend, Admiral Luther Averil Duncan, tall and forbidding beneath his shock of thick white hair, waited for him. Standing six feet eight inches tall with a Lincolnesque nose and an awkwardly assembled body, holder of the Medal of Honor from some war past—well, he expected Duncan to be there. He caught sight of that tall angular shape standing head above the crowd along the flight line as they swept by on the landing roll. Seavers strained to see Debbie and the girls but it was too fast and they were lost amidst the crowd of well-wishers, and he had no choice but to wait. He forced himself to breathe deeply and evenly. This would be no time to get giddy! He smiled when he thought of how the girls would regard the thick beard he had sworn not to shave off until he and his family were again together. His heart beat faster as they taxied back and the transport eased to a stop with the cabin door directly before the center of the greeting stands. Seavers sighed. He didn't need this protocol nonsense, but it *was* Navy and so was he, and he understood. But first, before all else, he wanted to grab all three of his girls, wife and daughters, and sweep them up in his arms.

He went down the stairway first, saw Duncan and another officer halfway to the plane. Damned official folderol. The admiral had his hand out and Seavers

39

snapped off a salute and grasped the firm, huge hand of his old friend. He tried to lean around Duncan to see Deborah, but there was this other officer, a four-striper, and he was in the way.

"Where's my wife?" Seavers asked the admiral. "What the hell, I can't see her or—"

The four-striper pushed closer. "Commander, I'm Captain Haggerty. And I—"

Seavers pushed him aside as politely as he could, but very firmly, looking for Deborah. The four-striper grasped his arm.

"Commander, that's also Chaplain Haggerty."

Seavers turned with a snapping body motion that was almost audible. Somewhere in the back of his mind a thin scream was beginning, a whispering primeval gibbering cry—

"Your wife and children are dead, Commander Seavers."

He stared. He tried to talk but he couldn't. For that terrible moment of no-time there was nothing, no talk, no racing thoughts, no pain. A no-time numbness. It fled.

"*What?*"

"Mrs. Seavers, Commander. She and your daughters were killed. It was an accident. On the highway. A drunken driver." The hand moved on his arm. Horrible, slimy.

"What?" A hollow word this time drifting from a slack lower lip. No air in his lungs. No brain to work. Slop for muscles.

"I'm sorry, Commander."

"What did you say?"

"I, uh, I said I'm very sorry, Commander."

From some remnant of peripheral vision he saw the admiral moving closer. But he ignored him. The world became only this simpering, uniformed *I'm sorry*. He gaped. *I'm sorry*. This was all he had left of Deborah and Karen and Missy and . . . He started forward, blinded with salt in his eyes, a roaring in his ears, a world of red, shrieking pain growing and leaping within him.

That goddamned hand again on his arm! "Commander, if there's anything I, we can do, just *anything* . . ."

Seavers' right arm came around in a devastating backhand to crash with terrible force against the side of the chaplain's face. He never realized the blow, the crushing force of his powerful arm, nor did he hear the cheekbone breaking and the splash of gore that exploded outward from the chaplain's face.

He didn't remember that. He had no memory of the next three days and nights. He wasn't there. Not in his body, not in his own mind. He was somewhere in a burning fierce limbo where all was pain, where there was nothing but pain.

"*No*, damn it!" Admiral Duncan slammed a powerful hand against his desk. "He's *not* trying to kill himself. I know Marc Seavers too well to believe that for a moment." Duncan swore to himself from the stinging in his palm. He rubbed his hands briskly and fumbled in his desk drawer for a cigarette. No one else in his office smoked. Duncan put a *Sailor's Choice* between his lips and realized he'd become the point of silent attention. He lifted bushy white brows. "Who's got a match, damn it?"

His aide flicked a Dunhill gold lighter to life and held it for the admiral. Duncan smiled. He'd given Lieutenant Atkins that lighter. The young man didn't smoke, never had, likely never would, but his admiral did, and who was going to tell a man who'd been wounded nine times in four wars that smoking was dangerous to his health? The Dunhill was a routine they'd developed between them just to keep everyone else off balance.

Duncan drew deeply, exhaled and then held the cigarette lightly but firmly between his teeth. "I repeat," he picked up where they'd left off, "suicide is simply not in this man's makeup."

A captain motioned his objection and Duncan nodded. "Sir, he's been climbing mountains. Wearing *sneakers*. Not mountain gear, Admiral. Sneakers, of all things! He—"

"Didn't he climb the Matterhorn?"

41

"Sir?" The captain did a quick swallow in realization of the corner into which he'd painted himself. "Uh, yes, sir, he did, but—"

"That means he's right and all you clowns are wrong, doesn't it?" Duncan pressed. "If the sneakers are so damned lethal, how'd he get to the top of that mountain and all the way back down again? Safely, I might add."

"What about his skydiving, Admiral?" Duncan looked at the grizzled old marine colonel. The admiral laughed and pointed at the man's chest. "You're a fine one to talk, Smitty. I see seven rows of ribbons on your ugly chest. *And* a combat infantryman's badge. *And* a set of paratrooper wings."

"Yessir," growled the marine.

"How many jumps, Smitty?"

"Eight hundred and sixty-four."

"Shut up, Smitty."

"Yessir."

Duncan looked about his office. "Anyone else with Seavers' plans for committing suicide?"

Commander Arturo Perez gestured and Duncan nodded to him. "Admiral, you know about *Spirit?*"

"Yes. The catamaran. Isn't he ready to shove off?"

"Almost, sir," Perez replied. "He's waiting for the weather to change."

"I thought the weather was fine."

"That's the problem," Perez said. "Commander Seavers—"

"Captain. As of tomorrow," Duncan broke in.

"Yes, sir. The problem is that Captain Seavers is waiting for the weather to *worsen*. There's a big trough working its way down the Pacific. It will be nasty for at least five to eight days."

"And he plans to get right in the middle of that mess."

"That's the size of it, Admiral." Perez hesitated. "He's going to try the Pacific in that catamaran on his own."

Duncan stubbed out the cigarette. "Not quite. Computer systems to run his toy, right?"

"Yes, sir."

"And Seavers is one of the best computer people in the navy, isn't he?"

"Yes, sir, but—"

"But *what?*"

"Computers don't have seamanship, Admiral."

Duncan smiled. "Well said. But Marc Seavers *does* have seamanship."

"Admiral, I'm really not being contentious—"

"Hell, I know that, Art."

"Thank you, sir. But the odds are lousy."

"Taking your way of thinking, Art, there are *still* those odds. You know what Marc Seavers is doing? It's not suicide, no matter what you may think. He's throwing the dice. Playing the odds. But it's not just a crap shoot. He's gambling on his own skills, his experience, whatever it is that makes him. San Diego to Nagoya, Japan, right? All alone in that catamaran except for his computers and his supplies, right?" Duncan offered the assembly before him a thin smile and then he placed both huge hands on his desk, leathery palms down.

"I got ten thousand dollars says he makes it. *And* that he sets a new record doing it."

His officers shifted uncomfortably, staring from one face to another before turning back to the admiral. "How about you, Smitty?" Duncan addressed the marine colonel. "You're a betting man."

"I don't bet a man's life, Luther."

"You're full of shit, too, Colonel. Do you think he'll make it?"

"Maybe."

"Put up or shut up, Smitty." The colonel answered with silence. Duncan locked eyes with each man in turn. "Anybody else?" The admiral leaned back and smiled. "Thank you, gentlemen. Oh, Art?"

"Sir?" Commander Perez stood before his desk.

"That other, ah, matter?"

"Taken care of, sir."

"Good day, Commander."

"Good day, sir," Perez said. Outside the headquarters building he left the others to make absolutely certain of that "other matter."

She came out of hiding on his second morning at sea, the western coast of California and Mexico already far behind and falling farther back with the quickening wind. Nancy Parks was a beauty, redheaded and spattered with light freckles and a body that would have satisfied either chorus girl or Olympic athlete. She slipped from the cabin to the deck in tight jeans and deck shoes, high full breasts thrusting tightly against her midriff tie shirt. She leaned easily against the cabin and smiled at Marc Seavers.

"Hi," she said brightly. "I'm for real. You're not seeing things."

Seavers looked at her without blinking or smiling, and she felt a pang of caution. "Who the hell are you?" he demanded.

"Nancy Parks. I'm twenty-two years old and your friends, your *best* friends, set this up and smuggled me aboard." She gestured to hold off what promised to be an angry outburst. "I didn't come here to intrude but to help. I'm free and white and sexually liberated and I don't care if we make love or not. That's up to you. But I'm a better wind sailor than you, Marc Seavers, and I've been sailing all my life. I—"

"You talk too much. You're not welcome aboard this boat." He'd sized it up in a matter of moments. He knew what was going on. That son of a bitch. Admiral or no admiral, he'd kill Luther Averil Duncan when he saw him. He shook his head. *No; the old bastard meant well. Have I been grieving that much? Is it that bad to my friends?* Too bad. This girl is beautiful and she's obviously for real. But that's her problem. *I'm not ready yet. Deborah is still too much a part of me. I can't stop seeing Karen and Missy.*

Seavers sighed. "It's not your fault. I know that. You meant well."

She was fighting back sudden tears. The pain came from this man like heat radiating from a hot stove. She tightened her lips and nodded in agreement.

"We take turns eating, we take turns sleeping, you do not bug me, you do not interfere with the sailing of

44

this cat, and you never, absolutely never, touch the computers. Understood?"

She forced her head higher. "Yes, I understand you. But I don't understand *why*."

"That doesn't matter. It's none of your business. I'm going by the Hawaiian Islands. You get off there."

Nancy Parks, he judged after another day and a half, was made of fine, pure steel. She was more beautiful than he'd realized and her body could easily have graced a Playboy centerfold. *And* she was a good cook and a good sailor and he was amazed she kept her silence. He spoke hardly another dozen words to her until they reached Hawaii and he hailed a coast guard vessel to come alongside. She was just about to leave *Spirit* when his powerful hand grasped her wrist. He held her eyes.

"Thank you, Nancy Parks," he said quietly, and then stepped back.

She wept until the sails of *Spirit* disappeared beyond the horizon.

He stood the violent night through, steel-cabled to the two posts on the afterdeck of the catamaran, pummeled and battered by wind and slashing sea, and the music played endlessly and on and on, the tapes running through to their final chords and the computer setting them around for another complete run-through. He slept standing up, slammed and punished uncaringly, and his eyes stared red and sore at the grey ghosting of dawn come the morning. Within the next hour the wind died to a ghost of its angry night passage. He unhooked the cables as the seas calmed and the first breaks appeared in the horizon. Yet the wind remained strong enough to keep *Spirit* hissing through the water at high speed. Seavers had heard the music all the night through until it was second nature to his thinking, and not until he sighted the distant thin plumes rising from the sea was he aware that his generators were still pumping a thousand watts of power through the amplifier and into the speakers, and with the shriek of wind

45

gone, the sound boomed away for miles across the open water and resonated through the deeps.

Those distant thin plumes. *Whales . . . whales answering the genius of Hovhaness.* He was stunned to see the life marching across the waters, more of the enormous creatures spouting until he saw them as far as the horizon. *And God Created Great Whales.* The music, and the cry through the deeps, and here was his answer.

Life.

He had pushed through the despair. He felt strangely at peace and infused with a new strength, his body uncaring of the punishment it had taken the night through. He went into the cabin and switched off the speakers, shut down the electronic control rack for the crashing music. Now he wanted the sound of wind and water and rushing hull, one with nature. No electronic call, nothing mechanical. He made strong coffee and he returned with the coffee pot and a heavy mug to the deck and sat cross-legged atop the cabin. He drank coffee and accepted the sea and searched himself.

Goodbye, Deborah. Karen. Missy. You belong in the memories of my heart. It's time to let you go.

The thunder brought him awake. He must have slept for hours atop the cabin, *Spirit* guided by the controlled force fields of her electronic helm. But the thunder . . . he looked about him, puzzled at the sky mostly rich blue and the clouds high and distant. He recognized the sound, then. Big rotors. Really big. Before he had them in sight he knew they were the huge battle helicopters of his navy. They boomed at him from out of the north, and for another puzzled moment that made no sense because they were too far from land.

They had to be from a carrier. They came in fast and deliberate, one standing off and the second coming in close, *USS Saratoga* brilliant and white along the fuselage and a crewman in the open side door signalling him to respond by radio. He went into the cabin and switched on his equipment and made contact.

"Please stand down your sails, Captain Seavers. This

is Commander Wright from *Saratoga*. I request permission to come aboard with a crew, sir."

Seavers didn't waste time with stupid questions. All this, whatever the devil it was, came with very good reasons behind it. He brought in the sails and the chopper slid overhead, riding its storm of downbeating air, and three men rode the cable sling down to the catamaran. Moments later he was talking with Commander Wright in the cabin.

"We're here to pick you up, sir. We'll leave a crew aboard to bring your vessel back to port. We're to take you immediately to the carrier."

It was happening too fast. "What's this about, Commander?"

Tod Wright was all navy and all business and as crisp as a newly starched shirt. "I'm not aware of the reasons, sir. Just my orders. To bring you as quickly as possible to *Saratoga*."

"*Whose* orders, man!"

Commander Wright answered carefully and deliberately. "Sir, I was instructed to tell you the orders come directly from Admiral Luther Duncan. I am also instructed to tell you this is a code seven five five, sir." The commander went silent, waiting for Seavers' response.

Marc Seavers stared at the officer who'd dropped in from the sky to the catamaran. He blinked several times. It all began to register in his skull. This was no game. Seven Five Five was the highest priority code in the business. It went all the way to the White House. Seavers nodded to Wright. "Okay. Let's go," he said and went topside to the deck. He hand-signalled the chopper crew to bring down the sling. Commander Wright was by his side immediately, shouting over the engine and wind roar of the big chopper. "Don't you want to take anything with you, Captain?"

Seavers gave him a brief, enigmatic smile. "Not any more, Commander. Thanks, but I've got everything I need right here," and he tapped a forefinger against the side of his head. He looked up and waved and lifted into the sky.

47

*   *   *

Two hours and twenty minutes later, a brief but high-energy meal in his system, clothed in a perfectly fitting partial-pressure suit and helmet, he was in the back seat of an F-14 Tomcat fighter racing eastward. To each side of him the great wings were folded back to make a huge arrowhead of the airplane, hurled along with huge engines at supersonic speed. The Pacific drifted below like a map unrolling. Seavers depressed his transmit button to speak by intercom to Lieutenant Bob Davis in the front seat.

"Lieutenant, how long will we be on the ground at Pearl?"

A chuckle came into his helmet. "The only way we'll see Pearl Harbor, sir, is from ten miles up. Look ahead of us at two o'clock, Captain. Just below the horizon. That's a KC-10 waiting for us at angels forty two. We'll hook up to refuel and keep right on going."

Seavers nodded to himself, then thought better of his silence. You don't leave the other man wondering whether you've received his words. "Got it," he said.

"Captain, we got quite a ways to go," Davis said over the intercom. "I'd sure recommend you get some shut-eye if you'd like. When they briefed me they said you hadn't had much sleep for a while."

"Thanks, Lieutenant."

He closed his eyes. He'd intended to watch the entire refueling rendezvous and hookup with the KC-10. He never saw that airplane again. When his eyes opened and he sat straight he looked to the dark—*dark? how long have I slept?*—horizon ahead of them. A soft glow diffused the horizon. "Davis, where are we?" he mumbled into his microphone.

A cheery voice boomed back to him. "Good morning, Captain! You're making a scenic arrival with Tomcat Airlines, courtesy of the United States Navy, to the west coast of the good old U.S.A. Directly ahead of us, sir, that's the Los Angeles area, and to the right San Diego's coming in pretty clear."

Seavers rubbed his eyes. The pilot up front must be a mind reader. "Sir, down to your left, by your knee.

Coffee thermos. The quantity is corrected for pressure differential in the cockpit, but I'd recommend the straw. It's a hell of a way for a man to drink his coffee but it's better than all over your lap."

"Thanks, Davis." He took several long sips and felt life returning to him. "We landing at Dago?"

The answer surprised him. "No, sir," Davis came back at once, crisp and professional again. He offered a quick explanation for a hammering conclusion to their flight. "My orders are to take this go-buggy straight to Ent."

"Ent?"

"Sorry, sir. That's Ent Air Force Base in Colorado, near the Springs."

Ent Air Force Base? In Colorado? What in the hell for! The echoes and questions repeated in his mind but he kept his silence with Lieutenant Davis. The man was a fighter pilot and nothing else for this moment. Besides, he knew even less than Seavers was already able to deduce, even if that deduction was skimpy. It was something big enough for the navy to find him in the middle of the Pacific Ocean, move two big choppers into position from the *Saratoga* to pick him up, leave a crew on *Spirit*, and— Sure, they hadn't gotten this fighter ready. It was ready *before* he hit the deck of the carrier. And then there was the admiral, *by name*. And above all that Code 755. He kept his words to himself and finished his coffee.

They raced over cities and mountains that reflected their haze-diffused glows and the lieutenant reduced his conversation to clipped phrases. "Captain, one hundred nautical out." A moment later. "Starting descent, sir."

They fell heavy and swift and controlled through the mild turbulence of night off the mountains, and Seavers watched the great wings swing forward to change the Tomcat from a supersonic arrowhead to a slower, more responsive locomotive with wings. Lights rolled and flashed, the gear bumped on the way down and flaps slid invisibly beneath him and magically they hung level, and he felt a gentle vibration and saw the nose of the fighter coming down and they were rolling down the long runway of the air force base, swinging off the active onto the taxiway and directly into a hangar behind a FOLLOW ME truck. His pilot shut down the huge fighter, offered the terse warning, "Watch your head. Canopy coming up. Please do not touch anything or move until ground crew safeties the ejection seats." It was all done, ladders thumped against the side of the Tomcat, men leaned in to unhook Seavers from parachute and survival gear and the machine itself. He stretched and climbed down and turned to stare into the statuesque face of Admiral Duncan.

A huge hand gripped his own. "Hello, Marc."

He shook hands, nodded briefly. "Admiral."

"This way." Duncan turned to lead him to a civilian van. At least it looked like a civilian van from the outside. When the door slid shut and lights came on, he was seated in a comfortable cushioned chair, facing Duncan. No sound came in from outside and even the driver was invisible behind a panel of thick smoked glass. Seavers had the feeling the glass was armored. He also knew they were moving.

He held Duncan's gaze. "Remarkable," the admiral said. "You haven't asked a single question."

Seavers shrugged. "I had the record, you know."

Duncan permitted himself the first touch of a smile in the hawkish, leathery face. "So you did. I had a bundle bet on you, too."

"Yes, sir."

"I'll fill in some of the blanks, Marc. We're driving to Cheyenne Mountain. You know what I'm talking about?"

"Yes, sir, I know what it is. That's NORAD headquarters inside the mountain. Also the bionics research center."

"It's also a very secure meeting place," Duncan added. "When we get there you'll shower and shave and get a decent meal in you. I want you sharp and clear between your ears for a meeting."

"Yes, sir."

"They told you the code?"

"Yes," Seavers said, nodding. "Seven Five Five."

50

"You know what those numbers mean?"

"Seven fifty-five A.M. The exact moment when the Japanese dropped their first bomb on the fleet in Pearl Harbor back in December of 1941. It means the balloon's gone up."

"That's right. Seven fifty-five. The air strike that whipped our ass at Pearl and put us into war."

Seavers felt a chill go through him. "Is the admiral telling me we're *at war?*"

"No."

Duncan fell into a heavy silence. It lasted less than a minute. Seavers sensed not to touch the moment, to leave it be.

"You're going to a very private meeting," Duncan said to break the heaviness that had misted between them.

"Do I know with whom, sir?"

"George Starling."

Despite himself, Seavers stared. "*President St*—you mean the president of the United States?"

Duncan gave him the barest nod. "Yes. The one and the same."

Seavers chewed on it for a while, then shook his head slowly. Very few moments caught him by surprise. This was bewildering.

"Admiral, what in the hell is coming down?"

Again the silence, but briefer this time. Not a flicker of emotion showed on the face of old leather. It seemed only the eyes were alive. Then he sighed, a deep-down gust of air carrying his words.

"The fucking world is coming to an end."

3 ———————

"Well, shit," Jeremy Gold said aloud, but as much to himself as any of the other shift monitors in Computer Central. He sat up straighter in his padded swivel chair, half-turning to the display panel. He blinked several times, took a long pull from the Coke can in his hand, placed the can carefully on a magazine to his right, still staring at the flashing display before him, and belched.

"What did you say?" Gold turned to Sarah Bleddington by his side. "I asked you what you said," she repeated. She lowered her copy of *Cosmopolitan* to afford her fellow monitor clearer attention. Gold made a mental note that Sarah would be a hell of a lot more attractive if she followed the advice in her magazine. Not that she wasn't attractive. Her hair fell long and flowing halfway to her waist and her breasts were disturbingly full and rounded beneath her sweater. She peered at Gold through granny glasses that she truly believed made her more attractive to men. Jeremy Gold wanted to hump Sarah Bleddington. He'd wanted to hump her for two years but she wouldn't put out. "No way, Jeremy," she'd told him with words of cold water. "What if it didn't work out? I mean, what if I turned out to be a lousy lay? Not that I am," she added quickly, "but *you* could turn out to be a lousy lay. We'd still have to come to work together the next morning, and from then on we'd be staring at one another and one of us would always know the other was a lousy lay, and that would make working here with each other pretty lousy. Thank you but no thanks." She pushed back her brown hair from her face, and when she did that her full lips seemed to beckon him on. "I like you and I intend to keep right on liking you, so we do not tumble in the sack together."

But that was some other time. Jeremy Gold rubbed his hand across his chin and offered up a weaker vestige of a belch from the soda. "Oh. Before? I belched. Sorry about that."

"I've listened to you belch for two years. I don't mind. My father always belched at the table," she said. "You said something before that. I think you said, well, shit."

"Did I?" he asked absently. "Yeah, I guess so. Sorry about that."

She hated that expression and pushed their exchange. "*Why* did you say that? Who were you talking to?"

"Oh. It wasn't anybody. I mean, no one in particular." He pointed to the display panel. "See there? It's the first time I ever saw the board lit up like that." They stared at the board. Jeremy is right, judged Sarah Bleddington. They had worked before this console for two years and never before had the bright red code behind 192X96 appeared. Old one ninety-two, as they called it, had lit up before, but it was always with the white light of scheduled remote station reports, and a few times there'd even been an amber light to let them know something out of the ordinary was happening. White or amber, they were used to that.

"It's *never* been red before," she said unnecessarily. They both felt somewhat awed by the red glow. It represented a major change in their routine. That was disturbing to them.

There really wasn't much to get excited about in the central data compilation for Project Dustbin. It was just one more of a dozen or two reporting stations for different research projects NASA and other science agencies from different countries had set up around the Earth. And on satellites, even deep-space probes. They had the sensors on satellites orbiting the moon and on the surface of the moon. They were even on the little moons of Mars and much farther out in the solar system. Jeremy Gold was surprised they sent up giant balloons that drifted around the Earth at higher than a hundred thousand feet with the sensor instruments. Why bother doing that with balloons when you could put up satellites a hundred thousand *miles* out into space?

"The red light, Jeremy," Sarah pressed him. "What does it mean?"

"It means we have to report what we're picking up, the stuff that's in the computers, I mean," he said slowly.

"Who do we report to?" she asked.

"You mean you've worked here for two years and you don't know who you got to report to?" He was acting superior and she sniffed her disdain.

"No, I don't. So you tell me, Mr. Smartass."

He had a sheepish look on his face. "Gee, to tell you the truth, Sarah, I don't really know. I mean, I know it, the report, I mean, we're supposed to report to the NRL. But I don't know to *who*."

"To whom," she corrected. He didn't know who was right so he didn't react to the correction.

"I guess we better tell the shift supervisor. He'll know what to do." He reached for the master instruction booklet. Sarah's hand shot out with surprising speed to grasp his wrist.

"*No*," she said emphatically. "Don't do that."

"Why not?" he protested. "We've got to follow orders and—"

"The red light's never come on before, right, Jeremy?" She watched him nod slowly in agreement. "That means it's something special. Maybe very special. It could be even super special. I mean, after all, Jeremy, we've been working here for two years and we have *never* seen a red alert before. But it's here," she pointed with agitation at the display console, "and that means something very special is coming down in here, at least it *could* be something like that, and," she gulped in air and went on in a rush, "if we call in the supervisor, I think it's Mamie Jenkins tonight, *well*, then she'll call report headquarters and—"

"Where's that?"

Sarah looked blankly at Jeremy. "Where's *what*?"

"Report headquarters."

"I don't *know*. But it's in the *book*, Jeremy, and we'll find out, and will you shut up and let me finish? If we tell Mamie Jenkins she gets all the credit and we get none, and why do you think they call us the Janitors? We're technicians, or we're supposed to be, and everybody looks down on us because we're technicians for this project they call Dustbin, right? Of *course* I'm right. Don't you see? Unless we break the routine and use that red light to make a *personal* report no one will *ever* know we're alive and we'll never get promoted and is this what you went to college for seven years for? So you could grow a fat ass and be a technical janitor? We'll mark down everything that's coming in and somewhere we'll find a good reason for breaking routine and we'll call headquarters, and," she snapped her fingers, "I remember now, it's Goddard, the Goddard base NASA has up in Greenbelt, Maryland, we'll call *their* shift supervisor and what do you say?"

Her nonstop plea left him winded. "Gee, Sarah, I don't know, I mean, we'll be breaking routine, you know how Jenkins always wants us to report to her and—"

"That's how she got to be supervisor!" Sarah hissed fiercely, trying not to shout. "She was just like us until *she* figured out how to get people to recognize her. Jeremy, I don't want to stay a janitor forever!" She leaned closer and took his hand and placed it firmly against a breast. She watched him redden and good gosh, that fast he was showing how he felt in his pants. She brought her lips to his ear. "I'll let you hump me, Jeremy."

He gulped and swallowed and ran a finger along the inside of his suddenly hot collar. He nodded. She knew he'd never turn her down for *that*. He motioned her closer as she gently removed his hand from her body. "We don't want anyone else to *know*," she said softly.

"I know. I want to try something, okay?" He went on before she could object. "At least let's get the old bat out of her office, you know, out of this section so we can say later if anybody tries to make trouble by saying we didn't follow our routine, that we tried to but she wasn't here and we judged this red light as being so important we felt we should call it in right away. *Then* Miss Jenkins can't say birdshit about what we did. Sound okay to you?"

Sarah Bleddington frowned. She patted her skirt and pushed out her chest just a bit more until Jeremy

55

reddened and shifted uncomfortably because his undershorts were binding him so bad now. "Okay, what do we do, wait for her coffee break or something?"

"That's a great idea, Sarah!" He looked at the wall timer. "Just another twenty minutes and she'll be gone. She *never* misses her coffee break."

"Okay, Jeremy. I think you better switch off the panel until she leaves. She might do a walk-through and see that red light—"

He moved quickly to open the access panel on the back of the display console and adjusted several controls. The bright red bar highlighting 192X96 winked out. They waited, fidgeting, Jeremy sliding his chair closer to Sarah and trying to move his hand between her legs. They spent eighteen minutes in hand-thrust and parry and Jeremy froze along her thigh. "There she goes," he said in a stage whisper to Sarah. They watched the supervisor exiting the control room to the coffee lounge.

"Hurry!" Sarah told Jeremy Gold. He slipped open the panel and reconnected the lighting controls. When he moved back into his chair by Sarah, Old One Ninety Two gleamed at him again.

"What do we do now?" he asked nervously, trying to look over her shoulder as she studied the instruction reference manual.

"It says here," she tapped the page, "that first we bring uplink all the stations reporting in on this code."

A frown creased his forehead. "Maybe we better call Miss Jenkins. I think this whole thing is sort of getting out of hand, Sarah."

Her look cut him. "Wimp!" she hissed. "You'll do no such thing. Now," she tapped harder against the page, "you do just what I tell you, okay? You *do* want to hump me, don't you, Jeremy?"

"Well, of course I do, but—"

"Then go to the activator panel. That's number five," she said with growing confidence. "Depress the STEADY REPORT button—"

"Okay. I did that," he said quickly.

"Next, there's a gang bar—"

56

"A *what*?"

"It's a master switch. They call it a gang bar because you uplink one switch and it brings a whole bunch of stations on the line. I guess they all feed into One Ninety Two, here."

He looked at her with awe. "Where'd you learn all this?"

"I guess when you were, you know, rubbing yourself, I was paying attention." She sniffed in offer of a superior air. "Jeremy, I *studied*. I really did. I studied what Dustbin was about and, oh, *not now*, Jeremy." She turned the page. "Check all reporting stations on line," she intoned.

He returned to the panel. "It's okay, Sarah. One through a hundred and twelve. They're all on—no, number twenty-seven is down. It's off the line."

"Hit the overdrive to bring it up."

"I did. It's dead. Probably it's off the circuit."

"Okay, forget it. Now, see that second gang bar? The amber one? That brings everything into central data receiving, and over there, Jeremy, the one that says MULTIPLE TRANSMIT. Bring that on line and then activate the bar marked GODDARD UPLINK."

"What does that do?"

"According to this manual, it feeds everything coming into here, into One Ninety Two, anyway, into a priority transmit line to Goddard. Not just to the station, but right into their computer. I guess when it all comes into Goddard their computer scans the reports and—*Mother of God, what's happening!*"

Dazzling light flashed from the master control console and a deep gong resounded through the huge control room. Jeremy and Sarah stared at one another in shock and surprise. They heard feet pounding on the slick floor and they looked up to see Mamie Jenkins looking past them to the display console.

"You assholes," she said more quietly than they liked. "Sarah, get the hell out of that seat." She dropped heavily into the empty seat, studied the data readouts, glanced at Sarah. "Hand me that phone," she snapped, pointing to a group of panel handsets.

57

Sarah was bewildered. "But I don't know which one!" she wailed. "I mean, there aren't any calls coming in!"

Mamie Jenkins sighed. "There will be. Any moment now—" She nodded as a light flashed and a quiet chime sounded. "Number three. That will be Goddard or I'll eat that phone."

Dr. Arthur Kimberly looked at the world beneath a mass of unruly grey hair, Einstein-style, that left on his shoulders, seat backs and the floor behind him a thin fallout of dandruff. "The son of a bitch manufactures the stuff," his fellow scientists grumbled, and all agreed it wasn't worth the temperamental rejoinders to get the professor to clean up his act. Or his scalp, anyway. At the bottom of Kimberly's long equine features, as if in jeering juxtaposition to the unruly, particle-extruding mop atop his head, appeared a delightfully trimmed salt-and-pepper beard that was the epitome of neatness. In between were huge horn-rimmed glasses, a nose pitted with acne scars, a smile of yellowed teeth, and behind the dandruff-flecked forehead, a brain of massive intelligence. Kimberly possessed the unfortunate body of a man who was put together of misshapen clay in one of God's lesser moments. Everything seemed out of joint, from an unbalanced jaw to angular hipbones to knobby knees to huge hands. However his throat had developed, he spoke with a gravelly whine. It would have been very easy, even greatly desirable once meeting Kimberly, to try to forget the meeting had ever taken place. Forgetting Arthur Kimberly was an act of kindness to oneself.

But it didn't happen that way. Behind his thick lenses (he refused contact lenses as an abomination of his time and a sop to vanity) his eyes seemed to glow, so fiercely a countenance did he present despite his faint resemblance to an old milkwagon horse. Genius he was, genius he acted, and it would never occur to Arthur Kimberly that he might be wrong about *anything*. He was as subtle in his professional associations as a locomotive going over a cliff, and his wife had been in a state of constant shock ever since awakening the morning after her marriage to realize she had committed herself to a man of utter brilliance who picked his nose in bed, made love like a snorting hog, and was never aware of when he farted in a wetly staccato eruption. He devastated her family, sickened her friends, forced her priest to vigorous praying for forgiveness from God for ungodly thoughts concerning Elizabeth Kimberly's husband, and at various early ages drove his three children from his home in a suburb much too close to Washington, D.C.

He held the Chair of Astrophysical Sciences at Virginia Technical Studies, where his presence cast a pall over anyone who had to endure his savage (but unintended) critiques, and where the parties to celebrate the government research contracts that took him frequently to research centers throughout the world lasted for a week of utter drunkenness and debauchery. He was a source of raw power with Stanford Research Institute as well, and gave fast, gravelly, but brilliant lectures at leading institutions and research centers throughout the country.

All this might have been endurable except for Kimberly's childish belief in the inherent goodness of mankind and that all wars great and small would evaporate from humanity if only all swords were beaten into plowshares. That there would then exist a planet of farmers behind horses would never occur to him. That most of his funding for research stemmed from government (i.e. military or quasi-military) sources was a fact he refused absolutely to believe. Thus Kimberly, in addition to cerebral magnificence which might have made him barely endurable, wallowed and stumbled through national politics and special interest groups. He was a leading figure for the Union of Concerned Scientists, whose leader, Eric van Loon, worked overtime to fit his verbal antics to his name, and behind whom Kimberly followed slavishly in the group's purported intent to "rid the world of all atomic weapons and delivery systems." Few, if any, of the national leaders of this so-called Union believed a whit of their platform, but there were enough frightened and impressed people out there to dump millions of dollars annually into their coffers. Dr. Arthur Kimberly was the perfect foil for their unashamed begging for personal profit in the name of science and survival.

"Throw his do-gooder ass the hell out of our programs!" That cry followed mention of Kimberly's name throughout the Pentagon. Rumor had it that Kimberly compromised security with his penchant for instant argument with anyone who disagreed with him. "The son of a bitch doesn't even know when he's breaking security. He'd as soon tell the Russians everything he knows just to win a goddamned argument." That was more hyperbole than honesty, reflecting intense personal dislike for Kimberly more than any belief in his being a security risk. Fred Smythe of the National Security Agency dismissed the horrendous tales of the free-swinging professor. "He's a horse's ass and he's a fool but he's *not* stupid, and he makes people believe he's careless with what he knows, but it's not true. Kimberly could win an Oscar any time he wanted. He's a brilliant, dedicated scientist who's scared the shit out of his wife and terrifies his students and browbeats everybody else, and it's all a put-on to cover the fact that his face looks like the south end of a horse going north."

"We need him in NASA," was the candid admission in the headquarters of the nation's space program. Marion Hughes directed NASA. Personally he thought Kimberly to be an unmitigated zit on the public face of space exploration. "But the bastard's got the ear of the president," Hughes warned his staff. "And the National Academy of Sciences, which doesn't give a rat's ass for popularity polls, also keeps him on their ladder's top rung. If we can keep Kimberly hot to trot in our interplanetary programs, then the Academy will back us to the hilt before the appropriations committees. All you people got that straight? He's *very* strong in Project Dustbin. Personally I consider that to be one of the all-time boondoggles ever perpetrated on a trusting public. But it provides the carrier vehicles for us to get our payloads out where we want them and *that's* what counts."

Jim Douglas shook his head. He'd been team leader of the Jovian satellite probes that orbited Jupiter and had landed on three of its moons and he'd had a running feud with Kimberly for years. "I can't say I agree with you," he said to contradict Hughes. "You're playing his value to us way out of proportion. I'll be damned if I'll treat him with kid gloves."

Marion Hughes smiled. "Hell, Jim, that isn't necessary. You know I'd never ask you to do that."

"I'm damned glad to hear you say that," Douglas said gruffly. "I'd refuse."

The smile washed away from Hughes' face. "I wouldn't ask you to treat him with kid gloves," he said slowly, "but if it's necessary I'll damn well tell you to kiss his ass. Is *that* clear?"

Douglas half-rose. "I'll quit first. I'm thinking of doing that right now, in fact," he snapped.

"Don't let the door hit you in the ass on the way out of your job," Hughes came back, still calm and collected in his tone. "I'm no scientist, Jim. In fact, I consider myself a farmer. But I've got what you haven't. NASA didn't have it when everybody lied to everybody else *and* themselves and killed all those people in *Challenger* back in eighty-six. We still don't have enough of it now. You know what we're in short supply for? It's common sense, Jim. Plain old everyday down-country farming common sense. You can't lie to your crops or your animals because your crops will die if they don't get nourishment and your animals will die if they don't get food and water. And our programs will die if they're not fed a measure of confidence to the appropriations committees, and they get that confidence from people like Kimberly. Even if he is an unmitigated pain in the ass. You'll still kiss it when I say or I'll take you up on your offer to quit *right now*."

To the right of Marion Hughes, Bill Lundgren was trying desperately to head off the worsening situation. Finally he just broke into their exchange. "Where's Kimberly now?" he threw into the middle of the verbal fracas.

Marion Hughes smiled to himself. Lundgren was

61

getting to be a pretty good politician at this business. He turned to his public affairs chief. "He's at the Cape. Got a whole bunch of scientists and eggheads with him." Hughes offered Jim Douglas a forbidding side glance. "The *top* people from our science agencies. They're counting down *Atlantis* for tomorrow morning's launch. One of the payloads—and you already know this, all of you—is the deep-space probe they're going to accelerate with the nuclear ion drive." Hughes shook his head. "It's still tough for me to accept that they're going to get that thing all fired up for six hundred thousand miles an hour."

Douglas was desperate to get back into the good graces of his boss. "It's just a matter of constant acceleration, Marion. All they need to do once they have a good orbit is release the damps on the—"

"Whoa! Hold it! Stop right there," Hughes said half in jest but serious. "Spare me. I'm just steering this here NASA boat, Jim. I don't need to understand the tech manual." He tapped a pencil on his desk. "Meeting's adjourned. Have a good day. Don't forget to wear your rubbers. Gonna rain tonight." He gave them a disarming smile and a wink and left the conference room.

High in the mountains of Alaska, anchored to a rock pinnacle scraped clear of ice and snow by scimitar blades of wind, a remote robot laboratory sniffed the taste and content of the atmosphere near the top of the world. After years of mindless measurements a marker had begun to edge upward slowly along a vertical instrument system until it nibbled at a sensor. The sensor trickled electrical current to a simple computer which, upon being "awakened" by the preceding events, interrogated all the instruments in the robot lab. The data collected, the computer flashed an accelerated-time signal to a communications satellite passing overhead in polar orbit. Eleven minutes later the satellite beamed that data, along with information collected from other assignments, to a huge antenna in Montana. The NASA facility routinely collected data and then farmed it out to various research centers programmed for such receipt. The engineer on duty glanced casually at the data receipt console and raised his eyebrows at a flashing red light. He tapped an ACTIVATE-DISPLAY *switch. Digital numbers flashed and raced before him. An electronic tone sounded and a computer voice spoke soothingly, yet with a calculated persistency to its timbre.* ALERT. ALERT. CODE 192X96. NOTIFY DUSTBIN. CONFIRM RECEIPT AND NOTIFICATION. *The message began again. The engineer followed his ordered procedures. Far off to the east an alarm sounded in a data office of the Goddard Space Center, Greenbelt, Maryland.*

The seven scientists walking slowly between the rows of television screens and control consoles in the huge Launch Control Center of Kennedy Space Center drew stares and murmurings of awe from the hundreds of technicians manning the monitoring and control facilities that would soon launch the great shuttle *Atlantis* on Pad 39A three miles east of the LCC building. Dr. Arthur Kimberly led the group in a strange disjointed waddle rather than walking in a familiar human gait. A sickening fragrance of rum-flavored pipe tobacco followed him. The sight and smell of anyone smoking in LCC was enough to raise a buzz of conversation. Ted Shiel, LCC Manager, started down the long aisle to tell Kimberly either to put away his offensive pipe or leave LCC immediately. A hand on his arm stayed his move. Travis Simmonds shook his head. "Don't bother. It won't work."

Shiel pulled his arm free. "Why the hell not?" His voice was almost a snarl. "This is *my* goddamned facility and no son of a bitch is going to smoke in it."

Travis Simmonds chuckled. "And *I'm* the director of this whole shebang, right?"

"You going against me, Travis?" Disbelief showed on Shiel's face.

"Hell, no. But I take *my* orders from Marion Hughes and you know who *he* is."

"Yeah, sure. What's the big deal? He's the administrator. I know that, for Christ's sake."

"And Hughes has given me clear and specific instructions. Dr. Kimberly wants to smoke, he smokes. He wants to sing and dance, he does it. He wants to fart and he can f—"

A muted razzberry drifted down the aisle to their station. "My God, I don't believe it," Shiel said slowly. "He did it." They looked at noses and faces wrinkling behind Kimberly, totally unaware of the immediate effect of his flatulence or its sputtering evidence.

Attention diverted to a young woman hurrying along the aisle in pursuit of Kimberly and his party of scientists. She swept through the offensive miasma, slowed, a look of incredulity on her face, producing waves of muffling laughter from technicians and engineers leaning against one another in near hysterics. The young woman drew herself up a bit straighter. "Dr. Kimberly! *Dr. Kimberly!*" she called loudly above the background din of launch control. "Sir! Please!"

Kimberly stopped and turned in a swirl of pipe smoke and ashes and dandruff. He towered over the diminutive woman and slowly withdrew the pipe from his mouth. "Yes?" It wasn't your *ordinary* yes. It emerged from Kimberly with the sibilant heavy breathing of a toothy python. In the silence that followed his single word he sighed, having encountered speech stumbles before from those trying to talk with him. "Who are you and what do you want?" he demanded.

"Uh, Miss Stewart, Jane Stewart?"

"Is that a statement or a question, Miss Stewart?" The look on her face, a mixture of dismay and fear, softened his tone. "What can I do for you, young lady?"

"Oh, thank you, Doctor. I'm *so* sorry to bother you at a time like this," she rushed on, almost curtseying to the scientists watching the exchange, "but there's a *very* important call for you. Its in the, uh, Goddard liaison office. Right around the corner from the end of the aisle over there?"

Kimberly was honestly puzzled. To track him down in LCC during the final stages of a countdown betokened something very much out of the ordinary. They wouldn't have called him *here* even if a garbage truck had crushed his entire family. It had to be official, then, but still— He stalled a bit for time. Jane Stewart looked up at fiercely bright eyes behind thick lenses. "And what could be so important, Jane Stewart? Did they tell you who was calling?"

She shook her head, hair whirling back and forth. "I don't know, sir." She fished a slip of paper from her skirt pocket. "But they said to write this down and show it to you as soon as I could reach you, and they said not to let anyone stop me, and—"

He gestured with a raised palm and under that papal movement she fell silent. Kimberly studied the paper.

192X96 RED. HOPPER FULL. DUSTBIN.

He glanced up. "That's all?"

"Yes, sir."

"You did well. Thank you, Jane Stewart." She stared up at him as if frozen to the floor. "You are dismissed, young woman. Thank you."

"Oh! Yes, sir!" She turned and fled down the aisle.

Kimberly rubbed his fingers across the paper as if some invisible message might spring forth. He passed the note to a thin, almost emaciated man to his right, Professor David Higgins, chief scientist of the Naval Research Laboratory. Higgins adjusted his bifocals and glanced at the paper. It took only that moment. He looked up at Kimberly and it was a case of two equals locking eyes. No diffidence here. "What about it?" Higgins asked with undue care.

"You are familiar with what you see?"

"I'm a damn sight more familiar with it than you are," he snapped. He didn't like Arthur Kimberly and he liked even less those moments when Kimberly acted the patronizing son of a bitch, which was right now. Even if the rest of the group didn't *know* that. To fill in the gaps brought on by the sudden murmuring from the group, Higgins kept his eyes stabbing into those of Kimberly. "I've been working with Kubasov's team on this since the early eighties, and I mean *working*." He kept his head turned to Kimberly but changed his tack. "This is not the time or the place, Arthur."

Kimberly surprised him, nodding agreement. "You're

right," he said. He took the cryptic note from Higgins and passed it on to the others. Dr. Jesse Markham of NASA's Lunar Facilities Office; Dr. Felicity Xavier Powell of the Air Force Office of Scientific Research; Professor Henri Saul Pietre of French Astronautical Sciences; Dr. Engineer Klaus Schoenberger of Germany's Office of National Sciences; and, Dr. Toshio Saito of the U.S. Department of the Interior all glanced at the note and passed it on. But not Dr. Forrest Reed of the National Oceanic and Atmospheric Agency. He held the note longer than the others and exchanged a meaningful glance with Kimberly and Higgins. He spoke in a hoarse whisper. "For God's sake, *not in here.*"

"Come with me," Kimberly announced in his usual imperious fashion, and launched himself into a perambulating march down the long aisle between the puzzled launch technicians.

Dr. Arthur Kimberly led his troupe of brainpower into the private office of Travis Simmonds. Simmonds held his usual meetings as Director of Kennedy Space Center in a large conference room. Beyond that room extended the "inner sanctum" for highest-level conferences, meetings with the president, and for maximum security. It was a room with lead-lined inner walls protected with electronic monitoring devices, and every phone and televideo line into and out of the Sanctum went through a code scrambler.

Simmonds had coffee and doughnuts brought into the room. Kimberly, Higgins, and Reed were each on separate telephones, and by the agitated sound of their voices, Simmonds judged that something very big was coming down. *Hard.* That the director, himself, of the Kennedy Space Center knew nothing of this Dustbin, whatever it was, gave him sufficient cause to start his own worrying.

He wondered if he was just growing old instead of being properly concerned. Then he heard the angry, strident tones of Dr. Higgins from NRL. He didn't catch it all, but enough to know that some of the most powerful intellects in the nation were reaching levels of agitation he hadn't encountered since they watched seven astronauts die in a crunching fireball so many years ago. Higgins' voice rose to an even higher, angrier level, and Simmonds listened this time. ". . . the hell do you mean that twenty-seven is off the line. Find out why, goddamnit, and find out now and get back to me here!" The phone slammed down with a bang.

Nope, it's not age, Travis Simmonds judged himself. He had the feeling he'd have plenty of reason to be concerned, if not worried. He looked across the room at Higgins, who broke a pencil in two and flung it angrily away.

What the hell is going on? Simmonds wondered.

4 ————

From one hundred and forty thousand feet above the Himalayas the highest peaks of Earth diminished to foothills. No human eye looked down from the huge pearly-white balloon riding the swift winds along the stratospheric top of the world. Dustbin Aerostat Three Seven One floated swiftly at two hundred and thirty miles an hour. Hanging far beneath the bloated gasbag at the end of a slim cable was a solar-powered instrument station. Dustbin 371 had been riding the tenuous but sometimes tumultuous edge of the atmosphere for eight months. Once-pristine gauges and sensors jutting like punk hair spikes from the instrument package had lost their former sheen. Many showed severe pitting. Dust had gathered in air so thin a man exposed lung-naked to this cruel environment would explode violently from the boiling of his own body fluids. Higher than the instruments, between the robot station and the main nylon cables of the aerostat, a miniaturized television camera looked down at the instrument station. The picture taken by the tiny camera appeared on the monitor of a scientific station on Hilo in the Hawaiian Islands. At a data display console Bob Novick leaned closer to the screen. He punched in the printout band to gain still pictures from the video image. "Jesus," he said aloud to himself, "I don't believe this. That's almost like mud." He readjusted focus and finger-tapped control keys to activate a glowing digital data screen. Above the data a computer-generated command appeared. PROJECT DUSTBIN CODE 192X96 IMMEDIATE NOTIFICATION. *"You got it, baby,"* Novick voiced his thoughts; *he tapped in the proper code and stabbed* TRANSMIT.

Arthur Kimberly replaced the telephone carefully with such detachment that his body moved in seeming slow-motion. His less-than-casual demeanor sent up warning signals to his fellow scientists. Nothing fazed Kimberly. So went the stories, so went their own experience with the Demon Professor, as he'd been named by students and fellow workers. Watching this extraordinary difference in Kimberly's behavior was enough to bring their sense of alarm to key pitch. Except for David Higgins and Forrest Reed. Dustbin was no stranger to them, but they kept their counsel to themselves. They would let Kimberly be the one to brief the others. He was so conservative that even a seemingly insane remark from him gained a level of acceptance that would be denied any "normal" scientist.

Kimberly turned from the telephone to face the others. He fumbled in his jacket pocket for his lighter and his fingers seemed to entangle themselves in pocket, pipe, and the sought-after lighter, with the result that the pipe fell to the carpet, spilling ashes in a semicircle on the floor. They glanced nervously at one another. *Arthur Kimberly's cage was being rattled. What the hell is this?* The message moved among them without a word.

Travis Simmonds stooped down to retrieve the pipe. He handed it back to Kimberly, who absent-mindedly tapped the pipe against the heel of his hand to dump more ashes onto the floor. Simmonds ignored it. He'd already recognized all the signs of big trouble. "Is there anything I can do for you, Doctor?" he asked Kimberly.

Kimberly drew a deep breath, found his pouch and

began tamping fresh tobacco into the pipe bowl. He spilled as much as made it into the pipe. Finally he looked at the space center director. "Uh, no, Mr. Simmonds. I mean, that is, I require a meeting, a very private meeting, with my colleagues here," he said with a sweeping gesture to take in the seven other scientists.

"Dr. Kimberly, this center is at your disposal. I would be pleased to seal off this room. I assure you it is absolutely safe for any confidentiality you may need to protect. No one else will be in here with you."

Kimberly looked about the room, caught the eye of David Higgins who barely moved his head back and forth. "Uh, Mr. Simmonds, I appreciate your offer," Kimberly replied. "But no. Not here. Not anywhere I have not been assured by my own security people—well, I hope you understand." Kimberly lied and he and Simmonds both knew it. Arthur Kimberly didn't believe in a shred of security. His career for years had been punctuated with verbal blasts at the binding ropes of government security. He didn't have any security team working for him. His words, his *lie*, spoke reams to Simmonds. He didn't press it. None of his damned business, whatever it was spooking the famous scientist.

"Tell me what you need and I'll do everything I can—"

"I need to be *outside*," Kimberly broke in suddenly. A sheen of perspiration on his face reflected the ceiling lights. In this final display of inner nerves, Kimberly summoned up his old strength. "You will see to it, Mr. Simmonds. We will leave this building and walk along the roadway that parallels the crawlerway to the pad. That will bring us along the banks of the turning basin."

"Dr. Kimberly," Simmonds said carefully, "that will take you within the three-mile fallback from the launch pad—"

"Really." Disdain was surging forth. Tension in the meeting room lessened. *This* was the Kimberly—insulting, unpleasant, cutting, wicked—they all knew so well. But Travis Simmonds wasn't put off so easily.

"Yes, sir. *Really*." Any subservience to Kimberly was gone. Simmonds was the man who ran this place. The absolute authority; and he was letting Kimberly know it.

Kimberly smiled. "You're fully aware of who I am and my position in government." He didn't *ask* Simmonds, but reminded him of what he already knew.

Simmonds sighed, a long exhalation preceding his spoken thoughts. "I know who you are," he said in a voice surprisingly free of emotion. Travis Simmonds had been through this drill before. With scientists, presidents, senators—the works. It was a routine with which he was familiar, ad he handled it with a steel fist within a fuzzy warm glove. "I know not only who, but what you are, sir," he went on. "You are one of the most brilliant scientists in this country. In the world."

"I am going to vomit," Kimberly said darkly.

To his surprise, Simmonds ignored the dangling bait. "And precisely *because* you are so valuable to science, to this entire country," the KSC director swept on, "I cannot permit you to expose yourself and your colleagues," he gestured to take in others, "because of your severe *lack* of knowledge of the dangers associated with your moving within the overpressure blast range of that vehicle on its launch pad. I know who you are, sir, and I am also aware that you know who *I* am, and that I have final authority on this installation as to who goes where and who does what. With all due respect, Doctor, I hope I make myself clear." He finished with as much deference he could mix with his stated authority.

To his surprise, Kimberly's smile might have sported canary feathers on each side of his mouth. The scientist pointed in the direction of the launch pad. "You are going to *have* to stop me," he said, showing his large stained teeth.

"Yes, sir, and I'll do just that," Simmonds said with a grave expression.

"You will have to stop me *physically*." Kimberly motioned his colleagues closer. "You'll need your bully boys to stop us. To stop *all* of us," he said without a trace of jest. "You'll need perhaps your people with guns, even your dogs. Oh, you have the authority. You can bash us physically and you might even end up

70

killing one or more of us, for I promise you we will struggle and we will shout and *we'll make certain that your people will hurt us most severely.*" Kimberly offered up a cold, thin smile. "A delightful scenario, don't you think? There's that press box in your launch center. *They'll* bloody well hear what's going on. And they'll report it, immediately, and I imagine, with lurid details." Kimberly raised his arm and motioned to point through a side window of the office. "Over there, on that press site. More than two thousand newsmen from around the whole world. *They* will have this marvelous story to relate. We shall make world news, Director Travis Simmonds, and it will take no longer," he snapped his fingers, "than *that*."

Kimberly turned and began walking to the far door. "Go ahead, Simmonds!" He held his right hand over his heart. "Have at us! Hurt us, detain us, arrest us one and all, *kill us*. We're here, as you *may* recall, at the specific request of the president of the United States. I'm certain he'll *love* it." He walked faster and turned to look back over his shoulder. "You idiot," he tossed behind him in a final call of contempt.

Travis Simmonds clenched and unclenched his fists. He knew he was turning purple. *The son of a bitch is right. I'd like to smash in his face and—* Instead, Simmonds motioned to the armed guard at the door to let the scientists pass.

The sun is a distant and tiny bright star billions of miles distant from Earth. Its light, diminished by distance and time, reflects weakly from a tarnished robot on which a pitted metal plate reads Voyager XIII. *Mindless, alive only by the warmth and trickling electrical current of decaying plutonium,* Voyager *bristles with antenna arrays, sensors, probes and recording instruments that sniff, taste, feel, pinch, smell, rub, measure, and otherwise gauge the radiations of the nearby and even more distant suns. The robot, rotating slowly when seen against the distant backdrop of celestial pinpoints, seems barely to drift through the space beyond the earth's solar system. It does not drift; all is relative and*

71

almost all is deceiving, and Voyager XIII hurtles from one measuring point to another at better than a hundred miles a second. Strangely, in this hard and unknowing vacuum beyond even the outermost bulge of Pluto's orbit, the robot's surfaces appear to be sandblasted. Dust lies airlessly on metal and glass alike.

Far, far distant, near the shores of an ocean called Atlantic, in a huge laboratory and data center within a human community known as Greenbelt, a large sign on a much larger building identifies the structure as GODDARD SPACE DATA CENTER. Within the multiple cubicles and enclosed spaces the locked entrance to one such set of cubicles is identified by its sign VOYAGER DATA RETRIEVAL, beneath which in smaller letters is the sign DUSTBIN. Inside this cubicle all data from all sources of PROJECT DUSTBIN is recorded, collated, examined, compared, tested, and extrapolated. This exhaustive, round-the-clock effort is the primary reason for a sense of unease and foreboding that haunts the men and women of DUSTBIN. Their casual dress, their long apprenticeship and servitude in the bowels of the complex data center, belie this unpleasantness of mood. They have lived with the remote possibility of what DUSTBIN foretells for so long that its burgeoning ascent to stark reality leaves them numb. So they continue as before, drinking coffee, munching on cookies and sandwiches, retreating to private rooms to smoke and even to brood but always to conceal their glumness when together as a group.

On this particular day their attention concentrates on one particular console display. A red light flashes as it has flashed on and off for just more than three hours. More and more people cluster about the digital display of data. As it sweeps across distant space and ghosts into receiving antenna, it is constantly updated and redisplayed. The men and women of DUSTBIN shake their heads in collective disbelief. Voyager XIII commands their attention. And, they are increasingly aware, threatens their future.

Cathy Gould is Prime Operator at this moment. She works computer controls. Deep in the bowels of the *computer central data is translated to picturization. What whispered across space at the speed of light as meaningless radio-frequency mutterings yields to the magic of computer interpretation and appears as a clear photograph on the large console sceen. Voyager XIII and its associated legerdemain takes its own picture. Cathy Gould leans back as murmurs arise from the group behind her at the pictures appearing before them of the incredibly distant robot.*

"Christ, I can hardly believe this," she exclaims as she points at the screen.

"That thing looks like its been in a sandstorm," a technician adds. This is Eduardo Farcon, an expert on metal structures, and he is dismayed beyond his words.

Beth Tarkington is a tough old bird who's been part of the space program since she was a child. In her lexicon V-2 and Redstone are as familiar as any of the new terms. No one remembers her ever being rattled by a mindless machine. "That spacecraft," she intones, "is seven billion miles away from us. It's supposed to be sterile out there." She glances from the screen to the others. "Did that hunk of tin cross a cometary tail anywhere?"

Cathy Gould shakes her head. "This whole thing is impossible!" Her voice carries the first touch of shrill. She leans forward. "I'm going to run a crosshatch from the rest of the system and—"

An amber light flashes and an electronic tone calls their attention. Gould touches the console speaker. "Cathy, top-priority call. It's from the Cape. Dr. Kimberly."

Cathy Gould sighs, glances meaningfully at Beth Tarkington, and places her headpiece against her ear. Beth Tarkington leans over her shoulder and gently depresses the SPEAKERPHONE *button so they can all hear what is coming down.*

"Follow them," Simmonds ordered his security chief. "But keep your distance from them, understand? You're not following them for any purpose but to keep everybody, and I mean *everybody*, away from those eight people. *No one* even gets close to them. Got it?"

73

"Yes, sir." Captain Ryan Tacker, Chief of Security of the Kennedy Space Center, cupped his hand over his mobile radio transmitter and spoke his orders crisply and quietly. Fifteen men moved on foot and by vehicle into position to maintain a protective distance from the scientists strolling—strolling, for Christ's sake!—toward the distant launch pad. Tacker felt uneasy. He keyed his transmitter again.

"Jolly Fiver Nine, you read? Come in to Team Leader."

His set hissed and a voice followed. That was young Tom Watkins, seated in their security jet helicopter. "Tom, fire up your bird. Keep it ready to hop on a single word command. Stay on this frequency at all times. Take your orders from me, and from me only. Confirm."

Tom Watkins read back the hard information and Captain Ryan Tacker relaxed. Not much. Maybe an ounce or two. He climbed atop his security van and brought binoculars to his eyes. The crazy bastards looked like they were cruising down the boardwalk in Atlantic City. Tacker didn't like what was happening. None of it *fit*. He'd *never* seen Travis taken apart, piece by piece, like that. He didn't understand what the hell was going on. And a good security man is supposed to be on top of everything, not stumbling about in the dark.

Arthur Kimberly led his troupe of scientific brain-power like children walking along a country road. The analogy met the conditions. Immediately to their left stretched a roadway of pure rock, Alabama river rock, smooth and rounded, brought to Florida at great expense and in huge quantities to be laid atop a deep foundation necessary to support more than five thousand tons of rocket, service tower, crawler transporter and associated massive and ponderous equipment.

In the humid Florida night air they could taste salt on their lips and tongues. "That's salt from the false Cape," commented Forrest Reed. "The salt here is the greatest concentration in ambient air, anywhere in the world."

"What is this false Cape?" asked Klaus Schoenberger. The German scientist was determined always to understand what these crazy Americans were talking about at any time.

Reed gestured beyond the shoreline. "It's just beneath the water. Out beyond the air force beach, over there. It breaks up the wave pattern so that wave action and the wind throws heavy salt spray into the air and—"

"Shut up, Reed." Everyone looked in surprise at David Higgins from NRL. "We didn't come out here for any damned tourist claptrap." He turned to Kimberly. "I want to walk along the crawlerway. Goddamn it, Arthur, I don't want asphalt beneath my feet. I want the same damn stuff on which all our big ships moved. Apollo and Skylab and the shuttles and—"

Kimberly nodded agreement and led the way to his left, off the asphalt, onto grass and then onto the crawlerway surface of millions of rocks ground beneath huge moonships that had come this way before. They stopped to look ahead of them, at the enormous searchlight beams and dazzling floodlights surrounding the launch pad where the enormous shuttle hulked on massive pinions. Lights of many colors and intensity blinked, shone, and flashed through the entire area, and beyond the pad, above the misty radiance of light reflecting salt spray, they saw the lights and heard the drone of helicopters and heavily armed gunships flying top security cover for *Atlantis* and its nuclear ion drive deepspace probe.

Felicity Xavier Powell stopped. The others walked on several paces until they noticed she was now behind them, unmoving, staring up at the monster package before them. Higgins walked back to her. "Anything wrong, Felicity?"

"Everything is wrong, David," she chided. "Or we wouldn't be out here after that ridiculous scene between Arthur and that fellow, um, Simmonds." She smiled at her old friend from the science battlements. "But you already know what is happening." She patted his arm. "We've worked together too long for those kind of secrets." She raised her hand to forestall the words she saw coming. "Hush, David. Break no confidences. Arthur will tell us soon enough. He is enjoying most thoroughly all the dramatics he has built up to this moment."

"There may be less *dramatics* than you think," Higgins said darkly.

"Perhaps," she said to dismiss the issue. She turned and studied the magnificent scene on the raised launch pad. "For this moment I prefer to be awed by what I see rather than to be either impressed or upset by Arthur Kimberly." She pointed, a tiny figure standing before the gleaming mountain of restrained energy. "It is—well, it is like a temple," she said finally. "Prometheus chained and awaiting his liberation. As soon as someone cuts his chains—"

Higgins took her arm with care and affection to walk with her to the waiting group. "The chains will be cut," he promised. "I have a man with a large axe hiding behind that truck, and when the time comes he'll dash out to the pad and give the chains a mighty whack and—"

Her laughter hung in the night air; a delicate sound from a small and elegant woman. "I hope he doesn't forget to kick the tires," she joshed.

"I'll be sure to tell him you said so, Felicity." He waved to the group they now joined. "Felicity was telling me," he addressed the others, "that what she sees before her is not a mechanical object but a temple."

"Well said, madam," Kimberly told her, as tender with this woman as he was almost savagely insulting with everyone else. "We may have need of such temples soon." He motioned for them to continue along the crawlerway.

Dr. Toshio Saito had run the gamut of his Oriental patience. "Arthur, I have thirty top officials from my agency waiting for me at the bleachers. Please, tell us why we are here." He looked about them, the gleaming launch pad, lights reflecting from the waters of the turning basin, the huge bowl of lights form the press site, and the monstrous Vehicle Assembly Building, the largest cube on the planet, rearing well over five hundred feet above the surface, emblazoned with an American flag and the NASA symbol, all of it imprisoned by miltiple arrays of floodlights turning night into artificial day. "I am lost," Saito continued. "I cannot tell if I am in some science fiction movie or a Grade B mystery suspense thriller."

"Hold your water," Kimberly snapped, ungracious as usual. "I still have some missing pieces to put in place. If your sniveling shoe clerks from the Department of the Interior are more important than what I may have to say to you, then I suggest you turn yourself around and march off."

Dr. Saito looked up and held Kimberly's gaze. "It is good that you have a reputation to overcome your poor manners," he told Kimberly. "I will grant you the time you need to rearrange whatever it is within your head. Then—"

Forrest Reed slipped between them, his back to Kimberly. He and Dr. Saito were old friends. "Toshio, he's acting this way because he's upset. And anything that upsets Arthur Kimberly has got to be positively monolithic. Put aside your feelings and—"

Saito gestured casually. "Tut, tut, my friend. I needed only this intervention to remind myself that we are supposed to be famous for patience." He leaned to the side to see around Reed's shoulder. "I apologize to you for impatience, Arthur. Even impertinence, if that will please you."

The tension eased, smiles appeared among them. To everyone's surprise, Kimberly seemed to banish his own imperious behavior. "If you would be good enough to walk with me to," he pointed, "that camera platform, we'll be off this road and somewhat in the shadows. I prefer that to being where we are. I feel—well," he said uncomfortably, "naked out here."

They were too astonished to respond. They followed him in silence to the girderwork at the base of a remote camera installation. Standing beneath a NO SMOKING sign, Kimberly filled his pipe and lit up. In the brief flare of his lighter flame they saw that rather than being obstinate or rebellious about the no smoking order he was simply unaware of it. He snapped the lighter shut with an audible click, took a long shuddering breath, and turned to his friends.

"I hate myself for this preamble," he began with more discomfort than they'd ever seen him reveal, "because I have always hated secrecy and censorship. *But*," and he seemed to bite on the word, "I must ask you to consider what we will say and discuss here in the most absolute confidence. If there is disagreement on this point tell me now." He looked at the seven scientists; they all nodded assent.

"You are all familiar with this code number we have been hearing tonight?"

Jesse Markham gestured. "Let me be certain. One nine two XRAY nine six. Is that correct?"

"You also call it," Felicity Powell added, "by a project name. Dustbin, I believe."

Kimberly nodded. "Correct on both counts. Dustbin is the seemingly innocuous cover name for a study of particles in vacuum. Dust, cometary debris, even atomic particles. The accretion of billions of years that escaped gravitational capture by the major celestial bodies. But it's quite a bit more than that. We began Dustbin as a long-term study back in 1985. That's twelve years ago, of course. In addition to my work with several universities I was also involved in scientific studies with both NASA and the air force—"

Professor Pietre was openly surprised and broke in without thought to his interruption. "*You*, Dr. Kimberly? You of all people working with the military? From everything I've heard you wouldn't even *talk* to those people!"

A wan smile met his remarks. "So people were supposed to believe," Kimberly said quietly. "Most of the work I did had nothing to do with military activities, but of course affected the military. As well as everybody else on this planet," he said wryly as a rebuke to the Frenchman. "Atmospheric research, hurricane tracking and control, wind shear effects and prediction, following volcanic and forest fire ash and dust clouds, measuring variations in the ozone layer, especially the reputed Antarctic breakdown—well, studies with which you are all familiar and which many other people were doing. Dr. Higgins, here, did a great deal of work with me. Several of you crossed paths with us. You, Toshio, because of Interior's involvement with every aspect of atmospheric phenomena. And, Felicity, your office in air force research funded much of our work. So. Some of you were even involved with what we were doing, and the others were aware of our activities."

He looked at each scientist one by one, and in the pause relit his pipe. "Forgive what appears to be a sophomoric rehash, but it is important we sustain continuity in our thinking. We're going to have to do a great deal more of *that*." He glanced at the great shuttle on its pad and gestured to take in all the launch sites nearby. As he turned, his gaze stopped with the sight of the moon on the low horizon. Kimberly thought back to his conversation hardly an hour before with Goddard Center in Maryland.

"Who took that call from Professor Kimberly?" Marv Coffin swung around in his swivel chair before his data panel deep within the Project Dustbin offices at Goddard. He nodded to Alice Mallory as she gestured. "I had the last one," she told him. "Any problems?"

Coffin nodded. "Yep. Not from the professor, though. You see the latest? No? Over here, babe, and hang on to your seat."

Alice Mallory rolled to a position alongside Marv Coffin, who activated the lunar monitor screens on his master panel. "Look here," he said as he pointed to Number 28. "That's the interior of the Ptolemaeus crater." They looked across the pitted dusty and boulder-strewn surface of the huge crater plain. "Now, I'll swing the observation camera around." Coffin worked his controls and a quarter-million miles away a robot camera moved obediently. The camera lens stopped at a sign reading Instrument Site Six. No Deposit on Bottles. *"Cute," Mallory said drily. "What are we looking for? Specifically, I mean?"*

By way of answer Coffin adjusted the distant camera

lens. They saw instrument spikes, antenna, solar collectors and cables and miscellaneous debris dumped during site construction. "Watch here," Coffin said, and brought the focus in close to the solar collectors that provided power for the remote instruments. Alice Mallory had seen these before. They were found on the moon, aboard satellites and the different space stations; anywhere solar energy could be tapped and utilized.

"I don't believe it," Mallory said slowly. "The last time I looked here those collectors were polished and . . ." Her voice fell away. What had been gleaming solar panels now showed a dingy surface of gray and brown. Coffin moved the focus in closer. "Holy shit," Mallory said, barely audible. At close range dust could be seen in whorls and clumps across the solar collectors. The picture began to fade.

"What's happening?" Mallory asked, bewildered.

"There was just enough juice left in the system for this look," Marv Coffin told her, but not looking at the woman. "Just enough electricity for a couple minutes' worth of looking. What happened? The whole damn instrument site's gone dead. There's no energy getting through to the collectors."

"Damn, I've got to get to Kimberly, then," Mallory said suddenly, starting back to her own console.

"No rush," Coffin told her. "I've already made the call. The professor went for a walk on the beach or something. We'll wait for him to get back to us."

Alice Mallory nodded slowly. She gestured to Coffin's control panel. "You getting the same conditions elsewhere?"

Coffin's fingers played expertly across his controls. "Let me run back the video and data tapes on the stations we've got on Phobos and Deimos. You won't believe it. It looks like someone dumped a vacuum cleaner bag on them."

Dr. Arthur Kimberly shook himself free of the immediate past and gave full attention to his colleagues. A distant horn sounded from the ocean; a passing vessel in the night, perhaps a coast guard cutter. *I must watch myself*, he thought angrily. *I'm letting every little detail drag me away from a reality I don't wish to admit. . . .*

"Go back in time perhaps twenty years," he said hurriedly. "The late nineteen seventies. You'll recall that was when Earth satellites and especially the distant planetary probes first began to encounter unexpected dust and meteoric particle densities. Nothing that unusual, of course. We were even able to chart gravitational patterns and prepare charts of where to expect such clouds. They were, after all, in gravitational capture of the major planetary bodies. But then," he closed his eyes briefly in search of memory details, "we began to encounter these same conditions in almost all sectors where we sent our probes. What captured our attention were the probes we sent to the major planets, probes that survived the asteroid belt and the terrible radiations of Jupiter and Saturn. What disturbed us, because it contradicted our extrapolations of dust conditions, was that *after* these probes went beyond the orbits of Jupiter and Saturn they were being reduced to junk by impact with dust particles."

Saito motioned to interrupt. "I fear I would ascribe such events to their velocity. Fifty and sixty miles a second—"

"That didn't do it," David Higgins broke in. "Accept if you will, Toshio, that all such predications have been taken into account. Velocity, unexpected bowl densities, gravitationally-held rings between planets, like an asteroid belt without sufficent mass for us to detect from Earth. You name it and we considered it. And none of the extrapolations fit. We were running into a phenomenon that simply had not been predicted."

"May I?" They turned to Jesse Markham. "I was on the lunar team as a young researcher back then," he added to Higgins' remarks. "I've remained with the lunar programs as my speciality ever since. I can be even more specific. We didn't pay much attention to an event that occurred during the last Apollo mission to and from the moon. That was Number Seventeen, back in 1972. The command and service module encountered a totally unexpected dust cloud during its return

81

to Earth. It was, oh, an event that covered some twenty thousand miles. An anomaly, nothing more or less. We considered it more a curiosity than anything else. When we examined the command module we found the windows severely pitted. We considered that to be an unexpected but still minor effect of re-entry. Later—much later, in fact—we had reason to go back to study just *what* and *how* those windows were pitted. They had gone through some severe effects *prior to* encountering terrestrial atmosphere on the return."

"Yes, yes," Henri Pietre said with a sense of growing excitement. "I was here as an exchange technician. We had some instruments on that mission and I went through the command module after its return. I remember how excited I was—I mean, to be moving through the very same ship that had carried men to and from *the moon*. I recall discussing the window erosion with Dr. Markham, here. We thought it might even be outgassing from the reaction controls of the spacecraft. But not everyone agreed with that conclusion. Outgassing, or even blowby of the reaction jets, produces a discoloration effect. This was not that at all. We were dealing with impact pitting."

They had warmed to the issue. In one way or another they had all been intertwined with their scientific research, and the pace of recollection and intermeshing picked up. "For years the only satellites we recovered," Kimberly took up the cudgel, "were military vehicles. The original Discover series, for example. Then the heavier reconnaissance satellites. But what we were recovering were payloads protected by shrouds while in orbit, and we were never able to tell from such equipment what might be happening to the outer shells. So they received little enough attention. It was in fact scant attention. Oh, we had failures of optical and sensing systems. Dr. Powell," he nodded to Felicity, "was disturbed by the degradation of optical lenses and other parts exposed to open space. Felicity?"

"There was not enough to provide the proper clues," the diminutive woman said softly. "When we showed alarm at the manner in which camera lenses were ground, as if by sandpaper, we were reminded that the reconsats had to be positioned properly for the cameras and sensing systems to do their tasks, and that meant, of course, firing reaction jets on almost every orbit. That, plus retrofire systems that sent out clouds of gaseous particles. The air force people concluded this to be the source of the problem and concentrated their attention, understandably, on the reconnaissance systems rather than our scientific pique."

"But—" As quickly as he spoke, the German member of the group cut off his own words. "I did not mean to interrupt. I have little to add, but I was curious about something."

Kimberly nodded to Klaus Schoenberger. "Please; your question?"

"There were other ships in space, no? I mean, Skylab is an example that comes at once to mind. The big American space station. It was in orbit a long time. Three different crews. I do not recall much being said about this problem with Skylab."

"That's because we didn't say too much," Forrest Reed answered. "Christ, there were windows on Skylab that had gone completely opaque on us. We had ready explanations. Outgassing of the glass surfacing. Ultraviolet radiation. Alternative heating and cooling for thermal expansion and contraction. Reaction jet firings. We had three Apollo spacecraft that rendezvoused with the station. That meant reaction control jets *and* some main engine firing. A hell of a lot of particle debris."

"Plus the garbage they dumped overboard," David Higgins added. "They dumped their piss—damn, I apologize, Felicity—"

"Urine is hardly a sensitive issue," she said. "Go on."

"Well, they dumped their urine overboard. Hell, it looked beautiful."

Schoenberger stared. "Beautiful? Human liquid waste?"

"That's right. Instant sublimation when it struck vacuum. It froze instantly to ice crystals. All those chemicals and acids. Whenever the station moved from darkness into dawn, crossing the terminator line, the low sun angles made the crystals explode with color, sparkling and shining like nothing else on or off Earth. It makes the most beautiful diamonds pale by comparison."

"The point," Kimberly carried on the issue, "is that there was enough junk and urine and gases and garbage out there with the Skylab to completely mislead us."

Henri Pietre motioned. "But you were flying the shuttle," he offered as a mild protest. He gestured at *Atlantis* glowing under its brilliant lights. "So many flights, and I remember," he smiled, "how we were so struck with wonder when your astronauts drifted away from their spacecraft. We watched the live television of how they recovered satellites, and those instrumented packages, and—"

"But we never went after any satellites that had been in orbit long enough, at that time, anyway," Higgins broke in, "to have had sufficient time for surface materials loss. Not with the shuttle flights we were making then, anyway."

"Yes, of course," Schoenberger added. "I was on the team to put a payload out for six months and then recover it, and . . ."

His voice fell away. They might all have shared the same unspoken thought. *Of course*. Challenger, *back in January of 1986. That terrible fire blossoming in the blue sky. Tendrils of flame and fingers of smoke and the pressure section falling for nearly three horrifying minutes all the way down from sixty-five thousand feet to smash into—*

"Well, we were misled even then," Kimberly said in a rush. "Do you remember when we first discovered that when the orbiter fell around Earth's darkside, the instrument packages taking films of the spacecraft showed it *glowing* in the dark? That famous glowing blue halo, all from the gases emanating from the ship and being ionized by the sun and by electrostatic fields?"

Toshio Saito offered a wan smile; he was still shaking off the stark memories of a great shuttle being torn to pieces. "There were even claims of angels, I recall. The spacecraft were blessed. They called the glow a heavenly halo."

"They called it many things, but none of it matters

now," Kimberly said, harshness tinging his tone. "You see, we were fooled by our own false conclusions, then."

"But not the Russians, eh, Arthur?" Higgins threw into the conversation.

Kimberly nodded. "Tell them," he said to the scientist from naval research.

"I was working closely with the Russians in the late seventies," Higgins explained. "Dubrov, Kruk, Yanshin; that crowd. Fortunately, I liked them and they liked me and events progressed into a permanent liaison. In other words, I had an open door with those people, and about ten years ago they were getting very upset about what was happening with their ships. They'd been firing both unmanned payloads and manned spacecraft into orbit with what *we* considered to be depressing regularity compared to our spits and sputters."

"They were putting up twenty-eight payloads to our one," Markham interjected with a scowl at the memory.

"He's right," Higgins confirmed. "They were firing their stuff all over the solar system, landing on Phobos and Deimos and then on Mars and the Jovian moons and—well, you read the newspapers just like everyone else. But they were flying some pretty important manned missions. They used their Salyut manned ships like buses. Up and back one after the other. They had a bunch of Salyut stations in orbit, and then they put up the Mir group of stations, and for a couple of years now they've had that Gagarin station in orbit. What I'm getting to is that they had a Mir constantly manned *for three years*. They kept changing crews, kept studying all the effects on those stations. And it was, um, I believe just about nine years ago when they sounded their first alarm to us."

"I do not recall any such alarm," Saito said, confused.

"They didn't go public with it, Toshio," Kimberly told him. "In fact, they asked us absolutely *not* to give any publicity to what they told us. David?"

Higgins picked up the thread. "To shorten a long and complicated series of events," he said, more serious than they had seen him, "the Russians discovered their windows were sandblasted, their antennae worn thin, their solar cells ruined. The amount of dust or gaseous particles they were encountering at orbital speed simply didn't meet their past experience. Five miles a second couldn't produce such effects based upon everything they had learned about near-Earth environment. Then *all* their spacecraft began to come unglued. The Molniyas, their weather sats and comsats, everything they had up there, failed one after the other. Since they had people up there in the Salyuts and Mirs they could do some hands-on testing. The answer, very simply, is that they were encountering extraordinary dust particle levels. Nothing fit the scenario. Wisely, they told us about it and asked for our input."

"What did we do!" Jesse Markham's question came out more as an exclamation.

Higgins replied with a short, nasty laugh. "What did we do?" he echoed. "Why, we acted like children sitting in a corner with our thumbs in our mouths—"

"Up our collective asses, you mean," Forrest Reed said nastily.

"We sulked," Higgins admitted. "I mean, *they* were making us look like incompetent idiots with hardly any flights while they were firing giant ships almost on a schedule. It was turnabout. Like the old days of Apollo, when we sent manned ships to and from the moon like express trains, and all the Russians could do was to blow up all *their* lunar boosters. Including a couple of them with men aboard. The upshot of it all was that we let it drop. We were desperately short of money. We didn't have the funds or the time or the people to listen to Russian grumbling about space dust. We were idiots. Stupid beyond all belief." He stuck his hands in his pockets and glowered at his own memories.

Kimberly's face reflected orange from his lighter as he rekindled his pipe. "Let me make it clear," he said as he exhaled a cloud of smoke, "that *I* was one of the scientists who should have known better. I did not. I adjudged the dust to be a normal aberration of flight. I considered the Russians as incompetents who enjoyed a temporary space superiority due to the old trucks they used for boosters. I was dead wrong."

Felicity Powell looked at him with a smile. "You, Arthur?"

"Me," he said emphatically.

"No wonder you brought us out here in the middle of this space Disneyland," she added with a touch of laughter. "To tell us your darkest secret deserves secrecy."

"You may remove your knife, Felicity," Kimberly said, without umbrage. "My point is that *I* was blind, but not Josh Arnold."

"Wait a moment," Saito motioned, startled with the name. "You are referring to *Joshua* Arnold? The former president of the United States?"

"Precisely," Kimberly snapped, irritated with the staccato burst of questions from Saito. "And you, Doctor, like most people, considered Josh Arnold to be a cornbelt politician without a serious brain in his head."

"A ricefield politician is what we called him."

"And you were all *wrong*," Kimberly spat. "Doctor Reed, here, and I worked with Arnold long before he set off on his political career. That cornbelt pose he affected was political wisdom. Josh Arnold had been a test pilot and then a weather scientist with the navy. He didn't use *that* as his platform. To compete with astronauts and other space-hero gadabouts would have been ridiculous. So he went back to the heartland. The cornbelt, or ricefield, or whatever the hell derogatory term you prefer. Let me stay with this, damn it, Toshio!"

Saito bowed slightly by reflex and kept his silence.

"Somehow, I guess when reading capsule reports that he read with absolute regularity," Kimberly went on, "he came across these reports of dust accretion. They disturbed him. Remember that he'd been a weather scientist. Being president doesn't leave much time for pursuing what the rest of us foolishly considered a scientific curiosity. Arnold called me into his office. I met with him. Dave Higgins was with us at the time. He'd done some report, I don't remember what it was—"

"Computer extrapolation of confirmed conditions," Higgins offered quietly. "When I got the computer results it scared hell out of me."

87

"What about you, Arthur?" Felicity Powell inquired. "What was your reaction to that report?"

"Me?" Kimberly laughed harshly and they recognized self-criticism in his retort. "*I*, like the other lofty members of my myopic profession—although not even before God would we admit *that*—had all sorts of precedence to shoo away annoying flies like young David Higgins. After all, we'd been hearing cries of danger in regard to ozone layer depletion, the greenhouse effect, nuclear radiation, raising ocean levels. There were bogeymen everywhere. So what if the solar system was moving through dust a bit heavier than what we knew about? Even at its thickest it was still a hard vacuum. Dust 'density' in this respect was meaningful only by comparison to prior conditions. We were too smug to recognize reality in the form of sandblasted metal and glass!"

"Are you saying," asked Pietre, "that you were—well, foolish is an expression kinder than—"

"Than stupid?" Kimberly threw at him. "What the hell do you want, Henri? A goddamned legal affidavit? Stupid? Foolish? Dumber than shit? We were worse. *We were blind by choice.* We were sulking, remember? It had become a national habit by then."

"Forgive me," Pietre murmured.

"For what? The truth?" Kimberly said, his teeth grating.

Forrest Reed touched his arm. "Go on, Arthur."

Kimberly shrugged. "I'll call any one of you or all of you unmitigated jealous liars if you ever breathe so much as a single word of what I've admitted about myself," he warned them.

"Goddamn it, stop the self-flagellation, Arthur!" Felicity Powell said harshly. "Get with it!"

"In February of 1987 Josh Arnold had a small group set up Project Dustbin," Kimberly went on.

"Wait a moment," Schoenberger interrupted. "What is this code one nine two, uh, xray nine six? What was that?"

"Nothing at all," Kimberly said with a smile. "Psychology. Public relations. A project with that kind of designation has mystique. It is a great assist in squeezing appropriations from a stubborn Congress." They shared a brief laugh, then Kimberly sobered. "I must add that I didn't agree with Josh Arnold that what we'd learned about the dust presented any meaningful danger. But that didn't mean we just passed it off. We *did* consider the possibilities."

"List them, please," said Dr. Saito.

"The theories went on and on," Kimberly reflected. "But Arnold—the president, I mean—and I spent hours about what dust thickening *could* mean. I'll do no more now than gloss over the issues we considered. If the solar system was moving along with the sun through a galactic region that was truly as heavy, dustwise, as we have observed in certain nebula, then obviously we would encounter severe interference with the solar radiation received by this world. That could produce all sorts of negative results. It might diminish the total radiated energy we receive and thus bring on a calamitous ice age. Conversely, as some of my colleagues argued, though more from a devil's-advocate position, the dust could act as a fuel to stoke the thermonuclear furnace of the sun. *That* would increase the radiated output of the sun, and this little world of ours would bake like a blistering turkey in some galactic oven."

Kimberly laughed, a memory of past moments about which the world knew nothing. "You wouldn't *believe* the postulations that went through our group. We ran computer extrapolations through the entire solar system. If the solar effect was a radiation increase, then likely the subterranean frozen oceans of Mars would liquefy, and despite some loss through sublimation the melting would be so rapid and extensive that once more, since billions of years past, the river of Mars would again flow down the old channels. The moons of Jupiter and Saturn, especially the frozen-atmosphere bodies, would heat up to an extent where life processes, once started, could begin again at their most basic stages."

Kimberly shook his head as if to free himself of the long-running list of potential events. "Let me not waste time on the scenarios that we found entertaining, possible, implausible, ridiculous—whatever. The point I wish to make is that *my* contention was that the solar system had in all likelihood passed through innumerable dust clouds in its history and we're still here. Mathematically, we should have had at least a hundred and thirty such encounters. That was *my* attitude. I thought the whole concept was, to quote a favorite phrase of Doctor Reed's here, as so much wasted pissing into the wind."

His untoward remark brought on brief smiles, then they again gave him their full attention. "Now, the other point is that Joshua Arnold wouldn't let go of this thing, and the fact of the matter is that I kept thinking of him as the president and I effectively, and stupidly, managed to forget that he had also been an extremely capable and experienced weather scientist. Josh finally drew the bottom line as the rule for us to follow. What was the worst scenario we might encounter from really heavy dust? And how long in time might we be exposed to the consequences of such—he called it an infestation of our little pocket of space."

"Let me break in here," David Higgins said abruptly. "I can't really believe Arthur Kimberly is taking all the blame on his shoulders. That's neither in his character nor is it the truth. We *all* rejected the concept of the grand catastrophe. I want to emphasize what Arthur mentioned before. We'd had so many scenarios of mass destruction. A meteoric or cometary impact that wiped out the dinosaurs when," he added drily, "a virus could have done the same thing. The nuclear scientists howled like wolves at the moon with their nuclear winter. You know all the others. We were convinced we were going through a replay of old bogeymen under a new title. But since it *was* the president of this country who ordered the computer extrapolations, we did it. That job fell on my shoulders."

"And what *was* the worst you found?" Klaus Schoenberger seemed to be hypnotized by clear revelations of what had so long been rumor.

Higgins seemed to slump, a scarecrow figure suspended from a pole behind his body. "First, a brief but devastating period of severely depressed temperature. Not an ice *age*. It wouldn't last that long. Soon after, a reversal as the sun gained trillions of tons of additional mass every second. Stoking the furnace, so to speak. A sudden and drastic increase in thermal radiation, and ionizing radiation as well. The sunspot effect would become—well, the worst we've ever known would be a sputtering match compared to an atomic bomb."

Professor Pietre smiled. "The end of the world, no?" The smile expanded to free laughter. "Invasion from Mars. Killer tomatoes. Body snatchers. Things and beings. Ah, how wonderful is your imagination. Jules Verne was a little boy in comparison to all this!"

"Hush, Henri," Felicity Powell chided the Frenchman. "What they told you was what the *computers* extrapolated, not what they believed."

"But, madame! It makes such a wonderful script!"

A dirty look from the small woman brought a rueful expression to Pietre and he nodded and kept his silence.

Arthur Kimberly had turned to look at *Atlantis*. Plumes of white vapor spewed forth from its sides from the pressure vents of liquid oxygen and liquid hydrogen. "Listen," he said. "Be quiet and listen. You can hear her singing."

For the moment they believed Kimberly had lost his senses. they remained absolutely quiet, straining, and then they heard it, rising and falling on the night wind. A chorus of voices, tenor and bass and soprano, some deep and others shrill, crying out into the night, phantom sounds that were real. "Good Lord," Felicity Powell said in awe, "it sounds like whales calling across the oceans." She turned to Kimberly. "Am I really hearing this? What is it?"

Jesse Markham placed his hand tenderly on her shoulder. "I've listened to that sound since as far back as I can remember. Those are the pipes you're hearing."

"The pipes?" echoed Saito, bewildered.

"Down here they call them the Pipes of Pan. They're the pipes carrying the cryogenics, the liquid hydrogen and liquid oxygen. The pipes bend at different angles and when the moist wind blows across them they react with a metallic shriek. This far away the night wind changes the sound. What we hear is singing."

"Incredible," Pietre said.

But Toshio Saito was fidgeting. "Arthur, *please*," he told Kimberly. "Go on. Let us finish what you have staged this evening!"

"All right," Kimberly responded, returning to the matter at hand. "When we finished our computer studies, Josh Arnold made Dustbin an ongoing project. It would be funded from other programs to keep its real purpose secret. Josh ordered us to keep elaborate records over the years. It was all low-key activity but with prime support. Remember, I wasn't asked to do this. I was *ordered* by the president. Arnold was as good as his word. We had excellent computer and records facilities, photographic and film labs; everything we needed. Stations throughout the world fed data on a steady basis into our central computer so we had a constant extrapolative update. But what always stuck most clearly in my mind was that President Arnold made it clear I answered to him and to him only."

Kimberly sighed, emptying his pipe of ashes against the heel of his shoe. "*That* should have alerted me."

"To what?" Markham asked.

"That whoever became president after Josh served his terms would also know of our arrangement," Kimberly explained. "That Josh Arnold intended the line of authority to remain unbroken. But what I never really understood all this time," Kimberly sighed, "was that I was never the hotshot in this whole picture. Far from it," he admitted ruefully. "I was simply the caretaker of the records we continued to gather."

Kimberly again lapsed into silence, staring at *Atlantis* and the multicolored lights drifting through the sky like fireflies of different flashing hues. "Until now, that is," he appended with an ominous tone.

The scientists looked at one another. Felicity Powell gestured; she would ask the obvious question. "You're referring to that telephone call a short while ago?"

"Yes."

They grew impatient with his silence. "Damn it, spit it out, Arthur," Markham snapped.

Kimberly drew himself up straighter; he seemed to gain in stature before their eyes. "Today is the twelfth of May and the year is nineteen ninety-seven. You, and I, and many more people, just about everyone on earth, are going to have good cause to remember this date. Those telephone calls were from central data of Project Dustbin where all incoming reports are collated, updated and then constantly analyzed by the computers." He drew a deep, shuddering breath, fighting to get out the rest of what he had to say.

"Earlier today, seven out of every ten stations and sites reporting on the increasing density of dust in and beyond this solar system went over their alert level. That makes the situation somewhat more than academic. It is now considered to be absolutely critical."

"Why so quickly?" demanded Schoenberger.

"Because most of those stations are already *failing*," Kimberly said, a touch of nastiness returning to his tone now that he'd cleansed himself of what he had concealed for so long. "And they will fail only when the dust density becomes so great it will literally sandblast a moving probe—or *cover* the surface of a probe stationary to a larger body such as a moon or asteroid."

"You are telling us, then," Henri Pietre said with great care, "that the Earth itself is now endangered?"

Forrest Reed laughed harshly. "In somewhat less than academic terms, Henri, you bet your sweet ass it is!"

"And what now?" queried Felicity Powell.

"A meeting," Kimberly told her.

She smiled. "Another meeting like this?" she said disarmingly.

"By no means, Felicity. This one goes all the way to the top. A meeting has already been scheduled with President Starling. I doubt we can go higher than *that*—"

"Well, there's always God," Higgins quipped.

"*Her* schedule seems to be full," Felicity Powell retorted, and turned back to Kimberly. "Are we invited?"

"You are *requested*," Kimberly answered immediately.

"When?" The short query from Schoenberger.

Kimberly glanced at his watch and gestured toward the shuttle on its launch pad. "*Atlantis* is to fly less than an hour from now. I suggest we relieve Mr. Simmonds of his apologetic feelings and walk back to the fallback line. As quickly as we can after that, when the traffic leaving here subsides, we shall leave for Washington."

Then and there they dropped the subject of Dustbin, an unvoiced consent between them to push it aside and give in to the fiery wonders of *Atlantis'* departure from the planet. The clock went through its backward count flawlessly and precisely at seven o'clock, against a brightening dawn sky, the horizon exploded in violent orange flame. A billion prehistoric voices howled as *Atlantis* crashed upward. Then it was silent, only the thick pillar of twisting white smoke etching the sky where a great vessel had fled.

5

Hank Marrows sat numb and dumb on the metal grating. Sharp points dug into the skin of his ankles and his buttocks and he knew he should have been swearing with pain but he couldn't feel a goddamned thing. He'd been numb for nearly two hours. All he had to do to return movement to his body, which acted as if it were set in hardened cement, was get off his numb ass and force his limbs to follow the commands of his brain. But his brain wasn't working. Not well, anyway. So Hank Marrows sat crosslegged on a metal grating that held a battery of cameras, and he forced himself to think. Not easy. He couldn't string one sensible thought after another.

Fuck it. I want a cigarette. But that's dumb. I quit smoking eleven years ago when that asshole sawbones told me I was getting lung cancer and if I didn't quit smoking all those coffin nails I didn't have a year left. So I quit. Now I know I'm going to die—ahead of

94

schedule, I guess—and I fucking well want a fucking cigarette and why won't my fucking brain work?

His hands moved. They hadn't done that in a while. Of course they moved stupidly. He found his hands patting his pockets searching for a cigarette pack that wasn't there. Not one lousy butt. *Stupid hands. But at least I'm moving a part of me.* He took command of his hands and used them to move his legs. Now he sat with his legs together and his knees drawn up to his chin and he wrapped his arms and hands about his legs and clasped himself tightly.

I'm acting like a goddamned kid. Jesus, this is crazy. How many wars have I been in? How many plane crashes? Jumps from planes in those stupid parachutes? Two ships sunk under me? Fires, explosions, epidemics, revolutions. Me, Hank Marrows. Best goddamned field reporter in the world. Pulitzer prize. Scooped the world a dozen times. Asshole buddy with presidents and kings and dictators and queens and— Oh, shut up.

But he couldn't help thinking about the past because it led smack right to this moment. Even that great scoop on *Epsilon*. Fed up with explosive Russian superiority in manned space flight, the United States had assembled a massive package to put up a jury-rigged eight-man space station and hurled the sucker into orbit. *No; that was four men and four women. Eight astronauts.* They'd nearly had a worldwide riot because of *Epsilon*. A plague erupted among the crew. Two men went mad. There was murder and assault and raging insanity four hundred and sixty miles above the Earth. The four survivors said to hell with this shit and prepared for immediate exit from *Epsilon* to return home, back to Earth for top medical treatment.

That's when the Big Fright erupted. Lurid news accounts of a spaceborne plague being brought back to Earth triggered a global spasm of intense fear. Evangelists and doomsdayers drooled with the opportunity. Terrified people overflowed the churches to such an extent that tent-city houses of worship sprang up throughout the world. A warning from God to keep man on Earth where he belonged, *that* was the message. The four surviving astronauts could not be brought back to Earth or plague and pestilence would ravage the land. *Blah, blah, blah.* An animal smell of fear and hatred swept a planet.

Hank Marrows broke the story. He had contacts all the way into the bowels of the space program. He had friends and where he didn't have friends he had people he could bribe to give him information. It was a hell of a story, and it got even bigger when riots broke out around the world. *Don't let them come back to pollute the Earth with the space plague.* That was the general idea. It sure as hell got out of hand in a hurry.

Marrows had been at the Kennedy Space Center, feeding copy directly from his typewriter into a computer hookup directly to his newspaper office. He didn't believe the *Global Times* would run his copy, but he wrote it the way he felt. That was his style. If they wanted to clean up his act that was their choice. But at that moment screaming mobs were outside the gates of the Kennedy Space Center and this was *news* time, boy! So Marrows wrote it the way he saw it, the way it really was.

"Today *homo sapiens* showed his true colors," he banged out on his typewriter keys, and the miracle of electronics swept his words into a distant office; Marrows didn't know that his top editor had already decided to run the copy just the way Marrows might write it. *Jesus . . .*

"Today the dominant race on this planet tucked its tail between its legs, shivered through its rump, and howled fearfully at the moon. Today the shit hit the fan."

He'd written those words with tremendous enjoyment, because he held most of mankind in utter contempt and he knew what they didn't. The space plague was nothing of the sort. One of the astronauts came from the Sudan, and just before the flight, he made a fast jet trip home to parade his black ass in his nifty NASA blue suit in his home village, downriver of some godawful swamp. He'd taken swamp fever of some bizarre and forgotten nature with him when he returned to crawl into the modified Apollo they used to put up four people in one shot. That was the program. Use the old Saturn IB boosters that had never failed, each kicking a four-man tin can into orbit to rendezvous with the bigger tin can they called *Epsilon*. Swamp fever, by Jesus! Oh, it was a hell of a story, and Hank Marrows had laughed and choked and spluttered at the idiocy of the human race. Smart enough to walk the moon and land robots on Mars and Venus and Phobos and Deimos and Titan and who the hell cared where else, but not smart enough to know the difference between swamp fever that had decimated African native populations for thousands of years and some frightful space plague that didn't even exist.

Two hundred thousand people died in maddened assaults against space launching centers. That a manned vehicle hanging beneath a big goddamned parachute didn't land from the same place it launched made no difference. *"Kill the fuckers! Destroy the unholy! Kill! Kill!"* They yelled that in thirty languages as they stormed the launch sites about the world, *and* the remote research centers, *and* the administrative offices, and for good measure they poured onto military airfields where defensive forces of the American and the Russian strategic attack systems had no choice but to defend where they stood, as well as themselves. They killed more people in one day than died at Hiroshima, Nagasaki, Berlin, London, Tokyo and a dozen other cities ripped up in World War Two.

When it was all over, and the morning came grim and smoking about the planet where chaos and fear had rampaged the night through, millions of people were dead, vast numbers of scientists, technicians, and totally innocent people had been burned, tortured, slashed, beaten and otherwise killed in gory manner, and nothing had been accomplished except to prove once again that prehistoric fears and animals still stalked the back regions of the human skull.

Hank Marrows had long been the archtypical newsman of old: thinning but still thick salt-and-pepper hair, a cigarette dangling from his lips with ashes strewn over whatever-it-was he was wearing, a limitless thirst for cold beer, terrific sense of timing with his copy and his willingness to go anywhere and try anything. With years of malaise tearing apart the guts of the American space program after what he described as the "suspended horror animation" of the *Challenger* crew as they waited, helpless and angry, to die from their long and almost languid fall from sixty-five thousand feet—no other newsman pointed out that their descent into the ocean from the lofty arch of their death plunge took place with the same speed of a heavy jet airliner *taking off*—he managed to keep alive his news reports from the different space centers of the country. And that was tough. Nobody cared any more. He couldn't blame the public. NASA had degenerated from a scrubbed-face image of the boy next door who couldn't do any wrong into a stumbling, irrational and utterly stupid mob of people roaming around and wailing, "Who's in charge here?" The air force spent nearly four billion dollars to package its Slick Six launch pad for its shuttle from Vandenberg Air Force Base in California and then mothballed the damn place *for seven years!*

When they shut down SLC-6, Marrows wrote that "the United States Air Force has just accomplished the most extraordinary building feat in history. For the approximately equal cost of building fifty-eight Taj Mahal temples, they erected a monstrous space-launching facility and then boarded it up. Imagine, if you will, a Taj Mahal in every major city of the world, and on the day of their completion, nail shut all the doors and windows. The builders of the pyramids must be rocking their burial chambers with hysterical laughter."

But there is now and the Taj Mahal and Slick Six are past events and I have got to get my ass off this god-damned platform and Jesus, I'd give a month's pay for a smoke. The first thing I'm gonna do when I unwind my ass from this godawful platform is buy a hundred cartons of cigarettes and get a dozen cases of beer and smoke my fucking brains out.

He rubbed his cramped leg muscles. He was sixty-eight years old and in damned good shape, but his legs cramped after a while and there'd been too many busted bones in the past and torn ligaments and smashed tendons and his body knew how to get even with him. He hurt like hell. He told himself the pain was sweet and wonderful, because he remembered all too well coming out of deep coma after the crash of a jet fighter in which he was riding—smack, crunching bone-twisting smack, onto the deck of an aircraft carrier—because when he opened his eyes *he couldn't feel anything*. He never again complained about pain. It took a month to get feeling back into his beat-up system then and pain had been a grimacing but good friend ever since. He slung camera straps about his neck and over his shoulder and lifted the trapdoor in the metal grating, and he climbed down slowly, taking the metal ladder rungs one by one until his feet touched asphalt. He took a deep breath and squinted into the morning sun and admired the snarled smoke trail of *Atlantis* where it had bared its fire teeth and hurled itself into waiting vacuum and the centrifugal slot of its orbit high overhead.

No one in NASA knew he'd been here for the launch. Well, *almost* no one. Sal Price from the communications team that monitored electronics transmissions at the space center knew. For a thousand bucks cash he'd slowed down and stopped for a moment in darkness along the roadway that paralleled the crawlerway to the launch pad, and he'd shut off his lights and covered for Hank Marrows as the grizzled newsman climbed the ladder and opened the trapdoor that let him onto the platform. He lowered the trapdoor, tapped on it three times to signal Sal Price that he was set, and covered himself and his cameras with a black canvas that blended him in with the equipment mounted atop the platform.

He had heard every word spoken by the eight scientists who gathered beneath the platform. He had switched on his pocket recorder as he heard the voices approaching. He had heard and recorded every word of Professor Arthur Kimberly baring his soul. He had heard in utter disbelief the questions and the back-and-forth conversations of the seven scientists with Kimberly. Heard it. Recorded it!

He had a tape recording of eight scientists discussing the fucking end of the fucking world.

He wanted a cigarette! He stayed under cover until Sal Price showed up in the communications van and Marrows slipped inside. "Hey, man, how'd it go?" Price asked, always jittery about what he did with Marrows until he had the newsman safely back at the press site and mixing with the crowd.

"Nice and easy," Marrows told him staring straight ahead. "Nice and quiet. Got some good pictures." He squeezed his leg to keep from shaking. "Sal, gimme a butt."

"Hey, you know I don't smoke on duty. They're real shitty about that here," Price protested.

"I'm not asking *you* to smoke the fucking thing," Marrows snarled. He grabbed the pack Sal Price held out. "Buy yourself another pack," he said, sticking a cigarette between his lips and stuffing the pack in a shirt pocket. He patted himself. "Jesus, of course I don't have a match. Sal, damn it, give me—" Price was already holding out a lighter. Marrows grabbed it and lit up and nearly coughed up half his lungs as the first deep cloud billowed into his chest.

It hurt like hell. It tasted terrific.

That was all that felt good.

Hank Marrows had the greatest story of his career. The greatest story of his life, for Christ's sake. He wasn't any ordinary newsman. He had two degrees in science. He'd been a pilot ever since he spent six years in the navy as a fighter pilot when he crawled forth from his teens. He'd spent a lifetime in the midst of advanced research, studying, learning, interviewing the greatest minds in all the world. He probably had a better overall view and understanding of the space program than any astronaut or scientist in the world. He had the enormous advantage of seeing that program from a span of more than forty years and from every conceivable angle. He had the even greater advantage of looking at things from the keen analytical and cynical

100

eye of the news reporter who's seen and experienced just about all there was to see and do in the business of space and astronautics and astrophysics. Hank Marrows was as familiar with the moon as the average Saudi was with his desert. He knew the features of the Martian landscape better than most locals knew their Virginia or Montana countryside.

He was comfortable with centrifugal force, apogee and perigee, liberation points, solar wind, quasars and relativity and time-space warps and black holes and galactic gushers and—

And with dust in space. With accretion and density and the so-called bowls, the planetary rings and cometary trails, and with outgassing and spacecraft acting as gravitational focal points for their own waste gases and astronaut urine and fecal matter and garbage and . . .

He left the communications van behind the geodesic dome of the press site headquarters. No one paid any attention to one more newsman walking behind the row of stinking portable toilets and their particular sickening brand of heavy chemicals and earthbound waste. Most of the news crowd was gathered out front of the bleachers for the usual blah-blah postlaunch press conference. He eased back into the normal routine with no more fuss than attended his unseen departure.

He fell heavily into a cushioned seat in the main press room and dumped his gear onto the floor. For several minutes he stared morosely at nothing, a vacant stare from a mind that wanted desperately to be vacant. But his thoughts wouldn't let him be.

What the hell am I going to do with this story? This isn't any theory. I know what's coming down, by Jesus Christ. They are really looking at the end of the world. Who the hell am I going to write this story for? Posterity?

A burst of laughter escaped him. He'd never really thought of that before. *There ain't gonna be no posterity. History is going to have a posterior, that's all. Looking backwards is all the world will have left. I can see it now. A world exclusive by Hank Marrows. I'll call it a really deepdown exclusive. Protoscope! by Hank Marrows and his Rear End View of the News! No shit, José.*

Old reflexes came to his aid. He knew he'd never write this story until the time was right, and that time would come only when governments could no longer conceal the truth. They'd need all the secrecy they could get if they were going to try to save a sliver of the human race. Unbidden his mind raced through a barrage of the possibilities and he forced down those thoughts. It was too much, too soon, too overwhelming. He didn't want to wrestle with it. He'd sit on it. He'd keep his mouth shut and his typewriter silent and he wouldn't go with the greatest story of all time because he couldn't. *But why? You're a newsman, Ace, and you gotta go with the story, baby.* Oh, he knew why. For the first time in his life he'd encountered the need to be a human being as a priority higher than being a news reporter.

He'd felt the reflex and he went with it, and he fished for the cigarette pack and stuck a butt in his mouth. No matches. He got up and walked to a row of offices. Empty. The NASA flacks were outside shepherding the newsmen through the blah-blah post-launch talk session. Someone had a pack of matches on his desk. Marrows stepped into the office and took the matches and returned to the seat with his gear. He slumped down and lit up and dragged deeply and blew out a long cloud of smoke.

The coughing brought tears to his eyes and he laughed at himself. Someone came over to him. "Hey, no smoking in this section. Can't you read the signs?" he admonished, pointing.

"Sure," Hank Marrows said, feeling slightly giddy and knowing he was the only newsman in all the world who knew the world was going to end a hell of a lot sooner than these assholes could ever imagine. "I can read your sign." He looked up and smiled. "Fuck you."

6

Vasily Iliych Tereshnikov wore the glittering insignia of a lieutenant general in the Space Brigade of the Soviet Air Force of the Union of Soviet Socialist Republics. When in full uniform he wore proudly his thrice-awarded Hero of the Soviet Union, the highest decoration of his country, as well as enough other awards, medals and decorations that covered his left chest most of the way to his waist. Gold, silver, platinum, diamonds, and other precious gemstones adorned his uniform as the more visible symbols from a grateful nation. Tereshnikov was every inch and every pound the most genuine of heroes in the finest of Russian and Communist traditions. The people regarded him as truly one of their own, a hero hewn from the thick forests of native peasantry, proof that even the lowest of the low, the poorest of the poor, could emerge from that lot in life to climb even to the stars. True enough, Vasily Tereshnikov had fought and struggled to emerge from a land called Siberia.

Despite the claim of Siberian peasantry, as far distant as the region of Altai, two thousand miles and more from Moscow, Tereshnikov appealed just as greatly to the privileged hierarchy of the Soviet apparatus who found in their national hero a true man of *Rodina*, the Motherland: courageous, brilliant, faithful, a dedicated Communist and a man addicted to spending long months at a time seven hundred miles above the planet. That, agreed the highest members of the Kremlin, was the best of all possible ways to laud a true hero of the Communist Party. One who is always visible—*almost* visible, anyway. But Vasily Iliych, he of the log cabin in the remote village of Polkovnikovo, former Olympic superstar, superb fighter pilot, musician, master of six languages, scientist, mathematician, the most dashing and appealing of all the cosmonauts, a veteran of eleven flights into high Earth orbit, Master Cosmonaut who had three times walked through the clinging dust of the moon, while himself not quite visible to the naked eye, was nevertheless at this moment aboard the great space station, *Gagarin*, gleaming in its swift passage seven hundred miles above Mother Russia. *That* is quite visible enough for the Party.

But not acceptably visible for the Russian women who swooned in their fantasies or yearned in their dreams that Vasily Iliych might share their sheets and plunder their bodies. Gazing into the heavens at a gleaming cold light warms no stomach and fills no arms. And was it not true that, when circumstances permitted, Russia's greatest hero would share his glory? Tall, broad-shouldered, heavy-muscled, unlike most Russians without a single hair on his huge chest, he was infamously wanton in his physical desires.

Parlor conversations regarding the maleness of Vasily were legion. *I spoke with Zemfira, who knows this Eevi, and it was after the banquet that by accident, of course it was by accident! she found herself in the room of Vasily Iliych. What is he like? They say he is the reincarnation of the monk himself! Rasputin's loins reborn. He is furious in the bedchamber, he has the same burning light of possession. Inexhaustible! He makes love like a locomotive roaring through a Siberian night! They say in Star City that the only women he knows in all of Russia with whom he has not fornicated are his mother and his four sisters, and they are too ugly for his taste!*

Ah, Vasily Iliych, moaned a million Russian women as their hands moved beneath their covers and their eyes turned upward, as if through the ceilings of their bedrooms and seven hundred miles up they could feast on the sight of this man.

Had they been able to do so they would have been rewarded quite properly for their effort. At this moment, seven hundred miles above the earth, Vasily Iliych Tereshnikov was buck naked. He wore only a huge grin. To the delight of Colonel-Cosmonaut Tanya Yevteshenka—veteran of a month of unbroken space flight, buxom, broad-hipped, and pubis damp from expectation—with Vasily's grin went an impressively huge erection. She smiled and reached for him. Easy enough in bed, but sometimes very frustrating in weightlessness.

"No, no! Do not use any handholds, Tanya," Vasily cautioned, pulling away his arms as he floated upside down before her, legs bent slightly. It provided an amazing angle for that erection. "Do not forget our agreement, little one. We are in zero g and we must remain absolutely that way. You cannot use any of the side grips or the clamps."

"But just my *feet*?"

"No!" he remonstrated. "We agreed—"

"Just *one* foot?" she pleaded.

"Not even one toe," he laughed. "Not a fingernail." She stared as his member swung up and down as if a heavy weight hid within the part she wanted so anxiously. "Remember, Tanya, if this is to be memorable as we wish, then we must be free of *all* earthly bonds."

She laughed and flung wide her arms in total capitulation. Giving in to her laughter was delightful, but it brought her no closer to Vasily and his marvelous instrument. Her sudden laughter with her expelled breath and the reaction of her limbs moved her *away* from her lover-to-be and left him hanging limply—well, not really, she sighed gratefully—in almost the center of the heavily cushioned cabin. She twisted and reached out anxiously for the nearest wall (ceiling? floor?) so she could push off to float back to Vasily. Ah, a hand grip. That lay within his rules. As long as their bodies weren't touching, she could use whatever she could reach to reposition herself. She swung her body about, one breast floating upward and the other pushing against her chest from the torque of the twist. There. She must aim properly. *Now*. She tensed her leg muscles and floated away from the wall, moving closer to him where he hung suspended, arms wide and legs spread. He was as anxious as she. Damn his silly male zero-gravity rules! But this time they would meet; she swore it.

They flailed wildly for one another, laughing hysterically. He managed to clasp a breast with a powerful grip. It swung her away from her float and down. Her arm moved instinctively, brushed against his thigh and grasped at him. Unknowingly she closed her fingers and mashed down on his testicle. He bellowed with the sudden pain and she bit her lip to keep from shrieking with renewed laughter, this time clasping what she had wanted for so long. Their faces came close and they grinned at one another, their faces glistening with perspiration. Their exertions had made them sweat like horses and most of their sweat collected glistening on their bodies. Sudden movement flung some of the liquid away from them. Clouds of vapor moved slowly about them from the fans of the cabin ventilation system.

Now, hands sliding across skin, they coupled face to face, her strong legs encircling his waist, but his weapon flat up against her stomach, reaching almost to her navel. They maneuvered a bit frantically and the interminable delay and crazy gymnastics became worth all the effort as she arched her back, constantly positioning herself, grasping him with one hand and then clasping him violently. They came together with a slippery bang, hands desperately sliding along slippery skin, and he could control himself no longer. "Now!" he roared. "Now we do it, my Tanya!" With the cry of a grizzly bear his body arched and he smashed their loins together. She shrieked with pleasure and a moment later cried out with dismay. You do not make love in weightlessness without forgetting, not for an instant, the presence of the third party to the lovemaking. Isaac Newton grinned at them from the musty pages of history with his law of action and reaction, and their bodies bounded away from one another, legs akimbo, their sexual liaison terribly brief. With that one mighty lustful lunge and reaction, her grip broken by their treacherous slippery skin, they managed barely to clasp one another with their arms but their lower bodies were well apart and their embrace became all the more ridiculous as they pawed and grasped greedily for one another. Vasily grunted in frustration and heat; Tanya smirked.

"You do not live up to your reputation as a Siberian locomotive," she needled him.

Vasily twisted his body, fanning the air with one hand in a ludicrous swimming motion, inhaling deeply and exhaling in the direction opposite to his intended passage. He reached a handhold, remembered his own rules and released his grip as if stung, and pulled himself to her along her arm, surrounded by a haze of beaded perspiration. Tanya noticed, almost with a separate sight, that the globules of perspiration shimmered and danced in the cabin air.

"Vasily, my sweet, my Rasputin of orbit, you will wear yourself out before we succeed. I shall be the first old maid of space, unfulfilled and broken in heart and with an aching and empty belly."

"Do not move!" he shouted. "I will come to you!"

"What you promise you have not delivered," she said acidly.

He glared at her, twisted mightly, and banged their heads together. They swung wildly from one another. Tanya snatched at a handgrip protruding from the padded wall. "Vasily, *enough!* Damn your rules! Save your acrobatics and your record books for some other woman. I want to make love! I want you inside me! *I will use the handgrips!*"

She locked her hands and feet securely in position, her arched back to him, waiting as he held her by one elbow and maneuvered himself carefully into position. "I feel like a dock," she said over her shoulder.

She saw the quizzical expression on his face. "A dock? What do you mean?"

"A dock for a very large submarine," she said sweetly. "Hopefully, its captain knows how to enter port, And— *Vasily!*"

She shrieked wildly as he gripped her pelvis and exhibited the seamanship she had wanted, penetrating deeply, thrusting madly with pent-up frustration and long-delayed lust. "Oh! Vasily! That is—" She gasped for air as her entire body quivered, breasts bouncing wildly in weightlessness, slamming against her chest and up against her chin. How marvelous! He crashed into her again. "Vasily! Oh, how marvelous! Love me, love—"

The emergency monitor crashed against their ears, the alarm clamoring angrily, an explosive outpouring of sound echoing painfully about them in the cubicle. "That's the fucking alarm!" Vasily bellowed. A stream of curses followed his angry shout as he pulled out of her, moving now with practiced skill, his body shooting quickly to the opposite side of the cubicle to the emergency communications panel duplicated in every section of *Gagarin*. Tanya was right behind him. Together they scanned the gauges.

"Nothing!" he roared. "Not a thing wrong with the station! No air leaks, no pressure breaches, no solar alarms, no loss of power! Then what—" They saw it at the same moment. The priority communicator. His hand banged against the ACTIVATE switch. In that moment he forgot that he brought to life audio *and video* systems. Whoever was on the other end of the line was seeing him floating naked and sweaty in the cubicle. To hell with that. But there was also Tanya, just as naked and sweaty and— To hell with that, too. "Tereshnikov! Identify!" he snarled at the microphone.

The video screen snapped to life. Vasily Tereshnikov stared disbelieving at the face of John Hastings. The American capcom, still the name they used at Houston for the communicator on the command line, also stared. But only for a moment as he broke into a huge grin at the televised sight of the two naked Russians swaying in weightlessness. "Well, shoot, I guess I interrupted something," Hastings chuckled. "Sorry about that, old friend. I could give you a couple of minutes, Vasily."

Tereshnikov's hand moved to cut the video. But he stayed the move. Naked didn't matter. John Hastings was an American astronaut and an old friend. They'd even flown a mission together in one of the older Mir stations, but *now* . . . And what the devil was an American doing on the top secret wavelength of the *Gagarin* station? Those thoughts flashed through his mind and dismissed completely any inhibitions at being unclothed.

"John, for you to call on this wavelength must be very important. Later you will tell me how you managed this, but for now, tell me *why*."

The grin faded from the American capcom. Hastings' tone changed imperceptibly but meaningfully. "This is Dustbin Priority," Hastings said. "Do you copy? And please confirm your full understanding of the priority code. I'll stand by until you check. And, Vasily, I seem to be having some trouble with my video. It'll be off for a few minutes, but I'll be on an open audio line until I hear from you."

"Thank you, John," Tereshnikov said automatically. He switched off his video pickup. Tanya was already on the other side of the cubicle with two towels and their jumpsuits. They patted each other dry and slipped into the suits. "Tanya, query the computer on Dustbin. I want the priority classification. I have the feeling that all this was arranged a long time ago. Moscow does not so easily give out our emergency frequency."

Tanya positioned herself before another panel, locked her feet in place, slid open the keyboard interrogator to the ship's main computer and typed in the data request. She hit the PRINTOUT button and the paper slid from the machine. A tone chimed to announce the end of message. She floated back to Tereshnikov and handed him the sheet.

PROJECT DUSTBIN. JOINT USSR-USA PROGRAM. CATEGORY UUA CLASSIFICATION. IMMEDIATE AND FULL COOPERATION AUTHORIZED USSR OR USA REQUEST. FILE REQUEST RECEIPT AND IMMEDIATE ACTION TAKEN. AUTHORIZATION LEVEL: PROCEED.

He read it several times and returned the paper to his chief assistant. "Tanya, encode and transmit to Starcomm on maximum security. Tell them we are on line with Houston capcom and they can listen—no; I'm certain they *are* monitoring. Tell them we will confirm to Starcomm whatever we receive and what action we will take. If there are any problems let me know at once."

He touched the pickup button to resume his exchange with John Hastings on Houston capcom. The video monitor came alive as well. Hastings didn't make any sarcastic remarks about seeing Tereshnikov in his jumpsuit. Could it be *that* serious?

"John, code and authorizations are confirmed. Tell me, in your own idiom, what is coming down."

Hastings moved aside a stack of papers on his control desk. He *was* serious. "I'm passing on an emergency-level request from our national space council, Vasily. We're requesting you to prepare for an immediate EVA— you personally, and at least one other crewman. As soon as you're ready, we'll uplink you with the specific request in detail. What I need now is verbal commitment from you for compliance as quickly as you're ready to go."

Vasily Tereshnikov didn't respond at once. All this was much too official. The Russian decided to switch to a personal exchange. "John, stop all this silly nonsense. What's behind all this?"

On the video monitor he saw Hastings' face relax. There are signs to look for: the corner of the mouth moving, the way John Hastings leaned back in his seat as if suddenly relieved of a burden. "Vas, old buddy, I really don't know. This has all the earmarks of the shit hitting the fan. But I don't know where or what or why. I don't even know what Dustbin means. Maybe we're going to sell millions of Hoover vacuum cleaners to Russia in exchange for vodka. I *really* don't know—but what I do know is that this priority goes all the way to the White House. From everything I can tell there's no problem between our governments. Just the opposite, in fact." Hastings let his face relax in a smile. "There. You got it all. Now you know as much as I do. Maybe even more."

Tereshnikov chewed swiftly on the words of the *Amerikantski*. There is a very special bond indeed between men who have floated together in weightlessness, their entire universe measured by the volumes of their pressure suits. He trusted John Hastings; yet the entire affair bewildered him. There are really very few emergency situations in high orbit other than onboard fire or breaching a pressure seal or a choking reaction engine that would require immediate action. Why, then, would the Americans go to such trouble to overstep all the bounds of agreement for contact between the two space

110

teams and not proceed through the usual channels? Normally John Hastings would have activated the hot line between Houston and Star City, requested the contact, and then Star City would either patch him through or give permission for direct contact. This way Gagarin Control appeared to have been bypassed completely.

And since when did the *Amerikantski* request—no, he corrected himself, since when did they *order* an out-of-ship excursion from a cosmonaut? And not just *any* cosmonaut, but specifically the commander of *Gagarin* station?

He picked up the thread of his exchange with Hastings in Houston. "John, I am thinking of what you ask. You offer me supposition and conclusions on your part, but that is not sufficient. I do not mean to sound so official but I am left little choice." He added a touch of steel to his tone. "For the record, Houston Capcom, by what authority is this EVA to be carried out? Over."

Tanya Yevteshenka had drifted slowly back to Vasily but, as she saw on their own monitor, she was not yet within reach of the video camera transmitting to Houston. Vasily motioned to her to remain out of lens range. She had been listening to the exchange and clearly she shared the confusion Vasily felt.

They watched John Hastings' blank expression as he pondered Vasily's question. Almost at the same moment they all heard a a communications annunciator. Hastings reached for a paper out of video range, brought it back slowly as he scanned its contents. A broad smile grew slowly across his face. He gestured with the paper.

"Here it is, Vas." *That* told Tereshnikov a great deal. The return to the old and very familiar name of *Vas* rather than an official *Vasily Tereshnikov* said torrents. Hastings obviously felt free of any problems or constrictions.

"Boris Zilotkin," Hastings went on. "Am I pronouncing that right?"

"No," Vasily told him and Hastings laughed. "Well, you know who I mean, though?"

"Yes, yes, John, I know him." There wasn't anyone

111

to know. Use of the name Boris Zilotkin meant the situation was not an emergency, but confirm details by scrambler wavelength as soon as possible.

"Very good, Vas. They're waiting to hear from you," Hastings said, unknowingly confirming Tereshnikov's own thoughts. His next words brought a frown to the Russian's face. "I'll be waiting for your call back, Vasily. Oh, yes, would you please switch to channel six two niner five?" There was a bare moment's hesitation and Tereshnikov's frown deepened. "Please confirm by hand," Hastings ended his message.

Vasily punched in the four numbers and switched off. He exchanged a long glance with Tanya. She shared his perplexity. All hints of sexual embrace had vanished completely; she was again a working cosmonaut. "Vasily, that radio frequency. It's our discrete scrambler code. What would the *Amerikantski* be doing with our secret channel? And how did he know of it? Even I have never had need to use that channel!"

Tereshnikov hung suspended in midair, swaying gently before the ventilator fans, as relaxed as a fish buoyed by its air bladder. "You have many questions," he said a bit distantly, still staring at the communicator panel. "Unfortunately, I have less than enough answers. But certainly all this is very strange." His lips tightened as he searched his memory. "Six two niner five," he said his thought aloud, then came to a sudden conclusion, his body bobbing gently as his hand muscles tightened his grip on the handle of the panel before him.

"All right. We shall talk with Zilotkin."

"Who is Zilotkin!"

"A code name. It means I am to make contact directly with Rauschenbach."

Her eyes widened. "Him I know. But he is the chief of all planetary sciences, the number two scientist in the Academy!"

Vasily scowled. "What does *that* mean?"

"But why would he want to talk to you?" She clapped a hand across her mouth. "Oh, I didn't mean it *that* way, Vasily. I meant only why he would want to talk to

112

you while you're up here, in the station, and we have no deepspace probes scheduled and—"

He held his forefinger against her full lips. "Hush, hush, Tanya. Because we are weightless it should not mean your brain has gone empty." She kissed his finger and for a moment he forgot whether to scowl or smile. He did neither as his thoughts returned fully to the issue at hand. "Tanya, interrogate the computer on this Dustbin. If it has nothing here within the station, establish direct link to Star City data banks. Bring a printout on whatever there is to the data room. I will make the call to Rauschenbach from there. Quickly, now, my dove. Go."

He swam past her, a space dolphin in human form, gliding weightlessly from a long-experienced gentle pushaway from the panel where he had talked with John Hastings in Houston. Tanya Yevteshenka watched him glide from sight along the exit tunnelway. She "swam" from the cubicle along a curving padded tunnel to the computer function cubicle, where she punched in her data requests. There would be a delay in data uplink from Star City. The circuits were jammed with unusually heavy traffic. She would have enough time then for a personal matter.

Her own personal compartment was barely a minute away, and she moved swiftly with hand-over-hand movements along the teflon tube that ran along the "top" of the tunnelway. She depressed the OPEN pad and the lightweight pressure door slid into its wall compartment recess, closing behind her at a wave of her hand that interrupted a photocell beam to trigger the DOOR CLOSE signal. One more need to meet as she bobbed and floated gently, her practiced toes wrapped about a padded bar, and that was to depress the OCCUPIED signal that would flash in personnel control, informing the crew on duty that at this moment Tanya Yevteshenka was specifically in her own compartment. You never knew, up here, weightless far beyond Mother Earth and moving at nearly three hundred miles a minute, when your presence could be critical to meeting an onboard emergency. But there was none now, at least in the mechanical sense. Tanya felt an urgent personal need.

She slipped from her jumpsuit, damp with the perspiration she had generated in that *almost* successful loving session with Vasily. She smiled to herself, a wan expression of unfulfilled desire. The crotch of her jumpsuit was maddeningly warm and damp as well. She pushed away the thoughts from her mind. *Not now, not now, little fool; you are to him first a cosmonaut and then a woman. Do not give Vasily reason to change his opinion.*

Suspended nude in air, she reached to her padded wall locker, braced a leg, opened the sliding panel and removed a plastic package from a box secured to an overhead shelf with velcro. She peeled away the wrapper, stuffing the plastic in the ever-ready disposal container, and opened a neatly folded, lightly scented towelette. Slowly and luxuriantly she removed the oily perspiration from her body. She smiled as the scent hovered about her. No Soviet quartermaster had ever issued *these* to the women cosmonauts who left the Earth behind! What she carried with her among her personal belongings were gifts from Susan Foster. It was difficult to think of Susan as just another *Amerikantski*. The lovely young blonde woman, with three space flights in their shuttle craft, had become a trusted friend.

Whatever their technical prowess, and Tanya knew it was most formidable, it was in the science of personal touch that the Americans were absolutely incredible. They were light years ahead of anything that emerged from Mother Russia. In the packages Susan gave her, concealed within a box supposedly filled with computer disks, were these sealed towels and their lightly scented fragrance, just enough to detect, and moist enough to clean and freshen her skin. It dried within seconds of its application and then you simply disposed of the towelette. She had hundreds of them. Some of the other women learned of her treasure and Tanya shared with them.

It made life infinitely more bearable after weeks and months in weightless orbit. It rendered personal hygiene a pleasure in a complicated, clanging, ear-stabbing vessel that reeked of oil, plastic, garlic and scallions and all manner of unpleasant body odors that soaked into the very "floors" and "walls" of the station cubicles. The Americans, Tanya smiled, demanded their little luxuries wherever they went, and their women cosmonauts were even more fiercely demanding than their men. *Hooray for you*, Tanya thought generously of the Americans. Long voyages into space within ships that stank left much to be desired, and if nothing else, the Americans were able to make of space adventure a mission that did not permanently wrinkle the nose.

"If the men wish to smell like garbage heaps," Susan had confided to her, "that's *their* business. I insist upon being not only female but feminine, *and* attractive, *and* clean, *and*," they were in near hysterics by now, "smelling lustful rather than being a woman who has an odor like a fish market. Besides, there is a certain heroic astronaut I intend to make out with and I need to be more of a heroine than a herring." She slipped a personal package to Tanya. "Take these aboard *Gagarin*. The women will love you for it and you might even get Vasily to *make* love to you."

"You know about, um, Vasily?"

"The space monk? Sure I do. Rasputin in a pressure suit."

Tanya shrieked with laughter. "The competition up there," she pointed to the sky, "will be much less crowded than down *here*," she admitted. "Down here he is besieged by lovely women young and old, by women and their sisters, by mothers offering their daughters *and* mothers and daughters together." She ran her fingers lightly over the package. "How many in here?"

"Four hundred."

Tanya's eyes widened. "Four *hundred?*"

"We're the miracle workers of folded fragrance."

Tanya lifted her eyes to look at her American friend. "And the men?" She felt embarrassed.

Susan leaned forward, conspiratorial in her manner. "They'll kill me if they ever learn I've even breathed a word about this to you."

"*I'll* kill you, Susan, *if you don't.*"

"All right, you've twisted my arm. Do you know about that marvelous French aftershave? Azzaro?"

"No. I have never heard of it."

"It's marvelous, Tanya. It makes a lover out of a man-goat. It makes *me* have wonderful animal feelings. Hugh Fitzpatrick, he's one of our engineer astronauts and a fanatic about hygiene, had the company make special kits for the crew, so they'll dispense in weight-lessness like these towelettes. You get into an embrace without weighing anything in space and, and . . . you know," she flushed, "all your senses are heightened, and it makes you want to tear the clothes right from his body."

Tanya smiled, gently this time. "I don't need your Azurus—"

"Azzaro."

"Whatever. I do not need it for Vasily. I *always* have the urge to tear off his clothes. But thank you. I will take this with me also and one night, or day," she shrugged, "it is all the same up there, when he is tired and I massage that magnificent body, I will use one of these and we shall see what happens. It is better than garlic and machine oil!"

And it is more than just his body I want, Tanya mused as she cleansed her body and slipped into fresh panties and jumpsuit. She had on several flights spent a total of five months in space in close quarters, in inti-mate exchange, with Vasily Tereshnikov. She had been in love with him longer than she wanted to remember, and it was maddening to continue meeting this man on separate but demanding professional levels. Tanya's ex-pertise lay in astrogation and computer sciences, in the exquisitely accurate orbital attitude positioning of *Gagarin* and its many cubicles and work stations, some of the latter disconnected from the main station and set adrift to float in formation for stellar research. In such work accuracy could never be compromised, and she was a mathematician supreme. Vasily appreciated and respected her versatility. He was no less impressed with her secondary talents as electronics technician and hands-on mechanical engineer, all skills critical to the safe operation of *Gagarin* as it plunged about the Earth at nearly five miles a second. Long before now Tanya had accepted weightlessness and the manner in which the lack of gravity stretched her spinal column and demanded payment in blinding headaches. The pain was worth the stunning view of sunrise and sunset every forty-seven minutes. The fact that the space station, weighing hundreds of tons, hurtled about the world many times faster than a rifle bullet had lost its meaning and slipped into secondary memory.

She could not feel the speed, and the Earth was far enough below that its features drifted by in a hazy, dreamlike slow motion. Far more important was Everyday. And, Everynight. Aboard *Gagarin* everything functioned by the digital numbers one saw everywhere. Day or night as she had known them all her life were banished. The clock in any and all forms dictated every moment of their lives and established the patterns within which their biological systems would function, intermeshed with those of the huge, ponderous, complex and yet delicate station.

Tanya Yevteshenka was the only cosmonaut—no; the only *female* cosmonaut aboard this station—who had three children on Earth far below. Three strapping boys. Their father had been an engineer, a test pilot, a daring cosmonaut. He had been many things at one and the same time. *Her husband Pyotr had been the first Martian.*

He was the first man to walk across the rocky reddish surface of Mars, the first to kick up its sand. He had walked with stunned wonder along the icy flanks of ancient Martian glaciers and he had discovered, fueling the dreams of scientists the world over, the great frozen seas beneath the arid surface. He had spread reporting instruments across the Martian surface with two other Russians, and then all three had died in the terrifying explosion of their space craft as it lifted from the terribly distant and lonely surface of Mars.

Oh, they knew what had happened. She had screamed then and she could remember herself screaming when she saw the live television transmission from the cameras Pyotr and his crew had set up on the surface to record their triumphant liftoff. What a miracle was this electronics! How wonderful to see her lover and husband and the father of her children torn to blazing shreds before her very eyes. In an instant she had become part of the large family who watched their loved ones engulfed in the red-and-white fireball over the Atlantic Ocean when *Challenger* died.

Tanya had been an airline captain then for Aeroflot, one of the first women to fly from the left seat, in command. As good as any man. She appealed directly to the president of the Soviet Union. She was as qualified as any man or woman to fly as a cosmonaut. "I do not want Pyotr's death to lose its meaning," she told the president of her country. "His sons one day will follow him into the cosmos. I must be the bridge between now and when they are old enough to wear his badge of courage. I beg of you. Let me take his place."

Ivan Merkulov listened. For several minutes he did not answer. He knew Pyotr well. And he had studied the file of this woman before she ever appeared in his office. Oh, she was qualified. She was also a cousin of Yevgeny Yevteshenko, their troublesome but tremendously popular poet. Finally he nodded, with tears on his cheeks. "I welcome you, Cosmonaut Tanya Yevteshenka," he said quietly, and embraced her fiercely.

It was done. Pyotr was memory. Strong, but with Russian stoicism relegated to history. He was as real as any statue in Red Square, but no more warm or human to her than a bust of Lenin. That was proper. It was history.

Now there was Vasily Tereshnikov, and Tanya Yevtenshenka meant to have him as her man. Fully dressed, equipment properly stowed, she propelled herself from her personal cubicle to the computer room to collect the data on Dustbin—whatever was that strange name—and bring it to Vasily.

Vasily Tereshnikov, like all commanders of a major installation, whether it be under the sea within a great submarine, or above the air ocean within a great space station, at one time or another found the need to decide between speaking truthfully or lying. Long before he ever left the Earth behind, in the command and staff schools of the Soviet Air Force and in the hammering political indoctrination of the Party, the need to speak other than the truth had been hammered home to him. Lying not for personal gain or for deceit, but to maintain control of a dangerous situation, to thwart dissension from within, to further the demands and goals of the Party itself.

"To carry out your duty requires rigid foresight. Only your duty matters. Do what needs to be done, say what needs to be said, but carry out your orders and your duty above all else." That was, essentially, the creed behind all the technical training he would ever receive. The creed arose from the hard Party doctrine that permeated every fiber and cord of the Communist apparatus, that was the backbone of Russian strength. Tereshnikov had found occasion to fault, at times, the *methods* of the system, but not the system itself. And that, he knew, was the basic flow of all major sociopolitical systems.

Vasily Ilyich Tereshnikov was unswervingly loyal to his country, his party, his duty. Fanaticism never entered his thinking. Conflict with other political or social systems never existed. Idiocy was to be found at any level in any system, and that was the only flaw that existed for him to uncover and boot out of his own operations. Where Tereshnikov chafed at times was not with the Party goals, but the petty grasping at power of political officials. "You will run into these maggots everywhere you go," an old line officer warned him. "They are part and parcel of every system. Never has there been a great forest where beneath the trees you did not find slugs and maggots. The key to success and the health of the Party is to uncover these vermin, to expose their own selfishness they disguise as political— well, commissars is the word we used in the old days—as political leeches, and rid yourself of them."

So the system demanded its pound of flesh in the

most distant reaches of the expansion of *Rodina*. Because not all of its people were strong or entirely trustworthy, the Party found it necessary constantly to drill faith and loyalty into those for whom it was responsible. None of this was new, strange or difficult for Tereshnikov; he'd lived and grown all his life with it. Was it not the Party who brought him out of the tiny hamlet of Polkovnikovo so close to Mongolia and China? Was it not from a crude log cabin fashioned by his father's own hands that the Party laid the path for him to grow if he were worthy? Log cabin, straw and mud, savage Siberian winters, education taught by candlelight and oil lamp, sleeping on a rack of straw on a thick shelf over his mother's bed, gaining his knowledge of the world from books more precious than any gold, from old newspapers and scraps of magazines. If there is spirit and intelligence, if there is yearning and drive, claimed the old Russians, it will always find its way upward and emerge into the light. And so it had happened with Tereshnikov. He had an uncle with a chestful of medals and a wooden leg who had fought valiantly against the Nazis in the Great Patriotic War and to whom even the highest members of the Party listened. He told Vasily to finish his schooling in the new communal building of his remote little village and then, "You will make your application, my nephew, to the Soviet Military Commission. You will ask to be a military aviation cadet. I promise you only that your application will be considered, and you will become both a great pilot and a good Communist." It happened as his uncle promised. Several weeks after submitting his application he was at the Ovchinnkov railway station, bidding his family and friends goodbye, and the son of an obscure Siberian peasant from a tiny village close to Mongolia was on his way to Kustenai in northwest Kazakhstan to report as a cadet to primary flight school.

So began the long and tedious ascent of grueling studies, punishing physical conditioning, and remorseless Party indoctrination. His uncle limped with a wooden leg but had sharp eyes for his nephew. He impressed upon the youngster that Party doctrine kept the nation going no matter how terrible the conditions under which its people might have to live. "There is reason behind what the Politburo does, my nephew. There is strength and continuity in the doctrine that has carried us successfully against all our enemies. Every officer in every service must know our doctrine as well as he knows his own heart and soul. Doctrine and law, law and doctrine. It brought us victory against the Hitlerites. It has both sustained us and given us strength in the trying times since then. The Politburo does not consider us to be at peace with the world. Especially with the Americans. Only because our political doctrine gave us strength did we find the means to catch up when we were forty or fifty years behind the Western world and perform the miracle that almost overnight made us the leading technological power in the world. It is not talk that stays the American missiles or their bombs. It is the Russian missile, the Russian winged machines, the Russian bombs to which they listen. You may not hear the gunfire, Vasily, but the guns are aimed and the hammers are back and they are ready to destroy us with their greedy capitalism, just as the Hitlerites followed that madman's fascism."

There was only one real problem with the Party doctrine. *After eighteen years it had become boring beyond all enduring.* It was the same old tune, repeated incessantly, rammed and crammed and jammed into their ears and noses and asses and stomachs until those who could really think, on their own, recognized the gravid pressure of blind repetition. They had nothing against Communism or the Party or its doctrine except that it bored them to tears and gave them a desire to smash things out of the frustration of hearing nothing new.

They discussed it among themselves, that and the growing unfairness of a system where the *zampolit*, the political officer always in their presence, could strip a man of his opportunity to soar into space or drift to the moon because he did not please that political officer personally. It was when their ranks thinned, when some of their best men were lost to them because of individ-

121

ual ingenuity and genius and spirit, that they came to recognize the heavy and unacceptable hand of relentless indoctrination.

"Are the Americans really any different?" they asked themselves. By now they knew enough Americans and knew the system well enough to recognize that the Americans certainly *were* different, but not necessarily because their system was any better. "They have the same petty jealousies, the same personal battles, the same struggle for power, that we do," Tereshnikov told them. "They also have their own solutions. They do not like to kiss American political ass any more than we like to kiss Soviet political ass." He studied his men and he grinned. "We have a problem. His name is Mikhail Perchenak. In case any of you are too dense to recognize the obvious, he is the *zampolit* among us."

His cosmonauts grinned at him. Vera Glagoleva laughed. "And all this time I thought he was just clumsy and stupid and nosy. Now I discover he is a brilliant political officer, which is the same as being clumsy and stupid and nosy!"

Vasily Tereshnikov left the matter up to his crew. They were in orbit aboard the Mir space station at the time. As advanced as was Mir over the Salyut, it was still cramped and crowded with cosmonauts and their battery of equipment and instruments. "He must become dangerously ill," Vero Glagoleva told the others, "before the next Proton supply rocket reaches us."

"Why?" came a chorus, accompanied with knowing smiles.

"He must return at once to Earth for medical attention. Every Proton has an emergency recoverable capsule. It has never been tested," Glagoleva observed. "Mikhail Perchenak shall make a major contribution to the development of our space rescue capabilities, no?"

"No?" they cried. "*Yes!*"

One day before the huge Proton closed in through its automatic docking system to the Mir airlock, Perchenak doubled over with savage stomach cramps. Slight but effective modifications to his food provided the intestinal agony. A slight misreading of the thermometer by

Vera Glagoleva led to her raised eyebrows and the exclamation, "Terrible! Everything indicates a touch of gangrene for a splitting appendix. You are most fortunate, Comrade Perchenak. The escape capsule in the Proton. It can return you almost immediately."

He looked at her with horror in his eyes. "But—"

A hypodermic slipped into his arm. His vision swam, his senses tilted. "See!" Glagoleva cried. "Not even the medication to settle your stomach does any good. You must return to Earth for surgery or most certainly you will die up here. Badly, too. From what I understand, weightlessness only increases the swelling of the appendectomal cervix."

Later, Vasily Tereshnikov, closely listened to by the others, asked her directly, "What the devil is an appendectomal cervix?"

She shrugged. "Some form of political affliction, I believe." They roared with laughter.

The unfortunate Mikhail Perchenak was provided with an emergency pressure suit, strapped into the uncomfortable but adequate cushioning of the capsule in the Proton emergency section, and his life was then trusted entirely to a rudimentary and rather stupid computer that sent the capsule on a free ballistic re-entry to scream through the atmosphere at eighteen thousand miles an hour. When last heard from, Perchenak appeared well recovered from his appendectomal cervix infection, but was still under heavy sedation in a mental hospital.

Now, despite his own fierce pride in the truth, Vasily Iliych Tereshnikov was prepared to carry on the Big Lie with the one cosmonaut he trusted more than any other. The lie had been going on a long time, and he had been the liar. It was both necessary and his duty.

He had been fully aware of every detail of Project Dustbin from the day it began with the Americans. He had also sent Tanya on a quest for information with which he was completely familiar. But it would give him time to think, to communicate directly with the special office in the Kremlin. There might be late updates on which he still lacked information; well, he was certain this would be the case. All the signals were clear to him. John Hastings making direct contact on the scrambler frequency meant that contact on Dustbin between the Soviet and American governments was already an actuality. Hastings would never have requested an EVA, most especially that Tereshnikov personally leave the station, unless that had also been coordinated. With Tanya absent he punched in his coded numbers, received verification of the priority, and six minutes later gazed upon the face of Academician Rauschenbach. He related the details of the call between himself and Houston capcom.

"When you finish with me, contact the Americans again. Use the discrete frequency, Cosmonaut Tereshnikov, that they have requested. We have already cleared it."

"Yes, sir," he said crisply.

"You will carry out the EVA."

"Yes, sir."

"Make certain that all your communications with Houston also are transmitted on the second discrete frequency. I shall be listening. And Vasily . . ."

He was startled by the familiarity. "Sir?"

"Who do you recommend as your companion?"

"Cosmonaut Tanya Yevteshenka, sir."

"Accepted. One more thing, Vasily."

"Yes, sir?"

"The General Secretary of the Party will be listening in on what you have to say to the Americans."

"Sir? *Yuri Fedov?* You mean—"

"I mean precisely that, Comrade Cosmonaut. Do not delay. This transmission is ended." The screen went blank.

Tanya returned with a printout sheet several times longer than he had expected. He eased into a seat in the suit cubicle, automatically locking his feet beneath the footclamps to keep himself from floating away. Such movements become instinctive after time in weightlessness. But Vasily spent no time thinking on routine matters. The hard data of Dustbin startled him. Probes failing, the lunar stations reporting *sudden* dramatic increases in dust impact levels, the loss of power from a Martian moon unmanned station . . . He needed only the swift scan. He switched on the seat communicator to station comm to talk directly with Nikolai Yashchuk.

"Nikki, you have my instructions. Use the discrete frequencies on channels seven and sixteen. Seven is for Houston and sixteen for Star City. Confirm the patch lines to the Academy communications in Moscow. I want all recorders running on this facility at all times. Cosmonaut Yevteshenka will make the EVA with me. While we suit up reconfirm at least twice all comm links."

"Very good, sir."

Thirty-five minutes later, breathing suit oxygen at reduced pressure, their pressure suits and equipment checked by astronaut technicians and then by each other, they floated slowly into the airlock. "Clamps before depressure," he said into his helmet radio. By way of answer Tanya floated to him and snapped a heavy dogclamp to his belt. He did the same from his suit to hers so that they were double-linked by very thin but strong metalon cables. "We will stay linked with the station," he told her, knowing that every word he spoke was being transmitted to station recorders and all station personnel, as well as to Star City, to Moscow and to Houston where he would have an open-line comm with John Hastings.

They went through the drill, the inner airlock door opened, pressure decreased steadily and they again checked their seals and equipment. "All is in order," he heard Tanya after inspecting his suit. He checked hers again and motioned with his left arm while talking. "Open the outer airlock door," he ordered. A haze of dust and crystallized air swirled past their suited bodies. Tanya snapped another clamp to the doorway of the airlock and they moved outside the station, gliding along handbars on the outer surface of the station.

Earth below lay swathed in darkness. Vasily knew they had nearly forty minutes before they'd come into another onrushing sunrise and eye-stabbing sunlight. He wanted to carry out his mission under artificial light for shadow effects. They had their helmet lights on. "Comm, give me perimeter lights rows three and four," he ordered. Above and beyond them bright floodlights came on to illuminate the exterior of *Gagarin*. "Do you have us on camera following?" Vasily queried.

"Affirmative, sir," came Yashchuk's reply. "Full video coverage all camera stations."

"Very good, Nikki. Stand by. Houston Capcom, do you read?"

Unexpected static. Strange, almost like static electricity as Hastings' voice crackled in their headsets.

"We have you four by four, *Gagarin*." Hastings' use of the station name let Tereshnikov know this was a lot more business than personal. There'd be less banter than usual.

"Go ahead, Capcom."

"*Gagarin*, we'd like a data readout and a video picture if you can, please, of Collector Panels Two, Nine and Fourteen. Over."

Vasily motioned Tanya to move with him. He saw she had the mobile video camera. Good. They'd get closeup shots this way. They moved along the guiderails, then swung upward and drifted freely to a long equipment beam jutting outward from research cubicles. Huge rectangular wings hung suspended away from the station. They resembled solar panels but were actually extremely sensitive dust traps, able to measure the impact of a microparticle. Of course, even a microparticle has an appreciable effect at better than seventeen thousand miles an hour. Vasily brought his hand floodlight to play at an angle across the traps. "Tanya, bring the camera in close, check the focus for a detailed slow scan."

"Yes, Comrade."

She came in closer, an expert with the video system. "Capcom, how is your picture?" Vasily asked.

"Very clear, *Gagarin*. But it seems fuzzy directly along the collector panels."

Vasily looked closer. He didn't believe it. He forgot the cool and collected data exchange. "John, I can hardly believe this myself. There's nothing wrong with

126

the video picture. Those panels *are* fuzzy. They're covered with dust and apparently the electrostatic effect is stronger than anything I've ever seen before. They, well, it looks like a yak-skin blanket out here. Over."

"That's affirm, *Gagarin*. It's how we read the video. The data display is clear off the scale. Vasily, uh, can you move on out to the next panel, please?"

They drifted further outward from the station. "Houston, *Gagarin*. John, I do not believe this. It appears as if someone struck this panel section with a shotgun blast. They have been scourged. Tanya, the camera here." He pointed to a spiderwork of cabling, signalling her to hold the camera on that target. "Can you see these cables, Houston?"

"Yes, sir, *Gagarin*, the transmission is holding up well."

"You will notice, John, even the cables have a collection of dust clinging to them. We have a dual effect here. Dust heavier than anything I've ever seen before and an intense electrostatic effect as well."

"Very good, *Gagarin*. Vasily, please turn your video camera down on the main body of the station. Bring your lights to bear if you can. We'd like, first, a broadview scan at full distance, and then, a zoom lens shot."

"We're doing that now, Houston." Tanya needed no further instructions from him, having listened to the exchange. He left her to handle the camera, loosened the cable clamp to play it out as he needed, and began drifting back toward the main body of the station. "Houston, there are collections of dust in different areas along here. Can you see them?"

"Not too well, Vasily. Please have the camera come in closer. We would really like a tight holding shot on those areas you mentioned."

Vasily motioned Tanya to come in closer and follow the request of the Americans. Several minutes later they heard a startled exclamation from Houston. "Vasily, if that picture shows what we think it's showing . . ."

"There's nothing wrong with the picture, Houston. We have a definite series of pitting on the metal, and the windows of the storage cubicles are—well, I can see the lights inside the cubicle but I can't make out details. The material has been scrubbed. It's as if someone scratched steel wool along plexiglass."

"We've got our people studying a large video monitor, *Gagarin*, while you're transmitting."

"Very good, John."

Tanya moved the camera closer to the windows. A sickly yellow light shone through from the bright lights within the storage cubicle.

One of the American scientists must have been on an open line with Hastings in case they wanted any additional views or angles. Unsuspecting he was verbalizing, he reflected the views of everyone watching the video screen picture of the pus-like light.

"Holy shit," he said.

I agree, Vasily Tereshnikov said to himself.

"Return to the airlock," he ordered Tanya.

He had just rid himself of his suit, preparing to towel down the perspiration from his EVA, when Nikolai Yashchuk came to him directly. "General Tereshnikov, I am ordered to give you this message personally." Vasily nodded for him to continue.

"Sir, you are to return to Earth. *Immediately*."

Book II

TROOPING THE COLORS

7

A great fist gathered in the midst of his chest and pain exploded in his lungs and arms. That was only the beginning. The fist gathered momentum and slammed between his chest and spinal column, wreaking spasms of havoc. Waves of pain choked off the air he needed, his throat swelled, his tongue turned darker, and Hank Marrows leaned heavily on the polished bar of the Surf Lounge in downtown Cocoa Beach, doing his best to resemble a man trying to cough up his brains and even his life. Hacking twisted his back muscles and strained his rib cage. His eyes teared as he rode the crest of the wracking spell of coughing. Louie Mangani leaned forward from the working side of the bar, close to Marrows' ear. "F'Christ's sake, Hank, y'sound like you're *dying*. Lemme do something for you, man! I got some syrup under the bar here—"

Marrows' right hand shot out like a striking snake to clamp about Louie's wrist. In between hacking coughs he offered up a crooked grin and bursts of words. "Nah, y'don't understand, Louie. I feel *terrific*." Spasms chewed through his frame and he choked down air. "Terrific. Never felt, ah, better." He sucked in a deep shuddering breath that dumped precious oxygen into his lungs.

"See?" he smiled. He had his body back under control. He sat up straighter and breathed deeply. "Wonderful, wonderful! That's how I feel!"

Louie had served drinks to Hank Marrows for better than twenty-four years. They were almost a team on the beach scene. Louie with the bionic ears that heard everything in the lounge and Marrows with the newspaper column that dripped acid in the form of printer's ink through the souls of so many who read him with dread. The Surf was their private kingdom, their watering hole, the beacon of their friendship. It had spawned and energized and preserved friendships in this fashion for more than fifty years after the Fischer brothers first opened its doors as a small seafood bar in a town with sand blowing in its streets. Those were prehistoric times at the very dawn of the space age. Cape Canaveral to the north along the curving beach was stirring the froth and flame and thunder of future dreams. Hank Marrows was there as a wet-behind-the-ears kid reporter eaten alive by mosquitos on a high sand dune when a captured German V-2 rocket roared off its slab of cement, fired by an engineering team huddled behind piled sandbags. The dawning of an age, the birth of a career that sprawled across some fifty years for Marrows. Louie Mangani was still a snotty little kid pissing on a fire hydrant in the Bronx. It had been a hell of a long road since then.

Louie thought his friend was going to choke to death. "When you go back to them fucking things?" he said with a snarl. He picked up the opened pack of cigarettes on the bar and waved them beneath Marrows' face. "This shit was killing you, remember? It ain't enough we saw Doug die in front of us? And a bunch of other guys? *You* look like you're dying, y'asshole!"

"I told you you didn't understand," Marrows said quietly, with a dignity and a sense of inner strength that pushed aside the tequila and the tobacco coursing through his system. "I *told* you it feels terrific. *I* feel terrific!"

"You can't see yer own face!" Louie shouted in exasperation. His arms shot up like an albatross trying to take off and came down with a slapping sound against his thighs. "Goddamn it, I can *tell* when you're in pain!"

Marrows laughed, quietly this time, without coughing. Then a slight spasm shook him again and his face reddened. He sucked in more air. "That's the secret. Sure there's pain. I love the pain. It feels so goddamned *good*. I love it."

"You," Louie said with a stabbing finger, "are crazier than a bedbug."

Marrows smiled, held up his shot glass in salute, drained the tequila in a long swallow. He belched loudly, set down the glass with a bang of triumph. "Fill it, Louie."

"You're crazy, you know that?"

Hank Marrows smiled and tapped another cigarette from his pack and lit up again in a renewed fit of coughing. Louis didn't understand. He couldn't. And Hank couldn't tell him that the pain *was* marvelous, that not even the cigarettes from which he'd stayed away so long would or could kill him.

Not before the Big One gets all of us, he thought with a deep inner smile. *Coffin nails can't hurt a man who's already dead, we're all dead and the only difference is that I know when they're going to ring down the curtain, you poor bastards, and you don't. So drink up, smoke any fucking thing you want to, and—*

"Phone call for you, Mr. Marrows." Hank turned to look into the beautiful face of a waitress. What was her name? Oh, yes; Ginny. "Sure," he said affably. "I'll take it here." He stretched his hand onto the bar. Louie had given him many a call here.

"Sir, in the back, please. The manager's office. They said it was *very* private."

"Well, shit. Thanks, honey." Nothing unusual. A lot of his tips and leads came from people who didn't want him talking in the public area of the lounge. He grabbed his cigarette pack and walked back to the office, sliding along the walls once or twice from the tequila. He turned down the short hall and pushed open the door to Morgan's office. A stranger in a dark suit sat behind the desk, looking up at him. Marrows heard the door close behind him. He hadn't touched it. He knew what he'd see before he turned: another stranger in a dark suit.

Marrows smiled at the man behind the desk. "I don't go out the way I came in, do I?"

"You're quick, Mr. Marrows. You're also right. No, sir." He gestured to the door leading outside. "We go that way."

"I have anything to say about it?" Marrows asked. He was incredibly calm. What the hell . . .

"No, sir. It's just a matter of quiet. We'd like to do this *very* quietly. But we'll do it whatever way we need." The stranger stood up. "It's not our intention to cause you any harm, Mr. Marrows."

"I'm glad to hear that. I'm not as good as I used to be." Marrows offered a very crooked grin. "Forty or fifty years ago, in fact." He chuckled at his own joke. He was past his prime before these people were even born.

"Sir, if I may say so, we appreciate your cooperation."

"Oh, sure. You've got it." Marrows lit another cigarette, went through another coughing spell, wiped his lips with the back of his hand. "Hell, I've been expecting you. Wondered what took you so long."

Hank Marrows was one of the finest experts in the world for reading a face. He couldn't read this one. *Jesus, this guy doesn't even know why he's picking me up. They have no idea. . . .* Marrows gestured idly. "By the way," he said with surprising good humor. "Just for the record, you understand. Am I under arrest?"

"No, sir."

"But I go with you no matter what I—"

"Yes, sir." *That* was very emphatic.

"Okay, let's do it," Marrows said, shrugging. He started for the door, stopped. "Hell, I forgot to ask. Do you tell me where we're going?"

"No, sir." There was just the hint of a smile.

"Do you even tell me who you are? What office you're from?"

"No, sir."

"Do I get three free guesses?"

Well, well, a chink in the armor. Two false starts, but they caught themselves quickly. So that's it.

"Sir?" The man behind the desk was confused, but he hid it well.

Marrows laughed. He held his hand over his eyes in a mock gesture of psychic seeking. "Don't tell me, don't tell me. . . . We're leaving here to Patrick Air Force Base down the road, right?" He peeked out between two fingers. "Then we get aboard an executive jet, probably a Canadian Challenger, that will have false company markings. I'll be the only passenger who's not supposed to know what the hell's going on, but you'll fly me to Andrews Air Force Base outside Washington, because National and Dulles are too public, and *then*," he concluded with a flourish, "a black car will drive me to the White House."

Both federal agents gaped at him. Marrows laughed and waved gratuitously to the door. "Shall we dance?"

He sat in a deeply cushioned executive seat aboard the Gulfstream IV (but that was the only point on which he'd erred) and he lit another cigarette as the sleek Grumman climbed out from Patrick Air Force Base and headed north. For a while the coastline was easy to follow: the glowing pearl necklaces of the beaches and causeways surrounding the two great launching centers of Kennedy and Canaveral, then the lights of Daytona beach and off in the distance the glow of Orlando. By the time they passed Jacksonville a cloud deck was thickening beneath them and he quit looking. One of the dark suits brought him black coffee and offered sandwiches that Marrow turned down. He wanted tequila instead of coffee but knew the futility of that request.

So they knew that he knew. It didn't take a computer genius to figure that out. Somehow they knew he'd learned about Dustbin or whatever it was they called this longterm space watch they were carrying out. Marrows had listened to his tapes several times and then burned them, personally poured gasoline on the tape

133

he'd unreeled and torched the sucker. He hadn't told a soul. The only change in his routine was going back to the coffin nails. He'd made an even-money bet with himself he wouldn't die of cancer before the whole planet cashed in its chips. He hadn't been the first bit concerned that the scientists might be wrong. Hank Marrows' business was news and what science dug up beneath the rocks of the universe, and you had to be deaf or blind and pretty damn dumb, if you stayed tight on covering the space probes, not to have at least picked up on this one. Having a concealed ringside seat to eight of the top scientists in the world spilling out their guts to one another was confirmation enough for him.

But even though they knew he knew, they must have judged he'd kept his mouth shut. They were giving him the kid-gloves treatment. Strength with courtesy. Authority with a plush seat and coffee. And even though they hadn't confirmed so much as a sneeze he knew he was on his way to talk to the top. Because he knew what he shouldn't have known, and he was a newsman who'd exercised some very heavy judgement in favor of silence, they figured it was time for a chat. Where *that* would go, he didn't know. He'd written scenarios all his life so it wasn't too tough to figure out the bigger details.

If they were worried about him he would have been dead long before this moment. When you know the world's coming to a grinding halt you've got to make your moves and damned fast. Your options are *very* limited. That means you control the government, the military, the news media, the public—the whole fucking world—with a grip of case-hardened steel.

So if he wasn't dead, and his cough-wracked chest convinced him of that, then they had use for him. "They" meant the highest levels of government. You don't go higher than George Phillip Starling, because Starling was the president of the United States. Interesting. Hank Marrows stubbed out his cigarette. And since he'd already made peace with himself, he had no trouble in closing his eyes and falling fast asleep.

134

* * *

George Phillip Starling never expected to become the president of the United States of America. Hell, he never *wanted* the job. Senator from Nebraska; a *yes* for that one. And one of the best ever. He'd been a Young Turk in his early days and brought strength with him into the political arena. Football star, wrestling competitor, tough and brawling yet imbued with a streak of sensitivity and hunch factor (the scientists called that one heuristics) that had women mothering him as long as he could remember. He left behind him the gridiron and the wrestling mat and plunged into intense studies of computers, bionic research, and genetic engineering at the University of Nebraska and came out second in his graduating class.

He married the top student. Martha Eddins had an IQ measured at well over two hundred, and Starling wasn't about to let a girl so smart and so beautiful out of his life. He pursued her in a whirlwind courtship so intense that it was years later she confided she'd made up *her* mind to marry *him*. Martha was more than brilliant in academia. She had an intuitive grasp of the future that let her plan that future molded to her private ambitions.

She wasn't simply the "lovely young college girl." Freckled, red-haired and with a body in a tennis outfit that he regarded as devastating, she dominated Starling's life. A dazzling, dimpled smile and penetrating green eyes that seemed to generate a form of brain-whipped laser power. Early in their mutual life (they married while still students; they'd be together a lifetime, she told him, and her plans didn't allow for *any* future stories about supposed promiscuous behavior) she began planning his career.

"George, I follow the Einstein program." He discovered what she meant soon enough. "Einstein didn't see things in numbers," she told him, "despite what the history books tell us. He had moments of intuition. Flashes of mental images. He locked those into his memory banks and pursued what he saw. The rest you know."

"What's that got to do with *me?*"

She laughed and kissed him. "Everything. I've got those same moments of intuition. You, my darling, are going to be the president of this country." He laughed. Then his laughter faded as she went at her "intuitive images" with consummate care. She studied computers, data management, history, politics, television programming, marketing, and the von Clausewitz school of war. She became proficient in trade, agriculture, and a dozen languages. She became a wicked chess player and a dangerous hand at poker, and she learned to commit almost everything to memory, as well as being so capable in nearly-instant data recall from the formidable computer programming she'd developed herself. With the touch of wizardry that rose from intelligence, intuition, and drive, and above all the ability to juxtapose so many different elements all at the same time, she maneuvered her husband into chambers of commerce, youth groups with heavy national coverage from the Boy Scouts to the Civil Air Patrol, and on into ROTC.

"You enlist," she told him as she explained her long-range program. "You do four years in infantry and armor. You get the perspective, feeling and respect of the grunt. The nuclear boys and the missile crowd will razzle-dazzle you with their bullshit, but when their shot is over there'll still be a war going on and it's the grunt who'll be around to pick up the pieces and help put the world back together." He did it all. Foot soldier, tank commander, ordnance specialist, and then flight training for both planes and helicopters. He got his paratrooper wings and when he was a real hotshot combat officer she got him to extend his duty for two years. He spent the first extra year in some real brain-busting stuff at the Air Force Academy and by the time he emerged he had a half-dozen degrees and she maneuvered him into astronaut training with NASA so he could earn his Ph.D. in Astronautics.

"Now you've got the young vote locked up. All shiny chrome and laser jazz. But you're going back to school. You do three months in maritime school, crash courses in economics and geo-politics, and *then*, my darling, you do six months of agriculture. *Including* three months of backbreaking sweat and stink on everything from wheat combines to hands-on pigslop farming. And I'll be right there with you."

She was. There came the day when he found he *enjoyed* the feel of dirt in his hands and his new understanding of animals and the odor, if somewhat less than fragrant, of what farm life really was about. He became a good horseman, and Martha took plenty of the right kind of videotape to use for her "intuitive plans for their future."

Not until he had his first seat in Congress was he aware that Martha had performed all her miracles with almost no attention from either the public or his newly impressed political cronies. He objected to the lack of credit she so richly deserved. He wanted her to be more than his elegant, beautiful, superbly-dressed perfect wife and hostess. She stilled his objections quickly. "I have no intention of being the power queen behind the throne, George. I'm a planner. The best there is, by God, but a *leader* I am not. Together we're better and stronger and more powerful than our individual parts and *that* is how you are going to sit one day in the Oval Office."

Whatever else Martha did, and she had a "skeleton in the closet" file he didn't want to know about, she was true to her images and her word. At fifty-two years of age, in splendid physical health, a brilliant leader of the republic's intelligentsia and a sworn friend of the everyday people, he was *in*.

History caught up with him and knifed through his euphoria when he reached the highest seat in the land. Nuclear horror still loomed on the horizon and Starling could never again yield totally to sleep. A part of his mind had to stay awake and ever vigilant. There were missiles in silos, in submarines, on planes, in trucks and on ships, in secret locations everywhere. No matter that the Russians would rather live with Americans than die with them, a feeling both sides shared, the dagger-sharp presence of guidance systems meant continuing

137

to spread out the weapons of terror, slipping them into trucks and trains, keeping them moving, always moving, always assuring enough missiles to survive *any* strike. Star Wars was a ghastly inheritance from the recent past, the most expensive array of glittering crap ever assembled by a frightened government believing in the quackery of electronic miracle cures. With a cost a billion times greater than all the ancient pharoahs had spent in their quest for "life in the beyond," the nation had cluttered space with crushingly expensive junk that slowly edged back into the atmosphere. All the triple-damned judgments and predictions of near-space atmospheric particles and meteoric dust had proven distressingly feeble, if not drastically wrong, and the rate of attrition from ghostly resistance became a landslide that wrecked the best hopes of Star Wars before it was ever tested.

Well, when you screw up you fall back and punt. Both America and Russia reverted to the tried and true. MADness had worked for many years and it was more reliable than strategic defense initiatives that buried a nation in crushing taxes. So the two great superpowers reverted back to the Doomsday Weapons. Each side had implanted deep within the earth and deep beneath the oceans hydrogen bombs with explosive force measured in the gigaton range—in multiple billions of tons. A pre-emptive attack on one nation by the other would trigger, automatically, the ultimately destructive bombs.

Dead Man's Trigger hung suspended over the entire world. The Sword of Damocles pricked blood from every throat. A single bomb of a trillion tons of explosive power could wreck much of an entire continent, cause unimaginable tidal waves, shatter even the heavens by eruptive atmospheric blowout. So the ABM's had failed and Star Wars was a grisly cartoon joke and the world turned every day with its buried cargo of bombs just short in their power of being classified as planet-busters.

It was enough to put the most optimistic of men in a deep funk from which he might never emerge.

But not the most wonderful of women. She sat with

her husband, the president of their nation, at Camp David and watched a glorious sunset. "It's not so bad, my darling," she told the man responsible directly for the lives and future of three hundred million people. "If it happens we will have perhaps a few seconds to watch the skies burn and to admire colors that will have never been seen before," she told her husband, "and then we shall be beyond the pale of life into the next great adventure."

She was truthfully, incredibly at peace with herself. He could hardly bring himself to tell her about Dustbin and what was happening. When she heard it all she burst into laughter. He stared at her with astonishment. "Don't you understand?" she asked finally. "It's the ultimate in cosmic jokes. Einstein was wrong—God *does* throw dice!"

Hank Marrows sat heavily in a chair of unidentified but clearly great historical significance. Having been selected for the Oval Room, it obviously cost a bundle. And it was one of the most uncomfortable chairs in which he'd ever placed his creaky old body. He squirmed to relieve a stabbing pain in his back. At least he could recognize the table by the chair. French Provincial. An original. Cost a bloody fortune. Piece of shit. On the table were two lead-crystal dishes. Another fortune. Where the hell's the ashtray? he wondered. None. He wanted a cigarette badly. He'd been waiting for fifteen minutes in this room. Screw this jazz. He lit up and graduated the closest crystal dish from priceless heirloom to useful ashtray. A secret service agent moved toward him. "Sir, there's no smoking in here, please."

Marrows gestured with his cigarette. "Obviously there *is* smoking. See?" He held up the cigarette. "I'm smoking. So you're wrong."

"You'll have to put that out, sir."

Patience evaporated. "Look, Dick Tracy, I didn't ask to come here. They sent me an invitation with a black border around it. So be nice to your guests. You want me to quit smoking in here? Tell me to get out. Go on!" Marrows enjoyed himself, punctuating his remarks with clouds of smoke. "Hell, man, *throw* me out." Marrows climbed to his feet and held his arms wide to each side. "I'm all yours, sweetheart."

The agent stopped, his face reflecting inner bewilderment. He was here to protect this man, even if Marrows didn't know it and wasn't being told. Marrows let his arms drop and grinned at the agent, who was saved by a door opening to his right. He stiffened as President and Mrs. Starling came into the room.

Not Marrows. He'd grilled George Starling at more than one press conference and he knew the president was a faithful reader of his news column. They were, in a sense, professional friends. Starling greeted the newsman with a firm and warm handshake. "Hank, thank you for coming." He laughed at the grimace on Marrows' face. "Sorry about our methods. You were treated well?"

"Exemplary, Mr. President. In fact, my friend here was just about to get me an ashtray." The agent swallowed hard but kept his composure.

Martha Eddins rescued him. "He already has one, I believe," she said, nodding to the crystal dish. She winked at Marrows and he smiled. "Please, make yourself comfortable, Mr. Marrows?"

"Ma'am, if its a choice of sitting in that Iron Maiden over here," he pointed to the source of acute discomfort, "I'd prefer to stand. No offense, but—"

Something sure as hell was up. Out of his view another aide was already rolling a comfortable armchair before the president's desk. The priceless table and the crystal dish-turned-ashtray appeared by his right arm as if by magic. He saw Starling make an idle gesture, the room emptied save for the three of them, and the last door clicked shut softly.

"Shall we get right to it, Hank?" Marrows looked at George Starling and recognized they needn't bother with any further amenities. Martha Starling sat to the side, stunning, perfect, legs together, slightly angled arms resting on the velvet sides of her chair. Marrows had to force his gaze away.

"Yes, sir," Marrows told his president. "We both know what brought me here but not *why*."

"You have any ideas?"

"Nope. I haven't done much thinking the last few days. I've been catching up on my drinking and my smoking." He gestured with the pack. "Do you mind, sir?" As quickly as he spoke the words, he frowned severely at himself. "Damn! And I swore I'd never again ask *anyone* about my smoking. They don't like it they can bloody well tell me to—" He turned with a guilty look to Martha Starling. "Hell, I apologize. Why am I acting like this to you people?"

She chose to respond. She flicked away an imaginary speck of dust from her knee. "I imagine that after all these years of abstinence from smoking you've gone back to it to filter out the dust."

He gaped at her, then exploded with sudden laughter. "My God, no wonder your husband is president!" he managed between a burst of coughing.

"The only question," she went on smoothly, "is if the cigarettes or the dust will kill you first. It appears to be an interesting race."

He nodded his respect. "*Touché*," he said with praise.

"I hope you live long enough to do a job for me," George Starling slid easily into their exchange.

"I didn't think this was a social event," Marrows said, slipping back into his professional stance. "You don't have enough time left for nonsense. You'll be tossing protocol and amenities out the window like dead rats."

"True," Starling confirmed. "You're here because you made a major decision."

"To keep my trap shut," Marrows finished for him.

"Precisely," Starling said with a touch of steel.

"How did you know I know?" Marrows asked. "Your usual security measures," he added quickly, "don't seem very important right now. Not as far as this room is concerned, anyway."

"The moment Arthur Kimberly threw his fit in launch control," Starling said bluntly, "our security people tapped him with longprobe acoustics. We recorded everything. We also filmed sensitive film and in infrared."

"And the IR picked up my warm body on the platform," Marrows concluded.

"There was a mass fit over that," Starling chuckled. "They were going to pick you up for busting all sorts of local regs at KSC, but Travis Simmonds has more than his share of smarts. Arresting you couldn't keep your mouth shut. We decided to let you go where you wanted and do what you wanted. Best test there is, Hank. You judged all the factors and you opted for prudence."

"Not too difficult when you're scared sh— when you're scared out of your mind," Marrows offered. "Not for long, though," he appended. "Guess a combination of a lifetime of nearly being killed so many times, and being on the short side of the ledger now—at my age, anyway—got rid of the frights. It doesn't bother me any more. Knowing I'm going to die. From something other than my own choice, that is." He started to light another cigarette and stopped. "May I ask you a sensitive question, Mr. President?"

He watched Starling nod. "What if I'd panicked and blabbed?"

"Very dead, Hank. Instantly."

"I thought so."

"We can't afford hysteria, panic, riots—you name it."

"No, you can't." He stopped sparring. "Why am I here?"

"Among all the other attributes you bring to your profession, Hank, you've just proven both prudence and wisdom." Starling glanced at his wife, and Marrows caught her barely perceptible nod of agreement. "We don't know how much time we have left before the cloud thickens," Starling went on. Marrows lit up instead of talking.

"I don't want all this to end without a record that's written without official bullshit, political meddling, or romantic posturing. I want you to write that record. We don't know precisely what will happen to this world of ours, but I'd like to leave a legacy of what could well be its final moments. We'll take that record and encapsulate it. Dozens of copies in titanium and carboloy cylinders we'll put deep into the oceans, in a mountain or two, deep within the moon. Those are details."

Marrows let out a pent-up breath. "Sir, you've got historians up the yingyang. Cameras, video, tapes; all of it. Why me?"

"You're the only one who's passed the test," Starling said with a smile that grew into a chuckle. "You *know* and you didn't tell. You knew what we would have to do."

"*Escape.*" Shit, yes, they'd have to try that.

"Could be. Maybe. Perhaps. Possibly. Plausibly? We don't know. Of course we'll try. We're about to start on those strategies in a day or two. I want you in on any and all meetings you can cover. You go with *my* authority. Where you want, when you want, nobody messes with you. You write it the way you see it. For the record, you're my official biographer. That covers all bases and shuts up the noisemakers. You'll have all the secretarial, recording, typing, computing help you need. An entire staff. Your own plane always on standby. Martha will coordinate all of it."

Marrows looked to her. "It works," she said succinctly.

"Who else will know besides you two?" Marrows asked.

"You," the president said. "And your own staff, of course. That's all."

Marrows ran a gnarled hand through thinning hair. "Jesus, Mr. President, I don't know. I mean, I figured I've missed a life time of sunsets and fishing and watching kids in playgrounds and . . ." His voice went slowly silent. "My God, sir, I feel hollow inside."

"I'll change jobs with you, Hank."

Marrows wanted to reach out and hold the president of the United States in his arms. He'd never thought of what this man would be going through from now on.

"Yeah, I guess you would," Marrows said after a shaky pause. "All right, sir, I'll do it but I don't *want* to. Writing obits is bad enough. Doing an epithet like this is—well, it's like digging a mass grave with your typewriter."

"See, my dear?" Martha Starling said from the side.

"It's as I told you. Anyone with the name of Henry O'Henry O'Rourke Marrows will do splendidly by us."

Marrows stared with open-jawed amazement. "Nobody knows that name!" he exclaimed.

"*I* do," she countered. "But since it appears that keeping your real full name secret is more important than the end of the world," she added with a laugh, a sound of crystaline laughter that might have come from a forest sprite, "our secret shall remain locked in this room."

"Yes, ma'am," he said, subdued.

"From now on, Hank, my name is Martha. His is George. We shall dispense with—oh my, you've already said it, haven't you?—with the protocol and the amenities. If it makes you feel any more comfortable, Hank, you remind me so much of my father it's almost scary."

"You ready to go to work?" growled the president of the United States. Marrows nodded.

"Martha will set you up. We already have your office and your staff ready."

"You were that sure of me?"

"How'd you think I got to the top? Blind guesswork?"

"I've got one question, sir. George, I mean." Marrows shook his head. "I'll get it, I'll get it," he promised.

"Your question?"

"You don't want this thing public. Okay. I buy all of that. If policy changes—"

"You'll be the first to know," Starling said impatiently. "The *question*, Hank!"

"This is my first official act," Marrows insisted, and saw agreement in the president's eyes. "This is a race against time, whatever it is you're going to try before they ring down the curtain on all of us. That means you need as much time as you can get with as little interference as possible." Marrows took a deep breath and suppressed a cough. "What happens if someone else—a reporter, a politician, a top government official, whoever—stumbles onto this before you go public with your plans?"

George Starling's face was stone. "Incarceration is preferable. It would be for a limited time only. If that's not possible, we kill him. Or her. Or them. I would hate to make that decision, to take away from anyone what precious little time they may have left."

"To kill them . . ." Marrows echoed what he'd just heard. "There's no other way?"

"Goddamn it, Marrows, switch seats with me and *you* tell *me* another way!"

Marrows rose slowly to his feet. A cigarette he wanted anxiously remained unlit between his fingers. "It's strange," he said at last. "Why is there so much pain and agony in meeting what's inevitable?"

"Because we're the keepers of this zoo, Henry. Because we opted to go for the brass ring and we've got it, and that makes us responsible for so many others who trust us and count on us. That's the Catch 22 in this job. You keep grabbing for the next brass ring. You try to find even a sliver of a future in what's coming down. Because it's better to end it all trying like hell than to quit now and meet your maker hating yourself."

Marrows tried to light his cigarette, but his hands trembled and betrayed him.

And I could have gone fishing and watched the sunsets, he thought miserably.

8

Yuri Fedov considered the Soviet Union's Doomsday Bombs to be wonderful. There is something very commanding about a single device that has, locked in its belly, malevolent and glowering, the power of three trillion tons of explosive force. The world pays even more rapt attention to the announcement that not just one but an unknown number of such devices have been constructed and emplaced in positions that, were they detonated, would guarantee the cracking of the Earth's crust, even the splitting of continents. How absolutely marvelous! The world shuddered and hurled imprecations against the Russians, and Yuri Fedov laughed because everyone heaped abuse in equal amounts on

145

the Americans because of *their* Doomsday Bombs. *Wonderful, wonderful*. Yuri Fedov was a madman, and George Starling was burned in effigy as a messenger of Satan. How fascinating: the outcries of that rubbery-faced actor-president, Ronald Reagan, that all Soviets were evil and satanic, had come full circle.

As the Premier of the U.S.S.R., Yuri Fedov knew very well the constitution, the history, and the fiber of George Phillips Starling. The old ways were no longer good enough. He spent hours watching films of the man who was now the president of the United States of America. He looked at pictures of the man from his childhood through his many schools and along the congressional and senatorial roads to the presidency. He listened to every speech, he watched the videos of Starling as a congressman and as a senator and the head of many committees. He studied his wife, the former Martha Eddins, and he smiled at the power he discovered in that woman. Then he had *his* wife, Yelena, study all the films and the pictures and the videos of both man and woman. He wanted nuances subtleties, mannerisms, reactions.

Yuri Fedov did everything in his power not to repeat certain critical mistakes of his predecessors. He and his wife, Yelena, the mother of their seven sons, bent every effort and broke with every tenet that had bound Fedov's predecessors to numbing and ponderous relationships with their opposite numbers in the United States. Yuri Fedov did more than break cherished traditions: he smashed the obstacles in his path by thundering roughshod over the cat-and-mouse protocol dictated by underlings and the guardians of past traditions. Like all those who are not merely successful within the Soviet system, but dominating in their power, he planned with exquisite care to move the right people into the most powerful of offices. No sooner was he thoroughly in command of the new guard that had evicted the old than he dispatched brigades of ministers and well-wishers throughout most of the world, bearing gifts in the form of agreements between governments, so long coveted by Russia's neighbors.

146

But he saved the best for his personal touch. Off to the United States he went, as he was fond of telling his compatriots, in the finest Arkansas-style. The world watched in amazement as rotund and beaming Fedov, with his charming smile and booming laugh, and the beautiful wife who could still model in Paris, *and* their seven strapping sons, flew into Washington in a blaze of red-starred glory and no little pomp and circumstance. Two large Soviet ships had docked quietly in Baltimore harbor where they were met with long rows of big semi-trailer rigs that carried its secret parade cargo from the waterfront to a military reservation just outside Washington.

Yuri Fedov was determined to make the world sit up and take notice of new Russian style. He reached back to moments of glory in ancient Russia, he studied films of British grenadiers and horsemen passing in review in England, and he made his appearance in Washington in a superbly timed and perfectly-drilled Trooping of the Red Banner by two hundred Russian horsemen in splendid uniforms. It was all there, brass bands and all, and on his first night the Red Army Chorus, making its first appearance in America, answered to sixteen curtain calls at the Kennedy Center for the Performing Arts.

As much as Mikhail Gorbachev had demolished many of the old and cloying institutions, so Yuri Fedov went several more steps forward. Fedov spoke perfect English without a trace of accent. He requested, and received, a special appearance before both houses of the American Congress, where he proceeded to sweep America off its feet. He brought forth to the podium Yelena, with a smile that won over every man and woman in the great domed hall. He signaled with a wave and his seven sons, following explicit instructions from their father given long before this moment, lined up to the left of Yelena. Finally he wrapped it up by requesting that the president of the United States, and the First Lady, share with them the speaking stand.

Then, without the first hint to anyone of what he had planned, he pointed his finger at his oldest son. "Leonid! Step forward!" he cried. A strapping youngster stepped forward one pace and stood at attention. Yuri Fedov turned to his audience and played to the television cameras. "This is Leonid, my oldest. Tomorrow he goes to the Massachusetts Institute of Technology where he becomes *an American student*. If he disgraces us by earning anything less than straight A's then I, his father, shall break both his kneecaps!"

When the roaring applause and laughter died down, the father's stern voice called out again. "Konstantin! For you, there is the College of Agriculture of the University of Florida." The appropriate pause and then: "Vitali! For you, the College of Bioengineering at the University of Washington!" Amazement, disbelief, delight, and wonder. Yuri and Yelena Fedov's three oldest sons had become students at American universities. A bridge was going up damned fast. He turned back to his enraptured audience.

"My dear congressmen and senators, an invitation to any and all of you," he called out in fine theatrical but humble Russian style, later reviewed as one of the more memorable performances before any political institution, "we wish your sons and daughters to join with us in pursuit of their education. Any member of this most august body is invited to send their son or daughter, as they may wish, as my personal guest to any Soviet institution of learning."

Forty-three American young men and women were soon on their way to the Soviet Union. It was a brilliant move, a stroke of genius.

It had been planned carefully by both Yuri Fedov and George Starling long before its presentation. It played and replayed to astonished audiences, in every language of the world, on the television sets of every country in the world.

But they, Fedov and Starling, were still condemned roundly as madmen. No amount of rhetoric or exchange of students could avoid the omnipresent horror of Doomsday Bombs implanted within the intestines of the planet.

Late that night Yuri Fedov padded in slippers, pajamas and elegant silk robe through the private guest

148

quarters of the White House, a snifter of fine brandy in one hand, a long slim Jamaican cigar in the other. He and George Starling sat together finally in plush armchairs before a roaring fireplace, where they were joined by one American, Dr. Richard Shaeffer, who lived in Moscow, and by the Russian Doctor General Gregory (Tretsky) Tretyakovich, who lived in D.C. It was a meeting which Starling's best counterintelligence teams made certain could not be recorded in any way. It was a meeting known to no more than four other officials of each government.

Shaeffer and Tretyakovich sat in armchairs facing the president of the United States and the premier of the Soviet Union. Theirs was a moment of extraordinary satisfaction, a tick in the time of modern events they hoped might be preserved forever.

"Is it really done?" Starling asked the two scientists. He spoke for himself and Yuri Fedov.

Shaeffer and Tretyakovich nodded almost in unison. The Russian gestured with his brandy. "Richard, have your say," he told his opposite number. Shaeffer took a long pull at his brandy. This moment had been years in the making. The brief pause gave the others time to reflect on him: a most extraordinary human being who had performed extraordinary feats about which the world likely would never learn any details.

Dr. Richard Shaeffer would have been the perfect undertaker if he were judged only by his physical appearance and morose attitude toward his co-workers. Tall and gangly enough to have earned the description "Lincolnesque," with the same gravelly voice and slowness of expression attributed to the long-dead president, Shaeffer was a human cage of rattling bones assembled loosely within sagging skin from which dark hair sprouted in unpleasant batches. He stood six feet seven inches tall and weighed barely one hundred sixty pounds and seemed physically endangered by even a mild breeze. His lower lip bulged forward with a bluish tinge and he moved with an ambling gait as if he'd never walked normally in his life. Behind his startling blue eyes and sunken cheeks, however, churned one of those minds that have baffled science since the first geniuses appeared on man's stage. Shaeffer was more than a rarity. Because of two dominant abilities, he had never scored less than a perfect hundred in his scholastic history from grade school through his Doctor of Science degrees. He remembered *everything* he learned, and he had the even more dazzling ability to retain and utilize everything in proper perspective. He was the closest human equivalent to a computer that not only keeps in its data banks everything fed into its unthinking maw, but can recall it instantly and then imbue any task with the peculiar human trait of judgment and decision.

George Starling selected Shaeffer after an exhaustive research effort, snatching him from his teaching position in Illinois. Every government agency poured data, as well as questions still in need of answers, into his skull. When they completed this staggering input, all of which Shaeffer took with his usual aplomb, Starling sent him with his wife, two sisters, mother-in-law and four children to Moscow, where he took up residence within the walled fastness of the Kremlin. It was a brilliant move. No matter to whom he spoke, Shaeffer had total recall of every detail. If what was presented to him contained gaps or disinformation, Shaeffer knew it immediately.

He caused tremendous consternation among the Kremlin occupants with the exception of Yuri Fedov. They accused him of having x-ray vision and the ability to read minds. They brought in their best bioscientists and their most touted psychic to study Shaeffer and discover whatever it was that gave him such superhuman capabilities. He had the ability, but it was in an area of cerebral freakishness no one in the world could even begin to understand. And it was all encased within a weakling's physical frame and an air of casual disinterest with which no one could find offense.

Tretyakovich had handed him the ball, Shaeffer mused. And Tretsky did *nothing* without a damned good reason. The power plays were still under way. *He wants the final word*, Shaeffer judged. *Richard, have your say* is how he had opened his verbal chess gambit.

Shaeffer smiled, a thin parody of pressed lips spreading. "It's not *my* say that's involved," he answered finally to their small group. President Starling wanted to know if they had really established their position, he in Moscow and Tretyakovich here in Washington. He turned from Tretyakovich to George Starling.

"Yes, sir, it really is done," Shaeffer said. "Unless the Russians break their word to us, I'll know every major decision they make. Even what they *plan* to make. I've learned their system so well by now that I can almost write scenarios of what they will do in any near future. What's more important is that if they break this arrangement, I'll know it at once. It's not magic or genius, Mr. President." Shaeffer threw out a spear to lodge within Yuri Fedov's thinking. Cage-rattling was a great art when no one really knew how you functioned between the ears. "It's—well, I'm tuned in to the Russian gestalt. I'm locked into their wavelength. Any time they deviate I'll know, and then *you'll* know, almost at once. As far as I'm concerned, they'll play by the rules."

Yuri Fedov sat ensconced in warm clothing like a gentle, somnambulistic bear. Gregory Tretyakovich offered the group the same smile a tolerant parent might give while watching his child perform a given task rather clumsily despite valiant effort. Richard Shaeffer never showed emotion once he'd had his say; he did not believe in chasing after the ball he'd just pitched. And that leaves me, thought President George Starling. Well, this little scenario is wound up just about as tight as it can go. I've got Shaeffer in the Kremlin, and by our agreement Yuri must permit him to listen to *anything* involving government, science, military or any other matter save connubial privacy and then *only* with his wife. If this works out, judged Starling, then I should always be one up on good old Yuri. There's no one else in this world who can perceive the Russians as a gestalt. They're all one mind to Shaeffer:

"Old Ichabod" is really tuned in and locked to their wavelength.

"Gentlemen," Starling offered, "one final round and then it's off to sleep for me. I'd like to have some bright eyes tomorrow morning instead of the red grapes my wife accuses me of showing her every day." They toasted their mutual health and separated.

George Starling was right about his one-upmanship over Yuri Fedov. Well, *almost*.

There's an old saw in the game of international contest: every weapon produces a counterweapon.

When George Starling first proposed the extraordinary and unprecedented move of each government permitting the constant presence of a member of the opposite country always at the side of the national leader, he was convinced "the Russians haven't got a thing to match Shaeffer. Hell, we wouldn't match him ourselves. We're talking about the level that produces Einstein, Galileo, Newton, Copernicus and that whole lot. Umpteen levels above the norm. The son of a bitch might just as well have come from another planet."

Lt. General Joseph Joshua Briand of the U.S. Air Force, one of the very few in government fully aware of Shaeffer's position in the Kremlin, smiled at the American president's appraisal. Briand was an old personal friend of Starling's and their wives were fierce opponents on the tennis court. At times the general spoke with the president as if they sat across a poker table, without inhibition.

"You watch it, George," Briand warned him. "I'm serious. Couple of my opposite numbers in Disneyworld East," the general's name for Russia, "were really put into a snit about Shaeffer looking over Fedov's shoulder. So they figured they ought to go one better with the man they're sending to look over *yours*."

"I don't believe there's another Richard Shaeffer on this whole planet," Starling scoffed.

"I agree. But sure as God made little green apples there ain't no other Tretsky."

"What in the hell is a Tretsky?"

General Briand had smiled. "I'm going to enjoy this. I really am, you know."

"Joe, get to it—"

Briand held up his hands to stem the attack. "Okay, okay, *Mister* President. Tretsky is not a what. It's a who. Doctor General Gregory Alexandrovich Tretyakovich. We got intellectual magic in Shaeffer? They got cerebral wizardry in Tretsky."

"You talk as if you know him personally."

"I'm the best goddamn gin player in the air force," Briand scowled. "Tretsky waxes my ass without even trying. In fact," the general's face darkened, "he even does the *New York Times* crossword puzzles *while* we're playing gin. He's ahead of me twelve thousand bucks."

"Ever play him poker?"

"I got killed. Listen, you familiar with the name of Admiral Isoroku Yamamoto?"

Starling nodded. "Imperial mucky-muck of the Japanese Imperial Fleet in the—" he smiled "—what your crowd calls the last good war."

"Right. Most people don't know that Yamamoto was the Japanese naval attache in Washington for a couple of years before they dumped on Pearl Harbor. He was also known as the best poker player ever to hit this town. And I'll tell you something, George," Briand said, stabbing a finger at the president to emphasize the point, "Tretsky could take our slant-eyed killer coming and going."

"Um." Starling chewed over what he'd heard. "Just tell me one thing. No, don't tell me. Don't tell me he *looks* like Shaeffer."

General Briand leaned back in his chair roaring with laughter.

Two souls, Shaeffer and Tretyakovich, could hardly have been more *un*like. There was Shaeffer, looming gaunt and cadaverous, croaking like a raven on a wintry night and with all the personality of a cobweb-stuffed computer.

"One thing you'll never forget about Tretsky," explained General Briand to President Starling, "is his voice." The Russian was the other side of the aural coin from Shaeffer. "He booms every time he speaks. *Booms*. He never speaks, he announces. He's like a row of Roman trumpeters heralding the arrival of Caesar."

Starling could hardly wait. When he finally met Tretsky, as he'd come to think of General Tretyakovich, he found all personal descriptions woefully inadequate. He first entered the president's office not loudly, but boisterous, rowdy, excited, bulging with life, grasping the world with his steely grey eyes and a huge smile with huge teeth beneath a huge shaven skull and bushy brows and a fierce moustache. He filled the space about him, a man of thick and bulging build, massive as the trunk of a great oak tree, snarling his clothes where his muscles corded and twisted along his body. He had arms as thick as Shaeffer's thighs, and without an ounce of flab on his frame he bent the scales at three hundred pounds.

He blew into the White House with his secretary, his press secretary, two researchers, and his doctor, and they were all of them women who were either beautiful or striking and all of solid physical stock. Tretyakovich was unashamedly wanton in his physical pleasures. "Drinking, eating, wenching, fighting, and thinking," he boomed. "These make the life worthwhile, no? *Yes!*" His philosophy, verbalized like a twenty-one-gun salute.

President George Starling began to appreciate the pleasure Yuri Fedov must have felt when he selected Tretyakovich for his assignment to the White House for "looking over the shoulder of the great American leader." Where Richard Shaeffer rattled the cages of the Kremlin power leaders with his hushed, shuffling presence and computer mind that never turned off, Tretyakovich rattled the White House itself. He ate like a lumberjack, sang with ear-hammering gusto, dressed in flashy silks and Cossack boots, caroused and laughed, caused feminine screams to echo thinly from his quarters at all hours of the night, and failed miserably to fool even for a moment either George Starling or his closest friend and confidant, Russ Corey, when the latter sailed in from the moon at presidential request.

154

Their first encounter, Corey and Tretsky's, produced a wholly unexpected result. The moment the two made eye contact it was like throwing a volume cutoff switch in Tretyakovich. "Talk about your Close Encounters," Starling later confided to his wife. "I guess this was an encounter of the Fourth Kind. It was like watching two giants colliding on a mental plane. For the first few minutes they never said one word aloud, either one of them. Just stared, and then each of them twitched at the corner of the mouth, and that became a grin, and they threw their arms about one another. I've watched Tretyakovich. Come to know what to expect. He's the original man with the bear hug. Picks up people and waltzes them through the air like they were rag dolls. He didn't even *try* that with Corey. I think I saw some honest, immediate affection there. I'm still baffled by it all."

Russ Corey had his private warning for Starling. "*Never* underestimate that crazy Ukrainian. Just because he can screw his way through a women's barracks in one night and destroy half a case of vodka in the process doesn't mean he's not packed just as solid between the ears as *our* boy. His methodology is different but he's just as sharp and every inch and pound as much a genius. Don't be misled by his showbiz. That's all Kremlin capers crap. *I know Gregory.*"

Corey smiled with his memories. "That bellowing son of a bitch is a ballistics genius. In fact, that's where he earned his rank as a general. You can give him the specific impulse and burn time of a missile and tell him the target, and in his head he'll compute different strata winds, declination and torque of the planet, rotational compensation and come up with burn times to the second, and he'll do it all standing there looking at you and scratching his balls. Armor, artillery, missiles; you name it, he's pure genius at it. Did you know he was a pilot?"

Starling shook his head. "When the hell would he have time?"

"He's a bomber pilot. Checked out in all their fighters. He's commanded an attack sub. He can design you a nuclear reactor between breakfast and lunch. Remember that with everything he can do, however, he is *not* like our boy Shaeffer, and it's critical that you understand the differences."

Starling smiled at the question he was about to voice. "Aside from the tap dancing and the unbridled lust, different in what way?"

"Shaeffer can whip Tretsky's ass all day and all night when it comes to chess. That's *pure* computer and you don't really need the kind of intuition Tretsky has and Shaeffer doesn't. But for those same reasons Gregory Tretyakovich can haul Shaeffer's ashes any time he wants if they ever play any serious poker. In *that* game it's bluff and psychology and intuition and daring—"

"I've played, remember?"

"Yeah, I remember, and you're damned good at it. But the Russian can clean your clock just as easily. Don't forget that. My point is, George, and I make this recommendation as strongly as I can, don't try to bluff this guy. Don't hide anything from him. It's not worth it and it won't work. He can smell a dodge or a lie a hundred miles upwind. All these tall tales about his being some kind of psych bloodhound are true. A lot of the top people in Russia are scared shitless of him. You just cannot keep secrets from Tretsky. This is not psychic bullshit. Some people would call his kind of intuition psychic."

"You don't?"

"Hell, no. It's a talent and he's developed it. He's a crazy bastard. He's called Fedov in the middle of the night to tell him a new joke he's just heard. Do you know what *you* would do if *I* called you at four in the morning to crack a new joke with you?"

Starling nodded. He learned back in his chair and dropped his feet on his desk. "Sure. I'd spend the rest of the night staying awake trying to figure out what you were *really* up to."

"And you know why the premier of the Soviet Union lets him get away with it?"

"Tell me."

"Because Fedov knows that all calls in and out of the

Kremlin are recorded. He also knows the best experts in the KGB and GRU and military intelligence end up going bananas trying to find the hidden message in Tretyakovich's calls. And there aren't any! It's just his style."

"It also shows me that Yuri Fedov has his own brand of humor if he goes along with it."

"Right on. Fedov does that, all right." Russ Corey studied Starling and made a sudden decision. "I'm breaking a confidence on this one. Do you know where Tretsky is tonight?"

"No."

"He's out there," Corey gestured to take in the outside world, "wearing a mask. He's using a false name. He's in Baltimore."

Starling's feet hit the floor as he straightened in his seat. "Why in the name of God would he—"

"Did you know Tretyakovich was famous for his parties in Russia?"

"What's *that* got to do with—"

"And his parties almost always ended up the same way." Corey smiled. "Tretsky's a madman when he drinks, which is often, but especially when he's drunk, which is not so often, but—" Corey shrugged. "He loves to fight. Knockdown, drag-out, barroom-brawl fighting. Pure redneck shit-kicking, head-stomping, good-old-boy fun, Russian style. And he takes on as many at one time as he can."

"Damn it, Russ, there hasn't been the first sign here of—"

"Fedov told him he'd have his balls on a silver platter if he pulled that shit even *once* over here."

"Then why—" Starling shook his head. "You've lost me. Pull me back in."

"Tretsky's got to get it out of his system. So tonight he's Abdul al Karim, and he's a masked wrestler from Turkey. That's how the card reads, anyway. Doesn't mean a thing, and—"

"You're telling me that the personal envoy from the premier of the Soviet Union to the president of the United States *is wrestling in the Baltimore Arena?*"

Starling went silent. After several minutes he leaned forward, a gleam in his eyes. "How's he do?".

"The son of a bitch wins every match. No one can figure him out. He doesn't know the meaning of the word rules. He gets in there and he goes berserk. Eats up the place alive. He's half-killed some of the best names in the pro circuit. The moment he finishes a match the secret service has a dozen of their biggest and best people rush him out of the arena and sneak him out of Baltimore."

Starling tapped his fingers on his desk. "Russ, are you aware that the man we're discussing, this wild man who at this very moment is trying to rip someone's head off in a wrestling ring, is one of the most important people in existence? That he's one of the absolutely critical keys to keep us, and the Russians, from cracking this planet in half?"

Corey's expression didn't change. "Let's just say I figured it. Let's just say," he added slowly, "that I know that Gregory Tretyakovich is a corresponding member of the Soviet Academy of Science, and that his specialty with that most august of bodies is thermonuclear fusion."

"Uh-huh. Let's just say that. But not for the record, correct?"

"As you and I used to say in the old days, George, you bet your sweet ass."

All that was far behind them now, mused Yuri Fedov. He sat bundled in a thick robe, feet wrapped in lamb's-wool slippers, a dusky cognac in one hand and his favorite cigar in the other. He thought of so many things leading up to this moment and he thought of his most recent order to bring General Vasily Tereshnikov down from *Gagarin* station. An order he had hated to give, because it meant the insanity of everything else pouring into the Kremlin intelligence compounds must be true.

If solving what faces us now were only as simple as ridding ourselves of our ability to destroy this world . . . He glanced up at soft sounds approaching him: Yelena and their two huge Russian wolfhounds padding by her side. She sensed his discomfiture, and like the good wife and woman she was, she knew when to communicate only with silence. She had heard enough of this thing they called Dustbin to know it was potentially the gravest challenge her husband had yet encountered as the head of the Soviet peoples. She understood this man and how he was turning back the years in his mind to set everything in its proper place. Around Yuri Fedov there were geniuses of all sorts. Mathematical, scientific; whatever. But there were very few men who could separate themselves from the physical reality surrounding them and look down on their nation, on the whole world, if necessary, and judge moments and events from the vantage of the gods. *And from what I am hearing, we will need them,* she told herself. She seated herself close by his feet, resting against his chair, and began to knit. It settled this man, let a part of him return to his own humble beginnings, when most of the clothes he wore as a boy had been handmade by his mother.

Who would ever have figured that the placement of Richard Shaeffer and Gregory Tretyakovich, pondered Yuri Fedov, *was a sham so carefully planned and executed?* For a moment he closed his eyes and thought back to that incredible moment when the American president caught him totally by surprise. It began with a seemingly innocent telephone call, not on the hotline between Washington and Moscow, but on a private line directly to the Fedov apartment within the Kremlin. Yuri Fedov years before had learned how to read between the lines of any conversation over telephone line or radio. Modern electronics meant capturing all unguarded moments for later reckoning. So you learned to understand the deeper meaning of what anyone might say, especially when the individual to whom you spoke also was capable of wielding enormous power. And George Phillip Starling wielded power sufficient to melt a planet.

"Yuri, I have good news," was Starling's innocent opening.

"The Soviet people are always happy to receive good news," Fedov responded, and he knew George Starling was also interpreting beyond their spoken lines.

"Our people have managed to get through the final committee meetings the cooperative deal for the thermo-fusion reactors. I know it's been a long time coming and very frustrating," Starling said with every word carefully chosen, "but the plasma container your scientists have wanted us to build for them is already well into construction."

Fedov's excitement was genuine but not for a reason anyone listening in to this conversation could possibly determine. "Wonderful, Mr. President! We are very well advanced in the fusion power program, as you know. Chernobyl will be much easier to put behind us, just like your Three Mile Island, the sooner we can get rid of fission reactors and go directly to the fusion method. Our Tokamak engineers will be most pleased, I am certain, when I give them the news. May I ask, Mr. President—"

"George; please."

"Of course. George, may I ask when delivery will take place? And where?"

"I understand your people would prefer to have delivery take place in Murmansk. Or Archangel, I am not sure; but wherever you decide, we will make delivery."

Fedov picked his next words with the greatest of care. Normally such a massive unit would be delivered through the warm-water ports in the Black Sea, but that meant passing through the constricting waterways of Istanbul, and there could be none of *that*. "I'm certain Archangel would be best, but we will leave such details to our respective committees."

"Very good, Yuri. I'm delighted we could go through with this arrangement. We will be able to have our scientists on site working with your people?"

"Of course. That is our promise. We do not break our word, George."

"Thank you, Yuri. Martha sends her best with me to Yelena and your children."

"Thank you, Mr. President. Goodbye."

Delivery was made before the next four months passed. A military cargo vessel carried the magnetic fusion equipment to Archangel. Four attack submarines shadowed the USS *Monterey* close to the Russian harbor. The equipment was unloaded with extraordinary care and its components moved by heavily guarded train to the Soviet research center. There, behind warning signs of radiation as well as maximum security sealing off the area, Yuri Fedov showed his prize to a select group of scientists and top members of the Politburo, an even dozen in all.

One scientist fainted. Two other men became ill. There wasn't any magnetic plasma container for thermonuclear fusion power development.

They stared at a thermonuclear bomb with the explosive power of three trillion tons of TNT. Right in the heart of the Soviet Union.

Yuri Fedov faced the twelve men with him, beset by fear, the white heat of rage, by all manner of emotion. Behind him rested a war machine that could rip out the heart of all Russia.

"This is a gift from the American president," he said softly, as if soothing words were required to keep the Beast quiescent. He raised his hand to stop any interruption. "This bomb as it rests here cannot be fired. All such devices are removed. They *could* be reinstated. But that will not happen. What *will* happen is—"

Sokolov could contain himself no longer. "How could you trust—"

"Be quiet. I trust no one but a Soviet with our country. Dzhermen Gvishiani and Anatoli Logunov personally dismantled the firing mechanism. It is in their possession. They have been with this monster ever since I made our pact with the American president."

"*What* pact?" Fedov didn't know to whom the quavering voice belonged.

"The Americans have nine of these emplaced. The Doomsday Weapons. The bombs that can destroy all civilization. They have given us this machine of death. It is harmless. We shall take it apart. We shall make certain it never, *never*, can explode."

161

Sergei Sokolov spoke in a hoarse voice. "What do they want in return?"

"We shall deliver to them one of our Doomsday machines. Two of their top weapons scientists will be with our ordnance people when we defuse *our* bomb. The American ship that brought us this terrible instrument will carry our bomb to them in exchange. They will take it apart themselves. And then they will bring us another. And we shall send *them* another. When we have delivered our seven and we have received their nine, we will all sleep better."

They'd done it. *That* had been the rationale behind Richard Shaeffer and Gregory Tretyakovich, each in the heart of the enemy's homeland. *Less an enemy than before,* Fedov reflected.

There came a summit meeting: Starling and Fedov and their incredible retinue of experts, advisors and the whole bloody lot that followed them about like locusts. The American president and the Russian premier let their lesser numbers haggle and barter. They went skiing, and when they had their opportunity, far from the following crowds, in sight of security teams from each government but unheard due to a nearby chain saw cutting firewood that blanked out their conversation, they could talk freely, even if only for a brief moment. Presidents and premiers do not have the luxury of true privacy.

"So," Fedov said. He and Starling looked out across valleys and peaks of blinding white, the mantle of Switzerland's winter snows. "It is really and truly done."

Starling nodded. There really wasn't very much he had to say. It was still so overwhelming. To think— No; he didn't even want to think that such things had been assembled and emplaced *and armed to go off*.

"Would you ever have used such a device?" Yuri Fedov asked suddenly, and as quickly as the words escaped him he gestured for the American not to answer. "I am no more insane than you. Who would so willingly incinerate an entire world?"

"Frightened people, Yuri. That's who."

The premier nodded. "Perhaps we are not yet wise enough. We still build warheads."

"As we do."

Fedov was more expansive than his companion. "Pinpricks by comparison. That is not so bad, my friend! George Starling, we have lived with these weapons for some fifty years now and we are talking to one another as friends. A pox on all these ideological arguments! You are not the evil monsters of money, and we are not the satanic empire. Both of us are good and bad, but above all we are different, and as much as it is rude to say such a thing, I am a good man. One day the world will know. One day they will take all the many letters of our two names and they will spell it, the new name, only one way. *Hope*."

Fedov let out a tremulous sigh. He wished to end this conversation as anxiously as did the man with him. He touched Starling gently with his fist. "Besides, your wife is engaged in espionage of her own kind right now." Starling turned with raised brows at the remark. Fedov smiled. "Your Martha is locked in a room at this moment with my Yelena. I know her questions."

Starling laughed softly. "I know," he said. "Martha is convinced Yelena has the most priceless secret in all the world. How a woman can bear seven sons and yet have a body with a flat stomach and beautiful legs. You're wrecking our fashion industry, Yuri. Our people are falling all over themselves preparing new clothing designs for mothers. There is an expression in our country being repeated everywhere. Flat is in and flab is out. Yuri, if you had to run for election in Russia against your wife, you would lose."

Most likely, thought Yuri Fedov with a deep and immense satisfaction. *But there can be no losing now. The machines to destroy this planet have been rendered harmless. If I were to die this very moment my life could not be more successful.*

Before the next year was behind him he knew he was very, very wrong.

Was there really a God? he wondered. If such a

163

creature existed, he had a most curious and twisted sense of humor. A sense of the grotesque.

When Vasily Iliych Tereshnikov safely returned to Earth from *Gagarin*, there would be an extraordinary meeting in the Kremlin. No secrets this time from the Party. None to be kept from the Politburo. From the people, yes. They would be kept in ignorance for the time being. Their turn would come.

Yuri Fedov felt crushing desperation. Right now, he knew, the Americans were holding their extraordinary meeting. It would be taped and the tapes would be hand-carried to Moscow. Doctor General Gregory Tretyakovich would be at that meeting.

They would talk about Dustbin.

Yuri Fedov already hated the word.

9 ─────────

Martha Eddins Starling studied herself in the full-length trifold mirrors of her dressing room. She liked what she saw, a woman in her early fifties with the matured but still sensuously curving form she had thirty years before. *Hard work, lady*, she told herself with satisfaction, *it's hard work what does it*. She smiled and patted the flatness of her stomach, the flesh-colored body stocking hugging her to slim perfection. She thought of Yelena Fedov and her superb form *and* her seven sons. *Yelena*, she mused, *if I didn't like you so much I'd hate you*.

Down to the business at hand. *The* meeting was set for today. "We're going to the sublevel for this," her husband told her. "It's going to be a pretty big bunch. A lot of hypersensitivity. We'll use the security conference room. It's the only one with a single table setup big enough for what we need, and it's got enough bathroom facilities, and do you know how much coffee we'll need?"

She nodded. "Yes," she added for effect.

"And some of them, you know, tea. Others will want just water. Or bottled water. Or Perrier, and—"

"George, stop it." He blinked several times. "Okay, okay," he said, nodding slowly. "I *am* dodging around it, I guess."

"No guess. Please leave it in my hands."

"Please?" He snorted with disdain at the thought of other people. "Damn it, Martha, without *you* handling all these details the whole thing could come unglued."

"I'll handle them," she said smoothly, leveling off his pre-meeting emotions. "Question."

"Shoot."

"I want this confirmed. You have no idea how long this meeting will last, is that correct?"

"It may explode in the first ten minutes and then it's all over. Or it can go on for a day and a night. Not too much chance of that. There aren't many people like Corey or Tretsky who can hammer out these things for three days and nights without sleep."

"Or George Starling," she emphasized.

"Okay, so I'm a lousy sleeper. But you better be ready for right around the clock."

She helped him choose the right clothes for what might be a very long meeting: loose, thin socks, loafers that would not bind after his feet swelled from hours of sitting, lightweight slacks with a thin belt. No necktie.

"Too constricting," Martha advised. "Even with the good air conditioning, that many bodies and hot coffee in the room will make it uncomfortable. If *your* neck is comfortable, the others will be more inclined to open their ties."

"Okay."

"George, get rid of your restrictions against smoking."

"Tough in an enclosed space."

"Tell them to increase the updraft suction. It'll take the smoke *up* and out. Won't bother those who don't smoke. Those who want or need to will begin to chafe after a while if they can't. They'll lose concentration. Nicotine will overrule even you."

"Excellent. Will you take care of it?"

"I will. Beat it, Mr. President."

165

"One last thing. What're you wearing?"

She smiled. "I'm going to knock your socks off."

"Uh, theirs, too?" he asked, referring to the people drawing together for the meeting.

"You bet. Bye." She kissed him and he left her in her dressing room. *You bet I'll knock their socks off . . .*

She'd selected her attire for this occasion with as much an eye toward the psychological effect as for social or feminine aspects. Her appearance was intended not to shock but to rattle those who expected otherwise from the First Lady. She knew also that many of the attendees would be coming into the meeting with horrible depression blanketing their minds. If they encountered the usual attire dictated by protocol or precedence, there would be the sudden judgement that the Starlings were emphasizing *status quo*. If Martha Starling emerged like a society queen or, she giggled, as a strumpet in bright scarlet, they'd be hysterical. So she wanted to give them the old razzle-dazzle but with a feeling of absolute self-confidence, and she knew just the ticket to fill that order.

First the body stocking she already wore. She'd selected as her main attire a Liz Claiborne outfit of denim designer jeans. She'd selected studded jacket and pants, the studs a brushed gold that accented the design rather than emerging dominant because of light reflection. She studied herself again in the mirrors. *No* pleats. The word *yuck* appeared instantly in her mind at the thought of pleats. Why have a pouchy tummy look when you'd spent most of your life keeping that same tummy well toned and flat? She was greatly pleased with the slim, neat look the fitted yoke of the jeans gave her. She selected and slipped into a silk buccaneer blouse, a Bill Blass original, in taupe, and set off the combination with a subtle but striking slim gold snakebelt.

Next, she worked into her Hana Mackler boots with a medium calf for cuffing and stacked midheel. The calfskin was the same taupe color as her blouse and maintained a perfect blend of coloration along her body. She'd kept her makeup subtle and effective. She studied her hair from several angles and decided it had been done perfectly for this occasion. Jean Harlow-style, framing the face just to the shoulders, turned under all along the back, classic style and parted on the left side.

She stood again before the mirrors, hands in half-fists resting against her hips, a wide-legged stance. *Lady, if I say so myself, you're a knockout.* Her alter ego answered with a bright laugh. *Damn right! Go get 'em, kid!*

President Starling sat at the far end of the huge conference table, a massive oak assembly fitted together with such skill by its artisans that, although it could seat a hundred people or more, it showed not a single seam or line within its rich deep finish. On each side of the room stood a security man, one in casual but neat sport suit, the other in a maintenance technician's jumpsuit. They paid little attention beyond protectively scanning the gathering at one end of the table, where the president worked with Jon Kleva, his best personnel intelligence man, and Marilyn Robins, the psych technician who'd been trained to anticipate his information needs when there was neither time nor opportunity for him to ask.

Kleva patted a raised dome before the president. "There are no visible switches or buttons, sir," he said. "Just press your foot by the side of the table leg, here," the president pressed down, "and the screen before you comes on." Kleva looked at Marilyn Robins. "Let's give the Frenchy a shot first." She nodded and studied the portable control board in her lap. "When your meeting is on, sir," Kleva continued, "we'll be in master control. We'll have full video and audio coverage of everything going on in here. Let's say that Professor Henri Pietre is talking with you, and, begging your pardon, sir, he's also giving you a hard time."

Starling gestured impatiently. "Dump the protocol, Jon. Don't talk up to me. We don't have time for it."

"Yes, sir. Okay, you're getting a snit fit from Pietre. If you knew something extra about the man, in reference to the subject at hand, it could give you just the edge you need to keep control of the situation."

"I'll be busier than a one-legged man in an ass-kicking contest," Starling observed. "How do I give you my request for a readout on Pietre?"

"That's when you hope Jon and I have done our jobs well," Robins said quickly. "I've spent two years establishing a psych gestalt between you and myself, learning how to anticipate your needs, how you think, where your train of thought will go in the next few seconds. If we observe you in a contest with Mr. Snit Fit from France, you'll have a video printout before you of Professor Pietre, along with any vital data we can uplink onto that screen. Let's say he once made a bad deal with the Russians, say on vital ore shipments, and that galls him. If he gets snicky or whatever, his bad deals, which he hopes you'll never know about or remember, will flash on that screen for you to use as you see fit. Also, whenever you want basic data on anyone, a tap of your foot brings that data uplinked to your screen. Now, I don't read your mind, sir—"

"I appreciate a few small favors remaining," Starling told her with a straight face. "You could be a very tough wife to live with." He was half serious.

Marilyn Robins shook her head. "No, sir. It doesn't work that way. Even if I *could* read someone else's mind I wouldn't, if they were important to me or I loved them. It would instantly destroy any relationship. What I have with you, sir, is the kind of understanding that goes into a good team. It's like a pilot and copilot of an airplane, Mr. President. After a while they know each others' thinking, patterns, moves, and decision-making factors so well, they can operate terribly complicated equipment without verbalizing."

Starling made sure to respect her feelings. "I'll buy that. All right. Let's see it and—" Before the sentence could be completed he was watching a video of Pietre in a laboratory, talking angrily but without sound from the video. Digital readouts flashed immediately across the screen. "We've eliminated the sound as being too distracting when you're otherwise occupied, sir," Jon

Kleva explained. "But there's what we figure is the pertinent data on this man that you might want during a confrontation."

Starling looked back to the screen. The video of Pietre in a laboratory had changed. Now he wore a hard hat and leather jacket and stood at the foot of an Ariane rocket. The digital readout brightened.

PROFESSOR HENRI PIETRE

FRANCE

DIRECTOR, FRENCH SPACE PROGRAM

DIRECTOR, NO PUBLIC CONNECTION, FRENCH BALLISTIC MISSILE PROGRAM.

BRILLIANT, PRAGMATIC SCIENTIST. PIONEER IN FRENCH ROCKETRY. OPPOSES FRENCH PARTICIPATION IN ESRO. WORKS CLOSELY AMERICAN AND SOVIET SPACE PROGRAMS. DIFFI-CULT YET COOPERATIVE

Starling didn't need the data readout for certain other points. He already knew a great deal about Professor Henri Pietre, and the video confirmed his memory of a tall, impressive man with a touch of insufferability in his expression. Almost as quickly as he recalled that and saw it on video, Starling read:

DE GAULLE COMPLEX. ALSO CONSISTENT OPPOSITION TO GERMAN ASSOCIATION. MOTHER AND FATHER IN WW 2 MEMBERS OF UNDERGROUND. BOTH TORTURED TO DEATH BY GESTAPO.

Starling hadn't known *that*. This cockamamie rig was already paying off.

George Starling took an hour away from everything else to study the looseleaf profile book his staff had prepared for the meeting. It contained a single complete page on each member of the meeting. Starling had insisted on that one page only: a small photo and the rest concise data. He had the natural ability, honed and refined through the years, to scan-read a page and recall almost all of it an hour later. If he scanned that same page several times his recall proved phenomenal. He knew he'd need every ounce of that talent. When he closeted himself in a very private room of the third-level sub-basement of the White House he had only one other person with him. They'd brought Russ Corey into the White House via service truck, and slipped him downstairs by the president's private elevator. Corey would attend the meeting with the same standing and distant position as any other member. But this private session let the two old friends catch up on events, and Starling would have the best psych-profile man he'd ever known to answer any questions.

They went through the pages one by one. Starling tapped his finger against the photo of Dr. Arthur Kimberly. "He's a strange duck," he mused aloud. "Publicly he's been a complete pain in the ass to the administration, a fly-by-night social do-gooder with that bunch of leftwing scientists trying to shut down our military establishment."

"My boys tell me," Corey said slowly, studying the end of his handmade cigar, "he's on your side."

"Oh, he is, but he's afraid to show it in public. Feels he's not simon-pure as a scientist. So he rattles his gourd and shakes his voodoo feathers at us. He's no problem."

Starling flipped the page. Professor Henri Pietre stared up at him from the photo. "Watch out for him," Corey advised. "Damned good scientist. Pushed their Hermes shuttle through almost on his own personality."

Starling thought about the test video he'd done with Kleva and Robins. "What it *doesn't* tell us here is that he hates the Germans. That's why, I guess, he's fought French participation in the European space organization so vehemently."

"You want my advice, Mr. Prez?" Starling waited.

"Get Pietre out of your hair. You'll have problems with him not only where the Germans are concerned but with the friends Germany's picked up since Hitler melted down into fat."

"That," Starling said unhappily, "and the fact that France told everyone in NATO to get stuffed a long time ago. There's no love lost with this man or his bunch." He paused but a moment, turned the page to Dr. Engineer Klaus Schoenberger. The data sheet brought them both up to date. There was something nagging about this one. The sheet laid it out hard and fast. Schoenberger was a beer-swilling, hard-assed German engineer who scorned pure science and took every opportunity to remind anyone within earshot that the great Dr. Wernher von Braun, the architect of the space age, had been trained not as a rocket scientist but as a locomotive engineer. A phrase leaped out at them.

"He has a genius for understanding machinery" said Corey. "A reputation that he talks to machines, they understand and do his bidding. He can fix anything and he considers himself the reincarnation of Wernher von Braun. Judgement call is that Schoenberger is fatuous, belligerent, difficult to work with. Heads program to establish major rocket launching sites in Germany proper. Married, three children. Abandoned his wife and children for Maria Klinger, registered whore from Hamburg."

Starling smiled. "There's a winner for you."

"Get rid of him," Corey snapped. "He's a fucking neo-Nazi who's seeking the greater glory of Germany. He didn't leave his wife. Your information is wrong. He's as queer as a three-dollar bill." Starling looked up, startled. "He married his wife and had kids to escape any stigma as a homosexual. His wife finally caught him in the sack with two young boys and she dropped him flat. Schoenberger pays that hooker through the nose to travel with him as a cover. Pick a fight with him or let one of us rattle his cage and *get him out of your hair.*"

"Duly noted," Starling said, as he went to the next page and studied the face of Professor Jorge Tierco Mendez of Portugal. Spent early life as farmer in Ponte del Gado in western Azores. Schooling in Lisbon, into Portuguese Air Force as fighter and bomber pilot, served as exchange pilot with U.S. Air Force three years, went to advanced maintenance and administrative schools in U.S., returned to Portugal as air forces' chief engineer and maintenance director. Retired from active duty and went on to earn doctorates in metallurgy and engineering.

"He *looks* like a farmer," Starling commented, not unkindly, on Mendez's olive complexion and rumpled clothes and teeth with gaps. "You'd never know he was as sharp as he is," Corey tacked on, and added, "Nothing on this sheet tells you about his land holdings in Brazil or his oil holdings in Venezuela. He's a millionaire a hundred times over."

"I wonder," Starling said slowly, "how he got onto this team that's meeting here today. Farmer, engineer, mechanic, big money man; that still doesn't put him on the first team."

"Dreams, sense of destiny, extreme intelligence; that and a bunch more. You want to hear it?" He watched Starling nod. "My recommendation is you grab this guy and hold on tight to him. He believes in the Portuguese bloodline. He's got all Portuguese power behind him. Sort of a religious leader without bearing the cross. The Spanish will follow his lead; so will Brazil and Argentina and—well, he's got a hell of a following. He's known about Dustbin for a long time, George. He figured out a long time ago what would come down on us if Dustbin turned out to be real. So he went to the monument of Belem in Lisbon Harbor. That's where the original Portuguese explorers shoved off to seek out and conquer new worlds. Not many people know about what *really* happened then. Mendez does. After Belem he climbed up the mountain behind the monument to the chapel where the King of Portugal always came to say mass with the crews leaving from Belem. You see, George, out of every thirty ships or so that left, they all knew that twenty-seven or twenty-eight would never return. That, my friend, makes Portuguese balls very heavy, indeed. Jorge Tierco Mendez had his Holy Grail. If Dustbin came to be, Earth would need a new breed of explorer. Mendez *knows* there are none truer, braver, more royal than those of Portuguese blood. So, being a practical man and understanding the leverage of the big stick, he's already formed a coalition of about a dozen countries. Just remember today that when he speaks, he speaks for *all* of them. He's also your friend. Has been for a long time."

Another page; a two-page spread. On the left Dr. Jiro Nakamura of Japan, and to the right, Dr. Zheng Fangkun of mainland China. There wasn't much said about Nakamura other than the obvious. Tall, slender as a reed, high forehead, contact lenses that gave his eyes a strange reddish cast. Director of the Japanese space program and its tremendous launch capability. "I know him," Corey said.

"Tell me what this page doesn't say," Starling asked.

Corey shrugged. "He's the Asiatic equivalent of Mendez but with more direct control of their rocket and space programs. Lot more militant, as well. Unlike Mendez, he believes that in a time of national emergency the top people take over the populace with an iron grip. He's simple to read, George. You give old Nakamura, here, a piece of the action and you got cooperation. You cut him out and you'll discover he still venerates the codes of Bushido, the samurai warrior caste, and *Hagakure*."

"Which is?"

"Their own special brand of honor. Nakamura interprets it as honor *to the Japanese*. Total self-interest. Can't blame him, I guess. But he comes from a very tough old Japanese family and that's got to be considered."

"How and why?"

"He comes here as an equal. His father was a big *hocker* with the old *Kempeitai*." He knew Starling understood: the wartime Japanese "thought police" who could make the Nazi SS look like nuns. "After the war, we hung the old man's ass in public. He was convicted of cutting children open while they were alive and eating their livers while they watched. He's going to be tough, this honorable son."

"Jesus Christ," Starling said softly, turning to Dr. Zheng Fangkun. "What's *his* background? Eyeball soup?"

Russ Corey laughed. "Who'd believe the Communist Chinese promise to be the easiest to deal with? Fangkun's the last of the international group you have today?"

Starling nodded. "But this sheet doesn't tell me very much about him."

"There isn't much to tell. Went to all the right schools, served his six years in the military, married, bunch of kids, brilliant engineer, dedicated worker, top scientist, and has the kind of magical aura that draws the other scientists and politicians around him to his leadership.

173

Zheng Fangkun is totally Chinese and for China and has no addictions to power. So the politicos don't mind backing him all the way. He's really a top man. He could become a priest tomorrow if that's what he wished. Or a farmer. Or a musician. Or just about anything he wants to be. His father was responsible for the Long March rockets that gave China its first ICBM's and put them into the space business. By the way, Zheng has four brothers. Two of them are astronauts. You"ll have to feel him out."

Corey stood up to stretch and walk around. He sat down again across from Starling. "Who's the top crowd from here? Besides Kimberly?"

"There's Dave Higgins. Good man. Heads naval research lab." Corey knew what he looked like; he didn't need the book. Competent scientist, five feet ten, 170 pounds, sandy thinning hair, bifocals, pompous, married to his computers. Decent enough, but uninspiring. Corey laughed suddenly, remembering that Higgins' wife had left him a few years back and in her divorce suit described her lamentable spouse as imposing on her an "utter, gripping, and desolate boredom." Enough said; one more faceless scientist with brains and lacking imagination.

Dr. Jesse Markham, on the other hand, was a pure, simonized, bootspit-and-polish bastard from the bottom of his manicured toes to the sharp edge of his military crewcut. Squarish in build and attitude, rock-jawed, a physical fitness nut, he terrorized his wife and was a runaway bulldozer in the normally placid environment of NASA's Lunar Facilities Division at Langley, Virginia. Markham was an old friend and supporter of Russ Corey, one of the best men in the astronautics business from anywhere in the world. "Count on Jesse for full support," Corey told the president. "He's officially the number one dude for the lunar bases, but—"

Starling broke in with a laugh. "Don't even bother to explain! You believe I need you to tell me that *you* run the lunar stations?"

"Well, damn it, George, I —"

"Don't 'damn it, George' *me*, you polecat. The word,

174

my fine feathered friend," the president whooped anew at his unintended pun, "is that if you ask anyone in a crowd who owns the moon, *everyone* answers, 'Russ Corey, that who!'"

"You want to play word games with me, George or you want to finish this list before—"

"Okay, okay," Starling broke in. "You said to count on Markham for full support. But what's not on this page and you're not saying is how and why Jesse Markham has so much power and play in *your* front yard."

"Good question, and the answer is simple. First, Jesse is the best damned lunar scientist in the business. Even better than me. Second, he gets along spectacularly well with the Russians. Third, he's got a reputation as the Ralph Nader of global ecology and he doesn't care what globe is involved. You dump trash on the moon, Jesse finds it and dumps it right in your bedroom. Except for the Russians and perhaps me, there ain't nobody that likes Markham, but everyone respects him. They even make him play golf alone," Corey finished with a smile.

"Golf? *Alone?* That's against the Geneva Convention, man!"

"It's been said the Jesse has never finished eighteen holes. Long before he gets through the course he's come to hate his clubs, the balls, the whole world. He always leaves a trail of smashed and twisted clubs behind him. He's *never* brought his gear back to the clubhouse."

"Okay, okay." The next page appeared. "You know her?" He pointed to the picture of Dr. Felicity Powell.

"She weighs ninety-six pounds and she's forty-three years old and fifty-eight inches tall, and if you add all that together you're still a couple of numbers short of her IQ."

"How will she fit in? She's the head of air force research but I don't know where her loyalties lie. With me, in the political sense, or her own crowd, which is the military."

"George, her genius doesn't end with science. Isn't she a good friend of Martha's?"

Starling smiled. "In this town they're known as the Terrible Twosome."

"Then why'd you ask me about her?"

"Because it's *your* opinion I'm after."

"No problems with her." Corey glanced at the next page. "But you may have problems with Reed."

The president didn't figure that way about Dr. Forrest Reed of the National Oceanic and Atmospheric Administration. By all accounts he and his scientist-wife, Helen, were known as the wild cards among scientific reserve. He was the first man to head NOAA by first-hand plunge into the real world. Forrest and Helen Reed were the best-known research team in the world. They knew the oceans and the tides and the forces of nature better than their own bedroom, in which they spent precious little time, preferring a boat deck or a tent or chasing storms in a van with the equipment to sniff out and lead them to tornados. They looked like two Vikings, big and strapping and blonde.

"They're one of the first to figure out Dustbin, Russ," Starling said, truly puzzled. "I mean, they never even knew about the longterm project when they both came to me. They insisted something was terribly wrong. Glaciers massing, icebergs changing, massive alterations of climate and atmospheric conditions due to drastic changes in the global forest picture. In fact, the Reeds went first to Felicity Powell, and she brought them to Martha, and my wife brought them to me. They could have come directly, but they felt what they discovered was so crazy they needed Felicity Powell to back up their story. So why should I expect a problem from them?"

"It's not their science or their loyalty. Unfortunately, it's bigger than that," Corey told him. "I know, what could be bigger than all that? There conviction that man has offended God and what's happening to us is that the Old Man in the Sky is pissed off and he's going to wrap up this little world and rid the galaxy or whatever of us pesky, rotten, irrational, destructive creatures. You've got plans, Mr. President, but *they* can get one hell of a backing among the scientific community

176

who may find their religion overnight, and *then* you got problems. *Kapish?*"

Starling glanced at his watch and stood up. "I'm not sure who I'd rather have on my side," he said after a long hard look at his best friend. "You, or the crazy Russian."

"You *are* having Tretyakovich at this meeting, I hope. For Christ's sake—"

"Never fear," Starling interrupted. "I wouldn't have it any other way. I just hope he's on *my* side."

Corey rested a big hand on the president's shoulder. "George, he's on your side, and so am I, and you are bloody well going to need the both of us."

"Terrific. Just what I need. Sodom and Gomorrah."

Russ Corey laughed. "Tretsky will appreciate *that*."

Someone tapped gently at the door, which was locked from the inside. Corey glanced at Starling, who nodded. Corey crossed the room, unlocked and opened the door. He stared at Martha Starling.

"Jesus," he said softly.

George Starling looked at his wife. "I can't lose," he said finally. "The angels are with me."

10 ───────

*B*ased on the assumption, the final evaluation, of the data we have amassed through the past several years, and more recently the rapidly accelerating mass of data, and considering the—"

"Goddamn it, get to the bottom line," Marion Hughes snapped at Dr. Arthur Kimberly. The NASA Administrator had left his patience at the door when he'd checked in. President Starling felt private gratification at Hughes' short fuse. They'd been in this triple-damned meeting nine hours. The scientific staff had made their presentations with extraordinary detail, droning on and on with exquisitely minute emphasis, until it began to dawn on all concerned that this searing dedication to minutea,

177

this nitpicking of the specific and the extraneous and the threadbare cousins to maybes and could-bes and perhapses, was the intellectual version of Cover Your Ass. Once that realization set in, patience for the continuing singsong shredded visibly, and the ladies and gentlemen attending this extraordinary session deep below the White House began to remove and throw away their kid gloves.

Starling had figured correctly that Marion Hughes would be one of the first to split from the niceties of procedure. He'd already kicked off his shoes and shucked his jacket, and his once-crisp necktie lay crumpled forgotten on the floor. Hughes had taken a shellacking for years, as had one NASA top man after another, and it was all winding down in this room. Marion Hughes had a wild streak up his ass and a gleam in his eyes and he was bringing things to a new head of steam quickly.

"This isn't an endurance contest, Kimberly," Hughes went on. "You've been saying the same goddamned thing a dozen different ways. Sum it up, man! Tell it like you got sixty goddamned seconds to live before the teeth close on you and you must get your message across. Will you for the love of God do that?"

"*If* our information is correct—"

"Assume it is, for God's sake!" That outburst came from none other than Helen Reed, who had murder in her eye.

"Then the solar system is moving into an area of space with an enormous accretion of dust. The density so far encountered is beyond anything ever predicted. Extrapolation on a sliding scale shows the density is increasing."

"Do you mean that the area into which this solar system is moving contains a greater dust density than where this system is now?" Heads turned to Henri Pietre, who looked at Kimberly with open disdain.

"Well, of course," Kimberly fudged, "I didn't mean that the area involved is increasing the total mass of the dust, but that we haven't yet moved into that volume of space where we'll encounter increasing density."

"Thank you," Pietre said nastily. "It always helps to

know with somewhat greater precision than I have been hearing, the density of your dust or space mud or whatever."

Starling's voice lacked the warm political tones to which they'd been accustomed. "That's enough, Professor," he said to nail the Frenchman. "Only one pound of flesh to each misstatement. Arthur," he nodded to Kimberly, "get on with it."

"If I sound upset, or if I mismanage my statements," Kimberly forced out, wiping his forehead, "I apologize."

"Goddamn, will he *ever* spit it out," someone groaned from the other side of the table. Dave Higgins, seated by Kimberly, nudged him with his elbow and whispered fiercely to him.

"Nothing we have ever anticipated meets what we're finding," Kimberly rushed on. "We've been gathering data for ten years. Most of that time the density increase has been steady but of little concern. In the last several weeks we've encountered density beyond anything we imagined."

Klaus Schoenberger snapped a pencil in two. He let the two pieces fall to the table in a move guaranteed to bring him attention. His manner and tone were grating and unctuous. Starling and Corey exchanged glances; both men shared the same thought. *Good; the faggot son of a bitch is making himself evident to this whole room.* "Forgive me, Professor," Schoenberger said, a touch of contempt deliberate. "I am no scientist—"

"True." Pietre smiled at the German.

Schoenberger went on smoothly: ". . . but even in high school they teach that in terms of mass there is more dust floating in space, in so-called *empty* space, than in all the galaxies put together. Even the great Horsehead Nebula is so great a mass of dust it blocks the light of distant stars, and—"

"What the fuck is this, a goddamned astronomy lesson?" Well, they knew that Jesse Markham had a short fuse, and between Kimberly and the simpering German the match had been held to Markham's temper. "For Christ's sake, Schoenberger, we're not here for high school or any of that other crap. Quit trying to make

179

yourself look important. And don't look so wounded, you silly shit." Markham pointed at Kimberly.

"Let's say normal density of dust in space, up to ten years ago, is a factor of one. What is it *now*? I mean specifically the disc of the solar system. The single big plate along the plane of the ecliptic. So that everyone knows what the hell I'm talking about, it's a dish. It extends from the outermost swing of Pluto's orbit from one side to the other. For round numbers we'll give it a diameter of ten billion miles. Now, damn it, we have a reference point of one up to ten years ago. What is that density *now*, for this disc that's ten billion miles across?"

"Factor of eight," Kimberly said.

"The density's gone up *eight times?*" The voice was incredulous. It belonged to Dr. Toshio Saito. Starling was surprised. Someone had screwed up. Saito was fourth-generation Nisei, not Japanese any more by a long shot. But his name hadn't been entered into the personnel log Starling had gone over so carefully with Russ Corey. *Forget it*, Starling ordered himself. He was more interested in Saito's reaction.

"Yes, Doctor," Kimberly replied, relieved to speak directly with someone who wasn't antagonistic.

"I wish to ask you something else. Very specifically," Saito went on. *Damn*, Starling thought, *I take it all back. He may be fourth-generation American, but he looks like he's reverted back to his ancestor*. Kimberly had nodded to Saito.

"What is important now," Saito said carefully, "is not what we have encountered in the past. Or even what we are encountering now. What matters is your extrapolation *of what we will be rushing into in the future.*" Saito took a deep breath.

Kimberly didn't answer immediately. Russ Corey sat at the far end of the table. He hadn't wanted to get into this, but most of the people in this room were in a state of shock, worse than he'd anticipated. So, to keep the situation under control when there's a vacuum, you step in.

"It means," Corey said in a rasping voice that cut

through the murmuring and exchanges, "that this old planet is about to buy the farm."

Bewildered looks appeared. "Buy the farm?" Dr. Zheng Fangkun stared blankly. "I don't understand what that means."

"My apologies," Corey said with the touch of a bow from where he sat. "It means that the planet is about to go under, be wiped. It means that everybody on Earth is likely to have the opportunity to find out just how right or wrong they are about heaven and hell."

"He's trying to say," Forrest Reed said impatiently, "that the world is in for a period of overwhelming catastrophe."

Corey laughed. "You're wrong, Doctor! It won't be a catastrophe. It'll be *the end*. Finished. *Kaput*. The Earth is going to be depopulated. You know? People dying? *All* of them."

"You seem very certain, sir," Dr. Fangkun said stoically.

"I'm willing to bet my life on it," Corey grinned back at him. "And so are you," he added with a jaunty air in stark contrast to their topic, "and everybody else."

Dr. Saito stood up slowly. "I still do not have an answer to my question, please. To what density do you make your extrapolation?"

The room calmed and they turned to Kimberly. "It could be double. It could be a hundred times greater than it is right now."

Saito blinked several times, then sat down heavily, lost in his thoughts. Kimberly took the moment to appeal directly to the president. "Sir, I feel it's important to make a statement."

"Good God, I hope so," Starling replied. "Please."

Kimberly motioned to take in the scientists with whom he'd worked for so many years. "Mr. President, I object strongly to the direction this meeting has taken. We are not here for jest or riposte, no matter how clever. We are deadly serious. You know the credentials of these people with me. On some details we suffer disagreement, but that is expected and well within the tolerances to which we're accustomed. What is absolutely

181

critical is that we all *agree* that even with taking into account the most extensive variations in our findings and how we extrapolate future conditions, that we may well be moving toward the end of life on this planet. As we know it, at least. As far as civilization is concerned as it exists on the surface, it appears doomed." Kimberly seemed shaken by his own words. "This sounds like a very bad dream, Mr. President. I can hardly believe I am speaking these very words. I'm—why, good God, I'm talking about *the end of the world*. It's like a very bad movie suddenly coming to life." He wiped the back of his hand across his eyes. "I can't believe my own words. I can't believe we're gathered in this room and people are more interested in," his voice rose shrilly, "making fucking brownie points with word-twisting and games!"

He looked stricken as he caught the gaze of Dr. Felicity Powell. That woman judged that Kimberly had never deliberately used a profane word before a woman in his life. She was right and she knew she had to help him back to an even keel, and quickly. "Well said, Arthur," she told him, holding direct eye contact. "The time for children's games is over. Please go on."

He gathered strength from her in a rush, stared around the table and turned back to Starling. "As I have stated, our disagreement is in some detail and continuity, but if our forecasts that the density will continue to increase are true, we shall go through alternating periods of extreme heat, to the point of surface incineration, to cold far worse than any ice age in the past, and the Earth . . ." He began to tremble as the enormity of what he, a renowned professor of conservative position, was truly saying. "The Earth . . . will. . . . it will burn, Mother of God . . . crushed . . . destroyed . . ." His voice trailed away into silence.

There was movement from Russ Corey's end of the table. President Starling looked at two groups that so far had maintained silence: his top military leaders and several members from the National Academy of Science, and the National Security Council. He had instructed these people *not* to make comments or otherwise

182

interfere with the meeting. "It's far more important for all of you to observe *objectively*," he had told them. "To put matters as bluntly as I can, you are not to interfere, criticize, or otherwise inject your feelings into what goes on. There'll be time for that later." Now he saw the muscles on Hal Eisenberg's face twitching; judging by the set of his jaw, the general was about to explode. Starling didn't want *any* of that. He glared at Eisenberg. The general didn't catch it, but the admiral to his left did and he clamped an arm down on Eisenberg's shoulder. The latter caught the president's eye and nodded slowly. And kept his mouth shut.

But not Professor Henri Saul Pietre of France, who looked to Starling as he jerked a thumb in the direction of the stricken Kimberly. "Mr. President! If you will permit me, sir, and there is no way other than this to describe what I have just heard from this simpering *coward*, this is, how you say in one word? *Bullsheet*." Pietre gave Kimberly a look of utter contempt and turned back to Starling. "What I just hear is what must be identified as a gross evaluation. What this crybaby talks about is a triggering of secondary effect *if* everything else is so bad as he says. And this man," he pointed to Saito, "is asking about extrapolation, no? That is a fancy name for more guesswork, and from guesswork, then *this* one," a finger stabbed at Kimberly, "is ready to die, to condemn us all, to give up. He should do us all a favor, Mr. President, and throw himself under the wheels of a subway train."

"I'll say one thing for you, Frenchy." Heads turned again, this time to Forrest Reed. "You're eloquent and you're strong. You're also a dumb son of a bitch. You haven't the first credential to contest Dr. Kimberly here, *or the fact that most of us who have worked with him for years are in complete agreement with him*."

George Starling felt they were finally getting somewhere. "Reed, just a moment. Professor Pietre said that Kimberly was talking about secondary effect rather than what could be initiated by solar system exposure to a dust cloud of greatly increased density. Is that correct so far?"

"Yes, sir, it is."

"Describe for me—no, Professor Pietre, you had your say and I want you to keep your seat and your mouth closed for now—those secondary effects as you agree with Dr. Kimberly. Do you understand what I mean? *Only those points on which you have all, essentially, agreed.*"

Forrest Reed offered a thin smile as preamble. "The sun will suck in, through gravitational attraction as well as its own galactic orbital speed of some two miles per second, enormous mass in the form of dust and other debris particle accretion. We are dealing with unknown trillions of tons. There will be an increase in solar radiation, especially infrared. Now, whether the Earth will initially be hit with this heat increase, or subjected to drastic reduction in heat radiation due to dust absorption of solar energy prior to an increase in solar output, is a matter entirely open to conjecture. Nobody here knows. We are dealing with unknowns."

Forrest Reed squeezed his wife's hand. "But the matters on which we have sufficient knowledge to talk sensibly make it clear that, notwithstanding the order of events, the Earth will suffer alternate heating and cooling of first its atmosphere and then the planetary crust, with such rapidity and in such extremes that the inevitable consequences will involve massive earthquakes, severe crustal disruption, unparalleled volcanic venting, tremendous evaporative processes and . . . Well, this world will know wind velocities such as have not been experienced since the great asteroids once hammered this world billions of years past."

President Starling didn't even blink. He'd known every word well before this meeting. He turned to Higgins of the Naval Research Laboratory. "Do you agree with what you've just heard?"

Higgins glared unhappily. "Damn it, sir, yes."

"Dr. Saito," Starling said abruptly to the man who headed the nation's Department of the Interior. "You're the master of geology in this room. Your position?"

Saito's face was granite. "My colleagues do not yet fully understand." He spoke quietly and without a trace of emotion or fear. "The effects under discussion shall revert us back in time."

"How so?"

"They have not been known on Earth since two hundred million years ago, when the supercontinent Pangaea broke up and started to become the world we know today."

Starling hadn't heard it that way before. "The beginning of continental drift."

"Yes, Mr. President. This will be the end of that drift, which continues to this moment. But now?" He smiled in the face of what he pictured as total devastation. "Likely even the mountain ranges shall break up. Many big rocks will be made into small rocks. They may even melt."

Starling's eyes burned into the face of every person in the room before they returned to Saito. "Doctor, a very personal question, if you do not mind." Saito offered a slight bow from his seat. His eyes seemed to have gone hollow, as if his mind had floated from his body to leave behind only a talking shell. "When this meeting is over, what do you intend to do?"

Saito offered a gentle smile, a beatific look that made it clear nothing in this room was of importance any longer. "When I leave here I will gather my family and while there is still time we shall return to our ancestral homeland. We will share what time is left."

George Starling turned again to Jesse Markham, who was having a fit trying to get his attention. "Jesse?" he opened the way for him.

"Sir, you've seen the films of the surface of Venus. Ours and those of the Russians." For the first time everyone seemed to remember that the only Russian in the room, Gregory Tretyakovich, had yet to say a single word. "That world has an atmosphere like ours, Mr. President, only much heavier and denser. In fact, at the surface of Venus it's like a couple of thousand feet below our ocean surface, as far as density is concerned. A long time ago something happened to break the balance of heat exchange between the Venerian atmosphere and the sun. So everything, so to speak, came unglued. Now they have an atmosphere a hundred times heavier than ours, and a surface temperature of about nine hundred degrees. No oxygen. No life. No water vapor worth measuring." He smiled thinly. "Sort of a longterm preview for our own world."

"*Bah!*" Felicity Powell stood up abruptly, fire in her eyes. "Listen to all of you!" she cried. "This sounds like a gathering of Hollywood producers prepared to make a great Cecil B. DeMille epic. Why don't you throw in the Ten Commandments, Godzilla, and a couple of UFO's for effect? I have never heard such caterwauling in all my life." She stabbed a finger at the president of the United States. "George Starling, you've given in to the miserable moaning of these so-called scientists. I have listened to this sort of nonsense before and so have you, and you should know better."

A motion of disgust by a sweeping arm gathered them all in beneath her contempt. "First we heard that the advent of the bow and arrow would destroy civilization. And then came gunpowder and *that* was the end of everything. When we learned to fly and could drop bombs, *that* was the end of everything. The machine gun spelled our doom. Poison gas would obliterate all life. Jet airplanes would wreck the ozone layer and kill us all with ultraviolet rays. And if they didn't do it, then the aerosol gases proliferating around the world from roach and hair sprays would finish us off. That wasn't enough? Well, my, my, *my*, we had biological warfare, and on top of that we've had the atomic bomb and the hydrogen bomb and the neutron bomb and the ICBM and Star Wars and we've had that nice young man, Sagan or whatever his name is, telling us about nuclear winter and marsh gas and— " She stopped for breath. "If the world had been listening to your prophets of doom for years past, then we'd all have been dead a hundred times over. Somehow I wonder about that, with all the wars and famines and the earthquakes and the pestilence on top of everything else, plus a thousand jealous gods, and how in the name of hell this planet has managed to bring its population up to almost six billion people in the face of all this ultimate destruction *is beyond me*. Or," she announced as she swept up her personal belongings, "any sane human being." Her finger pointed about the room. "If I want to hear this nonsense, I can do it at home with my shoes off and a martini in my hand listening to some *other* idiotic soap opera!"

She pushed back her chair and followed by a wave of stunned silence stalked to the exit, where she stared at a federal security agent. "Open this door or I'll kick your balls back up behind your navel," she said sweetly.

Starling nodded, the door opened, and Felicity Powell stormed out. The only sound in the room was Russ Corey applauding.

Starling gave them a break for coffee and the lavoratories. Before they stretched and dashed for the bathrooms, he held up a hand. "Understand something. Today's meeting is the first and the last you will attend on this matter. As you will see shortly, despite the commendable faith in our future on the part of Ms. Powell, we're going to have time for many things, but meetings won't be one of them." He stood up and left the conference room.

Thirty minutes later they were again at their seats, having relieved themselves, vented their anger or fear to one another, cursed some and praised others, and fortified their systems with coffee and food brought into the room. "All right," Starling announced, "no more sashaying about the bush. We get right to it. Before we get into any more contests you're going to see some special films that the rest of the world, outside of some scientific and government groups, knows nothing about." As he spoke, the room lights dimmed and a large viewing screen lowered from a ceiling niche. "I *was* going to say that this film carries the highest security classification, although that seems to be rather silly at this moment. To be certain that you are convinced that what you've heard about space dust, and to eliminate any conflict as to the extent that this has been examined, we'll show you some very hard results. We have been sending probes into deep space for some time

187

now and we have results sufficiently disturbing to have brought this assembly together. I've asked Dr. Markham to handle the commentary."

The room went dark and the screen came to life. A space shuttle drifted in slow high orbit, its great bay doors open and astronauts in EVA offloading a thick rocket cylinder. Markham's voice carried clearly to them all. "We transported the components for five deep-space probes into high orbit with a series of shuttle flights. You can see the specialists assembling elaborate instrument packages at the narrow end of the boosters. These carried American and Russian instruments. All this has been a cooperative venture." Different camera angles showed assembly procedures and then the completed rockets. The camera closed in to a single rocket booster. "We used six stages plus orbital speed to build maximum velocity." A searing blast of flame howled silently from the thick end of the rocket. It whipped out of sight, and the camera showed only a distant flare of light to indicate another stage firing. "Stage six burnout gave us nearly two hundred thousand miles an hour relative to Earth for departure velocity. The probes were all fired in a fan pattern ahead of the path of the sun in its orbit about the galactic gravitational center. The path the Earth follows, of course."

The scene shifted from space to a data room showing technicians receiving information from across deep space. All eyes were on the monitors shown on the screen. "You're seeing the real-time video we received as the probes moved far ahead of the solar orbital path. In terms of time they are between two and four years ahead of us. We're using time-lapse photography for the purposes of this film."

He said no more. They didn't need words. The time-lapse film showed instruments eroding, metal surfaces pitting, equipment disintegrating before their eyes. The monitors began to show streaks and meaningless patterns and the screen finally went dead. Immediately the room lights came on.

"How far ahead of us," asked Helen Reed, "is the most advanced probe?"

"Three years and four months," Markham responded. "There are some variations, but—" He shrugged. The variations didn't matter.

"It's too bad," Kimberly said suddenly, his first words in a long time. "I mean, *we won't be here* to confirm those figures." A shudder went through him. "Everyone in this room, everyone on this planet, will be dead."

"You are wrong, Dr. Kimberly."

They turned, startled, to face the president. Starling leaned forward, resting his weight on his elbows, a sudden energy suffusing his expression. "There is every chance you may be very wrong, indeed."

Kimberly looked for help from his fellow scientists, but they were just as perplexed and taken aback as he was. He caught the gaze of Russ Corey—and Markham, too!—who offered enigmatic smiles instead of blank stares.

Kimberly tore himself away from Corey's hypnotic gaze and glared at the president. Face flushed, agitation now beyond control, he gestured wildly and shouted. "You question what we've brought to you?" he cried in an anguished tone. "We've spent ten years gathering this data! You've just seen the films of the very probes *you authorized*. This is insane. I will not stand for this any—" His voice caught and he slumped back into his seat, a broken man. The president's next words caught him completely by surprise.

"Arthur," Starling said gently, "no one questions you, your people, or your findings. What you've all done is to confirm absolutely what other investigation established on its own. I am sad to say that your data is as precise as can be and your conclusions overwhelmingly accurate."

"But—" Kimberly was reaching wildly for balance.

"But everything we have been learning was so monstrous, *is* so monstrous, we had to investigate along wholly separate lines. We needed, I regret to say, the moral strength of your conclusions arrived at independently of other programs." Starling nodded to Gregory

Tretyakovich. "The Russian program, again unfortunately, matches ours with unerring precision."

Again George Starling seemed to pass through some sort of metamorphosis. As he moved to an area where he could exercise direct control, where he could do more than simply observe and study unnerving data, his inner strength came through. "Now that you have the background of knowing how extensive our studies have been, you'll better understand what I mean when I say to you that we are about to violate our oath of office."

Starling took a deep breath. "I am going to break my sworn word to the American people. I—we—are going to strip from them, and almost all this world, their favored position of being represented by their elected leaders." He made a steeple of rigid fingers and stared through them. "There's an old theme," he said with an enigmatic expression. "Felicity touched on it. It's a theme of science fiction. The end of the world is upon us, and there are feverish attempts to save a few specimens of humanity by sending them away from this planet. Unlike the popularization of this theme, however, *our* story is all too real. Our need is too great, and time is too short, for us to engage in public debate or to seek out public opinion."

A deep cough, almost the angry bark of a great bear, interrupted him. Gregory Tretyakovich was half standing with his massive fists on the table. "Nor do we have time to waste on long discussions any more!" he shouted. "You forgive me, Mr. President, but truth is I do not give a damn if you do not, but you cannot lecture like children all these people who come here to you. No time for this! *No time!*" He stood erect now, aggressive and powerful. "From this moment on we must always cut to the heart of the matter! Again you forgive me, George Starling," he stopped to shake his head furiously, "damn me for being polite! Double damn, Mr. President, but all this is academic, how the Frenchy call it, *bullshit.*"

He glared at the others about the table. "*You are not president any more!*" he roared. His fist struck the

190

table with a crash. "You are dictator! You are king, emperor, czar, tyrant, whatever you must be to be leader. You *tell* people to *do*! That way maybe a few of these weaklings will survive!" He dropped back into his seat with the sound of creaking wood.

Soft laughter came from the man with deep eyes and scarred face at the end of the table. Russ Corey smiled. "He's right, you know," he spoke with a voice amazingly abrasive for its quiet tone. "You're going to have to be one awful son of a bitch, Mr. President."

The scientists had been taken aback by Tretyakovich; Corey drove them deeper into their mental retreat. "I know, I know," they heard the president agree. "I'm just not ready to be a bastard. But I'm working at it."

"Well, you're no Hitler or Stalin, that's for sure," Corey told him, still smiling, his words bringing utter dismay to the scientists, "but the stakes are a hell of a lot higher now, and you need to be a mixture of the worst baddies this world has ever known."

"What are you all talking about!" Helen Reed shouted.

Starling looked at her with a whimsical expression. "We're talking about saving a piece of the human race."

"*What?*" She gaped. "But . . . that won't be possible!"

"It's possible. But it will be a very tiny piece, I'm afraid."

"But, how, I mean, what can we do? How could we—"

Starling motioned to Jesse Markham. "Helen, the films you saw didn't show *all* the probes. For a while we were so stunned that none of us thought straight. We forgot the structure of our own solar system. It's not, as everybody momentarily forgot, like a *ball*, with the sun in the center and the planetary orbits following paths that would mark off a sphere—"

"Of course not," she broke in. "You can't get much more elementary than that. It was said here before. You've got to think of the solar system as it is. A great dish or a platter with the sun at its center and the orbits curving gently upward the farther out you get and . . ." Her voice trailed away. "You mean—?"

He smiled. "Yes. We forgot that the galactic structure pretty well fits that same description. The stellar mass at the center is a lot more pronounced and the shape is somewhat different, a pinwheel with arms, sort of, but it's still essentially a disc shape."

Starling took over. "So we fired probes upward, so to speak. At right angles to the plane of the ecliptic. Up and away from this big platter that makes up our solar system."

"But we never—I mean," she protested, "I've never heard of these—"

"We fired them from the far side of the moon," Markham explained.

It all fell into place. They could launch almost anything from the lunar surface. Building the rockets as big as they want. No air on the moon, so no atmospheric friction. Go for maximum acceleration. Use the raw materials and production facilities of the lunar installations. Build monster boosters for the probes to sail not along the orbital path of the sun, but at a right angle. Most of them along a so-called northward path, some of them downward, "southward." "Our rewards came in firing northward," Markham went on. "Because it proved to us that the great dust clouds, like the greater bulk of our galaxy, follow the spiral orbiting along the flattened pinwheel outward from the galactic center."

Starling took up the description. "Now picture *our* solar system in your mind as a huge serving platter. The sun is in dead center. This is the lowest level of the platter. From the sun outward the platter rises gently until you get to the rim. From our viewpoint we have the sun at the center and Pluto's orbit making up the rim. Now, so long as you stay on this platter, or on the same level as the platter, you're in thick dust. And the dust extends beyond the platter for—well, we don't *know* how far," Starling emphasized. "But if you climb *upward* from the platter you find the density decreasing. And if you climb upward high enough, hundreds of millions, perhaps billions of miles, you seem to climb out of this enormous disc of dust. You're in, for want of a better phrase, clean space."

192

"Then there's *some* hope—?" Helen Reed had turned pale.

"What goddamned hope!" Kimberly shouted. "Do you know what in the hell you're saying, all of you? Obviously you're thinking of putting people aboard spaceships and firing out of the plane of the ecliptic." He was almost purple with sudden rage. "*But to where? What in the name of God do you think is up there? Out there? It's empty space! There's nothing there for trillions and trillions of miles! You're talking light years, for God's sake! You're dreaming, all of you!*" He took a deep breath and let it free in an explosive sigh.

"*There's nowhere to go!*"

"Yes, there is."

The voice was so soft, so gentle, so much at peace with itself that it had a greater shock effect than if the speaker had stood on the table and screamed. Silence followed the words of Dr. Zheng Fangkun. "There is a place to go," he said to them. "And now I understand."

"Where?" The one-word question came out like a rasp file from Klaus Schoenberger.

"Why, the future, of course," Dr. Fangkun said quietly. "A short distance into the future until the Earth passes through the dust clouds and calm returns. There will be drastic changes, catastrophes greater than any other known. But there will also be hope. That is more than I found in this room not too many minutes ago."

Jorge Tierco Mendez motioned for attention. "I gather the subject at hand is the building of great arks." He was suddenly in his element. Visions of Belem and sailing ships ghosted through his mind.

"*Arks?* You mean big boats? You're crazy." Kimberly was back into rage again, his scientific acumen threatened once more. "Didn't you even listen to what we said? The effects of quakes, volcanic eruptions, storms—"

Corey seemed to impale him with a finger from across the table. "Shut up, Kimberly. That's enough wailing like a miserable quitter. We're going to build something to try to save a chunk of humanity. Or a sliver, whatever. Call it Noah's Ark if you want. Hell, man, it doesn't matter. God may not offer meaningful advice on

193

how many cubits it should be, and we won't be taking seven pairs or even two pairs of every form of life, but sure as hell we're going to build those arks."

Dr. Jiro Nakamura leaned forward. "One, at least, will be American. Another is sure to be Russian. But there is no reason why many cannot be built. There will be a Japanese ark," he said sternly. "We shall build with all our industry and I hope with the help of the superpowers."

Kimberly sneered at the Japanese scientist. "Fell right into their trap, didn't you? Immediately you're part of the inner circle." Kimberly was back under control but sounded bitter. "I've heard American, Russian, Japanese. Does anybody else get tossed a bone? A few token races and colors? I wonder what all those nationalities you *haven't* mentioned will say when they hear your grandiose plans!"

"May I respond to that?" Corey saw understanding in Starling's expression as the president nodded. What was going to be said now was vital, and it was just as vital that it not be attributed to the president of the United States.

"Doctor Kimberly. All of you." Corey's eyes were almost glowing. He spoke with underplayed but inescapable impact. "*It doesn't matter what anyone thinks, or says, or does*. Only if they interfere with what we'll be doing does it matter. And then," he appended with a shrug, "they will die. Their death, in any event, will come only a short time before nature—or God if that's the way you look at it—finishes the job for most of the people on this planet. But there's a chance for a few and we're going to give them that chance."

"Even if you have to kill millions," Helen Reed said bitterly.

"No," Russ Corey told her. "Even if we have to kill *billions*. What the hell do you think this is? An Easter party to save the lemmings?"

"I wonder about something." Henri Pietre leaned back in his seat, one arm draped over the backrest. "President Starling, I am here from France. I see, in

194

national terms, Germany, Russia, Brazil, China, Japan. Not a soul from Africa. Or the Arab nations. Or—"

"Your powers of observation are duly noted," Starling said, specifically intending to be less than kind. "And I'm sure you would continue, if I did not stop you right now, with some sort of morose for-the-good-of-mankind humanitarian speech usually prepared for the sapsuckers."

"Sapsuckers, sir?"

"The tree called the United Nations. Where so many birds of a feather cling to its trunk and branches to suck the sap. All take and no give. If you have a speech about humanitarian causes, Professor Pietre, *do not give it here*. Save it for the East River. We have no intention of driving a snowplow through the accumulated drivel of the UN to save what we can of the human race. You're right. *Everybody* can't be here. There isn't the room nor do we have such an intention. They will gather in the UN and do whatever they wish. If you have a comment, let me hear it."

Pietre was stronger than indicated. "I am not so sure I wish to be associated with the manner of your thinking, sir." He sat straight now, stiff as a board, almost bristling.

"*Professor* Pietre." Starling's voice came at him like a lash. "This is the perfect time to set the record straight. *This isn't your party*. We are not the saviors of the world. You were invited here. You're aware that an invitation is *not* an obligation. I suggest that if you find our information, discussion, and future plans so much to your disliking, then I shall assist your indecision with a touch of crudity. In short, sir, don't let the door hit you in the ass on the way out." Starling didn't even pause. "If you wish to work *with* us—and we had hoped you would, and that is *why* you are here—you will let us get on with it and you will be pulling with us."

There was pause enough for a heartbeat; whoever might have had further comment was dissuaded as much by Starling's attitude as by his words, and the matter of woeful complaint did not again dominate during the meeting.

Jorge Tierco Mendez held aloft a hand for attention. His head remained down, his other hand a blur amidst a calculator and notes before him. He exuded a growing excitement. "Mr. Starling, from what I have heard here today, from what I had gathered before today," he smiled briefly and made it clear to all that he had been aware of Project Dustbin long before this moment, "and from what I now deduce, we have perhaps three years?"

"Three years for *what?*" Kimberly snapped.

"For the time in which to build the vessels. The arks." Mendez looked immensely pleased. "But there is more than one type of ark. We Portuguese are the sailors of old. With modern technology it should be possible to build enclosed vessels that can withstand any storm."

The French had long looked down on the Portuguese as swillers of anchovies and little else. "You intend to build enclosed arks and ride out winds of hundreds of miles per hour? Temperatures of hundreds of degrees? And then ice that may freeze to thousands of feet *thick?*" Henri Pietre rattled off the questions in staccato fashion. "You would do better to drink your very good," he made a face, "wine, as you call it."

Mendez nodded slowly and returned his attention to the president. "The French are pigs," he said calmly. "Every now and then a dog appears in their midst, such as this one," he jerked a thumb at the enraged Frenchman. "They are negative and have long been so, and I ask you, sir, why you have us all suffer this miserable person who offers us only a lack of solutions and an aversion to cooperation with *anyone?*"

"Hot shit," Jesse Markham exclaimed, bursting into laughter. "Promise a good Portuguese sailor three years to build a ship that can withstand anything and he's happy as a clam."

Kimberly was a sudden snowsquall of whirling arms and papers as he flung away the voluminous notes that had been laid out before him. "Is this some kind of macabre joke to you all?" he shouted. Papers swirled about like frightened quail. "You talk as if you *know* how much time before life can no longer exist on this world! None of you *know!* You people are idiots. *We* are the scientists and we are the keepers of wisdom *and we don't know!* You—"

He stopped as he saw Russ Corey rise to his feet. Whatever burned in Corey's eyes, his stance, brought Kimberly to silence, with his mouth still open.

"You, sir," Corey said with a damning tone to his voice, "are the very reason the president told you there would be *this* one meeting and no others." The rasping voice seemed to cut into skin. "You have lost control, Kimberly. You wail like a frightened child. *But most of all your feelings are hurt that we're not begging you for advice and leadership.* Your disappointment has led you to panic. Panic means squandering time we don't have to waste. It means throwing away energy we need to direct. It means losing coordination and teamwork which we need desperately, in the highest quality. If you panic, as you've already done here, then think of the effect you'll have on the people of the world who you want to look *to you* for leadership. You are the most convincing of all reasons why there's no time left for a caucus or—"

"Stop it!" Dr. Toshio Saito sat ramrod stiff, alive for the first time at this meeting. "That is really enough, Dr. Corey. You have made your point. Most of us saw it before you spoke a word. Your attack on Dr. Kimberly is an interesting psychological ploy, but you are wasting the very time you condemn him for losing."

Corey grinned and touched his fingertips to his forehead in salute. He took his seat, still grinning, as Saito turned to the president. "In this conversation of building certain vessels, referred to as arks, I am aware the term has certain emotional overtones, especially for Judean-Christian doctrine."

"Don't start on the Bible, man," Marion Hughes said, breaking his long and silent observation of the proceedings.

Saito ignored him. "Accepting the most advanced state-of-the-art technology and entirely enclosed vessels— and I will assume this was discussed before you held this meeting?" Starling nodded in confirmation. "Then why, sir, would you even waste your time when it is obvious no surface vessel could ever survive? You have a reason to practice this deception with us?"

"Professor Pietre summed it up well," Starling told him. "Winds, temperature extremes, ice; but would you wish us to make a final decision on such a matter? The history of the French as seafarers needs no further explanation here. Nor of the Portuguese, or the Japanese, or most of the world's nations. Let it not be said from the outset, Dr. Saito, that a few made a decision that should be adjudged by many. Let me ask you, sir, do you agree with Pietre that surface vessels will not survive what is coming?"

"Absolutely."

"Any other reasons than what he told us?"

"Many. The seas will run before winds of four to five hundred miles an hour. Even if a sealed vessel, no matter what its design, remained structurally intact, the violent forces of acceleration—the g-loadings, really—would kill all human and animal life within. Most internal structures would be destroyed." Saito paused, seeming to repress a thought he had clearly entertained for a while.

"But there is a way," he said so softly they strained to hear him. He looked about the table. "No one has spoken of it. *Submersibles*."

"Submarines?" Helen Reed's eyes were wide, begging more information.

"The word is inadequate," Saito went on. "Submarines like none ever imagined. Each of several hundred thousand tons displacement. Nuclear powered. Titanium, glassite construction. Able to withstand immense pressures, even of several thousand fathoms. They would be completely enclosed, submersible biospheres. They could remain beneath the ocean for years, even anchored to deep ocean rock strata." He caught himself in midthought. "I did not intend a speech. Only this thought," he added by way of apology.

Starling toyed with a pen as he made notes. His

doodling was for effect. "You seem convinced that could be the best way for us to proceed."

"Yes, I . . . *yes*," Saito said with sudden firmness.

"You heard the others. Dr. Kimberly and his associates. We don't know how much time there is. We'll say two years, maybe three. Could you build, equip, stock, launch, test such vessels in that time? It takes twice that long right now just to build an aircraft carrier."

"We shall never know until we try, shall we, sir?"

"Then, Dr. Saito, that matter is now your responsibility. As of this moment I relieve you from your post as this government's Secretary of the Department of the Interior. You will now direct the design, construction, and activation, and the selection of the people, for these undersea arks. I am familiar with your background, Dr. Saito. It is a most impressive one. Before you took your present position you spent more than twenty years in deep ocean research. I'd say you're admirably suited for this task."

Dismay and conflicting emotions appeared on Saito's face. "Sir, I do not know. I—"

"You still want to return to Japan and get shitfaced in some stinking rice field?" Jesse Markham shouted at him. He didn't care what Dr. Jiro Nakamura felt about his choice of words. Nakamura was Japanese. *Saito was an American, goddamn it!*

"You are insulting," Saito snapped.

"He's also accurate," Corey threw at Saito. "I notice you didn't tell him you *weren't* going back to rice and honeybuckets."

"I—"

"One more whimpering maggot among us," Corey said with biting sarcasm. "Mr. President, you'd better get some people with balls on your team."

The scientists stared at Russ Corey in mingled dismay and hatred. David Higgins rose slowly to his feet, a look of recognition firming on his face. He pointed a shaking finger at the rasping stranger in their midst.

"*Now* I know who you are," he said with almost a fierce intensity. "You're one of the world's richest and most powerful men. You own . . . whole industries.

199

Shipping companies, airlines, oil fields." Higgins looked with scorn at Russ Corey, swept his arm for everyone's attention. "Of course!" he said loudly. "It makes sense *now*. With all your money and your power, this government *needs* your cooperation. And for payment, you and some selected friends, I'm sure, will be guaranteed a place on one of those submersibles!"

Russ Corey laughed with genuine mirth this time. He threw almost everyone in the room off stride. "No, no, Higgins! You still don't understand. What does it take to get through to you people? No surface ship is going to survive, no matter how far back into history Jorge Mendez goes for his noble seafaring traditions. And despite what Mr. Squat, here—I beg your pardon; Dr. Saito—has to say, those submarine arks won't hack it either. The winds won't bother them *but that ocean is going to boil*. Do you understand what I'm saying? You'll steam everybody aboard those subs like they were clams. Sure, go ahead and build those big subs. It's a nice try, and it will keep people busy for a while. Certainly it will prolong their dying for a while. *But that's all*."

Corey drew a deep breath and deliberately paused to light a fresh cigar. He used it like a dagger when he leaned forward. "You haven't been listening to your president, Higgins. We're going to build the arks, all right. But they're space arks, man, not subs to wallow around in a pot of boiling water. And you're right about one thing. I'll throw everything I've got into the program to build them as big as we can and as fast as we can. Tretyakovich, here, can tell you about the arks the Russians will build. Maybe there'll be more. I can't speak for Nakamura and Fangkun. They'll do that for themselves."

"You son of a bitch!" Higgins yelled. "What's the difference? Space ark or ocean sub? You'll still *buy* your way aboard, won't you? You rotten—"

"Oh, shut up." Corey said it so casually it seemed to strike a physical blow against Higgins. "I'm not going on *anyone's* ark. If you know anything about me at all, then you know I've put billions into the moon base programs." He laughed quietly, a butterfly winging of subdued mirth, a rock of strength among frightened sheep. "I've got people up there," he gestured with his hand to represent the moon far above them, "who count on me. I'm not letting them down. The moon . . . that's *our* ark, Higgins. I don't think we have much of a chance surviving for very long up there without the Earth to support us, but what the hell, look at the view we'll have when this place starts to burn. I'm not interested in the space arks. If people aboard those things are going to make it, then it's the young ones who deserve their shot. Me? It's been a hell of a life. You see, Earth is your home. It isn't mine." He paused, and he smiled again. "My home," his finger stabbed upward, "is up *there.*"

The room went silent. Deep breathing rasped about the table. Then the sounds of bodies shifting in their seats. No one wanted to break the heavy silence. Finally Dr. Jiro Nakamura stood, a gaunt Japanese crane in what was now a rumpled white suit. "May I speak?" he addressed President Starling.

"Certainly, sir."

"I have not much to say. Like many here," Nakamura spoke slowly, his English still carrying a touch of hiss, "we Japanese have long suspected what Dustbin is about. Our own deep space probes. To the comets, to elsewhere," he shrugged. "That is not important. Everything now must emphasize the space arks. The launching upward." A smile appeared, vanished. "Out of the plane of the ecliptic. A stopping of the time our world will know. What I say to you I say with words of my government. You know our great rockets, our electronics, whole space program. We will join with those. We will ask no more than proper share of space for the Japanese who will go. But please understand. *We will go.*"

He returned slowly to his seat. His ending seemed premature to them all. His attitude said more than his words. He might as well have come right out and added, *and if we don't go we'll bring back the kamikaze and fuck every one of you, nobody goes. . . .*

But he didn't say it, and before anyone could lose his cool and vent the growing sense of fear and desperation, Dr. Zheng Fangkun stood at the table. "I will be brief," he said in flawless English. "I will not follow our ancient path of manners and courtesy that consumes time. I shall be forgiven, I am sure." Starling nodded for the touch of protocol.

"You speak, when you address me," Fungkun continued, "to the representative of more than one out of every five people on Earth. But in truth, since we are Oriental and there are many others of our kind, our numbers are more like two billion. We represent the majority of all human beings on this world."

He paused, closed his eyes, opened them slowly. "You must listen to us. We will say nothing about history or the saving of past art or such treasures. If the gods want these saved, they will be. They would have found another way to punish humanity than through lowly dust. So be it. What is, is, because it happens. We are given only our own means to survive. *Perhaps* to survive. The finest young people of China will be aboard the space arks. You are not to worry. We do not mean bloodlines. Nor do we include government. We mean our best. Our finest. We will help with engineers, with scientists, but also with those who will become the first true space farmers. Even aboard such great vessels as we envision people must eat to live."

He extended both arms, palms upward. "You know we have great rockets. Many of them. Even more than you know. Rockets to put up hundreds of tons of payload in a single firing. You will need such great cargo rockets. We have them and we will launch them with you to carry supplies and structures. And our people. And as many of your people as you wish."

Jesse Markham came slowly to his feet. No outbursts this time. Zheng Fangkun was well known to him. They'd worked together in years past. "Doctor, may I ask you some questions?"

The Chinese nodded.

"Sir, I don't wish to sound the least bit ungrateful, or unrecognizing of your people's ability to launch heavy payloads. But you speak so easily of carrying people. Once we assemble the first quarters in space to continue construction of the arks, almost every mission launched from Earth will have to include people. Those boosters to which you refer, Dr. Zheng, are not man-rated. But the ones we use will have to be, because of manned guidance needed in the terminal phases of rendezvous. There won't be time to develop fully automatic systems. The loss rate could be overwhelming."

"You see this as the major obstacle, Dr. Markham?"

"Yes, sir, I do. I cannot get away from the fact that they simply are *not* man-rated."

Dr. Zheng Fangkun smiled, an expression of infinite sadness.

"*Neither, sir, is this planet.*"

Book III

COUNTDOWN

11

Marc Seavers sat in a scientifically relaxed position, every inch of his body resting in a laser-contoured seat that almost swallowed his stocky frame. If a pressure point built up anywhere beneath a buttock or an elbow, *anywhere*, elaborate sensing devices sounded tiny warnings to a computer that knew Seavers' body far more intimately than did his mother or any other woman. So he was scientifically relaxed and comfortable and in a million-dollar electronic, computerized, cushiony, breathing seat and he was faking out the world. Comfortable, hell. He was almost as tight as a pulled bowstring. The seat felt like an encroaching cocoon. All that electronic gadgetry could always short-circuit, and then he'd be in a mad struggle to escape its clutches.

He sighed and looked through the titanium-ribbed lexitr-and-armorglas viewshield of the great vessel, every fiber of his being, body and soul, linked in living symbiosis to the gargantuan machine. His feet rested comfortably within strapdown pedals, heels against cushioned supports. The pressure along the back of his legs was just great enough to provide firmness and feel yet not interfere with blood flow. Each hand, arms resting to his sides in armtroughs, grasped and held lightly a fighter-plane-type joystick, a molded handgrip with a half-dozen switches and buttons beneath his fingers, thumbs and palms. Any one or combination of those sensors operated by any parts of his hands could nudge, maneuver, or blast thousands of tons into motion.

He wore a helmet that could have come straight out of a combat helicopter pilot's gear, with its many sensors, lenses, detectors and command controls. The headgear had a strange familiarity; it looked much too much like the oblong praying-mantis helmet worn by the astronauts in that old movie, "2001: A Space Odyssey." Seen from above, the helmet was the slick head part of a gleaming orange carapace. The oblong device fitted over his head and lowered a lexitr screen before his eyes. Just like the old HUD system he was accustomed to from the small attack submarines and that fighter pilots had used for years. Heads Up Display. All your instrument, operational and navigational data "appeared before your eyes" electronically so you could keep your head up and watch where the hell it was you were going and yet see everything your instruments were supposed to tell you. A lot better than the old system of constantly rotating eyeballs from the view ahead to the lower instrument panel where, in order to see whether your machinery was normal balls to the wall, or was about to come apart and explode right between your legs, you had to keep your head down. A bunch of good people flew into hills and mountains that way.

The lexitr screen was woven with invisible conducting threads so that it "came to life" with any presentation its computer was capable of generating. His living helmet brought Seavers all sorts of data. He received not only information, but constantly upgraded real-time data on motion, thrust, angular velocity, roll, pitch, yaw, tremble, grumble, shift, twist, bend, swerve, heel, tip: whatever. Lights and grid patterns glowed and trembled in a three-dimensional holographic HUD display that hung suspended before his eyes.

"Goddamnit, Seavers!" a voice thundered in his ears and vibrated through skull bones and stabbed down the back and sides of his neck. "Jesus, man, you're not just running this ship! You're not directing it or steering it or aiming it or controlling it! *You are the ship!* Do you understand? This ship *is you!* You feel every quiver, every slosh and every touch of pain. You know its every sensitivity. *Think ship, think ship, think ship!* You are Seavers-Ship. There's no Marc Seavers. There is no *Pegasus. There is only Seavers-Ship.*"

"Awright, awready," he grumbled under his breath. God, that voice was a pain in his ass. He stopped and felt mirth bubbling up in him. No; not in his ass. *Up my stern tubes, maybe . . .* He wet his lips and he had a godawful itch on the inside of his left thigh where sweat trickled slowly, antagonizing his skin, and—where the hell was the horizon? A light flashed and a woman's soft voice sounded in his ears, vibrated ever so softly through his ear and skull bones. "Pressure venting in section Four Delta. Pressure venting in section Four Delta. Emergency, repeat, emergency. Disregard biological hazards, repeat, disregard biological hazards. Undesired response, undesired response!" The voice grew louder, more anxious, frightened. *Remember, it's only a fucking computer, Seavers!* "Angular venting is producing dangerous roll-yaw combination, excessive delta V angle four-nine, study the gimbal situation indicator. Watch the indicator! Roll-yaw now an emergency, counteryaw

205

required immediately, *emergency action required immed-iately!*"

He worked his controls furiously and he knew he was over-controlling, he was being ham-handed on the controls, and he yelled back to the computer. "Tell the automatics to handle the emergency! Go to computer multihorizon axis! Damn it, go to computer auto—"

"The computer is out to lunch, Admiral Seavers," the electronic voice told him with saccharine sweetness. "You are an idiot, Admiral Seavers. It's been nice knowing you—" The world blew up in his face, stabbing intense white light and streaks of jagged red lightning bursting in his eyes, every inch of his body stabbed with electric needles, his ears ringing and eyeballs quivering and another voice from the computer roared at him, *"You're fucking DEAD, Seavers. You're fucking dead! You've lost it all, asshole. You've killed everybody—"* He leaned back and closed his eyes and listened to the computer tearing him a new ass and finally he removed his carapace *chapeau* and the voice cut off. He eased himself from the enveloping seat and looked into the grinning face of astronaut Susan Foster. "I've been meaning to ask you something, lady."

"After that performance, Admiral, I think you'd prefer to go soak your head."

"What's a beautiful blonde like you doing in an electronic nightmare like this?" he said to her. He took the towel she held out to him and wiped away the perspiration matting his hair and running down his face. "This thing isn't a simulator," he growled. "It's a torture chamber."

She smiled as she handed him a sealed plastcan. He snapped the flat straw and it jutted up from the drink. "Orange," she said. He nodded and drank deeply and the thigh itch attacked him again and he scratched furiously.

"Fleas, Admiral?"

He offered a grimace instead of a smile. "Crabs," he moaned.

"You destroyed your ship, by the way." She held the back of her hand to her forehead and groaned. "Two hundred and eighty thousand tons. Sweet, dear old *Pegasus*. Broken up like a wallowing old schooner on the rocks. I thought you were a hell of a sailor in your old days, but," she sighed. "Age, I guess."

"What went wrong?" he growled, crumpling the plastcan. A sharp edge bit into his hand but he'd be damned if he'd show it to *this* girl.

Suddenly Susan Foster was all professional. "You came in too late to counter the torque from that venting. You literally *twisted* your vessel. You're not sitting in any big bathtub, Admiral. *All* axes are involved here, as well as combination of axes."

"You do go on," he said a bit touchily.

She gestured with a flippant air. Blonde tresses glistened in the computer lights. "Maybe you're just spacey." Susan Foster could switch from girl to experienced astronaut back to impish woman without missing a beat. "Look, Admiral, I've been training with you now for nearly a year, right? You've made computer sim flights in orbit and to the moon and back. Hell of a record. A year ago you couldn't even spell astronaut and now I guess you am one. Am? Are?" She shrugged. "Maybe it scatters the brains. But if that were a real flight with *Pegasus*, and the number of people we computed were on that ship, you just killed two thousand eight hundred and seventeen of them."

"Don't forget the dogs," he added. "Have a cold one with me at the bar?" She nodded and they started down the long curving corridor of the training center deep beneath Vandenberg Air Force Base on the California coast. Hell of a deal. A billion-dollar training center resting on giant springs right on the edge of the earthquake fault zone. He dismissed the thought from his mind as they walked into the lounge. They went to the wall fridge and he took out two Coors Lites, opened one and handed it to her. They eased into comfortable lounge chairs.

"How's Rasputin doing?" he asked in reference to Vasily Tereshnikov. The husky commander of *Gagarin* station was even then going through the training simulation exercises to which Seavers had been subjected.

"He's a space-going dolphin," she said seriously. "An absolute natural. I mean that," she emphasized. "He is really the best space pilot I have ever seen. He's incredible. The other guys feel the same way. You know, I hate to give a Russian more credit than you, but Vasily—wow, man, he is but the greatest."

"You know, don't you," he told her, "that's the best news you could give me?"

"I'd hoped so. Want me to plug in?" He nodded and they changed seats so that they sat before a television monitor that made up a section of wall before them. For several minutes they watched in silence as Tereshnikov, wrapped electronically as Seavers had been, worked the simulator controls of a spacecraft, more a metal mountain than a machine, of nearly three hundred thousand tons. Marc Seavers reminded himself that's what such a monster *would* weigh on Earth's surface. This giant was an electronic extrapolation of the actual craft at that very moment slowly coming to assembled life seven hundred miles above the Earth.

"You're right," he said finally, leaning forward to switch off the viewscreen. "He really is incredible. The way he responds is so smooth and automatic that he seems to anticipate the problem before it ever reaches him."

Susan Foster finished her beer, sat back in her chair and lit up a chlorette. "I don't see how you can light one of those things in your face," he said, grimacing.

"This?" She held out the non-tobacco cigarette derived from hydrilla growth in water farms. "It *tastes* like tobacco, but there's no tar or nicotine and—"

"Spare me. I didn't mean to criticize and I certainly didn't ask for a lecture on the blessings of chlorettes. I simply pass on to you that if you're going to have a vice then enjoy it instead of circling the issue like a bladder-plugged hound searching desperately for a fire hydrant."

"My, how poetic!" She laughed as he bowed to her. "Want to pick up our conversation?"

"What's there to pick up? Vasily's the best man to operate the ship, and I'm damned pleased to say so." He meant what he said; she knew and understood that.

"I wanted to be certain you understand *why* you had problems."

He rested his chin on his fist. "Tell me."

"You reacted like you were moving in water. A vessel that displaces water has resistance against its momentum. Water cushions out, so to speak, certain macro movements of the complete vessel. Now Vasily, on the other hand, doesn't think that way. He knows—by now, in fact, it's instinct with him—that the only resistance to the movement along any axis of the big ship is its inherent inertia."

"Well, shoot, li'l lady, that's because I'm a sailor and he's a cosmonaut. It'd be strange if the results were any different." He watched her nod agreement, then remembered some bothersome details. "You taking complaints as part of the job?" She laughed and waited instead of verbalizing a response to the crooked grin he'd offered. "I need an extra pair of hands, Astronaut Foster. Every time I get into that rig I get an itch and I go mad wanting to scratch."

"Uh-huh. Left inner thigh, one point three inches from the scrotum." Her face was absolutely deadpan as his jaw dropped. "I didn't peek, Admiral," she went on. "We've got you wired coming and going. We need to know *any* physiological distraction that might interfere with what you're doing." She shrugged. "Ergo, we've got the kind of physio profile on you that lets the computer pick up what kind of itch and where."

"Okay, I'll play your game. What *kind* of itch is it?"

"Subliminal desire to escape."

He searched her face. He could pick out even the most subtle of cues if that's what she'd intended. But it wasn't there. Foster was playing it straight. He felt a wave of gratitude for small favors from the gods when she pinpointed the "desire to escape."

"It's strictly physical," she added. "You know you *can't* release those controls and you don't like the situation, and part of your brain agrees with you and says, hey, let's get the hell out of here and it delivers the message with the itch. It's natural and we expected it to happen."

He stared at her with mixed wonder and irritation. "How the hell did I get through the Antarctic without you guys to guide me through my psyche profile?"

"Easy. You itched, you scratched."

She smiled at his easy laughter. "And to answer your *next* question before you ask it, Admiral, we're through for the day. In fact, except for continued familiarization work, you're through trying to reach or pass goals in the command-sim. Frankly, your whole system is more dishrag than hero. You're a very different person from the man who once commanded an attack submarine, Admiral Seavers. What happened in Antarctica changed you forever. We have a saying in our business, sir . . ."

She paused and he knew she'd added that "sir" to disassociate herself from the personal. "What happened in Antarctica is that you learned how to suffer for other people."

"I don't get you."

"I had a Jewish psych professor when I was in college, and some of the things he told us will stay with me forever. We'd been talking about pain, suffering, the human tragedy—"

If you only knew. But he didn't say a word.

"—and this professor pointed out that some of the most fortunate people in this world were those who had been hurt, inside, because now that they were hurt so badly *they could relate to the pain of others*. In short, they had an overpowering empathy. It took them from the company of equals and made them leaders."

It began to dawn on him. Right then and there the first tendrils of what was really going on began to snake through his consciousness. He understood training programs. He'd run enough of them in his own time. You run all your people hard, even those you never intend to take command. It's the old stage drama of the Reality and the Placebo. Sometimes you even run a bunch of people through a training program just to get your parameters, especially in something that's never been done before. He felt a great release. He wasn't doing as well in that command simulator as he *should* have been doing. Susan Foster was right. He was a sailor and not an astronaut. *You're also a guinea pig.* But he didn't mind that, either. He knew the enormity of what was coming down, and anything that contributed to what needed to be done was all right with him.

"I'm not sure what you're driving at, Foster," he said after a long and thoughtful pause. "But I realize now how tough it must be on you to run me through this grind as a sort of placid test animal when you could be back on orbital missions."

"What? I don't understand—"

He rested a hand on her shoulder and his eyes gripped her. "It's just all come together," he said. "The training program here. The search for parameters. The whole shmear." All questions were gone from his mind. "Vasily's going to fly the *Pegasus*. Vasily, and the three astronauts who are duplicating his training syllabus."

"I, uh—"

"Don't feel put out, Susan. Vasily's obviously the best man. He'll have to have three execs for round-the-clock coverage of the flight deck. You're one of them. John Hastings is another. And the third one, he's British, what's his name?"

"Marcus Goldman." He saw that Susan wasn't offering any information.

"Okay. That's lead flight crew. You may not believe this, lady, but what I just realized is a tremendous relief." He started to leave, stopped. "Thanks for all the extra effort, Susan."

She had a *very* strange look on her face. "I'll add it to the bill, Admiral." He tossed her a lazy salute and left.

He went directly to the elevator that would take him to his quarters in Grissom Tower, a thirty-story marvel of engineering set amidst the high hills of the California coastline overlooking the tremendous launch complex that sprawled southward. In his apartment that also gave him a sweeping view of coastline and the Pacific Ocean beyond, he shucked his sweat-heavy clothes and scrubbed down in a fiercely hot shower. He turned the bedroom fans on medium and dropped into the bodyform lounge to air-dry his skin. *Even in his bedroom,* he seemed to notice for the first time, *I'm surrounded*. It was true. Bedroom, living room, studio, computer room. It didn't matter much. He was surrounded with books, training manuals, blueprints, computer programs. He was weary and bleary from it all. Day and night cramming, week after week, into months that had stretched out for nearly a year since his first meeting under Cheyenne Mountain with the president. Accelerated courses in astrogation, physics, metallurgy, psychology, astronomy, geology, sociology, paramedic training, basic agriculture and aquaculture, hydrodynamics, languages, social mores, religions, and then into integrated systems of all types. He was told, and a thick book dropped personally into his hands by President Starling, to study in the most intimate of detail the history of the Canadian Indians of Grassy Narrows, a small village in northwest Ontario. The study—he couldn't stop reading the damn thing once he'd started—had shaken him to the core.

It wasn't enough that they did their best to strangle his brain with subjects he'd long dismissed from the sphere of his life. They'd literally plunged him back into the kind of technical training he hadn't endured since his days as an ensign or a lieutenant j.g. He'd learned new terms, new technical expressions, whole new technologies. He was a pilot but he'd done all his flying within the comfortable grip of atmosphere, where great speed makes even a twitch of the controls turn a powerful slab of winged metal into a soaring dervish. Now they trained him in motion simulators balanced on compressed air so that even a cough imparted trembling movement to otherwise massive and stable devices. He sat in an observer's seat to watch Tereshnikov, and then Foster, Hastings, and Goldman, cocooned within an incredibly complex control system squeezed down to a single seat and the magic of the lexitr screen and holography. He watched them and read the manuals, and then they grinned and offered *him* that same seat.

"This is a full simulation, Admiral." He could hardly recall when his new rank had come in. So many things had been happening—and in his new training regimen it didn't matter whether he was a swabbie or an admiral; they came down hard on him and never relented. "You spend your first two weeks in here just sitting, receiving, judging what you get, understanding and evaluating it and making decisions in your mind. We want you to establish an empathic relationship with this system." He saw spots before his eyes even when they were closed in sleep. "You don't touch a thing, Seavers. You've got this huge ship under your command. Some things are right but now things are going to go wrong. *You do not touch anything.* You figure out what's wrong. You consider all the angles and the aspects and the effects of multiple choices and then you extrapolate what can or will happen based on all incoming data and your own knowledge of all systems and WAKE UP YOU DUMB SON OF A BITCH YOU'VE GOT A FIRE IN THE OXYGEN PLANT AND YOU'RE GOING RIGHT THROUGH MAX ALLOWABLE LINE PRESSURES WHAT THE HELL DO YOU DO NOW IMMEDIATELY!"

Terrific. Just terrific. They'd given him some real blinding headaches. But he was damned good and he cottoned to the routine fast and then he had it all down pat and he ran through a dozen sims—full simulations of a flight and powering up and maneuvering, and he still hadn't touched the sim controls. Then they gave him his first hands-on flight. Susan Foster had checked his seat and patted his arm. "Good luck, sir." "Thanks," he told her. She smiled briefly as she left the sim capsule and added, "You'll need it, Admiral."

So they gave him his first test and they threw in problems and he handled them with speed and precision and skill and when he was feeling real good about himself "YOUR CREW HAS JUST MUTINIED AND ARMED MEN ARE IN THE COMPUTER ROOM AND THEY'RE GOING TO CUT THE COMMAND CABLES AND DON'T JUST SIT THERE, DAMN YOU, TAKE CONTROL!"

After one particularly harrowing day—that damn command simulator at times was realer than life—he staggered back to his quarters in Grissom Tower and slugged down a sixpack that calmed his nerves and loosened muscles as tight as bowstrings. He looked to the south through his armorglas viewwindow. The launch area sparkled and gleamed with the flashing lights of pre-launch activity, and as he heard the thin wails of distant warning sirens the hot launch lights flashed in each room of his apartment. He shut off all the lights about him. Cold beer in hand he looked to the south and watched a star come to life amidst shackles of steel pins and girderwork. White flame shot outward in all directions from a mass of steel framing, splinters of eye-stabbing glare transforming along its outer edges to bright yellow and then orange and red, and as quickly as his eyes became accustomed to the still-silent explosion in the distance the fire genie pushed upward through the girders, flame lashing like a thousand dragon tails as it rose, and abruptly it was clear of all obstacles and the flame poured back in a streamer of blazing fire a thousand feet long. The rumble came then. Not a roar, but a deep cacophonous rumble that shook the world and all within it. The armorglas vibrated and he felt through his feet the shuddering of distant shock waves. The fire trail shortened as it gained distance and speed and it sped upward through clouds, alternately appearing and disappearing and then it was gone, and the hot lights in the apartment winked out and he knew another huge payload was on its way to orbit seven hundred miles high. That was the ninth that week. The giants were clawing away from Earth in a steady progression that made of computed ascents an invisible railway into the heavens.

The sight brought him to think of his simulated space-ship flights. Project Dustbin had been kept out of the public eye for as long as possible. But you couldn't shove that kind of story under any carpet. When you thought of all the ships ripping away from Earth, and so many coming back, it was a miracle they'd kept the lid on reality as long as they did. Japanese, Chinese, French, Italian, American, Russian, English, Brazilian, Indian, Arab—the list of countries sending up payloads was even longer because civilian groups were involved as well, and when hundred-million-dollar satellites begin to tear apart because of dust abrasion, there's no way to shut up angry, confused stockholders. The leaks began as drops and the drops became a torrent and some idiots preached disaster in space and it swept the world news bureaus like a prairie fire before a high wind. The doomsayers were out in full cry, and scientists throughout the world had chosen up sides rather than offering an agreed-upon statement to the public. The head of the Air Force Office of Scientific Research especially had put up a full head of steam. In an expression of public outrage and disgust, Felicity Xavier Powell had told the president of the country to stick his warnings of the world's end where the sun never shines. The genteel, charming and diminutive woman appeared to the world as an angered jaguar with sharp claws—and she led a contingent of scientists who ridiculed not only the American government, but the world body of scientists in general, for their premature, unfounded and outright stupid conclusions. The controversy overshadowed all other issues, commanded the headlines, and bloated the television tubes with constant news flashes of the "latest news" of the ultimate catastrophe.

Events tumbled along with a precision that Felicity Powell had predicted. She recalled the near-panic of the 1980s, when scientists warned that the alignment of planets with the sun in the so-called Jupiter Effect would result in continent-busting earthquakes, massive tidal waves, vast volcanic eruptions and a continuing string of disasters that would sunder the globe. "And the comets!" she cried on world wide television to vast audiences who wanted desperately to believe her and not that idiot Kimberly and his crowd. "Who can forget the comets! For centuries the scientists have told the people the comets meant the end of the world! They were the retribution of God, even if," she added acidly, "no one can understand why God wants retribution against his very own. Again and again the Earth has sailed through the tails and the thick bodies of the comets. Not only of dust! But of stones and rocks and dust and boulders and huge chunks of ice! Again and again we have done so and our atmosphere has protected us! Again and again the sun has raced through thick dust clouds, and which do you think will win? Dust, or a massive star with temperatures in the millions of degrees! We have been here before, again and again *and again*, and fear has never brought us anything but more fear! Have faith! God has chosen us and He will protect us, and Kimberly and his minions of disaster are the work of the devil himself!"

Well, it was one hell of a pitch, mused Marc Seavers. Felicity Powell and her band of faithful followers—counting among them some of the world's leading scientists, who condemned Kimberly as a foppish, self-serving pseudo-scientist trying desperately to get the world's attention in any way he could—could not have more effectively split scientific and public opinion right down the middle. Rather than whimpering in fear, as did hundreds of millions, most of the people on the planet chose the more sensible course. They lived their normal lives. They made love and went to dinner and swam in the ocean and bought stocks and did all the things they'd done for decades. Often they peeled one eye to the heavens (just in case) and found in the skies what had *always* been there, a variety of weather and the changing coloration of sunrises and sunsets.

Bitter political struggles leaped to the attention of the nation; to much of the world. Several governments chose to believe the warnings of Project Dustbin. Huge sums of money and staggering efforts were hurled into gigantic new rocket boosters, launch facilities, space programs. That the United States and the Soviet Union, supported fully by China and England and several other nations, were engaged day and night in the construction of a huge spaceship could hardly be concealed. Felicity Powell led the fight in the press to condemn the government: that this was their way of pushing through a great manned expedition to Mars, and damn the costs to the taxpayer. "Boondoggle! Fraud! Sham!" The accusations ran thick and heavy.

Marc Seavers had never fully understood the public eye or its mind—and most especially its collective actions. He'd studied every aspect of Dustbin. He'd seen at first hand the results of the accumulating dust, especially the steady increase in its density. He tried to convince himself that it was an awfully tough task to convince a planet it was going to die horribly, when your only evidence was a pinch of dust. Just like the dust that gathered in the corners of bedrooms and attics and garages. Dust that could be swept away with a vigorous application of the old-fashioned broom.

What he could not understand was that someone with the knowledge of Felicity Powell, who'd resigned from her federal position with a three-ring-circus press conference, could be so blind. She of all people who might question the accuracy of the reports still flowing in to Dustbin *knew* that *Pegasus*, as yet a huge skeletal whale slowly gathering shape and bulk and substance in its orbit seven hundred miles high, was never intended for any flight to Mars. Everything about such a judgment was *wrong*, and—

When he reached that point in his thinking, Marc Seavers understood the need to *just turn off*. To hell with the confusion and the contentious bickering of a world population. He knew enough of history to understand that, beginning with Sodom and Gomorrah, the arguments for living to the full—against the decried perils of the sins—had been part of the human picture. If all that was foul was to be burned (and frozen, crunched, besodden, split, twisted, and seared by some vengeful or uncaring God) then surely the Romans, the Gauls, the Babylonians, and the Turks and the Mongols and the Fascisti and the Samurai and the Nazis and— well, the list of those who plundered humankind and lived to ripe old ages with the spoils and the daughters of their victims was virtually endless.

Marc Seavers believed in man. He did not need to be fooled by the misadventures that plagued the race from Time Beginning. There was more to all this, he often thought, and perhaps this is some Supreme Being's way of forcing us away from the tiny clay world of our beginnings.

Thus able to push aside the arguments and verbal

assaults that raised clouds of contention as high as any thunderstorm, he could concentrate on the almost back-breaking demands of his training schedules. When first he began the computer simulation training for the giant spacecraft, he was painfully aware that such a vessel did not exist in any orbit about the Earth. He could read the programming of his own training computers! They were training him, and several carefully selected others—at least, those he knew about here at Vandenberg—to operate and flight control a space vessel of two hundred eighty thousand tons. Without the need for a heavy keel for support in Earth's gravity they were assembling a ship nearly two thousand feet long and at least twelve hundred feet in width in the shape of, well, a great football.

It seemed, at first blush, an impossible task. But the more he thought about it the less impossible it seemed. If you hauled seventy tons payload for every flight then in four thousand flights you'd have all the weight up-stairs for orbital assembly. That's a hell of a lot of spacelift, but the figures easily misled the casual observer. Many ships were kicking their huge booster tanks into orbit, and when you start assembling tanks that are over a hundred feet in length by forty feet in width, you are collecting both mass and bulk in a hurry. The new big dumb boosters were throwing two to five hundred tons a shot into orbit, and their lower casings were being kicked into low Earth orbit. Again, it didn't take a genius to figure out that manned ships flying low orbital profiles could rendezvous with the massive casings, attach small orbital engines, and kick the empties up into rendezvous orbit at seven hundred miles.

The word was out among the astronaut crews and space technicians that the winged horse—as they'd come to call the ship unofficially, and the name *Pegasus* began to stick—that the great space vessel was *really* being assembled as an emergency exit for a very small piece of the human pie, should Kimberly prove right and Felicity Powell wrong. Publicly the lead governments hurling their vast energies into *Pegasus* went for the low profile. Some even admitted the ruse to get a huge manned ship to Mars for settlement of that planet. Once again Marc Seavers found his own intelligence thrusting him into the contest, and once again he forced himself back to books and computers.

Yet something nagged at him. *For Christ's sake*, he startled himself with the realization, *I'm not even an astronaut*. And he wasn't. He didn't belong to the NASA astronaut corps; certainly the air force had never invited him aboard. He called Admiral Duncan specifically to ask him about that little matter. If anyone could tell him, and Duncan was both the chief of naval operations and a longtime personal friend, it would be the CNO.

"Do you want to be an astronaut?" Duncan asked.

His question was totally unexpected; it caught Seavers off stride. "Well, I suppose I am in training for a mission upstairs," he conceded.

"It took you long enough, son, to wake up and *say something*. What the hell did you think that computersim was for, a goddamned submarine?" Duncan followed his words with a long chuckle.

"Admiral, it might just as well *be* a submarine. I mean, it—"

"Hell, don't lecture me on boats *now*," Duncan broke in. "You've asked the right questions. The brass ring is clutched tightly in your fist."

"Admiral," Seavers said cautiously, "what's all that supposed to mean?"

"It means you pack when you hang up. Don't take much beyond your personal belongings. You ship out tomorrow morning. *Early*."

"But where—" The phone was dead. He knew better than to call back. Or ask anyone else at Vandenberg what the hell was going on. What had Duncan meant about his finally asking the right questions? *Okay, stop right there, Seavers. Let it rest. They want to play games? They pay the way, remember? Shaddup and go to sleep*. Good advice from his inner self. He fell into deep sleep to the sky glow and deep rumble of another huge payload boosting spaceward.

They got his ass up at five sharp in the morning,

pointed toward a military transport, and sent him on his way to the NASA astronaut training center in Houston. They didn't put him through the grind he expected. They shoved him into the computersim for the new and bigger shuttle, ran him through a series of "flights," opened the door and patted him on the ass. "Admiral," his instructor said, "Susan Foster told us you were hot. You are. You'll do just fine upstairs. Welcome to the club."

The next day he was on his way to the Kennedy Space Center. He couldn't believe his eyes when they flew in a wide descending circle over the military launch area of Cape Canaveral and then the vast sprawl of new facilities in the NASA-Kennedy area. Sixteen new launch pads and their road and rail approaches scarred what had been thick vegetation of Merritt Island. Playalinda Beach to the north was closed and filled with supply structures. The old administrative section of KSC seemed to have bloated in size by a factor of six. And the huge VAB that stood cubelike nearly six hundred feet above the ground now stood guard over long assembly sheds where the solid boosters were assembled and hauled to their launch pads. The manned ships still went out to the pads on the monster crawler transporters. Not the BDMs. The giant solids with their unmanned payloads went Russian fashion, horizontal on long railroad car sections and then raised to a vertical position for firing.

"You learn about Four Six Echo," they told him even while he stared at the pressure suit in his temporary quarters. "What's Four Six Echo?" he said dutifully, feeling like they'd pressed his button and he was responding in excellent walkie-talkie-dollie fashion. "That's your launch pad, Admiral. It's got the second-generation shuttle you trained on with compusim at Johnson Center. You launch almost immediately."

He reverted back to his times aboard attack boats. Go look at your boat. Get the feel, the touch, the sense of her. He went out to Pad 46E. Damn, she was a monster. They'd named her *Aquarius*. Strange name, but it *was* an ocean into which they'd climb. An ocean of emptiness, really. The boosters beneath this giant filled the massive launch stand, and the winged shuttle, much bigger than the first-generation ships, stood high above the ground. If these solid boosters blew, you had a chance to survive in the winged spaceplane. No more of the deathtrap that wiped out those people in the old *Challenger*. If something went haywire with the boost system for *Aquarius*, explosive charges would rip blow-out holes in the solids to diminish thrust and provide angular direction, a heavy shield between the boosters and the shuttle provided protection against blast from below, and four short-duration but powerful solids would hurl the entire assembly safely away from whatever blazing maelstrom might be occurring below.

Seavers crawled through the *Aquarius*. In the cat-walk of the cavernous cargo bay he met a powerfully muscled man in a NASA jumpsuit. He looked at him in surprise; he hadn't expected a black in the spacecraft. "The name's Archer Begley," came a deep voice behind an extended hand. "You must be Admiral Seavers. We've been expecting you. I'm glad they warned us first."

Seavers was disappointed. "Sounds like you've been told to give me the kid-gloves treatment," he said warily.

Strong white teeth flashed in a smile. "No way, man. We got the word from Admiral Duncan personally. It was delivered by Travis Simmonds. You know him?" Seavers shook his head. "He's the chief Indian here. Director of the whole shebang. Our orders, Admiral, are to ride your ass right into the—" Begley laughed. "I almost said right into the ground, but we're going the other way."

"I get your point, Begley."

The other astronaut looked him over carefully. "Lay it on me, Admiral. Is that white skin also sensitive?"

"Try me, mister," Seavers said softly. "Try me as hard as you can."

"God *damn*," Begley said, nodding. He pounded a massive hand against Seavers' shoulder. "I think we got us a real live new member of our crew. Which, by the way, is waiting most anxiously to meet you. Let's go."

It was a hell of a ride. They put Seavers in the right seat. He raised an eyebrow when he saw Archer Begley

221

take left seat as the mission commander and lead pilot. Behind them—surprise!—Susan Foster ran engineer duties, and there were three more people down below in the shuttle bottom deck. Seavers knew the routine and the controls. "Ride with me," Begley told him, all business. "I'll go manual on this turkey only if the automatics screw up. I'll call it out and you'll ride the controls with me. Otherwise we just keep our hands and feet poised and we ride this afterburner all the way on autopilot into orbit. Got it?"

"Yes, *sir*," Seavers snapped. Begley winked at him, they ran slickly through the countdown, and then they lit the fires below. Seavers hadn't expected the shaking and rumbling; he knew it was turbines spinning at tremendous speed and pushing thousands of gallons of fuel to the main engines. Then he saw the thrust stabilize and they lit off the giant solids. A roar hammered at them and he felt the holddown pins sheer and *Aquarius* hurled herself body and soul into the swiftly darkening blue. They went through Max-Q in the lower stratosphere and the ride smoothed out and went quiet because they were running upstairs faster than the speed of sound and most of the commotion was behind them. Begley patted the instrument coaming. "She's a sweetheart," he said, and she was. They kicked off the boosters, jettisoned the safety shield and ran out most of their fuel from the big tank. When they bounced it off he knew it would continue into low orbit, to be picked up later and boosted to rendezvous with *Pegasus*.

Now they boosted on their own engines and suddenly everything shut down and the flames and hustling booming sounds faded, and the engines crackled and sang as they cooled, but it was space music, symphony and ringing to him. Begley looked at him as he tried to look through his windows and also seem to be concentrating on the controls. "Go on," Begley urged. "I'll pitch her nose down. Take a good look, fella. You're going to be busy up here and you won't have this kind of chance again. By the way, sunrise is in twelve minutes."

He'd been so wrapped up in everything he realized he hadn't even thought about being in zero gravity. The body and seat straps also had him pretty well festooned. Begley grinned at him and patted his own straps; Seavers immediately worked the release. *There's no pressure on me . . . incredible. Nothing. Everything's gone. I can feel my clothing and that's all.* He didn't make a deliberate move, but his breathing, especially exhaling, imparted a definite motion to his entire body mass. He'd been warned about making any sudden head movements that would bring on giddiness until he became accustomed to the weightlessness of this fascinating new environment. He touched the forefinger from each hand to the seat armrest and pushed down as lightly as he could, and he began to float upward. "Hang on to the armrests a moment," Begley advised.

Begley worked his thrusters. Low-thrust engines spat before them. The nose glowed and cast off a dull-colored spray of gases. The sound came to Seavers as if someone had hammered on a large metal plate. Magically, the nose pitched downward through the horizon until they looked down at a steep angle. Begley's hands moved a fraction, more hammering sounds came from thrusters firing beneath the nose, and *Aquarius* stabilized. Begley chuckled. "You can let go now, Admiral."

Seavers glanced at him with a huge grin. "Admiral? I feel like the newest kid on the block. Like I did the very first time I ever went to sea."

Begley nodded. "I know," he said.

Seavers floated up from his seat. Below him a huge mass lay shrouded in darkness, and then he began to see the lights as his eyes acclimated quickly. He wasn't certain just where they were and he didn't care; he wanted the feeling and sense of this miracle rather than specific details. He knew they were falling around the planet; that was a truism but the whole concept was ridiculous. He floated in a dreamlike physical state and he had to counter that wonder with the knowledge that he, the men and women with him, this huge ship, fell with a speed of nearly five miles *every second*. A high-powered rifle bullet crawled like a maggot under a log in comparison. He shook his head in self-amazement, instantly regretted the move as his senses whirled, and held himself calm and steady for several moments.

Far below him a pearl necklace glowed and shimmered through the atmosphere. It wandered in a glowing tendril of light from the horizon until it disappeared beneath the nose of *Aquarius*. A huge shrouded pool of light sailed slowly toward them. He stared in fascination. He knew it was a city, the whorls and spirals extending outward like a glowing jellyfish of outlying suburbs and highways. Now he understood that thin tendril that ran from the horizon to disappear beneath them: a super highway running along the curving flank of the planet.

"Get ready. Let yourself drift a bit closer to your forward window." Begley's voice preparing him. He was already programming himself against sudden head turns or the instinctive nod to acknowledge a remark. One finger on the instrument panel to pull his weightless body forward. "Sunrise is a'comin'," he heard Begley say as an old dirt farmer might make the remark. "Don't look away even for a moment, Marc. It comes damn fast. About sixteen times faster than anything you ever saw before."

A quiet flash of rose appeared along the distant curving edge of the world. The flash came from their terrific speed as they hurtled eastward to meet the sun. There were a few moments of subdued rose stretching from side to side and then it brightened with a speed that surprised him despite his anticipation of quickly changing colors. Rose deepened to dark red, almost chocolate, and he saw the atmosphere as he'd never known it before, banded and layered, and the colors swam and drifted and floated into being. He had no other way to describe the yellow and orange and the sudden white and then deep blue coloration. He blinked suddenly as a dazzling streak of intense gold blossomed in the center of the color strata; the gold brightened even more and rushed to each side of its appearance toward the far curving drop of the horizon on each side of his view. Suddenly the heart of a blazing furnace stabbed at him and brightened so swiftly he squinted to avoid the pain of seeing the sun naked above atmosphere.

"Look down." Begley's voice. Seavers shifted his body, hanging head down in front of the instrument panel to watch daylight rushing in a vast silent breaking wave across the planet. The dark dissolved into long splinters of light where the newborn sun raced; the shadows were the momentary blocking of that light by mountains and hills and high clouds. Dark and light and shadows that ran, shifting and twisting before his eyes, for hundreds of miles. Then, in a long blink of his eyes, night was gone and he swept through daylight faster than seventeen thousand miles an hour.

"Show's over," Begley said with sudden authority in his voice. Seavers worked his way clumsily back into his seat and slid a belt loosely over his midriff and eased his feet into soft restraints. "Get the feel of things, Seaver. You got thirty minutes. Then we go downstairs—" He laughed with the look on the other man's face. "Lower deck. They've got a compusim waiting for you there. Duplicate of the system you were using at Vanny Farms."

He'd never heard "Vanny Farms" before. It's always surprising what people on the outside call the place you know only as Vandenberg Air Force Base. "Move around. Feel your way. Ask questions. Thirty minutes from now you go into the compusim, and we uplink the computers to provide a mass simulation from this bird to what *Pegasus* will be when it's done. That's going to be just about two hundred eighty thousand tons mass. Susan's waiting for you."

Susan Foster, he knew, would ream his butt through a rough session. He took Begley's advice. He drifted through the upper deck, took a look down below at the mental torture chamber waiting for him. He tried all manner of body movements, felt vomitus starting up his throat, remembered what he'd been told about the contents of his stomach floating freely and pressing against his intestines in a way he'd never known before. He got it under control and before he even started becoming accustomed to doing a fingerstand and floating absolutely free and unencumbered, his brief spell at

225

freedom was gone and Susan Foster grinned at him, an almost diabolical smile. "Let's get with it, Admiral. We're on a schedule." She might have gone too far, she thought, and appended a "Sir" to her words.

"Can that. You're the boss and I'm the student. Let's do it." He paused a beat. "Ma'am," he added. She helped him into the carapace helmet and its crazy holographic lexitr viewscreen. They were back in business. *In school*, he reminded himself.

"Admiral, this isn't a simulation. You're going to fly this tub. I mean literally control and fly the ship. The computer will translate our weight to the simulated weight of the final *Pegasus* configuration and accommodate for variations in mass, acceleration, and other factors. But you are going to bring us three hundred thirty-six point two miles from our present position with a change in orbital height and a shift in orbital plane so that we make a specific rendezvous with the assembly area for *Pegasus*. And if they haven't told you yet, that will also be close to the *Gagarin* station. Got any questions, sailor?"

He nodded and banged his helmet against the compusim gear. He winced. "Yeah, I got a question, ma'am. How do I get a transfer out of this chickenshit outfit?"

"I'll be monitoring your progress, sailor, and Commander Begley will also be ready to override you at any time you screw up. But I may as well tell you now. If he has to take the controls, when we get back dinner's on you for the crew. Now, shove off."

There *were* differences. Control action and reaction were exact. Thrusting and gimbaling and observing the myriad instruments and controls matched what he'd experienced in Vanny Farms. *Christ, it's catching*, he thought in an unguarded moment. The differences he found, first, were in his own body. No simulator built can provide the true effects of weightlessness, and he had to perform now with his stomach trying to float around inside his lungs. When the urge to urinate pressed upon him he pushed it down somewhere in the back of his brain. This compusim wasn't yet hooked up

226

to the hygienic systems and, although he had some sort of bastardized motorman's friend along the inside of his thigh and attached to his penis, Begley had warned him that "letting fly" wouldn't take the urine very far. "No air suction yet in the system. The stuff is weightless. It stays in the tube. You're liable to end up with a boot full of pee, Admiral." Begley had roared and slapped his knee with the thought.

Seavers flew the damn ship. He flew it right on the money, he felt the thrusters working to his every twitch and urge, felt the big orbital maneuvering engines come to life with a thudding explosion far behind them. "Bring us to a full stop based on inertial reference grid nine seven nine," Susan Foster told him. She'd begun to sound like a drill sergeant. He followed her orders exactly, the lexitr screen glowed steadily to show everything on the mark. Begley's voice came into his headset. "Dinner's on us, Admiral. You've dropped her perfectly in the slot. Consider yourself an astronaut. I've got the con, Seavers. You're disengaged from control. You on the line, Blondie?"

"I'm with you," Susan Foster replied.

"Suit up the new kid. Check him out yourself. Have him and yourself ready in the bay, compartment four. We're giving the sailor his first spacewalk."

It took forty minutes to suit up. Another twenty for a third astronaut to check out both Seavers and Foster. "You all set back there?" Begley called by radio to their helmets. Foster tugged gently on the thin cable connecting her suit with Seavers. "We're set. Let her rip, bossman."

"Doors coming open," Begley announced. Seavers felt the ship tremble as electric motors spun up, cables pulled taut and the huge clamshell doors of the long cargo bay eased open. Finally they spread out like folded wings to each side of the shuttle. Seavers stared in utter disbelief at the sight before him.

Space twinkled, gleamed, sputtered, shone, and glistened in a dozen colors, bright and subdued, sputtering and flashing. Before them, against the brightly curved horizon of a planet far below, was the growing assembly of *Pegasus*, spacewhale ribs showing gaunt and powerful. The whole thing was unbelievably huge and seemingly all the greater in volume because of the working cubicles drifting about the monster spacecraft. Assemblies and subassemblies, grotesque but efficient space tugs, rocket tanks, shuttles, Salyuts and the new Komarov winged ships of the Russians. Steel girders unfolding, titanium panels, gleaming solar panels, sprays of gas from thrusters. Units marked in colors and numbers, an incredible disarray that Seavers knew was very much in order and coming together as planned. He paid special attention to the separate unit assemblies. Entire sealed sections were self-contained cubicles, bolted together and then into position like a three-dimensional jigsaw puzzle. They drifted upward from *Aquarius*, secured by the safety cable.

As his viewing angle changed and the massive machinery drifted into darkness, he encountered the dustglow Susan Foster had warned him he would see. Along the edges of *Pegasus* a dim orange glow appeared. He saw it begin as a fuzzy light along the spacecraft as well, and it intensified before his eyes. He spoke aloud and his helmet radio carried his words to the others. "It's like neon light along the edges," he said, curiosity in his tone. "I expected, from what you told me, a hazy glow like a street light in fog, but nothing like *this*. Is it from impact with the dust? It's like a carnival out here!"

Foster laughed, a delightful sound in his headphones. "Dust and atomic particles. We call it chemoluminescence. The early flights encountered the glow on a much weaker level than what you're seeing now. It results from all this hardware moving at five miles a second. That's pretty good impact speed, and when a heavy mass strikes atomic oxygen it builds up an energy effect. Atomic oxygen atoms pile up, um, like the bow of a ship piling up water, and it all combines to form molecules of oxygen. It has to go somewhere and it shoves back from this hardware like spray comes back from a ship. When the oxygen molecules slow down, they shed some of their energy in the form of photons.

Now add the static electricity effects of dust mixing in with all this and you've got a—"

"It's like Disney World," he broke in.

"That'll do," she chuckled.

He was so overwhelmed by the sights before and about him he was only dimly aware of the panorama unfolding, unreeling beneath him on the Earth. He forced himself to take the moment to look down. They were rushing over a huge mountain range with its characteristic ribs and ridges, its dark streaks and fingers of white painted in snow and ice. The mountains ended suddenly, a river trickled from the peaks to a rust-and-sand-colored high plateau—it could have been a desert—and patches of green began to appear. He had no time for further sightseeing.

"Over there," he heard Susan Foster repeating. He turned in the direction of her upraised arm. A strange castle loomed out of darkness, illuminated from a hundred different points with onboard lights, the sun, and reflections from the massive construction and assembly nearby. The *Gagarin* station, he knew. "We don't have much time, Admiral. Everything up here is really drilled into a tight schedule. But we do have time for a trip to *Gagarin* and a brief visit. You set?"

"Go for it," he told her. They pulled together on the lifeline cable to bring their suited forms against one another. Foster held a spring-loaded crossbow in both hands, aimed through a laser sight, and squeezed the trigger. A small bolt snaked away, trailing thin cable behind it. "You always aim this well?" Seavers asked her.

He heard her laugh in his earphones. "Sure I do. All I need is a laser aiming-and-homing system like this. Can't miss." He understood then. In the bolt was a homer and it was locked onto a target laser beam from a docking port of *Gagarin*. The cable quivered and a green light flashed in the crossbow. Foster snapped it together. "*Gagarin*, we're ready for reel-in."

A voice with a heavy Russian accent spoke into their helmets. "Very good. Hello, Susan Foster! Do you have the greenhorn with you?"

"Hello, Mikhail. Yes, he's with me. We're hooked up and ready."

"Very good. Here we go—now." The cable stiffened and Seavers felt himself and Susan Foster being pulled toward the Russian space station. It expanded steadily in size as they neared the complex structure of girders, tubular sections and enormous solar panels. Several manned ships drifted nearby. "Prepare yourselves for contact," came the Russian's voice. The cable had gone slack, Seavers noticed. He followed Susan Foster's example and stiffened his arms before him. They touched the side of the docking cubicle with a surprising gentleness, grasped handholds waiting for them, and were drawn into the airlock. A five-sided iris closed steadily behind them, a light flashed, and Seavers could *hear* the air filling the compartment. Another door opened as a green light came on, and they drifted into an inner cubicle and turned to watch the inner seal close. A chime sounded and several Russians drifted to them. Seavers recognized Vasily Tereshnikov. He tapped Seavers' helmet in the signal to release the safety catch. Moments later Seavers' helmet was off and he and the Russian exchanged enthusiastic if clumsy bear hugs.

"So you have finally come upstairs to join the rest of us!" Tereshnikov boomed. "It is about time, Marc Seavers. Here, I want you to meet someone. This is Tanya Yevteshenka." Seavers held out a gloved hand to the dark-haired beauty suspended in air before him. She nodded. "Admiral, welcome to *Gagarin*," she said formally.

Tereshnikov laughed. "She is still too formal. But as the new commander of this station," he shrugged, "we can forgive her so much protocol." Tereshnikov turned to Susan Foster. "How much time do we have?"

Her helmet floated at her side on its safety line. "Just a few minutes, I'm afraid. They're unloading our cargo now, and we're scheduled for retroburn as soon as we return to the ship."

Tereshnikov nodded as if he knew their visit was to be abrupt. "Well, this is not going to be even, what do you call it, an eat-and-run visit. I understand that this qualifies you fully as an astronaut, however."

Seavers showed his confusion. "I'm not sure what's going on here, Vasily. I mean, I'm the greenhorn on this flight. Just along for the ride." He glanced at Tanya Yevteshenka. "Wait a minute. You said she's the new commander of this station?"

"That is so."

"But—"

Vasily Tereshnikov smiled. "We received the news only this morning. Or what would be morning down there," he gestured to the Earth far beneath them.

"What news?" Seavers asked.

"Why, we thought you would have been the first to know," Yevteshenka said to Seavers. "Vasily—excuse me, General Tereshnikov—was relieved of his duties aboard this station. He is to be the commander of the *Pegasus*."

Silence met her words. "I'll be damned," Seavers said at last. "No, I *didn't* know. Not a thing! But," he looked at his Russian friend, "that's terrific news. Vasily, my congratulations. I shouldn't be surprised. You're considered the best space pilot in the business."

"Thank you, Marc." Tereshnikov glanced at Susan Foster and then to Tanya Yevteshenka. "You mean," he said slowly to the two women, "he doesn't *know?*"

Susan Foster was struggling to keep a straight face. She shook her head. "He doesn't know a thing. It's not our policy to tell our rookies too much at one time."

"Tell me *what?*" Seavers asked, almost demanding an answer.

"Admiral Marc Seavers." Vasily Tereshnikov had drawn himself up as straight and formal as a man could in weightlessness. "Our two governments, and there are some others involved, have decided to build a second ship. An ark, I suppose. They have already named it. *Noah*. Some biblical name relating to animals. Whatever. They have not yet selected the commander of that vessel. From what I understand, it will be a Chinese. Or perhaps a Spaniard. They are both fit to command a floating barnyard, no?"

Seavers looked blankly at the Russian. He wasn't getting the drift of all this. "And?" he said finally.

"That means not one, but two great ships that will depart this world," Tereshnikov said with sudden solemnity. "I shall command one and another man will command the other. Two ships make a fleet. Or a mission. I'm not certain what they will call— "

"Vasily! Get on with it!" Tanya Yevteshenka shouted.

The solemn air of the Russian gave way slowly to a huge smile. "Marc, my friend. If there is a mission, then there must be a mission commander."

The silence hung heavy. Vasily Tereshnikov waved both arms and began a slow tumble and snatched at the arm of Susan Foster. "We have a mute, a dumbbell for a mission commander! Can he not talk?"

Seavers stared. He tried to speak but the words refused to come. Finally he forced out a sound. "You mean . . ."

"Yes! You have been chosen to lead the mission," Tereshnikov shouted.

With short bursts of the thrusters they eased away from the assembly of ships massed about the growing *Pegasus.* Marc Seavers was still in a state of mild shock. When they returned to *Aquarius,* he stopped Susan Foster before they left the airlock chamber. "Does anyone else know about this? Among the crew, I mean?"

"No, sir. I'm the only one."

"Then you keep it that way."

"Admiral, I'm going to burst if I don't— "

"Consider it an *order,* damn it."

"Yes, sir."

"And *don't* call me sir!"

"Yes, sir, uh, I mean, yes, sailor."

"Thanks." He hugged her and shoved them both against a bulkhead before they could float their way back into the crew compartment. Archer Begley grinned at him.

"I guess this means you've earned your space spurs, sailor. I'm sure going to miss calling you greenhorn, though."

Seavers strapped in. "I still haven't taken this thing down, Arch."

"No time like the present. Let's do a duet, sailor." Just like *that* they were a team. Two hours later, drifting slowly but steadily from the growing armada about the *Pegasus*, Begley issued a string of crisp orders to Seavers, who worked the computers and controls. A bellow of hazy violet flame broke the balance of her orbit, and *Aquarius* began her long fall home. Seavers turned her around with the attitude thrusters and they came back into atmosphere in a glowing envelope of flame, a huge glowing column trailing behind them. They plunged back into the upper heaving reaches of atmosphere, Seavers felt the aerodynamic controls grasping air and tugging at the ship, and they came down in a great curving spiral across the United States to the east coast. From twenty-two miles up they had the extended runway at the space center in sight. "I remember when that sucker was only three miles long. It was like landing deadstick on a carrier deck," Begley said. "She's all yours, mister. Take her in."

It's always nice to feather your ship onto a runway. Especially when she weighs one hundred and twenty tons empty.

Seavers checked through crew debriefing quickly and got to a telephone as fast as he could. He made a call direct to the office of Admiral Spencer Auchinschloss in navy headquarters.

"Marc, congratulations. I hear you aced your first flight," the admiral said with open sincerity.

"It looked that way, sir. Admiral, I don't know how high my VIP status goes, but I need a favor. It's personal, and it's damned important to me."

"Wait a moment. Before you ask anything more, you're scheduled to meet with the president in the White House the day after tomorrow. You'll get the details later. It's a hush meeting, so keep it to yourself. Now, what do you want? Or need?"

Seavers spelled it out. Auchinschloss was silent for a

moment. "I'll call you back within the hour. Where'll you be? Let me have that number . . ."

It took the admiral forty-two minutes exactly to call back with the information Seavers wanted so desperately. When he hung up, he studied the notes he'd written. He could hardly believe it was so close. He didn't want to waste any time driving. Hell, that's what admiral's rank is for, he told himself. Twenty minutes later he was in a navy jet helicopter, heading northwest.

"Land this thing on the helicopter pad at Shands Hospital in Gainesville. You know where it is, Lieutenant?" he asked the pilot.

"Yes, sir. We fly there for our burn cases. Been there a couple of times. I'll call in ahead so we can go right onto the pad."

He left the helicopter and a navy corpsman led him to the medical research center. "But you can't go in there without a pass, Admiral," he heard. He ignored it and went through the doors. Not in the lab. Not in the office. Finally he went to the coffee shop and stood before a table with several young lovelies staring up at him.

Nancy Parks spilled her coffee. She ignored it. He looked down at her, red hair and freckles and *My God, has she always been this beautiful?* He could almost see the wind in her hair again.

"Not very often in this life," he said slowly, "the old man upstairs smiles on us a second time. I have got to be the dumbest son of a bitch that ever walked or sailed a boat." He took a deep breath and said a silent prayer.

"Nancy, will you marry me?"

12

"When they come, it's going to be from the north, down from the highway. They'll be strung out and loose and they won't be much of a problem to stop. We'll be able to pick'em off without much trouble." Russ Corey eased the helicopter into a wide turn to the west and pointed. "*That's* going to be our real headache. A lot of these people, when they get all fired up, will go right for the air base. That means they'll have vehicles. All kinds, from pickup trucks to semis to road graders. It ought to look like a scene right out of *Mad Max*. And they'll come loaded for bear. There'll be no scaring them off. Do you understand that? Do your men understand that? You're going to have to kill and in big numbers."

Clete Marsh sat with a face of stone to Russ Corey's left in the front seat of the helicopter. Marsh ran the security force for the vast strip mines Russ Corey owned in the Arizona desert country. For a long time Marsh hadn't figured the reasoning behind such a move. The man was pouring hundreds of millions of dollars into a mining operation in shitpoor desert country, and to top off that wheelie-dealie, his mines were smack in the middle of the combat firing range of Luke Air Force Base. The whole damned place was a hotbed of fighters, bombers, helicopters, and God knew what else tearing up targets in an almost ceaseless cannonade of machine gun and cannon fire, searing napalm bursts, all kinds of bombs, explosive mists that rumbled the air all the way to the distant mountainsides. Sometimes they came through the areas where Corey's people were laying down long airstrips and even railroad lines and massive concrete foundations. To say nothing of the huge water tunnels they'd gouged from distant rivers and deep wells stuck into the ass of the desert.

He'd never seen mining towers like them before.

Everything arrived in a long series of truck convoys. Pieces of erector sets, they looked like. Hundreds of trailers for people. Restaurants, sewage facilities, power plants; the works. The trains rolled in steadily as well, and work crews began putting parts and pieces together with amazing speed. Towers going up everywhere. Long air-conditioned buildings and huge hydraulic rams to raise massive loads from horizontal position to the vertical. Damndest way to put up smokestacks and incinerators Clete Marsh had ever known.

He hadn't opened his mouth to ask a single question when they brought in miles of barbed wire. Damned tough stuff; made tough enough to rip open the hide of a damned grizzly. And they set it up concertina style. Not only the fences, but long rows of springy coiled wire of the type used around maximum security prisons. Real bitchy stuff. You got caught in that, it took you a day and a half to get out and you left your damned skin behind.

Clete Marsh was security boss for the Corey operation in this middle of nowhere, but he'd be damned if he really knew what was going on. "I'm going to pay you better than you ever got paid in your life," Corey had told Marsh and a select group gathered within a geodesic dome that had gone up with amazing speed in the desert. Amazing because Marsh and the others had read the instructions and, with one straw boss pushing them like a madman, they'd assembled featherweight metals and lexite and a plasticized curtain material into the dome about the geodesic framing. Corey then had them add separate lock systems in three different parts of the dome. You had to get through three separate air-pressure doors just to get inside the damned thing. When you came in from outside you first checked the pressure and temperature inside by gauge and by *looking* through a sheet of armorglas. You pulled three interlocking levers and the entry door opened. You got inside the first cubicle and sealed the door behind you, and then you went through the same routine for the second cubicle, and after that a third unit waited for them. And you did it Corey's way with no shortcuts or the man bounced your ass off his reservation—it was big enough for them to call it that—with your family and everything you owned. He paid anyone he threw off his turf and there was no coming back, but the man who'd been bounced couldn't holler too loud, not with six months' pay in his jeans and a bus ticket for him and his family to anywhere in the country to which he took a liking.

It was strange, but man, that Russ Corey was strange. Meaner than a damned viper when he took a pissing-off to anyone. The best and toughest friend in the world when you played by his rules. All sorts of rumors followed the man around. Big billionaire, they said. Owned factories all around the goddamned world. Ships and steel plants and airlines and he even had a goddamned factory *on the moon!* And he'd been there himself. Corey didn't deny it. Christ, he'd lived for a solid year on the moon setting up industrial systems and quarters for the people who worked there. Paid them a damn fortune, too. In fact, according to Charley Mankowicz, Corey had made a whole damn bunch of flights to and from the moon.

"Charley, he sure as hell don't look like no astronaut to me," Clete Marsh had said bluntly. "I seen them astronauts on television a whole bunch of times. You seen 'em, too. Clean-cut fellas. Them astronaut ladies. All of 'em got dozens of college degrees and they're smarter than hell. Does Russ Corey look like an astronaut to you? Not to me he don't! Hell's bells, that's a man's man. No sissyfoot shit with him. He's wildcatted oil fields and been a damned miner and he's tough as nails and he didn't learn all that stuff on no *moon*, that's for sure."

Charley Mankowicz just smiled. "You do your job, Clete, and that's all you got to do, right? Mind your damned business. But I'll tell you this much. You know them buildings way out by the towers? You been in there, right? You've seen them crazy ships like great big damn barrels with that rocket engine underneath, and them fuel tanks all around the outsides? He's got

237

dozens of them being built, and they can carry fifty people at a time if that's what he wants to carry."

"I hear they're for special cargo, Charley."

"You're right. *Very* special cargo. Seeds, plants, chemicals, fertilizers, all kinds of machinery, drilling gear, explosives, scientific crap. *And people*. Clete, do as I say. Just keep your mouth shut and do your job. That Mr. Corey, he's the best damn friend you got in this world, and you want to hope he keeps right on being your friend. Because what the hell do you think we're doing way out here turning this place into a fortress? You've heard what those science fellas are saying about the big dust clouds in space we're going to bump right into? Us here on the Earth, the sun, the whole blamed solar system."

"I've heard it," Clete Marsh allowed. He looked out across the desert floor of the firing and combat range. "But hell, man, look at the dust out *there*. It's all around us! Ain't hurting us none. Of course, when the wind blows real bad we got dust storms, but that's hardly new."

"You notice where he puts the families when we get them dust storms?"

"Sure. In those domes."

"And you notice no dust has *ever* gotten inside, no matter how bad the wind's blowing?"

Clete thought about that for a moment. "Now that you bring it up, you're right. He's developed one hell of a seal for those."

"And it means that if the dust can't get in, even with the wind doing a hundred or better and sandblasting the windshields off the cars and trucks out here, which means it's a mean son of a bitchin' wind for sure, *then the air that's inside can't get out*."

Clete Marsh had to ponder that one for a while. Not that what Charley said wasn't true, but he had never figured the *why* of it all. He shrugged. "Not my business, I guess."

Charley clapped him on the shoulder. "*That's* the ticket, Clete. Just keep thinking that way."

"Charley, you mind if I ask you one more question?"

He was taken aback with the disapproval on Charley's face. *"Just one, f'Christ's sake, Charley!"*

Mankowicz nodded finally. "Take your shot, man."

"The bossman—Mr. Corey, I mean—he's been real straight with me."

"You and everybody else," Charley said with a dark look of surprise that the subject ever came up for talking.

"Well, he's made it plain as the nose on *your* face, Charley, and it can't get much plainer than that, well—" Marsh kicked sand with a scuffing boot in his discomfort, "that he expects us to be *attacked*. You know, mobs of people bustin' in here and doing whatever they can to destroy this place."

"You better believe it, security man. You able to do that job?"

"Do it? *Do it?* Holy shit, Charley, I could hold off half the damned U.S. army with what we got here. We got missiles, and tanks and armored cars, and every damned jeep and truck and dozer's got a fifty caliber on it, and we got them M-27 autorifles that fire explosive rounds, and there's mortars and—" He came to a sudden stop, beginning to comprehend that Charley Mankowicz knew a hell of a lot more than he'd been letting on and that he was just letting Clete Marsh shoot off his big mouth, which was a very dumb idea when you got down to it.

"What's your point, Clete?"

"It's the fire stuff and the gas what disturbs me."

"How?"

"Well, if a mob tries to come in here, no matter what the angle and they ain't stopped by everything we got, Mr. Corey, he's set up what he calls his hellfire and puke defense system."

"Do tell."

"Yes, *sir.* Every bit of that ground out there," Clete said with a sweeping motion of his hand, "is honeycombed with plastic tubing and tunnels and it's got both that explosive mist and petroleum jelly in it, you know, that special kind of napalm. Plus the gas generators. Mr. Corey, he said he could be using phosgene or a choking gas like that, or even nerve gas, but it was

239

dumb just to kill all them people with gas when the puke stuff would make 'em so sick they'd *want* to die, and sure as hell they wouldn't want to come near this place. Mr. Corey, he said—"

Charley Mankowicz stepped closer to Clete Marsh until they were almost touching noses. Marsh was a big man and tough all the way through and he'd done a lot of combat in his time, so he recognized that this Mankowicz fella, despite his crazy Polack or Lithuanian name or whatever, was *very* special indeed. This was a man who got used to killing people a long time ago and—

"Clete, you want to keep your job?"

Marsh was so shocked he stepped back a pace. "Hell, sure I do!"

"Then I got some advice for you. Shut your mouth. You go on and on like a deep well that's busted clear out of the middle of the earth and just keeps spewing and spouting."

"Charley, goddamn it, I ain't talked to no one *but you!* Corey, he said—"

"*Mister* Corey."

"Mister Corey, he said to me you was his right-hand man, second in command so to speak, and that if I had problems and he wasn't around, I was to get you to straighten it out. That's all, damn it." Marsh took a deep shuddering breath and wondered what kind of hornet's nest he'd stepped into.

Mankowicz studied him carefully. "We let it go this time, Clete. We put your jabbering behind us, okay?"

"You got it, man. That's *fine* by me."

"You got a fine wife, Clete, and three fine boys, you know that?"

"What the hell are you getting at, man?"

"If you ever talk about this to anyone else, that fine wife is going to be a widow and your fine kids are going to wonder when their mama is going to get married again. Ain't no joy in growing up without a daddy."

Clete Marsh didn't back off that easy. "Charley, you threatening me, man?"

Charley smiled. He seemed to have become a death's

head. "No, man," he mimicked. "I never threaten, I guarantee." He put his arm around Marsh's shoulder and started with him for the messhall. "Just forget any of this ever happened, Clete."

Clete Marsh stole a glance at the big man walking with him. *You bet your sweet ass I will*, he promised himself.

Well, he'd had that private conversation with Charley Mankowicz some months back, and he'd never brought the subject up again. They had plenty of television with satellite relay feeds in the middle of the desert, and Clete Marsh began to take special notice of strange goings-on out there in the world. The scientists were still fighting and hollering among themselves, but that didn't matter much. Sheeyit, they'd been doing that ever since Eve cut Adam out of the first bite of that damn apple. It wasn't the chromedomes that bugged Marsh. People were getting scared out there. The first real sign that something was screwy was the sunsets changing. They'd become whole shows in themselves, the skies streaked with really shiny colors, and a lot of green in the evening sky, and dawn didn't seem to come as fast as it used to, and the teevee and the newspapers were starting to blame it on the dust in space. That it was getting heavier and heavier and maybe the good old Earth was really in trouble after all.

They heard about a television special that would explain the gorgeous sunrises and especially the sunsets, and Mr. Corey, he made certain his technicians recorded it so that all his crews and their families would have a chance to see it as many times as they wanted. There was this scientist woman, they called her a Doctor, and she had a real fancy name, Felicity Xavier Powell, what the hell kind of name was that? Clete Marsh and the others forgot all about names when she started talking. This woman had the power, all right, and she knew what the hell she was talking about.

She showed the damndest sunsets they'd ever seen. The sky was going crazy. Everything shone like mad and then it got dark and the sun was huge and irregular

241

in shape and it looked like blood dripping down from the skies. She showed a lot more. Great areas of Earth that were under huge sheets of dust laying in the air and they grew colder and snow stayed on the ground for years where it hadn't snowed for centuries. She showed a lot of stuff like that, and then she knocked them all right off their seats when she said the films they'd been watching were ten and thirty and sixty years old! They'd been watching the results of volcanic eruptions, like Vesuvius and Mount St. Helens and them funny-sounding Mexican names, and a bunch down in the Pacific Ocean, and she had special animation that showed how the volcanic dust and other stuff drifted around the world, and it scoured airliner windshields and even stopped their engines cold. She showed pictures of them big 747s and the even bigger 1290s with the paint scraped away and the engines chewed to junk, and the pilots had brought them in without power. There were films of Sahara Desert dust storms drifting over the oceans, taken from satellites, and how they made those terrrific sunsets all over the world. Then she showed what they were seeing now, and by God, that woman was right!

"See? See what she's telling us, Clete?" That was his wife talking, with their three real fine kids sitting with them. "It's been like this before. It's happened before. I bet it's them churches out there that's behind all this fussin' and hollerin'. You *know* what they're like," Janet Marsh said with absolute conviction. "They get the people all het up and they pour into the churches, falling all over themselves to throw money at the priests and make out like they're good souls. You know what they're doing, Clete? They're hedging their bets. They know they may go to hell for all the things they done and they been doing and they're trying to buy a ticket from God to get into heaven." She stood up suddenly, people looking at her, and she spoke in a loud voice. "I don't need to see no more. Mr. Corey, he's been straight with us. He's told us to look at everything there is to see and then just use common sense and decide for ourselves. Well," she announced primly, "I've decided.

242

I don't need to see this nonsense no more. *I* got work to do!"

Clete Marsh was real proud of her. He sure felt better, too. Somehow he had the feeling that Charley Mankowicz had never stopped keeping an eye on him.

That was now all behind him. Mr. Corey was on another of his unannounced inspections of the Luke range facilities, and Clete Marsh found himself back in the air in a chopper flown by the bossman himself. "We've got the pipelines finished," Marsh explained. "Like you wanted, they're covered with sand and most of them are invisible. They run down," he pointed to the east toward the military airfields, "from the hills in that area. Then we got a bunch from the opposite direction, from the Mohawk Mountains." Corey knew the details. He wanted to be certain his men knew the details. Corey had memorized every last detail of his Arizona complex. Their position lay almost due east of Yuma and in a line southwest from Gila Bend. The damned place was almost as desolate as the moon.

It was even scarier. Vicki Correnti had come up with a hell of an idea that would turn the Yuma area into a frightening deathtrap for the uninitiated. "Put up a nuclear reactor in the areas least protected by terrain and your defensive systems," she recommended.

He studied the maps where she'd marked her proposal. "What for?" he asked simply.

Vicki smiled, and he knew she'd studied this at length before saying a word. It was strange, being in a sixth-level underground beneath the moon and discussing what he should be doing in Arizona. But Vicki was a top psychologist and she never came up with a proposal that hadn't been thought through. "You put up the reactor with a hell of a lot of publicity. Then you add a lot of lights and make a big fuss over it, and *then* you have a meltdown." He studied her. Was she pulling his leg?

"Russ, it's the Chernobyl Syndrome. It's a lot more effective than any silly China Syndrome. Chernobyl's ghost stomps around the world. Any time there's a

243

radiation leak anywhere, everyone conjures up the horror of Chernobyl. To people it means horrible death and getting the hell away. And most certainly no one wants to go *into* the area!"

"Do you know," he asked slowly, "how long it takes to put up a nuclear reactor?"

"Uh-huh." She gave him the cat's smile again. "Seven years."

"There won't be a world in seven years, Vicki."

"That's why you build a dummy reactor. You can put up concrete and metal walls in seven *weeks*. You can store water in there with a direct pipeline feed to the flame buckets or the holding basins. In the meantime you blow up a part of this dummy building. You can get all sorts of radioactive trash to dump onto the ground, or spray it from planes so that radioactive readings downwind will scare the bejesus out of *anyone*. Then you put up more barbed wire and a lot of animal skeletons and radiation warning signs. You won't need a single sign that says Keep Out."

It worked. It worked along with everything else. It would even help funnel the screaming mobs when they came in thirsting for blood, as he knew they would when the time came. Funnel them right into what would be the killing fields of Luke Range. Too bad. *Tough shit is more like it*, he told himself, and with a shrug dismissed any thoughts of regret or hesitation.

He was setting up the Luke facility for a mass shoot. When the time came for launching, there'd be no leisurely breaks for long countdowns or fancy advanced rockets. It would all take place devastatingly fast. The hammer would come down and the birds would fly.

For nearly a year he'd been assembling the giant rocket sections. *No cryogenics*. That was absolutely the first rule. None of this nonsense for maximum engine performance, the specific impulse that engineers kept so dear to their hearts. Russ Corey knew his only chances for success lay in giant dumb boosters and one-time-for-flight electronics systems that went for maximum realiability over the short run. He also kept man in the loop so that expected breakdowns of electronics

244

systems wouldn't guarantee the loss of a ship and its crew.

Huge solid boosters for stages one and two, a massive liquid-propellant tank with storable fuels for the upper main stage. His liquid-propellant rockets of RP-7 and gasoline weren't nearly as efficient as the NASA birds that flew with cryogenic liquid-oxygen and liquid-helium, but they also didn't have to be babied and stroked and tested a thousand different ways just to make sure they were ready to fly. The boosters coming together at Luke could stand on their pads for a year and be ready to go within seventy-two hours of the decision to commit.

There *was* that little problem of where those massive first-stage solid boosters would land. His chief engineer wanted to get the record absolutely straight on that matter. When Corey met with Preiss in the latter's office, the engineer already had a complete electronic range display. "You're going to send up those things and they're going to come down," Preiss said with a grimace. "It's *where* they come down that's got me freaking out, Mr. Corey. Look here, sir. If we want polar orbit then we can dump the spent solids in the gulf waters, here, just south of the border, and—"

"You know we're not going for polar orbit," Corey said quietly. "You know what this is all about. Maximum performance of the boosters. You work on minimum orbital inclination. You slice these mothers as close to the equatorial line as it's possible to do."

"The boosters will impact in populated areas."

"So we'll kill some sheep and maybe a couple head of steer," Corey said indifferently.

"Sir, they're just as liable to come down in populated areas with *people*."

"That's not your responsibility, Sal. You stay ready, and when I say it's time to go, you launch."

"Sir, they're liable to try—hell, no, Mr. Corey," Preiss said stubbornly. "They are damned well going to try to stop the launches. And that means they'll try to come into this area. What will you tell them?"

"I won't tell them anything. We will kill those people

245

and that should discourage anyone else with the same ideas."

"Just like . . . just like that?"

"You seem to be aghast, Sal."

"I can't—I won't lie to you, Mr. Corey. Frankly, I'm amazed to hear that from you."

"Tell you what, Sal. You move your family out of here tomorrow. I don't want them or you mixed up in this. No hard feelings. And when the curtain starts coming down and this whole planet becomes a bed of coals, why, you can be real proud that you weren't involved in killing anyone who tries to stop these people we have here from getting to the moon where they will at least have a shot at surviving that dust storm waiting for us out there. Okay, Sal? I'm sure you'll feel terrific watching your kids die of heat prostration and if, just if, you understand, you have real good heat tolerance and you live a bit longer than they do, you might even be able to watch the fat melt from their bodies as the temp keeps on going up."

Sal Preiss looked like a man hung on a great steel hook with the barbed point going through the back of his neck. He didn't move, but cheek and lip and neck muscles twitched.

"I don't have time for this, Sal. When are you leaving?"

"When you say you're ready to launch, sir. When you tell me to get on one of those ships. Until then, I'll—" he swallowed, "I will do whatever you say."

"You're damned right, Sal. Nobody likes to see his kids' eyeballs sloughing down their cheeks, do they?"

Every ship that would launch, when and *only* when Russ Corey gave the word, would leave the Luke range and never return to Earth—unless the damn boosters had failed and it was falling back to crash. Any other plan would fail. One-way flights to the moon. Just enough power to get to the moon, with several minor midcourse corrections included in the fuel increment, and then that ultimate of all landings. His teams, working under Vicki Correnti, had been setting up radar and laser systems to guide the ships in. The crews would fly

246

them into curving lunar approach and they would then "lock on" to the automatic homing systems set up across a vast lunar plain. If something went wrong, everyone aboard the ship would die. It was that simple. If something went wrong that could be corrected by the pilots in the command loop, they had an excellent chance of making it.

The very first landing on the moon, way back in July of 1969 with Neil Armstrong on the controls, would have ended in a fatal disaster if the whole of the landing had been under computer automatic. Computers brought the old-fashioned Lunar Module down to the surface, but the computer was pretty damned stupid and about to drop the ungainly contraption holding Armstrong and Aldrin smack onto a huge boulder that would have toppled the ship and exploded its fuel. Armstrong took over and tweaked and nursed the controls and put them down safely with less than thirty seconds' fuel remaining in the landing module.

You didn't need more than thirty seconds. That was the game, that was the gamble. Corey knew that he might face tremendous opposition from the American government, backed by military force even he couldn't handle—if the political leadership of the country believed that his moon ships could be better used trying to save the "select few" who might use those same spacecraft to scramble aboard *Pegasus*. So Russ Corey set up his usual preparations long before the event. His ships wouldn't follow a direct lunar trajectory. Instead, their course would carry them into the same orbital plane and altitude of the huge *Pegasus* that would still be under construction. When the second-stage boosters shut down, they would be in high Earth orbit at least one hundred safe miles lower than *Pegasus*. But they'd be there for crews to move with space tugs up to *Pegasus'* orbit, and therefore they'd contribute materiel and mass to the assembling giant.

The world would believe absolutely that Russ Corey, firing out of his private Luke range, was adding to the substance and manpower of *Pegasus*. He wasn't doing any such thing. As soon as the big dumb solids were jettisoned in orbit, his flight crews would ignite the engines of the liquid-propellant stage and build to an approximate 24,500 miles an hour. There they would separate, the cargo or passenger ships to descend to a survival touchdown on the lunar surface, the big empty stage prodded by its basic but adequate computers and a few remaining small rockets to go into low lunar orbit at twenty to fifty miles above the airless mountain peaks. They'd orbit there just about forever—in human lifespan terms—and if things went well enough, it wouldn't be difficult to produce sufficient propulsion systems to retrieve their parts and pieces for use in longterm survival.

But it had to be done with exquisite timing. First, the mass propaganda campaign to convince the right people that the whole damned mission was to support the ark. If necessary, Corey had the best ace in the deck of the life-and-death poker game: there wasn't that much room on the ark. But space could be made available on the moonbound ships, *if* the men and women who were in control of political and military power went along with Russ Corey. Survival was such a sweet and simple game.

That, too, was a private touch of what he considered Corey Bullshit. Russ Corey was convinced that no one who was carried in a desperate escape attempt to board *Pegasus*—or the second ship he knew they'd build—would ever survive the flight. If the ships were completed in time to fire out of the plane of the ecliptic, up and away from the disc-shape of the vast dust cloud into which the sun plunged deeper every day, they faced a flight that at its least would be several years long—and most likely measured in decades.

Manned spacecraft didn't hold together that long. The existing shuttles had between ten and fifteen days in just Earth orbit, and those flights were riddled with problems before they ever got off the ground. Their fuel was limited, their supplies short, their power systems critically short-lived. Their systems broke down again and again, their computers ate themselves or just plain threw up; in short, they were totally dependent upon ground systems for final control and a place to return to for repair, refurbishment, resupply and often, reconstruction. The old Russian Soyuz and Salyut ships had the greatest longevity in orbit and had suffered more than their rash of mechanical measles and electronic mumps. The bigger Mir space station tested out the systems for *Gagarin*, and at best that newer station was a continuing nightmare of round-the-clock maintenance.

And now they were going to take a monster two thousand feet long with untried and untested systems, and load it up with all the necessities of life, and launch into some terrifying void with hopes of *surviving?* Their computers would break down swiftly and there'd be a limited supply of spare parts. Ventilator systems, air scrubbers, control systems, the problems of metal outgassing and corrosion and wear and tear would make the voyage a nightmare encroaching on every minute of the artificial night and day. And they'd top this off with the need to recycle food and water? And they planned to have thousands of people aboard, all of whom were supposed to obey orders and live out years in confined spaces, perhaps the entire time in weightlessness, and not puke and scream and cry and have the space heebiejeebies? Fat chance!

NASA had spent two hundred and eleven million dollars to develop a damned toilet that would work in space, and after ten years and more than a fifth of a billion dollars the damned things still jammed, clogged, and flushed backwards to dump their odoriferous contents in a nose-eyes-ears-mouth-lung-clogging stew of human waste.

Now there'd be people jammed bulkhead-to-ceiling, mass feeding problems, medical problems (God! when they started to give *birth!*), and psychological nightmares beyond all conception. No way; no way.

To Russ Corey there was only one real chance of survival. It already existed in basic form: the lunar installations. That was why he had his people drilling and gouging, setting off explosives and going for what might be considered a Lunar Mohole. Down, down, and still deeper down. If anyone was going to survive the radiation outpouring from the sun, even launching way above the plane of the ecliptic, they'd need a hell of a lot more protection against ionizing radiation than the thin walls of an overgrown space whale! There was only one way to make it through the terrible agonies waiting for the solar system.

You needed a rock into which you dug a very, very deep hole, and you pulled in that hole after you. There you would wait just as long as it was necessary while the planet a quarter of a million miles distant, that had birthed them all, screamed in its final moments and became a frozen cinder.

13

"*I* am a foolish man."

Jiro Nakamura stood with head bowed and shoulders slumped before the extraordinary meeting of the Inner Council of the Empire of Japan. Few people outside the Japanese home islands heard that phrase any more. The Empire had died in the blazing wreckage of Japan's cities, its final funereal pyres the twisting angry mushroom stalks soaring high over Hiroshima and Nagasaki. But the Japanese, the *real* Japanese who had created the enormous Empire of Nippon, never considered the war lost in the terrifying flash of two nuclear blasts that forever changed the world.

A world? *Ah, so.* The House of Nippon? *Never!* This was a war that would endure for a thousand years. There would be moments of blackness, even of devastation and defeat, but Japan would always emerge like some Oriental phoenix, gathering unto itself the glory of the ancient samurai and the power of the ancient gods. There was a strength in the past because the present was built on it.

"I am a foolish man because as one of our leaders I have ignored our traditions." Eighty-seven Japanese men listened with intense care to Jiro Nakamura's ev-

250

ery word. No women were present. Empires are not built by women, only toppled by them when they stupidly are allowed to assume power and then destroy their own institutions through bad blood and the wiles of feminine excesses. There is no such thing as a samurai warrior without balls.

"We struggle upward from the past," Nakamura continued, his head lifted slightly now as he gathered strength from stating his convictions to this distinguished body gathered deep beneath the Imperial Castle thirty miles northwest of Kyoto. "We exchanged our swords and our guns because the white man proved superior to us in battle. Superior in industry, superior in weight and numbers and armaments. We followed the ancient traditions. The industrial might of the Americans crushed us in the great fight for peace and prosperity in the Pacific and in Asia. They crushed us in the battle that ended with the sorrow of our destroyed cities. But our ancestors taught us that the secret to ultimate domination when you face a superior force is to yield, and then to utilize those same forces for your own good. We have done so. We are a small nation, yet we have matched even the American giant in industrial strength."

He paused to let his thoughts catch up with his words. He stood before his peers: scientists, political leaders, industrial giants, military men—the heart of Nippon. He wore a simple pair of cotton trousers and a cotton shirt. Nothing else. He needed nothing else. What counted now was neither pomp nor presentation but simple truth. *Reality*.

"We face a peril greater than any known in all our history," Nakamura went on abruptly. "You are all aware of this peril. The dust dragon swirling among the stars that threatens now to engulf us all. But it is not the end. It should not be permitted to be judged as the end, no matter what the scientists of the world are crying out in their fear. They are blind. They do not see or think with the wisdom of ancestors as do we. The peril we face is not fire, nor water; it is not ice or heat. *It is our own lack of faith*."

He waited for the murmuring to move among his audience like choppy small waves, then held up his hand. Tall, thin to being almost gaunt, cheeks hollowed, he seemed to gather substance and body mass before their eyes as he stirred the ancient feelings. "We must never forget that even we can be misled by our own great successes. We learned that not even our honored *kamikazes* could hold back the tidal wave of steel and fire of the Americans as they closed on our homeland a half-century ago. Then we learned how to use their own strength against them. We bettered their skills, their industry, their productivity. We never lost sight of the fact that family love and loyalty is a fierce and powerful tool of our industry." He looked about him, choosing every word carefully, building to the critical moments ahead. A slight film of perspiration glistened on his face. Nakamura made no move to wipe away the annoying droplets sliding down his skin. Maddened hornets could not have shaken his steadfastness.

"Even mice can nibble at the underpinnings of the greatest fortresses ever built. Mice with courage are preferred over the lions that retreat with cowardice. Why do I say these things?" For the first time his emotions moved along his muscles to his hands. They raised slightly, the first inkling of supplication to a higher authority he was recognizing openly. "We do not pay heed to our own history," he said with a touch of condemnation meant for himself and all before him. "We have many times before this moment faced annihilation. We teach every child that we faced the Mongol hordes and, when we had no hopes of physically withstanding the invaders set on savaging our hallowed land, we held true to our faith. Our ancestors heard us. The gods moved from heaven to earth and brought us *kamikaze.*"

A beatific expression carved his gaunt face. "The divine winds. Can anyone here doubt this divinity? Can anyone doubt the triumphant cries of our ancestors as hundreds of great enemy vessels were crushed and splintered and dragged down beneath the waters whipped to anger by the gods? Who can deny history? *We may*

forget history, but to deny it is to court ultimate disaster."
He took a deep breath, almost a sob, then went on.

"You have all heard the presentations for us to do our part to save some of the human race. The Asiatics, the Occidentals, the Negroid . . . each and every one. You have heard how we must feel ourselves honor-bound to send far into the northern stellar regions carefully selected representatives of humanity. Like diners at a sumptuous feast, the powerful government leaders shall stab their slivered forks into the writhing masses and pick here and pick there, and if Japan with its mighty engines of spaceships will behave, *if we will behave!"* his voice rang out in sudden anguish, "—then they, the round-eyes, will deliver to us their magnificence and allow a percentage of the refugees to number among them a few Japanese."

He stood head down, snapped his head erect, eyes blazing. *"Never!"* he shouted. "We cannot permit this to be so! We may not turn our backs on our ancestors! *We must not run like cowardly lions!"* Shudders wracked his frame as he struggled for control.

"We must stand like the true giants we are." He looked across the assembled faces. "Let me touch again on history. Let me remind you that the *kamikazes* of old gave us spiritual strength. At the turn of the century so long ago, the greatest fleet this world had ever known sailed around the planet to destroy us. The Russians met us at Port Arthur, and history records it all. We, the backward Japanese, destroyed the invincible Russians. We, the mongrels to the whites, met the round-eyes on their own terms. Our men fought with the courage of knowing their deaths would carry them to our gods and our ancestors. No one could stop us. Overnight all the world recognized this miracle that radiated white-hot from Japan. But victory brings with it false gods and weaknesses, and like so many others before us, we fell prey to the pride that leads all peoples to their own destruction.

"Hideki Tojo promised us the world. He promised us greatness and conquest. He told us we were invincible, and we believed him." A moment of silence for all to share the guilt of the past. "He told us we were invincible. The Empire was impregnable. We became mesmerized with our own powers. We saw in ourselves gifts that only the gods may keep. It is spoken in the Western world, and it is the Greeks who first brought us these words, that only the gods have the power to render their enemies mad before they destroy them."

His head bobbed slightly, a stuttering movement of a beaked dome atop a thin-shouldered stalk. "We also believed we had this power. We were arrogant. In the world behind us of Tojo and Yamamoto we believed we could blind the Americans with this invincibility. We would wield our ancient swords and the light of invincibility would gleam forth and destroy their energies. Ah, child's play? No. Our children play with wooden swords. We played with the lives of our people. And the gods turned their backs on us until we might once again learn truth. We came to know winds greater than any *kamikaze*. We came to know the winds born of the atom. We witnessed the deaths of a million of our men, our women, and our children in terrifying infernos *because we had come to judge ourselves as we wished the round-eyes would judge us*."

He brought up his hands slowly, the skin almost transparent, thin veins throbbing with pale blue, and he moved his fingertips across his eyes, dragging them down his cheeks and his lips so they might stir blood into his waxen face.

"Again we are being tested," he picked up slowly. "Again our ancestors and our gods move among us, whispering to our minds and our hearts to help show us the way in this new moment of peril. We are told this world is soon to die. It shall be ravaged and wracked, burned and frozen, hammered and split as the world has not known since the gods carved it from marble and fire and ice. The world will die from dust that will sorely test our sun. This is what the men of science have brought us to feed upon so we may not grow weak from the same fright that loosens their bowels.

"Oh, and they are frightened," he said with a burst of sudden energy. "They are terrified. They hold secret meetings. They call the two great ships they assemble in the sky by the names of *Pegasus* and *Noah*. *Pegasus* is a fitting name. Perhaps it shall leave behind it through trackless space a trail of celestial equine dung by which these terrified and whimpering cowards may one day return to a world they now hurry to abandon.

"Yes! To abandon! The round-eyes are feverish like rats swarming to abandon a dying vessel. This Earth! *This sphere created by the gods for man was not meant to be cast aside in a mad rush of fear!* Have there not been great storms before? Have we not known vast earthquakes? Tidal waves? The lash of the volcano? The sun twisting in its own belly from storms that spew forth a hellish inferno of particles that again and again have inundated this Earth of ours? Have we not had comets and meteorites and disease and famine and war and . . ."

He stopped in a sudden spate of exhaustion. Now he yielded to the reality of his own tired frame, and he reached for a glass of water resting on the table nearby. He took but a sip and the pink glaze left his eyes.

"Listen to me," he intoned slowly. "Listen to me, for you are the heart and soul of all Nippon. There can be no greater crime, no horror so unspeakable, as that we have all been about to commit."

Not even the stoicism of Japanese discipline could keep them unmoving now. They shifted in seats, rustled clothing and bodies, sucked air, and silently chafed for what they had assembled to hear.

"There has been dust before. There has been ashes before. And now there will be dust and ashes and fire again. The Earth will die," he hesitated a long moment, "but only if *we* ignore the gods and our ancestors and abandon our holy soil."

They were puzzled, astonished, bewildered; and Jiro Nakamura plunged into his ultimate of all calls to arms. He was the leading scientist of all Japan, the greatest mind the Orient had produced in known history. And from this mind they heard the cry of a battle unknown before in history.

"I implore you! We must defend this holy ground of

255

Nippon not against the dust from which the gods created all that exists, but against the fears the whites generate with such fury! We must defend Japan," his voice rose to a strident cry, "and we will defend this world!" Both arms shot out to his sides, fingers arched and so intense that he trembled from head to foot. *We must raise the shield of our ancestors against this new devil's work!* I implore you, all of you, to commit to the Shield. The Shield of Nippon! A powerful electromagnetic shield we shall erect here among the sacred mountains of Japan that will circle all the Earth, that will generate a force so mighty it will extend a billion miles into space! A shield to sweep dust aside as our mighty ships created bow waves where once they split the ocean waters!"

He was suddenly the scientist. "All our power, all our energy, must go into this single vast effort to place a cordon over our heads. We do not do this to save the world. They are rats tearing at their own bellies. *We are men.* We are men of Nippon and we must be worthy of our ancestors! We stand. We remain. We work, day and night from now on, to erect the machines that will generate the field. We will use nuclear energy, steam engines, hydropower, everything we have to create energy. And our prayers as well for our ancestors to assist us, to guide us, to bring the gods to show us the way."

His right arm stabbed forward. "We stay here. On our world. We do not cower in the dark of dust. We do not flee. We do not panic. We work, we fight. We will prevail."

Isoroku Tokugawa rose slowly to his feet. Instant silence met his presence. Tokugawa was no ordinary Japanese. He came from the northern island of Hokkaido, a burly man of incredible size for a Japanese, a rarity with a fierce, full beard. He wore a ceremonial robe, and the ancient curving sword of his family hung freely by his side. Slowly he placed his right hand on the jeweled hilt of the weapon and then he spoke.

"Enough talk." Two words, felt with tremendous impact in a room where he spoke for all. "Tell us what we must do." He looked about the room. Not a man doubted that a complaint would bring on a whistling song of steel as Tokugawa's sword would whip from its scabbard in search of cowardly flesh.

All eyes turned back to Nakamura. "First we commit ourselves to these islands," he said with an encompasssing gesture. "We help return to Japan our people wherever they may be in the world. They must be *here* if they are to join us and the gods."

His eyes pleaded with them to understand. "We begin to erect the shield. It will take all our energy. We begin at once. We work day and we work night. We celebrate our holidays by work. A vast undertaking demands only vast effort."

Another figure stood, white-haired, skin of olive hue, ancient and weathered. Every man in the room held his breath so this elder might speak with less strain to be heard by all. Koshiro Tanaka was ninety-two years old, a dozen wars behind him, his closest friend the macabre presence of death. He stood with a bamboo staff in one hand to support old bones, but his voice rang out with astonishing strength and harshness.

"Not enough. Work is not enough." He might have spoken directly with the gods, so certain was this elderly pillar of Nippon. "We must let the gods know. We must offer pride to our ancestors. We must commit as no others in all this troubled world can commit. Tell us, Jiro Nakamura. Tell us and we do this *now*. The gods are not spirits of patience." He remained standing, and as if by signal every man in the room rose to his feet to join Isoroku Tokugawa and Koshiro Tanaka. They stood in silence. The next words would decide the fate of more than a hundred million Japanese souls.

"We destroy the launching sites." Nakamura let his words reach his listeners. His words must settle on shoulders and move like smoke into ears until recognition appeared in eyes.

"All the launching sites. All the rockets. Every piece of machinery that can launch away from Earth, small and large. The fuel plants, the tracking stations, the control rooms. Utterly banished from existence. Then, the round-eyes will leave us alone. If we cannot help them in their frenzy, if we cannot suckle at their miserly teats in hopes of a corner of their vessels, they will leave us be. Japan will be freed from interference. This is the first step of purity. Then, and only then, do we begin. We no longer trade with our ships. We do not fly our machines to their lands. We stand together to face the devils that gather beyond this world, and that is how we will save it."

Koshiro Tanaka's bamboo staff rose and crashed against the marble floor. "Do it, then." All heads nodded in agreement.

Jiro Nakamura gestured. "That honor is for you, revered one," he said to Tanaka. "*Dozo.*"

Without a word of instruction, technicians appeared from side doors. They slid back panels at the front of the meeting hall to reveal television monitors and an elaborate computer control complex. Everyone recognized what they saw as the television monitors came to glowing life. On every one of the thirteen screens appeared the main launch areas and servicing buildings of every Japanese space center on the four main islands.

"Revered one," Nakamura looked at Tanaka, "the future awaits your hand."

Thirteen red handles jutted upward from the control board. Koshiro Tanaka walked slowly, with all the weight of his ninety-two years moving with him. Finally he stood before the first of the thirteen red handles. In that moment he was the personification of all that was the glory and the grandeur, the dignity and the strength of the long and turbulent history of Japan. Here, seemingly carved at this instant in mahogany with the mane of white atop his head, was the living personification of *hagakure*. Honor first and always above all.

He shrugged off the hands so eager to support him. Staff in his left hand, he reached to grasp the red handle before him. His fingers closed with astonishing strength for the old muscles and sinew. Koshiro Tanaka closed his eyes and met with all the ancestors of the past. His eyes opened, clear and fresh and seeing with the clarity the gods give only to their favored few.

He pulled the handle down and toward him. The circuitry in the board closed. The electrical signal flashed away from the underground chamber near Kyoto, the ancient capital of Nippon, and whipped through a thick cable southward to a microwave antenna standing on a high hilltop of southern Kyushu. The signal flashed with the speed of light outward from the parabolic antenna to a receiving dish high above Tanegashima Island. Here sprawled the Osaki Launch Site of the Tanegashima Space Center. Again the signal went through reception and redistribution within the Tanegashima complex. Electrical relays clicked, solenoids thudded against their stops, and thick packages of molded plastique instantly changed their molecular structure, to become savage heat sourcepoints of many thousands of degrees.

The Tanegashima Space Center erupted simultaneously from one hundred and twelve separate detonation points. Fuel farms exploded in monstrous fireballs, cryogenic farms shattered, fuel lines exploded up and outward from the ground and through the air. Assembly buildings, launch towers, fueling facilities, control rooms, tracking stations; all the myriad elements of assembly that together create a highly intricate functioning launch complex . . . vanished. In the fury bursting outward, Tanegashima became a slaughterhouse of twisted, torn, and flaming wreckage.

Koshiro Tanaka moved slightly to his right to stand before the second red handle. His right hand went up, his fist closed, and his hand came back toward him and down. The vast Rocket Engine Test Center of Kakuda, one hundred and sixty miles north of Tokyo in the valley regions at the foor of Mt. Zao, famed for its magnificent skiing center, transformed instantly into a series of explosions that became a single coalescing fireball that boomed skyward like a small nuclear blast.

The Tashiro Field Laboratory of Mitsubishi . . .
The great Aioi spacecraft factory . . .
The Tseubabeni Technical Center . . .

Mitsubishi's enormous Melco Spacecraft Works in both Tokyo and Osaka . . .

The Kita-Itami Space Sciences Center near Tokyo. . .

Every Japanese industrial, research, assembly, production, testing and launch center . . .

exploded.

14

"**O**h, God, I'm scared. Jeremy, *do something*. Please do something!" Sarah Bleddington clung desperately to the arm of Jeremy Gold, her partner from the data control system deep within the Goddard Space Flight Center. Greenbelt, Maryland, was quiet, rolling-hills countryside, home of NASA's data operations and research programs. Not any more. On this night, fires blazed in the countryside. Frightened mobs had overturned and torched police cars, fire trucks, and the vehicles of hapless innocents caught in the turbulent fury of frightened people led by diehard rabble rousers. There are some people who thrive on power, who thirst for it with devilish ferocity. They lack the true qualities of leadership. They are cunning rather than wise, sly rather than intelligent, and have all the instincts of a hungry fox wooing a nest of fledgling birds.

Zack Bible was one such man. He thirsted for power as a parched survivor of a desert trek slavers at the mental image of a cold foaming beer—or would slaver if any spit remained in his mouth behind cracked lips. Zack Bible had spent a lifetime preaching and thumping, shouting and screaming and exhorting frightened rednecks and dull-witted Baptists so that these droplets in the wastebuckets of American society would at least keep Zack Bible in bed and board. Now he led a huge force of frightened, drunken, crazed citizenry across the Maryland countryside in search of government space installations. He did so with extraordinary cunning. He made certain not to heave his assault against a launching center or a military bastion where he would face the dragons' teeth of professional armed forces that would cut his wild-eyed screamers to bloody chunks.

Oh, no; not Zack Bible, to whom God had finally responded after years of prayers, imprecations, curses and promises for the deliverance that would permit Bible to lead his people—whoever they might be at that moment—in the Good Search to serve the Lord. Now it was here. *Here!* In the past the Lord God had left His sign in so many ways. Locusts and famines, floods and droughts, disease and war and storms, and all the violence and havoc had taught man not a thing. Now God was through with the overt warnings, the hell and the destruction. Now He was giving man this one last chance, a sign from On Highest that He could signal with quiet dignity, with even this tenuous airbrush that whispered in space. Could there be any clearer evidence than this sighing of dust through God's ocean of vacuum? How could anyone doubt! No mountains grinding or oceans colliding or fiery comets ripping thunderously through splitting atmosphere. Just countless trillions of dust motes swirling and colliding in space yet making no more sound than the collision of two measly little snowflakes coming together in some Arctic night.

God was telling man to clean up his filthiness of despoiling his planet. It was long past time to end the worship of false idols. Rampant immorality and the hideous crime of abortion offended Him beyond all patience. Sodom and Gomorrah had been Easter picnics compared to the atrocities man committed day and night against the Holy Father who had created this world. *This was the final warning*, and He was giving that warning in the most gentle manner man could possibly imagine. And what was man doing?

Interpreting the word of God in the same old way, strictly from greed and covetousness, self-centered and selfish. Escape the world, indeed! God had created the world and the suns and the dust in space. He had laid down the mantle of motes to tell man, to beg of man, that he see the myriad error of his ways. If he did so, if man rejected the sins that twisted his mind and made slime of all that was good—why, that would be the act of faith God had waited for these many horrible centuries.

All that was needed was an act of faith. In the idiom so popular to the world, knew Zack Bible, that was easily interpreted as "cleaning up your act." That was all man needed to do. Reject sin and embrace morality. Cast out Satan and throw his arms wide to accept the Lord. *If he did that he need do nothing else to achieve salvation. The dust had always been there in space! Did mere man judge himself so highly that he believed God must work overtime to arrange everything on so colossal a celestial scale?*

God had no intention of destroying man or the world God had created in such incredible abundance that from only Adam and Eve there would grow a planet of many billions. He had given Man free will long before this moment and now, in a final moment of heavenly sorrow, He was once again offering the choice to man.

Believe in me and ye shall endure, and again ye shall prosper and wax with the good things in life. Reject me this last time and I will turn my back, and the world shall slide into the pit that has always been there in the void between the globes in the sky.

"All we got to do," Zack Bible said with absolute certainty, "is to stop shitting on the world that God gave to us. That is *all*. If we do that, if we respect our Lord, why, this little old planet will slide right through that there dust cloud in space like a burning knife right through butter."

But it didn't happen that way. Zack Bible was thunderstruck with man's audacity, the insufferable ego, the monumental love of self. Build a ship, *an ark*!, to ride out the dust storm in space. Could there be anything *dumber* than *that?* Oh, they could build the ship, even two of them, like they were right now. *Pegasus* and *Noah*. Even in their self-glorification he could understand using the name *Noah*, but the final insult was to name the main ship after a mythological creature of Greece, a nation that had shamed the world with its blatant homosexuality, that practiced the buggery of young boys by doddering old men, and passed on that hideous atrocity to the rest of the world that so stupidly twisted and distorted the sexual love God had created for man.

And where in Hell did they think those two stupid spaceships were going to go? The question answered itself. They would be launching straight to *Hell*. The netherworld of Satan didn't exist in the bowels of the planet, of *any* planet. Satan and his devils hovered invisibly about the minds of men, a sickly invisible fog working relentlessly, always, to invade through the nostrils and the ears and the mouth and take possession first of the mind and then of the soul itself. Did these fools really believe that by making this idiotic flea jump upward from the world that they would escape a retribution handed down so sadly by their Lord and Creator? God must be sad, judged Zack Bible, and the Devil must be laughing even more hysterically than on that heartbreaking day when he was welcomed into the Garden of Eden.

Well, by God and by damn, he'd show the Lord that not *all* men thought so poorly of their Creator. And if he could rally enough support to this final and holiest of all missions, then there was a chance, as thin as the most watery of gruel, that God might take notice of *some* of His children, who believed in Him enough to throw everything they had into the faith that their Lord would sustain them through their moralistic actions.

There was only one way. *Stop the ships*. Go after the control centers, the devil's own handiwork. Get to the launching sites scattered like dragonseed through much of the world, and enter with fire and fury and destruction. Kill. *Kill* swiftly and fully all those who would flaunt the Lord. Their deaths meant nothing. Were they not going to die soon enough if the Devil held sway and a handful of humanity scurried like rats to a ship that would sink in the ocean of ultimate dust?

Zack Bible was a huge man. He was big everywhere. He had big legs and big arms and a thick neck and a treetrunk torso and an oversized head with bulging eyes. He had never been seen without a florid expression on his face, waving his huge hands and stomping size-fourteen shoes, and he had a stentorian voice to match. In the backwater, horrid little town of Seviche on Route 17 in eastern Florida, where long ago time had stopped and the local populace had forever dabbled—hell, they'd plunged!—into miscegenation because they didn't know no better and it's God's truth that a hardon just ain't got no conscience worth a toot. Seviche had more slack-jawed first-cousin, sister-brother couplings, to say nothing of daddies and their wives and kids of both sexes getting in some, too, than the rest of the whole damned state of Florida. Zack Bible, and that was by God his real name, stormed into this serpent's den wearing a rumpled minister's suit and a stained collar, clutching a large sweat-spotted and worn leather-covered Bible, and both scared the living hell out of the town and intrigued its womenfolk, most of whom would have as gladly sported naked in the bushes with a wild boar as with their menfolk, who didn't really smell a lick better.

If there was one thing Zack Bible could do, it was get people to his church. Seviche had been without one since it was torched by blacks pissed off as all hell from local Klan outings hunting down dark meat, so Bible kicked in the door of the small old theater that also had been shut down forever, and he swore and did some more kicking and got a bunch of scraggly old-timers to sweep and mop and get rid of the cobwebs and dead animal skeletons and years of droppings. He came in; snorting and thumping with a magnificent revivalist outpouring. If he could have spoken without scorching the words of God he'd have been a smash hit on national television. As it was, he built an immediate and tremendous following in the poor country of central Florida, and the local politicians and businessmen jumped on his bandwagon, because if Zack Bible stood up on his pulpit and said that Jerry Brown by God ran the most honest hardware store by God in the whole sin-rotten state, then you by God bought at Jerry's Hardware. Fire and sulphur and brimstone, and he gave out a warm and helping hand to the lonely folk who'd had no one to go to and made them see the light. This screwing of your brothers and sometimes your daddy and all them cousins was in the past, y'hear? To show them the light, Zack Bible—who was just as big with that weapon hanging between his legs over steer-sized ballocks— provided the ladies (purely out of unselfishness and to protect them against sinful stirrings) with enough godliness to keep them both pregnant and happier than clams stuck in each other's shells.

His word spread quickly, to Bithlo and Frontenac and Christmas and all sorts of small towns to the south and the west. He reached out to Kissimmee, which was still backwater country but now surrounded by that goddamned mouseland and them huge whoring hotels with the fancy names and the painted women. He got onto a small Christian radio station in Kissimmee and he knew this was his chance, the moment to grab the golden goose and jab him hard under both wingpits and get that honking son of a bitch to lay some golden eggs. Zack Bible figured he might get only this one shot at reaching out to *someone* who might take up his cause, because sure as the Lord grew all them orchards with green apples, his own congregation couldn't even hardly read nor write, let alone what Zack Bible had to say about polluting the purity of space.

Well, the good Lord does play His cards in some strange ways, and heaven must have heard the deep honesty of this poor man, because when Zack Bible took the microphone in his hand he cut every which way but loose. The local minister who owned the station tried to cut Zack off the air, and likely it was the only radio broadcast ever done where the man shouting into the microphone held the station owner in a headlock of muscular steel, half-killing him in the process, but *nothing* was going to interfere with this special moment God gave to Zack Bible.

"God ain't gonna stand for this defilement we has all been doing to His heavens!" shouted Zack Bible behind the locked studio door with the gagging, half-choked-to-death station owner. "For years they been calling all this space stuff they doing to be science, all for the good of mankind, and you *know* it's a damn lie! You think that space station up there, or when them big shuttles fly, is nothin' but pushin' buttons and turnin' knobs and lookin' at all them fancy teevee tubes? Better believe in the Devil, because there's more truth in Lucifer than all these lies! There's all them menfolk and those women snugged together in them little cabins up in them ships and them stations, that's what! You know what menfolk and women do when they all snugged up! What the hell *else* they gonna do? They got no place to go. Man, you just can't step outside and look at the scenery, now, can you? They got this here zero gravity, they say, but how you can have something when you call it *zero* is mystifyin' to both God and nature."

His booming voice and deep intensity and the strange strangling sounds all had their effect, and suddenly wherever people could hear Zack Bible the televisions were going off and as quick as neighbors could call one another the radios were coming *on*.

"I'll tell you what they is doing up there over our heads! They are in God's own heaven, sailing through His space, and what they are doin' up there is *fornicating*." He said it again to drag the word right through his microphone and through the wires and right out of all those radio sets out there. "Forn-i," it sounded like *eh*, "cat-ing," and everyone listening felt the impact of the g. Oh, Zack Bible was an instinctive pro and he knew he had his finest moment at hand and that at any moment they might bust down the glass doors to the studio, so he made sure his hand was close to the big switchblade knife in his pocket, which he would just hold close to the throat of this here station manager, not intendin' to *hurt* him, you understand, but just to let him do God's work and give out the word.

"There they are, flyin' right over our heads, right over all of God's churches and all the good folk, and shamelessly, without a care in the world, buck naked, they is flying through all that space and they is *fornicating*. In them cabins they are rutting like two hogs in a holler. Let me tell you good folk something. Let me tell you what the Lord calls what they is doing. It ain't no damned zero gravity! *It be zero morality!*" He choked back a very audible sob and his tears near to squeezed through the radio speakers. "Zero morality! They keep sayin' to us that way up there in space they is no up or down, and you know, *you know*, you can't rut and fornicate without going up and down, and up and down, until it like to make the good Lord Hisself sick."

He switched tones like to pressing a button and his voice calmed and deepened and he was giving out *the word*. "A long time ago God give us a warning. Now, He most surely did just that. All you got to remember is those three young men who died in that there Apollo fire on the launch pad, them names you should never forget, because God burned up Grissom and White and Chaffee as a warning to the rest of us. And we wouldn't listen nohow. So to be sure we got the word, He scarificed some of them Roosian fellers. Killed a whole bunch of them, but that really didn't matter, because them Roosians is a bunch of heretics anyway and they claim there ain't no God, but they got to believe in *something*, so's I suspects, and I am sure God *knows* they are all in league with Lucifer. But He burned up three nice young white fellers, right here in Florida, and did we listen? *No!*"

Another sob, the perfectly-timed pause, and on he went. "Then He gave us a lesson we could never forget. He put it on teevee all over the world and we sent that sinful *Challenger* shuttle into space with men and women, and even a black man to fornicate with them young white women! And God was so upset with what we was doing that He really brought the hammer down, He did. They was seven in that ship, and God, He blew up and burned and chawed up them seven people and He made them suffer all the way down, from way to hell on high, keeping them alive to reflect on their sins before He smashed them all up when they hit *His* ocean.

"That wasn't no accident! That was a warning for the rest of us to stay the hell put where we belong! Right here on this Earth God gave to us. Ain't the world

267

enough? Ain't there enough land? Ain't there enough water? He even give us a whole ocean of air so we could fly like birds. Ain't *that* enough?

"Hell, no, it ain't! Oh, no, we has to be greedy and we has to interfere with His plans for other worlds, and it's Satan's work and it's all that zero morality—"

He never had the chance to say another word over the air. The night DJ had just come on duty and frantic station employees screamed their panic to him, and Jesse Holcum went up the station stairs two at a time, banged on the glass door, and drew his forefinger across his throat to signal Zack Bible to just cut it right there, man. Bible gave him a finger signal in return, an upward-extending middle finger, and he grinned at the people on the other side of the glass and squeezed the neck and head of the semi-conscious station owner just a bit tighter. Jesse Holcum wasn't a stranger to redneck conduct, being from a respectable three-generation Florida redneck family himself, and very calmly he withdrew a long-barreled .357 Magnum from his boot, because he *never* traveled the back Kissimmee roads without that piece, and with a single deafening shot he blew away the lock to the door and destroyed a radio control panel beyond, and he stepped inside the broadcasting booth and smiled broadly at the astonished look on Zack Bible's face. Jesse Holcum put the .357 muzzle against the side of Bible's head.

"The next word, mister, is your last. That's a promise. Now you let go that poor man and you turn that switch to off, right there, ah, that's it." Bible let the poor man go and he switched off the microphone and five minutes later the night crew had him so wrapped up in heavy electrical tape he looked like an overgrown Egyptian ready for premature burial.

"My name is Benjamin P. Stryker, and the P stands for Perspective, which is what my daddy named me so I might never forget that whatever a man does in this life, he'll never lose sight of God above or true values down here on earth. Don't be misled by my name, Reverend—" Stryker stared at Zack Bible, who looked like hell after a night in a slammer cell filled with vomiting, moaning, pissing drunks. Stryker had bailed him out and driven him in his pickup truck to the old-fashioned restaurant on the highway that, if you stayed put on the concrete, would lead you straight to one of them whoring palaces by Disney country.

"What do they call you? Reverend? Father? Pastor? What?" Stryker asked.

"Reverend will do fine." Bible wolfed down breakfast and sucked up coffee like a tornado funnel. He swallowed a huge mouthful of eggs and bacon, his right cheek puffed way out like the third week of one hellacious toothache. "I don't mean to seem, well, ungrateful, Stryker—"

"*Mister* Stryker," Bible heard, and the tone told him more than anything else. "It will *always* be *Mister* Stryker." Stryker smiled, and Bible had the sudden idea he was seated deep within a scorpion nest. "Trust to your instincts, Reverend," he heard in that same quiet voice. "Don't be misled by these farmer's clothes or that pickup truck. Your bail this morning was thirty thousand dollars. I paid it in cash. I could have bailed out a hundred like you from my petty cash. I also could have sent down any one of a dozen lawyers or even had the sheriff release you with no more than a phone call. Understand that, never forget it, and trust to your instincts as to what I really might be able to do."

Bible's knife and fork went down slowly to his plate. He finished a long gulp of coffee and wiped his mouth very carefully. Never let it be said that Zack Bible's mother raised a dummy.

"Yes, sir," he told the man seated across from him. "What can I do for you, *Mister* Stryker?"

"Specifically, I want to help you carry your message. That bit of zero morality," Stryker said, smiling—and Bible knew there wasn't anything even touching humor behind it—"now, that's pure genius. My own phrase was always outercourse, all that fornication in space, you understand. But this zero morality, that cuts it right to the bone."

"Yes, sir," Zack Bible said, and it was a minor miracle to itself that the Biblical Mouth of the South was keeping a very tight zip on his lip.

"I want you to lead the people," Stryker went on. "I'll buy you time on radio and television. I'll get you on video so we can repeat what you have to say over and over, day and night. And I want some giant, old-fashioned revivals, and I want you to say just what you're saying now. Whip up the people, Reverend. Whip 'em. Fire up their righteous indignation, scare the absolute living hell out of them."

Zack Bible beamed. *Hey, God, you listening? Thank you!* "Yes, *sir!*" he said to *Mister* Benjamin Perspective Stryker.

"Just about that time when you'll have an enormous following," Stryker went on, and it became instantly clear he'd had his ideas in mind for a long time, "things will be coming to a head with this space ark business. I don't want it to happen, Reverend. I don't want those ships to fly away from Earth like they're planning. I want those people to stay here and die like the rest of us."

"Well, now," Bible said, shifting in his seat and eyeing an apple pie on the serving counter, "I'm sure you *heard* what I had to say last night, and I'm real proud to be serving a man who believes as I do, and—"

"You ever hear of Jack Stephenson?"

Bible went instantly alert. The way this man had cut in on him, stopping the bullshit before it even had a chance to flow, said mountains. Whatever was coming down, this Stryker was offering him the opportunity of a dozen lifetimes, and now was time to pay attention. "No, sir, I haven't."

"He's one of the shuttle astronauts. A very rugged, good-looking type of man. All American. A regular Lothario as well."

"Yes, sir."

"I'm sixty-four years old, Reverend. I have a very beautiful wife who was twenty-three. I was very devoted to Phyllis."

"*Was*, sir?"

"She took up with this Stephenson fellow. The hero.

270

He seduced her. I didn't know about it. I would never have known about it except for that he gave her syphilis. I wouldn't have known about it except for the fact that she gave it to me. I haven't been with another woman for six years. She gave it to me. I gave her everything and she gave me a vicious venereal disease. Of course I've been rid of it for a long time now."

"And your, uh, wife—"

"I killed her, of course. God's will was given to me for her crime of adultery, only one of many."

Bible nodded rapidly. "I agree with you, sir."

"I don't want that astronaut to make it, Reverend. I don't want *any* of them to make it. So you start your sermons. You preach your damned heart out. You get the hell out of that pissy little town you're in and you come back here to Orlando. By tomorrow I'll have you a church and a congregation of ten thousand people for starters. You whip them up, boy, y'hear? Whip 'em up and get fire in their bellies, and when the time is right, you go for the jugular."

"Yes, sir, and how would that be done as you see it, Mister Stryker?"

Stryker looked surprised, glanced about him and leaned forward. "Not *here*," he hissed.

That was eight months past. Stryker kept his word. Reverend Zack Bible was a household word across America. His voice and his words reached out through all the world. Millions of people were frightened by him and they adored him. He could whip up a gathering of a hundred thousand people anywhere he wanted and any time of the week. Which is just what he was doing on this particular night in the rolling-hills countryside near Greenbelt, Maryland. Stryker had said that *when* was *now*, and sent Bible northward to test his mettle under fire—with fire and fury. Well, he couldn't have picked a better place. Hell, they didn't have no rockets here at this Goddard place. Just a lot of antennas and fancy buildings with big windows and pretty lights and real big parking lots. Their security force was a couple of guards with handguns and that wasn't worth a shit.

271

Still, this was a federal installation and there wasn't no use in taking chances.

"Tod, you get in there first with your people," he told one of his team leaders. "You work for Southern Bell so you knows just what to do. Cut all the lines, knock out them microwave towers and whatever other antenna you can find. I don't want these people in there calling for help." Bible turned to another man. "Zeb, can you handle their water supply?"

Zeb was another old-timer who knew his way around his chosen field. "Two big towers," he said brusquely. "Three main pipelines. I cut them and all they got left is a trickle. They couldn't put out a bonfire then."

"Where are the people with the flamethrowers?" Bible asked, looking about him. Several men and women in trucks with steel plating for shields held up their hands. Each truck was a rolling tanker with a high-pressure nozzle that could shoot an inferno of fire two hundred feet.

Bible checked the rest. Tens of thousands of people with rifles, shotguns, axes, hammers, pitchforks, clubs, and bats, likkered up. Bible climbed into the right seat of a Land Rover with its top down and a thirty-caliber machine gun mounted in the back. He stood up. He felt godlike. Power surged through him. He trembled from the excitement and the sheer enormity of so many thousands following him, looking upon him as a deity in his own right. He struggled to rid himself of such thoughts, but they persisted. He forced everything from his mind but the moment. He reached to his belt and withdrew his sceptre, that marvelous device one of his engineers had made for him. A tube, at the end of which flowered a bejeweled crown, each precious gem the receiving station of a laser system mounted within the tube. He turned on the switch and power surged and the crown of the sceptre lit up in dazzling glory, brighter than an airliner's flashing strobe. He needed only to hold aloft his sceptre and nod to his driver. The Land Rover started forth and the immense human tidal wave followed.

A battery of two trucks went in first. At full speed

into the main entrance, tearing it to splintered wreckage, jamming far inside, the men in the trucks killing every guard visible. A flame-throwing tanker took each side of the main building, its blazing shaft of fire as powerful as a high-pressure water hose, smashing in windows and doors from the first through the sixth floors, transforming the headquarters building into a blazing inferno. The water towers came down with devastating impact, every communications system went dead, and hundreds of crazed men and women with deadly weapons pounded into the computer labs, the control rooms, every room and system they could find. The death toll went up with incredible speed.

"Oh, God, I'm scared. Please, *please*. Jeremy, do something! My God, if they find us they'll—"

Jeremy Gold held his hand over Sarah Bleddington's mouth. He knew how terrified she was. He was scared to death himself. They could hear the thudding of doors being smashed, of explosives booming dully in the distance. They heard the flames, and the horrible screams of the men and women who staffed the Goddard center being murdered wherever they were found. Jeremy had run with Sarah through a side corridor within the computer banks. He knew a storeroom that hardly anybody knew about. It didn't even have a door, just a sliding panel. It was here they'd kept the secret tapes of Project Dustbin for so long before the story got out. Now he huddled with Sarah in the secret room. "Be quiet, *please*," he begged her. They both heard footsteps pounding closer and closer. "They don't know we're here, Sarah. Just stay quiet. Don't talk, don't move, please, for God's sake, don't say anything and—"

The sliding panel snapped open and brilliant light stabbed in. Sarah screamed as she clutched frantically at Jeremy, who looked up in fear and amazement at the huge figure with the blazing sceptre in one hand. In the other he held a fistful of woman's hair, dragging a bloody caricature of what had been a woman. One eye of her bloodied face was gone, trailing a gooey string down her cheekbone. The rest was covered in gore. "I

. . . I'm sorry," she choked out. "They . . . they made me . . . they made me tell . . ." She was flung aside. A man and a woman stood behind the wild-eyed man in black.

"Kill her," he said offhandedly. A shot rang out and brains and blood and skullbone sprayed the air.

Jeremy Gold tried desperately to shield Sarah with his own body. The big man laughed as he leaned forward and swung the sceptre at Jeremy's head. It split his cheek open to the bone and ripped away a chunk of ear. The sceptre swung past and came back with renewed force into Jeremy's mouth, slashing flesh, spraying teeth over the floor and the terrified Sarah. The big man reached down, grabbed the semiconscious Jeremy by the throat and hurled him like an empty sack behind him and out of the room. He turned to the people with him. "Leave me with this one," he said with the touch of a smile. "She is the devil's handmaiden, the keeper of the secrets that flaunt God's works. She must be taught that women like her are here to serve us. She must have her lesson before she dies."

Sarah Bleddington tried to scream as the Reverend Zack Bible snapped open his trousers and revealed an enormous penis. No one behind Bible had left. The woman licked her lips. "Let me hold her," she said, and Bible nodded. They tore away Sarah's clothes and threw her down on the dead woman and the unconscious form of Jeremy Gold and Zack Bible tore into her and tore her open, bleeding like a screaming stuck pig. Bible thrust like a maddened stallion, beating Sarah's face with one fist until she was no longer recognizable. He finished with a shattering lunge, screaming like a madman. He withdrew slowly and closed his trousers as he turned to the men with him.

"She's still alive," he told them. "She hasn't any teeth left. You better use her together. You have fifteen minutes and then this haven of Lucifer goes up."

He turned and left without a glance. The sounds of the choking girl meant nothing to him. Now he knew what *real* power was like. Now it was time to return to the south for the true measure of God's bidding. The first stop would be at Wallops Island in Virginia. Not a big launch site, but big enough. He smiled as he strode powerfully down the corridor, past the bodies crumpled like rag dolls. He felt he resembled the great conquerors of the past. He thought of the launch site in Virginia. He didn't give a damn about their rockets.

There would be more young ones like this girl to teach a lesson.

He tilted his head back slightly as if he could see through the ceiling and far beyond. His lips moved to his silent thoughts.

Thank you, God.

15 ———

Washington, D.C.

"I'm afraid not," she said. Felicity Xavier Powell toyed with the stem of her wine glass, her eyes downcast, looking vacantly for the moment at the curving lines of hand and glass as she reviewed a thousand possibilities. She brought up her head slowly, still physically childlike, still concealing behind that innocent facade the backbone of steel and rapier-like mind. For this single moment she basked in the pure luxury of the room paneled in Brazilian rosewood, adorned with masterful lighting and world-renowned paintings. Even the fireplace seemed from some marvelous Dickens work in this very private retreat of Russ Corey, and the fact that the waiters and the valets and the waitresses, so splendidly attired and meticulous in their manners, were all skilled professional killers and bodyguards. For *their* protection, Felicity knew. In this charming section of the national's capital and its rows of four-story brownstones, not even the anonymity of look-alike buildings could assure your safety in a world on the edge of madness.

Felicity Xavier looked up with a thin, sad smile on

her childlike face. What a shame, she thought. George and Martha Starling; two more splendid human beings had never existed. Theirs was a union carved sumptuously in heaven, theirs was a melding to stand as a shining example to the rest of the human race. And she knew that not very much longer from this moment they would die. *And so will I*, she added to herself as an afterthought. She shook herself clear of this maudlin nonsense afflicting her thoughts. This wasn't doing anybody any good.

"I'm afraid not," she repeated to keep her conversation clarified. "I've met with the real power behind the scenes at the U.N., and they are divided into three categories." The Starlings watched her with the aplomb of people well accustomed to news of idle society gossip or shattering import, with no change in their facial expressions. Russ Corey watched her with the barest touch of a smile in his craggy face, but his eyes still bedeviled and upset her. Yet the man was clearly warm to her. For the moment she ignored the others, knowing they would be affording her their full attention. She concentrated on her report of matters at the United Nations.

"The first group believes *me*," she said, unable to contain her smile. "Ever since I stormed out of the meeting with you, George," she addressed the president directly, "I've gathered a following that is convinced everything the scientists say about the Earth being consumed is so much sensationalistic rot, or a plot by us and the Russians to dominate the planet, or," she shrugged, "for some nefarious reason or reasons. Whatever the reasons, they feel it's a farce, stupidity, or a clever plan they can't yet figure out, and they won't have a thing to do with the plans for the great ships."

"And the second group?" Martha Starling asked.

"Oh, they hate me," Felicity Xavier said. "With a passion, I might add. I am the devil's mistress—"

"Good for you," Russ Corey offered, his smile a touch more pronounced. She bowed her head briefly to acknowledge the rare compliment. "And as the devil's mistress," she went on to the group, "I am the anti-Christ determined to foil the plans of good men who wish to preserve the human race and its history until such time as the Earth emerges from the great dust storm of space and once again becomes habitable for man."

"*If* it ever does," growled a husky voice from the other side of the dinner table. That pithy comment came from General Harold Benjamin Eisenberg, known to his staff as "Old Jutjaw."

"Hal, I asked you to hold arguments for later," the president chided him gently. Eisenberg bit down hard on a black cigar, shifted angrily in his seat, and obeyed his commander-in-chief by lapsing back into sullen silence.

"What about the third group?" the president queried Felicity Xavier.

"Numb," she answered brusquely. "Minds turned off, feelings turned off. The ostrich complex. Don't believe it, don't think about it, don't worry about it, ignore it, screw it," she finished with a snap to her voice. "They constitute the majority of the world. Most of the world doesn't even begin to understand what's happening. The idea is to keep them in sufficient confusion so they'd rather eat, drink, and copulate to their heart's content—"

"A primal urge? Instinctual conception for the future?" asked Martha Starling. Felicity looked at her friend and they both broke out in laughter. "It could be," Felicity answered noncommittally, "but what really matters is that they are not interfering with getting the ships ready in time."

Russ Corey gestured with a brandy snifter. "That wasn't any accident, now, was it?" he asked warmly. "In fact, I've never seen more *non*-interference. How did you manage it?"

Felicity Xavier felt a touch of pride from being addressed in this manner by Russ Corey. *He*, of all people. The Darth Vader of the president's inner circle. She knew much more of Corey than the man might ever imagine and she held him in awe as she did no other man. *Damn; stay with the subject*, she snapped at herself.

"The starting point was my storming out of the big conference at the White House," she related. "First, we had the attention of people sworn to silence whom we knew could never keep that silence. It's the old Washington story. Nothing here travels faster than a secret. Then we managed the open political split. I dropped the hammer, so to speak, on Arthur Kimberly. Like everything else, that was carefully arranged. We had enough doom-and-gloom scientists so that my voice wasn't needed. But what we did need was as much emotional stability as possible. No one really wants to believe they are utterly insignificant and they'll be snuffed out by a few trillion tons of dust. They want *not* to believe the worst. And I do have plenty of ammunition, of course. The comets, solar storms, the Jupiter effect. The old bit of slow down because the future is slippery when wet. Or dusty," she said drily. "Anyway, that was the basic plan, and then we implemented it. That's where Martha," she nodded to the first lady, "came in. *Her* contacts were critical."

Corey raised an eyebrow, and the military trio at the other side of the table also came a touch more alert. Martha Starling was lovely, social, witty, charming, even brilliant, but never involved. Felicity Xavier and Martha made eye contact and their smiles were barely noticeable. They were very good at having people believe what they wished them to believe.

"Television," said Martha Starling. "That was the real key. The world has come to believe in what they see and hear on television, especially if its repeated often enough. Didn't you wonder," she addressed her question to Corey, "how many new TV sets became available all about the world for the fabulous price of twenty-nine ninety-five? New germanium and silicon chip breakthroughs, we said. Plastic instead of glass. We employed a great deal of rah rah in this. Our biggest problem wasn't selling the sets, but in setting up production throughout the world so there wouldn't be a monumental distribution block."

"I made a small contribution. McElroy was my key," the president contributed to the explanation. "We did it by offering some really whiz-bang balance-of-trade deals. We, in short, lost our financial keisters on it. Everybody figured they were really giving us the shaft. So they bit, and that did two things. Because we were underwriting the dollar costs, they went into immediate production. They could also sell those new sets on credit. They were just about giving them away." He held up one finger. "First, that accomplished what Martha and Felicity wanted. Tremendous television reception throughout the world in the shortest possible time. Since we'd use direct comsat downlink broadcast we had no concern about electrical distribution in remote areas." A second finger went up. "Second, the very fact we were throwing all that money into long-term financial agreements convinced foreign governments and business leaders that this country was in business for the long haul. Why bother with long-term profits when you expect to be destroyed?"

"And," his wife added quickly, "we were then in position to have Felicity tear into the doomsayers with the greatest possible audience. If nothing else, it placed the scientists' warning of death and destruction in serious question."

General Eisenberg motioned to the president. "Sir, may I break in?"

Starling made certain not to smile at his four-star general. "Of course, Hal."

Eisenberg turned to Felicity Xavier. "Ma'am, tell me, after you managed to get all those television receivers where you wanted them around the world, what good did it do us?"

"Why, General, I've already explained that. If enough people *dis*believe in world destruction, they won't be rushing into fearful anarchy. People *do* react that way. When faced with destruction, they wreak their own destruction." Felicity Xavier sighed. "That's not simply phychological nonsense, either. It's *history*. It's the games people play."

"What I don't understand," Eisenberg persisted, "is

279

why people would believe you—and ma'am, I'm not being pushy on this, but why should they believe *you*—"

"A woman," she said quietly.

"That, too," Eisenberg said flatly and without hesitation. "In foreign countries, especially. I know women have led Israel and India, but sure as hell, beg pardon, most of the world believes what the men tell them and not their ladies. So how did you manage to keep everybody from tearing up their turf just by talking about it?"

Felicity Xavier nodded to Martha Starling. "We cheated, General," the first lady said. "We led them to believe anything we wanted. Subliminal messages in all the tapes, both visual and aural. Every show that went out, from news to sitcom to cartoons to soaps, *everything*, told them everything was fine, the future's great, eat well, make babies, laugh and be merry. They had no choice but to believe. Their own collective subconscious was telling them that."

"You see, their thinking is absolutely tied to video," Felicity Xavier explained further. "That's the world lifestyle. The tube is getting dangerously close to being their Godpoint. What we needed to develop even further was this voice and sight. What we managed to do was to establish a direct umbilical link between their skulls and those television sets. It's like feeding them drugs. They're hooked and they have stayed calm." She frowned. "Unfortunately, it doesn't work everywhere. We weren't able to achieve the same results in this country. Too strong a free video press, too much independent management, too wide a competitive base. But for most of the world, it's worked."

"I'll be damned." Hal Eisenberg leaned back in his seat and drummed strong fingers on the table. His face showed open admiration for the two women. "I will be damned," he repeated.

A chuckle came from Russ Corey. "That you will be, General. Like the lady said, her program doesn't work in this country."

Hal Eisenberg had never liked Russ Corey. "And what the hell is that supposed to mean?"

Corey glanced at the president. "He doesn't know?"

Starling shook his head. "I was going to tell him right after brandy."

"Tell me *what?*" Eisenberg demanded.

"A mob estimated at a hundred thousand strong destroyed the Goddard center tonight," Starling said calmly. "The local authorities and state police did their best to break up the mob—"

"Sir, excuse me," Corey broke in. "That was an *army.* Not a mob. It was led under a very careful plan."

"True," Starling acknowledged. "Thank you, Russ. In fact, General," he turned back to Eisenberg, "it was led by a religious fanatic. His name is Bible."

"Appropriate," Felicity Xavier said acidly.

"How bad is it?" Admiral Luther Duncan, one of the military trio at the table along with Eisenberg and General Joseph Briand of the air force, had listened and remained in stony silence. But not when this sort of information came out of the after-dinner sit, for Christ's sake.

"Was," Starling said, his face expressionless, and they knew he'd been expecting it a long time. "From what I understand, they used full demolitions. Everything is gone."

"The people who work there?" The question came carefully from the president's wife.

"No survivors."

"My God," Eisenberg said. "What the hell am I doing *here* then!"

"You can't do any good for Goddard," Starling told him. "Before you leave here tonight we will conclude our new program. Just bear with me for a little while, General."

"Yes, sir." Eisenberg was so taut he seemed ready to explode.

Corey leaned forward. "General, you ever kill any Americans?"

Eisenberg looked at Corey as if the man was crazy. "Mister, I fight *for* my country. I've killed Germans, Japanese, Cubans, Syrians, Palestinians, Russians, Vietnamese, Chinese—"

"And Nicaraguans, Libyans, Tunisians, Italians—"

"What's your point, Corey!"

"I asked you if you had ever killed any Americans."

"No, damn it! And I don't understand why you're asking!"

Corey laughed, a touch of humor along with the sardonic. "Why, because you're about to, you know." He laughed again at the look on the general's face. "Kill Americans, that is. *Lots* of them, General, a hell of a lot of them."

Moscow

Yuri Fedov studied the group gathered in the electronically shielded meeting hall of the Kremlin. They gathered once a week, late at night, for scheduled meetings. If emergencies came up and immediate consultation was required, every word spoken was recorded, and transcripts prepared immediately for the regular Special Committee. *It is a strange play on our lives*, mused the General Secretary. *For so many years our meetings have been ponderous affairs. We have been bedeviled by the KGB and the GRU and our military intelligence and so many factions seeking power. Now we are ready to give it away and everybody wants to cooperate. All is sweetness and light.* He made a face. *Of course. Everybody wants a seat on the bus.* The grimace changed to a wan smile. *No; not everybody. Not the Fedovs or the Starlings, at least. Our ships of state are sinking, and the captains will go down with their ships.*

The American was there, huddled with his Soviet counterpart who had just flown in from Washington. Dr. Richard Shaeffer and Gregory Tretyakovich made a most unusual pair. Two human beings could hardly be less alike, yet two human beings could hardly be closer than this pair.

Academician Josef Rausenbach represented the Academy of Sciences. Cosmonaut-Colonel Tanya Yevteshenka sat together with Cosmonaut-Scientist Boris Mikhailov. The Soviet air force was there in the presence of General

Yaroslav Goloborodko. Along with Army General Victor Gorbatko, they had ringed all the launching centers with fire and steel, as the Americans were doing. And there was Admiral Ivan Antonov of the Soviet navy. The surface fleets no longer mattered, but Antonov held the absolute loyalty of the submarine force. He could be a critical factor in the short time ahead.

They had been together for three hours when Fedov insisted on a break. Off to the bathrooms. Some food. What did the Americans call it? Ah; the seventh-inning stretch. Move the muscles and the limbs. Limber the body to freshen the mind. Now that break was behind them, and Boris Mikhailov coughed for attention.

"We agree to dispense with the protocol of the meetings. There is no time for such measures. I do not recommend such procedures. I make no comment on them except," he said very carefully, "to bring to your attention that the cosmonaut corps accepts and understands your orders. Our duty is to serve the Motherland, and as we have always done we will continue to do so. I am ready now to answer all your questions. After this meeting I will go to Star City to attend to assignments you have already given me," he patted a thick folder before him, "and then I shall fly to Tyuratam to coordinate your express orders at the launch center. I await your pleasure." As if throwing a switch, the heavyset cosmonaut, veteran of seven flights into orbit and one circumnavigation of the moon, dropped into expressionless silence.

Rausenbach studied the attendees. All his life the huge Russian bear of a man had pursued truth in science. His intellect had brought him through pogroms and mass assassinations and power changes—not because he was brilliant but because he simply did not give a damn for his life when political greed threatened. Josef Stalin had threatened him personally, and Josef Stalin had killed twenty million more *Russians* than all the Hitlerite brutes. Rausenbach had stood before the stocky, total ruler of all the Russias and said simply, "Go ahead. Do it, comrade. I am one man and my loss will be insignificant, like a man who is Josef Stalin cutting off his little finger. Pah! What is one pinky to a man like you! So kill me and you will cut off a pinky of the Motherland, and be damned to you."

By way of response, Josef Stalin had threatened slow, horrible death to any Russian who so much as harmed a hair of the Rausenbach head. He was still here through all the changes of government, ninety-three years old, still physically huge, still strong, still drinking his thirty or forty cups of powerful tea every day, still smoking his huge calabash and still the undisputed master of all Soviet science.

"We will continue the program to complete the main vessel with the Americans." He made the statement without intonation: flat, simple, unadorned. Yet his choice of words said volumes. They would *continue* in their program.

Yuri Fedov nodded his satisfaction. General Secretary or not, he had to go along with the Special Committee, with *all* the groups that sprang up overnight who demanded the Americans be tested. So far the Americans had known only full cooperation from the Soviets. Until this point, unless Tretyakovich were faulty in his evaluations from the right elbow of the American president, they had withheld nothing, had offered everything, and shared selflessly.

"There are the special interest groups, of course," Tretyakovich had reported to Fedov. "Just as we have them here in Russia. But theirs are somewhat different. Religious fanatics, political opportunists, survivalists; by the hundreds of thousands they emerge from the woodwork and the closets and from the alleyways and thrust themselves onto the public scene."

"I am aware of such things," Fedov said drily. "We are *all* aware of what took place at Goddard. That would not have been tolerated here. Not a single one of those madmen would have reached a critical building."

To Fedov's astonishment, Tretyakovich shook his head. "That is not true, Comrade Secretary. Picture, if you will, the most formidable air defense system our nation can devise. Surface-to-air missiles. Radar-directed, rapid-fire automatic weapons. Homing systems, men with

284

rapid-fire weapons. Computers; everything. Could you destroy all, or even most, or perhaps even half of a hundred thousand seagulls, or crows, or hawks, hurling themselves at a particular target? Or a hundred thousand wolves, slavering and mad with fear and hunger, rushing toward a single point?" The man who lived in the White House, who was Fedov's arm and ear with the American president, smiled.

"Share with me your amusement," Fedov said, a bit more brusquely than he intended.

"American intelligence knew of the attack to be made against the Goddard center," Tretyakovich told him.

"But that is astonishing! They are emotionalists, these Americans," Fedov protested. "They do not accept the inevitability of sacrifice as we do . . ." His voice faltered as he studied his man. "I appear to be missing a critical point, Tretsky, or whatever it is the Yankees call you."

Tretyakovich laughed. "The Americans are emotionalists, as you say, Comrade Secretary," he said. "But consider Hiroshima and Nagasaki. *First* they exploded their atomic weapons over the Japanese cities and *then* they spent the next fifty years emoting over it. But never forget that the emotionalism followed, and did not precede, the event."

Fedov considered what he had heard. "So the Americans sacrificed Goddard—"

"Precisely," Tretyakovich confirmed.

Fedov remained stolid in his seat but his thoughts raced. He had not become the General Secretary, despite his outward geniality, through a lack of knowledge, firsthand or otherwise, of the affairs of men who control power. Aloud he said: "The American president acted precisely as would I. Now I understand. They sacrifice a data center which they are convinced has no immediate role in the survival vessels, and is therefore of no real loss to them. And," he smiled finally, "they permit these dissidents to reveal themselves for future action by the American authorities."

"Yes, Comrade Fedov."

"What do you think they will do, Tretyakovich?"

285

"They are not so quick as we to dispose of vermin who endanger the state," Tretyakovich said. "But the American president has so many affairs on his mind, he will—and I am convinced of this, sir—he will simply turn over the matter to people who are more experienced in such affairs."

"You use many words to describe eliminating rodents."

"That is my assignment from you."

"How well do you know this Russ Corey?"

Tretyakovich blinked. The question nailed him expertly. He was off balance. For just that moment he blinked, and Fedov knew he had struck home squarely. One did not often catch the famed mental speed of Gregory Tretyakovich even a single pace slow. "I know him," came the answer after that flicker of hesitation. "I do not know him well, Comrade Secretary." Tretyakovich was neatly on his toes again. "The only man who knows him well, from everything I have seen, is the American president. They are, as one says, very tight with one another. Friends for many years. Both the Starlings have an unlimited admiration for this man."

"I wish you to cultivate a relationship with this man. Get to know him better. Be a confident of his. Earn his trust."

"That is easier said than done, Comrade Secretary."

Tretyakovich spoke with such care that he aroused more questions in Fedov's mind. "You never say such things without compelling reason," he came back immediately. "Why will it be difficult?"

"He wishes nothing from us."

"What is that?"

"The man Corey wants nothing from us. He needs nothing from us. He is damnably busy. His most precious commodity is time. He wastes none of it and he has none for idle acquaintances, which, under the conditions we endure, is what I would be."

Fedov wanted to smile but didn't. "I have never heard you deprecate yourself before."

"Nor am I now," Tretyakovich said without a shred of lesser ego or self-confidence. "And I bring to you only truth." He leaned forward, caught Fedov's eye, and the latter nodded. Tretyakovich continued talking as he spread caviar on black bread and poured a water glass of vodka. "It would help if I know your reasons," he said as he bit into a huge chunk of bread.

"This fellow has the moon," Fedov replied. "Not the American government. Not the Russian government. This man, Corey, *he* has control of the moon. Oh, we have some piddling bases," Fedov said in curt dismissal of such meager facilities, "but Corey is dug in deeply with a tremendous installation. Several, from what I understand. *We,* on the other hand, cannot spare resources from this space machine we build and must now supply. We cannot build in orbit and mount a logistics assault on the moon and prepare deep underground bases before the sun may burn our feathers."

Tretyakovich washed down bread and caviar with a wallop of vodka straight. "I understand."

"Tell *me,* then."

"You think of *Rodina.* You wish there to be as many Russians as is possible deep within the moon when the final days are upon us. Russ Corey is the only way to do that. His cooperation——"

"His invitation," Fedov said sharply. "Promise anything he needs or wishes. We will deliver. That is my word."

"Yes, sir," Tretyakovich answered. He saw Yuri Fedov's troubled look. He sighed and poured the Secretary General a liberal quantity of vodka. They toasted one another in silence.

What had he said? Yuri Fedov cursed himself for drifting away from the moment. Ah, yes; Josef Rausenbach. The elderly academician was speaking for the whole council body of Soviet science. Was he becoming a doddering old fool? Of course Russia would continue the program to complete this *Pegasus* machine with the Americans! What else was Russia to do? Launch its own program at this late time? Fedov had spoken with the younger scientists and the experienced cosmonauts. Their consensus made it appallingly clear. A Soviet ark—Fedov shuddered; he hated the word and its connotations—

would be distressingly small and ill-equipped compared to what they could build as a single force with the Americans. And they would receive help from any other governments wishing to climb onto the raft. *Aha!* There it was: what they should have called this damned thing all along. A raft. *A lifeboat.* Even better: a lifeboat to carry some survivors away from the sinking ship called Earth. Ark! What rot, and—

Fedov forced himself back to the moment.

"Do the Americans trust us? The question is well put," said Cosmonaut-Colonel Tanya Yevteshenka. "And the answer is yes. Here on Earth we deal politically. In space we have no time for that. Both sides are quick to accept superior command from the other when that is necessary. There has never yet been an argument on such an issue. I have lived and worked with the Americans. The manner in which they use *Gagarin* tell us that. Aboard *Gagarin* they accept all authority as Russian."

"Of course they do!" Admiral Ivan Antonov hunched his body as if he were a bear, glowering at them beneath a fierce walrus moustache of pure white. *Moustaches,* thought Fedov idly, *seem once again to be in vogue aboard our submarines.* He knew Antonov and his crusty manners. Now he made a minor gesture with his hand for the admiral to get it all out.

"Why should they not cooperate aboard the station?" Antonov went on angrily. "I return from a mission, and what do I find? The Americans shall command this stupid horse vessel, this *Pegasus,* and a Russian shall be subordinate. What madness is this? Who permitted such folly!"

"I did."

Antonov came up short, then bristled for another verbal assault. Fedov shifted in his seat and leaned forward, a clear body signal to the admiral to shut his mouth before Fedov became angry. Those moments were rare, but never forgotten. "I did," Fedov repeated, "because what you say is not correct, Admiral. This American, Seavers, shall be the mission commander. He is marvelously suited for the task—remember his

Antarctic experience. But he is an astronaut only for a short time.

"To run the ship, to command *Pegasus* itself, requires the very best in this business. It is the conviction of the Americans, as much as it is ours, that Comrade General Vasily Iliych Tereshnikov should be the vessel's captain. You of all people, Admiral Antonov, should understand the distinction between fleet commander and ship's captain. Seavers will command the main ship and the space barn filled with pigs and plants. *That* is the distinction, and I wish you to bring its full understanding to your entire command. Do *you* understand?"

Antonov sat rocklike. "Yes, Comrade. I understand."

"Comrade Secretary!" They turned to Army General Victor Gorbatko. "Do I understand you have agreed to a *Chinese* to be standby command to the American, this Seavers?"

"Yes."

"You will tell me why, please?"

"The Chinese offer enormous supplies, equipment, and what we need delivered to orbit for the mission. They offer us Chiang Biao as standby to Seavers. Biao is perfect for such a role. He releases us and the Americans from excessive control, in the eyes of others. He has no desire for actual command. He is not suited to it. But as standby command we can use best of all his skills as a scientist, a master of social dynamics. He is a Buddhist and of no conflict to the theological superstitions of the other races."

"But if something happens to Seavers then he will—"

"He will not," Fedov said. "If Marc Seavers dies or is incapacitated, then Tereshnikov takes over as fleet commander and retains his position of ship captain. Chiang Biao remains as standby command. In other words, his position as *second* never changes. And as second, in any capacity, he can give no orders to Tereshnikov. It is a brilliant solution to many problems."

"You have confirmed the top command?" This from General Yaroslav Goloborodko of the air force. Fedov nodded to Yevteshenka.

"Yes, sir," she replied to the entire group. "Seavers

has mission command for both *Pegasus* and *Noah*. Standby command for both vessels is, as you have just heard, Chiang Biao. Let me add that he has spent most of his life with the Tibetans more than he has with the Chinese, which makes his social and religious position even more compatible with the masses aboard the vessels."

"Enough of the damned Chinaman," Goloborodko snapped. "On with it."

Tanya Yevteshenka showed no ruffled feathers. She never failed to remember that *she* was on the ship's manifest, while most of the people dealt with were *not*. "Yes, sir," she said. "Doctor General Vasily Iliych Tereshnikov is ship commander of *Pegasus*. He will have three immediate executive officers. Two Americans, Hastings and Foster, and a Britisher, Marcus Goldman."

"No *Russians?*" Goloborodko was aghast. "We are giving away such control?"

"Not quite, Comrade General. There is overt status and covert control. I myself am on the manifest as Computers One. In short, I am in charge of all computers that run the ship. Clearly, then, my title is unimportant, but my position is absolutely critical and retains actual ship control between Tereshnikov and myself." She moved her papers about. "If you so wish, Comrade General, I can have a full complement—as full as we have decided so far—of primary commands and positions as soon as this meeting ends."

"Do it," the general said.

Academician Rausenbach motioned for attention and received it immediately. "I have been sequestered for some time and have heard little about outside events." He frowned. "But a story reached me just prior to joining you here in this meeting. Something about the Japanese refusing to join us and the Americans in the . . . the ships—"

"Lifeboats," Fedov suggested.

"Ah, yes. *Lifeboats*. Thank you, Yuri."

"I suggest we ask Comrade Tretyakovich. He has just

flown here from the United States." Fedov motioned for Tretyakovich to pick up the response.

"It is simple, really," Tretyakovich began. "They have gone mad. The entire nation is afflicted with a grip of total religious fervor. It is difficult for a Russian to understand. *I* find it difficult to understand. The Americans use phrases like 'that old-time religion' and born—" He turned to Shaeffer.

"It's called 'born again,' " Shaeffer offered. "It's a nationwide Baptist revival."

"This is crazy," Rausenbach said in wonder.

"Yes, sir," Shaeffer replied. He looked at Tretyakovich, who nodded for him to continue. "I spent several years living in Japan and I understand," Shaeffer said. "Things like the samurai code and *hagakure*, their system for honor. It's based as much on religion as it is on historical values. From what I gather, the Japanese feel their ancestors—all very dead, by the way, which in some way mix with their ancient gods, and I admit, sir, it can get very confusing very quickly—but to wrap it up, they have accepted that their ancestors feel that to leave the Earth in this time of danger is to act like cowards. So they make certain they will not run away. To the Japanese, if running is unacceptable and you may succumb to the desire, then the only thing to do is hack off your feet with a sword. That is precisely what they've done. By blowing up *all* their rocket-launching ability, they're chained to the Earth. They know we won't, and Russia won't, have a thing to do with them from now on, because if they've proved anything at all along with their self-immolation in terms of spacecraft ability, it's that they are a volatile and emotionally unbalanced people. It does pose a problem. We felt the Japanese were the best people to handle the entire *Noah* project. It would be a farm spacecraft, so to speak. More animals than people, jammed with crops, packed with frozen seeds and the stuff to make a world habitable when the two ships return, if it *is* habitable." He rubbed his forehead gently. "Forgive me; I am not responding directly. To sum up a response to your question, sir," he said directly to Rausenbach, "the Japanese in effect

291

have committed national suicide. From *our* viewpoint. From *their* position, they have assured themselves if not a place on Earth in the future, certainly a guaranteed berth in whatever heaven they envision."

Rausenbach shook his head in wonder. "And I had thought the Americans with all their wild religions to be mad." He nodded to Shaeffer. "My apologies."

Shaeffer laughed. "What ever you say about *our* grab-bag of religions is quite true."

"Who, then," Rausenbach directed his next question to Fedov, "will be responsible for the animal boat?"

"We shall build that vessel and its program on an international basis," Fedov replied. "We had hoped that Jiro Nakamura, the dean of Japanese science, would command the vessel. But he was the leader in this movement to have Japan cut its throat, as it were. To be specific, Comrade Rausenbach, we still search for a single commander who would be most acceptable to the greatest number."

General Gorbatko gestured angrily. "Move that Chinese fellow, Chiang what's-his-name, in with the animals! Then they'll all be at home with one another!"

Boris Mikhailov tried to choke back sudden laughter. "Thank you, Comrade General!" he said, almost shouting. "I do not know a single cosmonaut who would not agree with you." He passed a hand before his eyes, opened two fingers and looked at Tanya Yevteshenka. "Imagine, my dear Tanya, what it will be like after a month, six months, a year or more! All the smells of horror gathering within the ship, clinging to clothing, the bulkheads, above and below, to the instruments, coating the ventilator shafts, soaking our sleeping bags, cloying the food—*arrgh*," he finished, clutching at his throat. "Very good, Comrade General—"

"And the question," Fedov broke in with a voice of steel that snapped Mikhailov to instant seated attention, "is *who* we will find to command the vessel. Perhaps, my space-going friend, you would not find it at all objectionable if we performed a bit of nasal surgery on *you*. There will be no offensive odors then, yes? And you will be on intimate terms with all the beasts of the farms."

Mikhailov swallowed hard, and Yevteshenka busied herself suddenly with her papers to avert the smile struggling to break free. Rausenbach saved her.

"Make the commander of that animal boat an Asian or an African, he told Fedov. "I doubt you will find much opposition from the Americans. Likely it will fit their own plans quite admirably."

"Academician, you are a brilliant scientist, but a fool when it comes to dealing with the masses!" General Gorbatko glowered at the astonished elderly scientist. "Do you not know these Americans yet? Do you not read our intelligence reports on the problems they have with the blacks in their military services? The drugs, the fights, the rapes? And their cities, overrun with these animals in human form?" He waved almost wildly at Shaeffer. "What do they call them in your country, these niggers? Spear chuckers, hey? All manner of names?" Gorbatko turned back to Rausenbach. "This is the perfect time to clear out the human race once and for all of these inferiors! I *know* the Americans! I meet secretly with their generals to solve our problems. They hate their blacks." Again he turned to Shaeffer, but this time directed his attention to Tretyakovich.

"*You* have the ear of the Yankee president, Comrade! You know what he thinks! I want you to tell this doddering old fool here what the Yankee president thinks of sending the niggers into the future with the very best of their white race!"

"The American president," Tretyakovich said slowly, "cannot decide who goes and who does not go."

"*What?*"

"He can recommend. That is all. A secret panel makes the final decisions, and all first choices for crew are made apart from that panel." Tretyakovich spoke in a voice flat and toneless. "Admiral Seavers as fleet commander has absolute say-so. He picks his own crew. He permits his lead crew, his division chiefs and executive officers, to select theirs."

"Get to the point!"

293

"Please look at the list of lead crew for *Pegasus*, Comrade General. On it you will find the names of the commanders of the shuttle spacecraft to be used for the final return to Earth, if events permit such good fortune to attend the end of this mission."

"Yes, yes; so?"

"Commanding the shuttle program is a most experienced American cosmonaut. His name is Archer Begley. He was a fighter pilot in the American navy. In the Mediterranean war—or police action, if you will—he shot down sixteen Russian fighter planes flown by Syrians and Libyans. He is an engineering test pilot with many degrees and honors. He has made twenty-nine flights as a shuttle pilot. What you will not find on that roster of lead crew, Comrade General, is this man's nickname. The name his friends use in speaking to him."

"What is so special about this name? I do not understand."

Gregory Tretyakovich smiled. He relished the moment. "His name, Comrade General, is Captain Midnight. He is as black, if I may use an American expression, as the ace of spades. He is also the personal choice of Admiral Marc Seavers."

Richard Shaeffer sat with both hands cupped together, elbows on the table, his chin resting on his fists. "And let me add, General Gorbatko, that nigger is considered the best damn pilot in the entire American space fleet."

South Africa

"I suppose they are calling it disinvestment?" The speaker was bitter to the point of physically trembling.

"It is their idea of a cruel joke, perhaps. But yes, you are correct. The ultimate disinvestment. If you are an Afrikaaner, you are not fit to board that vessel."

"Ah, the ultimate disinvestment. That includes the children as well?"

"No. They will take children. A few, and none over

two years of age. Below what they consider the age of contamination."

"What other conditions?"

"For ever Afrikaaner child we deliver to them, we must send a black child."

"How incredible. They wish children whose parents are scientists, teachers, builders, and leaders and they want those numbers matched equally by babes from parents who still live in huts, scrabble in the dirt, and cannot read nor write."

"Sir, it is my understanding that what they offer is a lie."

"How so?"

"The children will be sent to the preparation centers as promised. They will be taken care of. But when they leave, it will be to other centers far from any launching site. What they do is a fraud not to anger us."

"I am beyond anger."

"I understand. I, also."

"Then we must follow an old rule. A lion dies with a roar, not with a whimper."

"Yes, sir. I do not mind dying, I must tell you. I will go even gladly if I can accomplish some redress for our people in the act."

"Then you will be aboard the ore ship."

"Thank you."

"Execute the plan immediately. There is less time than you might believe."

"Yes, sir. Destination for Number One?"

"Tampa."

"Number Two?"

"A diversion. The English Channel."

"Number Three?"

"Three and Four are decoys. Everything we have must go into One and Two. But Three and Four can do as much damage psychologically. Now, go."

"Yes, sir."

Highway I-95 Southbound

"Dr. Kimberly, I cannot tell you, the words are almost beyond me, and I am certain, absolutely certain, sir, that it is the will of the Lord that you have consented to be with us on this trip southward to the devil's own." The good Reverend Zack Bible, resplendent in a suit of brilliant white-and-gold leather, a heavy gold cross on a heavy gold chain about his neck, was sprawled in the lounge chair of the motor home speeding southward from Maryland to Virginia. He gestured expansively with a damned good cigar. "Yesirree, I must tell you, God's will is being done. We're going to Wallops Island, Doctor, and you know what evil is being done *there*. All them government whores and them government faggots what brought this terrible justice down on us, they is gathering there and they is performing *satanic* rights. They call these places launching pads, right? Damn it, you're a space professor, *you* of all people ought to know! But I'll tell you right now, Dr. Kimberly, they are holding them satanic rites, and the devil's with them, demons infesting their sick minds and they are killing the children and chopping up their bodies and quick-freezing them to take what's left of those poor little kiddies in freezer boxes into that demon-plagued ship they are building, did you know *that*? That is their food, Kimberly! They have figured it all out. The best way to get meat to those ships is not shipping carcasses from the slaughterhouses like decent folk do, but to take the children. Young, fresh meat. The demons cloud over the eyes and the minds of these people and they bring their children there, and they promise them all seats on the rockets to go up into space, and the devil grips their minds and they are killing those children, chopping off heads and feet and hands and gutting them just like a lamb or a heifer, and then they quick-freeze them and take what's left—the best parts, of course, what else would they take? They take the best parts because it don't require no energy to keep that kinda meat frozen in space, do it now, Dr. Kimberly? You're the scientist, *you know*, you know all about these things, of course. Why, I learned most of what I know from reading your articles and your books. It says so right in them very pages what you wrote. To store edibles, whether it be meat or vegetables or fruit or whatever, you quick-freeze it here on this good old Earth that God gave us to live in and procreate and prosper on, you take this quick-frozen meat up there, put it into a big container, a freezer, like, where the sun can't get to it directly, I think you described that as radiant heating, and it's where you say that on the sunlit side, why, the temperature could be hundreds of degrees, but on the shadow side, especially if you've gotten all the air outta that place, the temperature is hundreds of degrees below zero."

Zack Bible sat back in his seat with an expression of pure triumph at his tremendous intellectual accomplishment. Dr. Arthur Kimberly, he thought with amusement, looks like shit. His beard looked like the rumpled ass of a long-haired hog sitting in burrs, and his clothes was all rumpled. You got to know the signs, thought Bible, and this man is a whole forest of signs. Bible studied the hollow eyes with their pink glaze, the protruding, slightly blued lower lip, the slump of muscle and bone, the staring. It's almost time, he judged. He gestured with one hand, and behind him one of his people slid a hand into the pocket of Kimberly's jacket draped over a seat to withdraw the tobacco pouch. In a few deft moments the tobacco within was thoroughly mixed with bazuco and replaced. A hand tapped gently, once, on Bible's shoulder.

"Tell you what, Professor. A good stiff drink will do you a world of the rights, let you see more clearly and—"

"I don't believe a word of those terrible lies you told me," Kimberly snapped. "Not a single damned word!"

"Professor, why would I *lie* to you?" Zack Bible held a gold-ringed hand over his heart. "I am a servant of the Lord, selected by Him to do His bidding, and *I cannot lie!* I mean to tell you, Professor, even if I *wanted* to lie I could not do so. Why do you think I offered to *show you* what I been saying? It don't matter one whit to me or the Lord what you believes *tonight*. Tomorrow you re going to see with your very own eyes, with the sight the Lord give to you Hisself, and you will judge for yourself, and you will judge for the Lord, because *He* has given you this task to use that incredible mind and intelligence you got."

Bible sighed with understanding. "Professor, let us not dispute one another in contentious nonsense. Here is that drink," he gestured again and excellent scotch appeared in a glass held before Kimberly, "and now you drink up, and relax, and here's your pipe and tobacco, and I want you just to drink that one glass of scotch and smoke your pipe and just come down a bit, let yourself slide into the gentle arms of the Lord and feel better, and I won't say a word, not a single word to you, and my assistant, here, her name is Flower, it's Flower Sanchez, isn't she a beautiful child of the Lord? Flower will be here to get whatever you want or whatever you need, Professor." Zack Bible heaved himself out of his chair and went to the forward part of the private compartment. "We'll leave you to yourself, with Flower, here, you drink that scotch and smoke your pipe, Professor, and Flower, you take off the shoes and socks of this here good man, and gentle like, you anoint his feet with some oil, and rub them feet gentle like, just like that good woman Mary. Professor, I got business up forward and I will see you later."

Bible and the two men who had been in the compartment all went forward and the sliding teak door closed behind him.

"You drink and relax, Professor," Flower said. She was sixteen or seventeen years old and beautiful and her beauty forced its way through the dragging weariness of Kimberly's mind. "You smoke that pipe, I used to fill my daddy's pipe for him, here, let me do this for you." He watched in silence as she filled the bowl, tamped it, and held it up to him and leaned over him with a match to light up for him. He stared from inches away into beautiful cleavage, at those beautiful young full breasts and he took a heavy swallow of the scotch. It burned warm and then hot down his throat and it did make him feel better. He leaned back and sucked in on the pipe, that tobacco had never been better, and he watched her kneel before him, by his feet and she removed his shoes and his socks and just as Zack Bible had promised, my God, he wasn't so bad after all, she began to anoint his feet with oil and those supple, young, strong, beautiful fingers. Her face swam in a gorgeous halo before him as she bent lower to slide her fingers along his ankle, and her blouse was low and a breast slid out, God, it was marvelous, round and firm and full, bobbing ever so gently, the nipple erect, and he sucked deeply on the pipe and felt the wonder racing through his system.

They watched through the television monitor as his face took on a look of rapture, and Flower loosened his belt and his undershorts and slid down his trousers and shorts and her hand moved alongside and up his thigh and she moved closer and her mouth took him and the good Professor Arthur Kimberly arched his back like a deer shot in midstride.

"We got the motherfucker *now*," said the Reverend Zack Bible. "We own his ass, his body, and his soul. God's will is sure as hell going to be done tomorrow with this smartassed son of a bitch." Bible turned to Fern. He liked these names for his followers. "How much did you put in that tobacco?"

"Ninety-eight percent pure. Best damn bazuco there is. Three times stronger than crack, man—"

He winced at fiery eyes. "Begging your pardon, *Reverend*. As I was saying, he got enough in his system he's in heaven right now—"

Bible glanced up at the screen. "He's beyond heaven. He's pure rut now." They watched Kimberly astride Flower, thrusting wildly into her, his mouth open and screaming. "When that son of a bitch comes he's gonna pass out. They just about all do the first time," Bible said. "Get some food into him and then make sure he smokes another pipeful. By the time we hit Wallops Island I want him a zombie."

"You can put that in the bank, Reverend," Fern promised.

"Good man," Bible said. He made the sign over Fern's head and went into the next small private compartment. The two children were waiting for him there. Alice was nine and Kathy twelve and God they were ripe for him and he swelled immediately with the thought of their mouths and tongues and bodies all over his.

He stopped before the door to the compartment and raised his eyes to heaven. "The good Lord be praised," he whispered, and he went inside for a slice of heaven.

Camp David

"This could be the last time we walk together," Russ Corey said as he and George Starling moved idly along the winding forest path within the Camp David presidential retreat. The two men had made certain to be alone, fully and painfully aware of the sands of time rushing through the hourglass. It had also been the first few hours of calm in many weeks when they *could* be alone. Corey stopped to breathe deeply of the forest-scented air beneath the canopy of trees.

"These past few meetings," Starling said, in reference to sessions with all the people they'd butted heads against, "I must say you've been in top form. Glib, nasty, irritating, overbearing, confident—" He paused as Corey chuckled. "All the things you wanted to be, I know that," Starling went on. "But I know you, Russ. You're not *that* settled in your mind. You've come down on our scientists—with the exception of Felicity, I should add—as if they were the devil's own."

"They are," Corey said acidly. "Those bastards are almost grateful to God *and* the devil for what's happening. Damn it, George, this isn't like all the other doom-and-gloom scenarios. We don't have the scientists to blame for bombs and twisted biology. We're back to the gut-wrenchers this time. God and Satan and bullshit. I don't want you to forget for a moment that those who can't blame God need other people on top to hate. They hate *you*. They've *got* to hate someone, because all this is too overpowering. That means that you've got to become a lot less visible, and above all a hell of a lot less *available*. You see, you're a target for people who don't care if they're killed. When you get down to that level, like we had in Lebanon for so long, the only way to keep from getting your presidential skull blown off is to keep anyone from taking a bead on it."

"Thanks a heap," Starling said.

"You mind some business?" Corey gestured to take in the heavy cool night air and the forest about them. "I hate polluting this place, but—"

"Saito on your mind?"

"For starters. Like I said, this could be our last face-to-face, and I really do need your input. When did you decide to let Saito be top dog in the submersibles program?"

"Anything to keep him from running home to die in a tiny room filled with ancestral ashes. When Jiro Nakamura kicked off all those explosions to wipe out Japan's space launch capability, Saito was rocked back on his heels. To him, dying with dignity is not setting off fireworks. He believes in this electromagnetic shield program as much as does Nakamura, but to Saito the destruction of the means to save *some* children is unspeakable. He feels his ancestors, all the ancestral gods, should be venerated. That means going after every chance of sending living children into the future." Starling stopped for a glance at two bright-red cardinals whipping by. "It starts becoming too complicated for me at this point, so I've forced myself to ignore the Japanese and give extra attention to Saito and his subs."

"Before you leave that subject entirely, do you understand the Shield program won't work?"

Starling faced him squarely. "You *had* to tell me that?"

"You want lollipops, maybe?"

"You could irritate sandpaper, Russ."

"That's my charm. Okay, I'll shut up."

"And I'll kick your ass," the president said. "Out with it and quick and neat."

"The idea of an immense magnetic field, the so-called bow wave, preceding the Earth sounds just great. It will occupy a lot of minds and a lot of people are going to believe in it, especially because they want to believe in something." Corey sighed. "Damn it, George, it won't work. The people on top seem to forget the entire Earth is already a tremendous magnet. We generate a huge shock wave ahead of our orbital path, but that hasn't stopped even the *thin* dust. For all practical purposes, the dust constitutes the vacuum, the stuff of which space is made. *If* we had a place to anchor the Shield generators to create a meaningful static field, it might work. *Might*. But there aren't any skyhooks up there, because them satellites, they got to keep jiving like everything else in space, and something whipping or even crawling around the Earth at best is pretty damned tenuous. You see, when people think of a dust sweep, like the shield, they don't stop to think about where that dust will *go*. They imagine the shield as a prow, like a bow wave before a moving ship, but that ship isn't spinning like we were." Corey sighed. "But it'll keep the bastards occupied, anyway."

The president shook his head. "I've got a thousand scientists to advise me and not one of them has told me what you just said."

Corey grinned. "Being succinct isn't always a scientist's best qualification. What the hell, George, they're as scared as anybody else." He gestured and they started walking again. "Tell me about your final selections."

"You met them at your place, remember? Admiral Duncan will have overall command of our launch facilities."

"You made a good selection." Corey smiled. "I've butted heads with that old bastard a couple of times. Naval contract stuff. He'd liked to have run me over with a battleship a couple of—well, just about *every* time. He'd walk around his office stomping and kicking up a storm—"

"You're one of the few people who knows he has

302

artificial legs," Starling broke in. "He stomps to reassure himself he can still kick ass. More specifically, he's got the marine corps working closely with him. He's moving battalions into position to defend the launch sites."

"I'm glad to hear *that*." Corey frowned. "But it sounds like you're overloading him. Running the launch sites *and* protecting them? That spreads the man too thin."

"I know that," Starling acknowledged. "Hal Eisenberg has the security job. I chose him when he pointed out that site security doesn't begin at home. It's out along the roads and highways, the rail lines, airports, fields—"

"He's right." Corey thought of his installations in Arizona. "Damn, but he's right. Eisenberg's a good man. We've worked together. Shared a war or two. He's come up all the way through the ranks. If he could get away with it he'd dress like George Patton, pearl-handled revolvers and all. *Damn!* It's going to be very tough on that old man to kill our own people."

"*You* made that very clear, Russ. I asked him about that later. Killing Americans, I mean. Did you know his son *and* daughter are both officers in the army? I hated to do it, but I told him to imagine that his own son or daughter might hold a view opposite to ours. That what we were doing to save a piece of humanity might be wrong. For whatever reasons; it doesn't matter. So I asked Hal what he'd do if his own boy led a protest rally or a tear-it-down raid against a launch center. Would he shoot him? The general looked me straight in the eye and said only if he wasn't close enough to kill 'the son of a bitch with my own two hands.' " Starling shuddered. "I wonder what *I'd* do in a case like that."

"Same thing," Corey said casually.

"Easier said than done," Starling snapped. "You can order a thousand strange sons into battle by thinking of the numbers, but it's never the same with your *own*."

"Don't go parent-poetic on me," Corey dismissed him. "That's why you're made with a little switch in your head. You turn it OFF when you need to and you turn it ON when you want to gush. George, you want to go maudlin save it for your wife. We don't have the time."

Starling's hands turned into white-knuckled fists. He brought up his right arm to touch Corey gently on the shoulder. "I know, I know," he whispered. He forced himself out of the sudden funk. "How are you doing in your penthouse?"

Corey laughed at the reference to the lunar colony, growing fitfully but steadily. "We've got over seven hundred people up there," he said quietly.

"Seven hundred!" Starling's eyes were wide.

"George, there's not a flight goes up where we don't carry people. I mean *every* flight. Sometimes we know it's going to be so rough we drug them and strap them into capsules. They're scared out of their minds, but they're proud of it. They call themselves the Pod People. It's amazing how people absolutely love to give themselves identifying names. Ever think of that? Anyway, I'm preparing the Luke facility to run a steady flow of people, as many children as possible, out of there. The problem is we can't do it on a long, steady basis. We'll keep everything lowball until the shit hits the fan and then we'll just firewall the works."

"How many do you plan—"

"No plans for a top number. That's psychological suicide, George. How'd you like to know you're number one oh two but they'll cut if off at one hundred? We'll take them all. What the hell, man, they're going to die for certain if they stay here! Up there if we go down deep enough . . ." He shrugged. "It's the best shot. Anyway, damn it, and damn you and your maudlin wet nose, we've already started arranging marriages as rapidly as possible. Good old American pioneering tradition."

"Seven brides for seven brothers, hey?" Starling chuckled and stopped still with a look of surprise on his face. "I'm amazed at how we can still make funnies out of *any* of this."

"Another old tradition," Corey told him; "but that applies to *everybody*."

"You ever find your name yet?"

"Why, I thought you knew. *Hestia*."

"That's Greek."

"Mythological Greek, right. She was the sister of Zeus. Goddess of the hearth and the true symbol of the home, and her sign was always carried as an essential part of any new colony."

"Who'd believe it?" Starling said with a jaunty air. "Russ Corey, scourge of evil empires now the valiant defender of the weak *and* a poet at heart. A real softie."

"If you weren't so goddamned dignified I'd kick the shit out of you like in the old days."

"Compared to the crap I take every day as president I think I'd prefer a good knuckle-buster with you, old buddy," Starling said, a sad smile emerging with memories of the past. He sighed. "God, how the mind and heart rise and fall so swiftly. It's like emotional tides running at super-speed through the body."

Corey forced a change in tone. "How's Seavers doing?"

"Incredible. The Russians, the Chinese, everybody's accepted him completely. When he brought Nancy Parks with him to the White House for me to marry them, Martha cried the whole damned day—"

"What was wrong?"

"Wrong, hell! She was *happy*. Got to confess a few misties myself. Two shining examples of man's best. I'll tell you something else. When he announced Arch Begley as commander of the whole shuttle fleet, well, the effect was incredible. Everyone knows Seavers is color blind, that he always goes for the best man. Or woman, for that matter."

"Let him pick *all* his own commanders, George. Never forget the totally alien nature of what those people must do. Abandon Earth in some super-rowboat on a trip that will take only God knows how long . . . In other words, don't saddle him with earthly problems. They've got unique problems and they won't find unique answers in the past."

Starling chewed his lower lip. "Very good. I'll remember that. I can use it. But I won't tell anyone I got it from you. Somebody might say something nice about you." Starling sobered. "Russ, when . . . I mean, how long before you leave for good?"

"Soon," Corey said firmly. "When I go this time, I don't come back. I can't. The exact time of departure depends upon what happens here, and how things are coming along up there. We're working around the clock to prepare two major separate cities. One very deep underground base and the other, because of time constraints and other factors, either just beneath the surface or, tunneled within a mountain range. The latter is the quickest way to get as much additional space as we may want or need. *Hestia* will be the deep one."

"You really believe you can ride out what's coming?"

A flash of anger—at life, not the friend with him—came and went on Corey's face. "Who the hell knows," he said with the only touch of weariness George Starling had ever seen in him. "We can't predict tidal gravitational effects. We could be in for a hell of a ride with electromagnetic storms. We might get penetrating radiation from the sun. It's why I favor the deep base; deeper and safer, maybe. That also means—the solar and electromagnetic effects—we'll need nuclear reactors. Well, shielding won't be a problem. We'll go to remote location sites and run long power cables."

Starling nodded. "And the sperm program?"

"Better than we hoped for. Human and animal. The cryogenic units have been operating now about four months, and we haven't had the slightest hitch. I want *all* those units operational as quickly as I can, and keep using the best for reproduction. The animal banks are just as important."

"I didn't know you had gone into it that thoroughly. I *should* have known. I'm very glad to hear that."

"Among other things, it's going to be a bloody barnyard up there, George." Corey went thoughtful for a moment. "It's a lot more than saving *people*. We've become so people-centered in our thinking we've forgotten what really makes up man. What makes this human race possible. What *made* us possible and keeps us going. That's our environment, our ecology, our ecosphere. It's the creatures with which we share this damn world. We've been excavating huge caverns for them. Not orderly or cellular living like people will have to endure for a long time; I mean huge areas for the animals to graze in, live, reproduce, to satisfy that instinctive need for open spaces to some extent. Those radiant globes we developed? Well, we'll run them on a regular day and night cycle, try to reproduce what animals remember cellularly for millions of years. If we can do that on a big scale, and we already have on a small scale, we'll have streams for fish and air for birds to fly and we'll be able, hopefully, *hopefully*, to save animals like porpoises and seals, otters, beavers—well, it's one hell of a list."

"Russ, I'm amazed. I had no idea you—"

"You mean the animals?" He smiled as Starling nodded. "George, you ever hear of Chief Seattle of the Duwamish Indians? An American tribe?"

The blank look on the president's face gave his answer. "I'll *quote* him, George. I've lived long enough with what he's had to say about this. We're even naming our caverns after him. He said, 'What is man without the beasts? If all the beasts were gone, men would die from great loneliness of spirit, for whatever happens to the beasts also happens to man. All things are connected.' "

"That's an exact quote? When did you start learning at the knee of the Indian tribe?"

"Since I was a kid."

"You're not the only one, apparently. You know Joe Briand pretty well?" Corey nodded. Of course he knew him. General Joseph F. (for Firebrand) Briand, commander of the United States Space Force and the brightest of the bright, the man whom the young fighter and bomber pilot Turks would follow straight to Hell if he led the way. Corey brought up a memory of Firebrand. The cigar-chewing, round-faced general (his features resulted from the pairing of his American father with a Japanese mother) bore a startling resemblance to the cigar-chewing General Curtis LeMay, who'd bombed Japan out of the second world war and then built the huge Strategic Air Force of the United States. For years Briand fought to stay in the cockpit of the supersonic fighters and bombers he loved so much. But it wasn't to be. He was a terrific pilot, but the air force was fat on terrific pilots and lean on engineering geniuses. Magnetohydrodynamics, astrophysics, metallurgy, propulsion systems, robotics and bionics integration with cybernetics systems; these were all familiar grounds to Firebrand. Even more extraordinary were his doctorate in the humanities and his masters in anthropology, areas he considered as imperative as any other to man's survival in the super-rowboats they were building. His competence in those cerebral areas built solid bridges between his command and scientists throughout the land except for those backing SDI, which Joe Briand hated from his earliest association with the free-wheeling nuthouse creation of a bygone era. Star Wars had been an insufferable albatross about his neck for years, yet his own genius as a scientist and a manager kept him in his dominant position as chief design architect and leader of the space command.

And made him the chief designer and construction boss of *Pegasus* and *Noah*.

Starling jabbed a thumb straight up. "He's up there right now. He took three shuttles out of the pipeline and filled them with your kind of people. The best damned space construction men in the world."

"You mean—"

"Uh huh," Starling beamed. "The American Indian. The only son of a bitch who can walk high steel girders or platforms without having the first touch of vertigo. Height doesn't bother them a bit. It's an incredible characteristic, but that's why the American Indian has always been top dog in the steel construction business. He can look down from a splinter of steel hanging by a cable thread, and I mean three thousand feet straight down, and never bat an eye. So Joe got himself the very best of the best and he loaded up three shuttles for sixty Indians jammed into each one and he's now got over two hundred of what he calls 'his people' up there. I understand they're worth two thousand. Up, down, sideways; it doesn't matter to them."

They turned the last corner before the buildings where anxious security teams awaited them. Corey stopped the president. "One last thing." He waited for Starling's full attention. "We'll be giving you some headaches from up there, George. I'm sorry about that, but there's no way out."

"Saving people gives me a headache? You're not only a poet but you're also obtuse, Corey."

"You, sir," Corey snorted, "won't find a thing obtuse about the reaction when we start using atomic demolitions on the moon. To blast out caverns, for one thing. To create deep craters with heat-sealed glassine bottoms for water storage. Most of the blasts will be well below ground, but there's always the chance of venting the excess radioactivity as steam from below the lunar crust. It's the only way we can do everything in time. When the word gets out that we're blowing up atomic bombs, even the hydrogen weapons with their reduced radioactivity yield—well, there'll be a backlash here on Earth. The backlash won't have any real justification, but you're going to be saddled with a country that's helpless and frightened. Those mushroom clouds throw a long shadow."

"That's my problem," Starling said to dismiss the subject. "You get your tail up there to *Hestia*, Russ Corey, and save as many of us as possible. And, you son of a bitch, *you survive, hear?*"

Corey rested his right hand on George Starling's shoulder. "I hear. Yassuh, bossman." He studied the president. "You able to stand up to a short final speech?"

"Oh, no, Yorick, you back again? Shoot."

"I hate to do this, but I've got to leave you with a warning as strong as I can make it," Corey told him, his face, mood and tone telegraphing trouble. "Watch your back, your front, and both sides, my friend of friends. You have no idea how they'll come after you and everything you represent. All those bootlicking assholes who posture as psychiatrists and headshrinkers who know how everybody else thinks, right? They'll be wheedling every favor they can from every man and woman in government trying to get on that ship. They'll be bow-ing, scraping, currying favors, offering deals, threatening—and it's all bullshit, George. The best thing you ever did was to set up that panel that selects the people to go. But after a while even that won't mean a thing. Common sense and reality are going to be pretty damn scarce commodities around here. They'll wake up one day saying to hell with this crap of saving mankind for itself. *Save me*. That's all that will matter. They can't save the *world*, but they will sure as hell do everything they can to get a seat on the big bus. Last trip out, right? The ship's sinking. The ghost of *Titanic* sails again. When bullshit won't work, they'll use guns and blood. So either they get a seat from you and Yuri Fedov or—" He paused for a deep breath.

"Or what?" Starling said with surprising calm.

Corey laughed, an almost savage sound of condemnation for his fellow man. "Oh, it's not *guns* you're going to hear, George. It's light and sound. The sound of the nukes going off. You're on the brink of an all-out madhouse of nuclear warfare."

"We know."

"*We?* Who the hell is *we?*"

"*Komitet Gosudarstvennoi Bezopastnosti.*"

"The KGB? What the hell do they have to do with all this?"

"A great deal. Yuri Fedov comes across as a charming uncle. But he comes from the same school as Andropov and Viktor Chebrikov before him. Chebrikov and a group of top KGB men met with Shaeffer and then set up another meeting with myself and a few picked people. We met in Air Force One. In flight, I should add. Putting it all together, Russ, they offered us a deal. Made sense, too. They also anticipate nuclear strikes by madmen and governments. A final frenzy, so to speak. If we would take the children of the top KGB officials, who really rule all the others, then the KGB would use its private elite strike force—over half a million men with the best weapons there are—to control not only Russian nuclear arms, but to strike back at anyone they encounter who may be endangering the survival mission. In other words, our launch sites and the two spaceships as well."

Corey took the news in silence. "Damn, it makes sense. You bought their deal?"

"Of course! We're taking *children*."

"And you buy time and security for a while until those ships are on their way."

"Precisely."

"I'll do the same."

"You already are."

"I'm *what*?"

"You've been very busy. We approached Miss Correnti. Direct contact through a very secure comsat line. Jesse Markham set it up. They've already started. Three hundred and twelve children, ten or younger. Most of them are already at your Luke facility."

"I'll be damned."

"That," George Starling said slowly, his voice husky, "is precisely what you will *not* be." Starling looked at the lowering sunset. "Now, damn it, leave me. For the last time, Russ Corey."

They hugged fiercely, briefly. When they stepped back George Starling saw tears on Russ Corey's face.

"What's the matter, Russ? Didn't you ever hug a president before?"

He turned suddenly to walk away among the trees.

They knew they would never see one another again.

Cheyenne Mountain

"Well, that's about it."

Silence in the main data control room of Project Dustbin, patched together after the disaster at Goddard.

Men and women gathered before the main display console on a huge board once used by the Strategic Air Command to track Russian bombers. Twenty-seven white lights shone steadily on the board, standing out sharply against the amber, green, and red glowing in diminished number. The director leaned back in his swivel chair and lit a cigarette. Forgetting himself for the moment, he looked about for an ashtray. There wasn't one. There

311

never had been one in this electronics center so sensitive to concentration. Now it didn't matter. He flicked an ash on the floor.

A girl stood by his side. *"What's it mean? The white lights?"*

"It means that pretty soon the lights will be going out all over the world. Each white light . . . hell, I'm sorry. Each white light means that a Dustbin probe has gone dead. Dusted, so to speak. You'll see more of them before the day is over."

"There's no mistake?"

"Nope. Not when they start falling like snowflakes. Look; two more just came on line."

They stared at the gleaming white lights.

"What . . . what do we do?"

"Whatever you want, honey. It's all finished here. As of now, Project Dustbin is shut down. Finished. Dead." He swung around in the swivel chair. *"Go home to your family, girl."*

"Don't have one. I guess we're going to die soon, aren't we?"

"Yeah. I guess so."

"It's a lot of shit doing that alone."

The big man rose from his chair, dropped the cigarette on the floor, ground it out with his boot. He put his arm around the young woman. *"I got a wife, four kids, a mother-in-law, a dog, and four cats. One more will fit just fine. Come on home and join the family."* He turned to the others. *"Hey, don't forget not to turn out the lights."*

Nancy Parks sprawled on the king-sized bed of the lush suite in Disney World's Contemporary Hotel. They were just to the west of Orlando. The government and Disney crews had carved out dozens of helicopter pads and airstrips of varying sizes. They could take off in a chopper and head almost due east and in twenty minutes be settling to the ground alongside a launch pad in the great space center.

Every Disney facility, and the hotels surrounding Epcot, Sea World, and the Buena Vista resort area, were run by the government with the fortunate and whole-hearted support of the Disney work force. Nearby, Kissimmee Airport, just south of Buena Vista, had been transformed into a bristling military base with a hundred attack helicopters, vertical-takeoff jet fighters, and heavy combat strike jets. Along the eastern edge of Orlando, hugging Highway 50, Herndon Field was a command and communications center also under full control of the government. And directly south of Herndon, the great Orlando International Airport, with its two huge runaways each of twelve thousand feet, was now a full military and civilian government installation. It was a moment of the past catching up to the future. Many years before the huge commercial jet center had been McCoy Air Force Base. The Strategic Air Command had enough hydrogen bombs on that one field, had they all detonated at once, to blow the Florida peninsula clean in two.

Now, ringed by steel and containing massive firepower, the huge facilities of Disney World functioned as the interrogation, briefing, training, and preparation center for the people selected for the brief but terrifying ascent from the Atlantic coastline to the steadily growing structure of *Pegasus* seven hundred miles above Earth. Marc and Nancy Seavers were in the Contemporary to study the conditions under which the people-processing took place and above all to try to understand the grim psychological pressures on the children and lesser number of adults.

They were caught completely by surprise on their first day as they watched processing in the Polynesian Hotel. Mobs of bright-eyed children swarmed past them on their way to the Magic Kingdom, where all Disney entertainment had been modified to begin the psychological indoctrination. "Who would ever have thought that Mickey and Minnie Mouse, and Donald Duck, and Goofy, and the Chipmunks, and the Big Bad Wolf, *all* of them," Nancy said in amazement to her husband, "would be preparing children for the most incredible voyage anyone ever *dreamed* of taking!"

"Is that an expostulation or a question?" Seavers retorted, earning a finger-waggling nose-thumbing from his red-haired wife.

"You know very well what I mean," she told him. She grasped his arm and squeezed fiercely. "It's so *strange*," she said in a lowered voice as the children raced past them squealing and laughing. "This really *is* Fantasyland. Out there, beyond all that barbed wire and the fences they've put up, the world is grim and getting grimmer by the hour, and *here* the kids are singing *It's a small world, after all*, and getting ready to go on a space picnic!" She looked about them with a shadow across her troubled eyes. "If they ever get the chance . . ."

"What's that supposed to mean?"

"They won't *all* get the chance, Marc."

"Pick any part of the population in all this world and that statement is true."

"I know, I *know*," she said, trying not to be suddenly so miserable. "If I could save a few more of them, I'd gladly let them take my place."

Seavers sighed. He'd gone through *that* argument with so many people! "It doesn't work that way, hon. Children can't run the ships or—"

"*Stop*. Stop right there. Just because I know reality doesn't mean I can't get the sniffles every now and then."

"You've had your full ration, Nancy. Tears won't help these kids or anybody else. You have *got* to think that way from now on." She nodded as they stepped aside for a sudden rush of children, singing joyously as they went by.

"Well, I'm glad you let me have *my* program, anyway," she told her husband, wiping away a wet spot on her cheek. "Keeping the music alive is just as important as food, as far as I'm concerned." She shook his arm in mock anger. "I don't have to tell that to *you*, of all people. The first time I met you I thought I was going crazy on that catamaran with all that music blasting out across the water."

He smiled at memories of *Spirit*. She was right. Music had always been part of his life. But Nancy . . .

She carried it far beyond any such pale acceptance as *liking* or *enjoying* music. To her, music was life and life was music, and no sooner had they wed and the full impact of where the world was rolling with such finality hit her right between the eyes, when she took on the self-appointed task of "saving our spirits as well as our bodies."

He looked at her by his side and thanked God again for the miracle that let him love this woman as fiercely as he'd loved (and always would love) Deborah. Karen and Missy were no more, gone with Deborah, but now, through Nancy, he had hundreds of children whose lives would hang on his performance. "You know what they call you?" he asked suddenly, gesturing to the throng of children now behind them as they raced into the Magic Kingdom. "They call you the Music Lady. You're supposed to be the spirit of *Pegasus*."

"That's a tall order, Admiral," she said without committing to a true response. They entered the Polynesian and went through the security system to Briefing. Joe Briand had something to do with this group, Seavers understood, and when he saw the hundred dark-hued men and women, he understood. Indians, all of them. *Construction teams; steel workers on the ultimate girders looking straight down for seven hundred miles . . .*

They watched from a distance. Young bucks and their girls. Marc Seavers had made some very hard rules. No couples who were not married. No free love "up there." It was family time from the outset. No free love, no alcohol, no drugs, *and no exceptions* to those rules. Right now the Indians were having a bit of a hassle with the briefing teams. Marc led Nancy to the group to find out what was wrong.

"It's their ceremonial dress," Nancy explained, pointing. "They won't let them take it with them." She turned suddenly, her face stark. "Marc, *please*, don't let those people be forced to leave their things behind. Look: drums, clothing, it doesn't weigh *that* much. But I know what they're doing! They're taking their spirit, their history, their music with them. Marc, *please!*"

He caught her completely by surprise. He left her

315

with a shrug to free his arm and walked to the group. Nancy followed close behind, but not too close to interfere. Everyone turned to look at Seavers. A NASA technician came to attention. "Good morning, sir." Seavers returned the greeting. "Let's keep this casual," he said. "You have a problem?"

"Yes, sir. I understand *their* problem. They want to take those things with them. You know the rules, Admiral. Everybody leaves everything they can't fit in one small container behind them."

Seavers looked at one hundred young men and women. *They* were the true ancestors of this land. For several moments he remained silent, then gestured to the waiting, silent couples. He turned to the technician.

"Break the rules. They take what they have with them."

"But—"

"This is not a dialogue, Sanders," he said, reading the man's name from his security badge. "I'd appreciate your handling it quietly and with dispatch."

"Yes, sir. Consider it done."

Not one of the hundred spoke a word to Marc Seavers. They didn't need to. *There are more words in the eyes of man* . . .

"My God, how you amaze me sometimes," Nancy told him as they left the Polynesian. "One moment you're all steel and chrome and the next instant you show more understanding—"

"They hit a weak spot," he told her. He held his conversation as they entered the security van reserved for him. He leaned forward to the driver. "Take us to Buena Vista. Come around to the back parking lot by the paddlewheel steamer."

They settled down, Nancy studying him. "What did you mean by a weak spot?"

He leaned back in his seat and a long sigh escaped him. "I've been programmed," he told her. "One of my requirements for this job was too read a certain book. Hell, I can't even pronounce the author's name." He spelled it out for her. "Shkilnyk. Anastasia M. Shkilnyk. The book is called *A Poison Stronger Than Love*."

316

"Tell me about it. Please."

He stared straight ahead, but her hand reached across the space between their seats and found his as he spoke. "It's about a group of Indians, the Ojibwas. They lived in a place called Grassy Narrows. Up in Canada. I remember highlights; they won't leave me alone. It's why I did what I did just now. Anyway, of all the people who died before the age of nineteen among the Ojibwa, almost all committed suicide. One out of every four people in this tribe died naturally. The others all died from violence or suicide. And it was worse for the children. No one understood what was going on. These people were known for their love and kindness, and then within one or two generations they abused their children, beat them, starved and raped them or just abandoned them.

"The author of the study said it was a world turned upside down. A nightmare come real. A decent community suddenly became a nightmare day and night; she called it rape, incest, torture, murder, unchecked destruction. It goes on and on like that. In short, these people were self-destructing."

"In heaven's name, *why?*"

He turned to hold her eyes. "It's what they finally called a poison stronger than love. *Alcohol.* Rampant drunkenness. Total alcoholism. It became a horrible disease. The Canadian government back in the sixties relocated the tribe. They lost their faith, their spirit. They abandoned their relationship with the animals that had supported them and kept them alive for generations. The author also pointed out that they lost their music. They simply stopped having anything to do with it.

"I memorized her conclusion. I had to, once I read it, and I hope I'll never forget it." Nancy waited, silent. "She wrote that what happened at Grassy Narrows, and I'm quoting here, must 'serve as a warning that our own survival depends on restoring a sense of mutual responsibility for one another and ultimately for the fate of the Earth. Love has to become a stronger power than the poisons of self-interest and powerlessness or else we

317

will all perish.' End quote, Nancy. But that's become *my* avenue to the future and why I—well, why I broke my own rules and interrupted what was going on back there."

Captain Jack's Oyster Bar was still open and they gave themselves the disappearing luxury of crab claws and beer. They walked back along a winding path to where the security van awaited them. Their route took them alongside the *Empress Lily* paddlewheel steamer that housed restaurants and entertainment centers.

A young couple with two children, a boy and a girl, stood before them. "You're Admiral Seavers," the man said. Seavers watched him cautiously; there was no mistaking the look of desperation in the man's face. The woman was tight-lipped, her face white.

"They won't take our children," he said.

Marc and Nancy Seavers looked at the well-scrubbed brother and sister. "We've tried, Admiral," the man went on. "We've filled out the applications and we passed all the health tests and everything else, and we even said we didn't care if *we* went, but in the name of God please take our kids."

"I—"

"Nothing you say will mean anything, Admiral. I know that. I have to do what needs to be done."

Before Seavers could move the man jerked a heavy revolver from his jacket. In a swift movement, much too quick for Seavers to counter, he pointed the gun at close range at his wife's head and pulled the trigger. The back side of her head exploded and tore away in a grisly shower. It happened so quickly that Nancy was still screaming and throwing herself to cover the children when the man smiled at Seavers as he brought the gun around. "Maybe now you'll give them a chance." He pressed the muzzle against his head and squeezed the trigger. Another roaring explosion. His body whirled about violently as he crashed to the ground. Seavers looked at Nancy, stained with blood and brains and flesh, as she lay on the ground over the children, white-faced with terror.

"Move!" he shouted to his wife. He grabbed the boy, Nancy the girl, and they ran back to the van, pushed the children inside and climbed in after them. Seavers slammed the door. "Get this thing back to the briefing center," he snapped to the driver. "Take us inside to Processing. *Move it*."

The children were shaking, too terrified to cry. Seavers held the boy by both arms before him. "Tell me your name, son."

"T-Tom, sir." Seavers looked at the shaking girl in Nancy's arms. "How old are you, Tom?"

"Eight . . . my sister, Keesha, she's six." He swallowed. "Is my daddy and mommy dead?"

"Yes."

"He told us something bad was going to happen . . . and, and right after it did, there would be good. That you and this lady . . . w-would . . ."

Marc Seavers pulled the boy close. The tears came explosively against his shirt. "We will, we will, Tom." He turned to his wife.

"The madness is starting. We're going straight to Processing. You're no going back to the hotel with me. You and Tom and Keesha are going into Processing immediately and you'll be on the first ship in line to fly to *Pegasus*. Got it?"

She tightened her grip on the little girl. They were both crying. "Got it." She swallowed. *No tears, damn it!* "I love you. I'll be waiting for you upstairs."

Wallops Island, Virginia

The Righteous Army of God thundered down the highways, grouped for massed power at the causeways and lesser roads, hit the beaches north and south of Wallops Island Launch Center with beach buggies and tracked vehicles, and sent forty boats and swamp airboats along the canals, waterways, and beaches of the Virginia scientific launch site converted under emergency construction to heavy lift boosters to supply *Pegasus*. Zack Bible's storm troopers of the Lord, a motley, beer-swilling, coke-jabbing and -smoking band of terrorists in their ultimate element of frenzied rapine and destruction, tore against the hastily-erected barricades thrown up by national guard teams and SWAT units brought in from the surrounding communities. Unlike at Goddard, Bible's screaming men and women rushed into a heavy opening wave of defensive firepower. More than a thousand of the attackers fell from direct hits or the hard cracking blasts of mortars and recoilless rifles. But at best the defense was more hope than substance. Bible's troopers were too many and those who survived the initial assault were too crazed to care whether or not they died. They were zombies without real consciousness of self, let alone being capable of reason, even in concern for their own survival. They neither knew nor cared that one out of every three of their number was wounded or killed.

They were also unaware that their hysterical frontal assault was being maneuvered adroitly.

High above the ripping flame and tearing concussions an army air controller studied the scene. He zoomed in to a tight television closeup to a Land Rover racing amidst a group of trucks armed with heavy weapons. "I've got him, Big Tree," he called calmly into his lip mike. "It's the Land Rover within that bunch of vehicles coming along the Section Four Road. I've got that one they're looking for. Over."

"Eye Sky, you confirm the person of Zack Bible? Big Tree over."

"Sure looks like the reverend, Big Tree. White suit, gold stripes, standing up, holding a stick or a wand with a light at the end, pushing everybody on. If it ain't the reverend I don't know who it is. Over."

"Ah, roger, Eye Sky. Take him out. Over."

"Hey, you got it. Eye Sky confirming lethal strike against Target Able." Jocularity had vanished from the voice above the battle. "Please confirm, over from Eye Sky."

"Big Tree here. Go get him, ace. You're cut free. Over and standing by."

The A-12 Puma unwound its X-wing, a massive four-bladed rotor that had been locked into place as an unmoving wing for high speed. Now the wing began to turn and spun faster and faster to translate into a helicopter mode. The Puma swung down in a curving attack and came out level two hundred yards above the Section Four Road leading to the main launch complex at Wallops Island. The Puma came to a dead stop. The pilot-gunner cinched his sealed helmet, kept his view steady in the eyepiece, his fingers moving nimbly amidst the buttons and knobs on the control stick. Through the eyepiece the figure in white and gold stood out brilliantly in the crosshairs. The pilot selected automode tracking with a Penetrator wire-guided missile. "Bye-bye, Reverend," he said softly and squeezed.

The missile spat forward on flame, trailing the wire carrying guidance signals from the Puma computer system on target automode. Seven pounds of X43 plastique took the man in white and gold squarely in the chest. The plastique exploded instantly. The upper half of the body soared in a trailing-pink spray of torso and whirling arms for a hundred yards; the lower torso and legs were driven through the floorboards of the Land Rover that moments later vanished in its own fireball.

"Hey, hey, Big Tree from Eye Sky. Scratch the rev, babe. They're slowing it down there. Looks like the steam's out of that bunch. Over."

"Good deal, Eye Sky. Recover to two thousand and maintain battlefield surveillance on open line. Over and out."

"Ta ta, Big Tree."

Vandenberg Air Force Base, California

"This is Launch Control. I have a clear green board at T minus six minutes and counting." Gary Russel sat on a high podium in the launch control center of Vandenberg Air Force Base on the California coast, orchestrating the final countdown minutes for a huge new shuttle on the Slick Six pad. Three thick solid propellant boosters clustered beneath a massive curving dome atop the boosters, and above the dome rose another thick-bodied booster filled with liquid propellants. At

321

the top of the engineering heap the *Hap Arnold* bulged with its own fuel tanks, four air force astronauts, and a belly pregnant with volatile, high-performance rocket boosters and their intended deepspace probes.

"T minus four minutes and counting," Russel announced, his voice carried into every receiving headset and speaker throughout the base, to the search planes high overhead and to ships far downrange off the California and Mexican coastlines. "We will go to full autocount at T minus three minutes."

A voice came onto the line carrying with it the familiar crackle of a transmission originating from the air. "Slick Six Launch Control, this is Hiawatha Four. We have a cruise liner that's just entered a potential booster impact zone. Recommend a hold until we can clear them out. Over."

Gary Russel thought it over. Quickly and efficiently. The rules were that if there was more than one chance in a million of hitting a ship with booster debris, you held your launch. But those probes in the belly of *Hap Arnold* were critical to the future of at least a part of the human race and—

"Launch Control to all hands. We are overriding the problem of a target in a booster drop zone. All hands continue the count and continue to autocount at T minus three minutes."

"*But your procedures—*"

Russel didn't give the unidentified voice any chance to waste his time or mess up the countdown. "Whoever's on line, do you have a vehicle problem? *Answer immediately.*"

"Uh, no, but—"

Russel watched the digital numbers fleeing backward and vanishing. "Then shut the fuck up and get off the line. Launch Control here, T minus three minutes precisely," his finger depressed the control, "and we are on autocount. Cross your fingers and count your chickens, people. We are go. All reporting stations are go. Verbal confirmation, *Arnold,* please. Over."

"*Arnold* here. Everything's just hunky-dory, Control. Thanks for the boot in the ass. Over."

322

"Uh, roger that, *Arnold*." A momentary pause for continued board scanning. "Launch control at T minus two minutes and counting, we are green across the board, pressurization coming up, we have a live bird out there, rub them rosaries and rabbits' feet, we continue on line . . ."

Hap Arnold came alive with a scream and a lunge. With the huge solid boosters as primary thrust there were no massive holddown clamps. The great solids ignited to full thrust and threw the entire package upward. Trailing two thousand feet of fire, the new shuttle howled defiance at heaven and Earth and rejected the latter for the former. *Hap Arnold* kicked away her boosters and settled into the smoother ride with a big liquid-fuel tank providing the push. This mission had no time for booster tank modifications or small rockets to use the empty tank for the growth of *Pegasus*. Its fuel exhausted, it was dumped into a grazing atmospheric flight that would soon bring it back to Earth as blazing chunks of debris.

No one paid any attention to what had been discarded. *Hap Arnold* rode higher and settled into her orbit at three hundred miles, racing over the polar regions of the planet at nearly five miles a second. The bay doors opened and the astronauts went to work. As they came upward on a looping orbit toward the north pole they fired probes one through six, long-stemmed beauties of immense pencil-thin power, fanning out at varying angles up and away from the plane of the ecliptic. Three more passes around the world and they were ready for the next firing. Six more probes were aligned and held in position by their gyroscopes, the entire assembly fell southward toward Antarctica, and the probes ripple-fired on great fans of pale violet flame.

The astronauts nodded with satisfaction and jetted back to *Hap Arnold*, closed the doors and secured the bird. "Let's go home," the pilot said, and they did just that, slicing downward at eighteen thousand miles an hour toward the desert strip in California.

Far above and below the Earth, twelve probes hurtled silently up and down from the planet, seeking out dustless space.

St. Augustine

"The Lord God has spoken to me. He talks to me often, just as many times as *He* considers it to be necessary. He has told me that it is time to destroy the entire filthy place. Everything at the Cape *must* go. His legions, His hordes, must hurl themselves at the space demons who are trying to thwart His will."

"Yes, sir, Reverend—"

"Didn't God talk to me that night in Virginia? Do you all need any more proof than *that*? You was with me all the time, remember? Every blasted minute of the day and the night. I couldn't even take a piss without a couple of you watchin' me—"

"*Protecting* you, you means," growled a follower.

"Well, *of course* you was protectin' me! That's God's will. It's what I'm trying to tell you, ain't it? How else could I know, could I *know,* that they had a setup to kill my ass deader than hell at Wallops Island, unless God come to me in the night and spoke His warning to me? If any of you smartass churchgoers got any ideas that speaks to the contrary, lemme hear it *now.*" The God Reverend Zack Bible withdrew a blue-steel .357 Magnum from a shoulder holster and clicked the hammer back and laid the awesome weapon on the table before him. "Test yourselves, my friends," he said, smiling. "Your word against the hand of the Lord through mine own hands."

"Aw, shit, Reverend, that's hardly fair," Cal Tutberry complained. "Goddamn it, you got that there piece jes' waiting by yore hand and we—"

"*You* are fucking dead," were the last words he heard, as the .357 seemed to jump into Bible's hands and three rounds went off with shattering roars one after the other so fast they blended into a single ear-shattering explosion. The back wall of the Monk's Inn Restaurant in the historic section of St. Augustine turned from a pale beige to a new pattern: Spattered Blood, Gore, Bones and Brains. No one left the restaurant; they were

324

all part of Zack Bible's private armed guard. The men and women sat at the front of the restaurant or stood with heavy weapons in the narrow street outside.

Bible handed the .357 to an aide. "Clear the shit offen' it and put in all new rounds, silver bullets, now, you recall?"

"Yes, sir."

Zack Bible smiled. He didn't know jackshit about the voice of God talking to him, but it didn't take no damn genius to figure out after what they done up at Goddard, and how the body count of them young womenfolk must have been two hundred that they pleasured themselves with before cutting their bellies and their throats, well, you just had to know the people who really run the country, them FBI and CIA and all them types would be setting a coon trap to get his ass. Good old Kimberly. They'd snared all his brain into a little iron cage with that there really superfine cocaine and he was hooked just as fast as you can snap your fingers, and then Flower give it to him good, *real* good now, and the way he carried on and hollered, and even that time he plain shit all over the couch in that motor home, why, that must have been the very first blowjob that dumb damn scientist had *ever* had in his whole life.

No matter. The next morning when they got to Wallops Island, Bible dressed Kimberly in one of Bible's finest white leather-and-gold suits, made him stand out real pretty, and he made sure that Kimberly-come-Bible led the goddamned charge in that there Land Rover while Bible sat four vehicles back in an armored car, and whoowhee, but didn't they do a number on the honorable professor! They blew his ass to pieces, and *that*, Bible laughed, was telling it like it really was.

What counted now is that them government people, they figgered they had nothing to worry about. Zack Bible was in chunks feeding the scorpions and beach rats and the toads and the palmetto bugs and flies and skeeters and all them little critters, right? So they'd let down their guard, and all the next couple of days, why, Zack had his people gathering along the coast.

And soon they'd come together just off the rivers sepa-
rating the launch complex from the mainland, and God
would give the Reverend his greatest test yet. Zack
Bible smiled. Ain't *nothing* could stop him now. Not
when all them smart government fuckers just knew he
was deader'n shit.

16

Disney World

"Line up, please! Adults stay with the children but
we *must* have everybody in single file. We want
everyone to bare your left arm to the shoulder. As you
come to the table for your inoculations, stand in the white
circle and look straight ahead." Chief Petty Officer Bobbi
Mitchell, U.S. Navy, had moved thousands of recruits
through many such lines before, but *never* had she
known anything like this. A quiet desperation mixed
with a total lack of understanding. Relief at being selected to move through the line clashed with the realization that loved ones would never be seen again.
Exultation, numbness, fear, joy, exhilaration, terror,
hope, dismay; all about her, every day, she slogged
through the porridge of human emotions. The impact
was all the greater because the time of thousands of
recruits were behind her, in a world she knew she'd
never again know. The numbers had shrunk from young
naval recruits to what everyone hoped would be survivors of the worst storm the Earth had ever known.
Bobbi Mitchell was an old-timer, her two sons and
daughter grown and married and scattered about the
country. Too old, too distant to make it in here. Oh,
she could have done that. She knew the right people in
the right places, but her family had been navy these
three past generations and they had the inclination to

stay and fight it out. *Whatever it is we're supposed to fight,* she thought charily.

Most of the bodies shuffling through the lines now were children, anywhere from the little ones on up through teen-agers, with the adults obviously selected for strength and leadership. No matter how torn might be someone's inner feelings, she had never yet encountered any of the weepies or the gaunt facial expressions that spoke of inner torment allowed to spill out to affect negatively the children and people about them. And they looked for just that, CPO Bobbi Mitchell and all the others who moved amidst these ultimate of all refugees. When they found someone they thought might fold under the pressure or for whom the emotional upheaval or the fear was simply too great, that adult and all the children with that person were quietly edged from the main crowd. Never in front of the others. Never with a scene to dismay *anyone* here. They were tagged silently by look or name and, as the processing and briefing and preparations continued, they were "assigned to the next station" and sent to another, inland-distant briefing center where all proceeded as if there never existed the slightest hitch. And there they would remain, far from the launching pads carrying the brief acquaintances they had met in this mis-named Magic Kingdom.

Bobbi Mitchell stiffened when she saw the red hair. No mistaking Nancy Parks Seavers. *My god, it's the admiral's wife! What the hell is she doing here? She doesn't have to go through all this. She's supposed to go through astronaut indoctrination at Johnson or the Cape and* . . . Then she remembered. That horrible scene at Buena Vista, the murder and the suicide. They were still talking about the way Nancy Seavers had thrown her own body over two children she never even known to protect them from the gunfire she expected to tear into their bodies. CPO Mitchell didn't need any further explanations. As a navy noncom she might have questions. As a mother she already knew the answers, and she also knew enough not to say a word or make a special case of this woman. She caught the eye of the admiral's

327

wife, the young boy and girl clinging to her, and Bobbi Mitchell nodded, a barely perceptible motion—and received the same from Nancy Seavers, and that was their *only* communication of a personal kind.

They stuffed Donald Duck, quacking bitterly, into a vacuum-cleaner bag, wrapped latex gloves around his wrists, jammed a goldfish bowl onto his head and clamped it to the vacuum-cleaner bag, and shoved big galoshes with snap fasteners onto his feet. Within the goldfish bowl Donald quacked and spluttered and wriggled, but all they heard from the large video screen was muted muttering. Finally they attached a hose to the bag, the motor came on with a whine, and the suit popped out to send Donald floating at the end of the hose, quacking all the louder, but still not making a single sound that made sense. A hand appeared and quickly drew a microphone and headset on the screen and Donald's voice burst into screeching life, complaining bitterly.

The children giggled and squirmed in their seats and the adults either smiled or studied the screen intensely to be certain their cartoon-character introduction to a spacesuit was sufficient to really explain what was happening. The squawking feathered astronaut faded, to be replaced by an adult and a child on the screen. Now the figures the small audience watched were twice normal size, and small details became apparent. The unseen narrator kept up a running chatter to explain that everyone would receive instruction booklets for their equipment, but this was the best way to really learn what it was like. "Each and every one of you will be given a suit with your name already on that suit. You will spend two hours every day getting in and out of your suit until it's just as easy and comfortable as putting on a pair of jeans and boots. When you're real good at wearing the suit, we'll give you a special test. You'll wear your suit, with your oxygen pack attached and working, and walk into a chamber. Then we'll fill the chamber with an orange mist. You don't need to be frightened of it because it *is* orange. If your suit is on right, and it works just the way it's supposed to, you'll see the orange but you won't be able to taste it. Okay, boys and girls and moms and dads, here we go . . ."

Indoctrination took one week, no more, no less. There wasn't time for more. This wasn't a pleasure trip or even a space flight; this was *escape* and they had time only for the essentials. They gave up all their own clothing right on down to bare skin and received two sets of new clothing, from special cotton underwear to work thermals to easywear jumpsuits and slip-on boots and finally their own pressure garments that could keep them alive in vacuum. The whole idea was that they would never *be* in vacuum condition, but they had to be prepared to survive anything. The suits were intended to let the wearer survive an emergency, nothing more. They were taught to react to alarms, and not even the smallest children were spared. "It's like the smoke alarms in your homes, boys and girls. You were taught that if that alarm ever went off, you had to do certain things right and do them immediately. That's the kind of thinking we want you to develop with your new spacesuit . . ."

Nancy Seavers enveloped herself with the need to hover about Tom and Keesha. Both children clung fiercely to her presence, but they were still numb from their recent intimacy with the worst level of death, and both jumped at sudden loud noises. Nancy knew better than to baby them. That wouldn't do; the weepies meant that not even she could be assured of keeping these two children in the group that would soon travel to the Cape. And she was absolutely determined that they *were* going. She knew the real test would come with the way they reacted to the question and answer sessions where everyone seemed to have a thousand questions. NASA did it right. They used films of actual space flights, American and Russian, and made certain to show astronauts, both men and women, of many different races aboard the spacecraft and stations. Then the children gathered in a wide circle, informal and comfortable, to ask the questions bubbling within them.

"Is it scary to go up in a rocket?"

"It can be. It's noisy and the rocket shakes a lot

329

sometimes, and for a little while you can't move because of what we call g-pressure. It's like being in a car taking a turn at high speed, or in one of those teacups at the county fair that whirls you around. That's g-pressure. It pushes you down real hard in your seat, so we have comfortable seats for you. Besides, the whole ride from the ground into orbit to the ship that's waiting for you is only twenty minutes or so. Most of that ride is pretty neat."

"Will we get sick in space?"

"Well, *I* did. It happens to some of us, because when the rocket engines stop you're weightless, just like the people floating around in the movies you saw. The first thing you feel is like floating in a swimming pool. There's really no up or down except what you see with your eyes. So until you get used to things, the real trick is not to turn your head too fast or too suddenly, because that can make you dizzy and your stomach won't like it. If you do get sick it's like being in an airliner. You strap yourself into your seat and you use that nifty little bag they give you. It's free, too, and if you're real nice we'll even let you keep what's in the bag if you fill it with the cookies you weren't supposed to eat, okay?"

"You said your head gets, you know, like stuffed up? Is it real bad?"

"No way. You ever hang upside down from a bar in your gym or at home? Well, if you've done that you know exactly what it's like when you first get into space. We'll call you spaceheads. All of us know what it's like, but it goes away pretty quick."

"Do you really stretch in space? Get bigger, I mean?"

"You sure do. A person's spine, the backbone? Well, when you're weightless, with no feeling of gravity, the spine does two things. It gets longer and it straightens. A doctor tells you this is because the discs between the vertebrae expand. On Earth, they come back together again because of gravity. Up there," a finger jabbed at the sky, "it's *zero* gravity. There's no downward push on the spine so it stays extended. Some astronauts after a few weeks in orbit became several inches taller. Their pants didn't fit them any more."

330

Nervous laughter becoming honest laughter. One wide-eyed youngster with a hand up. "Do you ever shrink back to yourself again?"

"Absolutely, son. As soon as you're back on Earth in normal gravity you start becoming the size you were before. But in *your* case, being a little feller who's growing up so fast, you'll just keep getting taller."

Two hands in the air. "Let's keep your questions to what happens immediately once you're in orbit—or, on second thought, what really worries you. If it's interesting, and its *all* interesting, you'll have plenty of time to find out about it once you're on the big ship, okay?"

"Can you smell in space?"

"Sure, if you don't bathe or clean yourself. In fact," the astronaut speaker wrinkled his nose, "once I smelled pretty bad myself."

Giggles. "No, no, I mean, does your nose work?"

An astronaut's hand moved his nose back and forth. "Mine does. If yours works down here it works just fine up there. Next question?"

"I read that your face changes when you just get into space. Is that true?" The questioner couldn't really believe it could be at all true.

"That's a *very* good question and I'm glad you asked it because, *yes*, your facial appearance really changes, and if you don't expect it, wow, it looks like Halloween time and everybody's wearing a mask. If you look in a mirror shortly after you get in the big ship, why, you might not even recognize yourself."

A chorus of *wow, gee, golly, gosh, cool* and other phrases drifted about in response. "But it's not a problem. Feel the loose flesh on your face, like this. That's right, pinch it between your fingers. See, or feel, how it can move about so much? Well, once you're weightless, that loose flesh doesn't hang down any more. It floats upward and hangs around the cheekbones. Over there; you're Japanese, right? Would you please stand, miss? Now, see how high her cheekbones are? I hope you like the way she looks, because you're *all* going to look like that for a while. Also, you can expect your face to puff out a bit. We call it the Hangover Look. You get

331

bags under your eyes. Everything's floating around under your skin, and the veins in your neck, and a lot of times in your forehead, look like they're swelling up. About a week after you're in orbit most of this will go away. But for the first week, it's Halloween time!"

A woman with three children at her side raised her hand. Obviously she knew something of space flight. "Sir, how serious is the loss of calcium from the bones?"

"Not nearly as bad as we once believed. In fact, now that we and the Russians have had people in space for well over a year at a time, we've found it isn't that much of a problem. For a few months you do lose calcium. Then the rate of loss drops off and things return to normal. Good diet, supplementary calcium, and the body's own ability to compensate for a new environment make this an oddity instead of a problem."

"I had beautiful long hair. Why did they cut it off?"

"First, we don't want it getting caught in your pressure helmet. That could cause a leak and your face would really puff up then. Seriously, a suit leak is very dangerous. Long hair could cause that leak. Second, in space, long hair floats around like spider webs in a wind." Giggles. "It's easy to get your hair snagged and tangled in things. If you want to let it grow long again once you're aboard ship, you can."

"Do you wash with soap in space?"

"Yep. You've still got to wash behind your ears. You'll have the regular soap, you know, the bars you use now, and you can also use shampoo. It's a bit tricky, but then you're all here because you're smarter than the average bear."

"Isn't it real quiet in space? I mean, there's no air so there's nothing for sound to travel through?"

"Well, it's not *that* quiet. But if you're outside the ship and not wearing a suit, it's *very* quiet because you would be dead." *No* giggles. "That's why we're so strict about your suit training. But you're right. If there's no air around you there can't be any sound. But I guess you forgot that the ship is sealed, like an airliner or a submarine, to keep in the air, and so there's air all around you, and boy, there sure *are* sounds. All sorts of equipment will be working, so you'll be hearing pumps, gears, winches, fans, doors opening and closing, hatches clanging and closets banging, people talking, television and radio and—"

"Dogs barking?"

"I don't know the answer to that yet, son."

"It sure would be sad if we never could hold a doggie again."

"It sure would. We expect to find out real soon. Next?"

"Can I wear my contact lenses aboard the ship?"

"No." The astronaut hesitated for the effect of that emphatic *no* to ripple through his audience. "Keeping the air free of debris, specks of dust to pieces of dirt, is real difficult in weightlessness. We've tried contact lenses, so we're talking now from hard experience. You can take them with you, and you'll be allowed to wear them when you're not working or training. At the same time, and I'm glad you asked that, those of you who wear eyeglasses will need elastic straps or some kind of stickum to hold them on your face. Don't forget that they're weightless and without elastic or sticky stuff they just float up and down on the end of your nose." He brought his eyes together. "You'd look pretty goofy going around like *this* all the time."

"Who washes the dishes!"

"They don't *wash* dishes in space, silly. The water would just float away."

"Yes, they do!"

"Hold it, hold it. You're both right and you're both wrong. Most of the time you'll be eating from cans or bags. Sometimes, and we hope to get better at this, we can serve you food that won't crumble and float around. But whatever you use, we'll clean it with special ultrasonic machines—that's like supersound—"

"Hey, rock and roll!"

"Sure, why not. Rock and roll supersonics. Fans suck up the little pieces and carry them away into a container. We'll have special tissues with a soap disinfectant. There's lots of ways. But you *will* clean what you use."

333

"I hope we can wash our clothes. Can you imagine wearing dirty clothes all the time? *Ick!*"

"They'll be washed. Sometimes with ultrasonics. Maybe even in sealed washing machines. But yes, you can wash them."

"Can you sleep in space?"

"When you're tired you can sleep *anywhere*. Sure you can sleep in space. I did it for a couple of months. It's great."

"Did you snore?"

"Not in space. Maybe some people do, but I never heard them. If you look in a mirror with a bright light shining down your throat, you'll see a soft palate, um, just about here, *glug*, in the upper throat. When your parents sleep on their back here on Earth, this soft palate is hanging down and breathing causes it to vibrate."

"Boy, does *my* dad vibrate! He shakes the whole house!"

The laughter rose and fell easily. "Right. But in space that palate is weightless and it doesn't hang down. So very few people, if any, snore up there."

"Gee, that's a relief!"

"Uh, I'm not sure how to ask this, or if I should . . ." The young lady scuffed her toe and her face reddened, and the astronaut on the stage before the group came quickly to her rescue.

"You're going to ask me how to we go the bathroom in space, right? Hey, *everybody* wants to know that. They *need* to know it, because we have to go to the bathroom no matter *where* we are. So let's not be embarrassed about what's natural, okay? Now, let's understand that when you're weightless it makes no difference if you're sitting or standing when a person has to urinate. In zero gravity nothing falls down *or* up, so we've got to be sure we collect all liquids that aren't contained, and it doesn't matter if it's water, tea, urine, coffee, alcohol; whatever. The only difference we need to be concerned about is that men have outside plumbing and the ladies have recessed fixtures and that's all there is to it. When someone uses a seat we try to make it as airtight as possible. Beneath the person sitting down we have a suction system. That's a fan that draws all liquid into a collection compartment. That is it, no more and no less. And what's the difference for solid waste? Well, we use the same thing. We call it a john, a toilet seat, a commode, a potty, and they all mean the same thing and they all work the same way. The trick is the air suction that draws everything away from the person into the collection tank. Any paper or damp tissue people use for hygiene—our fancy word for cleaning our bodies—also is drawn by this same air suction system into the holding tank."

"Boy, that sure sounds like a lot of work!"

"It's a lot more work holding it for a couple of days, son."

"I don't think I could do *that*."

"So start learning how the system works and it becomes just as natural to go to the bathroom in space as it is here on Earth. Next?"

"If I can't take my doggie way up there can I have a bird, like a canary, for a pet?"

"Yes."

"*I can?*"

"Yep. We'll go into that later, but canaries and parakeets are just fine. Next question."

"Can I have a plant if I want?"

"Well, not only can you have plants, we *want* you to grow as many as you can. We'll teach you how to grow plants that provide food for us, like sweet potatoes, and other plants that change the air we exhale into fresh oxygen for us to breathe."

"Mister Astronaut?"

He looked down at her, all of six years old with that total innocence that never lasts long enough for any mother or father. "Yes, honey?"

"Can God hear me pray to Him when I'm in space?"

He knelt down to be closer to her from the low stage. He wanted to reach out to touch her curly hair, but he knew what she wanted most of all now was authority.

"Absolutely. God hears you down here and He'll listen to everything you have to say to Him up there."

"I'm glad, because I'm scared and I need to talk to Him."

335

* * *

"We've found it's best if you teach the children your-selves," Kay Deming told the adults assembled in the night lounge of the Polynesian. "*We* can tell them what to do in an emergency with their suits, of course, but experience proves this frightens them to the point where they'd freeze instead of performing. But if it's a family affair it seems to be much more effective. We've told the children their reaction to alarms must be *instant* and now we're telling you the same. It's life-or-death instant. A breach in a pressure seal almost always gives you enough time to get into a suit and seal it off, and we can pump air back in before you're in vacuum. But fear in zero-g breeds nausea, especially for the young ones. You need the practice first. If you throw up while you're wearing your helmet, you can force yourself to wait. A child can hardly do that. But let's stay with you people first. If there's any pressure you'll be able either to feel it or see the gauge in each cubicle, and *every* cubicle of the ship has a pressure gauge. Yet, even with some pressure, it can be so low that being out from the protection of your suit can kill you. Once again, if you toss your cookies in the helmet, keep in mind the suit pressure is considerably greater than outside the suit if we're undergoing a breach. That means when you open the helmet the air will blow out and so will the vomi-tus. There's a nose clamp built into the helmet. *Use it*. Grit your teeth and press your lips together very tightly, brace yourself and force open your faceplate. It will spring back by itself once you release the pressure. In the meantime a few pounds per square inch inside pressure blows out the vomitus. You can see how you can help a child do this when the child can't do it by himself. Now, at just one pound differential that face-plate closes hard. Make absolutely sure your fingers are out of the way. Now," Kay Deming sat straight and slapped her hands on her knees. "How are you enjoy-ing your space food and water?"

They reacted in different ways. Those who thought of their incredible rare opportunity for survival felt eating "space food" in cubes and cans and edible-plastic-sealed sandwiches was just great. The more delicate eaters found it a necessary evil. "How about the water?" Deming asked, and found unanimous acceptance of its sparkling purity and taste. "Great," they heard. "You've been drinking reprocessed urine. Your own. Collectively, that is."

Hands moved instinctively to throats. "Something wrong?" Kay Deming asked sweetly. "Anybody feel like gagging at the idea? If I hadn't told you you would never have known. Besides, what you're drinking is, first, far more pure than any water that comes out of a faucet around here, and second, it's what you'll be drinking from now on. They don't have any natural fountains where you're going."

One man asked the question they were all dreading to speak aloud. "Uh, Miss Deming, what about, uh, you know—"

"If *you* can't articulate how the hell do you expect the children to ask questions about eating their own reclaimed feces!"

"You mean—"

"We *are?*"

"Uh . . ."

"You're not," Deming said firmly. "Not in the same sense that solid body wastes are reclaimed as edible materials. We could do that, but we don't need to. Solid wastes will be used in several ways. Some of it is irradiated to kill much of the bacteria and viral content, and then it's processed as fertilizer by mixing with different chemicals. Understand, if you will, that hundreds of millions of people about the world use honeybuckets—that's unfiltered and untreated human sewage—as fertilizer just to grow enough food to stay alive. We don't need to do that and we won't. But the point is that if *you* hesitate and fumble, the children will take their cues from you. Knock it off, people, and grow up very damned fast or check yourself out of this ship. There won't be any room for you."

They took a coffee break and returned for a final brief session of hard questions and answers. *Ship's Rules,* their briefing astronauts called it. Last chance for questions on a no-record basis.

They had a hunch they wouldn't really like what they'd be told. In some ways they were right.

A mother asked the first question. "Why aren't there any children under six years of age? This isn't personal. My kids are all older. But it seems to me common sense would dictate saving as many of the youngest as possible."

Kay Deming took a deep breath before answering. She was a qualified astronaut with nine orbital flights behind her. She was automatically a crew member of *Pegasus* or, if she chose, *Noah*. But Kay Deming wasn't going to save her life aboard the lifecraft.

Kay had two children, five and three years of age. She planned to remain on Earth with their father so they could all die together. She didn't tell that to the people about her.

"There won't be any children under six years of age because they're too young to take care of themselves in emergencies. It's that simple. There's room aboard these v ssels for a very finite number of people, including the kids. In a real disaster, under the vacuum and weightlessness prevailing in orbit, it's almost certain that children who can't help themselves will die. That's it, pure and simple. We don't make these rules."

"Who does?"

"Reality does. We do *not* debate these decisions. Anyone selected to go has the immediate choice of quitting. For every person who's ready to quit, fifty thousand are clamoring to go. Next."

"Is there a ship's policy on sex? I mean, will we be given guidelines? I know this sounds terribly clumsy, and it *is*, but some of the teenagers have been asking me and I really don't know what to say to them."

"Strict morality is the rule. We insist on married couples as much as possible. We know that teenagers are normally active now by fourteen years of age, and keeping them apart in the confines of a spacecraft is going to be just about impossible. But *adultery* means

338

severe punishment. I don't even know to what extent except that there's only one way we can hope to survive this voyage, and that is to have the tightest grip on ourselves as possible. Even when we know we'll be prudish, that's the route we're going to take. Sex between adults and anyone younger than eighteen unless marriage is involved is absolutely forbidden. But we *are* encouraging—or we will—teenagers to marry. That way they pair off younger, they're not left to their own devices in a competitive world for economic survival—"

"But surely that means babies!"

"We surely hope so!" came the instant rejoinder. "But by then the parents will be experienced space travelers. And we'll be able to institute temporary artificial gravity for the period of childbirth so that the weightlessness problems are avoided. It won't be easy. Look, just trying to *burp* can kill you. There's no up or down, so gases collect along the interior linings of the stomach instead of rising. You can pat and thump all you want, but without weight and convection a belch is almost impossible. I threw that in to show you that we're anticipating as much as possible the problems that can arise with childbirth and infants. Let me get back to the matter of sex. *We will never make it a crime.* We're not taking those dark ages with us. What will be a crime is, as I said, adultery because it's a moral offense. Just as is rape, or abuse; you understand what I'm driving at. But if it comes down to two teenagers making love, we're not going to *punish* them. There are more intelligent ways, many of which we'll just have to work out after we're on our way. Never forget that this is naked survival we're after, not a pleasure trip. You can forget all about a moonlight pleasure cruise. Just staying *alive* will eat up all your spare time."

A pause followed these projections into the near future, and the next query seemed inevitable. "There will be a legal system, won't there?"

"Certainly."

"I'm glad to hear that. The democratic process should always prevail for—"

"Forget *that*. Forget you ever heard the word democratic or a publican form of government or the will of the people. All that is in indefinite suspension. You will live and function under what we call ship's law. The law of the sea where the captain is absolute master of one and all and there is no recourse to his final decision. His word is life and it is death or any combination of in-between. I'm making a canned speech so there will be absolutely no doubt in your minds. Your environment is going to be risky, dangerous, filled with unknowns, flimsy and alien to life and limb and all our futures. We don't have time for mucking it up with waving hands and secret ballots by people who really have little or no concept of what they're facing. A wrong decision here on Earth means giving up the bad and taking a new shot at another way. A wrong decision *up there* and we can all be very, very dead. I'm sure the captain of our space vessel will see fit to appoint tribunals, even judges' panels, but I can assure you of one thing. You won't find any jury system where you're going. We're running out of time. Let's get on with this."

"Is there any idea how long . . . I mean, how long this voyage will take?"

"Absolutely. Until the day it ends—well, or in disaster. Save those questions for *after* you're in orbit. They're innocuous if your shuttle fails."

"Good Lord, I never thought—I mean, could that really happen?"

"Yes. Live with it, but keep quiet about it around the children. If they persist with their questions, lie to them."

"If a child, or an adult, anyone, comes down with a disease, are procedures set up for that?"

"You bet. Measles, mumps, chickenpox, smallpox, rabies, polio, scarlet fever, diphtheria, encephalitis, blackwater fever, malaria, yellow fever, dengue fever, tick fever, anthrax—the list is incredible. We *hope* we'll be set up for just about anything. We have set aside isolation cubicles. They're attached to the ship's framework

340

but without a direct tunnel connection. You must wear a pressure suit and move in open space to get to the isolation airlock. Anything else could be utterly disastrous."

"What happens if someone contracts AIDS?"

"If they *contract* it aboard ship it means we are in very big trouble because it also means there's one or more carriers aboard. Instant isolation of anyone involved or concerned. Some large numbers of crew and passengers totally isolated from others, just as if the *Pegasus* became an island with groups remote from one another. I imagine you'd like to carry that question further in terms of someone actually *having* AIDS?"

"Well, uh, yes."

"First, instant isolation in a remote cubicle. *No direct human contact with anyone*. All treatment and life support systems will be remote by robotic or bionic and likely combinations of same. That's what the books says. That's what we're told and what we're supposed to tell you. I believe otherwise."

They studied Astronaut Kay Deming, mother, self-imposed earthbound prisoner. "Tell us what you believe."

"*Termination*. At once. Isolation in the cubicle and then slow lowering of ambient pressure to a mild hypoxic state, euphoric manifestations, then continued slow depressurization until death is assured. Quiet, painless, complete. Then, incineration." Kay Deming looked at the shocked faces about her. "I would do this to my own child. The risk of doing otherwise is to condemn to possible slow death what's left of the human race."

She rose to her feet. "You are never to repeat any of this to the children. If you do so, you, your associates *and* the children will be removed at once from any hope of every going on the ship. Good night."

They came for Nancy Parks Seavers at four o'clock in the morning. She didn't expect them. They still had three days of preparations to go through when the telephone in her room brought her out of a deep sleep. "Mrs. Seavers?"

"Yes?"

"This is Kay Deming. Are you fully awake?"

My God . . . Marc . . . something's happened . . .

She sat bolt upright on the edge of the bed. "Yes, Kay. Fully awake."

"Listen carefully, please. Get dressed and get the children dressed *immediately*. Talk to no one but me. No one. As soon as you're dressed, take with you only what will fit in the one small ditty bag we gave you. This is most important. I'll be there in five minutes and I want you and the children ready to move."

"We'll be ready." The phone went dead. She roused Tom and Keesha, half-stuffed them into their clothing, threw on a jumpsuit and slip-on sneakers, and grabbed for things that would fit within the ditty bag. She gave Keesha a small stuffed teddy bear to carry and at that moment she heard the knock on the door. When she opened it Kay Deming stood in the hallway. Practiced eyes scanned the room. "Let's go. Tom, you take my hand. Nancy, lock the door behind you."

Nancy Seavers knew when to ask questions and when to keep her mouth closed. She heaved Keesha into her arms and walked to the elevators with Kay Deming. They saw two women and one man and four children. Apprehensive looks passed between the adults but no one spoke. *Well, they've gotten the word also . . .*

On ground level they walked steadily with their NASA and navy escorts from the Contemporary across the sidewalks and onto a wide area of the parking lots before the hotel. The street lights had long ago been removed to leave clear spaces for helicopters. Two giant machines hulked in the parking area, giant rotors turning slowly with an ominous *blat-blat* and an ear-twisting shriek from their turbines. They went around to a rear loading ramp. Kay Deming stopped the group. "Go forward as far as you can and take a seat. Strap in the children and then strap yourselves in. Do *not* interfere with the crew." For the first time Nancy Seavers paid attention. This was a *Marine* helicopter, and all about them were marines armed with automatic weapons. They were in full battle dress and they appeared grim and alert. She didn't *want* to ask questions.

Kay Deming faced Nancy. They started to speak, then hugged each other fiercely. When her mouth was right by Nancy's ear, Kay Deming spoke to her. "All hell's breaking loose in the world. You're going straight to the Cape and right into your shuttle. Just try to keep these people calm and have a great flight and a wonderful future. I wish I'd known you better." She squeezed her fiercely and stepped back. Nancy led the children forward and strapped them in and took her own seat. Within ten minutes every seat was filled, the ramp came up with a powerful sound of electrical relays, and armed marines took up positions at scanning-door openings. Nancy held the hands of the children as the enormous rotor wound up and the great machine vibrated and then the world tilted and they were climbing up and rushing forward. They flew like that at high speed. She knew they were headed for the Cape. There wasn't anywhere else to go. The helicopter banked and she caught a glimpse of the highway below. The roads were jammed with vehicles. Through a window coming back to level flight she saw the flashing strobes of other helicopters.

It went with a rush. The big helicopter let down with a jolt and they were led outside. She recognized where they were: Pad Thirty Nine D for Delta on the Kennedy Space Center. Armed guards stood in the distance and the place seemed like Saturday night on Broadway with all the dazzling lights and activity. Several men and women she'd never seen before led them to an open tram like the ones they used in the Disney parking lot. It drove steadily toward the launch pad. They followed their escorts to big elevators and stood in rocking silence until movement stopped and the doors opened to a large all-white suiting room.

An astronaut stood before them. "You're going up in a few hours. We haven't the time to discuss what's happening, but it's important we speed up our timetable. Technicians are here to help each person into a

343

pressure suit. It will have your own name on it. You will wear the helmet closed, but only to keep it from banging into something. When you're in your suits we'll take you to the vertical room and you will be led to your position in the shuttle. This will be the *Odyssey*, by the way. Before you get into your seat, you'll have a fruit drink and two pills. One is for motion sickness to make things easier for you when you first feel what it's like to be weightless. The other is to let you relax. All this happens quickly and we know it can be upsetting. Okay, everybody, into your suits."

Dressed and arranged in neat rows, they shuffled to an open platform with a protecting cage. They looked up at the huge spaceship above them. *Odyssey* stood on its tail as usual, and the great cargo doors were open. Inside was mounted the passenger compartment that would be sealed before they moved the service tower from the shuttle. They could see the seats. Their turn came. Nancy led the children onto the platform, the cage door closed, and they were on the way up. They stopped midway along the compartment, and a ramp slid out from the cage as a walkway. Nancy saw that the seats rotated. They could climb into them and sit as if they were on an airplane on the runway.

A woman with short blonde hair in an astronaut jumpsuit waited for them. "Susan! Susan Foster!" Nancy said, in both disbelief and relief. The woman looked up and they hugged briefly. "You're, are you—" Nancy tried to speak.

"I'm pilot on this bird," Susan told her. "Arch Begley, you know who he is?"

"He checked out Marc—?"

"That's right. You've got number *uno* for your driver today. He's flying. Look, we'll have time later. Strap in. This is Tom and Keesha, right? Hi, kids. We'll keep you informed while you're waiting. Before we seal the sliding doors to this compartment we'll rotate the seats so that you're lying on your backs," she looked at the children, "just like the pilots do, okay?" They got the kids strapped down. The sedative was already working.

Susan helped Nancy close the helmets and hook up the oxygen lines to the suit. "Just in case. We won't use them unless—well, you know," she shrugged. "We haven't used them once yet."

Susan started to leave. Nancy touched her arm and leaned close to her. "Susan, just one thing." Susan Foster nodded. "All they told us was that they were moving up the timetables. Kay Deming mentioned something about all hell breaking loose."

Susan looked about them. No one was listening to a private conversation between two women. "Keep it strictly to yourself. Worry and panic grow like wildfire in a place like this. They've gone mad out there, around the world. It looks like war." She paused but a moment. "Take you seat and strap in, please." Susan moved on to the next tier of seats.

War?

Nancy strapped in, staring ahead numbly. She tried to think but it was all too much. Her head seemed jangled. Numbness began to creep in.

She awoke two hours later. A speaker carried a voice to them. "Tighten the straps of the children, please, and check the helmet seals. Now do the same for yourselves. We expect to launch in twenty minutes. The ground crew will move along the platforms and double-check your seats. Then the platforms will move back. Keep your hands on the armrests or in your lap. We're going to rotate the seats now so that you're on your backs. It will still be pretty comfortable but you won't be able to move around. Okay, now, when we count down to zero your seats will rotate. Five, four, three, two and a one and zero." There wasn't much to see. The seats rotated backwards and came to a stop gently. "All right, now we're going to seal the passenger compartment. You'll see the panels sliding shut above you." Curving steel doors overslid one another and they felt a thump as everything locked solidly in place. Green lights winked across a panel at the front of the compartment. There must have been seventy or eighty people with them, Nancy thought. She was grateful she could reach out to hold the hands of the children.

345

"We won't have much time to report to you," came the voice through the passenger compartment. "You can understand that we'll be pretty busy. When we can, we'll pipe in communications to you."

Sure; I know that one, Nancy thought and kept her knowledge to herself. If they had serious problems they wouldn't pipe it down to the passengers. Why scare the hell out of the children? She felt her belt chafing and moved to release the catch to get more comfortable. *The belt wouldn't release.* Moving as little as possible she tried several times. *My God, they've locked the belts. I couldn't get out of this if I tried . . .* She stopped her efforts. It made sense. If someone became frightened just before liftoff and climbed from his seat, acceleration would hurl him back with bone-breaking force and many people could be hurt.

"T minus fifteen minutes. TV monitors coming on."

She was amazed. She couldn't believe it. They weren't going to be kept "in the dark" through the count! The television monitors placed along the overhead came to life and they had a series of shots of *Odyssey* standing vertically, a mountain of energy. They stared at the ship from a distance, then at a closeup of the giant engines below, saw the plumes of supercold oxygen and hydrogen streaming away from the vents. Voices called *pumps coming on, fluid moving through lines,* and now they knew they were within the intestines of a living giant. *Odyssey* rumbled and groaned from building pressures, dull thuds came to them and would have been frightening except that they could *see* umbilicals pulling free and falling away, service platforms rotating free of the ship, and then they had a series of television shots of Arch Begley and Susan Foster and the other astronauts in the flight deck!

"T minus ten minutes and counting. We are into the final count and we expect to go automatic at T minus three minutes when the ship's onboard computers will take over the count and go into automode. Everything is on line and we are go for launch. T minus eight minutes forty-five seconds and counting."

Changing views on the monitors. Huge helicopters

with heavy guns and rockets patrolling the launch area. Contrails of jet fighters high overhead. A long shot from an aircraft showing *Odyssey;* beyond *their* ship other launch pads bulked with great space machines.

"*T minus five minutes and counting. Automode in two minutes.*"

What had Susan meant? War? What was happening?

More thumps, a solid bang. Another view of the cockpit. A dark glove raised from behind the commander's seat and an upraised thumb came into view for them.

"*T minus three minutes and we are in automode and the computers now control Odyssey. Full engine gimbaling in progress.*"

They felt the grinding rumbles, saw on the TV monitors the great engine bells swiveling about, cold vapors and particles of ice falling slowly downward.

"*T minus sixty seconds and counting.*"

Giant turbopumps building up to full power.

"*T minus thirty seconds.*"

Odyssey quivered like an arrow poised in a giant bow.

"*Twenty seconds.*"

"*Fifteen seconds.*"

"*Ten—*"

"*Nine—*"

"*Eight—*"

The Middle East

"*Four—*"

"*Three—*"

"*Two—*"

"*One—*"

"*FIRE!*"

The first missile blew up on its crude launching pad of concrete. One moment it stood gleaming in the sun from the wax of a hundred enthusiastic rubbings. In the next tick of time a great fireball writhed upward and downwind from the shattered concrete. No sirens wailed in the Iranian desert. No radiological teams screamed at

347

the missile crews to get the hell out of there at once from the spray of plutonium particles that had only minutes before been a crude warhead. The Islamic sword has no time for such childish nonsense. The missile crews sent in a band of four medics to attend to the dismembered, slashed, burned, blinded, torn, and dying missile team, and two hundred yards away counted down successfully with a second missile. Flame appeared instantly behind the missile designed by East German rocket technicians, built in Yugoslavia with a guidance system produced by Czechoslovakia, propelled by a solid rocket bought in quantity from Italy, and armed with a crude plutonium warhead assembled laboriously in Argentina by that cash-starved country and sold for a staggering price to the other side of the world.

Immediately that the thick white smoke trail leaped upward from the Iranian launch pad and arced over in flight in the direction of Iraq, a second, third, and fourth missile left the ground with a thunder never before heard in this seared and hapless surface. The guidance systems of the missiles were competent but less than fully reliable and the arming devices for the warheads neither competent nor reliable. The latter, however, albeit with some glitches, worked.

Sixty-two thousand tons of explosive force shattered the eastern half of Baghdad. The missile body, wobbling erratically in descent from a loosened tail fin, dove at over a thousand miles an hour into the city. The system was intended to explode the bomb at two thousand feet to maximize blast damage and minimize lasting radiation; indeed, to avoid altogether any meaningful fallout as had been accomplished more than fifty years before at Hiroshima and Nagasaki. All good plans to the contrary, the warhead penetrated thirty feet below the surface before it created, with the magic of the atomic genie, a fireball of millions of degrees that spread instantly to a diameter of more than twelve hundred feet, a shock wave of twice the speed of sound, and a wall of air punching outward from the explosion center with such ferocity, at a thousand miles an hour, that the air itself burned. The in-ground shock wave picked up the city and shook it madly and dumped it uncaring back to the ground. Baghdad vaporized, shattered, burned, exploded, collapsed, and otherwise met its doom in a horror beyond all words. Eighty-nine percent of the city was dead or dying before the mushroom cloud, thick and oily and ferocious with lethal radioactivity, really had a chance to show its stuff. A high wind blew across Baghdad when the warhead exploded, and there began the march of radiation that made of Chernobyl a feeble joke.

The second bomb detonated at three hundred feet over the main oil processing center of Iraq. Petroleum facilities do not well withstand an on-site temperature exceeding seventy thousand degrees nor a shock wave and succeeding blast wave of some twelve hundred miles an hour. The intense induced radioactivity from neutrons and gamma rays really didn't matter. Nothing was left alive; the earth lay helplessly pinned as all its petroleum orifices were raped by the downward and side-punches of the bomb, and a fire began that would burn unchecked for years to come—or until such time as the Earth itself crumbled and shifted and heaved and the ocean rushed in to squeeze the last breath of oxygen and ignition from the flames.

The third bomb was much more of a show for a wider audience. The white smoke trail zigzagged wildly across desert mountain country and impacted within a deep gorge to create a huge crater, a local earthquake, miles-long avalanches and a mushroom cloud boiling with radioactivity that soared to fifty-seven thousand feet.

Within two hours of the explosions both the Soviet Union and the United States, through satellite tracking, aircraft surveillance, and other systems, identified beyond all question the source of the missile launchings. The telephone lines ran hot between Moscow and Washington and immediate action, much of it preplanned, was agreed upon.

Four hundred killer assault helicopters and transport planes with paratrooper shock forces sped southward through Afghanistan to the flatlands of Iran, preceded by multiple waves of bombers and ground-strike fighters to cut off rail lines, communications points and roads. Russian electronic aircraft circled Iran at high altitude to jam all electronic frequencies and blanket the nation with screeching interference on all electronic communications facilities. Another wave of planes launched against every Iranian seaport and docking facility tactical nuclear weapons to melt and tear down petroleum docks and installations. Missile-firing Russian aircraft and submarines attacked and sank every Iranian ship that could be found. With Iraqi troops raging against the common border in a maddened human wave, Iran was quite effectively eliminated as a trouble source except to its own populace, which was hardly an event unknown to those hapless people.

Washington and Moscow were quite pleased. The scenario was going precisely as planned.

Paris

"We have named the new celestial object, this greatest of comets ever known, *Jericho*. There has never been anything like it known to astronomers since man first lifted his eyes to the heavens." Professor Henri Saul Pietre of the newly formed European Academy of Sciences stood before a packed house in the reception hall of the Great Science Museum of France. Dozens of television cameras picked up his every gesture to flash the incredible news throughout the world. *We're not going to burn up . . . we wont' turn into ice . . . we're going to live! The Earth is going to live!*

How could it be otherwise? Just listen to *this* scientist! "We have found the dust diminishing behind the path of our solar system as it revolves about the center of the galaxy. That means it has much more definite limits, much *smaller* limits, then we had reason to believe before we received the new data from the probes we sent out to precede this world. We are passing through the tail of Jericho. It is enormous compared to anything else known, and the thickness of the cometary tail debris will increase for at least a year. So we may

350

expect the effects we have heard so much about, but on a greatly reduced scale. Temperatures will rise. The tropics may even become uninhabitable for a while. The melting of icebergs and snow fields will increase the height of the oceans and contribute to greater rainfall. But we can prepare for these effects and live through them. We have endured wars, pestilence, famine; we can endure anything, especially the tail of a distant comet!

"And finally, you may ask why we have named this space traveler Jericho. It is simple. The tail of the comet is like a wall. We will strike the tail, the dust will thicken, and finally we shall burst through as if the dust were a wall that will come tumbling down about us, and then be gone forever.

"Thank you, and I share with you the renewed faith in our future."

Overnight, Felicity Xavier Powell became a renewed global celebrity. The French scientists had vindicated her every word. Ridicule and abuse were heaped on the leading powers rushing to complete *Pegasus* and *Noah*.

In Paris, Professor Henri Saul Pietre retreated to a private estate bordering Verdun. A select group of American and Russian officials toasted his performance. "How you feel now, Henri, that for so much of the world you have laid the bogeyman to rest?"

Pietre downed a snifter of brandy. His face was flushed from heavy drinking, and the dapper Frenchman had loosened his tie and permitted his clothes to rumple in a most unsightly fashion.

"How do I feel?" He laughed harshly. "When I finished that monstrous lie, I repaired immediately to the men's room and for twenty minutes I threw up. *That* is how I feel!"

Launch Pad 39D for Delta

The numbers were still vibrating in the speakers when Nancy realized the great engines were firing behind them. The roar swelled up from below, an uprushing incredible thunder like black water exploding upward from a deep well that burst all around them. She saw nothing clearly as vibration gripped *Odyssey* and then a tremendous crash struck all about them. She barely heard children and adults crying out from the jarring impact. They were thrown forward against their restraining straps, they hung there for an instant, and then the enormous power of the solids crashing free jammed them back down into their seats, and Nancy cried out in pure joy, because that feeling meant only that the thurst was ramming downward through her chest toward her back and they were *climbing*. Acceleration increased until she was pinned neatly to her chair as if by spikes driven through her body and limbs, and she knew the children also were helpless. *Odyssey* swayed and she felt rumbling and shaking all about her and she couldn't tell if they were rolling or in the familiar heads-down position. It didn't matter. The thunder became a deep crackling roar, the bullwhips of the gods snapping and smashing about them. She remembered something they called big max, or it was max something or other, and she forced her vision to the nearest television monitor and saw clouds whipping by. The acceleration eased off, it wasn't painful to breathe any more, and she held Keesha's hand and managed to turn her head enough to smile at the little girl's face within her helmet, a tear glistening on one cheek. She squeezed Keesha's hand gently and turned her eyes back to the screen. Now she remembered! They had to pass through a region where the air pressure was at its worst against the climbing ship—they called it Max Q, that was it—the air squeezing mightily against all the parts of *Odyssey* and that meant they were throttling back, and the sound eased off just enough for her to hear the voice in the speakers: *"Ah, roger, Odyssey, you're through Max Q and clear to throttle up to one hundred and nine percent. You are go for full-power climb. A real neat flight, you guys."*

The invisible fist shoved them steadily back into the seats and she felt the roar surging again, the thunder hammering at them and—*it was quiet. My God, the engines . . . have they quit? What's wrong?* She realized what had happened then because the acceleration was still shoving them hard into their seats. They didn't hear the roar from behind them because they'd gone through Max-Q thirty-seven thousand feet and ever since then they'd been supersonic and they were running away faster and faster from their own sound! How incredible! How marvelous! Nancy was laughing and crying and holding Keesha's hand and they saw a sign flash ahead of them: SOLID SEP IN 10 SECS. By the time the message had gotten through to her brain, that this was a courtesy the engineers had rigged up for all these passengers sealed within the belly of *Odyssey*, the huge solid boosters had burned out and smaller rockets exploded to shove them away from the manned vessel and now the ride became smooth and steady and they could talk and shout to one another through their helmets and—

Nancy Parks Seavers let it all go then. She let her head rest against the inner lining of the helmet. It was something beyond all believing to know they were now above the Earth's atmosphere and rushing wildly into black vacuum and *Good Lord!* she was thrown forward against her straps and everything was quiet and her stomach fell over on its side and *they were weightless*.

She heard a voice she'd never heard before and recognized it instantly, even before he identified himself. "Hi, everybody. This is your captain speaking. Odyssey Spaceways takes pleasure in reporting we're coasting right now on our way to *Pegasus*, and we won't be firing the engines again for at least forty-five minutes. So just relax, keep your seat belts on, please, and if there's anything we can do to make your trip more comfortable, why, just tell us about it after we get where we're going."

A hatch opened at the far end of the compartment and they watched Susan Foster *floating in midair* toward them. Her smile told them better than any words that the flight was going along just perfectly. Susan Foster held herself by one hand, levitating magically, and motioned for them to open their helmets. Nancy opened hers and then watched Tom open his helmet.

She leaned over to help Keesha. "My tummy feels funny," the little girl told her.

"So does mine," Nancy told her. "But it gets better."

"Will we be there soon?"

"An hour or two, I guess."

"You know something?"

"What, honey?"

"It doesn't sound right to call you Nancy."

"What would you like to call me?"

"I guess you're my Mommy now. Is it all right if I call you Mommy?"

Nancy tried to speak. She couldn't. She nodded her head fiercely, her lips so tightly together she tasted her own blood.

The Far East

"Pan Am Zero Three Niner, we advise immediate emergency letdown and landing at any available facility. Your best bet looks like Field Echo Tango Cocoa on Taiwan. You'll have some weather to get down through and we can vector you—"

"Blue Goose, Blue Goose from Zero Three Niner, we read you and we agree. Just tell us how close those bogeys are and what you want us to do. Let's get with it, guys, we got five hundred and thirty five frightened people aboard this barge. Over."

"Zero Three Niner commence immediate, I repeat immediate descent at maximum rate and commence turn to the right to a heading two two zero. This will put you in cloud conditions with heavy precip and should block the radar of the bogeys. Very good, Pan Am, we show you in turning decent. Your bogeys are three in number and they are approaching at supersonic closure. It's going to be tight. Over."

"Blue Goose, we need to know frequencies of Echo Tango Cocoa—"

"No sweat, Pan Am. They've already been patched into the line and are ready and waiting. You are cleared for immediate straight-in approach runway two-three with the winds strong and steady out of the southwest.

Any other traffic will break well away from you. Just keep on trucking, Pan Am."

"Ah, thank you, Blue Goose. Will you be staying with us?"

"That's affirm from Poppa Bear to Baby Bear."

"Blue Goose, where are you guys?"

"Pan Am, we're covering you from cruise at angels one hundred plus with full lookdown. Never mind the details. Turn right to a heading of two three five, I repeat two three five. You may expect to break out of cloud cover with a deck three thousand feet above highest ground. The field will be twenty miles directly in front of you. Advise max speed and descent all the way. Just dump it in, guys. Bogeys are in clouds now closing fast your position from dead astern. Over."

"Ah, that's great, Blue Goose. We're breaking out now and we have strobes in sight. We'll leave the garbage up until the last moment and then dump gear and flaps for—*holy shit!* We're under attack, Blue Goose! We're under attack! That was a missile that just went under our left wing and, oh, my God, they're firing at us from the left, I see one, three, no four missiles coming right at us and—" The voice rose to a scream of rage. "You sons of bitches, I—"

Blue Goose at one hundred three thousand feet watched the radar blips close. The controller in the high-altitude stealth reconnaissance control aircraft shook his head. "He's bought it," he told the pilot thirty feet in front of him within the slender fuselage. "Jesus. More than five hundred people . . ."

Far below, the 747 spun slowly in a circle to the left, the left wing gone, the fuselage ripped open and tiny figures tumbling out like stick dolls. The airplane whirled down like a leaf, struck a rocky ledge and completed its destruction with a roaring spume of fire and tearing wreckage and still more bodies spilling out down the steep hillside.

High above, Blue Goose received a coded message. The controller shrugged, punched in the coded numbers and letters, and transmitted a signal directly to Red Chinese fighter headquarters. There was a huge

Russian transport, one of those Antonov giants, flying in international waters off the coastline. The signal from Blue Goose was confirmation of standing orders for Chinese fighters to immediately attack and shoot down the unarmed giant transport.

The Mayday calls from the Antonov, as well as from the hapless 747, were heard in the cockpits of at least thirty-nine commercial airliners flying in that part of the world, as well as several major ships and ground stations. Some of the distress signals were picked up by Blue Goose and retransmitted so that Washington and Moscow could be certain the word of the attacks against helpless aircraft reached the outside world.

One hour later seventeen diplomats from China were attacked as they left United Nations headquarters in New York on their way to a favorite restaurant. Eight were shot down in cold blood. Three were beaten so severely they were blinded or crippled. The others lay in the street with broken bones, bleeding profusely until ambulances arrived. A TV cameraman got a terrific long shot of a police officer clubbing one of the injured Chinese to death. Blood spattered the camera lens.

In the next twenty-four hours, as planned, the Chinese embassy in Washington would be attacked by an enraged mob, its occupants murdered brutally and the building sacked and burned. American ships off the Chinese coastline would be struck and sunk with missile attacks. The Chinese embassy in San Francisco would be plundered and its women occupants raped publicly. Soon after, shrieking mobs in Peking and Shanghai would perform in kind against American and Russian embassies and consulates.

U.S. Naval Headquarters

"What was wrong? I'll tell you what the hell went wrong, you bungling idiot!" Rear Admiral Spencer Auchinschloss, head of naval intelligence and director of combined military intelligence for the Pentagon, gripped the telephone with white-knuckled anger. "It's like ghosts from the past! You fools always act on the basis of what your idiot computers tell you. You fudge on the human factor, you ignore all the basic and strongest emotional elements. Just like you've always done! Don't you have any agents who live among the population there? What the hell is Islam to you, another fucking planet, for Christ's sake?" Auchinschloss relented a moment in his blistering attack on the head of the CIA and cupped the telephone mouthpiece. Across his desk a tight-lipped Russ Corey tried to maintain a poker-faced look devoid of emotion, but the admiral knew him too well. "Goddamned idiots," he snarled to Corey. "They don't even have anyone living in Syria who belongs to us. In government, yes. In their army, yes. In their air force, yes! But not among the people! Not—"

He turned his fury back to the telephone. "You get your spooks together and put your asses together with Starbuck over at that pussyfooting NSA crowd, and in one hour—one hour, damn you!—I want a concise report not one damned word longer than three pages here on my desk, and an original delivered to me in the White House. Oh, you bet your sweet ass I'll be there." He dropped the phone as if it had turned to slime, sagged in his chair, reached into a drawer for a flask, unscrewed the cap and took a long pull. He held the flask out. "No," Corey said. "I want information."

"It's so bloody damned simple, I—" Spencer Auchinschloss locked down his temper. "All right, Russ. Pure and simple. Everything we'd planned worked faultlessly. The Chinese tore up some planes and the Russians did the same, and we had an escalation exactly along the energy guidelines we'd planned. Iran and Iraq have been at war for so long, *their* reactions were Pavlovian-predictable. But no one in Washington, or in Moscow either," he admitted grudgingly, "figured—"

"A holy war," Corey finished for him.

Auchinschloss glared. "Where the hell were you when they were feeding us predictions?"

Corey didn't bother to answer. "Give me the package, Spence."

"Cut and dried," the admiral said. "The bell-ringer

357

was Syria. There's Iran and Iraq really getting down to it. The Russians are kicking the shit out of Iran, so the Syrian bunch figures, and correctly, that some sort of deal is on—or under—the table, and the Russians won't go any distance beyond Iran. Iraq behaves itself because it's been nuked and the whole place is in collapse and all they want is a chance to find out how to stay alive. China's ringing bells and that occupies *that* part of the world. What does Syria do through all this? Nothing, absolutely nothing. They stand to gain in power and position by doing nothing. Let everybody else tear themselves to pieces, Syria stays intact and, obviously, it gains military strength on a relative basis."

"Then," Corey said slowly, "they had their grand-stand scene in Paris. Pietre."

Auchinschloss raised his eyebrows. "Damn, I knew you were good but I never figured you to ace that one. You're right, of course."

"Sure," Corey said, more easily now that he had a handle on why the world was going to hell on a rain-slick road, "the whole thing hung on just one word. *Jericho.*"

"What's crazy about this is that Salan didn't kick off the frenzy," the admiral added. "I mean, ever since he took over from the old Syrian government he's been trying to build up his power by staying *out* of these incessant wars."

"So there was a power play," Corey added. "Not too hard to figure out. There's a bunch of Syrian air force generals who see what they divine as the golden oppor-tunity. Iran and Iraq are tied up in knots. Russia is clearly exercising limits. *We* have China to worry about. And there's Israel ripe for the knife to the jugular because fast aid from us isn't in the cards at this moment. They overcome the official government posi-tion by screaming that the name Jericho is an insult to Islamic divinity. After all, what else can it be but a divine sign sent by Allah? The air force boys in Syria load up—"

"With nukes." Admiral Auchinschloss stared unblink-ing at Corey. "From what we've gathered, they put a

Mig Forty-One over Israel at eighty thousand feet and the pilot dove straight down. *All* the way. He stayed with the plane. Passport to heaven." Auchinschloss took a deep breath. "Tel Aviv is gone."

"How hard did the Israelis hit back?"

"Like you'd expect. Egypt turned out to be in bed with them, which really is no great surprise since they'd like to keep Cairo from turning into a crater. Egypt protected their flank. I don't think it would have mattered. The question of whether or not Israel really has nukes isn't a question any more. They had them and they still got them. But Syria is missing Damascus. *Three* nukes. The Israelis are *really* pissed. They put another four nukes into the mountain country to block all roads and highways. The Syrian army can move but it will have to be on foot, crawling over radioactive rubble. Besides, the whole country is in a mad panic. *Very* heavy fallout. And the Israelis have flat told all the other Arab countries to stay out or *their* cities will be on the missing list."

"If I know that part of the world, that war is already over."

"You are correct, sir," the admiral said. "All they're doing now is dying." He sighed. "In a way it fits the scenario we set up. We can go to full martial law right now in this country if that's what we need. The reserves and the national guard have all been called out, as you imagine. Full mobilization. The Chinese are cooperating. It looks like all-out war with them, which allows the president to press the panic button any time the situation calls for it."

Russ Corey stood slowly. "Thanks for the briefing, Spence. Use your phone? I've got a Starbird on the ramp at Dulles waiting to go."

"You heading for Luke?"

"Mach deuce all the way." Corey hesitated. "By the time we're in the pattern at Luke, I figure the blacks will be running straight at South Africa. Once again it's that great opportunity in the sky. God's talking in all languages to all people, Spence."

"What's *your* opinion on what happens with South Africa?"

"They are *very* tough people. They've got nukes. Spence. They'll use them. The blacks will mass on the plains like it's the old Zulu wars movies all over again. A few air bursts will incinerate a couple hundred thousand of them and leave another million praying they will die."

The admiral shrugged. "Well, just so long as the Big Lie buys us some time to get our ships upstairs, I guess it's all worth it. Hell, all we're doing is speeding up the timetable for those who die now. You know something? Maybe they're the lucky ones." Of a sudden, Spencer Auchinschloss had all he could handle of the subject. He extended his hand. "Will I see you again, Russ?"

"If you come to the moon, old man. I can still arrange for you to die in bed," Corey grinned.

"Hah! What a waste *that* would be!"

Brasilia

"Then it is decided. The *gringos*, once again faced with a choice of bedding down with the *Latinos* or chucking them off to die, have acted as always. We are second-class human beings. Even on our own land, the gringos use their muscle. The French are squeezing every last dollar and every drop of blood from the Americans to use the Kourou Arianespace launch facility in Guiana."

The Brazilian general held the gaze of the admiral who commanded the Venezuelan fleet. "They have accepted some of us for the ships?"

"*Some*. A tiny handful. Not at all in proportion to the total number who will go." The admiral smiled. "My children know the street language of the Americans. We are what you call the token spics. A few of us will be saved, but for those few to go, the many must sacrifice all."

The general did not smile. "You are prepared to lose your cities?"

"How will that happen? The French cannot invade. The range is too great for their missiles now trained against Russia. Their aircraft cannot reach us in any number. What do we need to fear?" The Venezuelan admiral pounded his fist on the table. "We move against Kourou. We send our people to the great ship above the Earth!"

The general shrugged. "You will lose your cities. But it may be worth it."

"But how—"

"Admiral, your intelligence is somewhat less than your oil. Four French missile submarines are already deployed off our coastlines. Each submarine carries twelve missiles and each missile has three warheads. And I repeat, it may be worth it. Do we proceed with the plan we discussed?"

"Yes. Full invasion from the sea with landing craft. Eight thousand men. And fifteen hundred paratroopers without warning."

The general nodded. He rose from his seat and walked to the picture window overlooking the hills carpeted with lush vegetation. The heart of Brazil is a world apart, he thought.

"What do you think of, general?" came the question from across the room.

"I wonder how these hills will look when they are black and no longer green . . ."

Earth Orbit, Seven Hundred Miles Up

A billion sparkling lights. All colors. Lights flashing, coded laser beams for communications, halos of thrusters, gases phosphorescent against backdrop sun, lights and stars and sun gleaming from metal. Searchlights, floodlights, signal lights, strobes, beacons, welding torches . . . Nancy could hardly believe the distant sight.

Susan Foster had come for her. In her place would be Astronaut Silvana Marinazzi, Italian-sounding but strictly lower-Manhattan in ethnicity. "Captain Begley would like you to come to the flight deck, Mrs. Seavers—"

"Nancy."

"Thank you. Silvana will stay with the children while you're gone. Okay, kids? You wouldn't mind your own

361

real-life astronaut to sit with you for a while, would you?"

"We're astronauts now, too!" exclaimed Tom.

"So you are," observed Silvana. She touched Nancy's arm. "Go ahead, ma'am. They'll be terribly disappointed if you don't."

The other passengers, still trying to figure out why their stomachs had turned into intestinal ogres bent on their destruction, watched in silence. No one had yet become accustomed to young ladies floating with such ease about the cabin. Between swallowing motion sickness pills and trying to concentrate on the nearest TV monitor, they were doing their best to acclimate to this not-so-brave but very new world.

"All right," Nancy announced. "Kids, you do as you're told, okay?" They nodded assent. "Just tell me what to do," Nancy said to Susan Foster.

"First, do *not* make sudden or violent head movements. You'll regret it if you do. Try to move in slow motion. That makes it a lot easier. Now, look down *slowly*. Move your hands to your harness release. That's it, push in and twist to the right. It releases lap and shoulder belts. Now, gently push down on the armrests with the forefingers of each hand. You'll float upwards. Your body will want to bend. Let it adopt what feels the most comfortable position."

It was incredible. A gasp of surprise and joy escaped her. "Reach up with your right hand, easy, easy, and grasp the guideline along the edge of the bulkhead, here, just like I'm doing." Instantly as her hand closed on something solid Nancy felt in control again. She had been a high diver for years; tumbling through the air was easy for her. This was different. No impact with water awaited her, but she had the feeling she'd adapt quickly. She realized of a sudden that every eye in the cabin was on her; they were using her for their cue as to what it would be like. Nancy held tightly to the guideline with her right hand, swiveled her body until she was vertical—feet to the floor and head to the cabin ceiling—extended her left arm outward, palm up, flashed a smile, and cried out, *"Ta da!"*

Cheering and applause. Susan Foster grinned at her. "I've got to remember that little scene. Okay, follow me along the guideline and just imitate my actions."

With every passing moment she was becoming entranced with weightlessness. What an incredible sense of freedom! Exhilaration, elation, wonder. Now she knew what the astronauts meant when they said that the entire history of man's fight against gravity was to reach this timeless euphoria.

She moved with the barest effort to the tunnel leading from the cargo bay of *Odyssey* to the middeck crew compartment. Two astronauts nodded to her. Susan drifted upward—oh, the magic of it!—to the pilot's flight deck. For a moment she stared at the dark features and broad white smile of Arch Begley. His voice carried to her with a deep honeyed timbre. "Welcome to your new home, Mrs. Seavers," he said quietly. His hand moved a switch and the flight deck went dark.

She felt as if the universe had reached out to hold her hand . . .

The sparkling lights, the colors, the sudden flashes and sprays of light seemed to float out of some unfathomable distance and whirl within her head. Utterly velvet blackness far beyond. Far below, a touch of the scimitar; abruptly she realized she was seeing the glowing curved edge of the planet itself. And ahead of her that incredible shape. No way to tell size yet. There was huge and there was tiny and mixtures of all kinds in between. She tried to move forward to get closer to the windshield, to see even better. She swayed in nothingness until a powerful hand grasped her firmly but gently and eased her weightless form forward as if she were the substance of shadow.

"I can't believe it . . . it's . . ."

She fell silent with the coruscation about her, the gleaming in so many colors. *Light of life*. Why did she think that? Ships and men and huge pieces of metal, structures of all sizes and shapes, an enormous space whale, some of its ribs still exposed, lights from deep within. Then . . . *those are cabin lights over there*.

Those are people living in there. My lover is waiting for me there.

She moved again, her own hand steadying her now. She could look down, down through the darkened space between the prow of *Odyssey* and the hulking mass of *Pegasus*. More lights came into view, sparkling spider-webs and glowing tendrils. She knew she saw cities and highways, soft hushed illumination of man on his world.

A sudden intense spray of white appeared, turning almost at once to gold and orange and red, tinged with blue along its edges, racing in utter silence across the darkened surface. She had never seen anything so beautiful.

"What . . . what was that?" she asked in a hushed voice.

It took a while for Arch Begley to answer.

"It looked like a moth in a candle flame, didn't it?"

His voice sounded so strange. He had leaned forward over the navigation computer and was still bending down when he spoke. He came up slowly, his body floating gently.

"That was Cairo." Silence for a moment. "Egypt. Egypt's still there. Cairo isn't. That light?" He shook his head in quiet inner disbelief. "That . . . was a hydrogen bomb."

17

Luke Range

"Starbird, better hang a wide turn to the left. Keep your inside orbit ten miles from the launch pad. Number Nine is hot and they're on terminal count right now. Over."

"Roger, Luke. Starbird confirms." Russ Corey leaned forward in the right seat of the supersonic jet, now cruising at a grindingly slow four hundred miles an hour in a two-mile-high circular orbit of the Luke facility in the Arizona desert. "Luke Tower, Starbird One here, what's the time on the count? Over."

"You're right on the money, Starbird. They've just gone to autocount and we are down through the minus three minute mark. Range safety passes on a warning to be ready for continuous ripple shock from the booster as it climbs past you. Over."

"Got it, Luke. Starbird's swinging wide to the north and we plan a run back starting at minus sixty seconds. We'll hit the burners and cob it. When radar picks us coming in tell them not to panic. We'll do a pullup and a vertical climb with the booster. Ought to be interesting."

"You got it, Starbird. The area is all yours."

"I'll take it," Corey told the pilot to his left. Tim Brooks nodded and held both hands just above the yoke. "You've got it," he confirmed. Corey swung to the north and the distant highways. For several moments he had a clear view of the entire firing range basin. In the distance loomed the shell structure of what was allegedly a nuclear powerplant and its spiderwork of roads and fences. He banked left to look to the south and east and the panorama of launching pads slipped into view. From this height the pads looked amazingly similar to the oil and natural gas fields of the great Permian oil basin near Midland, Texas. Hundreds of concrete squares and circles lay flat on the desert floor. Looming up from each was a high and wide structure with rounded shape to absorb the sudden powerful winds that could rip across this land without warning. He rolled to his right and began another wide turn. *"Two minutes and counting,"* came clearly into his headset. Corey judged distance and time with an eye and mental computer long attuned to such maneuvers. They flashed over the public highway and he frowned as he saw the antlike figures out in the open by hundreds—hell, no, there were thousands of vehicles on and off the roads down there. *It's already happening*, he told himself, then dismissed the sight and its consequences from his mind. He needed all his concentration for the next maneuvers and timing.

He steepened his turn to come back to the south,

heard the *"Sixty seconds and counting"* call, and tightened his left-hand grip on the throttles. The Starbird bobbled gently in turbulence as he pressured the throttles slightly to assure instant maximum power when he wanted it. Airspeed moved up slightly to four hundred sixty. Desert floor glided beneath them. It was all a matter of timing. Shrinking time for the huge booster on its pad, much clearer and more defined now, and shrinking time-and-distance for the Starbird. At such moments things and time seem suspended. Everything moves with an extraordinary slow-motion. *"Thirty seconds."* A touch more power, a slight pushback into the seat. Then the count went through ten and on down the shrinking remainder of time, and he resisted the urge to slam the throttles forward. The great rocket booster loomed upward in the form of a rounded building poised to laugh at reality and hurl itself away from the desert floor. *Buildings don't fly*, Corey told himself with a sudden behind-the-eyeballs grin. *"Zero, and we have ignition."*

The sun dimmed. It *seemed* to dim; Corey knew that was ridiculous. The effect came from the savagely intense yellow flame ripping out in all directions from the base of the huge rounded building on the concrete. Now it became clear that the monster rocket stood on a squared girder platform twenty feet above the concrete, that the flame tore downward. Memory filled in the picture: a needle-pointed teardrop jutting upward from the base of the platform, dead-center, so that the flame followed the curves of the steel teardrop and hurled itself away smoothly from the sloping steel base. Compared to the great launch pads at the Kennedy Space Center and the Vandenberg complex, this was crude and archaic. It *was* crude and archaic *but it worked*. They'd used this same "dry pad launch burn" system many years back for the old German V-2 rocket, *and* for the American Redstone and Jupiter and the field-combat Thor missiles and even the comparatively huge Navaho multiple-stage booster. What it lacked in useless finesse it provided in fabulous simplicity and reliability. No huge curving tunnels for flame buckets, no monster pumps hurling hundreds of thousands of gallons of cooling water. Just a simple, massive deflector that solved the problem of blowback shock waves. A twenty-foot differential between the three engine bells and the concrete was enough to give *just* enough time for the massive rocket to lift upward, the shock waves that could smash every face on Mt. Rushmore dissipating in crackling, howling thunder. The great booster to reach the moon outsped the bounceback shocks barely a second or two ahead of destruction. But it was enough.

The instant Russ Corey saw the Niagara of flame lengthen beneath the moving rocket he knew it would accelerate with speed faster than the mind could visualize for its enormous size. Now the timing of ascending rocket and speeding aircraft rested with Russ Corey. The rocket rose steadily, swiftly and with visible acceleration, seeming to suck up flame from the desert floor and transform it into that dazzling pillar. The flame in turn threw back a massive cloud of white smoke that swiftly obscured all the immediate world, a base surge of outward roiling, spilling, tumbling white that brought the scene into even greater clarity.

Now!

Rocket and airplane hurtled toward the same point in space and time, the rocket climbing almost vertically on its shattering pillar of flame, the Starbird streaking in horizontally. If one did not swerve, they would collide. Corey had no intention of letting *that* happen. Judging all the factors, he came back steadily on the control yoke and with a coordinated fluid movement his left hand moved the throttles past their full-power detent to emergency power as the nose kept coming up, the horizon fled beneath them and Corey pressured forward on the yoke and half-rolled the Starbird.

Rocket and airplane rushed upward together, an incredible formation, the Starbird just ahead of the massive ripple shocks beating out from the flaming booster. The sight was . . . There was no other word for it: *fantastic.* Other words crowded into his thoughts. *Unreal. Overwhelming. Incredible. They're all inadequate. That mother is heading for the moon, for a landing a quarter million miles away.* The Starbird shot upward at supersonic speed, the rocket chasing and closing the distance and now it was time to get the hell out of there, because that giant booster was gathering speed unto itself with a tremendous rush. A slight squeeze of hands and feet and the Starbird did a quarter-roll of its wings, presenting its belly to the booster and Corey pulled back on the yoke, bending the aircraft away and up in an arcing inverted climb. He held the maneuver for thirty seconds and they shot upward into thin, cold air but there remained plenty of power for Corey to half-roll her back to heads-up attitude and he came around in a soaring climb, the wings at a steep angle, so they could keep the moonbound ship in sight.

I guess we can call her the first of the last, Corey thought to himself as he watched the now pencil-thin stalk of smokespew punching through ever-thinning atmosphere. *"Coming up on solid sep,"* he heard in his earpiece. He heard the two pilots respond. "Ah roger that, Luke Control, we show everything in the green up here."

"Very good, Spider." Corey laughed aloud at the name. His pilots were picking up the names of the first manned lunar landers from the old Project Apollo. Snoopy, Red Baron, Gumdrop, Eagle . . . *"Ten seconds, Spider."*

A laconic "Rog," came back.

No need for further words. High, high above the now slowing Starbird, Spider's enormous solid booster system blew out its last gasp of raging energy. A great flash of orange-tinged white appeared on the edge of space to blow away the solids.

"Good sep, Luke," Spider called.

"Go get 'em, Cowboy," Luke radioed back. *"Ten seconds to throttle up. You're go for one hundred ten percent."*

"Gotcha." A long beat, then: "Throttle up to one one zero and this baby is hauling ass . . ."

Russ Corey turned the controls back to Tim Brooks. What he saw now materialized in his mind's eye. He was right a few moments back. *Spider* was the first of the last of the moonbound spaceships to leave the Earth. Perhaps the last for all time. All the power cords had been yanked on all the crystal balls, and the future remained murky. All that mattered now were the giant boosters and the remaining people waiting to go to the moon in order to survive.

Two hundred and twenty-six passengers were aboard *Spider*. Every manned ship would carry an equal number, every manned ship would be loaded in precisely the same manner. Not a single passenger on any of those ships would be conscious.

That was the real gamble. They didn't have the time, the rockets, the elaborate equipment, the ground support crews, the enormous far-flung system of Earth electronics and communications to play this game in the old way. If they had taken two hundred and twenty-six *conscious* passengers off the ground they couldn't have made the flight. The demands on the life-support systems would have been not merely staggering but overwhelming. There would have been problems feeding and watering them, providing sanitation facilities, keeping them under control while they were frightened half to death from the savage pounding of the solid boosters and the roaring ascent; then the open terror of falling toward the moon and praying that the thin bands of laser beam guidance would work right, and so would the attitude thrusters, *and* the radar and doppler altimeters, *and* the main engines, and the gyro gimbals . . . Well, it was one hell of a list.

So they became not only gamblers, but outrageous in throwing away the outmoded and wimpy concepts. To hell with providing all the amenities. That was a luxury-line cruise. This was steerage at the very bottom of the ships which sailed the ocean of vacuum.

"We need to get as many people to the lunar bases as possible," Corey had told his team. "And we need to get them there alive and functioning. That's two big numbers. *Alive*, and *functioning*. But in between launch and final touchdown all they need to do is to breathe."

Encapsulization. Fancy word for a simple concept. Each passenger compartment was fitted with pods. The entire compartment was sealed except for an airlock extending down from the minimal crew compartment at the nose of the ship. The people who were to go reported to a departure facility. They showered and spent several days eating a very special diet that would give their bodies full energy and reduce their need to evacuate waste material. Then they would don simple jumpsuits and climb—*willingly*, or they didn't go—into a capsule pod. Within the pod they were strapped down, secured against severe vibrations and other shocks, and shot with the drug that would keep them comatose for five days. Oxygen-nitrogen mixture was fed into each pod separately, and the entire compartment was filled with the same breathing mixture. If the large compartment suffered a pressure breach, each pod would keep its occupant alive with controlled oxygen, pressure, and temperature. If one or more pods failed, then *only* those passengers would reach the moon unbreathing.

"Solid waste can be stopped," a doctor complained. "But to expect the body not to pass urine that whole time?" He shook his head. "Uh uh. No way." He looked directly at Russ Corey. "How do you solve that problem?"

Corey answered with the stark simplicity of his entire program. "We don't. They got to piss when they're unconscious, they arrive on the moon with wet underwear. Next question . . ."

Simplicity kept the luxury liner concept out of the cockpit as well. Two astronauts flew the ship, with the help of a bunch of onboard computers. All manner of horror stories met Corey's insistence on final "locked design." No changes. Go with the simple. Follow the rule of KISS: *Keep It Simple, Stupid.*

"Where the hell are you going to get that many computers in the limited time you have?" an engineer demanded.

Again the answer was simple. Corey bought them from Radio Shack. When he encountered the expected uproar, he calmly presented the computer standards, and the equipment, for the first space shuttles to fly from the Kennedy Space Center. His designers were stunned. *The advanced computers at Radio Shack that*

*could be bought by anyone were more advanced than
the equipment in the space shuttles.*

The KISS concept was driven home with unrelenting
rigidity. They didn't need massive computers at Luke to
direct the moonbound ships to their lunar destinations.
They already had the computers on the moon. They
also had a huge landing grid built along the floor of the
enormous crater Ptolemaeus near the lunar equator.
The Russians had a small scientific station there but it
was existing on the barest of necessities and the Russians had unashamedly asked for help simply to survive. Corey met their request with a job offer. The
Russians laughed and accepted with open arms. The
Hestia station sent over huge loads of supplies and equipment: power systems to run the laser grids. Inflatable
structures to contain air, food, water, and living facilities for the surge of refugees from Earth. That was the
concept. KISS. Get as many people to the moon, alive
and functioning, as possible.

The entire interior of Ptolemaeus was the landing
field for the one-way ships from Earth. Landing coordinates with velocity increments and descent angles were
determined by the computers at Ptolemaeus, quickly
known as Grid Six, and flashed at the speed of light by
the laser communicators to the approaching ships. The
whole damned thing was automatic. The two pilots,
who had lived the three-day trip from Earth in their
cockpit, eating from tubed food, drinking canned water, and using the old Apollo systems for personal hygiene, monitored the spaceship systems. If something
went wrong they would take over manually. If the
system functioned as intended they'd hang on tight and
let the automatics take them down.

What no one discussed publicly was that of every
forty ships to leave Earth, thirty-seven would make it
and something would go awry with three. Those were
pretty good odds for bargain-basement spaceships. If
the prognostication worked, then the final Mad Dash
from Luke to the moon would see about seven hundred
people, passengers and crew, die.

Eight thousand three hundred and sixty-two would

make it. Not bad. Not bad at all, especially considering that if they remained earthbound they would *all* die.

There was also the matter of a maximum supply lift. Again Corey went with his ruthless application of KISS. Every spaceship that left Earth did so with computer-run controls and systems. At times a ship would have as many as twelve computers. The pilots went upstairs with their hands like claws over the controls, but unless something went wrong it was strictly a hands-off operation. The Russians *and* Americans had been landing unmanned ships on the moon since the sixties. Hell, the Russians had even put down a remote system that rolled about the moon like some mechanistic beetle. Other robots thumped down, opened their blind hatches, and scratched and clawed at the moon, stuffed moondirt in their bellies, slammed shut the hatches and came back to Earth with samples. *That was thirty years ago.*

"Who the hell needs a manned ship for a supply mission?" was Corey's question, to which the only answer was "Nobody, man. You can fly this kind of mission with a rubber chicken up front." The utter ruthlessness of Corey-applied KISS was never more evident. No crew controls, no pressurization, no food, sanitation, any kind of life support system, no more than automatic communicator systems. Except for the massive first stage booster, the whole package went to the moon, complete with cranes and derricks for loading and unloading. In such designs, without pressure containment systems, you needed aerodynamic fairings only for the first brief period of flight, after which the ablative material was unceremoniously dumped and the naked ship with open girders and cables containing its cargo boosted to another blind but by-now routine landing. And whatever made it to the moon was catalogued, placed in the inventory, and prepared for total scavenging by the Selenites, as the lunar populace had begun to call itself.

Blatting thunder pounded onto the runway as Russ Corey went down the short stairway of the Starbird. He looked up as thirty attack helicopters, still climbing out from "punch liftoffs," increased speed, noses down and rotors whanging away with everything they had. As he expected, thunder growled in the distance as the heavily armored gunships went to full power for takeoff. Six old turboprops, Lockheed C-130 Hercules, that had been around forever but were still the best machines flying. Direct descendants of Puff. He permitted himself a brief wan smile. The Magic Dragons, all right, first used in that role in a jungle potboiler called Vietnam. Each Hercules had been fitted with four Gatling guns, superfast-firing weapons with electrically rotating barrels that could each pump out between four and seven thousand rounds a minute. In 'Nam one gunship had proven itself capable of smashing an entire village to the ground as it orbited casually about its target.

"Get me to defense control, *fast*," he snapped to the van driver waiting for him. Inside the van he grabbed the radio. "This is Corey. I'm on the way in. Brief me on the ground situation. Hit it."

"Mankowicz here," came the almost instant response. "It's busting loose, Russ. All telephone lines are down but we still have radio comm. The mobs have taken down the microwave towers. We have fifteen remote choppers circling the main crowds for constant position updates and another fifteen covering the perimeters from eight thousand feet and up."

Corey nodded to himself. Aloud, he said: "Charley, I had a good look to the north. There must have been a hundred thousand people there. Most of their vehicles are roadside or offroad. Looks like they're getting up their snuff to come in. I don't want a human wave spread across the landscape. A few individuals with recoilless gear and homers can hurt us."

"Yes, sir. Permission to commence Zoboa."

How appropriate. The desert whirlwind that destroyed the Persian army gathering to destroy Cairo. That was four thousand years ago, something like that. The hands of time do come around.

"Charley, get Sal Preiss up to control immediately. Drag him out of wherever he is and no arguments. Where the hell is Clete Marsh?"

"He's on the line. Lead Dragon."

"Good. He's backed up?"

"Yes, sir. Don Watson's here."

"All right, my friend. Let's see just how good you people really are. Zoboa is it, buddy boy. Turn the dragons loose."

"Yes, *sir*."

By the time he was out of the van and running the short distance to the massive blockhouse where Luke Control held down its fort, he heard the unmistakable sound of the fat propellers of the Magic Dragons thrumming under full power. Seconds later came the first distant *THHHRRRPPPPP!* of the Gatlings firing. He had a mental picture of four thousand rounds per minute of twenty-millimeter cannon shells tearing up the highway. Despite himself and the absolute necessity for the move, he winced. Not even God had that kind of firepower . . .

To everyone's surprise, once inside the blockhouse he paid scant attention to the war erupting along the perimeter of Luke Range. That's why he'd picked the best men in the business for this job. *Their* wives and children were being podded at that very moment. Their families—and later themselves—would live or die based on just how good they were. Charley Mankowicz turned from his seat before master defense control. "Sal's on the way in. You've got a moment. Want a look?"

He stood beside Charley's chair. Rows of large television screens and grid monitors showed just about everything that was coming in. "North highway," Corey said. "Give me a high scan and pick up the zoom."

They looked at vehicles burning along the sides of the roads. Flames lined the highway for miles as the bumper-to-bumper cars and trucks leapfrogged their own fires. "There's the main bunch," Charley said, and the picture fell downward as the camera in the remote chopper zoomed in. A huge convoy of semi-trailers, armored cars, garbage trucks, and big flatbed trucks with heavy weapons rolled steadily southward. "Ah, there's the brains of that bunch," Corey observed as the increasing magnification showed an incredible array of motorcycles herding the heavy vehicles.

"We can't let them come south of the highway," Mankowicz noted aloud. "Those bikers will spread out on the desert and then we'll be swatting flies one by one." He pressed another transmit button. "Dragons, turn for that convoy with the bikers to the north. Choppers Four through Twelve, work them over from the perimeters. Dusters, I want that whole area in firemist right *now*."

They lost one Hercules and three helicopters to the weapons gathered by the invaders coming down to either get a seat to the moon or destroy everything before them. The spray planes went in low, dispensing a heavy aerosol mist that rolled like fog through the invading force. On the ground the bikers laughed. What the hell was *fog* going to do?

They didn't know about firemist: an aerosol that was napalm fog and could be triggered only in heavy concentration and by a specific electrical signal. Mankowicz had the concentration and he ordered a chopper to light it all off with one of the missiles that would send the electrical shock wave through the firemist.

For twenty-three miles along the highway and a mile to each side everything vanished in a single blinding sheet of flame. One moment there was power and mass energy and bikers and bloodlusting invaders, power-mad, confident, invincible. The next moment forty thousand human beings were burning to death, jumping, staggering, hurling themselves about in a frenzy of pain-induced madness.

"Dragons, Grid Seven, Grid Seven. They've got control of the trains. Take them out."

It was all business. Corey glanced up to see Sal Preiss come into the blockhouse at a dead run. He stopped by Corey and they went into a nearby situation room. A heavily armed guard poured coffee and placed sandwiches on the table. "Stay here," Corey told him. "No interruptions." He turned back to Preiss.

"Launch everything. Immediately."

375

"You saw the first one go. We're setting them up in one-hour intervals—"

Corey shook his head. "No good. Get them off *now*. Get them the hell out of here. *Now*," he repeated.

"The best we can do, and it's built-in safety in the circuits, is one every hour."

"Open the fucking door and destroy the circuits. I said to get them up *now*."

"Goddamn it, they can't land them in the flatlands that fast!" Preiss shouted.

"Stack 'em in lunar orbit," Corey said calmly. "You can do that. It's one of your contingencies. We don't have the time, Sal."

Preiss studied him carefully. "This isn't like you. You're Mister By-The-Book himself. What the hell happened?"

Corey was genuinely surprised. "You haven't heard?"

"I haven't heard shit," Preiss snapped. "I've been having people podded as fast as we could."

"Send them up podded or awake, goddamn it."

"Tell me why the panic button. We can hold off that mob out there and—"

"To hell with the assholes," Corey broke in. He eased off for a moment. "Sal, we got word on the way in here. Apparently Venezuela and Brazil wanted a bigger piece of the lifeboat in orbit. Too few of their people aboard *Pegasus*. So they invaded the Kourou site with paratroopers and a full assault by sea."

Preiss sat like granite. " Short and sweet, Russ."

Corey shrugged. "The French didn't like it. They resisted. The troops coming in went mad. They've killed most of the French and torched all their fuel farms. The whole place is a bonfire."

"Jesus fucking Christ . . . And the French—"

"They're pissed. They had a bunch of subs in the South Atlantic. MIRV'ed warheads."

"How bad?"

"For starters, Venezuela's lost Caracas, Port-of-Spain, and Maracaibo—"

"Goodbye, Venezuela."

"They identified four cities gone in Brazil. Rio de

376

Janeiro, Recife, Brasilia, and Sao Paulo. All of South America is waiting for the other thirty or forty shoes to drop and—"

Sal Preiss was already off his chair and on his way out the door.

Russ Corey finished his sandwich and coffee, refilled the java, lit a cigar and leaned back to relax. When you're up to your ass in alligators you don't panic. He'd finish the second coffee and then he'd go down to launch control and— He stopped his own thoughts. He wouldn't do them any good. Sal Preiss was the best in the business and Corey would only be underfoot. Well, what does the big boss-man do when everybody's got everything under control? Simple. You go where the action is, where the unexpected rules.

He'd get one of the Scarabs—the armored helicopter-airplane with the X-wing. It could fly at four hundred miles an hour or hover like a dragonfly, and it had thick armor plating and a hell of a lot of firepower, Gatlings and two hundred minirockets. One Scarab could kill a hell of a lot of people.

That's the way it goes, he mused as he walked back to Mankowicz's control panel. *You finish up on one world killing as many people as you can so you can take as many people as you can to live on another world. Too bad Shakespeare's not with us any longer. He'd get a kick out of this.*

Twenty-five minutes later Russ Corey gutted a convoy of a hundred buses that had been filled with armed men and women. He didn't enjoy what he did. He understood those people.

They weren't really bloodthirsty. Just terrified.

He rolled away from his last firing pass. Through the armored glass he caught sight of a daylight moon. The yearning to go home hit him with almost physical force.

Hang in there, Vicki. I'm doing everything I can to save us a chunk of the future.

Tyuratam

Vitali Krivitsky leaned over the situation map showing the sprawling manned launch center of Tyuratam and its seventy-four launching pads, servicing buildings, roads, fuel farms, living quarters, and all the other complex, massive, logistically back-breaking support facilities for the largest spaceport on the planet. He studied the outlying airstrips and helicopter pads that dotted all the area. He nodded to himself at the small model planes that identified the heavy transports flying into Tyuratam, bringing with them the finest of Russian youth, along with a sprinkling of highly skilled engineers, scientists, technicians, and a variety of specialists. They were all quartered, he knew, in three separate structures somewhat distant from the launch pads and the explosive fuel farms. One of the twelve-year-old boys in Building Three was his son, Oleg. Though the youth was but six miles distant, Vitali Krivitsky did not expect ever to see him again. What Russia needed now was time and distance between Tyuratam and the outside world, to get her best of the best into that high orbit where the two great space machines were being rushed to operational capability.

Vitali Krivitsky wore the insignia and the uniform of a full general of the Soviet army. He had the task of keeping Tyuratam isolated. He tapped the map. He did not turn his head an inch when he spoke to Yevgeni Udaltsov by his side. "Colonel, how many SAMS in place?"

"Four hundred on launch command status, sir. Eight hundred in lift position to replace those launched."

"Test the southern quadrant. Immediately."

"Yes, sir." Colonel Udaltsov picked up the telephone to his right. He ordered two MiG-41 fighters from an airfield a hundred miles distant to take off immediately from their "hammer back and ready" positions and fly due north over Tyuratam.

The general walked outside the security command center onto the roof. He brought binoculars to his eyes. "There they are, Colonel," he said to Udaltsov. "They are barely making contrails. What speed?"

"Mach one point six, Comrade General."

"Very good. I—" He spoke no further. Two lances of dazzling light ripped upward from a copse of distant trees. Two flashes of upper missile stages firing. With a speed faster than the brain could really comprehend, the two missiles that could intercept an incoming ballistic missile flashed to the two manned fighter planes and left a flash and then a smear in the sky.

"The system is effective, Colonel," General Krivitsky noted. "Change the procedure. *Always* launch at least two backup SAM missiles for every intercept. No deviation from that order."

Krivitsky went back to his situation maps. The plan was simple. The city of Baikonur, which had always supported Tyuratam, lay one hundred and fifty miles away. All roads and rail lines between Baikonur and Tyuratam had been cut and torn up for miles. *Every* road and rail line between Tyuratam and the outside world had been blown up. The only way in to Tyuratam was on foot or by air. If you came on foot, or tried on something like tank treads, you were attacked immediately, without warning and without surcease until you were destroyed. If you came by air, you had to go through five random computer checks of the defense system *and* confirm your identity visually and by voice-print. If you did not, well, the missiles were always cocked and ready to fire.

There had been a few problems. One transport with ninety-two selectees for the *Pegasus* had not complied fully with the security requirements. It was torn to shredded blood-and-metal confetti by a brace of missiles.

Major Arkadi Chakovsky approached the general. "Sir, you asked to be notified when we reached terminal count for the Lenin launches. We are approaching minus twenty minutes in the countdown."

Krivitsky nodded. "The people are aboard in the passenger compartments?"

"Yes, sir."

"What complement?"

"Tsiolkovskii Brigade. Complex Three, sir."

379

His son, Oleg, was in Complex Three. "The schedule called for Complex One. Titov Brigade."

"Sir, a minor outbreak of stomach disorders in Complex One. Procedures call for twenty-four-hour isolation and study. Complex Three was the next on the schedule."

"Very good. Come with me, Major Chakovsky. I wish to observe this launch personally."

"Yes, sir." The major hesitated. "Sir, with the general's permission?"

Krivitsky raised an eyebrow, then nodded. "Do you wish a message to your son, Comrade General?"

Krivitsky's face was cast in hard metal. Then, for a moment, only a moment, metal softened. "My son is gone, Major. In that ship there is no past. Only the future." He started to turn away. His arm went out and touched the major's shoulder. "Thank you, Arkadi. We will not speak of this again. Let us go."

They stood five miles from the launch pad. A mountain loomed before them. The *Lenin* booster soared six hundred and forty feet above its launch stand. Within the upper stage, as wide across as a huge jumbo jet passenger compartment, eighty-six youngsters and specialists lay strapped in their couches. Beneath them the *Lenin* carried three hundred tons of supplies. The entire upper stage would become a part of *Pegasus*.

The major leaned forward. "Six minutes, sir."

Krivitsky nodded. "Status for *Lenin Two?*"

"Nominal count, Comrade General. It will fly precisely thirty-nine minutes after liftoff of *Lenin One.*"

"Very good." Who would ever have dreamed we would carry out back-to-back launches of such monsters, mused Krivitsky. Nothing matched the *Lenin* boosters. For fifteen years they had been scheduled to carry a manned landing party to Mars. Now they would fire one after the other. *We are running out of time*, Krivitsky knew. The bombs going off through South America. The madness in the Middle East. More trouble brewing as the world hurled itself into a frenzy.

"Major, what of the Progress boosters?" the general asked.

"First launch at midnight, sir. Every two hours until all eight boosters are flown."

"Thank you, Major." The supply rockets. Big, unmanned, carrying the essentials for survival. They *must* get them off as quickly as possible. Time was running out. They were trying to keep it from the public, but the scientists had already detected the subtle but inescapable variations in normal sun activity. *Soon we shall know what it is like to be a close neighbor to an angry star,* thought the general.

A speaker intruded. "Sixty seconds. The vehicle is on final terminal count. All systems operating perfectly."

He forced quiet into his mind, gave his thoughts over to his eyes. With a start he realized it was early evening. Darkness moved furtively along the horizons. Krivitsky was looking to the east, to the darkness. So much the better for contrast. He—

The launch pad floodlights winked out. He had a brief retinal afterimage of the *Lenin* mountain and darkness settled into his eyes and mind. The seconds fled, swept along by the loudspeaker voice.

"*Tri.*

"*Dva.*

"*Odin!*"

Eighteen huge engines ripped into life. Flame stabbed out from engine bells. Light shattered the immediate world and dashed madly for the distant horizon. Rocket fire plunged downward into the manmade flame-dispersing cliff beneath *Lenin One.*

The giant stirred, shaking itself, rumbling and groaning with this first breath of the dragon. Slowly, ponderously, the greatest space machine ever heaved itself upward with agonizing firepain. The terrible glare rippled, flashed and tore loose. Light ripped into the eyes of General Vitali Krivitsky. He refused himself the relief of blinking. He would not yield a single instant of this moment. Standing on its blazing cataract, *Lenin One* whipsawed the thick, curving iron tubes deep within the bowels of the temple where it had been prepared for life, with fire that smashed into high-pressure water.

From each side of the launch mesa an orange-hued,

swirling, spattering rupture of steam howled at the sky and boomed up and outward.

Lenin One blew its icy breath downward and downwind, a swirling coruscation of ice vibrating from her thick flanks. Pressure built, thrust grew, power increased; flame snarled angrily at gravity. Columns of blazing, steel-hard fire tore at and gutted the throat of the launch cliff. The earth trembled, then rumbled and heaved in spasms reaching out for miles. The air before Vitali Krivitsky's eyes danced from the shock waves. The fury of sound bolted into the stunned observers and men and women opened their mouths in sudden pain as the deep-throated rumbles resonated in dental fillings. Men and women shouted as loudly as they could to relieve the pressure, their pitiful human cries unheard as the roar of *Lenin* sent sonic bolts exploding in their midst.

Lenin reached out for the heavens, umbilicals whipping away like fire-washed pythons drowning in falling ice chunks. Higher! Flame splashed madly along the edges of the launch stand and skittered with blind fury horizontally in all directions, a screeching fire broom that would make Lucifer recoil.

Heat rolled across the miles to the tiny humans as if a steel furnace had exploded a hundred yards away. Red fire became orange and then dazzling, exultant gold, shimmering along its ragged edges in free air, starting the pale violet glow of atoms stripped naked and discarded mindlessly. There was thunder no more. A billion torches shot upward, coalesced, invited eighteen engines to hurl forth their diamond-shaped shock waves so the sound became more than thunder, swiftly repeated terrible explosions, a machine-gunning of enormous bombs detonating, an acetylene-torch gasp of the gods.

The thunderwhip of Thor cracked, and earth and sky trembled. Now the flame metamorphosed, the gold returning to orange and then a new violet-red. The cataract lengthened to a half-mile of fire, its trailing edges ethereal, expanding as the ascent moved *Lenin One* into thinner atmosphere. A huge plasma sheath came into being and suddenly, as *Lenin* rose high enough to dive upward into the rays of the sun not yet fallen at that altitude beyond the Earth, the plasma exploded silently to become an envelope of glowing ionized gases.

Two minutes and fifty-three seconds after the first breath of the dragon, the eighteen engines of the first stage pushed the monster rocket upward at nearly three thousand miles an hour. The numbers had become meaningless. General Vitali Krivitsky knew the numbers. One hundred and thirty-two million horsepower burned back toward him. He murmured beneath his breath. There! White-hot gases spearing outward where the first stage joined the upper structure. The pyrotechnics severing connections, the retrorockets slowing the spent, useless dragon that had lived so briefly.

Don't breathe . . . watch . . . where is it? Where is—

New flame. Fainter, more certain of itself. High-energy fuels of the second stage, a monster unto itself that would soon soar upward into low orbit to be captured by waiting space tugs and carried higher to— But that was later. The general watched the upper stage bending over more and more in its flight, racing toward its rendezvous seven hundred miles high.

He watched until a tiny flicker of light flashed through a high cloud. The thunder rolled down from forever, regal in its descent from the heavens, a fitting sigh of departure.

A tear rolled down the cheek of General Vitali Krivitsky.

Goodbye, Oleg. Goodbye forever, my son.

The Middle East

There is no other silence like it. There can be the absence of silence, but even that is misleading, because within an anechoic chamber, where sound dissolves in midair and there are no echoes, a man *will* hear the blood pounding through the arteries of his ears. Silence where there should be bustle and sound and sharp reports and deep booms and coughing motors and laughing children and people shouting to one another and birds crying in the wind . . . *that* is silence.

383

So it was through the Middle East. Upon that hapless part of the world fell the terrible silence of radioactive fallout. Even men of singular hearing ability do not turn their heads at the hiss of white and grey ash drifting down from the sky, layering a pall of certain death that began in the instantaneous appearance of a fireball grubbing with atomic talons in the earth.

Neither the most virulent apostle of Islam, the most dedicated servant of Christianity, nor the tradition-steeped warrior of the ancient Hebrews held any heart to fight. Fight with gun and grenade and fist and bullet in a land sooty with lethal ash? To what purpose? To what end? *To walk across a field or down a road was to sign your own death warrant and that of many others. You do not wish to die? Easy to avoid! Don't breathe! That's all there is to it. Don't eat the food or drink the water or touch your beloved . . . just don't do anything. The wonder of this is that you need exert no effort to die. How efficient!*

They lay exhausted and dumbfounded, and the dead that had not been incinerated lay swollen and blistered and exploding in the terrible choking heat. No vultures came. The birds are particularly susceptible to nuclear radiations, and their feathered carcasses were everywhere. But not those of the flies and the grubs and the worms and the beetles and the scorpions and the mosquitos and all those horrid creatures. Science had long stated that the cockroach could absorb a million times the ionizing radiation that would kill a healthy man, and not be bothered a twit.

Ah, science. They were right. The roaches flourished and ate and gorged and grew fatter; this was *their* land.

Men looked through blistered eyes and tried to close oozing lips as they raised their heads painfully on weakened neck muscles to the sky. They looked for God. Islamic . . . Christian, and not a one of the Holy Trinity was to be found . . . Jewish, and forever, this time, He was gone.

So they all said the same thing in their different languages, and the words would translate to the same, if anyone would bother to do so. They would each and all of them ask the same question and there would be no answer this time, and there would be no answer ever again.

What have we done, oh Lord, what have we done!

And were God still about, behind some cleverly twisted drapery of time-space, and were He so inclined, He might this time have cut the biblical banter of thees and thous and wheresomefores and told them all: *You have really done it this time. Shit all over yourselves. And stop all that caterwauling and praying. You annoy Me.*

China

"I would prefer to call it the Great Farm. Or perhaps the Farm of Our Ancestors. But this silly old Jewish name, *Noah*? Do we pay homage to ancient superstitions of the Jews?"

The elder smiled. "We all have our superstitions. Theirs will do well enough. Their God covered the world with water and Noah saved the animals and the people. Now, fire will replace the water. It is not so different."

"But he would have had to build such an enormous boat!"

"Do we not do the same? Build an enormous boat that sails the orbital tides? That finds the streams of centrifugal force? That studies the position of the moon and the planets to best find its way?"

"Yes, but this is different."

The elder was patient. "It is always different and it will always *be* different." He eased to a more positive tack. "Does the work go well?"

"Yes, *yes*, Revered One! And not only with the great fire dragons, but also—"

"Do not patronize me. I know well enough we are dealing with multiple stage booster ascent, commencing with aluminum-nitrate-based solid first stages and storable liquids for the upper stages, that your new gods are pounds thrust and specific impulse and—"

"I beg your forgiveness, Honored sir. Yes, it goes well. And the round-eyes—sorry, the Americans have accepted Chiang Biao as the commander equal to—"

"Standby to."

"Of course, standby to the American Admiral Marc Seavers."

The elder nodded. "That is good. Tell me, the fauna that are our responsibility, have we succeeded? This absence of gravity could prove far more of an obstacle than anyone anticipates."

"I must be honest. We were *not* succeeding until the team visited us from America."

"Stanford?"

"Yes, Honored—"

"Get to it." The words came forth as an impatient, sibilant hiss.

"From Stanford and the Stauffer Chemical Company."

"I am familiar with the splicing. We have been using the natural soil bacterium, *Agrobacterium tumefaciens*, to infiltrate cells. But the plants resist and it takes time and it cannot affect corn and wheat, and they are most critical. The Americans have shown you the way?"

"Yes. Electroporation is the answer."

"Ah. Yes, yes. What do they call it in their idiom? Yes, zapping the plants with a jolt of electricity. That is it."

"Yes, sir. It opens the cell membranes sufficiently to permit the massive and immediate infiltration we induce. It has given us new crops with unbelievable resistance to every disease we have tested."

"What else?"

"We transfer genes between unrelated types. We are now in possession of entirely new species, disease-resistant, hardy, and greatly productive of new foods. It is, quite literally, two hundred times more effective than anything we have known before."

"I hope several generations are," eyebrows raised to the sky, "up there?"

"Oh, yes, sir. We have already produced our first accelerated crops. Rice, wheat, corn, all manner of grains, the vine plants, the new strains of bamboo, the kudzu, fruits—"

"Enough. I have eaten for the day."

"Yes, sir."

386

"You did not come here to gloat over your Trojan Horse plant cells."

"No, sir."

"You are a young scientist and yet you have come to see an old fossil like me. Obviously, you have a reason. If there is such a reason, it is also obvious you have a problem."

"Yes, sir."

"A problem you cannot solve with your shiny bright new uniforms, your computers—"

"Yes, yes."

"And you wish me to solve it for you."

"Please."

"The problem?"

"We have lost several large boosters carrying water to both spacecraft. The matters of mass, weight, inertia, slosh, imbalance; they drive us mad and we are far behind our schedule. The water does not behave as the computers predict—"

"Water cannot read computers."

"Yes, sir."

"You cannot overcome the slosh?"

"No. Even the compartmented systems, baffles and the like, give way from the high accelerations we have with the solid boosters. It throws the entire ship out of balance."

The old man in his silk robe stared at the haze-shrouded horizon. "You take many things with you, but you appear short of wisdom."

"Uh, yes, sir."

"Do you know what the Americans call wisdom?"

"No, sir."

"Common sense. And that is where the solution to your problem lies."

"I do not understand."

"Are you aware that I can walk on water?"

"*What?* Uh, forgive me—"

"You do not believe me. Be truthful."

"No, sir, I do *not* believe you can walk on water."

"Nor do you inquire how I can do this. Lack of questions presupposes assumptions, and that is foolish."

"Tell me, Revered One, how one may walk on water?"

"You freeze it, you dummy."

"Holy—!"

"Careful."

"Thank you, Revered One!"

"Oh, get out."

Grand Cayman Island

S.S. *Agalhus* steamed steadily through pleasant seas under a new moon. The powerful ore carrier moved out from her port in South Africa with all papers in proper order. She crossed the South Atlantic, maintained good radio contact and position reports, and maintained course that would take her through the Leeward Islands, directly through Guadeloupe Passage, between Guadeloupe and Montserrat, and then due west on a straight line running south of Puerto Rico, Hispaniola, and Jamaica. Past the latter island *Agalhus* would bear northwest to slide between Grand Cayman and Little Cayman Islands. Then a straight shot through the Yucatan Channel between South America and Cape San Antonio of Cuba and then taking a new course directly into the Gulf of Mexico, the final destination Tampa, Florida.

Beneath a thin layer of iron ore in the number four hold was braced an enormous squared object, as big as a three-bedroom house. The object bristled with electronic systems and massive cabling. At its heart was a plutonium warhead the function of which, inside this particular package, was to perform not as a destructive bomb, but as the detonator cap for a mass of lithium-hydride. The latter had been packed around an original small thermonuclear weapon with one point four million tons of high explosive yield. Respectable, but hardly different from the weapons common to the nuclear powers. But with lithium-hydride packaged about the original bomb, much as a child packs wet sand about a growing mountain at the beach, the potential explosive yield rose from the comparatively measly one point four megatons to seventy million tons.

A hydrogen bomb is like a bonfire. You can keep packing more and more burn material about the core and the power goes up in terrible quantum leaps. *This* bomb followed the old Russian design. Starting at the core was the plutonium bomb trigger, then the tightly packaged hydrogen bomb, *then* the mass of thermonuclear material patty-caked on to the hydrogen bomb, and as a final shell, the South African weapons scientists had fashioned a casing of radioactive dump material, U-238 irradiated in an electrical power reactor. Normally U-238 won't even fizzle when used as a bomb material. But in this particular contraption, where it would be drenched in neutrons outpouring from the fusion of lithium-hydride, it would have even more power than everything beneath its casing:

A bomb with an explosive yield of some six hundred million tons of TNT. Detonated as planned in Tampa Harbor, it would vaporize the entire area, throw up a fireball twenty miles in diameter, crush all of Tampa as if a giant mountain were dropped onto the city, do terrible damage for many miles beyond, and erupt from the sea bottom with a savagely radioactive column of water, steam and spray. With the prevailing winds out of the west *all* of central Florida, and much of the area north and south, would within two to three hours drown in radioactivity so intense a lethal dosage would be administered to any human being within six minutes.

Cape Canaveral and the Kennedy Space Center lay in the direct path of such an explosion.

The scenario, so explicit to the South African officials who ordered it and a second ore carrier even then steaming to the English Channel directly between England and France and the Low Countries, was hardly so unique that it could not be anticipated by the American military. From the moment S.S. *Agalhus* slipped through the Guadeloupe Passage she was shadowed by a high-altitude naval reconnaissance aircraft. Detailed photographs went immediately through naval intelligence files. The question needed asking only once. "What the hell is a South African ship taking iron ore to Tampa for? There aren't any steel mills in Florida."

Agalhus went to Priority Two. A swift nuclear-powered attack submarine took up station beneath and slightly

389

portside of the ore carrier. They were just off Grand Cayman Island when the submarine received its orders. CARRY OUT ATTACK FIRST OPPORTUNITY MAXIMUM NUMBER TORPEDOES WITH MAXIMUM YIELD WARHEADS. NO WARNING ANY KIND REPEAT NO WARNING ANY KIND. CARRY OUT THESE ORDERS IMMEDIATELY.

In naval headquarters they counted down the minutes. The attack boat captain would set it up by dashing ahead of *Agalhus*, turning, and coming back to set up a quartering bow shot with a full spread of torpedoes. He wouldn't take any chances. He'd fire three direct, two homers, and one wire-guided.

They didn't even dare question the skipper of *Agalhus*. This close to the southern United States, *any* suspicion could panic the man. Panic could mean a thrown switch and the monstrous fireball.

There was no panic. No warning. Six torps went their way and took *Agalhus* from bow to stern, breaking her back, chopping her into huge chunks thrown clear of the water to fall back steaming and grinding as they boiled into and beneath the water.

MISSION ACCOMPLISHED. SIX DIRECT. BREAKUP AND IMMEDIATE SINKING. NO SURVIVORS.

The computers hummed all night. Before dawn the *S.S. De Aar* was tracked off the Bissau delta of Port Guinea of western Africa by a killer boat of the soviet navy. The Russian commander fired six torpedoes from his bow tubes, deftly swung his boat through one hundred eighty-four degrees, and gave the *S.S. De Aar* another four shots. Three of the latter torpedoes went harmlessly through boiling seas where there had been a ship; the fourth struck a chunk of wreckage and provided a sudden pyrotechnic ending to what had been from its outset a sorry spectacle, indeed.

COMBINED HEADQUARTERS
UNITED STATES SPACE COMMAND
NATIONAL AERONAUTICS AND SPACE ADMINISTRATION.
US–USSR JOINT OPERATIONS COMMAND
CHEYENNE MOUNTAIN, COLORADO, U.S.A.

Hugh Fitzpatrick had the build of a hairless gorilla and the reddened face of a dedicated whiskey drinker, to say naught about a heavy spot of beer every now and then with the emphasis greater on the present than the perhaps. He looked out of place anywhere save an Irish pub, and his parents through years of verbal brawling had left him with a brogue as thick as a lumberjack's wrist. Behind his florid facial roadmap of red-creased highways resided a wellspring of pure engineering genius, which had prompted Marc Seavers to push the appointment of Fitzpatrick as Final Design Chief for both *Pegasus* and *Noah*. The position was a far cry from design engineer; there was little need for that to get the two giant lifeboats from concept to the first stages of physical assembly. Whatever was going to be done to create the two enormous vessels must be carried out with the building materials and supplies boosted at tremendous cost in time, energy, and lives. Moving huge chunks of material in zero gravity looked just fine on paper; in reality, with the pull and tug and sway and tremble of inertia and mass and wobble and still-new effects they were encountering, the space engineers considered building the pyramids to be little more than kicking sand into a pointed pile.

It was being able to adapt as swiftly as the ships began to expand into viable giants that was needed. Anyone who knew his onions about centrifugal flight and dancing in orbit understood without question that whatever design emerged at the beginning of the program must yield to the realities of inspace construction—which could not truly be anticipated until everyone was into the thick of it. Hugh Fitzpatrick had made his reputation not in strawbossing great construction tasks but in saving them from the incompetence and folly of others. Fitzpatrick had even been heard to admit that no man save himself could have carried through certain extraordinary tasks, and that no one who was booted from the construction site to make room for Fitzpatrick and his team could really be blamed. "After all," he twitted, "they're only human. And for a job like this, only human will not do, *no sair*, no' a'tall." After each lapse into brogue he might be seen ceremoniously sticking out his tongue and shoving it back into his mouth.

Marc Seavers knew Fitzpatrick and, more importantly, his skills and his brilliant adaptive engineering genius. Seavers left nothing undone to get the seemingly brutish Irishman, including a direct call from orbit to General Joseph Briand, who led the U.S. Space Command, appointed directly by President George Starling to run the staggering problem of logistical supply from isolated pads of steel and concrete on Earth to a theoretical point that could be found seven hundred miles up and fled about the world at nearly five miles every second.

Talking between orbit and Earth was no longer the ear-crackling struggle of the past—not with the great comsats in geosynchronous orbit that flashed voices about the planet like lightspeed will o' the wisps. With those aural signals went the video. Deep within Cheyenne Mountain, which Joe Briand hated fiercely as a truly stinking substitute for clean, high sky, the general and anyone else involved in the program could rest back in a comfortable chair and study a television screen born of flat computer chip elements—a screen fourteen feet wide and nine feet high with startling clarity. You saw and heard the speaker as if you were together. The only clue that this was not so was in the hesitation intrinsic to conversation. A lag of perhaps a third to a full second dogged every exchange. Man's need to talk to one another had already stretched the limitations of lightspeed, at which velocity communications ran the gamut of switching points of microphones, pickups, relays, conversations, transmissions, aural outplays, and then reversing the whole complicated process. But if you told yourself not to have a nagging concern about that briefest of hesitations, your communications were nigh unto incredible.

Joe Briand chewed on his cigar and stared into the face of Marc Seavers, who at that moment was on the other side of the planet in a nest of naked girders and drifting metal cubicles and the wild iridescence of orbital construction. No matter; Joe Briand puffed on his cigar and accepted the world's ultimate hero as sitting across the table. They had been going through their usual review at the close of each day—artificially timed, of course—of logistics, construction, progress and problems. Joe Briand didn't think of Marc Seavers as a hero; indeed, he pitied the admiral for his task. He looked down on Seavers as some form of space turkey who didn't know his own feathers from a wild goose chase: a chase after survival that could never be attained by running.

"Admiral, you want Hugh Fitzpatrick, is that it?"

"You going dense on me, Joe? I've been screaming for Fitz for weeks now."

"We got him for you."

"Where is he?"

He said he'd talk to you after he does the whirlwind tour of industry, transportation, launch sites, flight equipment, computer extrapolations of what the hell you're doing up there—you know." Briand shrugged again. "The usual."

"The *usual*?" Marc Seavers spoke the word as if in an echo chamber. The sudden stark look on his face and the bite in his voice brought the general upright in his seat. "Joe—*General* Briand—I'm going to say this one time and never repeat it again. If ever I see, hear, notice or otherwise detect in you this deliberate off-handed holier-than-thou attitude I'll have you off this project so fast you'll think you've been busted the high side of the mach. You read me, General?"

"Uh, Marc—"

"Never again, no matter how short or long the time left to what is swiftly losing its place as the dominant life form on your planet, do you refer to me as anyone but *Admiral*, and . . ."

Joe Briand didn't hear any more for a while. A snatch of conversation clamored between his ears, a massive ringing of huge bells pounding and thudding through every scrap of bone and folded tissue in his skull. With that one verbal thrust Marc Seavers had penetrated his defenses, crumbled his walls, struck down his casual contempt of death. How had he said it? In whatever time was left to him Joe Briand would never forget those words. "On *your* planet," he'd said. "*On your planet . . .*"

Marc Seavers and the others were gone. They were never coming back. They were no longer of the same planet.

Joe Briand felt stripped naked to his soul. It's a hell of a thing to realize suddenly that you're the ultimate outcast. That in whatever brave or terrifying new world awaited those people high above him at this moment, *there was no room for Joe Briand.*

He looked up finally at the screen, saw the concern in Seavers' face. The man with whom he'd been friends. Never again.

"Yes, sir, Admiral Seavers? We had interference," Briand lied about the connection.

"Get Fitzpatrick here as fast as you can. I want a full consensus—hell, General, I want a full congregation down there. Fitzpatrick, you, Travis Simmonds from KSC; who's in from Russia?"

"Anatoli Rubinov."

"Have him there for the meeting. What about Chiang Biao?"

"Unavailable, sir. He's at their launch site. We expect him to lift within the next two days or so."

"All right. See if you can bring in Marion Hughes."

"Yes, sir." Briand made a notation on his pad to get the NASA Administrator there come hell what may.

"General, be sure to have the entire session taped. Feed a copy realtime up here and to the Gagarin station as well, and make the usual feeds from your end."

"Yes, sir."

"Twenty-four hours, General. I don't care *how.* Just do it."

They brought in Hugh Fitzpatrick roaring with frustration and anger. Dead sober, although he looked and acted like a madman—a madman who understood the value of every word he spoke, every gesture he made. "There's no time for the president to *review* what we've got to talk about here tonight!" he shouted at General

Briand. "Don't you understand, you dumb starry son of a bitch? We're running out of time. Time, time, *time!*" he bellowed. "Now I'm ordering you, you tin asshole, get me a line direct to the president!"

Joe Briand was still back on his heels from those few devastating words from Marc Seavers in orbit; he had no cause to get between this Irish madman and the president of the country. To Briand's astonishment, the White House put Fitzpatrick through immediately to President Starling.

"Hugh, it's good to see you, even if it is—"

"Never mind the damned protocol, George!" Fitzpatrick shouted. "The next best thing to kicking your ass to get you *here* instead of staying in that pillared outhouse of yours is to make sure *you are part of this meeting*. Damn it, George, don't you understand what I'm saying? You're not going to do the future any good by saving lives and property for a little while longer, and—"

"What do you mean by that?" Starling iced his way into the harangue.

Obviously these two knew each other from way back, Briand judged correctly as he listened.

"It's just like I told soldier-boy here," Fitzpatrick snapped, jerking a thumb at Briand. "We are running out of time. The stuff is getting thicker than an alderman's tongue up there. In short, George, the heat's going to be upon us much sooner than we anticipated. *We won't have time to finish the ships*."

"I don't believe you," Starling said quietly.

"You mean you don't *want* to believe me," Fitzpatrick threw back at him. "But damn it, man," Fitzpatrick's hands waved great circles in the air before him, "I'm not saying things are hopeless or that everything is lost. Far from it. I am telling you that a decision must be made, three hours from now when we all meet in here, that will change the way we're going about saving this tiny pie slice of the human race. Do you understand? Stop beating around the bush, damn it. You're the president, for Christ's sake. Get the right people in your office. I'll see you in three hours, *sir*," he added for a fillip.

"That damned Frenchman told the whole bloody world a trumped-up lie and in the long run he's more accurate than anybody else," Hugh Fitzpatrick said by way of preamble at the meeting. "Though it's not a'tall a comet's tail. Or its nose, either. It's just that the dust is thickening so much faster than there was any indication." He looked about the room beneath the mountain at the people present, including the televised face of Marc Seavers. Behind Seavers he'd made out the features of that big Russian, Tereshnikov. That was good. He didn't know the woman with Tereshnikov. She wore an American jumpsuit. Little matter; she was with flight dynamics for the animal ship or something. They were also televising the meeting, but *without* two-way talking, to the White House and also to Moscow. Fitzpatrick had insisted there be no direct involvement of the political sector, as he called it.

"But you all know everything I'm saying about the dust," he went on, calculating his words for Washington and Moscow as well as the others more directly involved. "What you don't know for certain, and I don't know, and all we can do is to figure on the worst, is that we'll all be burning up a lot sooner than we hoped. In short, everybody, as I told our president a few hours ago, there's no way for us to be able to finish both ships before all flights between us here on the Earth's surface, and *Pegasus* and *Noah* in orbit, come to an end. Trying to enter the atmosphere from orbit will be like coming down through mud. Nothing built yet can withstand friction with that kind of sludge. So I've got some very important decisions to announce, I want every man jack to understand what I'm saying, and the ladies, too, I suppose," he added a bit ungraciously. "There is really no time for argument, a caucus, or a discussion. But I'll tell you this, all of you. Listen to me *and act*, or everything we've done will come very prematurely to an end, and the whole future of the race will depend upon that crazy bastard, Corey, on the moon."

Talker that he was, he knew when to cut the line and allow what he'd said to sink in. He didn't need to convince them about the thickening mass waiting to swallow the entire solar system—a thousand solar systems, when you thought about it—because they'd already been told that, and they also were all victims of the trap of hoping things weren't nearly as bad as they promised. There'd been nothing but rotten news for so long now that even a few months more of time had become a blessing. Well, b'God, they didn't have that much time. Hugh Fitzpatrick figured his longevity by the amount of whiskey he could drink before he departed this fair place forever, and the minimal quantity he found to be morally depressing.

Marc Seavers broke into his reverie of whiskey consumption. "All right, Hugh, short and sweet, lay it out for us."

Fitzpatrick also knew when to cut the mustard. He was all through with the long-winded verbiage that had so effectively occupied his audience to this moment. Of a sudden the Fitzpatrick that Marc Seavers knew so well was before them.

"First," Fitzpatrick said with a stubby finger jabbed into the air before him, "you concentrate almost entirely on the animal ship. You must, you absolutely no-arguments-about-it *must*, finish *Noah* as quickly as you can, even at the cost of leaving *Pegasus* as an uncompleted vessel."

"That's insane!" Marion Hughes cried. "Finish the ship for the animals and *not* the ship for people? Are you crazy?"

"My sanity is not the issue, bucko. People can adapt, people can live in crowded quarters and wear pressure suits and meet an emergency situation. They can do all this and survive." Fitzpatrick raised his eyes to the camera pointed at him. "Do you agree, Admiral?" he asked Seavers.

"Yes." There wasn't anything else to say—*yet*.

"Now, as to why you must complete the ark first, at *any* expense," Fitzpatrick went on. "Those creatures are dumb. You can *not* deepfreeze them, for Christ's sake.

397

They're going to be breathing, drinking, eating, defecating, pissing, farting, mating—hopefully—birthing, growing and whatever else bovines and those critters do. But they cannot wear spacesuits! And just as important, and I want you to understand I've talked with just about every damned expert there is on this matter—" He paused and took a deep breath. "Those animals, on which the future of man depends, cannot survive weightlessness."

The bomb exploded slowly in their midst as his words began to sink in, and he jumped in with both feet after the initial shock. "You're going to have to provide rotational centrifugal force in that bloody damned *Noah* to give some gravitational effect. If you don't—" he shrugged, turning to Anatoli Rubinov. "Hell, man, *you* tell them."

The Russian nodded unhappily. "What this man says is all too true. Sad, even . . . how you say—"

"Devastating will do nicely, thank you," Fitzpatrick nudged.

"Yes. It is so. We brought a variety of animals up to the *Gagarin* station. Separate cubicles. They float around, soon they are mad with fear because the animals are always feeling they are falling. They go crazy, thrash around. They break their legs, they bite and attack one another. So we test them with restraints. With harnesses. That keeps them from floating about but to the animal, he is *still* falling. It is a terrible thing to see a cow with five stomachs that are all falling at the same time. Animal throws up. Animal shits all over cubicle. In zero gravity it sprays everywhere and gets in everything, and since *all* animals do so it clogs up and jams life support ventilation systems. We try to feed animals, and each time they eat must be by hand. Animals bite their keepers. They must drink, no? How you get a horse or a cow or a sheep to drink water in weightlessness? It is not possible! The water floats around, the animals bang against the containers and breaks them, then they go mad and foam at mouth and, well, you now have idea of problems and there are much much more problems than I speak right now."

He wiped his forehead. "*Any* gravity make all the difference. Water stays in containers. Food stays what is floor to animal. The stomach does not float around. We had two cows die because they cannot belch. Gases choke them. But even with tests of one tenth of gravity from rotation, in small cubicle, is infinitely better. No shit is everywhere. No piss like yellow fog all over place."

"Enough with the critters, Rubi. The plants."

Rubinov winced when he heard *Rubi.* "Is much the same problem. We for years grow plants in stations Salyut, Mir, *Gagarin.* Americans do the same. We both growing rice, sweet potato, pumpkin, foodstuff that is concentrated, with strong vine, that give us oxygen as well as foodstuff from smallest space possible. Tough, hardy plants. Chinese have worked with Americans with new electrical genetic wonders, but not so good in zero gravity. With only ten percent gravity, is wonderful. With no gravity, plants seem confused, do not grow straight and strong. In time this can be corrected. But as Fitz Hughpatrick is telling us, there is no time." No one laughed at the mangling of the name. "We must have artificial gravity."

Fitzpatrick gestured that he'd heard enough. "All right, people, it comes down to this," he addressed them all. "We *can* set up Noah for artificial gravity. We've got to rotate the entire ship along its length. Think of a football that's in a slow spiral but balanced perfectly. We've got to do that and we *can* do that. Starting immediately—Seavers, I hope you and your Russkie buddy are listening carefully—starting immediately, we've got to weld the tanks from the shuttles and boosters together to form a long central core tube for *Noah.* Got that? It runs from the front all the way to the back, and for some time yet that core's got to be open at both ends. No pressure. Airlocks all the way down the damn thing along its interior curves. That will provide airlock safety and access to the main body of the ship. You can bring in the animals and your supplies through this central core where you'll have zero g. It will also be the slowest-turning part of the entire ship.

We'll have to go for something like two thousand feet in length, by the way. Ten tank cores gives us eight hundred feet alone, and we'll have a hundred or more to work with, so we're fat on that. We start the ship turning *now*. Everybody hear that? *Now*. That means we can move in all the soil and water and existing plants, crops, trees, flowers, and whatever else. It means that along the outermost wall of this ship, the farthest from the core, we might even get twenty or thirty percent g force, and that means the animals, the plants, and the water supplies will survive. You can double-hull the damn thing or even triple-hull it. For certain we'll keep full compartmental design for integrity of the overall seal of the ship."

He sat back. "The rest is detail. But you've got to do all this *now*."

Travis Simmonds stared at Fitzpatrick. "What about angular momentum effects? That could pose a real problem if—"

"*Goddamn it*, don't you understand!" Fitzpatrick roared. His hand smashed painfully, angrily, against the table. "If you don't do this *it's all fucking over!*"

"Hugh." The shouting died down with the sound of Seavers' voice from the screen. "You said we go with *Pegasus* unfinished. I'm not certain I get the entire drift of what you mean."

"It means," Fitzpatrick said slowly, meaningfully and with great care, "that unless you are powered up and on your way out of here in the next thirty days, you may as well shut down, come on home and learn what it feels like to be chicken fricasee, like the rest of us."

Only the hiss of beamed audio channels filled the sudden emptiness among the group gathered physically and electronically in the shielded room deep within Cheyenne Mountain. Finally Anatoli Rubinov gestured for attention.

"We must decide *now*. Engineer Fitzpatrick is absolutely correct," said the Russian. "There is another decision to be made, a part of all this, yet a separate decision. You people are launching as many shuttles as you have. So do we. Our ultimate goal, as we all know, is that one day these two ships will return. Earth will again be habitable. At least that is the hope we all cherish so dearly. To return from terrestrial orbit at that time, whatever number of years that may be in the future, means those shuttles will be needed to return as many people as possible, with animals and foodstuffs and supplies, to the Earth's surface."

Rubinov looked about him. "I recommend, with all the urgency I can convey to you people, that no shuttles be permitted to return earthside once they are in orbit. That we execute our standing plans to integrate them into the structure of *Pegasus*, and no longer risk losing such machines that we cannot hope to replace." Rubinov turned to General Briand and Marion Hughes. "I ask you this, gentlemen. How many of the large shuttles do you have available to launch and remain in orbit?"

"Fifteen for certain," Hughes answered at once. "Three more we hope to get ready in a month or two and—"

"If they're not ready to fly in three weeks, mister, stop wasting your time. Forget them," Fitzpatrick said coldly. "Put your energy into expendables, damn it."

Rubinov nodded slowly. "We have eleven smaller winged spaceplanes," he said slowly, "and four of the very large machines. We are prepared to commit them to the voyage. We are—"

He fell silent as the far door to the conference room opened and a young woman in army uniform stepped through the doorway, her eyes seeking out Travis Simmonds. The WAC mayor was obviously in a state of great distress at having pushed her way into so lofty a gathering. She took a deep breath and hurried to Simmonds to hand him a message.

"What in the hell—" Fitzpatrick was on his feet, glaring at the director of the Kennedy Space Center. "What could possibly be so important as to break into here?" he demanded.

Simmonds was on his feet. He glanced at the screen with Seavers and Tereshnikov, did the same to the others at the table. "Go on without me." He tapped the paper against his hand. "I have to leave immediately—"

"What is it, Travis?" asked Marion Hughes.

"We may not have those shuttles to launch," Simmonds said gravely. "All of the space center, the whole launch complex, is under attack. I've got to get back there at once. They've got a ship waiting for me." He looked around him. "You worry about tomorrow, all of you," he said. "I'll do my best to protect today." He left the room at a dead run.

18

SPACEPORT U.S.A.

Deja vu.

Whoo, boy!

What the hell was this? Delayed instant replay? He'd already written virtually the same lines *twice*. And now he was stumped for a new opening to the story. *Which might well be your final story, Marrows. You're getting awfully close to the end of the line.*

He grinned at the thought of the final byline. Not too many newsmen get to write their own final epitaph. *The Demise of Hank Marrows, by Hank Marrows.* Jesus, it was a crazy world. After years of abstaining from smoking and most of the really bad habits he'd acquired, after years of dire warnings about lung cancer and cirrhosis of the liver and fat in his cells and everywhere else, and hair growing from the palm of his hands from beating off too much (they'd warned him about *that* since he was nine years old), and eating too much red meat and—well, for nearly a year now he'd tried his damndest to kill himself by ingesting everything he'd ever been warned about—and he'd never felt better or was healthier in his whole damned life!

Well, he felt pretty damned healthy when he *first* wrote this story. Or almost the same kind of disaster story. When the word got out that the four astronauts returning from the small *Epsilon* station had space plague. When all hell had broken loose and a terrified world saw mobs attacking the launch centers, research laboratories, anything to do with space flight. The evangelists and doomsdayers led the mobs, the stink of deep fear permeated the air, and two hundred thousand people died in the frenzied attacks that wracked up a couple of billion dollars' worth of damage. Christ, they'd even trashed the space exhibits at the Smithsonian!

So how do we get a different lead for the latest wave to rise against Cape Canaveral and the Kennedy Space Center? *It's easy, Marrows*, he told himself. *Even God uses the same lines over again when they work.* He grinned with the thought and tapped the keys that set up the electronic system that would flash his copy throughout the world. An instinctive move brought his right hand down to his side, near the floor, where he had the portable electronic machine powered with nicad batteries, and he had plenty of batteries, and that little doodad would operate on a bunch of D cells as well. He knew he'd need the portable before this was through because the mobs would savage the power stations and cut the power cables and topple the microwave transmission towers. Marrows checked his pockets. Yep; the microcassette recorders were set and powered up. He turned back to the keys before him and just as easily turned back the clock to the time of *Epsilon*. The words flowed easily . . .

"Today *Homo sapiens* showed his true colors. Today the dominant race on this planet tucked its tail between its legs, shivered through its rump, and howled fearfully at the moon. Today, once again, figuratively and literally, the shit has hit the fan. And it's *everywhere*."

Not bad, Marrows. For an old asshole you still got a couple of good lines left in you.

"When *Epsilon* claimed four victims high above the Earth, maddened mobs gave in to their most primal fears and hurled themselves at space installations throughout the world. More than two hundred thousand people died because of naked fear. Four astronauts died because of swamp fever carried into space by one of their crew. The only plague that could be found writhed like grubs in the hearts and minds of men who were determined that their fellows should never return alive to Earth to infect them. We were treated to the ultimate leper colony."

Marrows rubbed his palms briskly, stuck a fresh cigarette in his teeth, took it out for a slug of *very* good whiskey, replaced the cigarette and lit it, and turned his fingers loose on the keys.

"The situation is in full reverse today. The mobs are stirring once again, the old fears rise high like the fires set by the KKK to burn the crosses of old, and men yield common sense and decency to have their own way. No longer are they determined to keep those men and women who are in space away from this world of ours. No; the opposite is true. Black has become white and white has become black. The fear today is that we, almost all of us, shall be left behind when the great refugee vessels hurl back sheets of fire to push themselves away from the contagion that threatens to destroy the last shreds of man's dignity. And it is a dignity he needs as our sun begins to render itself mad."

You're a fucking poet, Marrows. Have another drink, old buddy. He did.

"Today the goal is to get a seat on the bus. Today the driver is black and the passengers—the would-be passengers—screeching and killing to climb aboard are mostly white. They know, as you and I know, that they will not gain places on the bus. They will not, in truth, lift more than one single leg above the Earth, and then only a few inches high, like an old hound dog lifting his leg to leave his mark for some unknown future visit by a friend he doesn't even know."

Stick to the story, you dumbshit. You're not writing for American Kennels magazine . . .

He shrugged. *True enough. But what the hell do I really want to leave for posterity? Who's going to be around to read this crap?*

"Remember when we were kids?" *To hell with my better self. I'll write what the hell I damn please.* "We played baseball or football on the old empty lots or school grounds whenever we had the chance. And every now and then we'd face the problem of the one

404

rotten kid who had the only ball on the block and it didn't matter if he was a nasty little snit, it was his ball and if he didn't play, nobody played. Well, we've grown into adults since then, but it appears that most of us haven't learned a thing. We're playing the game for keeps now. The sandlot is the whole universe out there, and the tune has changed slightly. What the mobs are telling us now is that if they can't go, nobody goes. It doesn't matter that there isn't room for more than a splinter of the whole human race. Greedy, selfish people—and the future really won't miss them—don't care about that. Led by zealous egomaniacs posturing as servants of God so they may have their briefest of flings of power, they are determined either to get their seats on the space bus or they'll destroy the terminal *and* all the buses."

That deserves a drink . . . He took another.

"At this moment, the madmen, and their women who bear an amazing resemblance to the camp followers of old, are descending on the centers of man's greatest triumphs. The scientific laboratories, the astronomical observatories, the centers that bring in data whispering from other worlds, the control buildings for the satellites that tell us of our weather and help us talk to one another in words and pictures . . . all these are the targets.

"But most of these mental Neanderthals emerging from the dark forests of their little lives are moving against the launch centers that have turned night into day, ignorance into knowledge, earthbound into star travelers. For this is the bus terminal. Wherever the great rockets are assembled like ancient monuments pointing to the sky, the monoliths that represent the highest grasp of man, these are the candles for the blind-eyed moths of great number and little minds."

Holy shit, Marrows, you're really on a roll. If they could make a sandwich of your kind of eloquence you could feed a whole planet . . .

Shaddup, he told that inner voice and again unlimbered his fingers.

"I now know the feeling of being on a besieged

island. I write these words from the top row of the press site of the Kennedy Space Center, looking eastward. Many years ago I would stand on the grassy field edging the turning basin where the great rockets were brought to this launch complex. Stand there and listen to the rush of time forever behind us while the monuments stabbed flame hard against the Earth and rose to the heavens and beyond, to the moon with men, to other worlds. Today, as this world knows, this bus terminal for the great shuttle craft swarms with launch pads, with hordes of people, with new towers that have sprung up everywhere. To my right, to the south, a half-dozen new Titan pads reach skyward, and the now-ancient missile row of Cape Canaveral has been alive and thundering with rockets seeking out the new shape that is winged in name only. *Pegasus.* Our last great hope for the future.

"I don't look heavenward. Not now. Across the ocean, as far as I can see, the water churns with boats of all kinds. Cabin cruisers and speedboats and fishing boats and yachts, all of them filled with angry people, heavily armed, who have come here to do battle. To get a seat on the bus. Or to destroy everything they can reach."

Another cigarette, another slug of hard whiskey warming his gullet. Deep breaths. God, the words were rushing into his brain and—

"Marrows, if you want a seat on that chopper, *move your ass!*"

Marrows looked down the multiple rows of bleacher seats beneath the overhang roof. Gene Arinson waved at him. The NASA security officer pumped his right arm up and down in the time-honored GI signal to "Move out!" It had a more effective reach than words, although Marrows hesitated. "Leave your stuff!" Arinson shouted. "I'll have it brought to my office! C'mon, damn it, they're starting to take off."

Hank Marrows went down the concrete steps as fast as he could move safely. A tiny voice in the back of his head told him not to move faster. Too easy to lose his balance. *You're right, you're right,* he said of his own twittering counsel. *Killing myself falling down a flight of stairs when the whole Earth only has a short time to go really would be stupid.* He stood before Arinson and shrugged. "Where—" Air exploded before him as a dark shape curved around the sloping dome of press headquarters and powered to a fast chopping stop. "Go!" Arinson yelled, shoving Marrows. The newsman had already started. He stumbled, caught his balance, ran to the open doorway of the big Goldhawk attack helicopter. A powerful hand reached down, wrapped about Marrows' arm and hauled him aboard as if he were a child. Before he could say a word, a huge invisible hand shoved him down and backwards. Again he staggered and again that powerful hand held and moved him as if he were a child instead of an overweight, aging big man of over two hundred pounds.

The giant hand of acceleration held him pinned. Abruptly the Goldhawk's nose dropped and they raced ahead in level flight. The pressure fell away. "Put this on!" the crewman shouted in his ear, and helped Marrows slip into a parachute body harness. Not the chute, just the harness with safety cable clips locking him to the chopper so that no matter what happened he wouldn't be tossed out. The crewman leaned forward to shout by his ear above the scream of jet engines, the pounding of the giant rotor blades and the howl of wind going by the open doors. "Kanamine! Dirk Kanamine!" he yelled. Marrows nodded, seeing the name on the man's chest. He saw the paratrooper wings and the other insignia identifying Dirk Kanamine as one lean and mean hombre. Marrows shouted back, stopped with his mouth open as Kanamine handed him a headset and boom mike and plugged a thin wire into the chopper intercom. Talking became easy and amazingly clear.

"Who the hell are you?" Dirk Kanamine threw the question easily and casually. Marrows liked what he saw. A professional soldier in his twenties, a Ranger, he saw from the insignia. And a captain. Kanamine didn't wait for an immediate answer. "You sure pack a lot of weight from upstairs," he added.

Marrows stuck out his hand. "Hank Marrows," he

407

said. "I'm doing a special report on this square dance for the White House. Thanks for getting me aboard."

Kanamine grinned. "I figured you went all the way to the top." He turned to dig into a floor locker, came back with a heavy belt loaded with cartridges and a holster with a .38 revolver. "You ever use one of these?" he asked Marrows.

"I said I was covering this story," Marrows said, caught by surprise. "Not fighting it."

"Mister Marrows, if we—"

"Jesus, son, I was a corporal when I wore the uniform. It's Hank."

"You got it, sir. Hank. Anyway, if we go down I'd feel a lot better if you had this with you."

"I'm going to defend myself against a horde with *that*?"

"Nope. But you can cover *my* back. I'll be carrying the heavy artillery. Just consider any of us aboard this whirligig the modern version of Rambo."

Marrows looked about him. The Goldhawk was more than a flying arsenal. It looked like a small flying battleship. He took the belt and slung it low about his hips. Kanamine leaned down to tie the holster to his thigh. "There you are. John Wayne you're not, but you're tougher than you think. Those shells are hollow with plastic explosives inside them. You can kill a water buffalo with one round."

"Yeah, and the countryside is just chock full of water buffalo," Marrows said sarcastically. "Captain, where are we going and what's the situation?"

"I hope you can stand the sight of blood, Marrows."

"I've seen my share."

Kanamine pulled him closer to the doorway. "Look for yourself. Know where we are?"

"You're kidding, Captain. This place has been my beat for over thirty—no; over forty years."

"Then if we get lost you can tell *us* where the hell we are." He pointed out the doorway. "That's the NASA causeway?"

Marrows leaned out a bit, air slamming against him from the huge rotor above and the airstream whistling by. The Goldhawk bounced in rough air but rode the rapids easily. "That's it," he said into the lip mike. "Look, that's the shuttle runway behind us now. At the northern end you got two causeways. The one most north is a railroad line. Just south of it, angling across the Indian River, you've got a major service road. Now, closer to us, at the south end of the shuttle strip, you've got the main NASA Causeway. You can see Shiloh Field, we used to call it Ti-Co, over there. It's smack between U.S. 1 and I-95. Further south," he pointed again, "is the Bennett Causeway. It comes into this area from the Beeline out of Orlando. Then there's the 520 Causeway out of Cocoa into Merritt Island and continuing east to the beach. The next causeway is pretty far down, south of Patrick Air Force Base."

He looked about him, turned back to Kanamine with a troubled frown. "I had no idea the whole world was coming in here. I saw that boat traffic out in the ocean, but the rivers—Christ, it looks like Dunkirk down there."

"To hell with the rivers, Marrows. Better look again at the roads. There must be a half-million people or more on the move."

He was right. *Everything* was dark with cars and trucks, campers, trailers, vans. He looked a bit higher. There must have been a hundred armed combat choppers like the Goldhawk in the air. Most of them flew battle formations. "We belong to any special group?" he asked Kanamine.

"No, sir. We're cut loose from the others. If you look behind you you'll see another 'hawk. We're flying a hunter-killer team slot. We each fly wingman cover for the other."

A cold chill went down Marrows' back. "The last time we had a situation like this," he began, "a lot of people died. That was the *Epsilon* scare."

"Yes, sir. They briefed us on that. This one is a lot worse. We've had our people mixing in with the crowds. They're a nasty bunch and they're out for blood."

"They're scared, Captain. Scared."

"You think that's going to matter when they bust loose?" Kanamine didn't hide his scorn for Marrows' touch of apology. "Those people are armed to the teeth. And you, well, you were here before, right?" He saw Marrows nod. "Okay, sir. We don't harm a single hair on anyone's head until they start it with us. But hell, man, look down there. If they *wanted* to go back they couldn't! Look at those roads . . . there's no way back."

"Kanamine?"

Kanamine held up a hand to forestall any conversation as he responded to a call from the pilot. "Go ahead, Major."

"I think we've got our target spotted. The crazy bastard is wearing that white suit. He's up ahead of us." The Goldhawk was swinging around over the Indian River, headed north to the NASA Causeway. "See that group? We've got the scope on them. They have loudspeakers everywhere along that line of vehicles. They're stopped right now. It looks like they're getting primed to make their move."

"Got it, Major."

"Arm your gunners, Captain."

"Yes, sir." Kanamine looked about the cabin. Two troopers on each side of the 'hawk with powerful fifty-calibers. They had listened in and gave him the high sign they were ready.

"Major Burnett, our orders still the same?"

Marrows listened to the pilot through his headset. "That's a rog. We monitor the man in the white suit. Hawkins, go ahead and plug in the scanners and pick-ups on our target. Dead ahead six hundred and, ah, nineteen yards exactly."

A gunner-technician—Hawkins—in the back area of the cabin looked up at a television monitor as it flickered to life. "Major, we won't have to use the scanners. That guy is on every radio and television station in this whole area. I've run the sweep on him. All we need to do is watch the local station."

"Okay," Burnett replied. "Stay on him, be ready to go to our scanners if necessary. Can you pipe in a commercial feed with the intercom?"

"Yes, sir!" Hawkins paused to adjust his controls. "You got it, Major. Use your right headset volume

410

control to monitor. I don't guess you want video up front." There was a chuckle to Hawkins' voice.

"We can do without that. It sorta helps to watch where the hell you're going." Burnett paused. "Stand by, Nimrod One." They heard him talking now with their wingman.

"Nimrod Two, this is Nimrod One. You read our intercom?"

"Yep, One. We're also watching the follies back here. Is that guy the Zack Bible we been looking for?"

Burnett spoke back and forth between his wingman cover and his own crew. "Hawkins, get our scanner on him. Give me a facial pattern readout from the computer. I want absolute positive on the preacher man. He's put in a ringer before and we creamed the wrong party. Go to it."

"Yes, sir. Be back with you right away, Major."

"Very good. Kanamine, how's our guest doing?"

Marrows nodded to Kanamine and pointed to his mike. The captain gave him the go-ahead signal. "Major Burnett, this is Marrows."

"Glad to have you aboard. I heard your conversation with Kanamine. Your knowing this area could come in handy."

"Major, what's your plan?"

"Like Kanamine told you, we do *not* open fire on anyone until and unless it's absolutely necessary. It looks like that's the way it's going to go. I've got other channels up here. If you look south of us along the mainland—can you see that smoke?"

They looked at a greasy black column lifting into the sky many miles to the south. "I see it," Marrows said.

"That's Melbourne airport. There are six airliners on that field. There *were* six airliners. Every one of them is burning. So are the other planes, from what I can pick up. A mob took the field by storm. No real reason except that it was there. They're tearing the whole place down. Mr. Marrows, let me say something from experience. It's like a wave. It gets picked up and passed on and it gets worse. We're next. It's that simple."

411

"If they move against the launch area," Marrows said carefully, "then you'll—"

"I'll save you the time and effort, Marrows. *Everybody* up here cuts loose. No exceptions. We take *everybody* that's east of U.S. 1 out of the picture. Period."

"That sounds cut and dried to me. I got it, Major. Thanks."

"You upset over these orders, Marrows?"

"Major, I was here for the *Epsilon* riots. They had a lot of dead and wounded then and I never felt sorry for any of them. I see no reason to start now."

"We'll give them every chance. Those are our orders and I agree completely with them. In fact, Mr. Marrows, come on up here and look over my shoulder. I want to show you something."

Marrows worked his way forward to the pilots' cockpit, nodded to Burnett and the man in the right seat. The world spread out before them like a magic carpet. "See those helicopters up forward?" Burnett asked, pointing. "They're bullshit bombers."

"Loudspeakers?"

"Yep. They're talking to those people with megawatt speakers, begging them to get the hell off those causeways, to get back of the highways on the mainland. In a moment—there," Marrows saw the sky beneath the helicopters, along the causeways, become a blizzard of white. "Leaflets," Burnett continued. "We're dumping them by the tens of thousands. Same message. With maps. Telling them where it's safe to go. My personal opinion is they won't go. They'll stay. They'll think about what we have to say and then they'll listen to that muckraking son of a bitch in the white suit, and because they're already scared shitless and feel they haven't anything to lose, they will go mad. Like I said before, it's like a wave. It gets bigger and stronger as it sweeps along. You can't stop it. All you can do is to destroy it." Burnett turned to study Marrows. "I don't like any of this. Those are Americans down there. Our people. Frightened. They want out of what's going to happen to their world. But they can't go. So—"

"Major, we've got Bible. You can pick up the audio

412

on your right earset. I think Marrows ought to see this," Kanamine said on intercom.

Burnett nodded. "All yours, Mr. Marrows."

He returned to the cabin. They had a tight picture from the commercial station pickup. Bible wasn't into full swing yet. He was calling for the people nearby to gather about him. Marrows knew the routine. Don't let them be spread out when they're listening to the harangue. Tightly knit groups gather strength from shoulder-rubbing. Tight association builds the equivalent of neighborly courage—first cousin to bottle courage.

"Well, they're gathering. Moths to the candle flame," Kanamine observed.

"The worst of it," Marrows said after watching changing scenes on the monitor, "is that they're bored. This Zack Bible has a hell of a sense of timing."

Kanamine stared at the newsman. "*Bored?* That's the last thing I'd expect!"

"Well, *you* don't have to sell what you do. People like me," Marrows said, smiling, "need to know their audience if they want to stay in business. I've gotten to know mine pretty well." He pointed to the TV monitor. "Look at the faces. Tired, slack, some of them vacant. Many of them have been out here for a couple of days. They couldn't go back against the incoming tide. So they made a collective picnic out of being stuck here. On government property as far as they're concerned. Telling the authorities to go to hell simply by being where they were. Campfires, weenie roasts, beer by the case, a lot of hard drinking going on. By now they're about out of food and they're out of drink. Their portable toilets in the motor homes and the trailers are filled up and overflowing. Most of those people have been pissing and crapping in the river because they haven't got anywhere else to go. So *now* they're hungry, thirsty, they smell, they can't shower, they're surrounded with their own filth, they're feeling hemmed in, trapped, and Bible is ready to squeeze the trigger that'll set them off."

Marrows fished in his pockets. "Okay if I smoke here?" Kanamine nodded and Marrows lit up, then

413

used the cigarette to punctuate his remarks. "I'll tell you how it works. He'll make his fire and brimstone speech any moment now. The local stations will carry it. That means it'll be picked up on all the causeways and along the mainland. I'm not sure what his pitch will be, but I know what he wants to accomplish. To get to one of those launch pads, hold the whole damned space center hostage, and climb aboard with a few chosen stalwarts to get up to *Pegasus*. The next thing Bible will do is whip his crowd into whatever it takes for them to move ahead of him. We—all these war machines of ours—will cut the first waves to pieces, and Bible and his people will survive to make it to the shuttle. And right after—" Marrows gestured abruptly. "Okay, he's committed."

Kanamine nodded to their technician and he brought the audio feed into their headsets. ". . . and I have heard from the Lord God Himself! God is angry. He is to the point of rage that His children could be so incredibly stupid. Up there," the white-clad figure on the TV monitor jabbed his finger at the sky, "is the genius of God personified in the form of two great ships, but do you know what's missing? Do you know what satanic deviltry has been hurled against our God? Did you know that those who built those ships have abandoned the ways of the Lord? Let me hear your displeasure! Let me hear you!"

The roar shook the skies. A half-million voices calling out puzzled, but puzzled in anger, pounding over and over *"NO! NO! NO!"*

"Unless you all help me, unless you give me *your* love and *your* support, we are doomed!" Zack Bible screamed the words, waving his sceptre (a replacement, of course, his other one lost when Arthur Kimberly met his end) and its hypnotizing bright light. "Listen to me, my children. I'll tell you what has brought God to such anger, what He has asked me to set right, what He has asked you to help me do!"

The finger jabbed upward again, this time staying high. "There is not a single sworn man of God aboard those ships. Not one! There is no priest, no pastor, no rabbi, no reverend. There is not a single soul sworn to the love and service of our Lord! Help Him! Help me help Him! Let us do God's will! Let us go forward now onto the ground of the heathens! Destroy! Destroy! Kill! Kill! For the glory of God and your souls—*Onward, Christian Soldiers!*"

Kanamine switched off the audio. "Well, that tears it," he said calmly. He glanced at his men. "Gentlemen, lock and load." The gunners armed their weapons. "Major Burnett, we're set back here. Your orders, sir?"

"We stay high, Dirk, until we *have* to go down. We do not descend below two thousand unless we have hot guns."

"That's a rog, sir."

"Okay, you can see the first wave of bullshit bombers going down. They'll take up line abreast along every causeway, tell the people to knock off the shit, fire a few rounds into the water for effect, and—"

A flash of red rose up from the NASA causeway. They stared in disbelief as the red trail flashed toward the lead helicopter with its loudspeakers calling to the mobs below. At the last moment the pilot did his best to throw his machine out of the way of what was obviously a small homing missile. The Goldhawk whipped over into a vertical bank, clawing around under full power to slip under and to the side of the missile. There wasn't enough time.

The 'hawk took the missile immediately forward of its exhaust stack. One moment it was flying beautifully in its evasive maneuver, the next instant it flew in the center of a blooming rose that spread swiftly from its innards. The glowing red rose turned into a flash of dazzling yellow, and a huge fireball erupted in the midst of the helicopter formation. A second chopper, its pilots mesmerized by what they were watching, flew into the wreckage. A rotor blade snapped and the Goldhawk went wild, falling earthward in a violent swinging tumble, spilling several of its crew into the air.

"Jesus fucking Christ," Kanamine swore as he watched his friends die.

Burnett was already on open channel, his voice hard but holding a quiver only his friends might recognize. "All aircraft from Nimrod One. Attack along all causeways immediately. Fire at will. Fire at will."

No one had anticipated how well Zack Bible had prepared for this moment. Semi-trailer rigs and huge gravel trucks, mounting homing missiles and machine guns taken by storm from army guard and reserve armories and ordnance centers, raced down the causeway to tear past the first guard gates. They went through the defenses as if they were flimsy paper. Behind them poured the erratic convoy of every kind of vehicle, some of them spilling off at the Visitor's Information Center to vent their fear and anger on the museum-chained missiles and exhibits. The 'hawks went down with everything they had. In the first few minutes the repeated salvos of rockets and long bursts of heavy machine guns turned the causeway red with blood and dark with smoke.

Three more helicopters went down. Marrows hung on for dear life as his 'hawk, followed by the wingman, raced to the north and dropped to the water, hurtling just above the surface toward the causeway. "We want Bible!" Kanamine yelled, "He's ours! If we can stop him maybe we can pull the plug on this shit!" Bursts of machine gun fire drowned out his next words. Acrid smoke filled the cabin. Marrows hung on and looked ahead of them. Bodies and pieces of bodies flew through the air from the incredible firepower lashing up and down the causeway. He didn't see how they'd pick out Zack Bible in that smoking, flaming carnage. And if they did it wouldn't mean a thing. That wasn't a loyal crowd any more, but a mindless animal terrified with its own pain and blood but carried forward on the momentum of blind fear and weight of numbers from behind. As many of these people rushed ahead for safety as they did bent on destruction.

There was no surcease; there could be none. There was no way back. The helicopters rode up and down the causeways, firing until they ran out of ammunition. In the sudden lulls along all the causeways, from south of Patrick Air Force Base up along the beaches and Merritt Island all the way to the railway bridges up by Mims, the screaming mobs comprehended the sudden drop in firepower directed against them, and surged ahead. Heavy trucks with sheets of metal acting as armor plating and rolling barricades pushed the burning vehicles from the causeways into the river, and the mobs stormed ahead again. This time they began to break through, as the helicopters raced down to Patrick to replenish fuel and ammunition.

They had all seriously underestimated the heavy weapons of the attacking mobs under Zack Bible. The madman of the church had planned his moves exceedingly well. Fifty to a hundred thousand people died to absorb the full blow of the defenders. Now the second wave, protected by the deaths and losses of the first, stormed ahead. They ripped through the barricades of the second defense line, and thousands of screaming people drove their vehicles to the headquarters section of the space center, hurling sticks of dynamite from their speeding vehicles.

The main force thundered toward the huge Vehicle Assembly Building. Now the Launch Control Center and the roadways to the launch pads stood in terrible danger.

Ryan Tacker, director of security of the space center, had also prepared well for this moment. Buried beneath the roads and the grounds on each side of the roads were enormous pools of oil and incendiary chemicals. If the crowds got this far, he was prepared to unleash a hurricane of fire into their midst. Hank Marrows looked down from Nimrod One as they swung wide of the highway running north directly to the towering VAB. They had slaughtered hundreds of people trying to nail Zack Bible but without confirmation of his death. "Look at those trucks coming," Marrows shouted to Kanamine. "They're too well organized! Bible's still down there behind armor plate and asbestos! Damn it, he should never have gotten this far!"

417

He watched, fascinated and fearful at the same time, as the mass of heavy trucks drove toward the invisible defenses set up by Tacker. Helicopters appeared suddenly from behind the mass of the VAB, where they had been held in reserve for this moment. They raced overhead, firing missiles steadily into the oncoming mass. Explosions, fire, blazing trucks and screaming people—and *still* they came on.

They couldn't help it. They couldn't stop. The weight of numbers behind them pushed them on. No choice, no minds, no thinking. They plunged into carnage.

"There's Bible's truck!" Kanamine yelled into his mike. "Major, that gravel truck, third in line! It's got a false top to it! That's the one, with the angled prow in front! You can—"

Ryan Tacker put his plan into operation. The roadway before the trucks disappeared as a hundred tons of explosives blew huge craters where there had been a highway, and for two hundred yards to each side. Trucks and cars smashed like speeding trains into the craters.

Tacker held his own hand on the final controls. He pulled down the switches; one, two, three, four. The hidden tanks disgorged. Thousands of gallons of oil erupted like dark, swift-flowing lava into the craters. Still they kept coming from behind, crashing and slamming mindlessly into the screaming people before them. Tacker pulled the last switch to ignite the oil and chemicals.

The incredible explosion sent enormous fireballs a thousand feet into the air. Above the roar of exploding fuel tanks and deep rumble of the burning oil could be heard a thin wailing cry, thousands of voices screeching their last as the terrified people burned alive.

"NASA Control, this is Nimrod One." Marrows couldn't believe the measured calm in Burnett's voice. "You've stopped them for the moment, but the crowds behind can't stop. You're going to have to burn them where they are. That'll stop them back on the mainland."

"Ah, Nimrod One, do I read you correctly? You're calling for firemist control? Over."

"That's the only way, NASA. Or you're going to run out of oil a long time before they run out of people."

"I copy, Nimrod." A sound of resignation could be detected even through the radio transmissions. "Patrick, you read NASA One?"

They heard the orders going back and forth. The helicopters rose like lethal dragonflies, their rotors the sound of death. They fired no rockets, no machine guns. They flew three abreast along each causeway, spraying the heavy aerosol. The fine mist stretched from the beach areas, from Patrick to Cocoa Beach to the Bennett Causeway, along the NASA causeway.

"All aircraft from NASA One. Fire your charges immediately."

The helicopters lifted, swung off to the sides, fired their small missiles with the specific electrical charge.

Every causeway erupted instantly into a giant rope of explosive flame. Within seconds, every one of the eighty thousand people still on the causeways died.

That night the causeways still flamed with the fuel of human bodies, motor homes, vans, cars, trucks, trees, tires—anything that could burn. A heavy smoke pall covered the entire coastline, but from above the fires shone through like sparkling jewels.

Hank Marrows looked down from Nimrod One. They'd landed long before to refuel and rearm "just in case." No one could eat. They drank strong coffee, smoked hungrily, returned to the machine and took off again.

Now they flew at three thousand feet, through the still-rising smoke. Some crewmen gagged from the stench of burning flesh that permeated the whole world.

Hank Marrows stared numbly at the sparkling firechains beneath him. He stood at the edge of the open hatch, wondering about it all.

He stepped out.

Book IV

EXIT EARTH

19

*P*egasus drifted within a shroud of blackest velvet. From the cabin of the ugly spacetug only parts of the enormous ship were visible. Angled assemblies and girderwork reflected thinly the upper-atmospheric glow of the planet seven hundred miles distant, beginning another swift sunrise. But there were other lights, of varied hues and intensities. In the midst of the huge spaceship structure fireflies glowed, sputtered, drifted or flared briefly, intensely. Searchlights, running lights, windows, floodlights and headlights, welding torches,. signal beams, rocket thrusters and reflections turned the ship into a sparkling fantasia. The sight was dazzling; to a newcomer on the scene like Hugh Fitzpatrick, it was stunning.

Arch Begley worked the helicopter-like controls of the tug with smooth precision, judging his induced rates visually and above all by the instruments on the panel before him. Most critical were his velocity incremental rates and plots, distance from and closure with whatever target he worked, and the glowing eight-ball, a growth of the artificial horizon used for many decades in high-performance and acrobatic military aircraft. In space *all* horizons were gyroscopic. They were inertial frames built on a solid foundation of theory and displacement, always relative to other theoretical bases. Hugh Fitzpatrick glanced to his left at Begley as he rolled the tug. Cold-thruster reaction jets snapped and banged audibly through the structure. Everything in sight rolled—or that was the way it seemed. Everything out there rolled. The tug wasn't moving. The world was crazy. It had to be crazy. Begley moved his wrists and seemed to squeeze his toes, and God fell over on His side. Begley wrist-twisted and toe-squeezed, and thrusters fired and the crazy eight-ball stopped rolling around.

Hugh Fitzpatrick looked through the lexitr windshield—*how goddamned dumb can you be, man? Why do they call it a windshield? There's no wind in vacuum!* —and gaped. The Earth hung upside down in the top of his windshield—viewshield?—and *Pegasus* floated beneath rather than orbiting above the planet.

So Hugh Fitzpatrick did the only sensible thing. He threw up. This is neither the wisest nor the nicest thing to do in zero gravity. Vomit does not fall down, since there isn't any down. Puke does not arc over to a point on the floor; there isn't any floor. There is no up and there is no down and there is only this craziness of an upside-down planet and . . . Fitzpatrick shook his head to blow free the cobwebs. Begley, already severely distressed by the initial unpleasant spray of liquid and particles donated to him so freely by the gasping Irishman, yelled *"No! Don't!"* to prevent Fitzpatrick from going through the violent head motions that, far above his home world, had once worked effectively to dismiss the woozies and vapor locks affecting him after excessive drinking. Begley brought up his arms to protect his face when he saw he was too late to dissuade Fitzpatrick, who went from feeling ill to puking to complete vertigo. Which is a *very* rotten sensation. All balance snaps out of existence and there is no floor to stop falling and you fall and fall and *fall*, even if you are not falling, for a man's stomach is a terrible liar, and when the nerve endings within a man's body are floating freely, as they would be when a man topples off the edge of a thirty-story building and he by God *falls*, or when he's in zero gravity and feels like something left over from last week's breakfast . . . Fitzpatrick let out a cry of genuine, pure agony and flailed wildly with his arms, managing to catch Begley a thundering backhand across the side of his head.

Begley slipped the next wild blow and expertly pinned the arms of the big Irishman against his body. Heavy belt webbing kept them secured to their seats, giving Begley, an old hand at this moment of terror for the passenger, the leverage needed to keep Fitzpatrick from going completely wild. He drew Fitzpatrick close to him, squeezing him tightly, the sides of their faces hard together, holding Fitzpatrick's arms pinned. Begley spoke quietly and earnestly to the man who'd been swallowed by the Demon Vertigo. It really was *not* funny. Begley had seen men and women die from the terror racing through their hearts, bringing it to beat madly, to fibrillate.

"Easy, easy, man, very easy," he said close to Fitzpatrick's ear. "Take it slow, slow. I'm here, I won't let you fall, Hugh, I promise you I won't let you fall. Open your eyes slowly, *slowly*, look straight ahead, that's very important, very important, look straight ahead, *don't turn your head*, don't close your eyes, whatever you see lock your eyes on it, got that? Lock your eyes on it, stare at it, don't move your eyes, now breathe easy, deep and easy, don't breathe hard, man, you'll hyperventilate, nice and easy, hey, you're coming around, how you doing?"

A weak kitten answered. "Better." Fitzpatrick hesitated. "I've never been so scared in all my life. What in the hell happened to me?"

"Vertigo. Normal, to be expected, you get better control of it from now on, but you got to get through this first man, work at it, keep your eyes locked on one thing, don't turn your head, got it?"

"I'm okay there. Won't turn my head. Looking straight ahead. It's horrible."

Begley's brows went up. "What's horrible?"

"I'm looking straight ahead. What I see. Horrible."

Nothing Begley could imagine would bring on *that* reaction. "What is it?"

"Right in front of my nose. Maybe six inches away. Floating in front of my nose."

"What the hell is it!"

"Ball of vomit. God, it's horrible. Green and yellow and brown. Slimy. Disgusting."

"Jesus Christ, Fitzpatrick!"

"No, it's not, it's slime and puke and it's quivering in the air and I think I'm going to die if you don't get rid of it."

"You'll die if you don't shut up because I'll kill you myself. If I let go can you make it now?"

"Don't let go. I'm afraid I'll start falling again."

"The feeling will start to pass any moment now."

"I hope so. I can never tell anyone about this."

"Hey, it's no bad scene, man. Most people throw up until they become accustomed to—"

"Hugging a nigger in space who's covered with all your own cowardly vomit?"

"Did you know that Irishmen when they're real close smell like puke?"

"I didn't before. I do now. Hey, I'm starting to . . . that feeling is going away. My stomach isn't trying to kill me. *Can't you get rid of that slimeball?*"

"I'm going to let you go now, Fitz."

"Promise me you'll come back for the next dance."

"I promise."

"Don't move your head."

"If I have to fart I'll swallow it first."

"Good man." Begley slowly released his grip, pulled back, saw vomit-covered Fitzpatrick staring at the slimeball hovering before his eyes. The Irishman was right. The lumpy sphere of puke *was* quivering, in air being moved by cabin's ventilation fans. "God, you're disgusting," Begley said. "Is all dem white folks disgustipatin' lak yoo?"

"Only when they're on the way to the moon with a coon in June. Jesus, Begley, get rid to it! *Please!*"

"Cool it. It's not that easy. If I touch it it's likely to come apart and spray all over us and this cabin."

423

"*Guck.*"

"You bet. Now, stay still. I'm getting a damp cloth—"

"Where the hell are you getting a damp cloth in this rotten little ship?"

"It's a wet one. You know, what they use for wiping white baby's asses. *I'm* going to use it to wipe *your* face."

"Thanks."

"Hey, you sound as if you mean that."

"Bet your black ass I do. Thanks again." Fitzpatrick stayed calm, feeling infinitely better as Begley wiped him as carefully as he would a child. Then he cleaned his own face. He studied the collar ring of Fitzpatrick's spacesuit, reached out gingerly and wiped away a touch of vomitus. "Check my collar," he instructed the Irishman.

"You got a ring around—"

"I'll kill you, Fitz. Any slop on the ring?"

"No."

"Okay. I'm putting on your helmet. The oxygen comes on automatically and so does the intercom. Ready? Good. Here we go." Fitzpatrick saw and felt the helmet come down and watched Begley's powerful hands twistlock it into place. He watched Begley don his own helmet. Immediately the intercom was alive.

"I'm checking your harness. Just stay still where you are."

"Count on it, my friend."

"All right, my gear checks out also. Now, I don't want you getting alarmed. This cabin is small as it is and having your puke, spit, whitey sweat, and blood all over it is not my way of having a good first date."

"God, I love your approach."

"I'm going to blow the pressure."

"You're *what?*"

"I told you. Easy does it, man. I'm going to pop the main hatch. It'll be fast. Rapid decompression. You'll hear a loud bang, like an explosion, and see some fog from the condensation, and all that's normal. Your suit will also rigidize on you from compensatory pressure."

424

"Why are you doing this to me? I never even sang Al Jolson tunes in Catholic schools and—"

"Just *watch*." He hit several buttons rapidly and yanked down on a bright-red lever. Fitzpatrick saw the hatch snap away, he heard the loud BANG! and instantly his suit tightened, the world became sudden fog, the fog rushed up through the open hatch *and so did all the vomitus and other unsavory particles and wetness*.

"What a hell of a vacuum cleaner!" Fitzpatrick exclaimed.

"We'll wait a moment. Anything left in this cabin has already sublimated. All its moisture is gone and we may have a few ice particles left. But that's all. However, this is your first exposure to vacuum with a suit only. You're aware of that? Right now you have no cabin pressure protection from this tug."

Fitzpatrick felt naked. "Now I know what you meant when you told me to regard vacuum as a poison gas. Never let it in."

"You sound pretty good for someone who wanted only to die a short while ago."

"God's been good to me. Gave me a partner with rhythm. Close the goddamn hatch so we can go to work."

"Now, *that's* what I want to hear," Begley said with a grin. He banged a gloved hand against Fitzpatrick's arm, worked his controls and closed the hatch. Lights flashed across the console, the pressure safety light came on, bells chimed in their helmets and Begley removed the domed shape about his head. He motioned for Fitzpatrick to do the same. Fitzpatrick let his helmet float weightlessly before him and breathed deeply.

"Thank you," he said simply and meaningfully to Begley. "That is quite a routine you have for errant Irishmen with twisted minds and stomachs."

"You feeling okay now?"

"Sure as hell do. What are those for?" He looked at two orange pills Begley held in a small container. "Take these and swallow from this tube," he was told. "Think of these pills as stomach cement. They'll lock everything in place. What they really do is desensitize your stomach's nerve endings so they won't keep sending panic signals to you."

"Why the hell didn't you give these to me before?"

"Then you'd never have known the danger signs, good buddy, in case this happens again and you don't have these doodads with you. Wait about ten minutes and then it's time to work." Begley watched a communicator light blinking. "That's Tug Three-Six. Admiral Seavers will be aboard. He's got one of the Russians or Chinamen with him. Personally, I think it'll be Zheng."

"Zheng who?"

"Sorry. He's a late pickup. Like you. You didn't know you were joining us, did you?"

"Hell, no. I was all prepared to stay down there, *up* there, wherever the hell the Earth is, and drink myself to death, thank you. The next thing I know is a bunch of people in jungle fatigues move my ass into one of the fancy new choppers and they take away all my whiskey in exchange for a pretty blue jumpsuit and here I am. From the looks of things you're all going to need me. That ship is a mess."

"I know," Begley said carefully. "This Chinese? He's Dr. Zheng Fangkun. I understand he's the Chinese equivalent of you."

"Ain't no such thing as a slant-eyed Irishman."

"He's been running their booster program. Big solids that everybody else said wouldn't work."

Fitzpatrick's face showed sudden respect. "*That* Chinaman. He's pure bloody genius. A miracle man."

"Funny. He said the same thing about you."

"Aha! Did he now?"

"He did, and there they come." Begley turned the tug about to point it at a bright silver-and-orange box with knobs, humps, robotic extensions with clampclaws and tools, swivel lights, blinking warning lights, and a great bulbous shape on its top. The clamshell canopy for the ship.

"Three-Six, this is One-Four twelve o'clock low your position," Begley called. "Got us yet?"

"That's affirm, Arch. Eyeballs locked. We'll use names

426

now. Go to channel one two six one nine so we can keep the workbands clear."

They resumed communications. "Fitz was demonstrating to me how he understands your insistence on the American Indian for your steelworkers, Marc. Their habit of never getting vertigo."

"Did he throw up all over you, Arch?"

"How the hell did *you* know!" Fitzpatrick shouted.

"Everybody throws up. Except those Indians," Seavers replied. "Okay, let's get to it. Fitz, this your first time out?"

Fitzpatrick could hardly believe the easy conversation between two ugly spacecraft, floating in vacuum in the splintered shadow of a monstrous lifeboat seven hundred miles above a world that was—*knock it off*, he told himself. *Save the maudlin shit for when you're alone and drunk.* "That it is, lad," he replied to Seavers.

"All right, gentlemen," Seavers addressed the group, "for the benefit of Dr. Fangkun, who's been involved essentially in the heavy solid booster program that brought much of the material we're working with up here, we'll carry out an eyeball inspection of both spacecraft and all assembly procedures. Please feel free to interrupt any conversation with comments, notes, or questions. This entire session is being video and audio recorded aboard *Pegasus*. Each of these tugs has video camera pickup and transmission, shooting in several different wavelengths, including infrared. For the moment, we begin at the beginning. Arch, you have the best familiarity with these systems. Please take lead and we'll fly slightly above and to your right."

"One question, Marc."

"Shoot."

"Are we on live listen for anybody who wants to eavesdrop?"

"No. Why?"

"I recommend it, sir. That way, as we go along, anyone who's hit with their own thoughts or comments will be doing it on a realtime basis with us, and we can integrate it," he winced with a grin, "with our own observations when we're back aboard ship."

"I'll take care of it. Lead off, Arch, and comment to us just as if we were a congressional committee." No one answered for a moment. There weren't any more congressional committees. There weren't a lot of things any more. They found themselves caught up in little trips and traps like this one. Finally you stopped watching yourself, said to hell with it, and you spoke easily after that.

"Moving in," Begley radioed. He was back to that wrist-twisting and toe-squeezing ballet he executed with such exquisite precision. Thrusters spat a series of sprays about them, appearing like pale ghosts and fading to nothingness moments later. His innards put to peace, Fitzpatrick studied everything with both the serious concentration of the engineer, which is why he was here, and the delight of the child, which he was at heart.

He wasn't sure if they were drifting toward that magnificent display of girderwork and sparkling lights, or if the massive ship and all its loose component parts were coming toward them. His eyeballs lied to him and quickly he gave short shrift to dalliance, choosing what reason told him instead. Optical illusions could show up anywhere. He'd been warned they were much more severe in space, where lack of relative objects and familiar background made a mockery of what was real or unreal.

Pegasus began to block out the stars. The additional areas of utter black, from which new lights, shapes and reflections began to materialize, gave Fitzpatrick and the others a stark presentation of the vessel's enormity. Fitzpatrick had a different concept of the lifeboat—as he came more and more to consider *Pegasus*—than the others. All his professional life he envisioned his subjects in three dimensions. Nothing was ever *flat* to him. Photographs and blueprints and architectural drawings were only challenges for his mind to extend into a depth not immediately apparent. The ability of the computer to display three-dimensional views was like heaven to him, and the transformation of a computer view into a holographic image, about which he could walk to study from all aspects, was absolute delirium. Over the years he trained himself mentally to extend whatever he saw into the full three dimensions, so that, looking at the bits and pieces and part-bulk of *Pegasus* in the half-light afforded to him from this particular position, he was able to visualize the entire spacecraft. The small details where he could not see didn't matter; it was the *entirety* that commanded his study. To Fitzpatrick, the technique was much akin to a man looking at a full moon. If you could freeze the viewer's thoughts at any moment, perhaps one out of every two hundred really perceived the moon as the sphere it was and not a two-dimensional dish hanging face-on in the sky.

Pegasus came forth from direct view, memory of blueprints, and the Fitzpatrick introperspective in its true form. He knew this ship had begun its life as an enormous football (or an egg, depending upon whether you threw leather or cooked chicken embryos), and that it had doubled in size from its original design to what lay—floated?—before him now, a monster vessel fully a mile from prow to stern and some three thousand feet from side to side and through the belly upward to the humped top. Yet—and Fitzpatrick felt this as a marvelous psychological victory—as stupendous as this ship was seen from this vantage it was less of a shock to him than the first time he'd seen the blueprints and the actual photographs and films sent to Earth during early construction.

He had become familiar with the lifeboat. A ship five times longer than the *Queen Elizabeth* was infinitely more personal, warmer, more . . . *intimate*. He could glide effortlessly through the vast structure on a mental search, no matter what the direction. He had committed to memory the essential pathways and main structural elements, the power stations and the systems that brought life to the enormous vessel, *and he knew her weaknesses and her faults and he understood all too well that unless they continued the drastic changes he had instituted when he still lived on a planet . . . well, he hated the idea of the Last Hurrah for all the human race.*

Her keel was the same huge tubular core running the entire length of *Pegasus*. The castoff upper liquid stages of the shuttles, modified on the ground with crisscrossing braces within the tanks, provided the backbone of the ship. The later-model shuttles flew with extended propellant tanks, each stage a hundred and thirty feet in length. And that was after they removed the nose cap and let it "float in tethered storage" out of the way, and set up the tanks end to end so they would slide neatly together. Each tank joined another with long duralumin girders along the outer shell, six lightweight beams joining them together like railroad tracks. Duralumin offered extremely light weight with the strength of steel, a most admirable material for great structural reliability.

Ten stages end to end, keeled together, gave them thirteen hundred feet. Forty stages provided the required length for a ship fifty-two hundred feet—the mile they wanted—in length. So the logistics problem for the strongest part of the ship structure had never really been a problem once they were in orbit. By having all joining elements pre-formed prior to launch, they came together like a perfectly planned elaborate erector set. Laid tail to end after being flushed of residual fuels, each tank became a major ship structure. Its many subsystems unfolded within the shell like scissored accordians. The tubes for power cables, wiring, communications lines, and fluids transfer were all integral parts of the tanks and were quickly sealed by cold welds. Precut flanges and massive bolts added the strength that Joe Briand and Marc Seavers had demanded from the outset.

Hugh Fitzpatrick found no fault with this basic design. Simple, strong, reliable; he had no argument there. In fact, he would have demanded the massive bolts had they not been in place when he first joined this team. They'd had automatic seamless welding with largely robot systems since the Russians began messing around with expanding their Mir stations back in '89, and American astronauts were also well familiar with the technique. By leaving the tank ends in place, prefabricated

430

as pressure dome hatches even as the belly core of the ship was connected in the form of the single massive backbone, they created not only the great tubular tunnel with its pressure seals and safety systems but the single building keel for additional propellant tank sections to extend outward at right angles from the main keel.

"But it's not good enough," Fitzpatrick told the others after his first study of the structure. "It leaves too much to be hoped for in terms of reliability. You could take some unexpected angular momentum and the loads you'd put on that bloody keel will go beyond anything you'd ever anticipate. Not good enough, lads, not at all."

Seavers studied his old friend. "You're a bit late with major changes at this stage of the game, Hugh."

"The hell I am. Did you think I'd sit down with you to topple over your little house of cards without the proper solution? You know me better than that, bucko. Now, here's what we do. I've already programmed it into the computer for three-dimensional readout, proper scaling and all that rubbish. Here, take a look."

The television screen came alive with his design modifications to increase the keel strength and above all the reliability for *Pegasus*. Like most Fitzpatrick solutions to thorny problems, it went the route of least complexity—the simplest way to accomplish what was needed. "We use a whole bunch of those shuttle tanks. There's enough of them in the graveyard for certain, just floating around out there. We set them up at one hundred-twenty-degree positions about the main keel, like this. Now we've got four main sections for the keel. We attach through bolts along the girder connections, and rigidize the outside three new keels the same way. However, I'm not satisfied that's quite enough. We can crossbrace externally to this core, but we'll get a hell of a lot more strength by going to wrap-around cables of the whole affair. That's my only question: whether or not we have sufficient cabling."

Vasily Tereshnikov tapped the sketches prepared hurriedly by the engineer. The computer design would follow this "hands-on" feel that Fitzpatrick felt so necessary to his work. "What kind of cables?" the Russian asked. "Doesn't matter," he was told. "It can be steel, or that new type of nylon, or even power cabling. It's not the primary holddown, remember. As far as I'm concerned, you can wrap the whole bloody mess in duct tape. Use webbing if that's what you've got. So long as you wrap it enough it'll be as strong as cabling."

"Damn," Seavers said slowly, almost under his breath.

"Problems?" Fitzpatrick asked.

"No, no," Seavers said, looking up from the sketches and breaking into a grin. "It's just the opposite. This is marvelous." He looked around his group. Except for Fitzpatrick, who shared his grin, the others were stony-faced, not comprehending. Seavers wriggled his feet within the "floor" restraints and leaned back in his seat. "It's a matter of ship design," he went on. "Not too many people understand the problems of the really big ships—something the size of the *Queen Mary* or a modern supertanker. They're huge, enormous, massive, powerful; all the adjectives fit. But if you could pick up the *Queen Mary* at her bow and her stern, and lift that vessel clear of the water, it would break in two. The structure can't support its own weight out of water." He tapped the sketches. "Until this idea was proposed, we had much the same kind of problem: a spaceship designed along the principles of a ship in water. *Our* problem is going to be along the lines of angular inertia, shifting mass, whatever we call it. There's no way in the time we have to make *Pegasus* a truly rigid structure. When we're under way, even if we're affected by—well, an unexpected shift in interior mass, *Pegasus* is going to take distortion. She'll have twist, bend, all manner of problems. This should, *will*, answer those problems."

Pegasus' flight dynamics engineer, Michael Pruett, shook his head, instantly regretted the motion, held still a moment, then pointed to the sketches. "Sir, I've got to disagree."

"That's what you're here for, Mr. Pruett."

"This whole approach creates more problems. I really

432

hate to disagree with Mr. Fitzpatrick, and you, sir, but—"

"To hell with what you like or dislike, son," Fitzpatrick urged him on. "Tell us what are those problems."

"It has nothing to do with additional keel strength. God knows I'm all for *that*—"

"Son, tell me what you *know*," Fitzpatrick cut in. "And considering what's happening, um, down below, we'd better count on ourselves from now on rather than engineering proposals from the deity."

"Yes, sir. The way I see it, we have an inertial problem. You're going to have all that, well, balloon structure running down the spine of the ship. It won't be a problem when we're not thrusting or under acceleration. But with so much mass along assemblies farther from the keel, when we *do* thrust, or even go through major attitude changes, it's going to be a mess. We might be able to handle it, but we're dealing with so many unknowns in a ship this size, I'm starting to feel like we may be creating more problems than we are solving them."

"All points well taken," Fitzpatrick said immediately. "Now: what you want, then, is greater heft to your keel?"

"Yes, sir."

"These tanks are perfect for your needs, then. Fill them with water. *That'll* give you some heavy buckets for your inertial moments."

Pruett was aghast. "*Water?* You're not serious!"

"Never more, son."

"Do you know what the hell that will do?"

"Give you what you asked for, and that's as plain as the nose on my face—which is giving a hell of a lot, I'll tell you."

"Mr. Fitzpatrick, there's the slosh effect. Baffles won't take care of it. Long after we effect an acceleration change, that stuff will *still* be slamming around in the tanks. It can set up incredible mass shifts and—"

Fitzpatrick rested his hand on Pruett's arm. "Son, don't ignore the wisdom of the ancients."

Pruett's expression was blank. "What?"

"Take a page from the old people, Pruett. Listen to the Chinese."

"I'm not sure I—"

"Pruett, get the water in these tanks and then freeze the damn stuff."

Drifting closer, gaining visibility from floodlights within the framework, they had an excellent view of the lateral construction of *Pegasus*. Many of the payloads hurled into orbit had been fabricated from the outset as complete structural elements of *Pegasus*, and *Noah* as well. The great tanks and the spacecraft themselves disassembled easily and were then reassembled as they were moved into position in the huge spacecraft. One booster fuel tank could be made up of thirty-two separate duralumin beams, each ninety feet in length. So one shuttle tank was able to be adapted to *Pegasus* as almost one complete cross-girder structure, extending outward almost fifteen hundred feet in each direction from the bolt-on core section.

This was the widest diameter of *Pegasus*. In effect the great ship was coming together in its high orbit as an enormous skeletal structure, a space whale being constructed in reverse. One after the other the great "spokes" pushed outward from the keel to form the enormous ribs of the ship. Then began the task of assembling more sections lengthwise to provide running connections for the overall framework. As fast as the structure went through various stages of completion, hundreds of miles of massive ductwork went into place, bolted and ready with twistlock connections and then seamless welds to take the final cables, power lines, water and pressure mains, reclamation tubes, all the arteries and veins and capillary systems that would keep the lifeblood of the enormous vessel coursing.

But in no respect was *Pegasus* the adaptation of any naval design. A ship could never have survived space conditions. The closest thing to a spacecraft would be a giant submarine designed with pressure seals and the means to correct any leaks. Both submarine and spacecraft also had compartments that could be closed off from one another for survival.

Marc Seavers, working with Fitzpatrick and his team of engineers—but mostly with construction crews, for the time of engineering design was well behind them—effected a major change in construction philosophy. There was inbred acceptance of a design that in major respects followed naval ship layout. Crew compartments were set up to each side of long corridors. Fuel, oil, ordnance, cooking, medical and the like also were compartmented. That philosophy could be carried only so far with *Pegasus* and then they were in heavy waters, so to speak.

"The problem is that we've got to stop thinking in naval terms. Even in submarine or aircraft terms," Seavers told his design-construction team, laying down the sweeping new program. "We're paying lip service to the needs of the people aboard this ship. You provide compartments, but you know where you've failed?" He studied his men and women to make certain they understood just how serious he was. "What you've also done is to make each compartment dependent upon the entirety of this ship for survival. I'm going to stop that practice right now. You will modify *every* compartment aboard this vessel, small or large, so that it can survive for several weeks on its own, with its own supplies and power system, in the event the main ship systems break down and can't attend to the needs of all aboard."

"Do you know what you're asking, sir?" Miguel Rivera was Maintenance Chief for *Pegasus*. He came to the lifeboat with singing praise from the head of submarine design for General Dynamics: "He's brilliant, innovative, tireless and farsighted, and the kid's only thirty-two." *Which*, Seavers thought with a smile, *reflects generously on one's perspectives regarding age. But I guess the older we get the older others can be and still be regarded as "kids."*

"Miguel, I don't believe we're communicating," Seavers told the engineer. "I am *not* asking. Do you read me?"

Miguel grinned crookedly. "Yes, sir. You're telling."

"I'd prefer to think I was leading or instructing with some *oomph*."

"You got it, Admiral. If I read you correctly, you want a compartment, which is identified as a living or working unit, that can be identified as a section wholly separate from all other sections—" he paused to study Seavers, who nodded and waved him on, "—you want this compartment or unit to be able to survive a specified period of time if it is completely isolated from the ship."

"Just as effectively as if all connections were cut and it drifted off from *Pegasus*. That's right."

"And, um," Miguel Rivera frowned with his own rushing thoughts, "that means you'll want batteries, fuel cells, the works for air cleansing and reclamation, and supplies all stored with each unit—"

"And the idea, Miguel, is to rotate everything that's a consumable, from candy bars to batteries. Constant turnover. It keeps everything fresh and updated in the event of such an emergency, it permits improved control and accountability for supplies, it lets us sleep better when we find time to sleep, it lets us know that we can suffer a major breakdown of ship's power systems, let us say, without the usual consequences."

"Yes, sir, and that would also be a safeguard against the failure of any one compartment causing a chain reaction to the others."

"You're getting there. Let me take it a step further. Imagine yourself on a large ship. Transport, let's say. Like ours. What do you do if there's a sudden blowout and a shortage of air?"

Miguel Rivera went blank. "Sir?" He hesitated. "How can you have a shortage of *air*?"

"Your ship *sinks*. That's for starters." The others were listening intently. "The compartment is sealed and you have a massive release of smoke, carbon dioxide, carbon monoxide or any other choking chemical, or—"

"I get your point, sir."

"Where do you get replacement air?"

"Open the hatches, sir," Flip Paxton, one of *Noah's* engineers offered.

"Really?" Seavers countered. "Let's see you try that on *Pegasus*."

"Whoops," said Rivera.

"That's about the size of it," Seavers answered. "Now, let's go back aboard ship. What do you do with your garbage?"

"Dump it."

"You can't dump it from *Pegasus*. If you did, it would orbit about us and we'd be going through a cloud of sublimated urine and banana peels, for starters. But we don't throw away *anything*. Even if it can't be reclaimed, it can be burned in the centrifugal ovens."

"Yes, sir."

"If you're in trouble aboard a ship and you take to the lifeboats, where do you go?"

"Nearest available safe port, sir."

"There ain't none up here. I suppose aboard ship you could radio for help?"

"Yes, sir."

"There's no one out here to hear you."

"Yes, sir," very quietly, met *that* remark.

"Everything we have is limited or will run out aboard these two vessels," Seavers told them. "Except faith, hope, charity, self-confidence, ingenuity, steadfastness, love, loyalty, working toward a common goal or, in other words, if we do not fail ourselves we can survive *anything*. Now get the hell to work, you guys."

"Yes, *sir!*"

Hugh Fitzpatrick recalled that conversation as he and Arch Begley drifted in the lead of the two-spacetug formation toward the ever-increasing bulk of *Pegasus*. More and more of the starfield blanked out to give them a growing appreciation of its mass. "There was something else about that meeting," Fitzpatrick said suddenly. "Maybe we should have brought it up. Marc and I have talked it over many times and there are some people such as yourself who understand it. Ah, that's always the key, ain't it? Understanding instead of just knowing—"

"Damn it, Hugh—"

"Yes, yes. You're an impatient bastard. Anyone ever tell you that you bear an amazing resemblance to Darth Vader? His teeth are nicer—but *anyway*, did you ever consider the total number of people involved in the launch of merely one shuttle?"

"I hadn't *considered* it. Not specifically, no."

"You should have. It might give you better understanding of the nonsense we're attempting up here. It's no secret that the computers on the shuttles were really crude pieces of crap, that they came on line before microchips came into really wide use. But what most people never really understood is that it took the equal of an entire army division—*twelve thousand people*—to get the damned thing ready to lift." Fitzpatrick stared glumly at his astronaut companion. "We don't have that kind of support up *here*, Darth."

"Goddamn," Begley said.

"And there's no shop anywhere to send broken parts to," Fitzpatrick went on.

"And no supply stores for replacements," Begley added.

"And we have no idea of who's capable of milling or lathing parts and assemblies in a machine shop. *Especially* under zero g, I will add for greater effect."

"I've never heard it said that way."

"Neither had I until I lost a button on my shirt."
Begley blinked. "What?"

"You heard me. I was in my cubicle. You weren't there, which in a small way is a blessing since I'd never figured on launching into the celestial wonders of the universe with a teeth-tapping darky for company. Besides, you would have laughed at me, Commodore. There I was, trying to thread a needle. Easy enough. Child's play. *Not in weightlessness, it is not*. The goddamned thread has no weight! It snarls all about and within itself. Tangles like a briarpatch. Finally I remembered something I'd read about a cosmonaut. I held one end of the thread in my teeth and after about fifteen minutes I threaded my first needle up here. The point is, Arch, if just threading one lousy needle is such a bitch, can you imagine what machine shops and their like are going to be?"

"You have something in mind." Begley had learned that by now. Fitzpatrick had a tendency to run on, but never without a purpose.

"I need your help. No time to get a whole new program going. Have everybody who flies up here stuff tools in their pockets or their bags or anywhere. All kinds of tools. Hand tools, free-power tools working off batteries, inertial tools. Don't let them wait for the specially designed equipment for zero-g use. We'll *never* get it then. And Arch, you've been up here many times. You and your people—that's a nice turn of a phrase, that you and your people bit, but this time it means flight crews—know better than me what we'll need for the long haul up here. Pass the word, my friend, and pass it very fast. We're running out of time."

They floated slowly, majestically, up the slope of the ship and over the top into the blinding glare of the sun. The metal mountain hurled dazzling reflections and suddenly *Pegasus* snapped into startling clarity and definition, surrounded by a spiderweb of gleaming light. Moving objects leaped to prominence, small shapes of different sizes drifted and glided into and out of their frame of vision as the spacetugs and ships kept at their work. They had several occasions to move in close to the control jets coming into position around the girth of the ship, small nozzles that would nudge and tug at the mass of *Pegasus*, based on laser gyros spinning at more than a hundred thousand times a second, linked to computers and stellar navigation systems.

"Ah, there is what I wish to see," Zheng Fangkun told Marc Seavers. "The new multiple shells for the compartments." They moved in slowly, carefully, and turned on their floodlights. An open cross-section of the outermost shell of *Pegasus* lay exposed to them. "I see. Three layers. What gas between them?"

"Anything inert. Nitrogen, mainly. One of my engineers came up with a new idea, Doctor. Some of our waste liquids simply won't be reclaimable for use by our people or the animals. Industrial stuff, mainly. My engineer recommended we seal off these outer layers into flat, ultrathin compartments, like these before us, flood them with water under gas pressure, and then quick-freeze the liquids. It should remain frozen, it provides an extra barrier against micrometeoroids that may strike the ship, and it adds greatly to insulation for the compartments beneath."

"Excellent. Much cheaper than foam, so to speak. Also, Admiral, any penetrating object will vaporize the metal shell and also the layers beneath. Instant vaporization means enormous localized pressures that will consume the penetrant particle. It is good to see such thinking." Fangkun shifted in his straps. "I have a question, Admiral."

"Please."

"Have you set up the thrusters for— Forgive me. Not the thrusters. The main engines," Fangkun corrected himself. "The main engines for thrusting out of orbit, and then for deceleration when," he swallowed, "when we return home? To whatever home there may be, of course. Are these engines ready for this great vessel and," he pointed to a huge bowl of light in the distance, *Noah* also in direct sunlight, "and for the ark?"

Seavers frowned. "Not yet."

"May I suggest, urgently, Admiral, that you institute your contingency plan?"

"You do not say that lightly. I hesitated to use the shuttles as main drive engines, but—"

"If you do not," Fangkun said with a sad smile, "you may never use any engines."

"It has come to that?"

"It is beyond that."

Marc Seavers glanced through a thick visor at the sun. "I'm surprised," he said after a thoughtful pause. "There doesn't seem to have been any sudden increase in solar output, and—"

"Excuse me. The danger is not from the sun."

"Then—"

"There is a world group. It has gained, almost overnight, the support of many frightened people who still have great power about our beleagured world, Admiral. A madness sifts within their minds. We, up here, must not leave. Man stands together and he survives together. Or he must die together. They are twisted, but as I say, they are distorted out of fear."

"And—" Marc Seavers was starting to weary of ancient Oriental patience.

"I offer apologies for my dramatic approach. This group has seized control of several missile installations. Some in your country, some in mine. It happened also in the Soviet land, but there it was repressed at once. Not so in America and not so in China. Admiral," Fangkun said slowly. "We may be attacked with nuclear weapons. Every day we remain here our chances of leaving are reduced greatly."

Seavers found the news to be no great surprise. Joe Briand was, fortunately, a fanatic, and he was going to stick to his job of supporting what he considered a survival boondoggle because it *was* his job. The installations deep within Cheyenne Mountain had survived the screaming mobs trying to vent their terror on anything that smacked of officialdom, but Cheyenne Mountain was much too tough a nut to crack that easily. At one point the mobs had even doused much of the mountain with gasoline and oil flown in by aircraft and helicopter and then set the whole damned thing ablaze. Cheyenne Mountain's facilities had been designed to withstand the searing lash of heat generated by nuclear detonations. A puny fuel fire didn't rattle any cages within, and that kind of solid security left Joe Briand to pursue his job as long as he could still breathe. He'd told Seavers the same news that Seavers was hearing now from Zheng Fangkun.

"Say nothing, except to Vasily Tereshnikov," Seavers replied finally. "I'll put our best people on the propulsion modules right away. And yes, we'll move a number of the shuttles into position along the aft portion of both *Pegasus* and *Noah*. If we can't get our other systems and engines and tanks into place in time, we'll boost with the shuttles." He looked outside the spacetug for several moments. "What's next on our itinerary, Doctor?"

"What has a Chinese ring to it, Marc. The prow of energy, if you please."

Seavers laughed. "Let's go." He thumbed his transmitter. "Arch, lead on to the front end of this turkey. We'll follow."

In the lead spacetug Begley and Fitzpatrick stared at one another. "Turkey?" Begley echoed. "I've never heard him call this ship anything like *that.*"

"Well, it could be the Chink is giving him all the dignity that one man could possibly endure," Fitzpatrick smiled in return. "And that wouldn't be a bad thing a'tall, my friend. The admiral takes his tasks too seriously. He needs more time in the sack—or in the net, if you like—with that splendid young thing he married."

Fitzpatrick gestured impatiently. "Lead on, damn it. Let's go see the *real* turkey. This prow of energy, or whatever the Chink calls that damnfool nonsense."

Begley worked the thrusters and they fell slowly down the side of the metal mountain, past the already operational flight control deck, to a formation drift with *Pegasus,* holding position off the tremendous shape of the bow. Extending toward them from the enormous blunt nose were eight huge booms festooned with powerful energy grids and generators. Thick cables ran from the sides of the bow to the generators.

"Ah, a marvel of science," Zheng Fangkun said to Seavers in the second spacetug. "Pure electromagnetic energy to open a path for us through the dust storm of the void." He smiled. "A contradiction in terms, but nevertheless true." He gestured to the massive assembly looming before them. "Unfortunately, it will do us good in the psychological sense only."

Seavers was taken aback by the blunt statement. "You surprise me, Doctor. I have always believed you were fully supportive of this generator system."

"Oh, to be certain, I am. But not for obvious reasons." Fangkun leaned forward, moving floodlights along the boom generators. "The purpose of these machines is to create a mighty electromagnetic shock wave pre-

442

ceding our movement through the dust, to help us escape the great dust ocean into the empty void above the ecliptic. This will, one hopes, generate what we can describe as a bow shock wave that will send the dust away from before us, much like the bow wave of a ship, but in our case through a complete circle. It may be imagined as boring a tunnel through which we can slip without the grinding effect of dust friction. At our velocity that will certainly be a disturbing factor."

"I'm familiar with the system," Marc Seavers said, careful to be noncommital. "If it won't work then why did you—" He stopped for a moment. "You said your reasons for supporting this generator system were *not* obvious."

"That is correct, Admiral. They are psychological. A group of our best scientists and engineers, and by *our* I mean belonging to these two vessels, came to me with this concept. They were overwhelmed with their own enthusiasm. They were also deeply concerned about the dust resistance to our velocity. If this system would work, and theoretically it will, *but only in theory*," he stressed, "we gain much protection. I asked of them what would be their power source for such a mighty engine. That is the basis for the nuclear reactors we have mounted in the aft section of both ships, far from the living and working quarters of all our people and the animals. We need those reactors. We were seriously short of time to emplace and integrate them within the two ships. Few sources of energy, however, can match collective enthusiasm. I gave permission to build these systems, with your approval, because it lessened the fear factor by replacing its dominance with soaring hopes that these toys would work. In that respect, Admiral, we are most successful. Each ship has a nuclear reactor. Each ship will have power sufficient for its needs."

"Hopefully," Seavers said coolly. "Long-term reliability is far in the future."

"Yes. I agree. I spoke hastily."

"Why won't your gadgets work, Doctor?"

"I call it the rollback factor. As a man of the sea, you

443

are familiar with it. The effect is present also with such machinery as snowplows. When a ship rushes through the waters surrounding it, the bow wave spreads ahead and to either side and then it rolls back, *inward* against the hull. When a snowplow moves through the snow the same effect is visible."

Seavers gestured. "Even more so with a submarine. In fact, we use the side pressure—control it, actually, through heat rings—to reduce turbulent flow and actually gain a push from the effect."

Fangkun smiled. "A remarkable technical achievement. Which the dolphins have used for millions of years."

Seavers laughed. "Not too many people know that the navy borrowed that technique from the animals. You're right, of course. The porpoise generates heat along his skin wherever the pressure increases and this lets him slip through the water with less resistance." Seavers fell silent for a moment. "All right, Doctor. Let's put the rest of the cards on the table. No matter how badly your scientists wanted to put this gimmick together, I can't believe that their desire alone, even adding on the nuclear reactors that we need, would let you expend all the effort for these generators unless you had a specific need in mind."

"You are right, of course. When we first learned of the lifeboat issue," he gestured, "these two ships, we conducted a number of controlled experiments in orbit. Quietly. We created a dust cloud of our own. Perhaps ten miles across. Then we moved model spacecraft through that cloud. The static electricity was alarming."

Seavers studied his Chinese friend, the man they all called the Oriental equivalent of Hugh Fitzpatrick. The man with the astonishing ability to project himself into the future to "see" events and situations not readily apparent to others—what they called "programmed prevoyance." A stunning ability, as much intuition as it was scientific. *But intuition was the big thing with a man by the name of Albert Einstein,* Seavers recalled.

"This will counter?—eliminate?—that effect?" he asked finally.

"Until we are under way, I do not know." Fangkun shrugged. "It is as much, to use one of your expressions, gut feeling as it is based on data extrapolation."

"I guess that will have to do for now," Seavers concluded.

"You are kind, Admiral."

"Don't count on it, Doctor. If your ideas don't work I might just throw you overboard to swim home."

Hugh Fitzpatrick studied the other spacetug with the bright numerals Three Six showing clearly in a spray of light from *Pegasus*. "Wonder what the hell they're talking about?" he mused aloud to Arch Begley. "It's not like Marc to shut down his transmitter when he's made such a fuss about open line."

"You'll know when the time comes."

Fitzpatrick nodded. "To be sure, to be sure," he murmured. "Besides, we've still got to have a peek at—"

"Arch, we can head over to *Noah* now," Seavers' voice came into the speakers.

"Yes, sir. Top or bottom?"

"Um, come across the port flank to deck three, Arch. Go ahead. We'll follow."

"Bloody sailors," Fitzpatrick grumbled under his breath. He pressed his transmit button. "Admiral, I'll be begging your pardon, sir," he said with open sarcasm, "but did it ever occur to your highness that just like these scooty bugs run low on fuel, the same might be occurring to their occupants?"

A chuckle came across the radio. "Arch, I thought he'd tossed his cookies?"

"Flung is more like it," Begley answered.

"You miss the point, both of you," Fitzpatrick complained. "Nausea is a momentary thing for men of great taste and experience in the finer things in life. That regrettable episode is behind me. *Now*, following normal course of human events, hunger assails me from head to foot. 'Tis near starvation I am, and me stomach thinks our throat has been cut."

"Admiral, I can understand his problem," Begley

chimed in. "The way he upchucked he must have tossed from way down to his toenails. There can't be *anything* left."

"Hey, you guys. This is the flight deck." They recognized the voice of Susan Foster, second exec on duty. It was obvious from her tone that a lot of listening-in was going on. "Find something else to talk about besides the twisted intestines of that Irish freeloader. You've got half this ship—"

"Never mind," Seavers broke in to keep things from getting out of hand. "Begley, this is your captain speaking."

"I thought he was a bloody admiral," they heard Fitzpatrick say.

Seavers ignored the sidebar remark. "Begley, feed him," he continued. "If you haven't any food, give him his microphone to eat. He might even get fatter eating his own words. All right, everybody, off the party line and back to work. Begley, pedal to the metal, mister."

"Yes, *sir!*"

Zheng Fangkun exchanged a meaningful glance with Marc Seavers. "Very good, Admiral. When the nights are darkest, often the best light comes from our inner sense of humor. I admire your relationship with your crew."

"You mean *our* crew, don't you, Doctor?"

Zheng Fangkun was the first man Marc Seavers had ever seen manage a bow in zero gravity.

20 ────────

"**B**oy, just look at Smokey go!" shouted Tom Seavers. He moved his face so close to the plastic tube that his nose touched the curve of the tunnel through which the hamster raced with confidence born of successful experience. Keesha Seavers clapped her hands in glee, and Oleg Krivitsky looked with solemn approval as the hamster negotiated curves and turns without care for

446

his weightless state. The narrow tunnel, its inner surface ridged with the solid footing of grasscloth, enabled Smokey, whose back hairs touched the opposite inner surface of the tubing, to proceed without fear of weightlessness. The little creature sped around a curve, stopped suddenly to stare at the huge nose of Tom Seavers, twitched his own nose rapidly, and was off on another mad dash through the tunnel maze that comprised his entire world. One large chamber permitted Smokey to experience zero gravity. His first encounter with a lack of dropping to the chamber floor had brought on violent leg motions. Smokey remained unaware of the effect of such flailing, but it was sufficient in the air of his chamber to provide a clumsy action-reaction, and soon one frantic paw clutched at grasscloth. After a while Smokey learned to launch himself across the open space, and with amazing speed became as adept in the chamber area as he was running through his tunnels.

Smokey was also unaware, as were his masters, Tom, Keesha, and Oleg, that he was part of the Great Experiment: an assortment of animals popular with children as pets. Peter Nicholson from New Zealand was officially the veterinarian for *Pegasus*. Marc Seavers brought him aboard the lifecraft shortly after he received his own assignment to command the survival mission.

"What we bring back to this world, *if* we have a world to which we can return," Seavers told Nicholson, "will be in direct proportion to what we take with us. We can't bring back any greater variety of animals than we take."

Nicholson nodded. He was a short, wiry man who'd run a breeding farm and had an affinity for children and animals in equal amounts, which both returned. "You're not too keen on the *in vitro* stuff, I gather," he said.

"No argument with it," Seavers answered. "But that whole program depends upon how well we can sustain the laboratory conditions to keep everything alive and well; it depends upon temperature control that may be beyond our capabilities; it . . . Also, I can't predict and neither can anyone else how much ionizing radiation we'll be getting from an angry sun, and that could kill off or severely mutate the sperm and eggs we carry. Then there's the problem of weightlessness. You'd be amazed—or maybe *you* wouldn't—at the deleterious effects zero g can have on really sensitive life forms, and you can't get much more sensitive than life at its most basic levels. So the animals we take with us are the ones that have *my* priorities, and I want them to have yours. Any ideas?"

"All I have are ideas," Peter Nicholson told him. "I've looked into what the Russians and you Yanks have done with animals in the space stations, mainly the Olympus and *Gagarin*, and I'll tell you right off, sir, it isn't very much. In fact," he reflected, "it's downright skinny." He brightened. "But certainly I have ideas. And my first is to run as many experiments and tests as I can in zero g *before* we depart this local real estate."

Seavers frowned. "I can't spare many people for—"

Nicholson interrupted with a broad smile. "I already have plenty of help, sir."

"You have more secrets than I do, then."

"It's the children, Admiral. *The children*. I don't want any laboratory readings. I want real, live, warm loving care, and who better than to spend so much time, day and night . . . but we don't even have those naturally any more, do we? Well, not meaning to run on like that, but my plan is to supply pets, with the proper facilities, to as many children aboard this ship as I can, and see what emerges from their association. I have a hunch the kids will tell us more through their actions than any experiment we could dream up." Nicholson grinned. "Somehow it's a nice feeling, sir, to be involved in a project where the computer is utterly useless, and the gentle hug of a child is just as important as the food, water and air that an animal needs to live."

"To say nothing of what it does for the child?"

"Ah, I knew you'd understand . . ."

"Is there any real question?"

"No. We've now seen the pattern worldwide. We've registered temperature drops on a consistent basis. There

448

hasn't been enough time for glacial effects, but definite increases are confirmed in snow fields and the like. And we're seeing snow in areas it hasn't appeared in years."

"What abut icebergs?"

"Subtle. If we know what to look for we can see a minor increase, but it still falls within normal fluctuation range. But when you couple the effects with everything else we're seeing, well, it's getting hairy."

"Is the public aware of it?"

"The public is aware of everything. Including as much nonsense as reality. The facts are lost in the snowstorm of bullshit—so what they should fear is buried. I believe you meant that question in respect to awareness and reaction. If so, the reaction has not yet manifested itself."

"That helps. I suppose we should file our reports."

"Forgive me for laughing. File with whom?"

"National Weather Bureau, for starters."

"They already know. They won't say a word. It's nasty enough out there right now without adding— forgive me again—ice to the fire."

"Well, we're still part of the international group doing these studies. File a report with the United Nations, please."

"You're joking, of course."

"I am not joking, of course. Why would I be joking?"

"There isn't any U.N.! It's been shut down now for nearly a month. Haven't you read the papers? Or any of the magazines?"

"No. Absolutely not. Most of what I've been reading is trash, anyway. Why is the U.N. shut down?"

"They had no choice. Mobs smashed every window. What they couldn't reach with stones and slingshots they took out with rifles. They trashed the place and set it on fire—all of it. A lot of people were killed. Those who survived fled for their lives. I'm sorry to be the one to tell you this."

"Good God in Heaven . . . I had no idea."

"Do you want to shut down our reporting stations? Before too much longer the temperatures will swing.

The changes will come very abruptly and we'll have catastrophic meltings. Floods and—"

"I know what will happen. Do you want to shut down?"

"I have nothing else to do, nowhere else to go. I'm a scientist. All I know how to do is my job."

"Then we shall do it together. Right on to the end."

"Thank you."

"This is Admiral Seavers." The voice carried to every radio receiver, headset, and loudspeaker on two great spacecraft in high orbit about Earth, and into the spacetugs, spacesuits, and shuttles, to the dozens of men and women working on *Pegasus* and *Noah*.

"As of this moment all return flights to Earth are cancelled." Seavers stood on the bridge of *Pegasus*, velcro pads holding him easily to the deck beneath his feet. He wore a flyweight headset-and-boom mike. He spoke with his hands behind his back, staring at the glory of the planet curving below. He gave the statement time to sink in. He knew there'd be a chilling reaction.

"I won't keep you from your work," Seavers continued. "Full information will be provided on your teleprompters. All questions at that time will be answered. What I have to say now is not pleasant. We have been informed that certain groups on Earth, both political and religious, have been misled as to the purpose of *Pegasus* and *Noah*. These groups seek either our return or our destruction. A return at any time prior to our journey is not even worth dignifying with discussion. The ability to harm our two spacecraft and the people and animals onboard is, however, quite real. Steps are being taken to protect this mission. We are also convinced it is in the best interests of all concerned to accelerate our preparations and proceed with plans for early departure from orbit."

He gave a few moments to let *that* sink in. "All section chiefs will proceed immediately to their respective communicator stations for a video conference. You will receive your new instructions at that time and you can explain further to your crews. Generally, understand our new goal. It is to be able to leave orbit as soon as possible. All efforts will be directed toward that goal. Propulsion system readiness is our top priority from now on."

Again the careful pause, and again he continued. "I have no doubt you will hear from your own engineers and work teams that we may be committing to our journey before our two spacecraft are ready for the journey ahead of us. First, both *Pegasus* and *Noah* are far from complete. But they are almost ready to boost from Earth, and that moment is now rushing at us much faster than we had planned. Thank you for your attention, continue with the tasks before you, and I will expect section chiefs' contact precisely at oh two hundred Zulu."

"I don't think he likes the harness very much." Rodeina Quaid stroked the head of the Bernese Mountain Dog to calm him. It was a startling new world for the big dog. Huge brown eyes looked with gratitude at Rodeina. Fourteen years old, the Swiss girl had known mountain dogs all her life. She swayed gently, her feet held to the decking of the training cubicle aboard *Noah* by velcro spots.

"What's his name?" asked Bob Downey. He was only twelve years old, but the older kids liked him anyway. Bob's father was an aerospace engineer and the kids figured his son had picked up everything worth knowing. He could solve just about any problem there was. He also had a crush on Rodeina. He'd never known a girl from Switzerland before, and the long braided hair, in ponytails that floated and swayed behind her, contributed as much to his fascination as did her beautiful face.

"Brutus. I call him Brutus because it's a Roman name," Rodeina said. "Did you know that these dogs used to fight for the Romans? Not the foot soldiers," she emphasized with a slight sniff. "*They* got the mastiffs. But the royalty, they had these dogs," she patted Brutus, "to protect their families. That's because they were smart as well as ferocious."

Two other teenagers clustered with them about Brutus: Sean Talbot from England and Abdullah al-Ghanim from Saudi Arabia. "Our friends had two of these," Sean said, feeling important about his knowledge of the animal. "They were very good watchdogs, too."

"Never mind about what happened *down there*," Abdullah offered. The Arab youth was surprisingly pragmatic, but that came from being of a family of massive wealth. From his earliest days, Abdullah had been "saddled with the camel," as he put it, which was his way of explaining that his father had imposed heavy responsibilities on the youngster, with appropriate punishment for weakness or failure. "What I want to know," Abdullah said, pointing at Bob Downey, "is if his crazy contraption works."

"It works!" Downey shouted.

"We'll find out *right now*," Rodeina broke in, already accustomed from the past few weeks to the intense rivalry among the boys who swirled about her. "And if it works, then we can challenge that nasty Elizabeth Strickler to the contest." Rodeina lifted her feet from the floor, holding on to a guide rail surrounding the treadmill on which the dog stood nervously, then floated around so that she was in front of the treadmill and her dog. She studied Brutus. His great eyes stayed on her and she saw him starting to relax. That was very good. A nervous Bernese could drive you crazy.

She leaned forward to test the harness. Bob had designed it himself—or rather, had modified the harness they brought with them to orbit. He added four clips to the harness, two forward and one on each side of his back at the base of his tail, which she called the velvet hammer. With the harness on Brutus and the dog held down against the no-skid surface of the treadmill, they'd connected bungee cords between the harness clips and ringbolts in the decking. The downpull of the bungees kept the animal's feet securely against the treadmill. To move, Brutus had to shove hard in an *up* direction against the downpull of the bungees. When

452

he ran—*if* he'd run!—he would need extra energy just to keep his body erect. It would provide excellent exercise and— Rodeina forced those thoughts from her mind. She reached into her jumpsuit and withdrew a dog biscuit with the consistency of hard putty, which helped greatly to reduce the crumbs that would float about after the dog ground up the biscuit in his powerful jaws. Rodeina held the treat before Brutus, studying him carefully to see his reaction. For a while the dog only stared; then she saw the interest quicken in his gaze. She decided to wait just a few moments more until instinct brought him leaning slightly forward for the biscuit.

"One thing I just don't understand," Sean Talbot complained. "This stuff about weightlessness. Sometimes they call it that and sometimes they call it zero gravity and—"

"Sure, and they also call it free fall," Bob Downey broke in. "It's all the same, you know."

"Maybe to *you*," Talbot said testily. "Not to me, though. *I* think they're crazy, that's what. All this talk about mass and—look here," he said, trying very hard to sound serious, "do you remember we tried to move that big crate before? The one that had this treadmill? It's supposed to be weightless, right?" The three youths with him nodded. "Well, then why was it so bloody hard to move!"

"Because it has mass," Bob Downey told him.

"I know that!" Talbot shouted. "But I don't *understand* it!"

"It's weightless when you don't try to move it."

"That doesn't make sense."

"It does, too. It has weight only when you try to move it. Then it resists being moved. That's what we feel as weight. That resistance. Gee, all the kids in my class knew *that*."

"Well, I didn't go to *your* class, and you know what you—"

Abdullah was listening with rapt attention. "What is this free fall, then?"

"Huh? Oh. Well, it's us falling around the world," Downey replied. "You understand that, don't you?"

"I think so. I guess so," the Arab youth said quickly. "But why are we not feeling weight?"

"Because nothing resists our fall. We're falling *freely*. No resistance, no weight. See?"

"Okay , smartass," Talbot broke in, "then how come a skydiver *feels* his own weight? He's falling freely!"

Downey looked about him, uncomfortable. Rodeina smiled at him and he felt better. She'd already asked him these same questions. Bob Downey looked at Abdullah and then to Talbot. "Well, not really. I mean, he falls at over a hundred miles an hour and the air piles up in front it him. It's like invisible snow. It slows him down."

"I have never seen snow," Abdullah said.

"Well, *I* have," Sean Talbot said quickly, grateful to be one up on *somebody*. "I don't see how snow and air can be the same."

"So's water," Bob told him. "But it's heavier than air or snow, so it slows you down quicker. Don't you see? Any time something resists your movement, there's resistance to falling. Then you feel like you weigh something."

Sean Talbot screwed up his face. "How come when I was sitting on a chair at home I didn't just float away? Like I do up here?"

"The world drags you down. That's gravity, right?"

Sean nodded cautiously. "All right."

"What happens if someone jerks the chair out from under you?" Rodeina had finally gotten into the act.

"Well, if it happens right away, you . . ."

"Fall down," Bob said triumphantly.

"I get it!" Abdullah shouted. "Then you hit the floor and bang!"

"You stop, right?" Bob said. "Well, the faster you're going when you stop . . ."

Peter Nicholson stared at the television monitor with both hands hard under his chin, watching the youngsters work their dog and engage in their testy conversation about weight and mass and gravity. He banged his fist against the table, a sudden motion of triumph. The reaction lifted him from his seat and he lofted upward, grabbing for a handhold. Nicole Evans reached laughingly for him and dragged him back down again. Nicholson nodded to the dark-haired woman. He still didn't feel *that* comfortable in the presence of these superwomen who had trained for and been accepted as astronauts and cosmonauts. Nicholson had carried himself extremely well through his university years, but he knew that when it came to full performance in academics he didn't hold a candle to this crowd. How a woman who was shapely and beautiful could also be so skilled and capable remained a mystery to him. He knew he suffered from the childhood rearing of men who dominated their women, not from superior intellect or ability but through physical overbearing and economic control, and he hated himself for his own shortcomings—but damn it, it was marvelous to be beautiful and shapely and witty and talented, but did they have to be so incredibly *beyond* that?

Nicole Evans' voice brought him out of his sudden funk. "Peter, I do believe you're about to score a singular triumph with these children," she said, a smile on her dark features, beautiful high cheekbones, the hollow of her throat— *Stop it!* he yelled at himself. God, it was a bitch *being in love* with one of these— He forced himself back to the moment.

"I hope so," he said, wanting full vindication of his concepts but not yet daring to accept what was happening. "It's amazing. That boy, Downey, is only twelve years old, but his harness system and those bungees are as good as anything *we've* managed to come up with. There they are, yattering away about gravity and acceleration and mass and all that, not realizing how bloody marvelous they are, and that dog is salivating— Just a short time ago that dog was ready to *die*. He couldn't understand the helplessness of being unable to plant his legs solidly, his stomach was trying to turn itself inside out, he was dizzy—and in just a short time those youngsters rigged him up to where he at least *senses*

455

things are better, he's not floating about like a helium balloon. He feels secure with the children, especially Rodeina, and she's instinctively using a combination of Pavlovian response and the old carrot-before-the-cart trick by dangling a tempting biscuit before the animal. Now, if they can just—"

He stopped his conversation, his hand gripping that of Nicole, who looked at him with surprise and then a smile, because Peter Nicholson was glued to the monitor, rooting as hard as he could for those kids.

"All right, Brutus, *come!*" Rodeina prompted her dog. The animal lunged forward, extending the bungees. Immediately his forelegs slipped out beneath him, he stumbled, got his balance and moved his legs forward again. Rodeina held the biscuit within reach and Brutus gulped eagerly. He seemed to be coming to excited life before their eyes. "Come on, Brutus!" Rodeina shouted with laughter and held another biscuit before the dog, who again lunged, slipped, found his footing, *and began to run.* A counter clicked quickly past twenty miles an hour as measured by the rearward motion of the treadmill.

"It works!" young Bob Downey shouted, and threw his arms about Rodeina, who hugged him back and still managed to toss the biscuit to the dog. Sean and Abdullah jumped up with glee, expecting to come down as they always had but finding themselves floating toward the overhead, limbs flailing. Where only a short time before they would have been alarmed and frightened, now they grasped for one another and laughed.

"Watch this," Peter Nicholson said in a hoarse whisper to Nicole Evans. "If this is working out the way we hoped . . ."

The boy and girl with their feet still velcroed to the decking released one another. Each reached to his belt and unhooked a tube which they held up with arms extended, aiming at the two boys floating above them. Rodeina and Bob pressed down on spring triggers, and nylon line shot upward toward Sean and Abdullah. They reached out casually for the lines and pulled themselves back down.

Peter Nicholson was beside himself with joy. "They've done it!" he shouted to Nicole. "Full adaptation! They reacted by instinct . . . they're . . . they're . . ." His eyes widened.

"They're the first space children," Nicole Evans finished for him. He hugged her fiercely and as quickly pushed her to arm's length. "*Listen* . . ."

". . . and we can use the treadmill, you know, with an inertial gear, to turn generators and shoot electrical charges into storage batteries," Bob Downey was saying. "We had a rig like this at home. Dad used to teach us how to get energy from just about everything we did. So we'd run up the stairs, but when we came down we stepped on this platform that dropped alongside a pole, like they have in the firehouses, and when we came down it pulled a counterweight in the other direction, and that had a cable that turned a generator and charged batteries, and we used that to power systems in the house, and the electric company had a special kind of meter that recorded how much juice we produced ourselves in the house and we didn't have to pay that to the company, but Dad, he paid *us* instead and—" He gasped for breath and they were all grinning wide at one another.

"And it's exercise!" Rodeina rushed after Bob's words. "Not only for the dogs, but the other animals *and for us, too*."

"Is that how we will have a trophy?" Abdullah was confused. "I heard the men talking about a trophy, but it was one that was not good and we would not want it—"

"No, no!" laughed Rodeina. "They meant *atrophy*. Where you lay in bed for days and weeks and like months, and your muscles get soft and weak, they call that atrophy, and you've got to have lots of exercise in weightlessness like we're in now, *or else*."

"Hey!" Sean Talbot waved his hands for attention. "We can train our dogs and we can hold races with the other units! We could have prizes and—" His voice stopped as his face turned a stark white. The white brightened to a painful glare streaming in through a

457

triple-paned, thick circular window, and an instant later a beam of thick, savage whiteness stood out in the cubicle as if a laser beam had snapped into being.

"Oh, my God," Rodeina said, her lips trembling.

"I think," said Abdullah al-Ghanim, "that the sun has exploded."

Vasily Tereshnikov slammed a powerful fist against the master console of *Pegasus'* bridge. "I want a reading now, you blockheads!" he shouted. "*Now!* Not twenty minutes from now, not ten minutes from now. I want it—"

"Sir! *Sir, please!*" Kenneth Stewart, Chief Medical Officer of the spacecraft, tried as best he could to calm Tereshnikov long enough to get in a few words of his own. Finally, arm-waving achieving no results, he yelled louder. "Damn it, we have the readings! *Shut up, for Christ's sake!*"

"Where? What distance? What yield?" The questions snapped out like bullwhip shots from the Russian.

Stewart leaned past Tereshnikov and his fingers danced across the computer keys. The flat screen came silently to glowing life. "There it is, Commander," he said, moving back slightly so as not to block Tereshnikov's view.

"We are fortunate—" the Russian began, then stopped as Marc Seavers came through a hatch like a human torpedo. Stewart grabbed for him in a tangle of arms, and Seavers pulled himself around to the seat alongside Tereshnikov. They were already a swift team and needed only a minimum of prompting. Tereshnikov knew that Seavers had been on break in his quarters and that the crash alarm had brought him to the bridge as fast as he could maneuver. If he had seen that light—and it had been visible almost everywhere—then he knew that all hell had either broken loose or was on its edge. So Vasily Tereshnikov didn't wait for questions.

"It is what you think," he said to Seavers. "One nuclear detonation. First indications are fusion. Yield unknown, estimated four hundred kiloton. Distance at time of energy release, one hundred sixty-two miles."

458

"Too far for penetrating radiation effects," Seavers said quickly. "We take any damage?"

Tereshnikov shook his head. "None known yet. The thermal alarms triggered from the flash. No damage reported."

Seavers turned to the medical officer. "Ken?"

"Some temporary blindness is the best I can tell you right now. People outside with their visors up. Some looking through ports. At this distance they'll stay without vision anywhere from hours to days, but I've heard of nothing that won't recede on its own."

"Radiation cloud?"

Ken Stewart made certain not to shake *his* head. He couldn't handle zero g like the Russian. "If there is any, it's far enough away not to be a problem. Besides, the difference in orbital velocity will take it from us."

"How about *Noah*?"

"I spoke with de la Madrid," Tereshnikov said. "He had the con." The Russians, mused Seavers with a grip on his patience, must have seen too many Star Trek movies. They were infatuated with *Enterprise* idioms. "The Chinaman—"

"Dr. Fangkun?"

"Yes, yes, of course! How many Chinamen command that vessel!" Seavers kept his silence; he had placed Zheng Fangkun in lead authority only yesterday. "*Your* Chinaman," Tereshnikov said with a touch of exasperation, "is off the bridge. So is the Brazilian. So I spoke with de la Madrid," he repeated. "They report no injuries or damage."

Tereshnikov turned his seat to study Seavers. All traces of competition were gone from the Russian's face, replaced with the intensity Seavers had come to expect from his counterpart. "Tell me, Marc Seavers. That warhead, which most assuredly it is at this height, was aimed at us, was it not."

Statement. Not a question.

"That's my judgment. From what little I know."

"But . . . but you, we, were warned. You spoke with Firebrand—"

"Joe Briand, yes."

459

"And he spoke of the fanatical groups, and so did the Chinaman."

"Are you trying to get around to the subject of an ABM intercept?"

"Yes."

"If it was one of ours, Vasily, I'm damned grateful for it. If it was one of *yours*, I'm just as grateful. But I don't—"

"*Bridge, Camblin here. Priority override, please.*" Seavers and Tereshnikov exchanged glances and Seavers nodded. Vasily "had the con." He was running the ship.

"Tereshnikov here, Camblin. Go ahead." Gene Camblin was their Flight Dynamics Officer.

"Yes, sir. I've been running radar sweeps. We've got company on all quadrants."

"What the hell—" Seavers checked himself; it was Vasily's command.

"What do you mean by company, Camblin? Stop with the mystery games!"

"Sir, no games. We have radar targets in a wide circle around both us and *Noah*. They are matching our orbital parameters, thrusting when they need to in order to stay in position. I've also been running a spectrum sweep, and from what I can pick up they seem to be *manned*."

"That is crazy!" Tereshnikov said loudly.

"It sure is, sir," Camblin said.

Marc Seavers grabbed a headset and mike. "Gene, Seavers here. Are you getting voice transmissions?"

"It's tough getting anything clean, Admiral, but that seems to be the story. It sure does sound like they're talking to ground."

"Camblin, tell me," Tereshnikov broke in. "How many ships?"

"Six, sir."

"All six are talking?" Tereshnikov was incredulous.

"That's the size of it, sir."

"What language, Gene?" Seavers asked.

"Hold on to your hat, Admiral. They're talking computer."

Seavers stared at Tereshnikov. "Six manned ships talking computer," he echoed. "Vasily, you got any real swift answers?"

"Sure. Is bad dream."

21

"Yeah, those are my boys up there with you. Six of them, and I've got six more standing by to go if we need them." General Joseph Briand's voice warbled and faded in and out several times. That was a bad sign, and everyone on the *Pegasus* bridge, and those on duty aboard *Noah*, understood reality only too well. The sun was throwing off a bitch of a storm. Radiation storms were sweeping across space and tearing up the terrestrial atmosphere, drowning the air ocean in electromagnetic interference. It wasn't predicted to happen this quickly. *Damn!* thought Seavers. *We were supposed to have at least another month . . .* He clamped down on his thoughts and spoke anxiously to Briand.

"What happened with that warhead, Joe?"

"It wasn't a missile, if that's what you mean. The world's going mad, but . . . Anyway, those groups I told you about? The Holy Lights or whatever the hell they call themselves? They took over that launch station we all seem to have forgotten about—the one up in Greenland, way on top of the ice cap. Before everything started coming unglued, they moved a passel of boosters up there. The long and short of it is that this Holy Lights bunch gathered together a mob of engineers and technicians and they went to Greenland with a couple of planeloads full of people and equipment, including some pressurized cockpits and stuff like that. They threw together a real ratshit manned vehicle. A one-man ship *and* a warhead: that's what they sent your way."

Seavers glanced at Tereshnikov; the Russian motioned

for him to go on. "That sounds like a suicide mission, Joe."

"That's just what it was. I guess whoever took the job had some good reason for doing it. The pilot of that thing was aiming for you or the other ship. Didn't much matter to him. Anyway, we knew what was coming down. Barely in time, I admit."

"Are those really manned ships out there with us?"

"You bet your sweet potato, Admiral. They're Needles."

"I don't get it—"

"Ask the Russkies. *They'll* know."

Seavers looked to Tereshnikov. "One-man interceptors. High-energy fuel. The pilots, they are in liquid-filled cockpits to withstand enormous acceleration. They carry very high-velocity missiles for intercept of missiles or satellites."

"Joe, I thought we were about closed down with the launch pads. How did you get these guys up here?"

"Air launch, my friend. That triple-damned Orient Express that Reagan started back in the Eighties really paid off. We put the Needles piggyback on the Express, take 'em up to Mach Nine, and launch at a hundred grand. They scoot right on up to orbit after that."

"Vasily says they're missile-armed."

"They *were*. We stood down their warheads a while back. You know, that last space peace treaty. Damn thing like to gutted us, too."

"Then how did . . ." His voice trailed off.

"I see you understand the program, Admiral. You're right. The pilot closed on the target. The nice name for it is ramming."

Tereshnikov thumbed his transmit button. "General, I would like to express thanks for—"

"Forget it, Russkie. All in a day's work." Briand's tone changed. "Now listen to me, the both of you. We're coming apart at the seams down here. Those Needles pilots consider themselves *all* to be on a one-way mission. Their time up there is *very* limited. No replacements. It's a one-shot deal. We don't know who else is going to take some potshots at you, but anything

462

can happen. You people want my advice, you better start boosting damned soon. Like right *now.*"

"I wish we could. We still have—"

"Hey, don't tell me *your* problems, fella. I got plenty of my own down here. This isn't the world you remember any more, Admiral. You been reading your weather reports? We just went through the fastest goddamn ice age you ever saw. It hardly got started when it reversed itself. You can see the sun, Marc. Look at it again. Look real good, because it's going ape. I don't know what fell into it, but . . ." Static ripped apart his words. They sweated out the screaming static, the cry of demons riding the solar winds around the world.

". . . while you can. I can hardly read your transmissions, Admiral . . . maybe . . . more shot or two from the Cape, but I . . ."

A shrill squeal took over. Tereshnikov slapped the volume control. For a few moments, silence. Then the throb of pumps and the dull rumbling of automatic thrusters came to them. "I want full-time monitoring and recording of any transmissions," Tereshnikov said to his bridge crew.

He turned to Seavers. "This is time for you to make a decision. Now you really *are* admiral, my friend."

"Everybody is on round-the-clock duty," Seavers said without hesitation. "Everybody who's needed or can help is on the propulsion systems. Move whatever shuttles are still offship into their places, *now.* Move everything that's offship, supplies, whatever, back to the main baffle separators between the fuel compartments and the ship. Batten them down with cabling and the cable nets. There's no time to load. These orders stand for *Noah* as well. Have them either harness or net down their animals or sedate them; whatever's necessary to protect them during acceleration. Everybody on the bridge get all that? All right, pass the word."

He stood erect by the master panel. Tereshnikov sensed the moment and unbent his own body. "We boost in forty-eight hours," Seavers announced.

"But . . . that's impossible!" They looked at Betty

463

Haberman, chief of main drive propulsion. "We can't be ready for that, Admiral Seavers!"

"We can, we will, and it's not impossible," Seavers said with disarming quiet. "Pass the word to Ken Bergstresser on *Noah* that Cosmonaut Yevteshenka has prepared the computer programming for *Pegasus* and we'll feed the program to them in time to set it up for boost."

Tanya Yevteshenka moved forward. "The program is not yet ready. I—"

Vasily Tereshnikov looked daggers at her. "Nor will it be ready while you stand here making bleating sounds like a sheep. Everybody to work! Dismissed!"

Seavers insisted he and Tereshnikov take the time for a meal. "We need the energy—we're going to be going without sleep for at least the next two days—and we need this opportunity to talk without any pressure on us," he said. Grumbling, the Russian agreed and they retired to the on-duty mess. They had started to bring their packaged foods to their private table when a determined woman wearing a turban, a jewel in her forehead, and an astronaut's jumpsuit blocked their way. "Go sit," Beatrice Malhotra ordered, her dark eyes flashing.

"You are not commander. *Or* waitress," Tereshnikov growled at her. "So you go do things. We—"

"Take your seat, Commander," she repeated. "I'm the medical officer on duty. It's my job to look after the health of the both of you. Until you have a proper meal *and* your vitamins, you are under *my* orders."

"Do as the lady says, Vasily," Seavers said amiably. "She's right. She's the boss right now."

They watched Beatrice Malhotra preparing hot meals from the microwave, removing cold drinks with squeeze-straws from the cooler. "She is not American," Tereshnikov judged.

"She's Colonel Malhotra of the Space Command of India," Seavers told him. "Six missions before joining us. She's more than a medical officer. A brilliant surgeon. I'm damned glad to have her aboard."

464

"If I have appendix that yell for attention I will call her," Tereshnikov said, nodding. "Your doctor, this Ken Stewart, he is not nearly so pretty."

"Careful, careful," Seavers said mockingly. "Tanya's liable to reach down your throat and pull your appendix out by hand."

"Tanya wants very much for you to marry us."

"What's wrong with that? She's a winner, for certain."

"For certain. I am old-fashioned, Marc, my friend. I feel I should have at least *one* chance to ask *her*." He sighed. "But you are right. When we are under way, Marc, then you will do it? Ah, good," he said in answer to Seaver's smile. He looked about the mess. "Where is Nancy?"

"With the children. There's a lot of frightened kids aboard this tub. Ever since that bomb went off and we secured all the hatches, not being able to see outside has them spooked."

"So give them all hookup on televisions to main ship cameras."

Seavers stared. "I'm an idiot. I never thought of that." He started to leave the table. A powerful Russian hand gripped his wrist. "Children will wait for television. The admiral, he is under his own orders, no? Hot meal! Vitamins! We eat like good children, no?"

Seavers nodded slowly. He stared across the mess. "What is wrong, Marc?"

Seavers pointed. Beatrice Malhotra stood with her feet in the restraints before the microwave range, a tray in each hand, afraid to move. Tiny blue lightning danced between the microwave and her hair, sending it in all directions, making hissing and crackling sounds.

"St. Elmo's Fire," Seavers said quietly. "Static electricity gone crazy."

A loud *snap!* filled the air with the taste of ozone as the sparkling electrical snakes about Malhotra discharged and vanished. She turned, her eyes fearful.

"There'll be more," Seavers told Tereshnikov.

"I know. This is only the beginning. We are quick running out of time, my friend."

* * *

465

"I've never really imagined God as an angry and vengeful creature. But I've begun to think that way." Martha Starling looked grimly at the flickering scenes on their television in their Montana retreat, concealed safely in a blind canyon created by the Army Corps of Engineers a long time before this moment. *And for lesser pursuits than awaiting the end of the world,* she reflected. She looked at the changing pictures of burning cities, mobs trampling people underfoot, train wrecks, ship sinkings, garbage smouldering in streets and alleys, in— She snapped the OFF button.

"That's enough," she said to the president of the United States. "It doesn't do you or me, or those people," she gestured at the set, "a bit of good. You've served your country long and well, George Starling. You've earned for us the right to end our days secluded from all the anxieties you bore for them all these years."

He rolled to his side on the couch. "You don't think I'm copping out, old girl?" He slapped her gently on the thigh. The sound of the love slap was wet. Martha was soaked in perspiration, as was her husband. As was the world.

"No, I don't."

"What does our staff think?"

"Do you care?"

"Only that I hate to have them stuck here with us when they might be with their families. Or doing whatever it is people wish to do in the last gasp of life."

"No need for concern, my darling. They all left yesterday morning. I told them to go. I gave them all the cars and the vans."

"Damn glad you did that. Thanks. *I* should have done it."

"That was *my* job."

"Did they take the plane?"

"Uh-huh."

"That wasn't smart." He looked up through their skylight at a red-tinged, boiling sky. "Christ, think of the thermals! That air will tear their wings right off."

"If I didn't love you so much, and wanted more than

466

anything else to be with you right to the end, George, I'd envy them."

"Don't. All sailors go their own way down to the sea for the last time. They, theirs; we, ours." He looked up at her, grasped her wrist and tugged her gently close to him. "What was that you said about an angry and vengeful creature? Is that how you've come to think of God?"

"It is." She'd set her mouth firmly, he saw, and was grateful for the rush of emotion. It was too damned hot for anything else. "It's as if God was toying with the world, playing with people's fears and terror and dying for the sheer pleasure of it. I'd always read that the God of the ancient Hebrews was a jealous, vindictive, blood-thirsty and essentially, unforgiving deity. Then along came Christianity. Nothing seems to have changed. New role-playing in heaven, I suppose, but that's all. After all we learned and came to fear about the dust cloud, then God cranks down the thermostat and we're all dipped in ice water. We're not going to burn, we're all going to freeze our tootsies off and be frozen into human popsicles for some future race to find. People-brittle on an icicle stick."

She leaned forward as he slowly rubbed her back. "Then it's time for God to play some more of his games. Overnight he dips into his bag of tricks and twists the thermostat the *other* way. Presto! The temperature soars, the sun boils and our rivers and lakes and ponds and streams too, and pretty soon even the oceans, I suppose, start to vaporize. Steamed clams, that's us. God, I hate you, God.

"I'll get us some drinks," she said suddenly, standing, chemise clinging damply to the body he'd held so close all these years.

"Ah, a hot toddy."

"I have a surprise. Buried dry ice. A last package. Two drinks coming up. *Cool.* Maybe the last two cool drinks on Earth."

She returned in several minutes. He couldn't believe the vapor-shrouded glass. "No ice. But cold." She clinked his glass. "To us, my dear, on a bed of scotch, neat."

He smiled at her and drank slowly but without pause, knowing this *was* the last cold drink he would ever have.

Martha looked up. "Do you believe they'll make it?"

He followed her gaze. "Yes," he lied. "They have every chance. Better now than before because of those clouds. Damning to us but a blessing to them. No more missiles will be thrown at them. No one can see through those clouds, and they're so ionized radar can't even punch through them."

No one had seen the sun or the moon or the stars for days. As the temperatures soared, water vapor soaked the air, mixed with dust and industrial debris and the ashes of dozens of blazing cities, burning forests, fires unchecked almost everywhere. The clouds gathered and piled upon one another and formed a terrible canopy across all the world, trapping the heat beneath. The world was swiftly becoming a gigantic pressure cooker.

"I'm glad," she said finally. "Those few children who'll have their chance."

She leaned back against throw pillows. "George, I'm very tired. Will you hold me, please?"

He sat beside her, fluffed up the pillows and leaned a bit higher against the back of the couch so he could rest her in the crook of his arm, her head against his shoulder. He was tired as well. This heat . . . He kissed her gently on the forehead. She was already asleep.

As he was several moments later, deep in the sleep from which they would never awaken, in the sleep Martha had lovingly placed in their drinks so they might have this final sweet moment together.

"This is Twenty-Seven on a blind call. I'm four hundred yards beneath the stern of *Pegasus* and I need at least two more tugs to move this load into the storage area. Anybody free to work with Twenty-Seven? Over."

"Susan, you in Two-Seven? This is Begley in One Three. I've got Fitzpatrick with me and we can be with you in five minutes."

"That's great, Arch. Anybody else on line for Twenty-Seven?"

"Coming at you, Foster. This is Pruett in Number Eight. I'll come up right behind Begley. Arch, confirm you're One Three?"

"On the money, Pru."

"Okay, Foster to Begley and Pruett. We've got a mass of thirty-seven tons earthside. Four containers cabled together and snug. I've computed the delta V components, and three tugs will handle it fine. Cable pull, then run two of them out to each side and behind and the third tug for dead astern cable hookup and full reverse."

"Ah, roger that, Susan," Begley radioed. "You set for computer linkup with One Three?"

"Got it. Open the door, please, One Three."

"All set. Have at it, lady," Begley replied. He had opened his computer uplinks to receive full instructions from Foster's spacetug computer. Pruett did the same. Now all three tugs would operate under the lightning-fast senses and thruster reactions of a single computer rather than everyone trying to integrate three inputs, outputs, and adjustments. Begley, Pruett, and Foster would all be ready on their controls to take over manually.

Fitzpatrick watched it all with admiration for the team and professional fascination in the procedure. The three tugs slid into position along and in front of the cylindrical pallets carrying precious cargo for *Pegasus*. Normally they would have maneuvered the cargo to the forward or central bays. Not now. No more *normals* to work with. Now it was a matter of shoving everything into *Pegasus* and hanging on. There weren't enough storage holds for what had to be loaded. No time. Marc Seavers had made the only right decision. Shove it up against the aft bulkheads. Drape the cargo with steel netting. Sling even more cables around the cargo, and cinch it tight. In effect *Pegasus*—and *Noah* as well— became open-walled warehouses exposed to vacuum. But they didn't need protection in the human sense. Storage in vacuum was quite acceptable as long as the cargo didn't drift off in zero g, or get hurled backward when *Pegasus* lit its fires and thrusted. There would be another critical moment when the engines would be shut down and the ship would go through a fierce rebound, thousands of tons of cargo, the heavy pallets and other storage hurled forward with thrust termination. If the netting and cables failed to hold, huge sharp-edged boulders would hurtle forward into the forward compartments of the giant spacecraft.

Susan Foster worked her reaction thrusters in Two-Seven. All three tugs spat glowing haze behind them as the cables went taut and the cargo pallets began their glide toward the waiting cargo deck. Fitzpatrick watched the closure rate, distance and angular positioning on their computer display readout. The world became only the massive girderwork and perpendicular decks of *Pegasus*. "Coming up on thruster burn in ten seconds," Foster sang out quietly on the radio line. They watched carefully. "All right, three, two, one, burn time, check your delta V increments. Very good. We're in tight enough. Arch, Dick, hold your cabling positions, please. Loadmaster for Deck Nine, you read Foster in Two-Seven?"

"Five by, Susan. The cabler is on his way out right now."

They watched a suited figure gliding toward them, trailing a nylon cable. He stopped by the cargo pallet and ran a hook-and-eye lockbolt through a sling eye on the pallet. He waved as he called in. "All set, Loadmaster. Susan, you on the hold lines?"

"That's affirm. Loadmaster, start reeling in. I'll work the thrusters of the two tugs for you."

"Got it. Reeling in now." Within *Pegasus'* cargo deck a winch began pulling in the cargo pallet. Several times it began to swing around, a heavy mass at the end of a slender line. Susan Foster studied her computer readouts of the angular momentum and unwanted perturbations about the changing axes of the pallet. In the two tugs still attached to the pallet they heard and felt their own thrusters firing in short correcting bursts. "Okay, Susan. Bring the pallet to a stop, please." She worked the controls in her tug, thrusters fired in the others, and the pallet came to a stop, holding orbit drift formation with the mass of the spaceship. A boom telescoped outward from the cargo bay and pressed against the pallet so that it was held rigidly, the outward push from the boom matching the controlled inward pull of the cable. "Release tugs," the Loadmaster called. Begley and Pruett pulled their release controls, fired thrusters gently so as not to disturb the cargo, and drifted back from *Pegasus*. Another thruster twitch, they stopped the driftaway, and watched the pallet gliding in under perfect control of its lock-and-hold position. A heavy metalmesh net slid around the pallet and two cables snaked around the containers.

"That's it, guys," the loadmaster called. "Thank you and kindly get the hell out of the way. I got a bunch right behind you."

Begley turned the tug and they looked out upon a string of other tugs and cargo pallets being moved into position for lockdown aboard the spacecraft. "You know something, Irish?" Begley said quietly. "I think we may just pull off this cockamamie business of loadup. I didn't think it was possible. Seavers must have a crystal ball."

"If he does, then save your sympathy for his young bride," Fitzpatrick said with a straight face.

The lead team stayed on duty around the clock from the moment they lost contact with General Joseph Briand within Cheyenne Mountain. In addition to the many technicians and specialists running computers and life support systems, eight people made up the lead team on *Pegasus*' bridge: Marc Seavers, Zheng Fangkun, Vasily Tereshnikov, Jan Rosen, Tanya Yevteshenka, Betty Haberman, Gene Camblin, and Dieter Schroeder.

These eight ship's officers had real-time audio and video contact with the crew assembled on the bridge of *Noah*. Open microphones that could pick up whispers and amplify every sound formed an almost eerie aural connection between ships. Television scanners covered everyone and all equipment on each bridge and transmitted their scenes to large television monitors. It was a constant crosshatch. When someone from *Pegasus* spoke to *Noah*, the crew on the *Noah* bridge saw and heard the speaker from the other ship.

This was also the first time *Noah* had had a definite chain of command for such communications. Until a short time before no one had assumed, or been granted, absolute position of command. They lacked an unquestioned captain of the ship. They vacillated between ship's captain and mission commander, and suffered a classic problem of "Who's in charge?" Titular choice was acceptable only briefly; final decision was critical.

Marc Seavers and Vasily Tereshnikov had begun the selection process, then brought in Zheng Fangkun to arbitrate any deadlock. "Why do you not ask Chiang Biao? Why is it you select me for this most delicate of tasks?" Fangkun asked.

"Dr. Biao has withdrawn from the procedure," Seavers explained. "He told us that, as the representative of the greatest number of people from Earth, it would be inappropriate for him to exercise what must be a dominant position aboard *Noah*."

Zheng Fangkun smiled. "And it is any less inappropriate for me?" He saw their unease and added quickly, "I notice you do not include Dr. Gregory Tretyakovich. He is a most brilliant—"

"You know better than that," Tereshnikov broke in. "*Two* Russians making decisions? No; it would go down like vodka and strawberry pop. A very wrong move. Besides," he added, his face showing the edges of a smile, "the people of *Noah* have already asked for Tretsky as a coordinator between the two ships."

"Then I offer a suggestion," Fangkun said softly.

"Please," Seavers said.

"*They* must decide. Who is titular head?"

"First exec," Seavers told him, "is Benita de la Madrid from Mexico."

"And time runs away while they feel they cannot decide?"

"Exactly," Tereshnikov said.

"Time is everything to us," Fangkun went on. "A proper decision will never be made, otherwise they would have made it. Take their seven leaders. It must

472

be seven for the odd vote. Have them write names on paper and these to be placed within a jar, a box, a—"

"Ballot," Seavers offered.

"Yes. They vote one time and one time only for the vessel commander. *He* selects. Indecision ends."

Twenty minutes later General Mario Silva appeared on the television screens of *Pegasus*. "These people are fools," he said to open the contact. "They have voted me to be their *commandante*. I am a general of the Portuguese Air Force. I am *not* a politician. They would be far better with—"

"You are no longer a general," Seavers said quickly to break the logic Silva was establishing. "As of the moment the votes were cast, you became the Commander of *Noah*. Now, tell me your lead staff."

Silva blinked several times. Seavers well understood why they had selected this man of such quiet but enormous strength. He had moved Portugal through the labyrinths of NATO in a most extraordinary fashion. A nation suffering economic woes, its greater glory in its past, had been maneuvered skillfully into a position of voting equality within the highest power structure of Europe. General he might be, but he was also a pilot, a master diplomat, and a brilliant engineer whose skills would be sorely tested in the months to come. They watched the change come over Silva as he judged his own thoughts and the expressed wishes of those aboard *Noah*. He glanced at a paper before him and never referred to it again; he had already committed his command establishment to memory.

"Standby commander is Pablo Martinez, Mexico. Our First Executive Officer is Benita de la Madrid, also Mexico. Both are highly experienced in logistics and engineering. Ron McKenzie, Australia, second exec. Willy Henson, United States, third exec. Chief Engineer is Hans Dornier, Germany: he has been the lead engineer of the European space community. Flight Dynamics is Helen Chandler, U.S. Two Maintenance Chiefs: Flip Paxton, U.S., and Jaime Ogpin, Philippines. Shall I continue with the full list, Admiral?"

"If you please, just the immediate operational staff

for spacecraft operations," Seavers replied. "We'll get onboard lead personnel later."

"As you wish, sir. Ken Bergstresser, Canada, is chief of main drive propulsion systems. Flight dynamics is Carol Shaw, U.S. Computers under Duane Chen, U.S. And, um, we then have Henri Dufour, France, and Boris Mikhailov, U.S.S.R., for the spacetugs and the shuttles. That is the list, Admiral Seavers."

"Thank you, Commander Silva." Seavers turned and nodded to Vasily Tereshnikov. The Russian leaned forward to address the group aboard *Pegasus* and gave full attention as well to the TV cameras carrying his audvideo to *Noah*.

"Mario Silva, is your vessel prepared for boost on our command?" Seavers groaned inwardly. Vasily had jumped with both big feet squarely onto Silva's chest and, almost as much physically as figuratively, had knocked the breath from the man. But then, Seavers told himself, there wasn't any time left for the niceties of breaking a man into his new command. They were moving swiftly to a do-or-die threshold.

But Mario Silva came back immediately. "It is not possible, General, to answer your question since you fail to tell me *when* you are ready for boost."

"Nine hours twenty-four minutes," Tereshnikov glanced at a digital counter nearby, "fifty-six seconds and counting. Ignition at zero count."

"*Nine—!*" Silva's eyes went wide. They heard gasps and exclamations behind him from *Noah*'s bridge. Silva glanced offscreen at someone not identified. He nodded, looked at the video picture before him of Tereshnikov, spoke as if the man were seated across from him. "My flight dynamics crew informs me we require at least twenty hours until—"

"Then you will be left behind." Tereshnikov was as warm as a block of stone. But he wasn't icy. All professional, not cold or antagonistic. "Do you understand, Commander Silva? The choice of timing is not mine, nor that of the computer. It comes from the grinding wheels of celestial mechanics, my friend. In less than nine and a half hours, this ship will fire its engines and we begin the burn to take us out of orbit and translate. There is no other way. Since *Noah* will uplink to our computers for its firing commands, I suggest you ignore everything but preparations for that moment."

As if an omen had been hurled into their midst, at that exact moment the lexitr shields looking out to space from the *Noah* bridge glowed blue-white. Heads turned, and emerald fountains of crackling, hissing fire raced along the nose of the enormous ship and forward to the great booms installed to form an electromagnetic tunnel through the thickening dust. The braided ropes of fire swelled and collapsed within one another, and an eerie ghostlike glow sped ahead of the huge spaceship. Suddenly, like some great generator, the booms stabbing forward hosted an eruption of blue and red spasms of electrical fire, and there was a dazzling flash as *Noah* discharged the tremendous static overload. On *Noah's* bridge the smell of ozone permeated crew and machinery alike.

Commander Mario Silva turned from staring through the forward shields and nodded to Tereshnikov. "General, I will be the first to say you have a most persuasive argument. While we were occupied, my crew has matched countdown timers. We will be ready. Our preparations up to this point do not matter. *We will be ready,*" he stressed, more for his own bridge crew than for Tereshnikov or Seavers. "I, for one, have no desire to die with those poor souls imprisoned on what remains of our world. If there is nothing else, I would appreciate having our bridge crews coordinate operations."

"Thank you, Commander," Tereshnikov said. "This meeting ends now. From this point on our two bridge crews operate as a single unit." Tereshnikov turned to Seavers. "Admiral, anything—"

Seavers surprised him. He paid no attention to the courtesy of command shift offered by Tereshnikov. Instead he glared with unconcealed anger at Logistics Officer Janette Rosen. Tereshnikov floated closer to the exchange. ". . . the hell authorized such an insane move! Goddamn it, you're in charge of logistics. You *must* have known what they were planning! And where the hell is Pruett?"

Janette Rosen bit her lip. "A-Admiral, none of us knew." She was trying desperately to screw up her courage in the face of raw anger. "M-Mister Pruett . . . sir, he's with Cosmonaut Tanya Yevteshenka. They've been trying to talk them out of it, and—"

"Marc!" Tereshnikov insisted.

Seavers half-turned. "Damn dumb son of a bitch," he growled. "It's that crazy bastard Fitzpatrick. He's on *Gagarin*."

Tereshnikov's eyes widened. "He is *where?*"

"You heard me, Vasily. On that damned space station."

"But we abandoned *Gagarin* days ago. Stripped her of everything we might need aboard this ship and—" He stopped and studied Astronaut Rosen. "Woman, tell me. Who is with Fitzpatrick?"

"Cosmonaut-Scientist Boris Mikhailov—"

Tereshnikov groaned. "I should have known. If ever a Russian should have been a wild Irishman, it is Boris." He looked again at Rosen. "Anyone else?"

"They seem to have some other people with them, sir."

Seavers looked at her in disbelief. "*Seem* to have other people with—" He cut off his own words and went *very* icy. "All right, Rosen. Who's missing from this ship?"

"N-nobody, sir. All personnel are present and accounted for, sir. Except, uh, for Fitzpatrick. Mikhailov belongs on *Noah*."

Seavers looked at Tereshnikov. "Do *you* know what's going on here?"

"No. And if I am correct, we removed *all* communications equipment from the station."

"*Damn*. Wait a moment. If they're on *Gagarin*, they needed a way to get there. One of the tugs. That means we can try a patch through the tug to their suit radios."

"*If* they have them on," Tereshnikov cautioned. "But we shall try."

Twenty minutes later they had radio contact. Seavers had cooled down enough, accepting the possible loss of one of his closest friends, and Tereshnikov was showing typical Russian stoicism, as he accepted that Mikhailov was as crazy as his American companion and could easily die with him. Somehow both Seavers and Tereshnikov knew that both men planned not to return before the insertion burn into what would be the start of the long, looping elliptical orbit away from Earth.

"All right, Fitz, I'll keep it calm," Seavers promised Fitzpatrick. "Now you keep it straight with me. What are you two doing on that station when we're getting set to thrust here? And who else do you have with you?"

"Aha! First things first, laddie. For the record, we've taken possession of this derelict and abandoned vessel, aboard which we now reside. Law of the sea, but you'd know that best of all. I just wanted to be certain you understood, you and that Russian granite block Vasily, that you have absolutely no jurisdiction over me or Boris here, and a fine fellow he is, too. This be a statement for the record-keeping aboard *Pegasus*, unsolicited by anyone save myself and Boris, that neither the captains of *Pegasus* nor *Noah* have any authority over what Boris and I are doing. Now, what else did you ask? Who is with us? A fine question, that."

"Fitz, *get to it!*"

"Of course, of course, lad. Ah, who could we possibly have aboard this sorry derelict of a station as it whizbangs around the Earth? It cannot be anyone from *Pegasus* or *Noah*; I'm certain you have all personnel accounted for—excepting, of course, me and Bolshevik Boris."

Abruptly the tone of impudence faded from Fitzpatrick's voice. "You've all forgotten a few things, it seems to me, Marc. Perhaps that's why you brought me into this whole affair. To *think* of things others are too busy to recognize."

"Fitz, you can't—"

"Don't waste our time with nonsensical objections, *whatever* they might be, lad. Be quiet and listen to me. Is Vasily listening? What you forgot are the pilots of those six Needles. You see, Marc, they can't go back to

Earth. There's thick cloud cover everywhere, the winds are gusting well over a hundred knots almost everywhere, and most of the computer tracking and guidance stations are shut down and the airfields scoured clean. *So they're up here to die*. And letting good men die without purpose, or at least a fighting chance, isn't my way of doing things. Or yours, or Vasily's, for that matter."

"Jesus, have them rendezvous with *Pegasus*! We can transfer what fuel they have left and—"

"Ah, that's piddling away an opportunity on which we all agreed. Give the credit to Boris, in truth. Both *Pegasus* and *Noah* are short of materials for finishing off a lot of work. You're boosting in a few hours. You're leaving with ships not much more than half done. Boris suggested, and I agreed, that if there was *any* chance of giving you a great big bonus to get this expedition better on its way, we should take it."

They heard him take a deep breath. "So! We've managed to bring five of the Needles into rendezvous with *Gagarin*. I wish it could have been six, but we lost one man. His engine exploded on ignition the last time. Lights out very quick that way. But to bring it all down to the nub of things, the pilots, along with Boris, have been lashing up the Needles against the *Gagarin* main structure. We'll be calling in directly—who does the computations? It's Yevteshenka, isn't it?—to feed the main computer left here when they stripped this place. We'll wait until you people boost and when you're on the other side of the planet, we'll fire—"

"You are idiot!" Tereshnikov shouted into his microphone. "Boris Mikhailov is bigger and dumber idiot! Structure of *Gagarin* could never take acceleration of five such rockets! Station was never made for more than minor low-thrust attitude and height changes. Whole place will smash down around your ears!"

"Maybe, maybe not, Vasily," Fitzpatrick came back smoothly. "It doesn't matter what you say, bucko. We're going to try to boost this whole station into a formation flight with you. These Needles have a hell of a bang to them. Lots of power. There's no question there's enough juice to boost the station along with your own velocity. We won't fire all five at the same time. I agree that's a wee bit too much for this tin castle we're in. We'll fire one to burnout, then two, and finally two more. If we're not aligned properly when we shut down, why, you've got all them lovely tugs to nudge this station where it belongs. Think of it, gentlemen. All this structure to use for your two ships. Now, we are running out of time. If you'd like to give us a chance to live a bit longer with you, then kindly get to hell off this line and patch us into the main computer."

Seavers exchanged a long glance with Tereshnikov. The Russian sighed, then shrugged. "All right, Fitz," Seavers told him. "We'll do it your way. We'll patch you in."

"A commendable decision, lad."

"Fitz, before you go."

"Yes, bucko?"

"You idiot . . . thanks."

"Good luck, laddie. Keep your feet dry."

22

The hammer came down on Earth with mind-numbing suddenness. A pall of dust ninety-three million miles thick between Earth and sun dimmed solar radiations by a fraction of their normal strength, but the world of man exists on a delicate balance. The fractional temperature drop was sufficient to tilt the world thermostat downward and to squeeze savage cold southbound from the Arctic. Similar cold spilled northward from the refrigerator at the bottom of the world. The successive waves of bitter cold were short-lived but so turbulent that the temperature variations whipped up screaming gales devastating everything in their path. Winds steadied at better than a hundred miles an hour and gusted frequently to a hundred and sixty, tearing apart everything from isolated farmhouses to the towering monoliths of the larger cities. Millions of people fell before the wicked onslaughts of a winter never before seen on the planet.

Then winter that should not have been was gone, leaving only a memory of cold air swiftly vaporized by the thermal crunch of a belly-swollen sun. Normalcy crumbled along the horizons of the world as sunsets transformed into terrifying deep yellows and then a grisly Halloween orange-red-blood that lasted for hours, the thickening dust extending twilight long after the sun had fallen beyond the horizon. It had become the ultimate haze, stretching all the way from sun to Earth.

Long before now the need for artificial crises had gone. It was no longer possible to avoid the obvious. The Zack Bibles had come and gone; their flicker of glory could not have been sustained for any greater length of time than when they prospered with fat bank accounts of fear and prayer. During the opening panic that swept much of the world, when the mobs still answered the calls of their priests and howled like packs of mad dogs against "the establishment" no matter what the political entity, there had been enough time for the military forces in the United States, under the command of General Harold Eisenberg, to ring most of the launch sites with walls of fire and steel. But only for a woefully short time.

Wallops Island in Virginia was the first to go, its beaches drenched red with blood, its crabs feasting on chunks of human flesh spattered along the ocean line. Then, down the east coast, came the turn of the Cape, the all-encompassing entity of Canaveral and Kennedy. As Hank Marrows and other newsmen noted of those gut-ripping moments, the enraged mobs more than anything else felt betrayed by news of animals being launched into orbit. *Animals! And my kids are being left here to die while they take them goddamn dogs and snakes and sheep* . . . The animals became a blazing ember in the psyches of people who had nothing else at which to strike with true feeling. Betrayed, lost, helpless, and terrified, they threw themselves into the cauldrons throughout America, Russia, China, and anywhere else the rockets rushed into the sky.

Vandenberg Air Force Base in California endured longer than the others, protected by strict military discipline, heavy weaponry, trained defenders, natural protective terrain, and its very isolation. Air force troops sealed off the hills and mountains, blocked access to the sea and managed to keep its boosters flowing from a great underground stockpile of launching vehicles. Yet even here the days were numbered, and the death knell sounded when a determined group of pilots, convinced their families had been abandoned to politically-motivated selection, led not one but four huge airliners, fuel tanks full, in suicide dives into the heart of the launch complex. So died Vandenberg.

Luke Range did not need to endure as long as the rest. Operations there had been escalated to massive intensity once the need came down that it was time to go. As simple as that. Fire the great birds once every hour, more often if needed. The moon beckoned; Russ Corey's people went. It was that simple. The mobs that tried to wreak destruction? *Kill them or die with them*. Rocket flame and buckets of blood gave Godspeed for the lunarbound.

The last ships to knife into orbit from the United States bore upwards not from launch pads, but piggyback on hypersonic airlines: seven spike-nosed Needles flown by men dedicated to their final mission and lofted into the fringes of space by jetliner crews equally as dedicated. Then it was *Shutdown*.

The Russians launched until they ran out of boosters. It was that simple. Every rocket that could lift, from every launch site through the Soviet Union, carried manned and unmanned payloads. Finally there could be no more launches because there was no longer any true guidance. Even the spaceships that could fly on inertial guidance, on dead reckoning, on hope, prayer and to-hell-with-its, could not go, for there was no way to tell *where* to go.

Between Earth and heaven, between launch pad and *Pegasus* orbit, great barrier reefs had sprung up. The winds made launching impossible. The only boosters that could break from the surface were solid-propellant rockets that lunged fearfully from their launch pads, each with so great an acceleration that the g-forces would have killed anyone committed to such flight. Unmanned ships might have flown against such wild winds, but high above Earth where the jetstream raced, the winds were flung by uprising thermals and clashing fronts to five and six hundred miles an hour. Where man had defeated gravity, he now found old enemies waiting: the same winds that for centuries had destroyed his ships, now tortured with electricity that flashed and danced in the heights above Earth. Air thickened with water vapor and dust, soaked with massive clouds; thunderstorms rose on thick columns like hydrogen bombs above the atmosphere. And the miles-thick mantle soaked up and made a shambles of electromagnetic transmissions. Except for his most powerful search radar, the gods had blinded man. Through the entire spectrum he could no longer see. Blinded rockets do not fly well through multiple gauntlets of destruction.

The last manned ships to leave were the seven Needles that formed a thin but effective cloak about *Pegasus* and *Noah*; they and the single manned suicide mission that sprang spaceward from the Greenland ice cap. There were no more; there would be no more.

Seven hundred miles high, the men, women and children of *Pegasus*, *Noah*, and *Gagarin* fell around a world that had become a sister globe to Venus—shrouded in impenetrable clouds. The clock raced backward aboard the three ships, and Marc Seavers spoke to Vasily Tereshnikov, by audvideo hookup to Mario Silva, and by radio line to Boris Mikhailov: "Notify all hands to remain on station. We are one hour from ignition. All computers uplink to *Pegasus*. Gentlemen, you are now in direct command of your ships."

There was, essentially, silence. Men and women called out the needs of the countdown. No cheering, no jubilation, only a feeling of blind commitment to an unknown future; and great sadness for the world enduring a violent death far below.

The ultimate heat wave responded to the spasms of the sun. Temperatures soared to one hundred and forty degrees in midcentral America and Europe through the corresponding latitudes in Asia and the Orient. They seemed to rise with every hour. Soon Canada and its global neighbors that had for so long known bitter cold began to come apart under the onslaught of one hundred and twenty degrees, and then a hundred and sixty degrees. The calamitous winds gave no relief as they transformed the crushing heat to hurricanes that blew from a planetwide blast furnace. Millions died quickly; tens of millions fell every hour. Human life and almost all animal life vanished from the equatorial zones almost immediately, and as the temperatures continued to rise, an invisible wall of death moved north and south. Pockets of survival existed briefly in underground shelters and high mountain redoubts, but with temperatures soaring swiftly to two hundred degrees, death could hardly be kept waiting by sealed doors. Water supplies evaporated. Streams, lakes, rivers, reservoirs steamed and churned and began to vanish. Fields and forests shriveled and then began to burn wildly before the winds no one had ever known before and in the face of which any hope of survival flickered to incandescence.

The vast killing raged.

The glaciers and snow fields of the Arctic and Antarctic yielded to the blowtorch of cyclone-fed heat. With a terrible irony in a world where water was the most precious commodity, the oceans began to rise with relentless speed. Former tides became great curling walls of devastation, inundating shorelines and roaring inland. Where civilization had built its great coastal cities now swirled angry, hissing, debris-spattered oily liquid. Millions of square miles vanished with each thundering encroachment. All of Florida and much of the southeast, the great basins of the Gulf of Mexico that made up the scimitar underbelly of America, vanished. The island chains of the Caribbean and the

South Atlantic, the lowlands of Europe and Africa and the Mediterranean all yielded without resistance to the rising waters. The Strait of Gibralter, and all such narrowed passageways, turned into horrendous tunnels of water under enormous pressure, water boiling and steaming and as powerful as steel ramrods.

A madness fell upon the Earth. The most terrible punishments of all the gods of all the world's religions paled to puny weight before the great storms that rose and carried with them everywhere the thundering hooves of the Four Horsemen—and worse. The balance of water vapor and heat, of moisture and winds, shattered forever; the air oceans of the planet became a charnel house of fury. Cyclonic storms hurled before them winds of three and four hundred miles an hour. Survival became a grisly joke. The anicent prophesy of the living envying the dead became insufferably true. Across an entire world the air shook with ceaseless blasts of lightning and an endless cannonade of thunder. So great were the storms, tearing away coastlines and inundating the higher lands, that natural geologic faults were strained to their limits and then beyond. Earthquakes rattled and pounded the continents and tore open volcanic vents to bring on eruptions not known since the formative days of the planet billions of years past. Vesuvius and St. Helens and Krakatoa a thousand times more violent sundered the world, and Time raced backwards to match the fury of upthrusting continents when Earth was still cooling from its creation.

Supercharged with electromagnetic forces, a vast global generator of electrostatic energies, the dense planet began to cast off the burgeoning electrical fury flickering across its tortured landscape. Lightning flashed between the wracked surface and the high clouds. Thunderstorms cast down naked bolts of energy that made a hollow mockery of any hammer of Thor. One form of energy compounded another, fed upon each other. The dust through which the planet swirled was like that in a sawmill which has been stabbed with a burst of electricity; it has nowhere to go but to explode.

Thus did the energy contained in the violent high

storms. Lightning bolts no longer shot to Earth or traveled from cloud to cloud or even reached upward from the surface. Now they exploded, erupted, and flung themselves upward as enormous rivers of pure electrical fire, tearing into the stratosphere and climbing ever higher. The thick cloud mantle covering Earth sparked, and then enormous forked tongues racing for hundreds of miles with the blue-white lash of energy run amuck. They ran higher and higher until they were above all the clouds and near to space itself. They sought natural outlets for their fury—and there were still some heavy satellites remaining in low Earth orbit, dustblasted and lifeless but providing a natural beacon to the energies far below searching for release.

Lightning forked upward a hundred and two hundred miles, exploding silently but with mind-numbing fury, churning the electrical atmosphere into planet-girdling aurora. In their last hours chained to the orbital bonds of Earth, the on-duty crews of the two great spaceships and the once-abandoned Russian station looked down in disbelief as satellites far below, invisible to the eye, beckoned as receptors to the blindly searching rivers of lightning and then exploded with the fury of contact.

Long since gone were the many programs, those valiant and desperate efforts to create survival refuge on and within the earth itself. The enormous submersibles of Dr. Toshio Saito, magnificient spherical vessels of thick walls and multiple levels and nuclear power, survived longer than any other refuge, but not without a terrible penalty. Above them surface ships cracked open like brittle eggshells before the winds that turned spray into explosive pistons. Mountain strongholds endured the worst of the early storms, ensconced as they were within granite fastness, riding out the shock waves on enormous coiled springs and hydraulic shock absorbers, sealed against weather and wind, drawing sustenance from great supplies of food, water, air, and energy. But only for a little while. Against the sliding of granite walls, the cracking open of the planet, the crumbling of mountains, the savagery of volcanic pustules torn open to erupt fire . . . against this fury there were only screams heard no farther than the cracking walls, and then only for the briefest of moments.

That left only the submarines and the deep ocean habitats. Those secured to the ocean bottom soon realized that futility as the great mountain ridges within the oceans tore apart, exposing volcanic vents into which cold water poured, there to meet fury erupting upward from beneath the crust of the world. Fire and water, steam and explosive fury, shock waves that vibrated water to steam . . . and crushed the last anchored cities of man.

Saito's dreams of survival took the shock waves well enough, but only in the structural sense, and then for a pitifully brief time. Pressure lines twisted and writhed like wounded snakes and, finally, buckled, pouring radioactive steam through living and working quarters. The hammerlike blows hurled humans about like so many soggy, leaking dolls, breaking limbs and burning flesh. Long before the thick walls of the floating cities yielded to relentless pressure, the last men and women of Earth were no more.

All such events had not yet come to pass when the people of *Pegasus* and *Noah* girded themselves for the final moments of waiting. They heard the intoned countdowns of their great lifeboats through speakers in every compartment and cubicle. It might yet be weeks before Earth would truly be an uninhabited planet, but all that was only a matter of time, and an event that would never be seen by those who had fled to a vacuum plateau seven hundred miles high.

And where time mattered, none was left for the lifeboats. Time shriveled away in the heat gutting the Earth and in the crackling roar of stupendous lightning bolts reaching for the last free survivors of the world.

Pegasus counted one thousand four hundred and eighty-nine men, women, and children within its great rounded flanks, as many of that number as possible separated within sealed cubicles and compartments. Half this number had risen from the United States and the Soviet Union, the others from as many parts of the world as could be safely dispatched to the vacuum plateau. Of that number nearly seven hundred were young children. Aboard *Noah*, stuffed with its animals and its flora and soil and "the good things of life," another four hundred humans shared the capacious lifeboat with perhaps a thousand animals, plus birds and the insects so necessary to life. There were aquatic animals and there were fish, the latter kept alive at this stage of flight only precariously, in huge tanks with constant aeration, with nutrients provided under great air pressure to keep the water from becoming bubbles and froth in weightlessness. In some tanks only fish and sea flora were to be found. In others, where the air barrier and enriched oxygen was especially critical, were the surviving mammals of Earth's oceans, small porpoise and seals, walrus and orcas, all now kept alive by the tenuous threads of technical ingenuity stretched to its limit.

Of the four hundred humans within *Noah*, ninety-two men and women comprised the crew of the great vessel. After shutdown of the huge stern engines in readiness for "escape flight," those engines would not again be fired for . . . *No one knew for how long, but if they were fired again as intended it would be at the end of the looping elliptical swing back to Earth and a roaring blast of engine flame to decelerate back into orbit about the home planet. If, if, if . . .* If the *ifs* worked no further than thrusting *away* from Earth, successfully, the duties of that crew would be consumed almost entirely in maintenance, upkeep, and repair for the other three hundred and eight human beings and all the animals. *All* would become keepers of the menagerie, the first space-dwelling farmers, working to keep alive human, fauna, and flora for some future return to Earth, *if* . . .

Aboard both lifecraft all crew members slipped into pressure suits with backpack life-support systems. Disaster teams stood by their stations ready to conduct rescue missions within the vessels each as large as a small town: close off pressure breaches, extinguish fires; whatever might be undone must be repaired *immedi-*

ately. As many children as could be accommodated were also ordered and helped into survival suits, cumbersome affairs that lacked the technical niceties of the fully adaptive outfits worn by the experienced spacefarers and crew, but just as capable of keeping alive their occupants if ship systems shut down temporarily.

No one knew beyond generalities what would be the effect of engine ignition on the huge lifeboats. There was always the looming spectre of immediate disaster in the form of engine failure or exploding fuel tanks. No one really harbored those nightmares. Engine systems reliability was far beyond the Eighties. *Pegasus* and *Noah* would thrust on storable fuels from which wicked instabilities had been removed. No supercold fuels under huge pressures, no lines taxed beyond their limits to burst, and the whole system designed from the outset to ignite and thrust at only sixty percent of rated power, and to continue normal operations despite any engine-out emergencies.

But the structural integrity of both vessels had far from a clean bill of health. Neither ship had ever been under acceleration. Were there faults in construction, assembly, fabrication—*what?* Where? How? In what manner? There comes the time when you face all the questions that cannot be answered, but make certain the questioners know they're prepared to counter what cannot yet be identified in the failure mode, and then you get on with the tasks at hand. *Period.*

A spaceship that has never gone through ignition and thrust is unborn. A hundred television scanners throughout *Pegasus* and *Noah* could be trained on any area of the two vessels. They would record its moments of birth and its first squalling cry tinged with the violent fire of first motions of life.

Aboard *Gagarin*, painfully aware of the fragile structure of the Russian station, Hugh Fitzpatrick and Boris Mikhailov checked their pressure suits and those of the five Needles pilots. The American pilots each returned to his respective craft, sealed in, and monitored the countdown. They would be ready for manual override of their propulsion systems "if all things proved not to be equal."

Marc Seavers placed the homebuilt hourglass on the control display panel before Vasily Tereshnikov. The Russian eyed the strange contraption and looked up at Seavers. "Is bomb, maybe? Strange people are known to fly these days."

"It's an anachronism, Vasily."

This time the Russian chose silence and raised eyebrows.

"It's an hourglass. I started it at T minus sixty minutes. You can see that it's thirty minutes since I activated it." They looked at the hourglass rotating steadily. "You might say," Seavers went on, "that in here we've captured a sliver of gravity. It spins by battery power. The wheel is attached to the inner boom so that where the hourglass is located at the inner rim, centrifugal force gives us exactly one g." Tereshnikov watched the sand thrown by rotational force through its narrow opening. "When all the sand from the core is in the glass at the rim our engines will fire." He placed a hand on Tereshnikov's shoulder. "The gods willing, we'll be safely on our way." He withdrew his hand, the whole moment earning him a studied look from Tereshnikov. "Twenty-eight minutes, Vasily. I'm leaving the flight deck now. With your permission, of course."

"And where do you go, Marc Seavers?"

"To join my wife. She's in compartment Thirty-One. She has twenty or thirty teenagers under her care. I'm going to join her." Seavers looked about him. "You see, Vasily, this is the toughest part of being mission commander. Admiral or no admiral, my friend, at this moment I'm dead weight up here. You're the captain of this ship and Silva runs his vessel, and all I can do when you're maneuvering is get in your way. I will be with Nancy and the children until our engines shut down. Then I'll return. Until then—" He snapped a salute to Vasily Tereshnikov and the flight deck crew, turned on the velcro pads beneath him, and floated smoothly from the control deck.

He was right, he realized as he swallowed the hard lump in his throat. This was the toughest part of this job.

He pushed his way down the tunnel to the suit room, slipped into his emergency pressure garment, opened the flow valves, checked the gauges, then went through the triple airlock doors. Five minutes later he slipped into Compartment Thirty-One and knew he'd done the right thing. Nancy's smile of gratitude for his presence, and the expressions on the faces of the youngsters, answered any questions about his decision to come here. The only younger children, he noticed, were his own. His and Nancy's. Tom and Keesha, as close to their new mother as they could get.

He studied the compartment. Nancy had placed the children in restraints against the aft bulkhead. Right now they were weightless and walls were floors and floors were the ceiling or whatever you wanted. But when the engines ignited and thrust came to the great vessel, there would be an up and a down and a forward and backward, and the aft bulkhead would become the floor, and they didn't want the kids slamming back suddenly against the hard surface. He noticed that everything loose had been secured, for the instant the engines fired anything that was loose would fly backward as well. But everything was in order and—

"Admiral Seavers?" He turned to look at the girl, pigtails floating to each side. He judged her to be fourteen. She was lovely, and like most of the other children, she was frightened. "Sir, are the engines going to work okay?"

Seavers didn't equivocate. "Absolutely. That's why I decided to come down here and be with you. Everything is going so well on the flight deck they don't even need me there."

Solemn nods, a bit of the wild-animal look in eyes dimming. A hand lifted. He recognized the boy: Josh Batiste. His mother was crew; a doctor. He nodded. "Admiral Seavers, do we really have to leave Earth? I mean, for good?"

"Son, we've got to leave, that's for certain. You all

know what's happened to the world. If we don't leave here and get out into space where there isn't any dust, well, things could get pretty rough for us."

"Are we ever coming back?"

"I'm *planning* on it. Why? Did you have some other place in mind?"

They're smiling . . .

"Do you ever pray, Admiral Seavers?"

"That depends upon how scared I am. And I've been pretty scared in my time, so I guess the answer is yes."

"Are you scared now?"

"No."

"Really?"

"For sure. Somehow I get the feeling that life is an experiment," Seavers said carefully, "and we're just one small part of that experiment. If we've learned anything from our history, it's that there are always some pretty grim moments for the human race, like now. Maybe we're selected as the ones to make a fresh start when we return."

To his side, Nancy had started a small tape recorder. This moment, these words, were unplanned. She had the feeling she would want to remember every word, that they would all look back one day on this moment.

". . . and civilizations rise and they fall. When you look at all of man's history, we're latecomers to the scene. Maybe it's time we learned better ways of getting along with one another."

"Tell us, please, what you're thinking right now? *Please?* This won't be . . . it won't be so scary, then."

He had searched a long time for something appropriate to bring to this moment and rejected almost everything as trite and contrived. Suddenly he let his thoughts free and an old memory welled up from the recesses of his mind, a vision of a white-haired professor.

"All right," he told them. "Try to imagine all the millions of years before this moment. Now let's use a scale we can understand, okay? Let's imagine that human life appeared on this world of ours only one year ago. Got that? Mankind showed up on Earth just one year ago. Now we can put things in scale." He paused only an instant. "Then Neanderthal, the first true man, made his appearance on Earth only fifteen hours ago. Still with me?"

Heads nodded, but only for a moment as they were reminded instantly of being weightless. He knew the seconds were speeding through that hourglass and he wanted to say the thoughts now pushing to get out before ignition.

"Cro-Magnon, *us*, showed up six hours ago. The first farmers, the men who settled in villages and raised their own crops, came on the scene, oh, just about ninety minutes ago. Men began assembling the Bible, the Old Testament, less than a half-hour ago, and seven minutes later, Mohammed appeared."

He offered a fleeting smile. "It gets better, kids. Man made his first flight less than one minute ago. He developed the computer and the atomic bomb only twenty-five seconds ago. He walked for the first time on the moon just about ten seconds ago. We looked at the first closeup pictures of Saturn and Jupiter *two* seconds ago.

"We just got to *now*, you, me, all of us here in this ship. All of us, all of this, happened in our past in less time than it takes you to blink. But I don't want you to do that. From now on it's time to keep your eyes open, to remember the good things about our world, and God and time willing, we'll come to know again."

Silence fell behind his words. Silence for them, but a far-off orchestration to his trained senses. The life sounds of *Pegasus* filtering down with its vibrations of pressures, currents, shifting loads, radiative heating and cooling, great pumps far behind them spinning at full speed, ramming fuel down thick lines, the huge ship coming into a new life, a fire birth—

"*One minute,*" the speaker said suddenly. "*One minute to ignition.*"

They stared at one another.

"*Thirty seconds.*"

Lightning hurtled upward, flickering angrily, blue-white and yellow and crimson red. Their skin tingled from the enormous charges seeking the ship.

"Everybody hold hands," he told them. "We're all going *together*."

"... *three, two, one, this is it*."

Thunder erupted behind them.

Pegasus groaned.

A child cried out in fear.

23 ——————

*F*ar behind the pressurized living compartments, work stations, huge water supply tanks and the control decks, beyond cargo storage and the docking bays for the spacetugs, past the massive lockdowns for the great winged shuttles, on the other side of the enormous fuel cells, beyond the bowels and the knees of *Pegasus*, twelve giant engine bells and six lesser engine nozzles extended on thick steel girders into vacuum. For several moments white mist poured aft from three of the lesser engines as a cleansing agent rammed backward from a pressurized tank through fuel lines, flashed away from the engines and vaporized instantly into a retreating gruel of thin ice crystals. The engine bells trembled and shook from some inner force racing through the stern of *Pegasus*, a rumbling vibration felt and heard through all the ship. Those who'd flown the great rockets before knew the rumbling: the powerful turbopumps whirling at full speed to smash fuel backwards through the lines to the engine bells. In the throats of the three lesser engines a dazzling spark appeared in the midst of spraying fuel. Instantly the igniters converted the cold outpouring of fuel to immense blazing energy.

Pegasus was coming alive—but carefully, slowly, even timidly, with only a small fraction of her enormous power, not yet the mighty blast of flame of which she was capable. That kind of blow on the untested *Pegasus* and her sister lifecraft *Noah* could have sundered the ships. Now the three engines of *Pegasus* burned steadily. From *Noah*'s bridge they watched the intense opening flash of engine ignition, a blowout of collected fuel and gases in the form of a great orange fireball spreading swiftly and fading from reality, followed by a flame combination utterly beautiful to the eye. From the engine bell centers, each blazing inferno hurled back a thin spike of blue-orange flame; at its last visible point, the spike fluttering in its own shock waves, it was three miles beyond the stern of *Pegasus*. From the rim of each engine a ghostly radiance flashed outward at right angles, incredibly glowing flowers of wavering violet flame through which the stars could be seen. There was more beauty than angry fire, more control than explosive energy.

And then, six seconds after successful ignition of the *Pegasus* engines, *Noah* also came to life, shoving herself forward with ponderous slow motion.

One minute more and the long sleek chamber of the rearmost Needle lashed to *Gagarin* burst into shocking white fire. The entire space station trembled, then swayed dangerously, its structure bending ever so slightly but unmistakably like the first motions of drawing back a great bow, and its bulk stirred from the orbital balance it had known so many years.

"Why is it shaking so much! I'm frightened!"

"Me, too!"

Teeth chattered as the children squeezed the hands of their friends, frightened by the deep rumbling sounds and then the cannonade of thunder, the swaying and creaking and the building vibration that already made falsettos of their voices and blurred their vision, all the while increasing acceleration pinned them back against a bulkhead that had suddenly become a floor.

"Mrs. Seavers, c-can I go home? I'm scared! *I want to go home!*"

The woman's hand reached out against a gravity they hadn't experienced in weeks, struggled, found the child's hand and hung on tightly.

"You *are* home, Betsy . . . we're all home now . . ."

* * *

494

The children remained unaware that the crushing acceleration they endured in the stirring birth pangs of *Pegasus* was but the lazy step forward of the giant. The three engines increased the speed of *Pegasus* relative to the writhing world below and began to lift the height of its orbit. But the thrust administered to the massive space liner was minimal for what was needed. Any greater lunge away from Earth, at this moment, could have been disastrous.

Marc Seavers had expounded the danger long before. Just as an ocean liner is a thin eggshell creature buoyed by the sea and kept from destruction by its ocean support, so *Pegasus* was an eggshell giant vulnerable to sudden strong forces that could twist its spine and crack its ribs and tear apart its vulnerable tubes and tunnels and inner structures. Acceleration was now their lifeline to the future, but it was also a heavy and dangerous stranger in their midst.

Liquids moved ponderously to the aft end of their tanks. Whatever was closest to the stern of *Pegasus* became, in the first magic of acceleration, a floor or an aft bulkhead. Acceleration means movement until that movement is stopped by a resisting surface, and resistance to acceleration means *weight*. The zero gravity of all life aboard *Pegasus* vanished in the first snap of the firewhip from its three blazing engines.

But not even the blazing thrust of the three engines meant a sudden departure from weightlessness to high-g forces. The ponderous mass of *Pegasus* had to be displaced from its exquisite orbital balance between inpulling gravity and outreaching centrifugal force. The three engines broke that balance, added velocity to *Pegasus* and began to nudge it along an invisible line breaking away, outward, from Earth. As the engines maintained a steady firing rate and acceleration permeated every atom and mote of the great spacecraft, things moved. Liquids settled within their tanks, shoved against the aft end of fuel lines. Heavy equipment moved backward from the direction of thrust and strained structures, netting, and steel cables. Everything became a matter of obedience to thrust and acceleration, and resistance to that acceleration. *Anything* not secured commenced a slow backward slide, watched by the anxious crew through the scanning video cameras. Except for minor breakage—eggshell fractures, the crew called it—*Pegasus* was clearly holding her own during the "thrust settlement period."

The great vessel creaked and groaned through every beam and plate and girder, every fastening, every weld, every enormous bolt locking metal to metal, every piece of plastic—*Pegasus* was *alive* as it gave off a deep throbbing basso intermixed with squeals and cries of metal, chitterings and sighs and crackling sounds, metal knuckles and joints pushing one against the other, seating themselves, pushing aside weak connections or incompleted settlings, rubbing and rasping and grinding gently. She shuddered, an effect like a breeze wafting through solid molecular structure. It was a faint swaying, the sigh of the giant disturbed in its hibernation.

Aboard both *Pegasus* and *Noah* were men and women who had sailed the polar regions of Earth and felt and heard enormous wedges and sheets of ice pressing against the flexible metal plates of their ships. There were men and women who had sailed submarines small and large, research subs and giant nuclear killers. In one fashion or another they had gone deep enough for the massive metal and glass structures of their submersibles to yield to savage pressures all about them, and a boat under that kind of crush is *not* a solid mass of resistance. It bends, admits creases to its structure, flexes and in so doing makes the groaning, sorrowful, living sounds the occupants now heard aboard *Pegasus* and *Noah*.

The rocket engines of both ships had settled to their steady beat, the silent crash of energy in vacuum; behind each vessel three needles of pure fire coalesced as they expanded in vacuum and became a single great tube of blazing energy, rippling throughout their length with glowing, floating diamond-shaped shock waves. The crews on the flight decks of *Pegasus* looked at *Noah* and *Noah* looked at *Pegasus* and each ship was the mirror image of the other. Each ship stabbed vacuum with lances of fire, each spewed the loveliest of shock waves, the great feathery peacock plumes of ionized gas. Each came alive with a startling, incredible bow wave of electrostatic icy flame, whipped into life by the soaring energies their passage was creating so close to a planet already saturated with more energy than it could contain.

From *Gagarin* both spacecraft were no longer visible, bending as they were around the other side of the planet. Yet *Gagarin* plunged into the trail of thin fire spumed back from *Pegasus* and *Noah*, for their paths away from Earth were inexorably intertwined, and the space station, perilously close to structural failure, accelerated through the ionized plumes left behind by the two giants.

No need for lights aboard *Gagarin*! Electrical fury stalked the metal flanks of the station, danced and sang and whirled along cables, spattered through windows and vents and soaked into the metal of the ship itself. *Gagarin* began to glow from within and without and formed an astonishing pale star a hundred miles across, an ethereal star of cold energy painting its way across the heavens with the most gossamer—and frightening—of brushes.

"I've never seen anything like it." Vicki Correnti stood with Russ Corey and a dozen men and women from the deep Hestia base on the moon. The rounded curve of lexitr sheltering them from lethal vacuum gave them a sweeping view across the lunar surface and beyond a darkened horizon so that the canopy of stars fell from the black sky in an unmoving shower past the curving edge of their small world. But the stars held no interest at this moment. All eyes were riveted to the glowing streak moving with painful slowness before the darkened face of Earth. Several people held powerful binoculars. Jesse Markham sat in a bulbous protrusion above the treaded lunar bus, tracking with a ninety-power scope. "It looks like they're getting into a real nasty situation," he said to the others as he kept his own gaze locked on the scene painted across the distant planet. "They're collecting a tremendous charge from the big ships ahead of them. It's like they're plunging through a tube of—well, a force field . . . I don't know if you can see it yet, but *Gagarin* is creating its own plasma field. It's getting brighter."

Even without the scope they could see the glowing streak begin to brighten. Vicki moved closer to Corey. "They can't take that much longer. They're turning into an electrical bomb."

"No one's ever done what they're doing," Corey replied. "I don't know if they can discharge what they're soaking up, but if they can't . . ."

A torn and tortured Nature finished his words for him. Appearing suddenly along the rim of the distant planet, a single flash of light grew upward through the clouds, poised for a moment as if it were an intelligent creature seeking its prey, then dashed along the glowing trail of electrostatic forces, spreading, brightening, swelling in energy.

"My God . . ." Vicki Correnti said aloud, unhearing. "It's a lightning bolt . . . and we can see it *from here*."

Russ Corey's words came to them like a small thunderbolt about to explode in their midst. "And it's *chasing* the ships."

On the flight deck of *Pegasus* the ship's commander and his immediate staff took the pulse, temperature, heft, and feel of their lifeboat. Vasily Tereshnikov orchestrating all that happened, Michael Pruett watching every heave and change in flight dynamics, Betty Haberman monitoring the engines, Tanya Yevtashenka and her team hovering over the computer readouts . . . Checking constantly temperatures, fuel flow, backpressure, yaw and slip and skid and roll, a thousand sensitive instruments and sensors touching and feeling, sniffing reflex actions, judging the steadily changing center of gravity of the huge craft, nudging the thousands of tons of accelerating machine with small reaction thruster flame, keeping the vessel accelerating steadily through its computed and always changing slot of time and space, raising height above the Earth and velocity away from it, an inexorable and desperate drive for survival. Twelve minutes into thrusting they notified Tereshnikov that all was proceeding as computed, that they should commit to the program worked out so carefully before. Vasily Tereshnikov took only a moment to stare at the violent electrical storm erupting constantly off the long booms in front of *Pegasus* and he gave them only one word: "*Go.*"

Marc Seavers held hands with a youngster to each side, all three of them pressed hard against the bulkhead that had become a floor. After more than ten minutes of steady thrust following weeks in weightlessness, the children felt wearied and exhausted. Seavers and Nancy did their best to revive flagging spirits by talking to the youngsters almost too tired to talk for themselves.

"Are we . . . almost . . . through?" Seavers looked at Chrissy Trenner. The fourteen-year-old was pale. The others shook gently in the rumbling ride of *Pegasus* at the head of her three blazing rocket engines. Seavers knew the initial thrust period of twelve minutes was almost behind them, but—

"No, Chrissy. This is just the beginning of what we have to do."

"Oh, God," said another girl. "I can't take this—"

"Of course you can take it!" They turned their heads with great effort to Nancy Seavers. "You'll take it, just like us, because we *have* to take it. Do you know what's happening? Every second, *every second*, we're faster and higher above Earth than we were before. Every second we're that much closer to safety, and—"

"*Sixty seconds to ignition main engines. All hands, secure yourselves. Fifty-five seconds and counting to ignition main engines.*"

They stared at the "wall" speakers. "W-what does that mean, Admiral Seavers?" The speaker was Charles Berry, fifteen years old.

Seavers didn't soft-pedal what was about to happen. "It means . . . the big engines will start to fire. They'll burn for just over six minutes. Kids, it's going to be a rough ride. It's almost time. Everybody, press back hard against those pads behind you. Got it? Now, look straight ahead. Fix your eyes on one spot and keep looking at that spot. *Do not turn your head.*"

"*Ten seconds. Nine, eight, seven—*"

"Hang on tight, boys and girls!"

At three seconds the heavy pressure eased. Smiles started, faces lit up. Marc Seavers groaned to himself, glanced at Nancy. His wife had her head pressed hard behind her and she looked straight ahead of her. Her upper lip twitched ever so lightly as she also felt the pressure ease off, but she knew from talks with her husband that the relief was false hope, that—

The main engines lit off with a savage bellow that rang like enormous gongs through every fibre of the metal being of *Pegasus*. Marc Seavers from the corner of his eye saw blood start from the nose of Chrissy Trenner. He couldn't help her. Not with all fiery hell loose behind them.

As the last seconds of the first twelve minutes of booster firing slipped away, the computers throttled back the three engines, slowly and smoothly, so there would be no sudden violent rebound if they stopped firing before the main engines ignited. Body pressures eased, heavy forces waned slowly, but there remained sufficient acceleration forces to seat fuel in tanks and lines for six huge engine bells.

They "lit off" almost perfectly. Five engines flamed within one second of computer-control ignition, the sixth only four seconds late. Engine gimbals moved two huge bells to compensate for the minor off-thrusting of the system, returned to nominal position as the sixth engine lit and threw back its fire to join the others. A flame tongue twenty miles long screamed in vacuum silence, but the roar within *Pegasus*—and then *Noah*—was shattering.

A plasma sheath expanded swiftly behind both giant spacecraft, that lovely pale violet mist of excited atoms and gases along its edges, caressing the diamond shock waves within the thick tube of flame from the main engines. The ponderous thunder of steel dinosaurs crashed through the decks and beams and substance of the spacecraft as the acceleration built to a force four times greater than the living creatures, human and animal, had ever known on the surface of the Earth.

Children of eighty pounds suddenly weighed more than three hundred. Their facial skin pressed back in gravity-mashed distortion. Capillary systems broke under the sustained pressure. Blood trickled from noses and mouths, and after thirty seconds the pain became acute. Few cried out. Their lungs had turned to lead, their limbs to mercury, their hearts to sluggish meat. Even their brains changed to reservoirs of murky, thick, heavy fluid trying to circulate and carry oxygen within flattened tubing systems. They still had to endure an eternity of punishment. Resonances built within the engine chambers, shock waves roared back against the structures of the ships, vibration and shaking and pounding and hammering became ever worse.

On *Pegasus'* bridge, Michael Pruett tried to focus on his instruments to keep up to the split-second on flight dynamics. Abruptly he abandoned the effort. He couldn't read the gauges, he could barely move his arms under the squeezing g-loads. He let his body ease back to even pressure in the semi-supine position of first-position crew and glanced at the forward windows, where an electrical maelstrom reigned in a maddened light show of electrical fury.

He caught Tereshnikov's eye. Under even this heavy pressure the Russian remained his old self. He forced his facial muscles into a grin and raised a lead-heavy hand. "You enjoy the ride, Michael? You do not pay attention to your instruments!"

Pruett couldn't help himself as he returned the grin. "What the hell, Vasily, I can't read the gauges and even if I could I wouldn't change anything! We can't go back, we can't stay in our orbit, so we're on a ride to hell or heaven and either way there's no stopping!"

"Good for you, Pruett! I thought you would never understand!"

"*T plus two minutes and counting. All systems are*

nominal," intoned the all-too-human voice of the propulsion systems computer.

"Stop talking, you son of a bitch!" Tereshnikov roared above the hammering thunder. "Just shut ups and drive!"

"It's getting closer."

"Holy Jesus. I can't believe I'm really seeing this!"

"If we could only warn them—"

Russ Corey turned to glance at the people with him in the lunar bus. "You can't. We can't warn them about anything. And if we could, what would you say to them? A lightning bolt as big as the Mississippi is about to slam into their ass?"

No one answered. They strained better to see, and Russ Corey turned back. Behind *Gagarin* station the jagged streak of lightning tore ahead, stumbled at invisible force fields lying in its path, swirled and danced madly as it gathered energy, a Walt Disney dervish of mountainous proportions: raw, naked energy howling after its prey.

It stumbled again, tripped over its electrical feet, bunched its mass into a great irregular sphere and then burst free, an energy werewolf of space. The enormous mass and bulk of *Pegasus* had wedged a tunnel through the dust. Invisible at slow speeds, the dust at better than twenty thousand miles an hour was the equivalent of a powdery sludge, actually building up before the prow of *Pegasus* into waves of resistance that could have crushed the accelerating vessel. But the long booms extending forward of *Pegasus* and *Noah*, performed as advertised, hurling aside the electrically-attracted or -repelled dust particles. Dust swirled about and rushed back from the nose and flanks of *Pegasus*. Behind the spaceship stretched its screaming fire, creating another violent electrical field. And for miles to each side of the hurtling giant machine there appeared an enormous banded tube of electrical attraction.

On the opposite side of the planet Boris Mikhailov and Hugh Fitzpatrick readied themselves for the increase in booster power for the space station. *Gagarin* swayed and rattled and shook as if it were a drunk suffering from a palsy affliction. "Hugh, I am concerned about the structure holding together when we increase thrust," Mikhailov said to the American.

"You're a phlegmatic son of a bitch, I'll say that for you," Fitzpatrick retorted. "You're concerned and *I'm* scared shitless."

"I can understand that!" Mikhailov shouted over a rattle of metal bulkheads. "But we have no choice, do we? We must go to the thrust of two Needles, whether we like it or not."

"Balls to the wall!" Fitzpatrick shouted. "Hey, you guys in Two and Three listening in?"

Voices sputtered back to them on their headsets from the two waiting Needles. "Two here. We're ready, man. I just wish I knew what the hell that glow is. My ship is all lit up with St. Elmo's."

"Number Three here. Same thing, guys. But it's worse where you are, Fitzpatrick. I mean, your part of the station is spitting fire. It's like a Van de Graaff generator. And do you guys see that trail we're moving through? It stretches ahead of us like a damned tunnel. I guess it's the aftershock of the two big ships, but it sure gives me the willies."

"Willies, shmillies. You're coming up on thirty seconds to ignition. You all set?"

"Gotcha, sweetie. Number Two counting."

"Number Three ready. Call it out at minus ten, Fitz."

Fitzpatrick waited, looked at Mikhailov who nodded, then held up ten fingers. "Ten, nine, eight . . ." Fitzpatrick reeled off the numbers and at zero, in perfect timing as Number One shut down its engine a split-second before running out of fuel and finishing off with a sputtering cut of power, the next two Needles lit off their powerful rocket engines. *Gagarin* shot ahead, trembling and shaking wildly. Fitzpatrick and Mikhailov lurched against their straps in the main control room.

"Hey, the . . . behind us, it's as bright as day out there!" came a shout from one of the Needles pilots.

"Whatever it is," called another, "it's coming after us like a runaway locomotive!"

503

Fitzpatrick and Mikhailov struggled to a viewport to look directly aft. The sight immediately outside was frightening enough. Several of the station's living cubicles had broken their supports and flopped around wildly. Support cables snapped like bullwhips. *The goddamned place is coming apart. But just so long as all these pieces stay tied together, it doesn't matter*, Fitzpatrick thought angrily. The bulkheads about them shimmered with constant vibration, and they felt sharp shocks through their booted feet. But the worst was the electrostatic field and what it was doing to them. Bolts of electrical fire arced between station sections, blue flames running up and down rounded flanks like demons on skates. Electrical fire sputtered angrily, whipped around the larger sections, and cavorted along the cables now writhing like demented snakes.

Mikhailov lifted his arm to point behind them. Fitzpatrick half-turned to see a lightning bolt bigger than an ocean liner tearing toward them, its size and glare and fury impossible to tell, its speed horrendous, beyond all belief as it hurtled in pursuit and as fast as they could follow its path it was upon them like all the furies of hell.

No time to cry out, to curse or to pray. The universe was light everywhere, inside metal, inside flesh, all-encompassing light. Fitzpatrick stared, stunned and horrified, as Boris Mikhailov glowed and a split-second later stood with his legs wrapped in blinding electrical fire. Light streamed from his eyes and nostrils and his mouth within his helmet, light filled the bowl of the helmet, hesitated barely another moment, and Mikhailov opened his mouth, perhaps to scream or to shout, they would never know, and a searing blade of pure electrical fire knifed upward through his boot beneath the skin of his leg and punctured his groin, up through his belly and his chest and ramming upward through his throat as if it were unresisting tissue paper and the lightning tore through his open mouth as water rips from the nozzle of a powerful fire hose and the energy bolt flashed through his lexitr faceplate and for another instant it poised as Boris Mikhailov exploded in a vast

504

eruption of pure light energy. Hugh Fitzpatrick started to reach out his hand to help his friend, started to speak, started to feel the horror of the moment, started to think of what was happening, *started* all these things and more but there wasn't time, the bottle of Time was drained dry, sucked away by the immense electrical forces raging through *Gagarin*. A human thought begins with chemical-electrical mixtures, a flow of free electrons with a speed of twenty-six thousand miles a second, but then it must traverse so many switching points and synapses and jumps and leaps and twists and turns within the brain that the speed of human thought slows to two hundred miles an hour.

Two hundred miles an hour was a groveling crawl in the face of pure lightning run rampant. Too slow for a single one of those thoughts to be completed before the lightning *snapped* from the blossoming eruption of what had been a Russian cosmonaut into the eyes of Hugh Fitzpatrick and melted his eyes and his skull and his brain.

Electrical forces greater than an atomic bomb gathered within the compartments, cubicles, workshops, control stations, every part and piece and parcel of *Gagarin*, and exploded.

A quarter of a million miles distant, looking up through the lexitr shield of the lunar bus, Russ Corey and his woman and their friends stared at the silent, awesome fireworks, and Russ Corey knew a dread that flashed instantly across space to him.

"Shut down! Shut everything down!"

Russ Corey spun about within the lunar bus and pointed his hand to Jesse Markham in the blister. Markham had a second master control panel before him that duplicated the system before the driver, but Milt Irving was in the center of the vehicle, too far from the driver's control panel. Time was vanishing swiftly for them all, and only Russ Corey was aware of that terrible fact.

"The electrical system, damn it!" he shouted again. "Do as I say—*shut it down!*"

Markham needed no further prompting. His hand

flicked across the panel, killing the switches. Lights went dark at once. "It's all down save the life support system—"

"Cut it off. *Now*," Corey snarled.

The people with him stared in disbelief. "But—" started from one engineer and got no further.

"Everybody listen to me!" Corey said with controlled fury in his voice. "Shut down your suits. Goddamn it, *do it!* Shut down all your suit power and do it right now. Jesse! Pull the circuit breakers on everything, right across the panel. *Pull everything!* I don't want a drop of juice moving in this thing. Everybody, listen to me. If you want to be alive a few moments from now, make sure your suits are *off*. There's plenty of air and heat in this thing to take care of our needs for a while. Everybody's suit off?"

He watched them nod, heard their murmured confirmation. "Now, settle down. Don't move around this vehicle, understand? Stay where you are. *Do not move*. Don't scratch your nose or your ass or touch anything. *No movement*." He glanced up. "That's about all you can do. Look up. Look at where you saw *Gagarin* and hold your breath and hope it misses us."

Then they understood. Until they were shut down, all power off, they were a tremendous source of electrical attraction: battery power great enough to move the tracked vehicle six hundred miles across the lunar surface while supplying all their needs for oxygen and ventilation and radios and lights. That's why he'd ordered Markham to pull all the circuit breakers. Cut the cords; not even any leakage. Why he'd ordered their suits shut down. No battery power, no surges or currents of electricity. That's why he told them not to move. Slide your hand across the back of a seat and you create static electricity, you start sparks, you produce a conducting attraction. Russ Corey didn't explain any of these things. They were all engineers, technicians, specialists; they knew how such systems worked.

One glance into the lunar sky told them without words that the genie was out of its gravity bottle, malevolent, wild, destructive, blindly furious, hungry for anything that attracted its awesome power. Earth had become a supercharged sphere of electrical energy, far exceeding its capacity to contain such naked fury. The great ships above Earth firing their engines to escape the planet, to put maximum distance in the shortest time between themselves and the dying world, had created the equivalent of an enormous arc attracting burgeoning energy from far below.

The call was answered. Lightning surged and roared and gathered in a single hellish outpouring that hurtled toward its siren call. *Pegasus* and *Noah* were blindly and unknowingly targeted for destruction as they burned an electromagnetic wand in their fire-lashed run for freedom. A lightning bolt beyond imagination, beyond comprehension, such as had not been known on Earth since billions of years before the first drops of water ever fell on the planet, searched for and reached out to that bristling electrical wand. High above Earth the river of electrons bent to follow the powerful arc around the world and raced after its source, two ships with the remnants of humanity aboard. They were doomed.

A swaying, rocking, failing, disintegrating mass of metal with seven people, six American and one Russian, hurtled through space between the ultimate engine of destruction and the two last ships of man.

Cagarin vanished into free atoms and a vast field of stripped subatomic particles, into hurtling electrons and ionized gas and swirling fields of plasma. For a moment, immeasurable in terms of man's clocks, the energy paused, sated for an instant, and then answered its own blind call to expend its energy.

Pegasus and *Noah* were on the other side of the planet, now several thousand miles high but with an entire world blocking their siren call of electromagnetic energy. There was another source, closer than any other. Electrical energy was there in abundance. Nuclear reactors, solar generators, fuel cells, lights, radios, motors and engines, moving vehicles supercharging lunar dust with electrostatic forces, tall radio antenna, great fields of searching antennae, air conditioning and life-support systems, aeration motors for great tanks filled with liquid, external vents and louvers, hot and cold and all of it soaked, drowned, charged with energy that threw off a tremendous signal.

The genie searched and instantly it found. It gathered unto its braided river of pure electrical fire all its strength and reached upward and the attraction held. At twenty-six thousand miles a second the lightning bolt hurled itself far beyond the last vestiges of terrestrial atmosphere, knifed with contempt through radiation belts and electromagnetic fields and shot straight and true for the sweet lure of energy beckoning to it from the moon. Positive to negative, negative to positive, like two planetary batteries, and they were sparking now.

It took nine seconds for the electrical Mississippi to leap the distance from high Earth to surface moon. The tracked lunar vehicle was fifty miles to the lunar southeast of Ptolemaeus Station where newcomers from Earth had joined with the small Russian base to create a thriving surface and underground city. The river of pure energy passed overhead at a distance judged at five miles. It did not bend downward to the tracked bus that had no electrical systems operating. To the lightning bolt, Russ Corey and the others and their vehicle did not exist. In the spectrum of electrical silence the lightning bolt was blind. The genie could not see or feel.

Ptolemaeus was vibrant with electrical energy, rich and fat with power, saturated and—

The bolt went through the southeastern rim of the crater wall, vaporized rock as if it were thin fog, struck the closest vertical antenna, consumed it, and then splintered and sprayed out and downward across the surface, into the ground and deep beneath the surface. All of the interior of Ptolemaeus changed. Whatever it was one instant, the next it became boiling, furious electrical soup. Metal, rock, flesh, plastic, bones, glass, thought, water, dreams . . . no matter; all became equal. For another two hundred miles the electrical fury raged, the genie consumed, the moon glowed and shone and

508

then the bolt backed up against itself, unable to go further but still needing release.

An electrical bomb with the power of mass fusion let go and horror stalked the moon.

Moments later the first deep underground shock waves cracked the outer shell of Hestia's surface installations.

24

Sixty-three farm animals vital to the future of the human race died when the huge engines of *Noah* shut down simultaneously. *Were* shut down simultaneously. Chief Engineer Hans Dornier and Flight Dynamics Officer Helen Chandler, strapped into seats with propulsion system master controls at their fingertips, looked with alarm at their display panel showing rising temperatures in the massive engine bells and fluctuating pressure in the lines.

"Stand by for emergency shutdown," Dornier said in a toneless voice, his words stabbing at Chandler and, carried to the flight deck, sweeping that capacious area with instant dread.

"We *can't* do that!" Chandler protested. "If we cut off now we may not get restart in time and—"

"You would prefer," Dornier said coldly, "for the engines to explode, I suppose." He flicked switches and cut off control from the distraught woman. "I have master override," he said in the same flat tone. "Standing by ready for emergency shutdown." His expert eyes scanned every gauge. He could hold off on reacting to the temperatures. Those were climbing but on a steady grade, which meant the problem in the engines was not yet dangerous. Pressure fluctuations were something else. If they went offscale they could blow wide open and they'd have a massive explosion through the entire aft end of the ship. He kept his hand firmly but gently on the master switch. "Do not just sit there, Miss

Chandler," he said in his most positive tone. "Pray. Bite your nails, but—

"Cutoff!" he shouted, and his hands snapped the switch toward him. The needles had swung erratically and he knew there could be no more waiting. But at the same time he had cause to know exultation. The countdown timer for burn period had swung to zero a split second before he'd hit the switch to shut off the fuel valves to starve the engines.

"Hang on!" Chandler yelled. For an instant Dornier had forgotten what was coming. Their plan had been to burn full thrust for six minutes and then to fire up three lower-thrust engines and shut down the main engines. This would mitigate the sudden loss of thrust and prevent violent rebound within the ship. Now that danger leaped among them, and as the engine flame vanished they felt and heard the tremendous CLANG of all the metal structure rebounding in the direction opposite to thrust, slamming forward. For all that could move aboard ship it was the same as standing in a bus that without warning comes instantly to a stop. Whatever is loose is hurled forward. Whatever is secured by straps or cables or netting is hurled against the restraints.

The sudden loss of acceleration threw Dornier hard against his straps. Unprepared for the violent forward thrust, his head snapped ahead and down. Globules of red, shimmering and trembling, floated past his startled eyes. He reached up to touch them and one globule spattered softly. It dawned on Dornier he was watching his own blood. He must have torn something in his nose. He tasted salt. Maybe in his mouth as well. To hell with it. He forced his attention to Helen Chandler. She was the one person now to know if they had reached their magic numbers.

"Helen, how did we—" One look at that radiant smile told him everything.

"Nine point one three," she said, filled with pride at the reading. "Bridge! Chandler here. Over."

"Chandler, McKenzie here. What are—did we make it?"

"On the money, Mac! Niner point one three miles

per second right on the button. We're on our way, my friend!" She heard muffled cheering from the bridge and she leaned back in her seat, or tried to, anyway, in their return to weightlessness. She grinned at Hans Dornier. "It's a free ride from here on out, Hans," she said after a studied pause.

He laughed, the tension flowing from him like adrenalin through a hose. "Case of beer," he offered.

"I wish!" she said gleefully, feeling her own pent-up emotions flowing from her. *My God, we did it,* she thought with a sense of wonder that kept rising up about her. *We really did it. We're moving away from that hell planet beneath us. More than nine miles a second. Away from—*

"I don't have any beer," Dornier was saying to her, "but I did save something very special for this moment." He reached into his suit and removed a flat squeeze bottle. "Pimento liqueur. I have kept this secret many, many months." He removed the safety cap and handed the bottle to her. "Drink up, Helen. *We are alive.*" He laughed, this time with less mirth. "And we shouldn't be."

"*Prosit,*" she said quietly and took a long, burning drink to an uncertain future.

Jon Gierek wiped bloody hands on his jumpsuit. "All right, we can report now," he said, his face reflecting the misery he'd known since they started finding the animals that were already dead and those they had to put down. Sixty-three of the farm creatures! What a terrible blow! And who would have expected such a disaster at the very beginning of their flight!

Gierek looked at the carcasses in the netting, wafting to and fro slowly in the strong breeze of the ventilator fans. Dairy cows, three of them. Their straps had broken in that murderous rebound when the power stopped. They were hurled forward into the nearest bulkhead. One cow broke its neck and died immediately. Another broke its two front legs and kept bawling in its terrible pain, tongue extended, frothing at the mouth, its eyes wild. The poor thing in its pain-frenzy had shit and

511

pissed without control and the stuff was everywhere. Mixed with blood, too. The third cow had ruptured internally and poured blood from what seemed like a dozen orifices. What a way to start a trip that only God knew how long would last. Shit, piss, blood, phlegm, froth, stink, and mess.

Jon Gierek had attended animals for years. He was Master Farmer for the sprawling State Farm Six of the National Farm Combine of Poland. He'd spent his entire life with such animals as these, all kinds of farm animals. He knew them better than he knew people. When they were brutalized like this he knew an almost uncontrollable anger. Who could have used such inferior materials for the webbing and the straps? Didn't these fools know any better? And they'd lost some of the hogs, and other animals as well. They *needed* these. More than sixty. It was so hard to believe.

And more could die. He had animals all over this damned space farm choking and throwing up. Bad enough for them to have been in this insane weightlessness. The animals had bile to the point of agony. Gas bubbles choking them, their stomachs heaving and twisting. They sedated as many as they could but that still didn't stop the gas. *Then* they fired up those damned engines! Out of nowhere the animals were hurled back until they weighed many times Earth weight. But to be shot like out of a gun into such heaviness . . . it was all too much. And that collection bin that had ruptured. Terrible. They had worked for weeks to modify the animal waste collection. You couldn't put a diaper or such device on the rear end of a cow or a sheep! That was ridiculous. So they kept the fans working at full speed, and they tried waist-circling diaphragms. Sometimes it worked, most of the time it didn't. And when the engines fired and they were all thrown so stupidly into heavy weight, the bin filled with urine and shit broke open and the stuff weighed four times normal and it was *everywhere*.

Now the fools were arguing with one another. That idiot from England. Rudyard Gyn. What was he? Life Support Officer. Some fancy title like that. Naturally.

512

He had to be called an *officer*. Jon Gierek hated all officers. He'd spent four years in the Polish army. Communist pigs for officers. For those four years Gierek had butchered their meat animals and attended their horses. At least he'd made a good name for himself and had gone on to achieve the status of Master Farmer. And he knew the animals so well, and was such a good veterinarian, that they'd selected him for this crazy flight. He had hesitated about going. All those stupid stories. The end of the world, indeed! Russia and Poland were filled with these end-of-the-world stories. All he cared about were the animals.

That fool from the Sudan. A crazy name, also. Chuks Ileogbunam. He had a crazy title like the others: Reclamation Officer. *Another* damned officer. He spoke in a crazy singsong nigger voice. How did they ever let such a blind black fool like him into this ship? He stood before Jon Gierek, did this crazy Ileogbunam in that bedsheet wrapped about him and tied up through his crotch, his magnetic soles planted on the gridwork of the hooved animals section, and he acted like some damned skinny black pope. "You cannot dump such vital materials into space like that," he told Gierek.

"It will clean out the pen!" Gierek shouted. "Dump all that stuff out into space."

"Yes, it would do that. But we need the body products of the animals. We must make fertilizer and we can reclaim the urine to make drinking water for them."

"Are you crazy?" Gierek had shouted, almost losing control. "That place is full of shit and blood and piss and vomit and *that* is what you want to reclaim so we can grow food in it and water these animals? You are mad, nigger!"

"First, I am Sudanese and I am not negroid *or* a nigger. Second, you Polack idiot who is the son of an idiot and who has an idiot for a mother, because you do not understand our methods of reclamation does not make them crazy or stupid. And third, you will do as I say because I am the Reclamation Officer."

"And I," shouted Jon Gierek, "am Jesus Christ and I will have none of eating and drinking your stupid shit

513

and piss!" He yanked down hard on the emergency pressure dump handle, through the thick lexitr ports they saw a condensation cloud snap into being, heard the muffled thump and roar of the outer port opening and the air—along with its stomach-turning contents— whip out of sight. Whatever remained was instantly frozen.

The other people in the farm animal section, frightened and upset at the screaming and banging and thumping, put in a call for reinforcements to quell a situation promising to become dangerous. Mario Silva groaned. They'd hardly had time to settle down into a routine and already he had an international fracas on his hands. He sent Flip Paxton and Willy Henson down to the animal bay. They took four very large men with them. They were persuasive. Paxton, who had practiced law for the Royal Navy of England, acted as judiciously as possible.

To Jon Gierek he said: "You will dump nothing overboard from this ship again unless it is on fire and you can't put out that fire, do you understand? You think you've rid us of that mess. You've done no such thing. Instead, we now have a loose cloud of frozen animal wastes and vomit orbiting this ship. Much more of that and we won't be able to see anything outside. Do you read me, Gierek? If you violate these orders I'll slap you in irons for the next two years."

To Chuks Ileogbunam he said: "You are no longer a tribal prince from the Sudan. You are an officer aboard this vessel and you will either conduct yourself like one and refrain from calling these skilled specialists any names now or in the future, or I promise you that you will be chained right next to Gierek and you can both curse me until you have no more strength to speak. Do you *both* understand me?"

He prayed this was precisely the manner in which these two men were accustomed to being chewed out, and they were, and they quickly nodded assent to everything he'd said. "Good. We waste nothing. *Mister* Ileogbunam, you are Reclamations Officer. You have sixty-three animals to reclaim. Collect your teams. These creatures are to be properly butchered at once and their meat preserved. You will save *everything*. Not a scrap is to be disposed of, understood?"

"I have a question, sir."

"Well, what is it?"

Ileogbunam screwed up his face in distaste. "Save everything, sir? Entrails, eyeballs, the contents of the bowels and—"

"*Everything*. In case you have forgotten, we are a small planet. There are fish to be fed. Insects of all kinds. They will feast on what you save, my good sir."

Day 3

This is the third day after the engines of this incredibly huge ship were shut down and we were told we had all the speed we needed to escape from the dust cloud that's caused our sun to go haywire and the Earth to be scourged by heat and fire. But I'm not going to go into that, because there are plenty of historians who'll have a lot of time on their hands to write things down.

My name is Nancy Parks Seavers and I'm aboard *Pegasus* with nearly fifteen hundred other human souls as well as all manner of animals and birds from Earth. My husband is Admiral Marc Seavers and he's the mission commander of this ship and our sister ship *Nouh*, which people here have already started to call the Animal Farm. At my husband's request I'm keeping a daily diary. It's a good idea and I believe I've found a way to make it more than we planned. Each day, whenever the moment becomes available or something special comes to mind, I record my thoughts by speaking into a battery-powered tape recorder. We're still close enough to the sun for the great solar cells all over this ship to generate lots of electricity and recharge the batteries we use for things like this.

Anyway, when I complete my recording for each day, I give the tape to the children in our group of cubicles. They're not really children but young people. Young adults. Christy Trenner is fourteen and when she was in school she wrote for her school paper. She types very well and I've had her working on a manual portable

515

typewriter to transcribe my tapes. The other boys and girls help her. Christy uses the portable machine because we can't expect to have so much free power as the months go by and we get farther out from the sun. Well, when Christy types up the notes all the young people in our cubicle read what I've said. That way we keep no secrets from them and we expect the same courtesy in return.

Okay; enough of an introduction. I should say a few words about that hellish ride away from Earth. Almost everybody was bleeding. Several of the girls had their periods and the severe gravity forces hurt them. They bled heavily, but they're okay now. Weightlessness has eased their recovery. We were all frightened. I know *I* was! I was scared out of my mind, which doesn't make sense because there was no going back or anything like that. Go back to what?

After the engines shut down and Vasily passed the word from the bridge—that's Vasily Tereshnikov, captain of *Pegasus*—that we were now flying away from Earth at 33,000 miles an hour, everybody cheered. We'd been through the gates of hell on those rocket engines and not only had we survived, but we were on the exact course planned for us, and we had all the speed we needed, and the ship had really held together quite well. There are plenty of problems but Marc tells me there's no sweat; we'll solve them.

Anyway, when the engines shut down and we were thrown forward and found ourselves weightless again, there were a bad few minutes while we collected our thoughts and unstrapped ourselves and stopping the bleeding, and then we just settled back into the routine I'd set up while we were still in Earth orbit.

For the first time I really understood what Marc meant when he said the big ships were alive. He asked all the kids to hold it down and listen. *Pegasus* was groaning. I couldn't believe it. It sounded exactly like one of the great sperm whales when it sounds, a deep basso grumbling. As it faded away, we all heard the medley and chorus of metal settling down, stretching back to its shape before acceleration, of tubes popping.

516

I once sailed an old wooden three-master, and when it was tied to its dock, rubbing its sides against the bollards, it talked and it groaned and it sang, and so did this giant new ship of ours.

One of the questions everyone asks, and of course it's natural to ask it, is how long will this trip be? How long before we'll return to Earth? Will we *ever* return to Earth? The best way to answer these questions is to answer the last one first. Of course we'll return to Earth—for better or for worse. There's nowhere else to go! Everybody *must* understand that fact. It's just like birth and death. It can't be avoided. What we'll find is open to debate, and that helps answer that other question: how long will this flight take?

We don't know. Period. We'll be firing probes back to Earth to see what's happening. We'll be checking all the time on the dust cloud. Marc has already told everybody that as soon as it looks as if the Earth has cooled down and can again support life we'll be on our way back. But he also warns us that the only thing we can expect back there is the unexpected.

I spent a few hours on the bridge this morning (that's "morning," "noon," and "night" as judged by the ship's timing system, since there isn't any day or night up here) and I've been able to talk with the children a bit more sensibly about our flight. When our engines shut down and we sailed away from Earth at well over nine miles a second, we were in the kind of balance we needed to keep going for a long time. It's a fixed race, so to speak. We're in an iron balance between the outward thrust of our engines (our centrifugal force, a rock tied to the end of a string a boy whirls about his head) and the steady but diminishing tug of the sun pulling us back. So we're really slowing down all the time, but quite slowly and just the way we want to slow down. We're like two small footballs thrown very high upward through the gravity well of the sun. We don't ever escape the sun with our speed, and we slow down all the time, but we're lofting higher and farther every day. The trick is to make sure the sun doesn't lose this celestial tug of war. That's why our speed and angle of flight stretches but doesn't break the sun's elastic gravitational cord. And, going back to the analogy of two small footballs thrown high in the air, we'll finally slow down to the point where we'll no longer be leaving the sun. From then on we'll be starting back. They call this a free-return trajectory, but that's fancy verbiage that doesn't explain any better what's happening. Once we no longer drift away from the sun we'll be starting to drift back, increasing our speed slightly all the time until we arrive at the same point we stopped firing our engines, and with the same speed.

That's the simple explanation. There are all sorts of minor variations to the theme but this overall view will do just fine.

Now, how long will it be before we stop our escape and start back? Big question, that. If we don't tweak the ships' engines to push us farther out into space, then fourteen months from now we'll be at the top of the gravity hill and starting back, a round trip of twenty-eight months. Strange: to us that seems forever, but for the Earth it's an incredibly short time to settle down so it might just welcome us home.

But, there's something else even more important. We, the kids and myself, can't affect what happens with *Pegasus*. There's schooling to be done, and everybody has to work, and we have to figure out ways to not only conserve energy, but also produce as much as we can. We'll work on that problem soon enough. But what I consider as important as anything else, right after the complicated issue of surviving, is our heritage. In the mad rush to get into space and aboard *Pegasus* and *Noah*, we appear to have forgotten something not only very dear to all of us, but critical to our nature as an advanced species.

It's the effort to save something so precious to all of us. Our music. Oh, I've managed to have children and their parents, anybody and everybody I could, carry something of music with them. Instruments, notes, sheet music; anything that would bring forth the sounds of man's history. But in all the programs to train and study, to keep alive our past and to prepare for that moment when, God willing, we return to a world that will welcome us, no one thought to include music! There's that old saw that life is made up of more than bread alone. Well, the future is more than computers and engineering and architecture and farming and whatever. It's music as much as anything else. And I intend to make sure that it not only stays alive, but that these young people with us are inspired to create their *own* music.

Hi. My name is Chrissy Trenner and I'm fourteen years old and I feel silly talking into a little machine, but I've listened to my voice on this tape recorder and I guess it comes out okay, and anyway, everything we say on tape is going to be transcribed and made a part of the diary Mrs. Seavers is keeping. I'm helping her with that, too. Oh, I forgot to record when I say these things into the recorder. This is *Day 14*.

I don't think I like weightlessness very much. I don't like the way my face puffs out, even if everybody else has the same problem. My back hurts, and I had a lot of trouble with my period. Being weightless, the blood didn't flow anywhere but just collected inside me. Mrs. Seavers helped me in the shower, in the special room all sealed off, and she used that soft plastic tube with its suction to help me clean myself. I never thought I'd be using a vacuum cleaner for personal hygiene. And I still can't believe they're saving everything, the blood and whatever sloughs off from within me. Mrs. Seavers explained they'll take anything that's of a biological nature and mix it with special plants and yeast we brought along in the ship to make food for the animals. That's what we hear about all the time. Everything on this ship is to be used. Nothing is to be wasted. But the idea of some fish eating a part of me is—I think *blech* is the way you spell how I feel about *that*.

I wonder how George feels about it. That's George Larson. He's fifteen and I think he's got a crush on me. I like him *very* much and I think this could really turn into something special. But the way he looked at me today means he must know what I was just talking about. A vacuum cleaner hose (even if Mrs. Seavers said I shouldn't call it that) in my vagina for personal cleanliness isn't the most romantic thought in the world. Oops, I forgot. In the world or *off* it. We'll see. Things aren't the same for George or the other boys either. It must be strange having to lock your feet in stirrups and then poke your thing into a tube when you have to pee. There's air suction in the tube and the way the boys have been giggling I guess it feels good to them. But if they didn't use the tube they'd have pee all over the place, and if they didn't use the stirrups the reaction to their peeing would send them floating in the opposite direction. It's really weird up here.

Commander's Log, *Pegasus*.
Day 17.

If I ever missed and sorely needed someone who's no longer with us, it's Hugh Fitzpatrick. We all need his free-wheeling engineering spirit. We've been learning, *very* fast on this ship and our sister vessel, *Noah*, that the one-two-three rules of engineering acumen, experience, and slide rule solutions don't work up here. We've never had a situation like this before, never known problems like these. And when we faced problems even remotely related to what we now struggle with as an everyday occurrence, there was always the possibility of shunting the problem aside and looking to Earth for postponement, replacement, solution, or permission to forget the whole thing.

There's no Earth to turn to any more. Whatever problems we face we must solve and solve them immediately. If the problems get out of hand then they become dangers, and danger escalates swiftly into disaster and after that there's catastrophe and after that— Well, I can't remember who said it, but whoever it was said that Einstein was wrong. God does throw dice, and *we're* on the biggest roll of all time.

Today's meeting was the best example of the Einsteinian Faux Pas, as I call it. I've begun to appreciate the Russian attitude now that I'm living with it. They're pragmatic to a fault and we desperately need that approach to everyday survival. I have never referred to the future as an issue of long-term survival, because the very words beggar themselves. Obviously, long-term is meaningless unless we solve our most critical problems *right now*. For a long time the Russians have regarded their space program as a steady, plodding, hardworking, knuckle-busting effort. We spent years deriding it as unsophisticated in comparison to our exquisitely advanced (and horribly complex) systems. And both sides of that coin have been true. But when we suffered a tragedy, its impact was so devastating it knocked us out of the box for a period of time that really twisted our noses. If a Russian booster failed, they at least had the advantage of knowing the damned thing had fired successfully the past ninety-seven launchings and they could narrow down the problem quickly. And while they searched for what obviously must be a random failure, *they could keep launching*.

Fitzpatrick spent a lot of time with me trying to reinforce that attitude. He used to drive home the point that the Russians were simply using tried-and-true methods *just as the U.S. had done for so many years* and then abandoned to the siren call of complex systems intrinsically more vulnerable to failure. Let's face it. A Land Rover can always get through where a Maserati bogs down.

I'm getting carried away. Back to today's meeting: what I should call the Cold Water Session. I dumped enough of it on those people. We had fifteen of the top staff from *Noah* tugged to *Pegasus* so we could rattle cages in a face-to-face confrontation. The little things are critical here. The night before the meeting I met privately with—belay that. Vasily Tereshnikov and I met privately with Marilyn Robins, who'd been for several years the power behind the scenes of much activity at the White House. She was the psych technician for the president and she can unscrew the top off anyone's skull to see what goes on inside. Between Robins and Gregory Tretyakovich, we had an excellent chance to find the handle that would pump some sense into the top people of both ships.

The hard nut of all this, and Vasily backed me to the hilt to get across the message, is that all of us must think of our two vessels in terms of lifeboats. That is what they are, pure and simple. *Pegasus* carries most of the people and the heavy packages in the form of technology that we'll need if ever we find Earth hospitable to us again. *Noah* has already been named the Animal Farm by the occupants of both ships, and the name fits. But, and again I digress, the hard nut of our conversation was that *we are not flying through space in spaceships*.

Or, for that matter, in two great technological lifeboats. It's much simpler, and much more frightening, than that.

We are aboard flying junkyards. We are passengers and crew aboard huge garbage trucks that were never completed before they were flung away from Earth. The moment the engines stopped and both ships were on their way on our free-return trajectory, *both ships started coming apart.* Our breakdowns began immediately: breakdowns among a crew who must operate in as close to perfect harmony as it's possible to achieve but who were never selected on the basis of being able to cooperate with, work with, understand or consider one another. In this mad rush to escape we were forced to pick and nab and grasp a representation of the human race, our intellectual decisions often distorted by political and power needs that had to be satisfied in order to get these ships ready in the all-too-short time that was available.

So we have ships never completed. Systems never really designed or built to function as integral parts. Systems that in many instances have never been tested under the conditions we now face every minute of the day. A crew that never trained together. Hundreds of people critical to everyday and long-term operations who received jury-rigged, slapdash training and don't know beans about what they're doing, but *must* carry out their duties very well indeed, or we all suffer the consequences. We didn't bring the finest of humanity with us. We brought splinter representation that we *hoped* would endure. We brought with us vastly differing and sometimes violently opposed ethnic, racial, personal, and social mores, religions, habits, customs, and God knows what else. To say nothing about the stumbling blocks of languages!

And they must do so much more than simply get along with one another. That is a concept so ridiculous that it should never even have been entertained at any meeting. *To hell with getting along.* I don't care if they all hate one another just so long as these ships endure and we endure and we get back to the surface of the Earth and they can begin that long, miserable on-going conflict once again.

All right. Back to the heart of all this. We'll never make it for a flight of twenty-eight months, what we need for a return trajectory. The ships won't hold together long enough. They're going to need a massive infusion of work that was never done. They're going to need building, let alone rebuilding and restructuring. There can't be any letdowns for this job or we may all die.

Which means hard, harsh, unremitting leadership. I thank our lucky stars we have Tereshnikov at the helm of *Pegasus*. After faltering briefly, Silva has started to run *Noah* in the same manner his ancestral captains ran the great sailing ships of old Portugal, with unwavering discipline. This problem of enforcing the law can only be solved if we keep it simple, if we base what we do on the old and established rules of maritime law. The captain—in this case, the captains, plural—are the masters of their vessels. I have a responsibility, as does Chiang Biao, to put aside our own personal feelings, no matter what they are, and absolutely support Vasily and Mario. We made a most meaningful decision before we left Earth: *no firearms*. Projectile weapons aboard these ships are as dangerous as a greased bottle of nitro in the hands of a drunk. Firearms or longbows or spears or crossbows or anything of that nature were, and are, forbidden. The laser bows for EVA work are important but we cannot permit the existence of *any* weapon or device of that nature. One breach of pressurization will kill a great many people and our animals, and that is suicide.

So we came to a decision today that was a sore point to everyone but couldn't be avoided. Discipline is critical, rules must be obeyed just as in any lifeboat situation, and the punishment for infraction of rules must be immediate and absolute. No one had discussed openly before today whether we should have brought the death penalty with us for certain crimes. There's no easy answer. What do we do if someone murders another person in a fit of anger, or because of lust, or due to plain cabin fever? What about child rape? What about the many heinous crimes that can stalk our numbers?

They cannot be left without response. They cannot go unpunished. Yet we are in such a finite system that the deliberate loss of a life is a grave matter. Executing a man means losing his sperm, his energy, his ability to work. Just as executing a woman means losing a mother, a worker, a human being. Yet, if we do not deter, how do we prevent anarchy? And on these ships anarchy is worse than an explosive fire!

We made what I believe is the right decision. In truth, Vasily made the decision, Mario Silva went along with it, and Biao and I kept our mouths shut. The day-to-day business of running the ships fell on the shoulders of Tereshnikov and Silva. They took the heat. It was their move. Vasily is pretty hard in these matters. Russian history, I don't know. But he must have had a touch of Solomon in him. He abided by the rule that to take a human life deliberately is an act of total desperation. If he found someone guilty of a serious crime that deserved serious punishment, he made certain the punishment *would serve the needs of the survivors of the human race.* Us!

The treadmills were part of the answer. The treadmills for cleaning out sewage, working in the reclamation vats, cleaning up after the animals. If a job was dangerous and dirty, so much the better. The convicted man or woman would carry out his sentence, or be confined to solitary.

Now, Tereshnikov knew better than to waste food and

water on anyone under punishment. That would only hurt those who abided by the rules and worked for the common good. So he devised solitary. They'd used it on *Gagarin*. I didn't know that. The prisoner was drugged so there wouldn't be a need to physically suppress him. He was then stripped naked and sealed in a flexible plastic bubble. The bubble was attached to a cable and pushed away from the ship.

The man or woman inside had no food, no water, no replacement of air. It could be viciously cold or suffocatingly hot depending on what side of the ship they were on. It didn't require a fancy IQ to realize this was really a rotten way to die, which they most certainly do if they stay out there. The way back was to promise to fulfill whatever punishment had been meted out. If they came back in and resorted to their former ways, out they went again, and this time they were left there until they *were* dead. They knew that after being returned to the ship their bodies would be plucked and picked clean to serve the rest of us. Organs, arteries, veins; all went into medical cryogenic storage for someone who might need them to stay alive in an emergency. Whatever couldn't be used would be ground up and mixed with animal feed for additional nutrients.

Does it really sound as horrible to the person who may be reading this as it does to me? Well, if you're reading these lines it means our mission was successful and that our system worked and we returned to Earth, after all, and generations followed us. I hope so. I hope dearly you're reading these words. It doesn't matter what you think or feel just as long as you're here to think and to feel.

But remember one thing, please. All the resources of all the universe to sustain us, to keep us alive, to hold out this last remaining spark for the future of the human race, were contained in our two ships. For a long time we held out hope that the Hestia base survived the violent electrical forces playing between Earth and the moon. We know that titanic energies must have created havoc beyond our imagination. Yet Hestia was deep beneath the surface. So were other facilities. If

they were deep enough and shielded well enough, they
could have survived. But as we were finally forced to
admit, survivors would certainly have rigged some kind
of radio communication. They could have sent us tight-
beam signals of *some* kind. Anything of a pattern would
have confirmed to us they were still alive and functioning. We have heard nothing. The silence is ominous.
The only sounds of human life are those from *Pegasus*
and *Noah*. I—all of us—wish we had more to offer. We
do not.

There was nothing else. There could be nothing else.
That was, *this is*, the way it is.

If no one reads this, then all will be darkness. If
someone does read this, it means there will still be light
by which to read.

*This is how we kept the fire burning for you, whoever
you are.*

Day 22

Helen Chandler floated "down" through the connecting tunnel from the bridge of *Noah* to Schoolhouse
Four amidships. On the way she opened and closed six
separate airlock doors, each with a teenager monitoring
the pressure gauge readings and controls. That had
been her own idea. As Flight Dynamics Officer for the
Animal Farm, she had been trying to bring the youngsters more and more into the daily operation of the
great vessel. The worst thing they could do was to
consider the children as wards or passengers.

She smiled as she eased into the training compartment marked with a tree symbol on its outer airlock
door. Ages six to ten. They were marvelous. These kids
had adapted faster to weightlessness than any other age
group. It seemed to come as naturally to them as flying
had to her when she was a youngster living on the
airport her folks owned in Montana. Chandler was thirty-
one years old and she'd been an astronaut for eight of
those years. Experience as a test pilot and several months
in orbit aboard a prototype space station of the United
States had guaranteed her selection for *Noah*. Now her
task as Flight Dynamics Officer was largely in limbo,

relegated to working with the computer and navigation teams to update constantly their position relative to Earth and sun already far behind them. *Now* she had a rare opportunity to teach the children how they could best work for their own future, first in space, and, hopefully, when the time came to return "home."

Chandler removed her pressure helmet. She floated with the casual smoothness of long experience to the "floor" of the Tree Room, where several children watched two youngsters in room center deeply engrossed in an experiment of their own making. She recognized Carey Randall, dark-haired and with huge eyes. Carey was nine years old. Her constant companion since entering *Noah* was Tim Foote, ten, and they were among the most promising of the "special" youngsters. At the moment they were building what they called a free blob, and it hung between them, quivering gently from its own instability and air currents in the room. Their blob was already five inches in diameter, bright pink and with the appearance of a Jello that had not come out right in the kitchen. Chandler noticed this blob differed from others. It was bigger than any she'd seen and had bright yellow spots through the quivering mass.

Carey saw Chandler floating nearby. "Hi! I'm glad you're here," she said brightly. "This is our best one so far. See how big it is, Miss Chandler?"

"It's a record," Tim added.

"So I see," Chandler said. "How'd you get it to stay together like that?"

Carey screwed up her face in thought. "We never got more than three inches across, you know? They would break up then. So we figured we needed more adhesive—"

"Adhesion," Tim corrected.

"Uh-huh. So we mixed in some pink food dye, see? That gave it color. Then Tim added vegetable shortening. Those are the yellow spots. Then we have this Blob Control—" Chandler saw a severely modified blower with four openings pointed in to a common center and a thick cylinder at the bottom. "Tim and his friend, Mike, they made this. They made a hand pump to compress air inside this part, see? And it's got a squeeze grip at

527

the top that releases *just* enough air for control so I can keep the blob in the center as it grows, you know, as we add the pink water. And that's how we got it so big. What's the biggest one you ever made, Miss Chandler?"

"Three and a half inches, Carey. I used a hair net to move it around. Before it broke up, that is. Yours looks much better." Her admiration for such ingenuity was real.

"We're going to let it free float now," Carey announced. She moved the Blob Control carefully away from the water sphere until it floated by itself, just over five inches in diameter, shining brightly. A small finger moved in to touch it gently. "See how it spins?" Carey cried out in delight as the blob quivered and began to rotate. She blew on it carefully and it spun faster. Tim blew from the other side so it wouldn't float away. "We want to make it spin faster," Carey said. The blob began to oscillate in different motions and its speed of turning increased.

"Watch out for peanut instability," Chandler warned.

"I know. That's the problem we want to solve," Tim Foote said solemnly.

"Damn damn!" Carey broke in as the water sphere began to shake and then broke into two blobs. "Bring them back together!" she called to Tim, and they blew carefully on the two drops until they joined. "Boy oh boy," Carey said, "I think it's going to work."

Laughter broke out as the two smaller spheres came together and then spattered into a hundred lesser globules. Immediately two other children held up vacuum hoses to suck in the free-floating liquid and keep it from splattering through the room.

"Well, like the big people say," Tim said with a smile, "that's close enough for government work."

Chandler laughed easily with them, then noticed the laughter was dying out quickly among the children. They were watching her in a sudden silence and glancing from her to Carey. *Uh oh. They've been waiting to get one of the big people alone like this*, Helen Chandler judged. She was right.

"Miss Chandler, can we ask you something?"

We. Not *I.* "Of course, honey. What is it?"

"When will we be going home?"

The question came forth so seriously, so direct, that Helen Chandler knew better than to answer in anything save the same vein. "None of us know, Carey," she said matter-of-factly. She eased herself to the deck and secured her feet to a velcro pad, then lowered herself so she could sit cross-legged and be on eye level with the children. She didn't want to leave her last response in a vacuum so she offered more. Carey was as solemn as a statue.

"We have limited fuel aboard this ship. Both ships have the same problem. That helps determine the minimum time we'll be away from Earth. It all ties in with our speed, how long we believe it will take the earth to be okay for us to live on, things like that. So from this information we come up with what I guess we could call a minimum time."

"That means we've got to be out in space for at least that much time, right?" The questioner was Tim Foote.

"Yes," Chandler said.

"How long is a minimum time?" She couldn't tell which one of the children had asked. They had moved in slowly until they sat before Chandler in a semicircle. *Like a jury*, thought Chandler.

Aloud she answered: "At our speed we'll sail outward for at least fourteen months. If we don't do a thing with the engines we start back then. It'll take us as long to get back as it did to get up that far. So we're talking at least twenty-eight months. I think it will be longer."

"What if we want to go back sooner?"

She no longer tried to identify any of the children from their questions. Let her answers be immediate and speak for themselves, she decided. "If we did that— and we could—we'd be signing our own death warrants. Do you understand what that means?" Heads nodded, and she went on. "If we burn fuel to slow down to start back sooner, we'll arrive back at Earth without enough fuel to get into low orbit about the planet. That would be stupid. And it's why I told you it

529

would be at least fourteen months before we'd even start back."

"But what if we find out," asked a dead-serious Carey Randall, "that we can't go back for, oh, let's say, well, twenty years, okay? That means twenty years going out, right? And twenty years coming back. Gee, Miss Chandler, I'll be about fifty years old by then."

"Me, too," said Tim Foote. "It would sure help to know what's going on."

"I've given you a very honest reply," Helen Chandler said. "An absolute minimum of twenty-eight months. I personally believe it will be between four and ten years."

Murmurs drifted among the children. "Miss Chandler, will our Earth ever be the same again?"

"No. *Nothing is ever the same again.*" Her eyes searched among the children. "Did you really mean to ask whether the Earth will again support our kind of life?"

"Uh, well, I guess so."

"The dust cloud that brought us out here won't last forever. It's like a desert sandstorm but much, much bigger. It has limits. Our solar system will move through it. When the sun is again normal and settles down, I believe our Earth will spring back and will definitely be a home for animal life."

"Does that mean us, too? People?"

"We are an animal type of life. Our existence is tied to the animals on these two ships. If it's okay for them, it's okay for us. I hope so. *You* hope so. That's the best we can do. We simply cannot predict everything."

"We're so far from home and we're still going out. How—uh, when, too—will we know it's safe to return?"

"Every month, starting just about eight days from now, we'll be firing a very fast rocket from us back to Earth. It uses special fuels—well, it's a very special kind of rocket. Its computers will slow it down when it gets to Earth and place it in orbit, just like we were. It has powerful cameras and radios and it will examine the Earth in detail. Or," she made a sour face, "as much detail as it can get. We don't know how thick the clouds still are, or how bad the storms are. That's why we'll be

530

sending back these probes. When we get the pictures and the information we need to know it's safe to return, that's when you'll be hearing those big rockets booming."

"But what if it's not safe to go home for a long time?"

"Then we keep right on trucking, boys and girls."

"How long could that be?"

Chandler shrugged. "Twenty years. Thirty. Maybe forty."

Carey Randall's mouth opened in a soundless O before she found her voice. *"But I'll be old by then!"*

"Yes.' You'll be old by then. And so will everyone else who left Earth on these ships."

"Will you be dead by then?"

Helen Chandler laughed quietly. "I think so. Sooner or later we'll all go that way. It's a necessary part of life."

"But . . . what happens to us, all us kids, if you and all the other grownups die!"

Helen Chandler offered up a silent prayer for this incredible moment. "You'll take over," she said softly. *"All* the children will take over as they grow older. That's why we're teaching you to run the ship, to take care of the life support systems, to clean the air and run the power generators. How to work the computers and the rocket engines, and repair the ships, and be space farmers who take care of all the animals and the plants. *And each other.* Don't forget that. You've got to take care of each other. You'll be the only ones left. That is, of course, until the new children are born and then you can pass on that same information and skills to them. You see?"

"Are you going to have children, Miss Chandler?"

"I hope so. I hope that if I have a girl, she'll be just like you, Carey. And I'd like my son to be like Tim."

"Thank you. Will you teach me how to fly *Noah?*"

"You bet I will!"

Day 47

Interim Progress Report of Cosmonaut Tanya Yevte-shenka, First Computer Officer, SS *Pegasus*

This American, it turns out, is not the fool I had taken him to be. He is crafty, even cunning, beyond anything for which I gave him credit. I was against the selection of Marc Seavers as the mission commander of these two vessels. He is an American admiral, but that does not match the years of training and preparation that we cosmonauts have behind us for so ultimate a flight as that which we now take. There is no substitute for experience. General Vasily Tereshnikov has that experience and his skills were recognized by all when he was made the captain of this vessel. Giving command to Mario Silva is a horrible decision. Why anyone would confer upon the little general of a militarily bankrupt nation like Portugal the command of such a vessel as *Noah* defies all reason. That was the ship that should have come under the command of Gregory Tretyakovich, who is beloved to the people of all nations. To maintain this record in strict accuracy, it must be recorded that Tretyakovich, when approached by us on this matter, lost his famous temper, told us he would never accept such a position, and forbade us ever to bring up the matter again. He was truly angry. I do not fully understand, although it is my conviction that he hoped the details of his refusal would reach the ears of the people from the third-world nations who crowd these two ships.

Where I found Marc Seavers cunning is in his genius for conferring responsibility on his subordinates. He considers Vasily Tereshnikov to be one of those lower-class members of this crew. Vasily dismisses my feelings with a curt motion of his hand, but I know and love this man, and I also know better. Seavers spent the high moments of his career in Antarctica. Clearly he is a brave and a courageous man, but all the courage on or off a world will not replace the experience our people have gathered.

Marc Seavers sustains a most lofty position. He is almost a pope on this ship, and that strange Chinaman,

Chiang Biao, appears to function as his high priest. They plot together very well. Seavers makes decisions and issues orders, and Biao wears ceremonial robes and dispenses pearls of wisdom which few people understand but which seem not only to placate those under Seavers but even to inspire them. It is a remarkable combination.

Seavers has been entirely successful in unloading technical problems on the shoulders of Tereshnikov. Poor Vasily! He awakens one morning to take his duty shift and he is immediately burdened with the problems of that idiot nuclear reactor we have on this ship. We have been experiencing load-up problems. Unusual pressures arising from the formation of superheated gas bubbles in the lines, most likely due to the effects of weightlessness on such machinery over this long period of time. Several times now the entire vessel has felt the grumblings of the nuclear genie mounted amidships near the stern. Everything has rattled, and fear stalks the control rooms and the corridors. Seavers in his infinite wisdom, I confess to sarcasm here, has ordered Vasily Tereshnikov and all technicians to prepare for shutdown of the nuclear reactor and operate for weeks, if necessary, on standby power. We *could* rig long power cables from *Noah* to us and avoid so complicated a task, but the decision is made on the highest of levels and Seavers has the authority. We spent nearly three days and nights without sleep computing the shift to non-nuclear power, and then everything was kept on standby. I suspect Marc Seavers did not lose any sleep. I suspect further that he spent his sleep and rest periods enjoying the charms of his woman. Vasily does not have that pleasure. I want to pleasure him, but of all people he must not set what the American calls a "poor example." We must first be married. Seavers has no idea how long I have waited for such an event!

Day 51

"We are ready for the test, Marc Seavers." Vasily Tereshnikov looked haggard. He'd caught a few naps

533

during the past four days while technicians modified the boom generators at the prow. Seavers had ordered the electromagnetic deflectors to be shut down.

"They're draining our energy," he insisted to Tereshnikov, "and they aren't doing a damned bit of good. We're being hit with as much dust as we were—"

"It is less," Tereshnikov insisted.

"Only because we're starting to escape from that damned cloud," Seavers shot back. "But it's *not* less because of any current those booms are kicking out."

"That may be so," Tereshnikov said, not yielding an inch. "I do not know and *you* do not know. You suspect, you theorize. But I must agree with you that we need greater results for the amount of energy we expend. All right, then. Our computer studies have shown that the problem lies in how we have spent our energy. We need to reverse the field."

"That's so much Russian bullshit, Vasily."

"Yours is of no higher quality," Tereshnikov retorted. "We will talk forever and accomplish nothing. You agree?"

He watched Seavers nod, then turned to his staff at the power controls on *Pegasus'* bridge. "Commence the test," he ordered. On the bridge the crew crossed fingers. They all knew both ships had been taking a terrible scouring from the long passage at great speed through the thinning but still dangerous dust cloud. The boom generators had not reduced the sandblasting effect by any appreciable amount. Even the lexitr screens were showing signs of scraping.

Marcus Goldman held his hand firmly on the heavy switch, looked at Tereshnikov, saw him nod, and hauled down. A deep thrumming sound built up at once as enormous energy fed from the nuclear reactor into the boom generators. Green electrical flame arced from one boom to the other, sputtering and snapping. *It worked.* For the first time, they saw a flow pattern in space vacuum as the powerful electrical field acted as a great plowblade.

And a devastating static electricity field leaped into being within the ship. Limbs jerked as sparks shot between ship structure and human bodies. Static electricity crackled audibly, streamers began to extend from hair and fingers, and little beads of electrical fire appeared above the control panels. Alarm bells clamored through *Pegasus* as electrical systems began to overload, and soon the cries of alarm from the human occupants were met with a horrendous uproar from frightened and pained animals as static electricity shocked across fur and feathers and skin.

"Shut down! Shut down!" Tereshnikov shouted. Goldman had already reversed the switch when he felt the shocks and saw his master panel needles swinging into yellow danger zones. He gasped from a final surge of current through his hand. He felt release from the current, turned to Tereshnikov. Goldman rubbed a hand that still curled stiffly.

"Sir, if we try that again we'll blow every resistor and circuit aboard this ship," he said to Tereshnikov.

The Russian nodded. "Disengage the system," he ordered. Tereshnikov turned to Seavers. "It seems you are right. We must find another way to protect us for what you call the long haul."

"I'll set up a meeting right away for—"

"*No.*"

Seavers blinked. Neither had ever said that to the other. They locked eyes in their first confrontation. "You have more important and less technical matters to attend to," Tereshnikov said. "Commander Silva wishes you to meet with him on *Noah*. There is a leadership problem there. *That* is your first responsibility, Admiral Seavers."

"We make our decisions jointly. You and I," Seavers reminded him.

Tereshnikov did not smile. "Authority is not something one bandies about, my friend. *You* will decide the issues that affect how we live, how we work, how we plan for what we both fondly call the big picture, all those things you will come to hate soon enough. But where you run your ship of state, Marc Seavers, *I* run this vessel. You may select its course but not its operation. You must understand this. I ask it of you. The admiral commands the fleet, not the ship."

"You're the captain," Seavers said finally.

"Good!" Tereshnikov boomed. "Now I will oversee the dismantling of the system."

"After which," Seavers said slowly, "you and your engineering staff will meet with me and you will then explain to me what you will substitute for the force field." Seavers rose quietly to his feet, controlling his body movements with practiced ease. "To continue this growing collection of witticisms, Vasily, the captain's work is never done. Please have a tug ready for me to transfer to *Noah*."

He winked as he floated by.

Day 62

These are the, uh, I guess you call them the minutes of our, uh, first meeting. Oh. I'm, uh, not used to working one of these things. This tape recorder I'm using. I'm supposed to keep a record of our club. My name is Charles Berry. I'm fifteen and most of the guys are about my age. We're keeping our club a secret. I guess the older people would call us a gang. Maybe so. We call ourselves the Eagles. You know, for the biggest birds of prey. The guys on *Noah*—we all agree that's a stupid name—they're the Wolverines. They like that name. Would you believe they actually got some of those things on that ship? Six of them, in fact. Man, they're nasty, all right. Two of them ate through the screening in their cage and got into a bigger cage. It was filled with goats. All of them tethered. The guys said there was blood everywhere. Them wolverines killed nine of 'em. Just tore their way along, hanging on to fur and chewing as they went.

This whole club idea started when the Elders, that's what we call the old fogeys, well, when they made us all go to meetings to talk about religion. We know better'n that shit. They didn't want to *talk* to us. They wanted us to attend some kind of religious services. Not all the elders. Them Russians, man, they got a real hardon when it comes to this praying stuff. The captain of this ship, this Tereshnikov, I hope I said his name right, he blew up when he found out. Said none of this was ever to happen again without his permission.

This God stuff is a lot of shit, believe me. Anyway, if God was real I hope they shove it as far up his ass as it will go. I mean, what are we doing here in this stupid ship and the whole Earth and all them billions of people back there are dead. Man, there ain't no God what would do that.

So we decided we got to look out for ourselves. Tereshnikov told us that. He warned us that both ships were full of these religious nuts. They all believe that they're right and everybody else is wrong. That can't be right, so what Tereshnikov tells us got to be true. He told us to think for ourselves, that the history of the world is filled with fanatics like these and all they ever caused was a lot of killing and slavery. We set up a secret radio frequency between the two ships. We can hold meetings here and the Wolverines, they can do the same over there, and we can sort of meet at the same time by radio. The guys been ripping off some stuff from the storage bins. They're building teevee transceivers from our clubhouse to theirs, you know, send and receive at the same time. If some of our real smart guys work it out they'll build a special kind of laser beam design for the teevee signal, so we can all see and hear each other.

We got to hold these meetings. We're starting to keep a list of these fanatics. The ones that Captain Tereshnikov said want to brainwash us. If ever we get back to Earth, he told us, they'd control our minds before we ever got there, and then they'd be the masters and we'd be their slaves. And all the time we'd believe we were doing it for God.

Boy, what a crock of shit.

Day 71
Report of Peter Nicholson, Veterinarian, *Pegasus*, and Jon Gierek, Livestock Chief, *Noah*, submitted jointly to Captains Vasily Tereshnikov and Mario Silva, further

distribution of copies to be made by Executive Command each vessel:

The experiments conducted with centrifuges have worked beyond our greatest expectations. In one stroke we have found the means to overcome the almost one hundred percent death rate among animals during birthing. The problem, as expected, has been weightlessness, with only a few surviving animals among those sedated and tethered. But at the rate we have been losing our animals, the future has been bleak.

We made the centrifuge experiments with the smaller animals. This permitted us to assemble the materials quickly and minimize energy expenditure. Mice, hamsters, rabbits, cats, and small dogs were used. Some of these animals were pregnant. Others were among the more serious cases of calcium loss, blood cell breakdown, consistent vertigo, stomach disorders, and similar problems, all of which are included in the appendix to this report.

Note: Many of these same physiological disorders are already being encountered in increasing numbers with the human passengers aboard both vessels. This matter must be, in the opinion of the signers of this report, addressed immediately. To continue:

The centrifuges were built up with a complete outer tube much on the order of an innertube. Lexitr construction material was used due to its nonelectrical properties, strength, visibility, and resistance to corrosive fluids, including animal wastes. At various locations within these tubes we placed drinking water, food bins, material for making nests, enclosed areas for complete privacy. We built the centrifuges so that we could resupply food and water. Elimination of waste material while under operation has yet to be worked out.

The animals were placed in this outer rim. The compartment in which the centrifuges were mounted was set up with ultraviolet fluorescent lights timed to normal Earth day-night cycles. The wheels were then spun for seventy-two hours at a rate imparting a thirty percent Earth-surface g along the outer rim. The outermost inner wall surface, once spinning, became the "floor" of the compartment, and the design "pushed" the animals to accept it as such.

After the first three days of .33g we increased for three additional days to .70g and, after this period, increased rotation to 1g. *Almost all of the deleterious effects indicated improvement almost immediately.* Anticipating this level of success, we had already begun work on the tanks for marine creatures. The same system as noted above was employed and special aeration was used for high oxygen flow to the water. Initial success has again been on a level we judge as extraordinary.

We make two immediate recommendations. First, that larger centrifuges be constructed at once for the larger animals and for human reacclimation to responsible g-loading. Such large centrifuges understandably may cause perturbations of the multiple-axes stability of a vessel even as large as *Pegasus/Noah*. Prior to submitting this report we met with John Hastings, Gene Camblin, Kenneth Stewart, Lester Rejani, and Archer Begley of *Pegasus*, as well as Benita de la Madrid, Hans Dornier, Helen Chandler, and Hans Motubai of *Noah*. We bring to this report a unanimous declaration of agreement.

We further recommend an immediate conference on imparting a responsible g-loading to the entire *Noah* vessel.

Please consult the appendices for specifics.

Day 94

Preliminary Confidential Report. Commander Mario Silva to Dr. Chiang Biao, Admiral Marc Seavers, Commander Vasily Tereshnikov. Further distribution at this time is not recommended. Group discussion among those named is considered imperative. The following is a tape-dictated transcribing:

We are faced with our first murder. That is my immediate reaction to the situation aboard *Noah*. It is true my words are a prejudgment, but in the position I hold it is an acceptable fault. Tradition commands that the captain does not hold trial by jury. I will review briefly and then I respectfully request group discussion to establish precedence in fact rather than in only principle.

What I describe as murder may not be, in that the act may have been based on such emotional outrage that some would consider it self-defense. That is not my feeling. I face a killing of a human being by another human being in a situation where no lives were imperiled. In brief, CHUKS ILEOGBUNAM of Sudan, charged with Reclamation responsibilites aboard this ship, became embroiled in a most serious emotional dispute on ethnic and religious grounds with the Israeli, YESEF HARIF, who directs *Noah*'s Genetics Laboratory.

The dispute centered about the use of reclaimed and reprocessed human urine as pure water for human consumption. With most of our initial water supply consumed, this is the only method we possess for sustaining critical water source until we make Earthfall at an uncertain time in the future.

Yesef Harif appears to consider this fact of our collective situation of less importance than his ethnic and/or religious background. In sum, he has declared that it is against the word of God to drink one's own body waste products. He refused to accept any such water that is being consumed by everyone else aboard our ship, and demanded drinking water from the supply brought aboard this ship during orbital supply operations. This insistence, and unkind words directed at Chuks Ileogbunam, who demanded the Israeli perform as everyone else, led to a serious confrontation between the two men. Ileogbunam solved the immediate problem by seizing Harif, along with several of his coworkers, and, holding the Israeli against his wishes, force-fed him the reclaimed liquids.

The Israeli considers himself unclean and, according to the dictates of his religion, can cleanse himself only with the blood of the tormentor who violated God's laws. As captain of this vessel, I do not judge theological beliefs. My concern, as you will agree, involves Harif's reaction to this incident. During the next sleep period he strangled the Sudanese until he was dead. Harif has not attempted to hide his act or deny being directly and deliberately responsible for the death of Ileogbunam.

I am not Solomon. I am distraught with the concept of deliberately taking a life. I can accept killing through passion or fear or other intense emotional crises. But I now face a most serious disciplinary situation. I cannot permit the crime to go unpunished. I am horrified at compounding the matter by ending the life of a human being when there are so few of us left.

Help me.

Day 110

"You have completed your studies? Your meetings?" Marc Seavers felt like an idiot, posing the questions to Chiang Biao. On the plane the Chinese scholar and scientist functioned, Seavers knew he could only rate as the lowest order of novice. Yet Biao didn't appear to feel that way. *He sees something in me I never saw*, Seavers thought warily.

Biao sat before him in midair. He had taught himself this remarkable position, legs crossed and feet beneath his body. Adroit motions of his hands and controlled breathing, all on a subconscious level, enabled him to float within a prescribed area. *If we were back on Earth he'd be just as comfortable as he is now, except that he'd be levitating*.

Chiang Biao nodded agreement to Seavers. He did not turn his head, but his eyes moved to acknowledge the presence and importance of Nancy Seavers seated with her husband. "Yes. I have done so," Biao verbalized his response.

"I want to get something very clear," Seavers said. "This is not an official meeting. It is, as you requested, a philosophical overview between," Seavers smiled, "friends and scholars. To give us a perspective we would not achieve merely by considering material responsibilities of who and what we are."

"Yes."

"You specifically requested my wife to be with us."

541

"Yes."

"I appreciate her presence—"

"Why?"

"Why?" Seavers echoed. "Because you honor her!"

"I'm grateful to be here," Nancy Seavers said quickly. "I hadn't expected—"

"Forgive my rudeness. Do not be grateful for what is not so, Nancy Seavers. There lies nothing personal behind your presence. I do you no honor. I wish to ask you questions for something you do that is remarkable. I would not have expected it without long tutoring at a monastery. In *that* respect I honor you. But it is for your thought, not your most cherished personal company."

"I detect a touch of a smile, Doctor Biao."

"You are a discerning as well as beautiful person. May I commence?"

Nancy smiled. She felt marvelous in the presence of Biao. "Of course. Please."

"You have, in the vernacular, been driving people up a wall with your insistence on preserving music. This is remarkable for one so young. It is even more remarkable when we understand there is no particular music that you seek to preserve. Do I speak accurately?"

"You do. My interest is in the music of man. Of the human race."

"Nancy, do you know why human beings evolved music?"

She smiled at Biao. "Yes, I do."

"How marvelous. Our scholars have spent centuries trying to discover that secret. Would you care to tell me?"

Her smile was a touch more reserved, more secretive. "I am delighted, Doctor. Human beings evolved music because they wanted to do so."

Biao's eyes widened which, for him, was equal to shouted exclamations and a St. Vitus's dance. "Incredible," he said, so softly they barely heard him. His head leaned a bit closer to the Seavers. "I speak now in true search. Your opinions, your judgments, are remarkable. Would you venture your opinion on two other questions? Ah, thank you. *What* is music? And, *when* did music originate?"

"The answer to both questions, Doctor Biao, is simple. I do not know. I don't believe anyone knows. I cannot believe we will ever *know*, as we judge knowledge in terms of measurements. Music transcends and evades all such measurement. It emerges from conscious and subconscious. It is," she hesitated before going on, "the spirit. It's also like a closed loop of understanding. Like the difference between brain and mind. What *is* the difference? When did the mind emerge from the physical brain?" She laughed. "*That* answer is easier than music! When the brain perceived itself it had already become a mind. Music in its whys and whens is much more difficult. However, I am convinced—without proof, I'm quick to admit—that I believe this part of the human spirit is as essential to growth and survival as is speech. In many ways it *is* speech. If we let our music die, a critical, intrinsic part of us dies. We must not permit this to happen. It is why I am such a—"

"Fanatic?" he offered.

"Yes," she said firmly. "A fanatic. Like all those who believe as strongly as I do."

Marc Seavers looked at Nancy as if he were seeing his wife for the first time. "Good Lord," he said slowly, "I had no idea. Not a smidgen," he went on. "When did you start all this?"

"Back at Disney World, Marc. I made certain that musical instruments, everything from harmonicas to lutes, were brought to the briefing areas, and whoever could do it, I had carry one of those instruments with them. If I'd tried to get them on a cargo manifest I know I would have failed. Who's going to put aside medical supplies or food for trumpets or a clarinet? Your astronauts also helped. They slipped instruments everywhere in the shuttles. Even in the cargo loads."

"Jesus," he said. "You *do* know how to keep a secret."

"So did the astronauts," Nancy grinned at him. "That's in addition to the sheet music and the tapes and—well, you get the idea."

"Be grateful to her, Marc," Biao said. "She has saved what may be more valuable to us than any technical knowledge."

"Doctor, why do you consider this music so critical?" Seavers asked.

"It is our spirit captured," he was told. "That simple. It is not technical, mathematical, a thing to put down in formulae. Music emerges from physical motion as compression in air. Waves of pressure flow outward from their source. A man's ears detect these pressure waves, detect their infinitely subtle variations. The miracle that is our body and brain transduces the pressure waves of a fluid medium, the air, into incredibly complex electrical impulses. Bundles of fibres shoot these to the brain. Yet the man or woman who hears a particular strain of all this subtle and complicated affair recognizes a chord, a melody, and instantly a vast orchestration of memory and association is triggered within his mind. Our response is totally, absolutely emotional. We live, vicariously and actually, the experiences of *all* our species through its music."

Biao turned back to Nancy. "How is your concert coming along?"

"How did you find out!"

"What concert?" Marc Seavers broke in.

"The children. They've been practicing. Listening to the tapes and practicing. We're going to assemble them in groups aboard both ships. They'll coordinate by sight and sound—audio and video hookups. They're planning a concert to be played for everyone."

"I'll be damned," Seavers said.

"Saved, not damned," Biao told him. "Marc, are you familiar with the name of Hippolytos?"

"No."

"Einstein quoted him with almost forbidding regularity. Hippolytos lived nearly two and a half thousand years ago, and he in turn was fond of quoting Pythagoras. Behind all this quotation is the written belief of Pythagoras that is it is not man who sings, but the universe itself; that all the universe was constructed in absolute harmony. Music, therefore, is an expression of universal order. It has always been with us; indeed, billions of years before man was even considered in the universal scheme, music existed. Harmony does not result from music. The universe evolved with its many parts and the whole in harmony. Much, much more recently, as you stated so eloquently when we departed Earth, Marc, man arrived to observe, perhaps even more to sense and feel this harmony, and produced his music. I consider music to be this universal harmony now available on command through our instruments, voices, and our electronic devices."

Nancy shifted uncomfortably. "You make me feel . . . well, almost sacrilegious to dare to walk among such giants," she said.

"Ah, but you are wrong, Nancy Seavers. It is the other way around. It is I who listens to the teacher. It is you who has the instinctual understanding. If the fates smile upon us, if we make our own future as we have the capability to do, we shall endure; but we shall continue to endure only if our music goes with us. Otherwise we shall be struck deaf and blind and it will be our end."

Marc Seavers pursued a thought dropped by Biao, tantalizing and yet difficult to grasp. "Chiang, wait a moment. Something you just said. I'm not sure I understood what you meant. You said that we would make our own future? That *we* would *make it*?"

"I am pleased, Marc. You heard and you remembered correctly."

"How do you mean that?"

Chiang Biao's eyes seemed hollow, pools without measurable depth. "Some call it fate. What will be, will be. I do not so subscribe. We must become part of the harmonics of the universe. Then we do not fight all the forces that make up existence. We glide through obstacles. If we do not, the friction makes all things impassable and we are no longer fit to harmonize with the future. Thus we never achieve it. The universe, my friend, is littered with unharmonic failure." Biao closed his eyes, seemed to leave a hollow shell of a body with the Seaverses. His body trembled as he returned to occupy its space.

"Ah. I believe, my friends, that the gods have planned all that has happened to us, most carefully. I do not believe as you do, Marc Seavers, that this flight may last a hundred years. These ships will never endure. You know that; now we share that knowledge openly. We will return much sooner to Earth *but we must will this to be so.* That is the law of Anthropic Principle."

Nancy stared at her husband. Marc's expression was blank. Biao had struck a chord somewhere in his thoughts and again, as he'd already done several times, he found himself pursuing what seemed always to lie just beyond his mental fingertips.

Marc Seavers studied the older man. He wasn't prepared yet to consider Chiang Biao a *friend.* The walls between them were still mysterious and many, although they seemed to be thinning. Biao could drive a sane man crazy with his dipping into philosophical pools, and just when you were prepared to jump his ass on ignoring reality in favor of philosophical doodle-dipping, you had to remind yourself that he was for many years one of the world's most accomplished scientists and theoretical physicists. But Seavers had something few other men had enjoyed—what amounted to virtually Biao's full attention to Seavers' future.

"You've been pushing me in this area," Seavers said aloud. He glanced at his wife and returned his eyes to Biao. "First it was Heisenberg day and night. Now it's Anthropy. Why are you dragging that in here at this point?"

It was the first time Nancy had ever seen Biao smile openly. "Wonderful! You have been to the well, Marc."

"Damn it, yes," Seavers said impatiently. "Now let's put all this together. Music, harmony, challenge with a different face: you're trying to have me push and prod all of it into a single package with an anthropic label on it."

"You do very well. Do you yet understand that you must pay your dues to Heisenberg's Uncertainty Principle before you may proceed to the next step?"

"I've sure as hell been trying," Seavers said, almost with a growl. Nancy looked at him, astonished. She had had no concept that her husband had ever plunged so deeply into the abstract— *Whoa; stop right there, lady. This isn't abstract to them. That's the whole pitch from the Chinaman. He's talking about reality on a level you haven't even dreamed of yet. Shut up and listen.*

". . . if you have hewed to the Uncertainty Principle," Biao was saying, "then you cannot ever measure more than one specific, or quantity, at a time. The specific may be motion or position or momentum; whatever it is down in the field of subatomic particles you are trapped. The measurement of one forbids the measurement of another because the act of measurement in the first sense precludes the other."

Nancy felt her head swimming. She was amazed as Marc moved smoothly through the thickets. "Yeah, well, that figures easily enough," he said in response. "It's like trying to measure the forces of an aircraft in flight. Each measurement must be taken separately; all others become and must remain theoretical. If I want to measure lifting force at any one point, I have to 'stop' the machine in flight. But to do that I must stop forward movement, which means I've also stopped airflow across the wing, and if I do *that* I've killed the lift. Yes, Chiang, Heisenberg is just as familiar in the everyday molecular as he is in the subatomic."

"Please," Biao urged. "Continue."

"Well, everything has to relate to or be related to. If you take pairs of subnuclear particles from a single source and separate them, they'll continue to match or influence each other. Somehow, if you measure one of this pair, the measurement determines the properties of the second particle, no matter how distant it might be from the first."

"Relate what you have said to where and what we are and must become," Biao prompted.

"Whoo, boy . . . Okay. If the 'uncertainty principle' becomes a part of everyday life, *observable* everyday life, then whatever we see in the universe or of the universe *depends upon the means we use to observe that universe.* If our observation changes what we're observing, then the act of observing or measuring makes the very act of observation a creative element of what's being observed. So when I observe a particle, I imbue it with certain properties that exist *only* because I'm viewing or measuring it. Therefore," Marc Seavers plugged on doggedly, "we all play a critical or even dominant role in bringing into existence something of what we see or observe."

Nancy stared at her husband, at Biao, then blankly. "If I'm not here to be affected by compression of the fluid medium, as you two said before, and I can't judge the timing of compressions, and my biological system doesn't convert varying pressure into electrical signals . . . then, then there's no music."

"Ah, marvelous," Biao said very softly.

"Without me there's no music?"

"That is so."

"Who established what they call the anthropic principle?" Nancy Seavers asked of Biao.

"His name is Robert Dicke. A physicist. He repeated many times," Biao related, "that the universe is the way it is only because we are in the universe."

Nancy giggled. "Certainly. If I'm not here to observe you two, then you aren't here?"

"That's the general pitch," her husband said, grinning. "The crazy thing is *that it's true.* We couldn't conceive of the universe unless we, all of us, were here to observe it. But what gets stuck in my mental craw is that the community of thinkers, all of us, aren't possible *unless* the universe is adapted from its very start to give rise to life and then to mind. Sort of gets you in the gut, doesn't it?"

"You're both making me quite dizzy," Nancy said in self-defense.

"Well, it's a closed circle, hon. You can't have any laws of physics unless there are minds, sentient beings, to observe those laws. No observers, no laws. *No nothing.* But what grabs you is carrying that one step further. Once we as the observers create the laws of physics, we become trapped by them. They're like free-flowing concepts until we give them form. Once we do that they become rigid and we're now controlled by the laws we created. What Chiang is trying to tell us, I *think*," Seavers rolled his eyes, "is that what happens to us from now on is determined more by what we decide to do and then *do* than by sitting back on our collective butts and waiting for something to happen."

"There is another way to say it. We have been saying it for thousands of years," Biao offered. "We are the masters of our own destiny."

"Where would our destiny be," Nancy said, irritated by what she considered lofty pretensions, "had we stayed on Earth and died with everyone else? What would have happened to our observing anything out here?"

"You didn't stay on Earth. You're here, affecting everything about you. If you weren't here, you would affect nothing. You would not *be*." Biao smiled. "But since you *are* here . . ." He concluded with a shrug.

"Maybe I can help with that one," Marc Seavers offered his wife. "Think of merry old England. Robin Hood trots along a country lane on his horse. He sees a bunch of horsemen and figures he's really in deep stuff now because they look like the local sheriff and a bunch of his not-so-merry deputies. Robin kicks his horse in the slats and takes off at a gallop, going cross-country. But the horsemen aren't from Nottingham; they're actually Little John and more friends of Robin Hood. They wonder where Robin is going so hellbent for leather, and they ride after him. Robin is galloping alongside a cemetery when his horse pulls up lame. He jumps off and hides behind a gravestone. There comes Little John and Robin's friends. They see Robin hiding behind the gravestone and they ask him, 'What's up, man? And what are you doing behind that gravestone?'

"Robin sighs, gets up, dusts off his clothes and stares up at Little John. 'It's more complicated than you'd ever believe,' Robin tells him. 'I'm here because of you, and you're here because of me.' "

Day 111

Keesha Seavers held the furry little body in her hands. A tear started from her eye and drifted before her, glistening-quivering in midair. "Smokey's dead," she told her brother Tom.

"I know. But Mom said we could have Bullwinkle."

"Bullwinkle's a rabbit. I don't know if I want a rabbit."

"Maybe we'll like him."

"I *love* Smokey!"

"Me, too."

"I think we should bury him."

"You *can't* bury him. How are we going to bury Smokey in space?"

Keesha's eyes widened. "But if we don't bury him, where will his soul go?"

"Gee, I don't know."

"Me, neither." She clutched Smokey tighter. "I *won't* put him in the garbage!"

"Maybe we can bring him to Reclamation, Keesh. That way he'll still be here. You know, like a part of the other animals."

"Will it hurt?"

"Nah, I don't think so."

"You think Mommy will say a prayer for him?"

"Sure. You and me, too."

Day 146

"Control, Begley here. Tug Twelve is in position off the starboard bow. Over."

"Five by five, Arch. You ready for your inspection report?"

"You better believe it, Control. Record this, please."

"You're on. Go ahead."

"Okay. Begley in Spacetug Twelve. I've completed my visual of the forward sections of *Noah* and *Pegasus*. Right now I'm a hundred yards off the nose of *Pegasus*. I've made a detailed observation of the prow shield. It's in terrible shape, pitted and worn thin. It will stop dust for a while, but any micrometeoroid particles will punch right through. If we want to prevent a big hole from appearing in any of the forward sections of this ship, or in *Noah*, we'd better get some kind of a shield in place or we got real troubles. Over."

"You got pictures, arch?"

"Color and three-D."

"Bring 'em in, babe."

"Gotcha."

Commander's Log, *Pegasus*
Day 158

Married Vasily Tereshnikov and Tanya Yevteshenka today 2200 hours. Sonia Barkagan was maid of honor and Gregory Tretyakovich best man. Nancy Seavers and Susan Foster produced a fresh bouquet of flowers for the bride. God only knows how they managed that small miracle. Costa la Perez of Argentina sent over from *Noah* a bottle of wine that appeared as if by magic. Six children played the wedding march. A wonderful, spirit-enhancing occasion. I have forbidden Vasily to return to the bridge or any other ship's duties for seventy-two hours. After that we'll all have our hands full. We must produce a solution that will protect both ships from the abrasive effect of dust at our continued high speed. We are also losing animals at a disastrous rate aboard *Noah*. We have no choice but to attempt to rotate the entire vessel for artificial gravity. It will be like rolling a mountain.

25

*M*ichele Crawford had long blonde hair twisted into ponytails and wrapped behind her head. She was of that rare breed, the veterinarian astronaut: her training and experience had been directed toward keeping animals alive, healthy, and functioning aboard orbiting animals alive, healthy, and functioning aboard an orbiting space station. Aboard *Pegasus* she shared that re- ists worked closely with their equal numbers aboard

Noah, Jon Gierek and Rudyard Gyn, who were near to desperation trying to save the lives of the hapless domestic creatures and "wild" animals on that giant craft. Michele Crawford became the natural leader of the group due to her degrees in mechanical engineering as well as husbandry. They met aboard *Noah.* Crawford noted in her log that they had been away from Earth now for five months thirteen days, and things were going to hell in a handbasket.

"The four of us *must* function as the tightest team possible," she told the others. "While we attend to the miracle they want us to pull off, I want you all to feel confident that the animals in your charge are taken care of properly. Sonia Barkagan will become director of all animal life support for *Noah* with Costa la Perez as her standby. Andres Segovia and Lester Rajani will fill those jobs here on *Pegasus.*

"Now, let's review. Nice and fast. No one's ever faced our problem. We have no precedents. This is a make-or-break shot. Anybody find any fault with *that* let me hear it now." No one said a word.

"The animals have suffered, most of them, from the moment they were shoved into zero-g. We've had them in harnesses, all kinds of experimental restraints, we've wrapped them nose to ass in velcro, but none of it works. That young girl, Rodeina Quaid, set the pattern for animals with her dog, but we need a lot of hands and time to rig up the harnesses and treadmills and the rest of that lot. It doesn't work when you've got weightless barnyards and terrified creatures in wholesale lots. Now, the animals aren't adapting, and we can't handle even a fair share of them in the centrifuges. We've beaten a lot of birth emergencies and other problems with the whirligigs but at best it's a lousy solution because of all the logistics—feeding and cleaning, for example—that simply won't go away. There's only one answer to preventing us from losing these animals, and let me make it clear that if we lose them half the people on these ships will be dead before we ever return to Earth. Okay, I'll stick to the issue at hand. Our only answer is to impart artificial gravity to a very large area of *Noah*. If we do that we can even move the more sensitive creatures from this ship to the Animal Farm. Any questions?"

"What level g are you talking about?" Gyn asked.

"Minimal at first. Ten to twenty percent. No more than that. The physiological transition could be very brutal after this much time in zero g. We'll also have physical problems with the ship. I'm absolutely certain of that. We're going to load up that tub in a way it was never designed to handle. A lot of things could come loose. It's going to be a three-ring circus before we're through. But once we get through the first rotational periods I believe we'll be able to build up rotational speed. Along the outside of *Noah* centrifugal force should give us some very decent weight factors."

Michele Crawford tapped her notes. She didn't need to refer to them. She'd been working on these problems a long time, ever since it became clear to the command group that the animals would never survive a prolonged flight under weightlessness. Yet they couldn't do the job hastily. They had to figure in the dynamics of rotation, accelerating the great ship around its axis in lateral motion, imparting a gentle spin that at first would produce along the outermost walls of *Noah* a small fraction of terrestrial gravity.

"When we start up," she warned the others, "we'll need every hand we can get. Fluids are going to shift and we've got to control that shift or it will punch right on through the hull. That tub could develop a squiggle that could carry through with a resonance bounce and break up the strongest beams in the structure. We're not *that* certain that everything is squared away properly. I expect we'll snap some lines, strain the hell out of others, and make most of the cabins on that ship a real mess. So we do everything very gently and give people a chance to stay on top of things. Above all, with the hooved animals, we've got to have people right there to shift them from harness positions to where their own legs will support them. That means different restraints, no-skid surfaces under what will become floors. Questions?"

553

Jon Gierek looked doubtful. "You talk of fifteen percent gravity, no?"

"That's the minimum once we're spun up, yes."

"How do you know this will work for the animals? I am very concerned."

"I respect your concern, Gierek. But we know one-sixth grav will work just fine. That's what they had on the moon bases and the animals did great there."

"Is good," he said gravely. "Thank you."

A lot more was required than simply placing reaction thrusters angled at ninety degrees to a line from bow to stern. The motors had to fire smoothly, each one in concert with the others, and all of them must be ready to fire in the opposite direction to their initial thrust to correct any overspeed or to damp out oscillations or wobbles. There was always the danger that rotational thrusting about the wide girth of *Noah* would impart an undesired pitching motion that must be stopped immediately before swing forces built up to start breaking up the ship and its contents.

Finally all was in readiness. People were poised and animals were restrained and the children and their caretakers harnessed but ready for immediate movement in the event of any danger. Everybody wore a pressure suit. A twist to *Noah* could breach the hull and explode their atmosphere into vacuum.

They all listened to the countdown on speakers and helmet headsets. This time it would be different than when they'd fired the huge aft rockets . . .

"Three—two—one—we have ignition." A brief pause and then, *"Confirm ignition and burn all amidships thrusters."*

Everyone listening grasped handholds or jammed feet into stirrups or relaxed within restraint harnesses. A hollow, distant thunder swept around *Noah*'s enormous girth, sound trembling in the structure, booming gently through the air of the vessel and casting clouds of slow-moving dust and debris inward from the hull.

Under the bright floodlights of *Noah*'s external hull the first duststorm anyone had ever seen in space drifted gently away from the metal mountain, a swirling storm dazzling under the spotlights of the spacetugs following its lazy, lofty expansion. The dust would become a great sparse cloud orbiting about both *Noah* and the in-view *Pegasus*.

Limbs relaxed and people looked with surprise at one another. No one had really believed Michele Crawford when she explained to *Noah*'s occupants that this time there'd be no crushing pressure—no discomfort at all, nothing except surprise to the first inklings in so long of faint, whispered gravity.

The girth rockets burned with measured low thrust and long patience. With the passing minutes the change began to manifest itself. People standing on the decks they had used as floors for more than four months found themselves leaning and then slowly toppling to one side. If they lifted their feet from velcro constraints, their bodies drifted slowly to the nearest wall in the direction of the outer hull. Soon it became possible to stand in a field so weak it was heady and gossamer, *but it was gravity*, the bulkheads resisting the tendency of whatever was free within the ship to travel in the "outward" direction. Some people exulted, others felt dizzy and confused, but they all loved what it meant. The bawling of animals feeling this strange and mysterious force resounded through the enormous interior, a sound welcome to all their human attendants. Loose articles slid or floated slowly, water shifted its angled level in its tanks, and along the outer hull, beyond the triplehull safety construction, amazed people looked through helmet visors or triple-paned windows and saw stars moving by. Finally *Pegasus* came into view, moving with magical motion from the top of the windows to the bottom.

Noah would continue to turn at this speed, in this manner, until a force greater than the mass of the vessel interfered with that motion. Except for damping motions causes by liquids or minor structural rebound, the motions of *Noah* were now "permanent!"

But this was just the beginning, the "stop and lock" maneuver to permit inspection crews to move swiftly but thoroughly through the ship. Along *Noah*'s inner "tube" rotational gravity was just about nonexistent. It increased steadily as someone moved toward the outer shell, just as the "inside" skater in a long turning line on ice has virtually no outward momentum but the "outside" skater is going hellbent for the snowbanks and hanging on for dear life. The initial burn period produced the desired breath of gravity: three percent Earth's surface. Several hours later minor glitches had been attended and *Noah* pronounced ready for speedup. This time the girth thrusters brought the outside swing force to just under nine percent of terrestrial.

The crews rushed to prepare the animal pens. It was an incredible moment for them all as they packed down slabs of dirt and sod and watched them remain in place. Feeding troughs and water tanks were shifted carefully and secured, hoses and lines and tubes rerouted where necessary, additional support provided for structures and liquids that now had weight and would soon weigh even more. The heavier hooved animals were carefully rotated until their feet and hooves rested against resisting floor. Now they stood with far greater comfort, their backs in the direction of ship center and their hooves pointing outward. A five-hundred-pound animal now "weighed" forty-five pounds, still far less than on Earth but ponderous and even crushing compared to zero weight.

Michele Crawford moved the crews into a twenty-four-hour "wait, see, attend" mode. This gave everyone time to carry out a meticulous inspection of the spaceship and its animals. It also provided time for bodies and minds to acclimate to the blessed sensations of weight and to begin adaptation to the angular motion producing that weight. Side forces could cumulatively become disorienting. Graduated increase and the slow spinning speed made possible by the long "arm"—the distance from ship center to outer hull—greatly mitigated the unpleasant side effects.

Twenty-four hours later the girth thrusters sped up the roll to the desired level. When the rockets snapped to silence and the last thunder echoed away within *Noah*, animals and humans in the outermost compartments weighed what they would have on the surface of the moon. At this level they had hard and meaningful experience. It was marvelous weight, yet marvelous freedom from weight they remembered. A man of two hundred pounds Earth weight on *Noah* moved the scales at thirty-five pounds, and the animal of seven hundred twenty pounds now weighed a most respectable one hundred twenty.

Sonia Barkagan and Costa la Perez moved with hand-clapping delight through the great Animal Farm. They *walked* through *Noah*. They *climbed* up and down ladders instead of floating magically. And la Perez slipped, tripped, fell, skinned his knee, and chortled with laughter at the marvelous sensations.

But the best of all was what they saw of the beasts in their care. Animals ate at open troughs or in open feed bags; only hours before they had haplessly bitten air as often as food that floated weightlessly. No longer did even a slight nudge send them reeling against harnesses with terrified bawls and cries, legs dangling stupidly above a floor that wasn't a floor. Water flowed decently through pipes and rested safely in open troughs rather than spreading wildly in every direction as huge spatters of spray.

"For a while I thought the people left behind on Earth were the lucky ones," Sonia Barkagan said with a sigh after their rounds. She had met Marc Seavers and Vasily Tereshnikov in the spacetug chambers of *Noah* for their inspection of the now gravity-rich craft. The angular motion produced dizziness and other problems, but as Barkagan emphasized, "Now, at least, when you are dizzy there is a place for you to fall to. *Down*." Mario Silva, accompanying the group, smiled at her enthusiasm. She had brought tremendous new life and excitement to his beleaguered Animal Farm.

"I want you all to understand the problems we have had and those we still face that we may yet be able to avoid." She led them down through airlocks into a huge hall. "Until we rotated this ship, we were on the edge of violence." She laughed at their looks of surprise. "You haven't *lived* here and that is why you are caught so unaware," she went on. "What I tell you now, and you must listen, is that the problems we had before with our people will soon be back." She led them to aluminum-walled stalls where cattle fed dumbly but now without alarm.

"Look," she said, pointing, "what color is that metal?" The query was outlandish, but Seavers fielded it. "Pale bronze. Copper. Why?"

"It is bright duralumin," she said firmly.

"Any fool can see it is not duralumin," Tereshnikov snapped.

"Then wipe the shit from the metal, Commander," Barkagan retorted. "The color is from farts spraying from the animals and from urine and dung splattering and splashing for as long as we have been off Earth! Do you realize how close we came to losing our animals? Or that we almost lost them because the people were starting to refuse to attend to them? That it was almost impossible to breathe in here with farts and belches and dung and piss and vomit day and night and night and day? Zero gravity, aha! The ventilator fans seemed only to make it worse. They swirled this muck everywhere. Bovine farts are no respecter of technological 'solutions.' It has been on our skin and in our noses and mouths and in our clothes and it has not been at all funny."

"There is a point to this, Barkagan?" Tereshnikov wasn't amused *or* patient.

"Yes, there is a point to this," she said, almost snarling. "It is time to end the preferential treatment we have endured all this time."

"In what way?" Seavers asked.

"In addition to feeding these dumb creatures there has been the task of milking, shearing and, worst of all, butchering. Where do you think your food has come from since the cans were emptied? From *here*. From people soaked in blood and bile, in all the wastes, in snaking guts and—" She shook her head. "You are not amused, I see."

"You are right, woman," Tereshnikov growled.

"You will be less amused when I ask you when *you* will take your turn cleaning out this shithouse."

"*What?*"

"You, and him," she stabbed a finger at Seavers, "and the little general," Silva almost recoiled from the stabbing digit. "When do you share the equality of survival and take your turns shoveling shit! Before you answer, understand this. Your precious scientists and technicians, your computer experts and your mechanics, your brilliant lovely people, they are *all* to come here, and they are *all* to clean out this entire ship."

"You give orders quickly," Tereshnikov said in warning.

"Oho! The czar speaks!" she mocked him. She stood toe to toe with the powerful Russian. "You will all come here and clean up all this shit and piss and blood and vomit and the rest of the slop or," she shook with pent-up fury, "we shall refuse to come back into this sty, and *all of you* may become the warders and the farmers!"

"I'm warning you—"

"Do not say it, Vasily Tereshnikov. You will regret your words and you will eat them instead of the rice and potatoes and wheat we grow for you and the meat we butcher for you. The warning is on the other foot, Comrade! Do not test me again! Do not test *any* of us again!"

She took a deep breath. Not one man tested her. "When you have done this work, when you know what is involved here, what this calls for, I want one more thing from you." She let silence fall.

Marc Seavers took up the cudgel. "All right, Sonia. Tell us what you want."

"I want the children."

They gaped. She had caught them totally by surprise.

"The children?" Mario Silva repeated.

"Look about you again," Sonia Barkagan told them. "You all think of this ship as the earth we know *and you are all wrong*. Look and touch and *smell*. Picture yourself taking care of these animals for perhaps *the rest of your life*. It is not truly inviting. Think of caring for them, feeding them, attending their pregnancies, caring for them when they are sick, butchering them, controlling their genetic lines—well, you understand, I believe. You are good men and now I wish you to think most carefully of something else.

"These are the last creatures of their kind in all the known universe. Not a single beast lives on Earth. Not one. What is left is in these two vessels, *and our time is sorely limited.* Do you believe I do not know our ships are falling apart? That the engineering systems are failing and you make desperate repairs? That is what occupies your minds, and it is not enough. If these animals do not survive, man is dead. And to survive we need much more than computers and sensors and all your fancy machines.

"Those are Band-aids to keep us alive for a while. Nothing more. When our rations run out, how will we eat? Will your machines make food out of smelly air? And even if they could, the air is beginning to fail us. Did you ever think about *that*, my admiral, or my big bad Russian here, or the general who wrinkles his nose at the stink in here? Have you ever talked among each other about our air running out?"

They looked at one another, uncomfortable with this woman and her words. "No," Seavers said finally. "*I* have not. They will speak for themselves. But I'll tell you this, Sonia Barkagan. I am listening to you most carefully, and you make more sense than anyone else I have ever heard."

Her burst of laughter startled them. "For an American scientist that *is* a victory," she chortled. "For a Russian it is, well, unbelievable," she added tartly. She walked several paces to a grassy knoll assembled only the day before. "Sit here, all of you," she commanded, patting the grass beside her. She gestured to take in all the ark.

"When we return to Earth we shall be the only people on that world?" They nodded. Tereshnikov said, "Yes."

"So," Barkagan went on. "Perhaps we will be old by then, or even dead. These two great ships, ah, fancy junkpiles very soon. But . . . the youngsters of now will be the elders of tomorrow. There will be, the saints willing, new babies. A new generation. If they walk again on Earth, what will they be?"

Her hand moved. "There is no need to answer. I have been a cosmonaut and a scientist a long time. I have lived with computers and marvelous machines and all the wonders that made our survival possible. But it is but a short step until tomorrow, *when our time is over*. Returning to Earth for these children means living without computers. There will be no factories, no steel mills, no chemistry labs, no ready-made electricity or medicine or plumbing or canned food or trains or aircraft. *There will be only the struggle to survive.*

"These children must be farmers! Woodsmen, *if* there are trees for wood. They must milk cows and shear sheep and attend the fowl and build homes. They must be one with the earth and increase their flocks and learn to survive in a world that may not even know forests. Is that not why we carry all these miracle seeds for swift-growing grasses and wheats and the seed of the fish and the frozen eggs and . . ." She let her voice trail away, and when she spoke again it was almost to herself. "They must be midwives and doctors, parents and priests and historians and farmers, and all this new world will be a terrifying and a lonely frontier." She looked up. "Tomorrow has no room for cosmonauts and computer scientists. That will be a far and distant future once we touch Earth's soil.

"Bring me the children. We must teach them the nature of nature. We must teach them that without their animals man is nothing. I prefer that you, I, all of us who are the elders, will one day be mourned by these children. If we are not, it will mean we have all died together, and all this will have been stupid and useless."

She rose to her feet. "I have nothing more to say." She walked off and left them staring uncomfortably at one another.

Tereshnikov found his voice. "Well?" he demanded.

"Well *what?*" Seavers answered harshly.

561

"What do you think, of course! You heard that damned woman!"

"Oh, I don't need to think about anything, Vasily. When Tom and Keesha wake up tomorrow I'll bring them personally back here. Right to that damned woman."

Day 172
Ship's Log, Vasily Tereshnikov, Commanding

Today was one of the more ridiculous episodes of this flight. At the engineering staff meeting we heard proposals as to how we may protect the ships from continuing dust abrasion and the impact of meteoroid particles. Both have become a serious danger. The electromagnetic wave front on which we once relied is a sad memory. We have been welding and bolting together whatever metal we could cannibalize from *Pegasus*. Almost none can come from *Noah*, which now rotates and needs full structural integrity. So we have a very serious problem.

Lester Rajani dominated the meeting. He is an expert on agriculture and forest growth. He is from Pakistan, and among the people in that part of the world he is famous as Mr. Bamboo. He has performed miracles in genetic alterations of bamboo plants. I never expected to be talking bamboo in my report logs, but there is a reason. Rajani may have saved us all. This man with dark skin and the deep, brooding eyes of a Russian poet is a genius. I am glad he fought me as hard as he did. For a while I judged him to be crazy.

Rajani had performed brilliantly with food plants. It is important that this truth be remembered. Our food supplies would have been sorely tested without him. He perfected a strain of the sweet potato that not only made our survival here possible but will be critical when we return to Earth. His Rajani strain gives us all a continuous food source of amazing variety and also a means of reclaiming and regenerating human waste products. The Rajani potatoes grow in huge vats and have proven greatly effective in absorbing waste carbon dioxide and producing fresh oxygen. As food, the Rajani potatoes are roasted, fried, souffled, and mixed into breads, cakes, rolls, and pot pies. All of them are excellent. The Rajani food strains also include sugar beets, lettuce, snap beans, scallions, wheat, soy beans, white potatoes, and pumpkins. The genetically altered Rajani pumpkin plant gives off twenty-eight times as much oxygen as the carbon dioxide and other gases it takes in. We all breathe sweeter air because of Rajani.

The day I married Tanya and adopted her children was the same day I became intensely interested in Lester Rajani's work with bamboo growth. I write these extra pages so our sons may read them one day and pay homage to this man from a backward country who may have saved the future for them.

Rajani has a most extraordinary perception of the future. Apparently he has always had this trait. Marc Seavers tells me he considers Rajani the embodiment of a famous name in American history; he calls the man from Pakistan the Johnny Appleseed of the future. All nations have their Johnny Appleseeds; in the future our young ones must honor Rajani. Somehow he knew that our single greatest tool and supply source, while we were in space but most especially when we returned to Earth, would be bamboo, the giant grass that built and sustained so much of the world before our ultimate disaster. Let me emphasize that the Soviet, like the other technological societies, abandoned bamboo in favor of metals, ceramics, and plastics.

How foolish we have been! How utterly stupid we are in our present situation, to rely upon materials that are so limited to us! Ranjani spoke to me as he would to a child. He taught me that bamboo is the only truly *renewable* source of a thousand goods and uses. He spread his plants everywhere in *Noah* and in many parts of this ship. How can one argue with a man who uses space no one else does and grows his giant grass in incredible speed and profusion? It is strange to be a student to this man, but so be it. Rajani had me learn about the Giant, a bamboo native of Burma which grows more than a foot thick and better than one hundred and forty feet high. He pestered me so much that

I gave him a full afternoon for his teaching. He seized on this fiercely. Among things I was *ordered* to learn was that, in the Giant bamboo, columns of living tissue are scattered throughout hollow culm walls, and that its joints, or nodes, provide tremendous strength. Why do I persist in writing all this? I said that Rajani might be the one who saves us all; I repeat it now. Who else but Rajani could grow a plant that becomes a building and construction material, a dozen tools, a variety of containers . . . the uses are boundless.

"You will need this giant bamboo, along with the more critical plants, when we make planetfall," he told us. "The Earth will be stripped of its precious fertile soil. There may be nothing growing but grass and weeds and bushes. Without the insects there will be no flowers. What we bring back will determine our future. There will be no trees. We must bring instant trees to Earth for the future generations, and it is the Giant that will do this. See here? It never takes from the soil, but enriches it. It binds loose soil together and firms it. Do we need scaffolding? Paper? Medical supplies? Heat and energy? Furniture? Wagons and boats? Drinking vessels. Conduits for water. For *anything*! And look how it grows! Aboard this ship seven feet a day! Under Earth gravity, crushing and relentless, it is still four feet *every day*."

Lester Rajani spoke also to the children. They must learn to work, plant, harvest, respect and love bamboo as he did, he told them, and he told them stories. I will repeat one here as he told it. The American woman-astronaut, Stacy Thorpe, has typed out the moment—

"Once upon a time, long ago and far away, so far away that no one knew where it really was, there were dragons who lived in Ishmoteer. This was a fabled and a truly marvelous land. Now the dragons here were considered to be magic, because with only the great bamboo forests about them, they did wondrous things. Using only their bamboo, they grew food and they built houses, they made their own furniture and floor mats and even their cooking utensils. They made wheels and wonderful chariots, and little cages for their pet crickets, because dragons have pets, also. They made paper for writing and telling stories and for very fine painting. They made all sorts of marvelous things. They made drums and flutes and fifes and pipes and clarinets and bongos and laughing music with their instruments. They made perfume, and fine jewelry, and even crutches for the dragons who stubbed their big toes. They made vases for their flowers and long tunnels to carry water and ovens and stoves for cooking and baking. They made writing pens and combs and shoes and when they went high into the mountains where there was snow they made sleds and toboggans and even skis. These dragons of Ishmoteer built soaring bridges and wonderful temples, they made candles from bamboo, and on warm summer evenings they sailed their bamboo boats and played music and sang songs."

"Were the dragons *really* real?" an excited little boy asked.

"And was there really an Ishmoteer?" cried a young girl.

Rajani smiled upon the children who had glided through the bamboo thickets of *Noah*, growing tall and straight under the ultraviolet suns crafted by man, glistening in the light of charred bamboo in the decorative lamps, looming over the bamboo chairs and benches, holding drinks in bamboo cups and gourds. Rajani brought a bamboo flute to his lips and an airy tune flew forth. He lowered the flute and his eyes shone.

"Of course the dragons are real," he told the children. "And do you know where Ishmoteer is?"

"Tell us! Tell us!"

"Why, look around you. *This* is Ishmoteer, and we are its dragons."

Day 172
Ship's Log, Vasily Tereshnikov, Commanding
Continuing the Special Report

Lester Rajani understood that with every passing "day" aboard the two space lifeboats the forward sections of the ships became ever more vulnerable to breakdown or collapse. We had already begun to move the control decks and all their equipment farther back into the ship. Dust is not at all dangerous. But we moved through dust, as thin as it might be, with great speed, and that speed transformed dust into a scouring sand. We had used metal plates, glass, anything to protect us; but everything wore down with frightening swiftness. Then, too, at any time we could move into meteoroid material. A tiny chunk of rock slamming into the forward section of either ship would penetrate like an armor-piercing warhead and go through the ship like a bomb. There were many solutions offered. Fly the ships stern first, for example. Coasting along a centrifugal arc in weightlessness, it didn't matter what attitude we held along our line of flight. But that would expose the engines and fuel cells to possible collapse, and we simply could not tolerate that danger. Still others suggested we fly the ships along our trajectory in sideways fashion, but that would only expose the weakest and most delicate parts of the ships to danger, like a cur dog lying on his belly and exposing his flank.

No, to survive we needed a physical barrier across the front of each ship, wide enough to span the vessel's full diameter and more. A barrier that could cause an incoming rock particle to disintegrate and somehow break up its force before it struck the main structure of a ship.

"I can build you such a barrier," Lester Rajani said to me. He entered my command office and calmly told me he could do what our engineers, scientists, technicians, construction crews, metallurgists—the whole useless lot of them—could not. And he could do it quickly, without damaging or weakening any part of our two ships.

I asked him how long it would take to perform this miracle. He told me four to seven days. I almost threw him from my quarters but he was too quiet, too confident. Give me your construction teams and all the extra hands, the spacetugs, and in one week at the outside he would have the needed barriers in place. And, he added, he would be able to replace the barriers and keep replacing them as necessary. I would have thrown him from my sight except that in my sudden anger I lost my temper and my feet spun out from beneath me and I could barely move. But even as my hands groped for his throat he smiled at me. Never will I forget his question.

"Commander Tereshnikov, are you aware that in many instances bamboo is stronger than steel?"

Stronger than steel! Of course I did not know any such thing and I told him so in most unpleasant terms. He informed me he had already been preparing the barriers. None of this made much sense until I told him to speak with greater clarity and take each move one at a time. Here, as I recall it, is what he said:

"Bamboo can be made stronger than steel. It is much lighter than steel, so it is easier to handle. I start all this maybe fifteen days ago. Much of our Giant bamboo is ready for cutting. So we cut the tall grass, and we have been heating and drying them until two days ago. Then we have been containing them in a heat-soaking oven. This enables us to straighten them and cut them to any length we need. Have you ever been to Hong Kong? Of course not. If you had then you would recall that in that city *all* the scaffolding for building construction, no matter how tall, is made from bamboo poles tied together with strips of bamboo. After a typhoon you would see steel structures twisted and smashed—but not the bamboo. It endures, just as it has endured for centuries. I do not believe you have seen the most famous of all historical bridges. There is a great suspension bridge at Siuchuan in China that spans the Min River. The bridge is suspended by bamboo cables. The cables are wound about capstans and are tightened when needed."

I asked this madman from Pakistan just how long the bridge had lasted before it fell into the river. Again, I quote to the best of my ability:

"How long has this bridge lasted? When we left Earth it had been standing for more than one thousand years. Since five centuries before Columbus crossed the ocean. It still carries—I beg your pardon, it carried until the final destruction—full convoys of trucks. And it was still bamboo. A thousand years, a thousand years."

How would this man make us the barriers we needed? To him it was simple. The engineers adapted machine shop presses to create a pressure oven within which they laminated bamboo with plastic. What emerged were great woven and plasticized sheets, one layer over the other, of a thick and strong shield. How was he so certain all this would work? He and his people had been producing these thick sheets for weeks. He would never have wasted a minute of my time unless he was absolutely certain everything would work the way he said. His plan that he gave to me was that construction crews in pressure suits would bring the plasticized sheets to the bow of the ships. There, using scaffolding made of bamboo—he smiled as he called it the Hong Kong Treatment—the crews would build huge bow plates. The full growth of Giant bamboo, he explained, requires only sixty days. He had brought enough seedlings to produce bamboo for a hundred years.

Of course I gave full permission for Rajani to commence this critical work immediately. I notified all engineering and other personnel who would be involved that Rajani was the project chief and that I would consider any hesitancy in cooperating with him to be a direct challenge to me.

After this amazing farmer from Pakistan left me, I thought greatly on the meeting. I marveled at our incredible good fortune. I do not know how many times I worried myself to the bone about meteoroid strikes. Of course it meant much more to me than to the others. I was aboard *Gagarin* when we took such a strike: perhaps a fist-sized piece of rock. It carries such tremendous inertial energy, striking us with a speed of perhaps ten to twenty miles a second. When it strikes something, a ship, a station, anything, it is pulverized, converted to terrible energies, and becomes a lance of superheated gas, harder than any steel, tearing into its prey. On *Gagarin* we lost twenty-nine out of forty of our people aboard that station. This is what the bamboo shields will prevent. Multiple layers will absorb the initial blows and transform kinetic energy from the velocity of the rock into heat. This in turn will pulverize the rock to tiny fragments already greatly decelerated by impact and instantaneous heating.

I have not felt this good in many—

Commander's Log, *Pegasus*
Day 174

I hope, and I truly believe, that my closest friend on these two ships that carry all we know that is left of humanity, died instantly and without pain. "Lights out" and it's over. Vasily Tereshnikov was working in his quarters, which lie directly aft of the main flight deck of *Pegasus*, when the meteoroid struck. As best we can determine, it came in a trajectory almost identical to the longitudinal axis of the ship. The shields we had up before the prow were worn thin and provided only the barest of resistance to the particle that hit us. It went through the shield with a speed the engineers judge at between forty and seventy thousand miles an hour. Fragmentation began the instant it impacted with the triple screen of the flight deck, a bullet through paper, in effect, vaporizing the lexitr. By the time it entered several feet of the flight deck, along a line through the main computer banks for the control system, expansion and violent heating was definite. Instead of a solid rock, however, we now faced a ball of incandescent gas harder than steel and with tremendous driving mass. Violent fragmentation was well along when it pierced the flight deck and smacked internal atmosphere, instantly creating a pressure of thousands of atmospheres and thousands of degrees. Fourteen members of the standby shift were vaporized and the particles ejected with the explosion. The ball of gas yielded its substance in a final explosion alongside the cabin where Vasily Tereshnikov was working. He died instantly. His remains, whatever could be found, were gathered in a plasticoffin and under my orders placed in the unpressurized area of Cargo Hold Forty Seven, in shadow for frozen storage and to prevent sublimation. When the time comes I shall carry out his final moments of physical existence as he made me promise before we left Earth orbit.

Much against my wishes I have assumed full command of *Pegasus*.

Nancy is with Tanya Yevteshenka Tereshnikova. The children were with Sonia Barkagan at the time of Vasily's death.

We were only a few days from erecting the Rajani Shields that would have prevented this disaster. Several hours from now I will carry through my first orders as ship's captain. All children remaining on board *Pegasus* will be restricted to the amidships area for maximum protection. We will also maneuver *Pegasus* so that we take up lead position in line trail, precisely ahead of *Noah* to provide maximum frontal coverage for the vessel that carries most of our children, and the animals.

Commander's Log, *Noah*
Day 251

We are not in the best of shape. This great vessel has become like a leaky boat. *Pegasus* has much the same problems. We have been gone from Earth now for more than eight months in ships that should never have survived beyond six. These vessels were built from scratch and their many parts slapped on. There was no development time, no superior design input. As much cross the ocean in a leaky rowboat.

The systems are breaking down. Motors are burning out. We have now traveled far enough from the sun that we must depend upon the nuclear reactors for power, but the reactors have experienced so many problems that we are becoming starved for energy. We get some energy through the solar cells, but they are old and have been damaged by dust and other particles, and we have no replacements for them. We use every energy source possible. Fuel cells, even the treadmills we use for exercise when our people trickle-charge the batteries. Power is more valuable to us than food. There is no way out of it. We are starting to shut down some systems to save power for others absolutely essential to life.

Both ships are losing their internal heat. Cold seeps through metal. Cold begins to reach everywhere. We lack the power to heat many parts of the ship and conserve in every way we can. Our people sleep in warm clothing, or sleeping bags, or their pressure suits. Bundling two or three to a large sleeping bag is accepted.

Even our ventilator fans are starting to break down. We have about used all the spares and we work day and night to devise treadmills and other systems that will allow human and animal power to turn the ventilator blades. Much of our food we now eat cold. Cooking ovens impose a tremendous drain on the battery systems.

We cannot long endure under these conditions. Never have I felt so helpless. Once I judged these ships to be giants. Now they are tiny motes drifting helplessly through a sea of space and time which we cannot even begin to comprehend. I pray the probes being fired back to Earth will bring us good news soon. Unless we begin our return soon, none of us will ever walk again on its surface.

I add a postscript. Since we boosted from Earth orbit we have tried, every day, every hour of the day, to make contact with the underground cities of the moon. We have not succeeded. Our long-range cameras showed signs of destruction to the surface installations, and our scientists theorize that the enormous energies being released by Earth in some way or another damaged or destroyed the surface installations. We have failed, as well, to detect any electromagnetic emissions. The scientists of Hestia knew our planned trajectory and how to send a tight beam to us. But we know only dead air. Commander Seavers tells me that we cannot afford the energy to keep transmitting messages. Today was the last day we made such an attempt. I feel very sad.

Day 267

I've stolen him away. I feel guilty about that but to hell with it. Everything is coming apart so quickly that Marc hasn't had a single moment to himself for weeks. He's been exhausted that whole time. He's been losing weight and hasn't been following his exercise regime,

*the same one he insists everybody else must never miss.
I'm afraid for him. Muscle atrophy, bone marrow loss,
calcium deprivation—the whole damn rotten biological
business. He hasn't been eating well, either. And his
sleep is atrocious. I remember what he told me about
that terrible time in Antarctica. Every now and then
(that was the best he could do; they told time that
winter strictly by the clock just as we do) he had to get
away from everybody and everything. To be alone, to
bury himself in silence. I prefer music. So does Marc,
most of the time, but he insists there are times when
silence is the greatest of all insulations. I knew that if I
could give him a total rest, a perfect sleep period, it
would be like a month's vacation. The others helped
me. Arch Begley rigged up a battery-powered heater he
"borrowed" from a spacetug so our compartment could
be warm. I don't know how Susan Foster managed, but
she and the others saved their rations to prepare a feast
for us. They went hungry during their eating period so
they could give the "old man" a break. Lester Rajani
and Sonia Barkagan, bless them, sent over from Noah a
drink I couldn't identify. It tasted like coconut milk but
it wasn't. It went down smoothly. I didn't know Marc
was drinking a powerful fermented plant drink that
would knock him into the middle of next week. He
didn't pass out on me but faded away. I had the heater
going and I put on a tape, low but just loud enough to
absorb the sound of the fans and ventilators, and I
stripped Marc down to bare skin. Not difficult when
your man doesn't weigh anything. I got all his clothes
from him and crossed his arms across his chest. He was
in very deep sleep. I floated back to a bulkhead to
watch him. The lights were on dim and I knew he was
stoned asleep but I saw him moving. I couldn't believe
it. Very slowly his body, floating in cabin center, was
moving to the left, then to the right, back and forth
that way. I didn't understand and tried to time the—I
had it. His heartbeat. That marvelous engine beating
within his chest. Action and reaction. Newton chasing
us across the universe. His body was moving to the*

pumping action of his heart. It was the most incredible demonstration of life I've ever known.

Commander's Log, *Noah*
Day 291

It is done. We apprehended the criminal, trapping him with infrared videotape that left no question of his crime against his fellow man. A Canadian, of all things. James Griffin. And from the Arbitration Panel where he sat in judgment on so many of his fellows. Sonia Barkagan reported in secret that they had a short headcount of sheep. Suspicions were confirmed. Several animals had disappeared. We set up the cameras and did nothing to alarm anyone. Within two days we showed the videotapes to Griffin so there would be no doubt. The man had stolen the animals, taken them one by one to a storage room where he slaughtered them. He drank the blood of the creatures and skinned them. Somehow he had stolen an oven and a supply of rechargeable batteries and cooked himself weeks of fine meals.

There was no trial by his peers. There is no room for such luxury. Griffin appeared before me. I did not sit alone. I could sense generation upon generation of my seagoing ancestors with me. Hard men who had braved a harsh world. Men who lived and died by the rule that you sail together or sink together. There could be no other way in emergencies. I made certain that what I said to Griffin would be known throughout the ship.

"You have stolen food from the mouths not only of your companions but most of all from the children. You have robbed your fellows here and now. You have stolen from all of us a part of our hopes for the future. Indirectly you may have condemned many people. Yours is a crime of selfishness, of greed, of contemptuous self-indulgence. You have no place among us for you would fill your belly before sacrificing for the common good."

Griffin said not a word in his defense. He did not fear the consequences of his acts. The ruling by Admiral Marc Seavers was still with us. To take a life now

573

denies us all the value of that life when we return to Earth.

If we return to Earth. Our privations will become much worse before that happens. Our discipline will be sorely tested. All the elders will have to go on short rations to feed the children. We need these animals desperately. This contemptible creature would deny us all.

The ruling of Admiral Marc Seavers be damned.

This is my ship and I am its captain and I am responsible for all!

I would have had Griffin locked in a chamber and the air removed. That would have killed him through explosive decompression. But it would have blown his blood and other fluids out of his body. We can afford to waste nothing, not even as an example to the others.

But I could not impose so grave a conscience on anyone else. Griffin was tied securely to a chair for his trial. With sentence passed I ordered everyone from the chamber. I locked the door. I used the silk cord to strangle him myself. His blood is on my hands. I am now the executioner as well as the captain. Griffin's remains are to be ground up and mixed with grain to feed the same group of animals from which he stole to assuage his greed.

Day 302

Rodeina Quaid hugged her huge mountain dog. Brutus sat beside the girl, stolid and protective, relaxed with the presence of children familiar to him. Yet something kept him alert. The dog reacted to their tone, and their voices were becoming angry.

"They killed him, you know," Rodeina told her friends, Sean Talbot, Bob Downey, and Abdullah al-Chamim. They had been inseparable since they drifted together soon after boarding *Noah*. Rodeina was now sixteen years old. Bob Downey, from California, was the youngest at thirteen, and the other two boys, fifteen years old, never understood why Rodeina would sextime with Bob but never with them. Well, it wasn't important.

The others all shared. Right now what Rodeina was saying meant much more to them.

"They had to kill him," Abdullah said, blinking. "My father or my brothers, or anyone in our family group at home, would have done the same. Stealing the food that feeds the children is a crime that is never forgiven. But," he smiled, "they would not have done it so kindly. A cut here, and there," he gestured. "It would take a long time."

"I'll bet," Sean grimaced.

"I heard the elders talking," Bob Downey said quietly. "A lot of them were mad because Silva refused him his rights. I think that's what they said."

"It's not what they said. How you spell it is what counts," Rodeina said.

"Yeah," Sean added. "Is it r-i-g-h-t or r-i-t-e?"

"Oh. I think they said last rites."

Rodeina made a face. "The elders must have been the Weepies, then. They're *always* complaining about something."

"They're always pissing and moaning about God, you mean," Sean added.

"God's stupid," Abdullah said suddenly.

"No. It's the Weepies who are stupid," Bob told him. "What they believe is stupid. Even this ship, man, that's *dumb*. All that horsepoop they tell us about Noah getting a call from God. Build a boat. Gather animals and things from everywhere. So Noah is supposed to build a boat a whole navy could hardly build. He sounds like a real asshole. Whoever wrote his story is another asshole. He kept praying and thanking God for destroying the world. And then he had to have seven pairs of clean beasts—"

"Why clean?" Sean asked, puzzled.

"So he could cut their throats or bellies or something like that to please God," Rodeina explained.

"That's dumb!"

"You think *that's* dumb?" Bob went on. "How about he had to get matched pairs, fertile male and female, of everything. How could Noah get pairs of viruses? How could he even tell male from female?"

"Maybe God gave him a big magnifying glass," Abdullah giggled.

"Sure, especially for the animals that change their sex."

"Maybe he took video pictures to compare them later."

"Well, he was supposed to take flies and mosquitos and larvae and grubs and microbes and all the dirty germs, too, I guess," Bob Downey said.

"The elders say that God loved his people."

"Sure! You mean, he loved to beat up on them, cause them misery, make them sick. If he didn't, why was Noah supposed to take two of *everything*? That means the stuff that makes malaria and dysentery—"

"What about polio, and scarlet fever and mumps?"

"Ringworms, measles, cancer, AIDS, syphilis, dengue fever, typhoid, typhus," Bob Downey called them out one after the other.

"Boy, we really need that *here*, don't we?" Sean said, shaking his head.

"I wonder how Noah got blue whales on his boat," Rodeina offered.

"I wonder how these dumbhead elders believe all this bull."

"What about that rain? It was supposed to cover the whole world," Abdullah said. "That means the water level was higher than five miles. That's crazy. The whole earth would have been a *sponge*."

"I don't think there ever was a Noah."

"If there was, then the rest of that crazy stuff has to be true. You know, demons and angels, heaven and hell—"

"We're *in* heaven and hell!"

"Boy, that's dumb."

"God's dumb."

Day 314

Taped Report of Probe Team. Members present are Mustafa Nabil, Dieter Schroeder, Susan Foster, John Hastings, Archer Begley. This is an open tape. The team members contribute freely to chamber pickup. Report approved and submitted as a group.

The team has launched probes every thirty days to Earth, commencing on the thirtieth day after ignition cutoff. As reported previously, the first three probes were lost and no explanation has been found. The next four probes established the thinning of the dust cloud through which the solar system moves, essentially along the plane of the ecliptic. The last probe fired, a Mark IX, carried increased transmission power and the improved Beltor antenna imaging system. We now confirm a rapid diminution of the dust mass. We are in the process of computer-enhancing the images received from the Mark IX, but in this preliminary report we confirm unexpected breaks in the hitherto solid cloud deck about the Earth. We cannot confirm the reason or significance of this observation.

Uh, do you want to field that one? Sure; I'll take it. We, uh, appear to have detected some sort of electromagnetic transmission in the higher frequency range, well above Ultra. It wasn't possible with the equipment on the Mark Niner to determine where these transmissions originated except general Earth vicinity. We're also stymied by our inability to break down the signal as to its source and transmitting power. We'll stay on this, of course. Uh, Arch?

This is Begley. I've got to sound a warning here. There's no way to determine what that radio signal might have been. With the crazy atmospherics in Earth vicinity we could have had solar howlers or an EM whistler. Interference in terrestrial vicinity could be anything. Then we might have had a freak transmission from what's left of an old satellite. Maybe it came from the moon. No way to tell. That's the point I wanted to make. Don't look on this signal as anything special. We'll stay on it and see if we can pick up anything else. Okay. Susan?

Please be patient with us until we have a chance to get some additional photography and multispectra scans of the terrestrial cloud cover. We'll be better able to determine if there are actual breaks in that deck or if what we saw was something on the order of a super cumulus that pushed up through the deck and cast a hell of a shadow. The shadow could give us false readings. We're more hopeful on this matter than on the EM squawk. We plan to initiate another probe within twenty-four hours.

Anybody else? Okay, gang, that's it. End of probe team meeting, day three one four, time twenty-two-forty hours.

Day 339

"Call the roll."

Marc Seavers sat comfortably, no sign that only the press-cling strips on his chair kept him from floating above the big oval conference table. He looked as confident and secure as he did back on Earth at such meetings. *Earth . . . Once upon a time on a world long, long ago and far, far away . . . Knock off the shit, buddy-boy. This is the big one.*

Marilyn Robins tolled the names. "*Pegasus*, please. Chiang Biao; Command. Susan Foster, Michael Pruett; Flight Dynamics. Ted Snow; Maintenance. Betty Haberman, Gene Camblin; Propulsion and Trajectory." One by one they responded by verbal call or hand gesture. "Lars Anderson; Life Support. Tanya Tereshnikova; Computers. Archer Begley, Dieter Schroeder; Flight Operations."

She ticked off the last name and flipped to the second page of her clipboard. "*Noah*, please. Captain Mario Silva; Commanding. Gregory Tretyakovich; Arbiter. Hans Dornier; Engineering. Helen Chandler; Flight Dynamics. Ken Bergstresser; Propulsion. Rudyard Gyn; Life Support. Jon Gierek; Fauna. Lester Rajani; Flora. Monica Marlowe; Reclamation."

Marilyn Robins knew her boss. She knew his moods and when the time had come to cut through all the buzz and nonsense and get with the issue at hand. She lowered the clipboard, looked about the conference chamber, and spoke in a flat and impersonal tone. "This extraordinary session of the command leadership of the space vessels *Pegasus* and *Noah* is called by Admiral Marc Seavers under emergency priority. This meeting is to be considered an emergency session. Video and audio taping is under way for official records." She turned to Seavers. "Sir, the meeting is yours."

Seavers leaned forward slowly to rest his elbows on the table. The elbow patches of his jumpsuit were imbedded with magnetic threads and he had secured magnets beneath the duralumin of the table. It was a small but important touch. He seemed to be incredibly free of weightlessness, pushing down against the table and not floating away. Then he dismissed everything from his mind but the burning issue at hand.

"Gentlemen, ladies, we'll not waste any time for this meeting. We will make a decision before any of you leave this chamber. A decision that affects all of us, and all other people aboard our two ships. I am making it very clear that I do not require permission or agreement. I do wish your information on this matter to be as complete as possible so as to eliminate any troubling reservations on your part."

He let silence fill the chamber for several moments. The distant drumming of turbines, pumps, regulators, solenoids and other machinery vibrated through the chamber bulkheads and floor and furniture. As if in response to an unspoken prayer by Seavers, a grinding rumble sounded and increased in intensity until it was felt throughout the chamber before fading away. Marc Seavers knew only too well the source of that disturbance: the main air shaft ventilator pumps. The bearings were shot, the metal was failing, the whole goddamned thing was coming apart. Well, that's why he had all these people here.

We must turn back for Earth immediately.

No need for false dramatics. That was heavy enough. A murmur began and swept through the room much as had that grinding rumble from the distant pumps. It died away with a sudden fading whisper as Seavers gestured.

"Our ships are wearing out," he said slowly and carefully. "To cut through all the words that would waste our time, our ships are coming apart at the seams. Make no mistake about it. *We are in trouble and it is*

579

serious. We have begun to race a new clock. That race is stacked against us from the beginning."

His hand moved in an arc to take in both ships. "These ships we're in weren't designed to go traipsing around the galaxy. Pure and simple, they're lifeboats thrown together in one hell of a hurry. They are not the best workmanship. The truth of the matter is that without a few geniuses working on our equipment our ships would be crippled where life support systems are concerned. And without the incredible accomplishments of Lester Rajani and Sonia Barkagan, many of our people would now be dead.

"We are, or will be in a few hours, three hundred and forty days out of Earth orbit. Based on our fuel use and all other factors it will require at least that period of time to return to Earth orbit. At that point we require still further fuel for near-Earth maneuvers and orbital insertions. But it will take us at least those three hundred forty days to get back.

"These two ships will not last another year. The numbers speak with great eloquence. Either initiate deceleration at once or we compound our problems. We must act immediately to start the trip home."

"If there *is* a home," Rudyard Gyn said moodily.

Just like it was in Antarctica . . . defeatism sets in. Some of these people are ready to quit right now. Maybe they'll pass around the gas pipe. Jesus goddamn Christ . . .

Seavers' hand slammed against the table with a flat cracking sound. Just about everyone in the chamber jumped. Seavers' hand stabbed toward Gyn. "That's the first and the last time I want to hear any of that defeatist crap. You start brooding on all the negatives about this miracle that's kept us alive and it'll spread like an epidemic. *Shut up, Gyn.* If you can't work yourself and lead other people on to work, just keep your mouth shut or I'll put you where no one can hear you. And if you can't handle *that* just take a walk *outside.*"

Betty Haberman gestured slowly and Seavers nodded. "I don't need to apologize for anything," she said with suddenly growing confidence. "But I'll put this in the form of a question. What if there *isn't* a home for us, what if Earth is still poisoned and—"

"Give me a course to your alternate destination and we'll set it immediately."

Betty Haberman seemed to shrink a little. "Yes, sir, I get your point. I just didn't think."

"No apology needed. My point is that I simply don't want to hear that kind of talk again *from anybody*. We're going to have to fire our main engines. That's going to raise hell with the systems of the ships. We still have at least three hundred forty days before orbital insertion *back home*." He stressed those last two words and paused a moment. "It's going to be tough sledding in these buckets. I know that; we all know it, really. But tempers are going to shorten with every passing day, and unless everybody pulls for the long haul *we will not make it home*."

He looked at them all and in that look invited, *dared*, their comments. The iron was hot. Time to strike. "It's not all tough news," he said. He looked at Archer Begley. "Arch, if you please."

Begley rose to his feet, hooking his toes in the stirrups before his chair. He didn't want to make like a drifting balloon. "About three weeks ago we received news that is more than encouraging. I consider it sensational. We haven't said anything about our Earth probes because we weren't certain what we were seeing. But with the latest supervel probe, and computer enhancement of photo transmission, I've got something very specific to say." He took a deep breath. The people staring at him were trigger-poised. He couldn't blame them, but Seavers had told him *not* to blurt out what he had to say.

"The cloud cover over Earth is breaking up." He heard the sucking in of air, a complex vacuum of human emotions tumbled off balance. "We've confirmed major breaks in the clouds. Light patterns, differentiation of spectra; that sort of thing. Even more important, the last several probes have revealed—at first we weren't even sure of this, but we are now—we've seen a drastic reduction in thermal radiations through the cloud breaks.

If that tells us anything it's that the solar system must have come through the worst of the dust cloud. The sun itself is or *has* been calming down. Solar storms and heat fluctuations may already be a thing of the past. In short, we have a real shot that the Earth is returning to normal. And since we've got a full year before we're home . . . well, I don't know. I'd hate to be a prophet and be proven wrong. But as far as I'm concerned, those temperature readings are the best sign that the atmosphere is returning to something like acceptable weather patterns."

"Acceptable for what?" someone called out.

"The emergence of plant life, for one. Acceptable temperature bands within which we can live. The ability to plant and whip growth along. We don't have to wait for nature. That's why we have those balloons and those biovats stored so preciously."

"We'll go into all that later," Seavers broke in. "None of it will mean a tinker's damn unless we commit to the return, *now*." He took a few moments to study his stunned audience, to try to fathom what lay behind either impassive or tortured faces. He thought they understood. Everything that he, Marc Seavers, was doing here was window dressing, nothing else. There was no need for these people to be here. He was recognizing their positions—but they would not affect the decision that he, Seavers, *had already made*.

But I haven't made it, he tried to reason with himself. *It's the old syndrome of time and tide wait for no man. Now it's a case of dying machinery and broken parts that will die on us without warning. The decision was made by sick machinery and stale air and an angry nuclear reactor and the laws of orbital mechanics and the knowledge that we have, at best, a year before our ships fall apart.*

He seemed to grow cold before them. "Ladies, gentlemen. Prepare for full thrust seventy-four hours from *now*. Cosmonaut Tereshnikova will coordinate all timing systems. All other personnel are on full operations or standby from now on. *No excuses*. Full deceleration is going to be very rough on everybody." He pointed to a group from *Noah*. "Gyn, Gierek, Rajani—as of this moment your boss is Sonia Barkagan. You will do absolutely everything she demands. She's the lady who's giving us tomorrow."

He glanced at a note reminder slipped before him by Marilyn. "One more thing. We'll do a dry firing run at T minus twelve hours. Everybody in pressure suits, full preparations just as if the big ones burn. And I don't believe it will hurt anything if we all cross our fingers. That's it; this meeting is over."

Marc Seavers and Gregory Tretyakovich stood together by the lexitr viewport in the navplot compartment. They stared through the port as if intense study might bring a far distant planet called Earth into view. Tretyakovich did not turn to Seavers when he spoke. "A ruble for your thoughts, my friend. Are you troubling yourself about the engines?"

"No. I don't give that matter any thought at all. Hell, Tretsky, that's in the hands of the engineers. They know more about that stuff than I do. They've been cleaning and flushing out lines, running the turbopumps— hell, you know. So far I've heard a lot of grumbling but not a single complaint. That's all good news."

"Then why are you so worried? It is written across your face."

"We're about to have a caller. *He* concerns me. Worry is the wrong word. You worry about things you can't fix."

"Who comes?"

"An idiot. Arrigo Levi. Italian. An idiot in everyday life but apparently a genius in construction, survival engineering, that sort of stuff."

"You are annoyed by an architect? You amaze me, Marc."

"Not because he's an architect." Tretyakovich smiled and waited. "He's become a religious fanatic. Maybe he was one all the time. I don't know, but— He's here. Want to stay?"

"I wouldn't miss this for all the world. No pun intended, my friend," the Russian chuckled.

Arrigo Levi floated through the doorway. He was a big and florid-faced man with a thick beard and bulging eyes. He knew the established routine in Seavers' command quarters. You get into a seat and hunker down. The admiral had a distaste for people floating about like balloons when he talked with them.

"Admiral, I am grateful for this moment," Levi began expansively. "I—"

"There's no time for that now," Seavers said, a bit more sharply than he intended. He didn't like what he saw: the cut of Levi's clothes. *He's only one step from wearing a priest's frock; damn!* "Please state what you want."

"I have heard about the news. The meeting yesterday? That is a miracle, Admiral. No one ever knew whether the Earth would accept us again. But it is a miracle not of our own making. A world from which man was banished is being returned to us. God in his glory and his mercy is showing us the way to—"

"*That's enough.*"

"But—"

"I haven't the time for arguments, councils or anything else on this subject, Levi. I've heard your routine before. Next you'll want a mass prayer by everybody to deliver thanks to your god."

Levi looked bewildered. "Why, yes, that's just what I was planning to—"

Tretyakovich moved forward, his hand suddenly on Seavers' arm. "Admiral, if I may?"

Seavers hesitated. He wanted to shove Arrigo Levi back where he belonged, and Tretyakovich was justly infamous for his response to whimpering theology, and it *could* precipitate a hell of a problem . . . *but how much worse could things be? Hell, turn him loose.* Seavers nodded, and eased back in his seat as Tretyakovich impaled Levi with a look of ice.

"Whatever you were planning for your mawkish prayer meeting is denied," Tretyakovich said with the voice of a grizzly. "You will not spread your poison in these ships. Be quiet!"

Levi had started to interrupt and was iced down

before he could utter a word. He knew little of the devastating aura of this man, only that he sat in the highest councils of the two vessels.

"We have avoided your drivel since boarding these ships. We've kept peace among our people and I will not permit it to be destroyed by your babbling. You *know* our rules! You wish to pray, do so! But you do it privately, to whatever god or idol or icon you wish. No pushing, no pressure of any kind, either by orders or by your deviant psychology. There are more than twenty religious denominations on our ships. We respect them all and they must respect the others without pushing against them. So keep your praying very private, Arrigo Levi, or I'll have you thrown in irons or worse. Get out and from now on mind your step."

Seavers stared at Tretyakovich in the silence that followed Levi's departure. Tretsky was right. The last thing they needed when ship discipline was going to be tighter than a bowstring was a mass devotion to the god who had destroyed life on their home world and now, by some miraculous cerebral twitch, perhaps, would shed a relenting tear to save the people aboard these two ships. It had nothing to do with belief in a supreme power or a deity. Seavers had spent half his life plumbing the depths of the universe and on his philosophical wanderings never failed to be humbled by the spectacle of beauty and harmony he found everywhere. But personal gods who were kept handy to dispense good and evil were so much claptrap.

"That was neatly done, Tretsky," Seavers said at last. "A bit vehement, but—" He shrugged to deny any criticism.

Tretyakovich surprised him again. "I have studied man my entire life, my friend," he told Seavers. "This year aboard these two ships I've had much time to think of our race." He gestured for them both to consider the universe. "There are different gods out there. Gods for all men for all reasons. I believe in the being who gave us the miracle of mixing a soup of chemicals and electricity to give us life and mind. The trickle does not dash to and fro within our brains? We are dead.

How marvelous, that the spark races through a biological sponge and we comprehend the universe. To me, Marc, *that* is godlike, and it is not our creation. We were given minds to think *and that is all*. There is no god out there to repair our engines or the reactor *or us*. If we return safely to the world we left, then our Italian madman is free to rub ashes on his forehead and skin his penis and make sacrifices. But in the prayers of that man are the demons we have kept at bay in these ships. I want them locked up until we deliver these people safely on Earth. Then Levi may scrabble in the dirt."

Tretsky took a deep breath. "But not on *my* ship!"

Seavers held the eyes of his friend. "Amen," he said and they both broke out into laughter.

Tretyakovich rose from the table, poised in midair. "We are how long from ignition?" The laughter was gone.

"Four hours."

"Then we should do it now."

"Yes. Let's get our suits. I'll have Begley bring his tug around."

"Good. Vasily liked that crazy darky very much."

"The feeling, my friend, was mutual."

26

*E*ngine Number Three trembled from the alcohol purge in its lines. Far upsystem turbopumps shifted from throbbing idle to howling fury. Fuel rammed down the lines to the nozzle throat of the three main engines of *Pegasus*. A white flash of purge appeared within the third bell, followed instantly by the explosive eruption of fuel. Before the fuel could move more than several inches a supersensitive monitor detected its presence at the throat of Number Three and spat energy to the igniter. The doors to hell blew away in a gush of pure flame.

Only for an instant could the plasticoffin be seen

secured by thin wires across the mouth of the engine. Only for an instant as the dragons screamed.

In that instant the mortal remains of Vasily Tereshnikov were cremated. Dust among the stars, as promised.

Engines crashing against an invisible wall, *Pegasus* began to slow its headlong rush away from Earth.

Security One Record Notation, *Pegasus*
Eric Hughes, OS
Day 347

Much to everyone's surprise the plan worked. It took a bloody great deal of patience, and we had to enlist the services of people I never believed would know the ins and outs of this sort of business, but what counts is that it worked. The lads never had any idea we knew about the gangs that sprang up in both ships. After all, they are sharp. They know electronic systems in some ways better than the professionals. Their system of laser television transceiving was brilliant. The whole time, of course, we were on to them. After all, these ships were rigged to detect any kind of anomalous radiation; the spectrum didn't make a hang of difference. But they were, really, harmless. Oh, they went their own way and got in a bit of devilment, but they never hurt anyone and never loomed as a risk to the machinery or the ships.

What we watched for the most was that they would take after each other. The Eagles from *Pegasus* and the Wolverines from *Noah*: that could have been a nasty scene. Of course, it was worth letting them plot and plan just to see how they'd figure a means of getting across the vacuum between the two ships. They considered it. We played their tapes back—our tapes, I should say, from the mikes we had everywhere; got to do that sort of thing when the lives of so many people hang by a thread—and we were in near hysterics.

I mean, they considered hurling themselves from one ship to the other by bloody slingshot! It didn't take them long to work out that this sort of thing would have flung most of them off into space forever, or that if they did reach the other ship they'd whack into it at high speed and that would be the end of them. They designed some strange compressed-air guns to shoot themselves across, and the more they got into it the more they realized that the idea of a confrontation between rival gangs in the last two spaceships in existence just didn't have much smarts to it.

The break came when the Wolverines bit off more than they could chew in trying to "walk the fence" a bit smarter and trickier than the Eagles. Their competition had finally boiled down to videotapes they passed back and forth of derring-do on their parts, each gang trying to outdo the other. Well, the Wolverines broke into the wild animal compound with steel netting and the nits actually bagged themselves a real wolverine! Unfortunately for them, on the way back to their clubhouse the nasty little creature ate its way out and made a feast of the foot of the leader from their bunch. His big toe disappeared in a flash. There was a lot of bloody yelling and screaming and by the time we latched on to what was happening that animal had tore up four more boys and was trying to eat its way through a bulkhead. We got into the tunnelway in time to pop a few narcdarts into the wolverine and put it to sleep in a hurry. It was off to the dispensary for the lot of the boys and hospital time for three of them.

Well, there was no hiding anything from that point on. The admiral had told us from the start of our surveillance that leadership always emerges at the top, and leadership is what all of us would need when we again walked Earth. So, following his orders, we watched but let them be. The animal's feast settled that, though.

How the admiral was right! Those kids in their forays and sneaking about had got to know these two ships better than anyone else. They were absolutely perfect for inspecting areas we didn't even dream of. The admiral made them all full-blown astronauts, gave them rank and responsibility, their own quarters, and put their hides to work. They go through the ships looking for damage, breakdowns, trouble spots. We don't deal with them as kids. Not any more. They're full-fledged members of the crew.

That works both ways. Not only are they given responsibility, they're responsible for themselves. And it's terrific. Enthusiasm at this point of the flight, with everyone wondering whether we'll make it home before these wheezing boats come apart at the seams, is something we all need very badly.

God bless those boys. Those *men*.

Commander's Log, *Pegasus*
Day 370

It is Antarctica all over again to me. We're down to raw survival. Staying alive. Keep ourselves from freezing. Ration food, water, and above all heat and power. Keep defeatism at bay. If these people quit between their ears we've bought the farm. I hate many of the steps I've taken. Once again I've become a brutal taskmaster and disciplinarian. If I'm not we won't make it. I hardly see Nancy. God bless her, she spends almost all her time with the children, working day and night to keep up their spirits. The music; how the music has made such a difference! When they're too tired or hungry to be worth anything in school, music is their escape. Music hides the thumping and banging and clanking of machinery breaking down. The kids clutch music for their safety. It lets them take one day at a time. Nancy is a slavedriver with the kids and their music.

Commander's Log, *Pegasus*
Day 374

Damn, damn! Our first rape. Incredible that we've avoided it this long, but the conditions must have favored self-control. That and the *non*puritan life. Not free-wheeling, but sexual affairs and relationships with circumspection, most of them leading to marriage. Not this time. This was rape pure and simple. I would be glad to let it go with some sort of Solomon-like decision that under ordinary circumstances would be acceptable to the victim. We're *all* victims here, in a way, but that doesn't excuse this sort of assault and crime. The victim was a girl only twelve years old and I cannot let this pass. I don't even want her name in the records and it won't appear. The rapist is Norman Henke, until this crime a quiet, dependable Dutchman. I don't know what happened to him. Off the deep end or whatever. We can't leave him go free or unpunished, of course. Too many people are too close to snapping their self control as it is. The girl's parents are up in arms and the father has asked me to let him carry out the death sentence.

I can't even wait for a trial. It's got to be immediate. If the man isn't guilty, put him back in the mainstream as a contributing member to our survival fight. If he *is* guilty then there's no way I can continue to permit him to consume air, food, water, power—all of it—that might be denied children before this flight is over.

Tretyakovich, Begley, and Fangkun took matters out of my hands. Henke confessed to them and on this ship that's tribunal enough. The word of those three is unquestioned. I don't know how they did it but somehow they convinced Henke the only way to avoid a really terrible death was to go out by his own hand. He did just that.

They took him to Loading Bay Six and left him alone in the outer air chamber. They remained behind two other chambers with airlock control of Bay Six in their hands. Henke stood by the final door and they saw him look up when the red light came on. He reached to his right and turned the three switches and then yanked down and sideways on the handle. When you do that there's still a sixty-second wait before the Bay breaks the seal. Begley told me Henke stood facing the outer door, not moving, not turning around, not saying a word. At sixty seconds the bay door flew open. There was immediate explosive decompression. Henke's body lost its blood and other liquids and the blast of escaping pressure hurled him away from the ship. He was unconscious almost immediately, of course. Begley calculated ejection velocity and mass. The corpse will fall into orbit about this ship at about twenty to forty miles. Hell of a satellite.

I regret losing his biological matter. Reclamation was

real angry. Marlowe raised hell with me but it was half-hearted. As much as we need his nutrients and liquids for the animal feed, no one even wanted the idea of a rapist contributing to our own bodies, even for our survival. I don't blame them. You reach a point where you look death in the eye and refuse to yield your own principles one iota more. I'm proud of these people.

Captain's Log, *Noah*
Day 393

Cold. The cold is our whole life. We do everything we can to keep the people warm. And the animals as well. We are in a race between the cold and the sun. Every day we sail closer to the source of all heat and light and life as we fall down the great heights back to our solar system. In the meantime our power shortage brings the cold to live with us. I have ordered tighter gathering of people. We can do without huge compartments housing only a few people. The more people in a compartment, the more they benefit from body heat. Many of the caretakers live with the animals, sharing warmth. This makes for fetid air but that is a small price to pay to avoid frostbite. By reducing the total volume we need to heat we have eased the problem. Lester Rajani once again has come forth to help save the day. He sealed his vital bamboo growths in plastic hangings to retain heat. In the compartments adjoining those for the children he and his teams packed insulation against the outer walls. The engineering teams set up low-thrust ventilator shafts. In those compartments Rajani and his teams have been burning bamboo in special ovens. It produces enormous heat. The walls heat up. Sealed pipes are heated and carry water in the form of giant radiators beneath the floors of the compartments where we have gathered the children and the women, and the animals most sensitive to cold. In those same compartments we have moved the sweet potato and the pumpkin plants. This protects them against the cold and makes the air sweeter with fresh oxygen and gives the children something to care for.

We shall prevail.

No time to keep up the log. Maybe we'll do it later when this survival flight is over. Three weeks ago all hell broke loose on this ship. We lost our nuclear reactor and avoided total disaster only through the knowledge, bravery, and sacrifice of our engineering and construction crews. The first sign of trouble came with huge air pockets in the piping system carrying steam from the reactor to the turbines. We have no way of knowing what caused these problems, but the moment they started our people began shutdown. Susan Foster had the con and once again she proved her tremendous worth. Sam Vance and Ted Snow had been keeping close tabs on the system and together they saved the ship when flow turbulence developed and the temps started out of sight.

When they shut down the reactor we lost seventy percent of all power in this ship. Immediately we began transferring people and the smaller animals to *Noah*, where their reactor is in good condition. We've been using fuel cells and anything else to keep up power and heat in the critical areas of our ship. We may be able to do better than that. The crews are running a cable from the generators of *Noah* to our system. We can bypass the regular hookups and take the electrical power supply directly. It looks like it will work. Every day, of course, as we get closer to the sun we're starting to pick up power in the solar cells. We've lost a good many of those to dust impingement and other problems. But somewhere along the line Fitzpatrick—God, how we miss him!—had laid in a good supply of accordian-fold solar collectors and we'll start putting those outside the ship in the next day or so.

It's crazy. We abandoned Earth because it was burning up. Now we're freezing.

Probe Team, *Pegasus*
Report by Begley, Archer
Day 440

Great damned news! Not much time to do this report, and pardon the scribbling, but I had to get this in the records for this day. The latest probe has sent back clear pictures AND WE CONFIRMED THAT THE CLOUD COVER OVER EARTH IS BUSTED WIDE OPEN! The atmospheric pattern doesn't seem one bit different that the one I've looked down on from orbit all these past years. It's tremendously promising. I'm not sure from these first photos, but there's some changes in continental outlines. We expected that. The way these ships are coming apart there's no question now that as soon as we get back into Earth orbit we'll have to transfer down to the planet just as fast as possible. Until today we really didn't know if we'd have to do that *blind*. Now we know that won't be necessary. We can photograph and videotape the potential landing sites. It's fantastic, wonderful, incredible news. The first real break in a long, long time. We'll be sending out two big probes to insert into Earth orbit with real-time transmission of their video systems, one in equatorial and one in polar orbit so we can have a damned good idea of where to try to put the shuttles back down. The balloon and biovat people are out of their gourds with joy. With that sunlight and ultraviolet bathing the atmosphere and the surfce they'll have a chance to strut their stuff.

One last item in this log. We picked up that crazy EM transmission again. All we know is that it originates in the general vicinity of Earth. Nothing more. Still comes in pulses. It doesn't really seem to matter. We're all so jazzed with the news.

Commander's Log, *Pegasus*
Day 518

Cold. Writing by hand. Most of our people are aboard *Noah*. We lost only eleven people in that reactor accident, six of them not related to the reactor. Doesn't matter; they're still dead. I made the decision not to send the bodies to Reclamation. The emotional bond is overwhelming. Even the idea of—eating is a rotten word but it has to do—surviving by using these people in the food chain is simply not acceptable. Our people made their feelings clear. They'd rather follow the dead than be on top of even a long chain that smacks of even the slightest traces of the dirtiest word of all: cannibalism. I vote with them. We keep our dignity even if the thread of survival is worn thin. Anything I ever knew in that long Antarctic winter has been far exceeded by these incredible people. The bodies were wrapped in flags sewn by anyone who wanted to volunteer. Full funeral services were held. Prayers and final words of farewell were spoken in seven religions and nine languages. Fitting. The bodies were ejected from Airlock Sixteen. They will orbit slowly about this ship. When finally we deboost for orbital insertion our speed will drop by more than eight thousand miles an hour. Our friends will continue at full speed into Earth's atmosphere to be consumed by friction. I think I can feel the touch of whatever power it is that gave us life. Our return to Earth will be preceded by eleven shooting stars. The first people to return.

Shuttle Report to Commander, *Pegasus*
From Shuttle Team; Dieter Schroeder, Lead
Day 542
Preparation of the shuttle craft on both *Pegasus* and *Noah* proceeds on schedule. Some mechanical and electronic systems problems have been encountered but they fall within the parameters of what was expected. Repairs and updating are under way. We will not load propulsion units for orbital deboost until Earth orbit is achieved, as per your orders. We have made several more loading runs. Several shuttle craft can accommodate 170 people or more, depending upon their size and other cargo. We load each shuttle with maximum people capacity plus all the minimums as specified in orders (full survival capability each shuttle). We have extrapolated schedules and loading. We have sixty-one shuttle craft available. Larger animals will be the major

594

problem. J. Gierek recommends the animals be sedated before loading for protection to the animals as well as permitting maximum capacity loading on the cargo "floor." All shuttle flight crews are updating proficiency in the simulators. When this phase is complete they will be run through shuttle control simulator in Tugs Two and Nineteen. End of report.

Commander's Log, *Pegasus*
Day 560

No major events to report. Shuttle preparation on schedule. Dry-run loading tests on schedule. Nuclear radiation from reactor shutdown within acceptable limits. Everybody hanging in tight. The biggest game in town is calendar-watching.

Commander's Log, *Pegasus*
Day 571

Dr. Chiang Biao met with me, Gregory Tretyakovich, Benita de la Madrid, Lester Rajani, Sonia Barkagan, and Hans Motubai to review the potential for plant growth on Earth prior to our return, and what hopes we may honestly entertain resulting from our own activities.

There is much to be pessimistic about. What with the heat that scoured earth, the catastrophic floods, fires, volcanic eruptions, thick cloud cover, poisonous gases, nuclear radiation, winds, shock waves, we don't expect any plant or animal life to have survived.

Chiang Biao and Lester Rajani took sharp issue with us on this matter. It is most important I record their heated, even angry, opposition to our conclusions. It is their opinion, based on far more intimate knowledge than the rest of us have, that we are unduly pessimistic. How wonderful if we are wrong and those are right! But wonderful is not the issue. In short, Chiang Biao said we lacked understanding of the inherent survival nature of many plant species.

Many plant spores, he emphasized, will have been thrown into the air in a pattern the Earth has known for billions of years. Those spores will drift in the very high atmosphere, free of the severe conditions closer to the surface. Spores such as these have been sealed in rock, denied water, air, sun or any nourishment, and after thousands, even millions of years, have been exposed to the elements and *flourished*. Biao was absolutely convinced the high atmosphere of Earth was filled with billions of such spores and that as the temperature waned and the clouds parted, with a drastic tailoff of winds, the spores would descend like rain and trigger new growth in most parts of the world. Rajani agreed completely. He told us of plants that take root inside the lips of giant volcanic craters, enduring many hundreds of degrees, poisonous gases venting from the crater, eruptions, howling winds, massive ash falls—and survive and flourish even under these conditions. In the Himalayas, they stressed, were trees and flowers that have learned to survive in winds of two to three hundred miles per hour.

Biao was especially critical of the way we had ignored the many plants that would be buried because of changing surface conditions and would still emerge fertile and seeking growth. Mud flats, alkali beds, deserts; saline pools, lava beds—the worst conditions develop the hardiest survivors. Also, and here he was most adamant, we were woefully ignorant of conditions in the deep oceans. Turning the ocean beds completely under and rolling them over, he told us, would not harm the ocean flora that grow and do splendidly under enormous pressure, in terrible cold *and* exposed to volcanic events that heat water to hundreds of degrees. There are plant and animal beds flourishing in huge colonies sixteen and twenty thousand feet beneath the ocean surface. He reeled off the types of sea worms, scallops, shrimp, sole and other forms of life that thrive under a pressure of four tons to the square inch.

"A minor disturbance of the surface world—and to these creatures that is all that has happened to Earth—means nothing. I expect many forms of fish and other ocean life to survive. Fertilized eggs can be buried for centuries in ocean mud and suddenly begin to develop when conditions are right. There are fish that live in volcanic waters that would kill anything else and they are healthy and happy . . ."

In short, surface vegetation (I hope). Extensive plant life in the sea (I hope and feel better about). Animal life in the oceans (that would be incredible), and in lake beds and streams and where rivers once flowed.

Biao and Rajani made two other points; obviously they had spent much time on this matter before our meeting. Rajani used as his example the theoretical situation of unchecked growth by a single blip of bacterium. If such a creature had plenty of food, he said, and could dispose of its own body wastes, then it is capable of dividing every twenty minutes. "Do you know what that means?" he asked. Only Biao seemed to know and he only smiled. "Theoretically," Rajani told us, "in forty-eight hours these bacteria would multiply to a mass that would be *four thousand times the size of the Earth.*"

"Fortunately," Biao added, "that is only theoretical, so we need not be overly worried about being drowned in life." The old devil was actually enjoying himself.

So was everyone else. I've ordered copies of this meeting to be distributed throughout the ships. Let them chew on some good or at least hopeful news. First the cloud cover breaking and now this completely upbeat prediction.

Executive Officer Two, Flight Deck Report
Day 592
Submitted: Astronaut Susan Foster
Earth is visible!

The flight deck seemed to *sparkle!* With the naked eye our home world is a bright light in the sky, but with the deck scope—well, I cried, almost everyone on the deck was crying or swallowing pretty damned hard. For the first time we can see our world is still there. And to look through that scope and see that incredible, wonderful, marvelous blue-white sphere leap into prominence . . . the feelings simply cannot be described. I set up an immediate uplink through both ships to trans-

597

mit a camerascope picture to the TV monitors. Let everyone share this fantastic sight!

Noted in the log that we have again detected those strange radio signals from Earth-moon vicinity. We still do not know what they are and even computerscan drew a blank. They come in bursts. No pattern. Almost like unrelated pulse signals. The electronics people are convinced they're not solar in origin.

Commander's Log, *Pegasus*
Day 620

Two months to go. The single greatest change has affected all of us. We're now close enough to the sun for the voltaic cells to be charging our batteries at and to full strength. Power is no longer a critical factor aboard *Pegasus*. The construction teams did some modifications of their own. They stretched black cloth fiberglas and metal along the sunward flanks of this ship, soaking up solar-radiated heat. It was like a boiler coming on line slowly but with great effectiveness. Blower systems jury-rigged within the immediate hull distributed the welcome heat throughout the ship. It really does look like we're over the hump. Now if these ships will just hang together a bit longer . . .

Captain's Log, *Noah*
Day 646

Every day life is better, brighter, bigger! We have flown through the Valley of the Shadow and drifted high from the world of man with Death and we have fought and we are winning. Men, women, children; all of them on a mission that stands as tall as any sailed by the Portuguese armadas and explorers and settlers at their very best. Or anyone else's expeditions, for that matter!

There is no way to describe the salutory effect of the sun. It is the destroyer of the human race, but who can blame the magnificient giver-of-life for the devastating avalanche of sand some uncaring gods poured into its blazing furnace? What fire does not flare up when you enrich it suddenly with a blast of air or throw gasoline

598

into its curling flames? The sun we have known from birth and that birthed our race did no more than perform as was intended. What better proof of our constant need for its warmth than sailing beyond its reach? Perhaps the Aztec and the Maya and so many of the older races were right, after all, to worship the sun. We might as well be doing the same on this ship as we shake off the cold that bit and chewed at us. New life moves among us. Eyes lift up instead of casting down.

And there can be no greater exercise, no performance that gives more joy, than the repeated rehearsals in loading the shuttles. The crew has set up a mock shuttle that serves to rehearse the loading of human passengers and, by moving internal structure about, prepare the mockup for animal or cargo loading. We have no shortage of volunteers. They are practicing to go home!

Commander's Log, *Pegasus*
Day 650

Beautiful, precious, incredible Earth. We know of no other world so bountiful, so rich, so luxuriant in life and plenty. To look through the lexitr sheets at the velvety darkness and find that shining blue-white marble suspended in ultimate blackness is more than can be described. Earth hangs in the forever sky like a keyhole to another universe where life awaits us all. It is not and cannot be here in this black emptiness. It must be the gateway to Elsewhere. To Life. The feeling grows and surges. It is absolutely amazing.

One month to go. Everybody hangs by the windshields and the ports every chance they get. The television monitors throw a huge picture of Earth on the great screens. Our people stare in wonder, drinking in this incredible world. To have ventured forth into nothingness and now to return . . .

The last time I looked in this direction at the Earth-Moon system there could hardly have been regrets for a world charring its inhabitants, and to imagine that the moon, for so many billions of years the lifeless stepchild of Earth, *now* harbored the last remaining higher life forms of the planet . . . well, it was simply too much. The twists and turns of life are just so incredible. Do we duck the next time God throws his dice? How could Einstein have been so wrong to deny that! All the time we've been gone the Earth has been burned, drowned, smashed by winds and quakes until all its people no longer existed—but now it's awakening again to life, gathering new spirit to itself, opening its arms to new *and old* life forms, and the moon—well, obviously dead again. Had they made it through that terrible time, we'd have heard from them. If any man could pull his people through hell and damnation it would be Russ Corey. But I shudder even to think of the radiation storms they had to endure, the electromagnetic battering, whatever tidal gravitational effects may have spun out from the sun, perhaps even Earth. It would be so marvelous to know there had survived on the moon, *in* the moon, another brotherhood of man—

I've got to stop this. Those crazy high-frequency radio signals aren't that rare. I had whistlers and howlers in the Antarctic. We all did. The intense cold, the grinding of subpolar air masses, the static electricity that sent radio waves screeching and screaming everywhere. Now add the sun as your antenna and *wham!* You've got signals racing out beyond the galaxy.

Commander's Log, *Pegasus*
Day 671

Nine days to go. Nine days counting down to ignition. We've made a last-minute decision to modify the burn times and procedures to decelerate. We're back to almost 33,000 miles an hour, we'll be at that velocity in just nine days, and that means one hell of a burn with the main engines to drop us into the orbital slot we need. At T minus four days we'll separate the cables from *Noah*. We've got electrical energy pouring into the batteries from the solar cells, more than enough for what we'll require from now on. The engineers agree that to burn with the big engines is to invite tearing this ship into great big pieces that may decide to go their own way. We've programmed the burns with the six lesser engines. We'll fire two, let everything settle, then two more, and when we get the kind of readings that satisfy us we'll go to the six lesser engines and just let them blaze away until we've deboosted right to the numbers we require.

With our master computers twisted wreckage from the meteoroid strike that killed Tereshnikov and the others, we've had to depend on the system aboard *Noah*. Again our tight little world offers up its twists and turns. Leaving Earth, we computed for and controlled *Noah*. Now the Animal Farm is going to return the favor.

Tomorrow we reverse ships' attitude to place the engines into our line of flight and the flight deck to the rear.

No time now for the log. We're all going day and night to have everything ready. Day and night . . . . if all goes well that phrase will return to its original meaning for us all.

Commander's Log, *Pegasus*
Day 679
THIS LOG ENTRY IS FROM A REAL-TIME RE-CORDING MADE ON THE BRIDGE OF THE SS *PEGASUS*. NO EDITING HAS BEEN DONE. THIS IS A VERBATIM RECORDING.

We're on the w-way in . . . shaking and rattling from the long engine burn . . . dust in the air with sunlight streaming in the ports . . . it's beautiful! . . . *Pegasus* is creaking and groaning like bones rubbing together in an old body . . . feels strange . . . all this gravity after all this time . . . rough . . . on children . . . on women . . . very rough . . . but I bet they're laughing while . . . they hurt . . . we've got systems . . . failing everywhere . . . red and amber warning . . . lights . . . flashing across the boards . . . as long as the main . . . systems hang . . . in there we'll . . . be okay . . . our engine burn has . . . *uh* . . . burn has been . . . terrific . . . right on the . . . money . . . *Noah* reported . . . number five engine had sudden . . . overpressure . . . shut down number . . . brought in one of main . . .

601

engines and . . . compensated for thrust var . . . variations . . . both ships in loose . . . formation . . . th-
three m-miles apart and . . . continue deboost . . .
until we lock in to. . . . Earth . . . orbit at two . . .
hundred miles . . . What? That's . . . it can't be . . .
real! . . . radar picked up . . . now have radar lock on it
. . . impossible . . . have visual . . . have visual. . . .
impossible . . . *a flashing light coming up . . . from
. . . astern!* My . . . God . . . it must be . . . it's got to
. . . be a ship of . . . some kind. I have visual . . . have
a visual on the. . . . target. Holy Je . . . it's real . . . its
really out there! Radar plot says . . . it came up very
. . . fast and now it's . . . decelerating. . . . formation
between us and . . . *Noah* . . . getting radio transmission . . . from . . . s-ship . . . see only . . . reflection
. . . too bright . . . engines or whatever the hell. . . .
engines firing . . . let me have that radio . . . report,
damn it! They're calling out . . . coming up on . . .
shutdown. . . . here it is . . . two, one, SHUTDOWN!
Bingo! . . . we've got it made . . . two hundred ten . . .
miles . . . preliminary. . . . you're damn right I . . .
pipe it through . . . speakers . . . yes, yes, I understand . . . English and . . . Russian . . . let me hear it
. . . be quiet I want to . . .

27

. . . *N*ot interfere with the craft between your
two ships. It is a Beltor Mark Six strongly
modified for remote communications and heavy payload. The Mark Six will maintain precise formation
position between *Pegasus* and *Noah*. When you respond to this message, direct your transtenna at the
Beltor. Your transmission will be relayed automatically.
Now listen carefully for your instructions. Follow them
exactly. If you have doubts as to your willingness to
comply, you shall soon understand how unwise that
would be.

First, do not deploy any shuttle craft for deboost. This is an order. Do not deploy any shuttle craft for deboost. This delay will not be extensive.

Above all else do not interfere with the Beltor Mark Six. I cannot repeat that instruction with more emphasis. I repeat, there is to be no interference with the Beltor Mark Six. If you do so, or if any shuttle craft deboosts for reentry, the Mark Six will detonate.

We repeat. Violation of those instructions will cause the Mark Six to detonate. The entire procedure will be automatic. We repeat, the entire procedure will be automatic.

Between your two vessels you now have a twelve-megaton thermonuclear bomb. Neither of your two ships can survive its energy release.

Prepare to copy frequencies. Following this message will be your instructions for audiovid exchange. We will communicate with *Pegasus*. All communication at this time will be on tight secure beam.

Please stand by.

Welcome home.

"This is the captain. Gregory Tretyakovich and Chiang Biao to the flight deck immediately. Gregory Tretyakovich and Chiang Biao to the flight deck *immediately*. All other personnel continue your computations and preparations for shuttle manifest. Navplot teams continue full reconnaissance coverage. Navplot teams continue your Earth scans and readings. Propulsion teams bring the engines to standby, bring the engines to standby. Captain out."

I should have said commander, not captain. I'm rattled by all this. But then who the hell wouldn't be!

Marc Seavers almost threw himself into his wide chair behind the work table in his conference chamber. He forced himself to quench the white heat of anger surging through him. Now more than at any other time he needed the tightest control possible. He had been so engrossed for so long with mechanical and other ship's problems that the concept of what was happening right now hadn't come within a light year of his consideration. Again and again his anger boiled upward and he forced it down. He must not react. That could be the end of them all. The situation they faced, even with as little information as they had, was going to demand as much cunning as it did original thought.

He watched Chiang Biao and Gregory Tretyakovich come through the doorway. Seavers motioned to seats and waited as they settled down with velcro strips to hold them securely. For several moments no one said anything. Their heads turned irresistibly to the thick ports and through the radiation-streaked lexitr they strained to see the unwelcome company holding formation with *Pegasus* and *Noah*.

"All right," Tretyakovich broke the silence. "Let us first determine what is that monster machine out there. I heard it all. A Beltor Mark Six. We had nothing like that in our stocks."

"Nor ours," Biao added.

"It's one of ours. American, I mean," Seavers confirmed. "But we never had them as weapons. The Mark Six is a powerful deep space probe loaded with heavy instrumentation, cameras, the whole lot. Obviously what these people have done is modify it with an advanced computer brain. Damn, it's rough even saying it! They've shoved into that thing a fusion bomb. Twelve megatons, they said. And at this distance the radiation pressures and the rest of the energy release would take us out."

"You are referring to, when you say 'they,' obviously the lunar base people?" Biao looked puzzled as Seavers nodded. "What would they be doing with so powerful a bomb?"

"If Russ Corey had anything to do with it, Chiang, he had a bunch of those things up there. Corey's from the old school. Smile, be nice, and carry a hell of a big bang in your hip pocket. The way the world was going, that's how *he* judged things. Insurance for their survival against power plays from Earth. I'm sure they never figured to use one like *this*."

"You're certain it's from the moon?" Tretyakovich asked.

"Yes. Nothing with that kind of capability survived on Earth. And if it had been left in orbit as part of any strike or defense program it wouldn't have the capability we witnessed. Uh-uh. It's been modified and it's been waiting for us. It's from the moon, all right. It also fits right into whatever plan they cooked up for us."

Tretyakovich hadn't accepted Seavers' ready answer. "There could have been another group that left the plane of the ecliptic."

"And had the room and the weight ability and the rest of it to lug along hydrogen bombs? No," Seavers said flatly. "Forget the rest of it. It's got lunar base stamped all over the damn thing."

"Then," Biao concluded, "since they are sending us the audiovid frequencies, we should soon be hearing directly from—"

A soft chime interrupted, confirming his words. They turned to the television communicator. Three cameras trained on them individually and the viewscreen flickered and spat for several seconds. It cleared to show a snow-spattered picture of Russ Corey. He looked, not haggard, but drawn and tested, like battle-hardened leather. Seavers recognized Vicki Correnti seated behind Corey, and, yes, there was August "Mother" Mason. Seavers ignored the other faces to concentrate on Corey, who nodded and then spoke.

"Jesus, I am glad it's *you*, Seavers. I can't tell you how good it is to see you *live*, let alone alive. Who's that with—ah, the Cossack madman made it with you." He nodded to Tretyakovich and then his eyes narrowed as he studied Chiang Biao. "I wasn't sure if he . . . I didn't know you were aboard, Doctor." They saw him trying to see any other faces. "Where's Tereshnikov?"

"Dead," Seavers said. He felt distant, cold. "Meteoroid strike."

"I'm sorry to hear that. Really." Corey's eyes closed a long second, opened again. Somewhere in that time he had opened and closed a door. "He's the kind of man we need now. All right, Seavers, let me get to the point of all this right away."

"*No.* You hold all of it, Corey." Seavers' voice came out hard and strong, unemotional, unavoidable. "There doesn't seem to be any sense in our talking while you threaten us with a thermonuke between our ships. That's insanity."

"There's very little enough insane about a fifty-mile fireball." Corey didn't twitch or flicker a muscle. His eyes bored out from the screen as if he had projected himself among them. "Oh, it's real, Seavers. Don't think of it as a bomb." Corey smiled, a widening of hard, thin lips, a touch of additional crease to his eyes. "Think of it from this side of these television screens, my friend. Think of it as a club. Very big, the biggest one we could think of."

"Why, damn it! There are better ways. Jesus, I know *you.* I know you can—"

"Admiral, Admiral," Corey said softly, disarmingly. "It can't be you don't understand, can it? You're the only train left in the station, Admiral. The last ride out. You're the only way left for us to reach Earth. Only a fool would let that train leave before he got aboard. I haven't heard you offer to sell us a seat, Admiral."

"Why didn't you contact us sooner? Damn it, man, you're talking pretty damn good to me right now. Why'd you wait so long?"

"We didn't." The smile didn't leave even a trace. "We've been trying for months. Apparently we were a lot worse off than I thought. Antenna aiming problems. We didn't know what transmission strength we had. Didn't know how you were receiving. So we let our power build up and then we shot messages to you with all the transmission boost we had. Pulsed messages. Figured, hoped, you'd receive. Obviously, you didn't. We never got any calling cards from you."

"We received EM bursts we couldn't identify. We'd have answered you otherwise."

"Well, nice to know the welcome mat was still out."

"You're treading pretty heavy on it right now," Seavers glowered.

606

"Spare me your wounds, Admiral. Let us get right to it, shall we?"

Seavers was listening to a stranger. Damn, he'd known Corey, admired him tremendously. This man was someone he'd never encountered. Hard as leather nails. He forced his attention to the screen. He nodded. "Go ahead."

"This is a case of numbers, friend. How many shuttles do you have capable of carrying people, animals, cargo, whatever, through reentry to a controlled landing?"

"Sixty-one."

Corey remained expressionless. "Your planned capacity?"

"Twenty to thirty people average each ship. You know how this sort of thing works. We don't load up topheavy with people in any one ship. We need best mix at all times. People, animals, food, medicine, supplies, tools, seeds, and as you say, whatever, carefully selected. If the ships separate on the way down and any of them lands in an isolated area, cut off from everybody else, then each ship has enough supplies to last a year. Time enough for the super grains, wheat, and other food plants to take hold. You know how this works. Why are you so interested in the details? And especially right now? We came back here much sooner than we planned, Corey, because our ships are falling apart. Every day we spend short of getting those shuttles on their way cuts down our chances."

"I know that, Admiral. I can't help your problem unless you work with us."

"Oh, come off it, Corey! So far this has been a one-way deal. You drop a hellbomb between our two ships. There hasn't been even the smell of a negative toward you or the people you have in Hestia and yet you give orders, you demand obedience, and you've got this ridiculous setup for this *tête-à-tête*. It's not terribly impressive, Corey. I always knew you as a man of tremendous efficiency. You're slipping badly. You haven't even told us *why* you've done all this."

"Admiral, being stupid doesn't become you. Nice ploy, Seavers. You've already figured it out. You didn't miss the reference to the last train in the station. Stop playing dumb."

"Then tell me *why* you're going this route!"

"We're dying up here, Seavers."

Silence met his words. Seavers and the men with him exchanged glances, decided on silence. But it was time for further involvement rather than just this one-on-one exchange.

"Mister Corey." Tretyakovich stared at the camera. "Be so good to tell us. What do you mean you are dying up there? Is it too much penetrating radiations? A disease, perhaps—"

"Tretsky, shut up and listen. I'll tell it to you all very straight. We lost just about everything we had up here. But it wasn't a war. No fighting. No disease. No problems with radiation. It happened to us like it happened beneath your feet. Nature tore us up, ripped us but good. Nearly two years ago. To be specific, at precisely the time you people were busting out of here. Whatever electrical charge your ships set off triggered a release down below. The answer was the lightning strike of all time. That's what destroyed the *Gagarin*. You were on the other side of the planet when it happened. But that bolt kept growing and it jumped us here. *I saw it happen*.

"We took it full force. We might as well have been hit with a whole bunch of nukes. It tore the hell out of us. We had over four thousand people up here. I want you to think about that number. Four thousand. We have just over four hundred left. Nine out of every ten are gone. Okay; that's history. The people still here, alive, are *not* a matter of history. They've got a slim shot at staying alive, at some kind of future. *You're that future, Seavers*. We've got supergrains, the whole ball of genetic wax to help make a go of it. And these people are real survivors. I want them to have their shot, mister. You're their tomorrow."

Biao didn't let a second lapse between Corey's last word and his own question. "You have the ships to depart the moon with your people?"

"Yes." For someone who just made a hell of a speech, Seavers thought, Corey knows how to clip the language.

"What, then, is your problem?"

"It's pretty damn obvious, Chinaman. We can get to Earth orbit, but our ships are strictly pogo sticks for vacuum operations. They can't survive reentry."

"But you can bring all your people here to rendezvous with us?"

"Yes. But to finish the trip the right way we've got to use the shuttles. *Your* shuttles."

"There's not enough room," Seavers said from the side.

"You said that before, Admiral. *Make room.*"

"It's not that simple. I—"

"It's a lot simpler than waiting to die."

"Corey, damn it, this isn't the answer. I've been going over the numbers ever since . . . ever since you sent your little gift to fly with us. You know how it works out? If we take all your people down then we can't take all our people down. I cannot and I will not condemn any of the people aboard these ships to die in orbit—"

"And I won't let my people sit here and die while they watch your people going down to Earth to live." Corey's face was a mask, but Seavers knew the man was doing exactly what he had to do. *Anything* to save his people.

"Sounds like impasse," Seavers said.

Corey showed a twitch in a cold, hard face. "Right. Let me give you something to think about in the next half hour or so, Seavers. We're about to lose contact until you come up again around the other side of the planet. So you keep this in mind. You start sending your shuttles Earthward while we're up here watching, the game ends then and there."

They heard Tretyakovich suck in air. "End the word games, Russ Corey. Speak plainly!"

"Why, it's simple, Tretsky. I blow the bomb. Big bang. You get it? All of you buy it right where you are. *We* stay where *we* are. The name of this game is Everybody Dies."

The screen began to flicker as line-of-sight contact began to break up. "That's the only way you'll play this set?" Seavers asked.

Ice across space. "You bet, mister."

Seavers leaned back in his chair. He closed his eyes for several moments, opened them and leaned forward as if he could get closer to Corey.

"Go ahead, then."

"What?"

"Go ahead! Explode your damned bomb." Something hot and surging welled up in Seavers and he no longer tried to fight it down. He found himself on his feet, fists pressed against the table, feet instinctively locked in the restraints, temper flaring and yet absolutely under control. "If the human race has got to go right to the end fighting and squabbling like this, under threats and coercion and blackmail, then screw it, friend! Go ahead, damn it! *Set that thing off and we'll wipe the slate clean once and for all!*"

He didn't wait for *Pegasus* to slide down the far side of Earth. He cut the connection.

"Bridge, this is Seavers! Shut down all radios. *Immediately.* You copy?"

"Yes, sir, shut down all radios. Stand by, uh, where's— got it. Okay, master for antenna, master for—"

"Kill the main transmitter," Seavers ordered. "Notify all hands to shut down all radios, all radio *and* television freqs, use lines only. While you're doing that, tap me in to line-carried speakers for the ship."

He heard switches snapping. "You're on, sir."

"This is Admiral Seavers. Listen closely. I've ordered all electromagnetic communications shut down. If you're working with any kind of electronics communications, *shut down immediately.* Do not use suit radios, tug radios or anything else. Use phone lines, lights, hand signals, but I want this ship to be electronically dark. *No exceptions.* Seavers out."

His hand flew across his control panel. "Bridge, contact the shuttle loading and flight teams. Commence initial loading at once. Confirm."

Bridge called back his orders. "Get on that immediately. Now, anyone on the bridge know how to handle the Aldiss?"

As he expected there was no immediate answer. If you knew how to handle the Aldiss it meant you were still proficient in Morse code. "Skipper, this is Goldman. I served on a destroyer and I've kept up my Morse. Over."

"Stand by, then. How about *Noah*? Anyone there you can talk to with the lamp?"

"Carol Shaw. Flight dynamics team on the bridge. We've practiced. Just in case everything went to hell."

"It's done just that, Mister Goldman. Give it your best shot. Contact her by Aldiss. Order *Noah* to shut down electronic transmissions just as we've done. And Goldman, make damned sure neither of your lamps is directed at that robot out there between our ships. We don't want Baby upset or anything. When you've made contact and passed on those orders, get back to me at once."

"Yes, sir."

"Bridge from Seavers."

"Sir!"

"Get Gene Camblin on the horn immediately."

"Yes, sir."

Seavers glanced at Tretyakovich and Biao. The Chinese scientist smiled.

"Something is funny here?" Tretyakovich asked, puzzled.

"I believe the admiral is about to do Earth a favor," Biao said. He stopped short as the speaker came alive again.

"Admiral, this is Camblin."

"Gene, how fast can you pop those biovats out of here?"

"They're on standby, sir. All on thirty-second counts."

"Can you get them away and into atmosphere in, ah," Seavers glanced at the bulkhead time counter, "twenty-five minutes or less?"

"Can do, Admiral."

"Do it, *now*. Don't waste a second, Gene. Pop 'em."

611

Seavers leaned back, closing his eyes. He'd always had the ability to project himself into the future, into a situation where everything appeared in any detail he wished to extrapolate. He was doing that right now, looking at the belly of the great spaceship as if he floated nearby in a tug or his suit, seeing the huge metal flank. With the magic of his ability to dart and drift in his mind, he watched the cover panels roll back from the probe airlocks. Cold vapor flashed out, danced and gleamed and vanished from sight. The spray of compressed air pushed out thick-bodied probes studded with antennae and knobs. A mile beneath *Pegasus* they flashed as small thrusters locked in their proper attitudes relative to the planet below. Now Seavers looked down, saw the probes reflecting golden sun, in the distance watched the onrush of the glowing terminator line heralding nightfall.

All this was still unfolding as his mind raced ahead, at first only minutes into the future as the biovats within the probes came to life, poised, waiting for their moment. Then the timers counted through and small wasplike rocket engines screamed, only for seconds but enough to break the balance that poised the probes so delicately between gravity and outward spiraling force. The probes now yielded to gravity and fell Earthward on a long slanting descent. A panel opened in the lead probe and a thick package ejected. Seconds later another, and then another and another and still more. Each probe clicked and shuddered and hissed and released panels and springs, and the thick packages fell blunt-nosed into atmosphere. At five miles every second the probes soon glowed red with frictional heat and then spattered chunks of blazing ablation material from the thick nose cones. The heat dissipated rapidly, never reaching the precious payload behind the shield. Finally the speed fell to something sensible, friction was far behind, and more relays clicked in each probe.

The first probe began to tumble. Small tubes extended and a thin spray whipped away by centrifugal force from each tube. For two hundred miles the probe tumbled, ever lower, ever slower, still spraying its cargo of superseeds, genetically altered seeds for grass, wheat, alfalfa, corn, hay, all manner of plants, all mutated for swift growth under the most hostile of environments.

All along the flight path of *Pegasus* the larger probes fell away and spat flame and fell, the thick packages ejected and began their entry into the high atmosphere of Earth. The Tumblers kept spraying across an area of Earth fifty-nine degrees north and south of the equator. Much of their payload would fall into the sea. Just as much would fall to ground in a gentling rain of life.

Beneath the Floaters, the ablation heatshields fell away to lighten the load. Springs snapped out stiffly, blowing away door panels, ejecting long ribbons of nylon. Parachutes slowed down descent, valves opened, and helium gushed from containers into flyweight plastic. The balloons filled and halted descent and now the Floaters went to work, riding the high atmosphere, easing their precious cargo into the thicker, lower atmosphere in a long-lasting trickle to cover the greatest area. Eggs, billions of eggs of spiders, honeybees, beetles, butterflies, earthworms rained gently to the largely barren land below.

The Tumblers and Floaters separated. The Tumblers, their containers finally empty, continued their madcap descent all the way to impact against the ground or disappeared forever in some faceless body of water. Not yet the Floaters. They would drift for days and then for weeks, releasing their spore at timed intervals until, at last, the helium would seep through the balloon plastic and lift would decay. Those still aloft, having escaped storms and lightning and cold, would then descend silently, also to be absorbed by earth or water and disappear: unseen, unnoticed, unheard, but with an impact that could not be measured.

Marc Seavers knew that after their swooping curve about the Earth when they came back into direct observation of what remained of Hestia on the moon, no sign would be visible of the biovats that had left *Pegasus*. When again they fell down the farside of the planet in relation to the moon, *Noah* would send forth the flowers and plants and insects of the future.

613

If not a one of us lives we have still returned to this world of our birth an assurance of new life. And if none of us lives, that is enough. But this tea party ain't over yet . . .

He opened his eyes to find Tretyakovich and Biao staring at him. "You, ah, go somewhere?" the Russian asked.

"Quick trip to tomorrow and back. Trying to think things out," Seavers evaded. "Okay, let's rub our brains together," he said to both men. "We don't have much time to come up with a game plan."

"Then you are open to comment?" Biao asked.

"Of course I am."

"That was a terrible risk you took with the man Corey," Biao said sternly. "You saw his face, his eyes. He is on the brink. Anything could push him over."

"Bullshit," Seavers said immediately. "You, my friend, confuse philosophy with seven-pound balls. That man wasn't close to being pushed *anywhere*. You turn off, Chiang. People like Corey get tougher and harder. They dig in. He's a survivor: for himself, but much more importantly, for his people. He is *not* going to blow up the very last chance his people have for getting to Earth. *We* are that chance. Besides, what he wants *us* to do is simply not acceptable."

Biao's eyes widened. "Even at the risk of all the lives on our two ships?"

"*Absolutely.*"

For the first time since they had departed their tortured world, Chiang Biao saw the Marc Seavers that the president had in mind when George Starling selected him to head the survival mission. A Seavers that had been laid aside all this time. Now here before Chiang was a man he hardly knew. *But that does not mean the American, this Seavers, is right.*

Biao looked to Tretyakovich. "Do you believe the man Corey would set off the bomb?"

Tretyakovich chewed his lower lip. He laughed suddenly. "The first question is whether or not there really *is* a bomb in that machine out there," he offered.

Biao was stunned, and his expression showed his feelings before he could draw a mask over them.

"But if there is a bomb then, yes, I believe he would. I knew Corey in Washington. I do not know of anything he would *not* do," the Russian concluded.

"Then you must cooperate with him!" Biao said with a flash of anger to Seavers.

"The hell I will," Seavers snapped. "You may hold the world record for Tibetan staring into space, Chiang, but I don't think you'd make too good a poker player. You're both wrong. There is one thing that Russ Corey absolutely would *never* do. I don't give a damn what anyone says. *Russ Corey would never commit suicide.* He'd be doing exactly that if he blew up our ships. And he's a hell of a poker player. He's convinced I don't have the gumption to stand up to his threat and that's why he made it." Seavers studied the two men with him.

"But there's something else I want to make clear to you. I meant every word I said to Corey. If we've got to start all over again on Earth through blackmail and—"

"Include the word compromise!" Biao shouted.

"Then compromise with the devil himself!" Seavers shouted back. "You'll get nowhere just as fast. Can't you understand *yet?* Can't you even see what's happening? Corey knows that if our positions were reversed, that if it was *me* on the moon and he was here in this ship, *then I'd be doing exactly the same thing he's trying right now.* If he *asks* for our help, the numbers provide the answer. We're going to turn him down because it means condemning some of *our* people. And you know damned well we're not leaving anybody up here in orbit just to take care of people from the moon. So he *can't* ask, because then he's nowhere if he's turned down. Begging is another level of asking, and he would *never* beg. Not because he's too proud, but because he knows it's a useless, sniveling act that never changes anything. He's left with one way to go and he took it."

Seavers' hand stabbed to the window. "It's out there. Oh, I don't doubt for a damned minute that there's a hell of a nuke in that thing. Why should he bluff when he has the goods?"

"Marc, my friend," Tretyakovich spoke softly, "what is there that is so wrong with compromise?"

"Because my first responsibility, my sworn oath, everything I stand for, is to the people of these two ships first, foremost, last, always and above—*almost* above—everything else. There is only one devil I will not worship, and that is Compromise. *If we do that we must condemn some of our people to death.*" His face took on a mask of grinning death. "Tell me, oh wise one," he glared at Biao, "which children will *you* pick to stay here and die so another child now on the moon can live? Who will you choose? Will you enjoy playing God? Do you have some infinite wisdom the rest of us don't know about? I'll spell it out for you, Chiang. Your compromise is the death sentence for many people here. Will you ram the knife in their chests to stave off a slow, lingering death?"

He laughed coldly, with mingled pain and sorrow, and his voice fell to a sound of weariness. "Do you want full-screen titles for this replay of the Garden of Eden? Do we need to go back to the beginning of Time? Not with just two characters from the book, but now with almost two thousand in our ships alone. Don't you even see what's happening here?" His hand jerked downward. "Do you know what's waiting for us down there? A world that is unspoiled because there's been no one alive to screw it up. As tough as it's going to be, it's a brand-new start, and if you understand anything, the *both* of you, then understand that we're making our choice right now, here and now, to come back as men undaunted, strong, moral, *our ethics uncompromised*. Or we start off with one knee bowed to blackmail and the whole rotten story starts all over again."

He shook his head. "No. I'll be no party to that. I—"

"Skipper, Goldman here." They looked up instinctively as the bulkhead speakers came alive.

"Go ahead," Seavers called out.

"Full Aldiss contact with *Noah*. Carol Shaw's a beaut

with the blinker lamp. But we've increased our speed. You can communicate with *Noah* fast as you can talk."

"Quick and dirty, Goldman."

"Yes, sir. The main computer on *Noah's* programmed for Morse. So is our backup. We have people typing direct to the computers, they translate to Morse and flash it by blinker between the ships. We stuck to your orders, Admiral. We've bypassed radio, TV, all electronics systems except direct line and blinker."

"That message on shuttle loading—"

"Under way, sir."

"Contact Camblin personally. Tell him to pass on to *Noah* the same orders I gave him for the biovats from this ship."

"Yes, sir."

"I'll be on the bridge soon. Make sure that any call from Hestia comes in to me here at once."

"Got it, Admiral."

"We don't have much time to work out a solution to this mess," Seavers said to Tretyakovich and Biao. "I have an idea but I'm going to hold off on it for a few minutes. First, let me define what we're facing.

"The survivors on the moon have been through a long winter of dread. Clearly, their only real hope for survival has been *our return*. Now we're here. Those people have got to join us here in Earth orbit, *and* get seats on our shuttles. If they can't do *both* they're as good as dead. Okay so far?"

The Russian and Chinaman nodded.

"They can handle their first problem. Getting off the moon and joining us here. They can do the deboost and rendezvous. They *can't* go through atmospheric reentry and land. So we become the train station. Without us they're stuck. If we make room for them then their chances are as good as ours—but ours are suddenly less.

"And we can't give them their chance because there aren't enough seats for everybody. We can't even leave the supplies, equipment, or the animals, yes? If we do that, our people, and theirs, have a poor chance of surviving," Tretyakovich said.

"That is what you Americans are so fond of saying," Biao added, "is a Catch 22."

"That's it in a nutshell. Catch 22. Dead end. They can get to us and we can take them but if we take them we can't take our people and everything else they'll need, which means a slow instead of a fast death, and *that* isn't acceptable."

"And Corey will not send that bomb away," Tretyakovich said slowly, "until we accept the unacceptable."

"I have a solution."

Seavers and Tretyakovich turned to study Chiang Biao. A look of serenity suffused his face. "Tell us," Tretyakovich prompted.

"The solution is Catch 22, that is, it is unacceptable, *only if everybody insists upon returning Earthside.*" Biao smiled.

Tretyakovich scowled. "Of course! Who would stay up here willingly!"

"*I will.*"

"Chiang, that's crazy!" Seavers half-shouted.

"Not crazy at all, my friend. We have all lived under the sentence of death for a long time. In my mind I ceased to resist two years ago. These last two years are a gift. I have drifted among the stars. I am a very, very rich man. I will stay. I will not be the only one. There are more who will think like me." He raised his hand, palm out. "Please do not interrupt. We will free enough places for the young ones, the mothers, the specialists and the farmers and woodworkers . . . ah, they are all more valuable than the old people. Marc Seavers, I have never before considered myself old, but I have been known to age swiftly. You will place my name on the list of the volunteers to remain behind. I am certain the news will be received with great jubilation on our moon."

Tretyakovich burst out with laughter. "Ah, the ways of the Orient. Always the urge to be first. You usurp the Russian position, old man."

"What the hell are you talking about?" Seavers demanded.

"I have never yielded an inch in my life for any cause," the big Russian said. "And I will not change *now*. Not for anyone. However, this stupid Chinaman has challenged me to a chess match. It seems our match will take many years. We have no time for, what do you call them? Yes, yes; no time for joyrides. So this ugly person and I will engage in the first unlimited zero gravity chess competition in history. We shall keep you informed on the surface."

Seavers stared. He started to speak with these two men who had caught him so completely unprepared. Instead, he turned to his comm panel and snapped a switch. "Bridge! Seavers here."

"Sir?"

"You about ready for lunar contact?"

"Any moment, sir."

"Expect Russ Corey to show on the screen. Hold off a moment in patching him through to me. Ask him, first, at my most urgent request, to get Vicki Correnti on the horn. You got that?"

"Yes, sir. Vicki Correnti. Will do, Admiral."

"I'll stand by. Get to it."

Seavers turned slowly, looking first at Biao and then at Tretyakovich. "Goddamned heroes," he said finally. "You're assholes. Beautiful, but assholes just the same. Both of you, cross your fingers. I think I have the way out of this. It's risky, but it *is* a way. I'll know better when I talk with Correnti."

"You are keeping this a secret *from us*?" Tretyakovich said in disbelief. "I make the first grandiose gesture in my whole life and you talk in riddles? Marc Seavers, I think that if we all get out of this alive, I will kill you."

"Later, later," Biao said impatiently. "Your plan?" he asked Seavers.

"A couple of things I remember from some years ago. I was just a kid when I saw the first one. I've seen it several times since. Then there was an interview I saw on television. From the moon. It was about Vicki Correnti and the Hestia base."

Biao and Tretyakovich again looked at one another. The Russian shrugged. Biao turned back to Seavers.

"But what could you remember that would change everything?"

Seavers smiled. "A movie. A movie and a boobwalk."

28

*T*hey peered across the space between *Pegasus* and *Noah,* barely able to see the long and menacing torpedo shape of the Beltor Mark Six. But even the faintest glimpse of that cold metal and the terrifying device within its belly was enough to bring a person to nausea. The thoughts rolled within and among them and—

It happened faster than their eyes or minds followed. Golden flame appeared, snapped abruptly to red, and the space torpedo was *gone,* its existence reduced to a fading sparkling glow. The trail swept across the curving horizon of the planet and needled straight out, its destination the sun, where it would flash only once more as it was consumed, and then the last bomb would be gone forever.

"Admiral Seavers? Sir, we confirm a series of rocket exhausts from the lunar surface, normal burn times, each of ten boosters reporting nominal climbout and acceleration to required velocity."

"Can you stay in contact yet?"

"Yes, sir. We've deployed the three comsats equidistant about Earth in our orbit and we've tested comm bounce. We're on the money with them, Admiral."

"Which of those ships have crew only and heavy cargo?"

"The three lead ships, sir."

"Okay. Keep tabs. Good work, son."

"Thank you, sir."

Marc Seavers took a few moments out for hot coffee from his pressurized mug. He sipped slowly to savor the taste. He had an incredible, sudden urge for a whole wheat doughnut. He was amazed. Where the hell had that come from? Earth and his past tugged at him. *Not yet, not yet*, he told himself. He tapped a comm button on his chair.

"Navplot here, Admiral."

"Nav, how go those new charts?"

"Very well, sir. We're making up copies for all ships, full coordinates and pertinent data. We're also feeding in all the new data to the memory banks of each shuttle."

"How about probes video?"

"Got it, Admiral. Damned good, too."

"Have them played on constant basis on all monitors. Both ships, Nav."

"Yes, sir. You can review it yourself any time, Admiral. Just punch the button."

"Thank you. Seavers out."

Nancy Parks Seavers had refused to be put off this time. "I don't care how busy you are. The worst is behind us as far as I'm concerned. I've hardly seen you for months!"

"Damn it, Nancy, you know what I've got to—"

"You've got to slow it down, Admiral baby. Slow it down and have a decent meal and see some people for dinner who are your *friends*."

"There'll be plenty of time for that when we're on the ground," he growled.

"Marc, I'm going to make a scene."

"Would you? Really?" He was astonished.

"It's time you met the other me, love. I'd prefer you didn't. Dinner and candlelight and music, that's much nicer."

"Candles? In zero g?"

"So I'll hold a flashlight in my teeth."

"Okay, okay."

She felt great. He hadn't laughed this freely since—she'd *never* known him to let it just bubble out.

Tanya Tereshnikova and Peter Nicholson joined them in their quarters for the "candlelight" dinner. Amazing what a woman's touch can do, Nancy mused. Even if the silverware has got to be slightly magnetic to keep it from floating away . . . Nancy placed four pressure containers of dark, hot coffee in the magholder before each seat, content to sit back and listen.

"We've had excellent tracking with our scopes," her husband was explaining to Tereshnikova and Nicholson. "That gave us good leads to zero in with some landers that also sent back live video. Then, we hung cameras on some of the extra biovat floaters. Now we *know* what awaits us."

Nicholson sipped coffee and peered over the edge of his container. "Pins and needles, Admiral, pins and needles."

Marc Seavers offered a rueful smile. "Sorry, Pete. I didn't mean to be so dramatic."

"All American admirals are dramatic, I think," Tereshnikova tweaked him.

Seavers nodded. "Short and sweet, that world below was pretty well scoured. Maybe cleansed is a better word. There isn't a trace of a city or a highway. That's amazing. All that steel and concrete. Gone. Just *nothing*. Swallowed up or covered over; whatever. It's like there never were five billion people down there."

"But it's acceptable for us?" Nicholson asked.

"I sure as hell *hope* so," Seavers told them. "One thing's for certain. The planet is making a hell of a comeback. I've been marking the charts— Here." He spread navplot charts across the table and his finger tapped the plastisheet. "See this lake? It's really an inland sea now. High hills around the area, good rivers, and the beginning of what's clearly heavy grassland and new forests. *This* used to be the Great Lakes between the States and Canada. It's one of the most promising areas. We've targeted it for seven or eight shuttles; they're working out the details now.

"Okay, now to the south. Florida and the entire gulf coast *are gone*. I mean, vanished. So are the island chains of the North Atlantic and the Caribbean. That chain that curved down to South America? Strictly memory now. Whatever's left is sand. However, see here? This is the new south oceanfront of what was the United

States. This is a huge bay carved out of the land where Atlanta used to be and it's choice. Or it sure looks that way. We got two landers down there and I don't think we'll find anyplace better on the whole planet. The most exciting news we've had is that the cameras appear to show definite signs of sea life."

Nicholson's eyes widened. "Any details?"

"Not yet."

"I think I'd like to put in for that site."

"Do it." Seavers moved his hand westward along the charts. "If it works out here's where Nancy and I would like to try for. Eastern Colorado. We've confirmed running water and grasslands. It sure looks like new forest growth as well. This kind of mountain country usually survives well. It gets tumbled and shaken up pretty good, but when it settles down the soil is rich and whatever was growing there before somehow comes back very strong."

"Do they have the charts for Europe yet?" Tanya Tereshnikova had been waiting patiently. North America held little interest for her. South America was a jumbled mess. Europe still had its siren call.

"Southern England went through a hell of a change. The seas did a real number on England, but in the southern area the land appears to have lifted. It's high out of water and it looks real good. The British contingent on *Noah* has opted for here. Um, the mainland— well, the lowlands are *gone*. We expected that. To the north, whatever's left of the Scandinavian area will take a long time to come back. We've rejected that for a landing. Parts of France and Germany, especially the high plateau areas, they have the best possibilities."

"Russia?"

He held her gaze. "Whatever came down from the Arctic, Tanya, wiped everything before it. Maybe in a couple of years. Not now. It's barren." His hand moved again on the charts. "The Mediterranean has good possibilities. But there's no more sea there. It's all a bunch of big lakes now with high hills mixed in. The ground must have been ploughed up and it settled into what it was many thousands of years ago.

"West Africa looks promising. And, here, well, the major land mass got chewed up by whatever tore up central Russia. The Himalayas seem to have raised a whole bunch of new peaks and ranges. Tough country."

"How did central China do? That was wonderful farmland," Nicholson observed.

"We haven't had a good look. Major weather system there for the past few days. We're still trying to get some probes into there."

"Australia?"

"Flat and empty."

"How about India?"

"Swampland. Sri Lanka's *gone*."

"It's not the same world any more."

Seavers pushed aside the charts. "Nope. It isn't, and the sooner we accept that the better. I'm not involved in deciding who goes where. It's best for the people to work that out for themselves. Let their responsibilities begin right now. But the closer the main grups end up on each land mass, the better it promises for everyone. That's my feeling, anyway. We'll be able to stay in touch with each other for a while. There'll be plenty of radio equipment. We've already put out navstar satellites for reference points. Everyone will know *exactly* where the others are. That will help. The urge to be able to travel between the new population centers will be strong. A damned good driving point for everyone. So by the time we lose the navstars, well, I hope it doesn't really matter by then. We should have a whole new generation of navigators."

"Mario Silva's ready to drag out his old uniforms," Nancy Seavers said, laughing. "He's reminded everyone he was a sailor as a youngster before he went into the air force. He can't wait to rebuild the Portuguese traditions on the high seas."

"I don't want anyone to think we've got it made yet," Seavers warned. "Those shuttles will be touching down anywhere from two to three hundred miles an hour. It's a one-time only shot putting down on skids and using braking rockets and parachutes. There aren't any airfields any more. The four-man spaceplanes will go down

624

first since they land slowly. We've got six of them. Each will go to a landing site and the crews will search for the most promising touchdown sites for the shuttles. They'll set up homing beacons to guide in the shuttles and they'll be able to pass on to the pilots weather information, prevailing winds, that sort of data. They'll need all the help they can get."

The next day the spaceplanes left, *never to return*. That's how it would be for all of them. They crowded the viewports or watched video monitors, knowing their turn would be soon. The wedge-shaped spaceplanes drifted slowly away from *Pegasus*, spots of bright flame winking on and off from the thrusters. Then they were at a safe distance, glistening arrowheads, and they spat fire from their main engine. They were *gone*.

Aboard the ships everyone listened to the radio transmissions of the crews. The spaceplanes punched through the violent heat of reentry, slowed, and then they rode atmosphere, wings grasping lift. Each ship operated better than they had a right to expect, but the crews had babied and ministered to their ships with exquisite care. From each spaceplane a small turbofan engine extended into the air. Wings swept forward to provide maximum lift for low-speed operation. Now they had become great dragonflies, their video cameras holding audiences high above in orbit hypnotized with the moving sights of a new planet awaiting their arrival.

Five ships landed safely. The sixth descended in new mountain country of southern Germany. The wind was tricky. Three men died; one survived, badly hurt. He set up ground cameras, triggered the homing beacon, and became the fourth man to die on New Earth.

No one could remember who had first used that name.

Three cargo ships fell swiftly from the moon, accelerating in answer to the gravitational pull of Earth. A hundred miles out from *Pegasus'* orbit they flared great umbrellas of flame, shed eight thousand miles per hour of their speed and fell into their own orbit. The pilots began their maneuvers to refine speed and altitude to join up with *Pegasus*.

Fourteen hours later the remaining seven ships from the moon blossomed flame, burned off their speed, slid into matching orbits. As they approached *Pegasus* and *Noah*, Begley's spacetug crews moved them carefully into the big loading bays. Airlock doors closed, pressure built up, and the crews of the two great ships hurried to transfer the lunar refugees to shuttles. Children, adults, small animals and precious cargo for the future moved quickly to waiting shuttles. Two hundred and four, young and old, moved to their seats, were strapped in, and waited, numbed with the hopes of survival that had seemed impossibly far away so many times.

Russ Corey piloted the last ship off the moon. He came out of his ship in a loading bay, half-floating, taking long gentle bounds as he approached Seavers and Tretyakovich waiting for him and Vicki Correnti. They studied each other for several moments, and Seavers and Corey extended their hands at almost the same moment. They clasped firmly, their grins speaking for them.

They moved quickly to the flight deck of *Pegasus*. Through the lexitr shields several shuttles moved slowly away from the great ships, pushed with spurts of flame by the tugs.

"When do we shove off?" Corey asked.

Seavers gestured to the shuttles. "When they're gone. They've all got video scan of their approaches and where they land. We'll know a lot more about our landing site after they're down."

Vicki Correnti pushed forward to the lexitr shield. "You know, as fancy as those things are," she said in reference to the shuttles, "I think I prefer *our* ship."

"That isn't a ship," Seavers told her. "It's an abortion."

"Don't be too hard on Moonbeam, Admiral Seavers—"

"*Moonbeam?*"

"Moonbeam Three, to be exact."

"Charming. Going down to Earth in an abortion of a ship called Moonbeam Three piloted by an ornery son of a bitch name of Corey. Hell of a finale to this trip."

Corey clapped him on the shoulder. "That's better than *no* finale, Admiral."

"Holy Jesus, what an approach!"

"Look at that bay!"

"Man, they've got a beach that goes on forever . . ."

"They lucked out. Who the hell could expect a *flat* landing site!"

The shuttle pilots still aboard *Pegasus* crowded together on the broad flight deck to watch the large television monitors displaying the realtime transmissions from the first group of shuttles committed to landing in what the other pilots had already christened the Culpepper Coast. They fell silent as the lead shuttle banked steeply to provide a crystal view of a tremendous beach and a long sloping grassy plain to the north. They watched two screens, each with its siren call for attention. To their left was the scene from the camera set up by the spaceplane crew; to the right they saw out of the shuttle making its approach with the same view of the pilots at that moment committing to the life-or-death touchdown.

Shuttle One arrowed in with precision, the two pilots talking steadily to one another, judging their speed and altitude in a crosshatch between their own experience and the information presented to them by their onboard computer. They hardly breathed as they watched and listened.

"Nose coming up."

"You got it. Seven degrees up on the eightball."

"Okay . . . and we show three thirty."

"Let's bleed it off a bit. Nose up to nine degrees, speed coming down, okay, we're at three ten now."

"Very good. Let's hold that."

"We show four miles out. Right on the money for the approach."

"Roger. How's the wind holding?"

"Fifteen knots slightly from our right. No real factor."

"Uh, that's good to hear."

"You got the flasher?"

627

"Yeah. Right where it belongs. Nothing like a good old VASI approach."

The camera showed a brace of red and white lights that gave the pilots an accurate display of their continuous approach altitude. The trick was to get the two top lights on white and the bottom on red. They'd touch down one thousand feet beyond the VASI system if they held to that attitude and descent rate.

"Confirm skids out."

"Three green. We're a tad hot."

"Got it. Spoilers working."

"Roger. Okay, here we go. Nose up to ten."

"Very good. You got two eight zero, two seven zero, bleeding off nicely, that's two fifty, you're one hundred up, seventy up, holding nicely, speed two thirty and we're sixty up, speed two twenty, fifteen up, hold it, hold it, hold it, that's five up, we got a little prestall shake, very nice, ready for touchdown—" The voice rattled and vibrated and the screen shook for a moment.

"Skids down, skids down—"

"Chutes!"

"We have chutes, we're shaking pretty bad, full chutes, hit the reverse—"

"Hang on, rockets fired—"

A roar overwhelmed everything. On the right screen flame stabbed the world, smoke and dust blanked everything. They locked their eyeballs on the left screen for the ground camera view, saw the Shuttle One nose coming down hard, it slowed, then touched and flame speared ahead from the retrorockets, the parachutes billowed wildly and Shuttle One plunged into the smoke and dust of its own making, then the rockets shut down and the great winged craft emerged through the boiling clouds, sliding ahead into clear air, *and came safely to a stop*.

The uproar on the flight deck was overwhelming.

It became worse as Shuttles Two, Three and Four skidded and hammered to safe stops. *The first colonists of New Earth walked the soil of their planet*. It was incredible, marvelous.

Shuttle Five landed farther to the north, along the

grassy plain. On the flight deck voices cut off as if sliced by a knife as they stared, horrified, watching the nose skid dig into a hummock and tear free in a spray of torn metal. Shuttle Five dipped to the right, the wing caught and spun the ship wildly to the side, tearing loose the chutes, bouncing the ship violently up, then slamming it down. The shuttle cracked in two amidships, the two sections tumbling wildly, spilling people, animals and cargo in a screaming cloud of destruction along the ground.

They didn't have the luxury along Culpepper Beach to abandon their jobs for the moment. Into the terror of silence on the *Pegasus* flight deck they heard the spaceplane pilot who had set up the ground equipment talking as if he'd never left Earth. "You're on the money, Al. Keep her right in the slot with the VASI. You're looking good, looking good. The wind's shifted a bit from the south, bring your nose left ten degrees, very good, very good, hold it right there, you're coming down right in the slot, that's it, you're about to touch, hold it, hold it, just beautiful, baby, you're number one for the runway, the field's all yours, and we have . . . *touchdown*."

A plume of sand and dust, parachutes billowing, rocket flame and smoke, then silence. Number Six was down safely.

They lost two ships going in to southern Germany. Four others made it unscathed, one landed hard and the stuff inside broke loose. Three dead, nine injured. Pretty damn good.

Howling winds appeared out of nowhere to nearly wipe out the flock of shuttles trying to land in southern England. Two ships landed clean, four smashed up and only thirteen people survived from the one hundred and eighteen aboard.

All nine shuttles landed with only minor incidents in France.

Two out of eight crashed in west Africa. The others did fine.

Sixteen headed for central China. Thirteen made it

with varying degrees of success. Three crashed. Chiang Biao died in the first ship to be lost.

Seven went for eastern Colorado. They had a big fat plateau to use for a landing field flat as a paved runway. All seven made it down, one with damage, the others unscathed.

The last three to leave orbit had the luxury of pick-and-choose. Culpepper Beach took the honors. One didn't make it, dropping into the water and exploding.

Sixty-one shuttles made the attempt, following the six spaceplanes. Five spaceplanes dropped in safely, one crashed.

Forty-six shuttles put down intact. Fifteen shuttles either were lost or suffered catastrophic damage. Four hundred and four people died.

One thousand seven hundred and twenty-four lived.

Three modified, ugly Moonbeam ships with two hundred and nine lunar colonists, three crew from *Pegasus*, Marc and Nancy Seavers, and Marcus Goldman, waited their turn.

"Name your poison, Admiral," Corey told Seavers.

"That's a nice beach at Culpepper, but I don't think the elk hunting will be very good down there."

"*Elk* hunting?"

"Yeah. I'm damned good at it, too."

"For Christ's sake, Marc, there ain't no damn elk any more!"

Seavers smiled. "I *told* you I was good at it."

Nancy Seavers moved between them, looked directly at her husband. "For two years I haven't asked you for anything, have I?"

"No, you haven't."

"I'd like something now."

"Name it."

"Colorado."

"Elk country it is. But Moonbeam, here, has a voice in this, too. So does Vicki."

"I'll bet he can't shoot worth a damn," Corey said.

"One way to find out," Seavers retorted.

"Yeah. Colorado. We might have to wait a bit. You can't raise an elk herd overnight."

*   *   *

A red light glowed brightly in the loading dock. "Okay, let's do it," Russ Corey said from the left seat of Moonbeam One. He glanced through the flat wind-screen of the cockpit at the other two lunar ships that had been drastically modified for their last flight. Their landing legs had been cut away, the outer shape of the moonship bulged with domes and casings and jutted awkwardly at odd angles. "God, they're ugly," Corey muttered. No one disagreed with him.

"Let's get outside," Seavers urged. He looked about him with a sudden expression of distaste. "I'm getting claustrophobic in this damned tunnel," he added, refer-ring to the loading bay. "We can drift off and hold for them outside."

Behind the cockpit seventy adults and children, sur-rounded by small animals and all the cargo that could be crammed safely in their midst, waited anxiously. They were strapped in tightly, clumsy and uncomfort-able in pressure suits and helmets. Had they been able to see themselves, their faces haggard behind the curv-ing lexitr globes of their helmets, they might have been startled at the resemblance they bore to other, similar refugees many decades before: refugees from another killing mass of dust, in the great American west and southwest, immortalized in an old novel, *The Grapes of Wrath*. A resemblance of weariness, of homelessness, and yet, a difference. An all-important difference. *These* refugees had lost their homes, state, a nation, a world, an entire civilization and way of life. And still they carried their heads high, buried or not in curving lexitr, and they had absolute confidence in the people at the front of their ship, Corey and Seavers. They were ready to attempt *anything*. They knew this was their final do or die. They knew that if *this* final of all flights suc-ceeded they would have their chance to renew all of life again. They hated being strapped down, locked in and helpless, unable to perform any service, uncomfortable and clumsy.

As were the flight crew. Russ Corey in left seat, Marc Seavers in right. In the aft section of the cockpit Vicki

Correnti held down the engineer's seat, Marcus Goldman backing her up, Nancy Seavers watching wide-eyed. Seavers worked a remote control on *Pegasus'* frequency. Moonbeam One shuddered slightly as a powerful loading arm moved the ungainly spacecraft from the loading bay. The great airlock doors were already back. Seavers tapped the button that released them from the loading arm grip. "Take her out. We're free," he told Corey.

Corey worked the thrusters. Moonbeam One drifted away from the great spacecraft. Behind them Two and Three spat clouds of thruster plumes, drifted slowly. The three ships spread out, each three hundred yards from the nearest companion in a loose line-abreast formation. "Computer drive to ON," Corey called out. "Vicki, you on monitor?"

"On monitor," she confirmed. "Everything's up as programmed."

"Two and Three from One, are you on computer?"

"Two here. Roger. Heads up and locked. Waiting on your word to initiate."

"Three here. That's a rog, One."

"Okay, boys and girls," Corey called back. "Confirm set for three-second interval burns?"

"Two set."

"Three set."

"Very good. Check your passengers."

"All set."

"Snuggled up and ready."

"On my mark we will be to computer auto and counting to minus sixty seconds. Auto sequencer all the way. If you do not have ignition on schedule you will hold for your next pass around the block. Confirm."

"Two has it five by. We're waiting to punch the little red button."

"Three is go."

"Okay, now, coming up for auto sequence, on my mark, we are three, two, one, *mark*."

"Two confirms auto sequence."

"Ditto for Three."

"We're in the slot with One. Have a good trip, you guys," Corey called out.

"Yeah, watch out for those Sunday drivers, fellas."

"I think I forgot my driver's license."

"Thirty seconds for Three."

They fell silent, listening to the count. "Three is coming up on ten seconds. *Ten*. Everything's in the green and, ah, we're at three, two, one, *uh*—" Flame needle, an umbrella plume and Moonbeam Three whisked out of sight. Moonbeam Two fired and was gone. Before they could say a word their sequencer closed its relays and fire punched away from Moonbeam One. Sudden acceleration slammed them back in their seats. *"Whoo-eee!"* Corey yelled after he'd caught his breath. "That *is* a kick in the slats!"

"Ten seconds to cutoff," Vicki Correnti said, voice a touch tremulous from the vibration of the firing rocket engine.

"We have c—" Bam! The shock of engine cutoff was almost as great as ignition. They were thrown forward against their straps. "Confirm deboost on time, on the money," Correnti said. "You're free to rotate to reentry attitude."

"Got it," Corey answered.

"Hold it a second, Russ." Corey understood before Seavers needed to explain. The man who'd commanded *Pegasus* leaned closer to the lexitr panel before him and looked up and out as the great ship receded swiftly. Seavers didn't say anything. His gloved hand came up in the best salute he could manage in his pressure suit. When he leaned back, Corey worked the thrusters and rotated the ship to reentry attitude and position.

They waited. The fast conversation was put aside. Finally Marcus Goldman broke the silence. "We have the point zero five g light," he announced. Moonbeam One was treading the upper reaches of atmosphere. They were beginning to push thickening air aside and they had begun to decelerate. They couldn't feel the first whisper of g-force. Moonbeam One began to shake gently and then the shaking became strong buffeting. Instinctively they cinched their straps as they plunged into atmosphere riding backwards, taking the growing forces of deceleration back-through-chest.

"Jesus, in this bucket it's going to be a rough ride!" Seavers said loudly, fighting the pounding that rattled them severely.

"I'll turn off the meter!" Corey shouted back. "Damn, what a sight . . ."

Riding backwards, their windshield looking back along their line of flight, they stared at the huge column of blazing gases streaming behind them. "That bamboo sure burns good!" Corey sang out. "I hope your Rajani boy or whatever his name is has a money-back guarantee!"

"It works, it works," Seavers reaffirmed. "With the plastic steel and baking—"

"Never mind the sales pitch, Admiral! If it doesn't work we'll all be bamboo fricassee!"

Three thick layers of superhardened, baked bamboo with plastiseal covers took the brunt of reentry as the loads increased to four times the force of gravity. "We should be losing the first one any moment now!" Seavers called.

"There it goes!" Goldman shouted.

Huge blazing chunks whipped past the sides of Moonbeam One. Shock waves hammered and tore at them.

"Damn, it's burning away!" Corey shouted.

"It's *supposed* to burn away!" Seavers yelled. "The second shield should let go any moment now!"

A thousand flaming pieces tumbled and whipped out of sight. "One more to go!" Seavers called.

"Four g's holding steady." Vicki Correnti's voice was incredibly calm. "Speed dropping steadily."

"Man, I didn't believe that bamboo crap of yours would hold as long as it did," Corey said through chattering, bouncing teeth to Seavers.

"We're not out of the barrel yet," Seavers reminded him. "Ready on the bottles?"

"Ready," Corey snapped.

"Okay, the last shield is starting to go. It's lasting longer than the others. I don't think we can wait any longer, Russ! If that thing breaks up before we have the next shield out—"

"You got it!" Corey shouted, and his hand yanked down on the jury-rigged trigger. Behind them huge bottles of nitrogen released their pressurized gas, plunging into the spaces between four layers of thick plastifoam, snapping the layers into a thick heatshield.

"There it goes!" Goldman shouted. The third and last bamboo plastisteel shield broke up and was flung away by the howling, superheated wind. The color of the flames and gases streaming behind Moonbeam One changed from the bright red of burning bamboo and plastisteel to a darker red from thick plastifoam ablating away slowly. The inflatable heat shield yielded material in exchange for sloughing off heat, spreading it to the outer edges of the shield protecting the pressurized bulk of Moonbeam One.

"This is a hell of a ride!" Corey sang out. "Thirty seconds more and we'll be through the burn and home free!"

"Home, James!" Seavers laughed. "Twenty seconds!"

"Where the hell did you get the idea for this rig, Admiral?"

"From a movie and from you!"

"What the hell are you talking about?"

"When I was a kid—ten seconds!"

"When you were a kid, *what?*"

"We're coming out of it! Jesus," Vicki shouted from behind them, "we did it! We really did it!" Fists pounded against arms and shoulders.

The flames were gone. Moonbeam One fell freely through atmosphere. Thirty seconds of free fall coming up . . .

"When you were a kid?" Corey prodded Seavers.

"I was still a kid when I saw that movie, "2010" . . . you know, that classic about going to Jupiter?"

"Yeah, I remember it."

"And the only way they could slow down to get into orbit about Jupiter was to use an inflatable ablation heatshield. They blew it up just before smacking into the Jovian atmosphere and it soaked up and ablated away the heat, and when they were through they jettisoned it—uh—like *right now.*"

Correnti's arm pulled the dump switch. Latches pulled away and springs snapped taut, air whipped beneath the burned and still-smoking shield and hurled it back from Moonbeam One. "Just like that," Seavers laughed.

"Pyros set to fire," Correnti announced. Dull thuds, sudden tiny gouts of flame as a protective cap blew off the opposite end of the ship. A small drogue parachute flashed up and away.

"Ten seconds," Correnti announced.

Another cap flashed away to free the restraint on the small drogue chute whipping wildly high above them. The drogue pulled away from the canister atop Moonbeam One, hauling with it a huge parachute assembly. The lines pulled taut, the drogue broke free, and three great parachutes, tightly reefed to keep the big canopies from deploying at what was still high speed, whipped and fluttered wildly above them, slowing the ship, stabilizing the fall.

"Confirm drogue away, confirm three clean chutes and reefed," Correnti said. "Five seconds to go . . ."

A small plastic charge cut the reefing lines. Three enormous parachute canopies spilled and tumbled outward as they captured air. They filled with a jolt that banged them hard against their seats.

"Good chutes! Good chutes!" Goldman shouted.

Cheers and shouting came forward from the main cabin.

"We have a good descent," Correnti confirmed.

"I see the other ships!" Nancy screeched, banging her helmet against the nearest port.

"Helmets off, everybody!" Corey told them. "Vicki, open the ports."

"The first ship is on the ground! It's okay!" Nancy shouted again. "The next one is about to land!" Sudden flame and smoke obscured Moonbeam Two as its retrorocket fired just above the ground.

"Seventy seconds to touchdown," Goldman announced. "We have the landing bag coming down, *now*," he added. Another sudden jolt as beneath them a plastifoam bag extended from the girth of their ship, long spikes pushing downward from the base of the landing bag punctured with small holes, an updated version of the old Mercury spacecraft landing bag that American astronauts flew back in 1961. When it hit ground the bag would collapse upward, ramming air through the holes and performing like a great hydraulic lift to soften ground impact.

"Okay, okay, finish your story, damn it," Corey urged Seavers. "You saw the movie and it gave you an idea for the inflatable ablation shield. But how'd you figure in this plastifoam?"

"You did an interview from the moon to show what Hestia was like," Seavers said. "Vicki demonstrated the flooring she'd developed for the personnel quarters. Plastifoam. Stronger than metal. Impervious to chemicals, made to last a lifetime, inflatable, completely fireproof. And you, *Mister* Corey, looked straight into the camera and you told the whole world that walking on Vicki's inflatable floor on the moon was just like walking in a room with a floor filled with tits. Those were your exact words."

Corey exploded in laughter. Giggles from Nancy. Vicki's voice came to them all. "Knock it off . . . Twenty seconds to go. All electrical systems for cabin and flight deck off. Fifteen, slight left drift, ten seconds, *hang on!*"

Marc Seavers had a brief glimpse of rolling hills, a green slope nearby, people in the distance waving, watching—

"Contact!" Vicki called.

A sudden roar as the contact wire touched ground, set off the braking rocket, they felt the landing bag hit, Moonbeam One lurched sharply, settled, grumbled through its flanks, *stopped.*

"My God . . . we made it, we actually made it," Nancy Seavers said, eyes wide, disbelief flooding her mind. She threw off her straps to hug her husband, Russ Corey, *anybody*.

"Open the hatches! Somebody open the hatches!" Metal clanged, hatches flew open, sweet, cool mountain air washed over them. Nectar to breathe . . .

They saw animals in the distance on the ground among the people. Dogs barked.

They climbed down, brought their people out. They

all emerged to a world heavy with its gravity, and some of them fell beneath its ponderous drag, and they lay on the ground and breathed heavily, feeling pain, and they smelled the sweet ground and the air and they rolled onto their backs and felt the wind on their faces and looked up at the clouds, and weak as they were, they laughed, and from their ship, Vicki Correnti and Marcus Goldman, keeping the pact they had made on the fiery plunge home, opened bamboo cages and released their captives.

Wings beat furiously as two falcons raced away for the nearby hills.

Marc Seavers stood with his arm about his wife, hugging her fiercely. Then he stared. In a million years he never expected to see what was before him, a sight that said it all.

Russ Corey looked at his falcons flying free.

He wept.

HE'S OPINIONATED

HE'S DYNAMIC

HE'S LARGER THAN LIFE

MARTIN CAIDIN

Martin Caidin is a bestselling novelist, pilot *extraordinaire,* and expert on America's space program. *He's also a prophet of technological change.* His ability to predict future trends verges on the psychic, as when he wrote *Cyborg* (the novel which became "The Six Million Dollar Man") and *Marooned* (which precipitated the American-Soviet Apollo-Soyuz linkup mission). His tense, action-filled stories are based on personal experience in fields such as astronautics, aviation, oceanography and the military.

Caidin's characters also know their stuff. And they take on real life, because they're based on real people. Martin Caidin spent a stint as a merchant seaman in Europe and Africa, worked for Air Force Intelligence in the U.S. and Asia, and has flown his own planes to many parts of the world. His adventures can be yours in these novels from Baen Books.

— — — — — — — — — — — — — — — —

EXIT EARTH—Just as the US and the USSR have finally settled their differences, American scientists discover that the solar system is about to pass through a cloud of cosmic dust that will incite the Sun to a paroxysm of fury. All will die. There can be no escape—except, possibly, for a very few. *This is their story.* 656 pp. • 65630-9 • $4.50 _____

KILLER STATION—Earth's first space station *Pleiades* is a scientific boon—until one brief moment of sabotage changes it into a terrible Sword of Damocles. 55996-6 • 384 pp. • $3.50 _____

THE MESSIAH STONE—"An unusual thriller . . . not only in subject matter, but in the fact that the author claims that the basic idea behind the book is real! [THE MESSIAH STONE] concerns the possession of a stone; the person who controls the stone rules the world. The last such person is rumored to be Adolf Hitler. . . . Harrowing adventure and nonstop action."—*Science Fiction Review*. 65562-0 • 416 pp. • $3.95 _____

ZOBOA—It started with the hijacking of four atomic bombs, and ended with the Space Shuttle atop a pillar of fire. . . . "From the marvelous, cinematic opening pages, Caidin sweeps the reader along in a raucous, exciting thriller."—*Publishers Weekly* 65588-4 • 448 pp. • $3.50 _____

To order these Baen Books, check each title selected and return with a check or money order for the combined cover price. Send to Baen Books, 260 Fifth Avenue, New York, N.Y. 10001.

Distributed by Simon & Schuster
1230 Avenue of the Americas • New York, N.Y. 10020

Have You Missed?

DRAKE, DAVID
At Any Price
Hammer's Slammers are back—and Baen Books has them! Now the 23rd-century armored division faces its deadliest enemies ever: aliens who *teleport* into combat.

55978-8 $3.50

DRAKE, DAVID
Hammer's Slammers
A special *expanded* edition of the book that began the legend of Colonel Alois Hammer. Now the toughest, meanest mercs who ever killed for a dollar or wrecked a world for pay have come home—to Baen Books—and they've brought a secret weapon: "The Tank Lords," a brand-new short novel, included in this special Baen edition of *Hammer's Slammers*.

65632-5 $3.50

DRAKE, DAVID
Lacey and His Friends
In Jed Lacey's time the United States computers scan every citizen, every hour of the day. When crime is detected, it's Lacey's turn. There are a few things worse than having him come after you, but they're not survivable either. But things aren't really that bad—not for Lacey and his friends. By the author of *Hammer's Slammers* and *At Any Price*.

65593-0 $3.50

CARD, ORSON SCOTT; DRAKE, DAVID; & BUJOLD, LOIS MCMASTER
(edited by Elizabeth Mitchell)
Free Lancers (Alien Stars, Vol. IV)
Three short novels about mercenary soldiers—never before in print! Card's hero leads a ragtag group of scientific refugees to sanctuary in Utah; Drake contributes a new "Hammer's Slammers" story; Bujold tells a new tale of Miles Vorkosigan, hero of *The Warrior's Apprentice*.

65352-0 $2.95

DRAKE, DAVID
Birds of Prey

The time: 262 A.D. The place: Imperial Rome. There had never been a greater empire, but now it is dying. Everywhere its armies are in retreat, and what had been civilization seethes with riots and bizarre cults. Against the imminent fall of the Long Night stands Aulus Perennius, an Imperial secret agent as tough and ruthless as the age in which he lives. But he stands alone—until a traveller from Earth's far future recruits him for a mission so strange it cannot be disclosed.

55912-5 (trade paper) $7.95
55909-5 (hardcover) $14.95

DRAKE, DAVID
Ranks of Bronze

Disguised alien traders bought captured Roman soldiers on the slave market because they needed troops who could win battles without high-tech weaponry. The leigionaires provided victories, smashing barbarian armies with the swords, javclins, and discipline that had won a world. But the worlds on which they now fought were strange ones, and the spoils of victory did not include freedom. If the legionaires went home, it would be through the use of the beam weapons and force screens of their ruthless alien owners. It's been 2000 years—and now they want to go home.   65568-X $3.50

DRAKE, DAVID, & WAGNER, KARL EDWARD
Killer

Vonones and Lycon capture wild animals to sell for bloodsport in ancient Rome. A vicious animal sold to them by a trader turns out to be more than they bargained for—it is the sole survivor of the crash of an alien spacecraft. Possessed of intelligence nearly human, it has two goals in life: to breed and to kill.

55931-1 $2.95

DAVID DRAKE

"Drake has distinguished himself as the master of the mercenary sf novel."—Rave Reviews

WILL *YOU* SURVIVE?

In addition to Dean Ing's powerful science fiction novels—*Systemic Shock, Wild Country, Blood of Eagles* and others—he has written cogently and inventively about the art of survival. **The Chernobyl Syndrome** is the result of his research into life after a possible nuclear exchange . . . because as our civilization gets bigger and better, we become more and more dependent on its products. What would *you* do if the machine stops—or blows up?

Some of the topics Dean Ing covers:
* How to *make* a getaway airplane
* Honing your "crisis skills"
* Fleeing the firestorm: escape tactics for city-dwellers
* How to build a homemade fallout meter
* Civil defense, American style
* "Microfarming"—survival in five acres
  And much, much more.

Also by Dean Ing, available through Baen Books:

ANASAZI
Why did the long-vanished Anasazi Indians retreat from their homes and gardens on the green mesa top to precarious cliffside cities? Were they afraid of someone—or *something*? "There's no evidence of warfare in the ruins of their earlier homes . . . but maybe the marauders they feared didn't wage war in the usual way," says Dean Ing. *Anasazi* postulates a race of alien beings who needed human bodies in order to survive on Earth—a race of aliens that *still* exists.

FIREFIGHT 2000
How do you integrate armies supplied with bayonets and ballistic missiles; citizens enjoying Volkswagens and Ferraris; cities drawing power from windmills and nuclear powerplants? Ing takes a look at these dichotomies, and more. This collection of fact and fiction serves as a metaphor for tomorrow: covering terror and hope, right guesses and wrong, high tech and thatched cottages.

Here is an excerpt from the new collection "MEN HUNTING THINGS," edited by David Drake, coming in April 1988 from Baen Books:

IT'S A LOT LIKE WAR

A hunter and a soldier on a modern battlefield contrast in more ways than they're similar.

That wasn't always the case. Captain C.H. Stigand's 1913 book of reminiscences, HUNTING THE ELEPHANT IN AFRICA, contains a chapter entitled "Stalking the African" (between "Camp Hints" and "Hunting the Bongo"). It's a straightforward series of anecdotes involving the business for which Stigand was paid by his government—punitive expeditions against native races in the British African colonies.

Readers of modern sensibilities may be pleased to learn that Stigand died six years later with a Dinka spear through his ribs; but he was a man of his times, not an aberration. Richard Meinertzhagen wrote with great satisfaction of the unique "right and left" he made during a punitive expedition against the Irryeni in 1904: he shot a native with the right barrel of his elephant gun—and then dropped the lion which his first shot had startled into view.

It would be easy enough to say that the whites who served in Africa in the 19th century considered native races to be sub-human and therefore game to be hunted under a specialized set of rules. There's some justification for viewing the colonial overlords that way. The stringency of the attendant "hunting laws" varied from British and German possessions, whose administrators took their "civilizing mission" seriously, to the Congo Free State where Leopold, King of the Belgians, gave the dregs of all the world license to do as they pleased—so long as it made him a profit.

(For what it's worth, Leopold's butchers *didn't* bring him much profit. The Congo became a Belgian—rather than a personal—possession when Leopold defaulted on the loans his country had advanced him against the colony's security.)

But the unity of hunting and war went beyond racial attitudes. Meinertzhagen was seventy years old in 1948 when his cruise ship docked in Haifa during the Israeli War of Independence. He borrowed a rifle and 200 rounds—which he fired off during what he described as "a glorious day!", increasing his personal bag by perhaps twenty Arab gunmen.

Similarly, Frederick Courteney Selous—perhaps the most famous big-game hunter of them all—enlisted at the outbreak of World War One even though he *wasn't* a professional soldier. He was sixty-five years old when a German sniper blew his brains out in what is now Tanzania.

Hunters and soldiers were nearly identical for most of the millennia since human societies became organized enough to wage war. Why isn't that still true today?

In large measure, I think, the change is due to the advance of technology. In modern warfare, a soldier who is seen by the enemy is probably doomed. Indeed, most casualties are men who *weren't* seen by the enemy. They were simply caught by bombs, shells, or automatic gunfire sweeping an area.

A glance at casualties grouped by cause of wound from World War One onward suggests that indirect artillery fire is the only significant factor in battle. All other weapons—tanks included—serve only to provide targets for the howitzers to grind up; and the gunners lobbing their shells in high arcs almost never see a living enemy.

The reality isn't quite *that* simple; but I defy anybody who's spent time in a modern war zone to tell me that they felt personally in control of their environment.

Hunters can be killed or injured by their intended prey. Still, most of them die in bed. (The most likely human victim of a hungry leopard or a peckish rhinoceros has always been an unarmed native who was in the wrong place at the wrong time.) Very few soldiers become battle casualties either—but soldiers don't have the option that hunters have, to go home any time they please.

A modern war zone is a terrifying place, if you let yourself think about it; and even at its smallest scale, guerrilla warfare, it's utterly impersonal.

A guerrilla can never be sure that the infra-red trace of his stove hasn't been spotted by an aircraft in the silent darkness, or that his footsteps aren't being picked up by sensors disguised as pebbles along the trail down which he pads. Either way, a salvo of artillery shells may be the last thing he hears—unless they've blown him out of existence before the shriek of their supersonic passage reaches his ears.

But technology doesn't free his opponent from fear—or give him personal control of the battlefield, either. When the counter-insurgent moves, he's likely to put his foot or his vehicle on top of a mine. The blast will be the only warning he has that he's being maimed. Even men protected by the four-inch steel of a tank know the guerrillas may have buried a 500-pound bomb under *this* stretch of road. If that happens, his family will be sent a hundred and fifty pounds of sand—with instructions not to open the coffin.

At rest, the counter-insurgent wears his boots because he may be attacked at any instant. Then he'll shoot out into the night—but he'll have no target except the muzzle flashes of the guns trying to kill him, and there'll be no result to point to in the morning except perhaps a smear of blood or a weapon dropped somewhere along the tree line.

If a rocket screams across the darkness, the counter-insurgent can hunch down in his slit trench and pray that the glowing green ball with a sound like a steam locomotive will land on somebody else instead. Prayer probably won't help, any more than it'll stop the rain or make the mosquitos stop biting. But nothing else will help either.

So nowadays, a soldier doesn't have much in common with a hunter. That's not to say that warfare is no longer similar to hunting, however.

On the contrary: modern soldiers and hunted beasts have a great deal in common.

APRIL 1988 * 65399-7 * 288 pp * $2.95

To order any Baen Book by mail, send the cover price to: Baen Books, Dept B, 260 Fifth Avenue, New York, N.Y. 10001

ROBERT A. HEINLEIN

"Heinlein knows more about blending provocative scientific thinking with strong human stories than any dozen other contemporary science fiction writers."
—*Chicago Sun-Times*

"Robert A. Heinlein wears imagination as though it were his private suit of clothes. What makes his work so rich is that he combines his lively, creative sense with an approach that is at once literate, informed, and exciting."
—*New York Times*

Seven of Robert A. Heinlein's best-loved titles are now available in superbly packaged new Baen editions, with embossed series-look covers by artist John Melo. Collect them all by sending in the order form below:

REVOLT IN 2100, 65589-2, $3.50 ☐

METHUSELAH'S CHILDREN, 65597-3, $3.50 ☐

THE GREEN HILLS OF EARTH, 65608-2, $3.50 ☐

THE MAN WHO SOLD THE MOON, 65623-6, $3.50 ☐

THE MENACE FROM EARTH*, 65636-8, $3.50 ☐

ASSIGNMENT IN ETERNITY**, 65637-6, $3.50 ☐

SIXTH COLUMN***, 65638-4, $3.50 ☐

*To be published May 1987. **To be published July 1987. ***To be published October 1987. Any books ordered prior to publication date will be shipped at no extra charge as soon as they are available.

Please send me the books I have checked above. I enclose a check or money order for the combined cover price for the titles I have ordered, plus 75 cents for first-class postage and handling (for any number of titles) made out to Baen Books, Dept. B, 260 Fifth Avenue, New York, N.Y. 10001.